KU-321-071

Praise for Paula Volsky and

THE GRAND ELLIPSE

"Stylish . . . truly magical . . . convincingly exotic . . . and rich in the small details that invite the reader to enter [Volsky's] world completely. Turn off the TV, put on your slippers, and curl up in a fat armchair by the fireside with this book. You won't regret it." —Robin Hobb

"Fresh and fun, a picaresque page-turner that reads like a collaboration between Jules Verne and Jack Vance." —George R. R. Martin

"Harrowing, bright, inventive, romantic and above all entertaining." —*The SF Site* Featured Review

"Fantasy writing at its best." —*Tampa Tribune and Times*

"[Volsky] excels in portraying fantasy worlds steeped in quasihistorical authenticity and convincing 'period detail.' . . . Recommended." —*Library Journal*

"Those who want humor and adventure in their reading are strongly encouraged to read Paula Volsky . . . a vivid and imaginative writer." —*The Washington Post*

"Richly inventive and breathlessly paced . . . brimming with vibrant, exotic settings and Volsky's knack for utterly convincing dialogue . . . this lively adventure makes for unflagging reading enjoyment that should appeal to a wide swath of SF and fantasy fans." —*Publishers Weekly* (starred review)

"Volsky serves up adventure laced with humor and romance and brings it all to a literally pyromaniacal conclusion." —*Booklist*

"A spine-tingling, heartwarming delight." —*Kirkus Reviews*

"Provocative . . . wonderfully enjoyable." —*Publishers Weekly*

THE GRAND ELLIPSE

Paula Volsky

BANTAM BOOKS

New York Toronto London Sydney Auckland

This edition contains the complete text of the original hardcover edition.
NOT ONE WORD HAS BEEN OMITTED.

THE GRAND ELLIPSE
A Bantam Spectra Book

PUBLISHING HISTORY
Bantam Spectra hardcover edition published October 2000
Bantam Spectra paperback edition/November 2001

SPECTRA and the portrayal of a boxed "s" are trademarks of
Bantam Books, a division of Random House, Inc.

ISBN 0-553-58012-4

Published simultaneously in the United States and Canada

Bantam Books are published by Bantam Books, a division of Random
House, Inc. Its trademark, consisting of the words "Bantam Books" and
the portrayal of a rooster, is Registered in U.S. Patent and Trademark
Office and in other countries. Marca Registrada. Bantam Books, 1540
Broadway, New York, New York 10036.

PRINTED IN THE UNITED STATES OF AMERICA

OPM   10   9   8   7   6   5   4   3   2   1

THE GRAND ELLIPSE

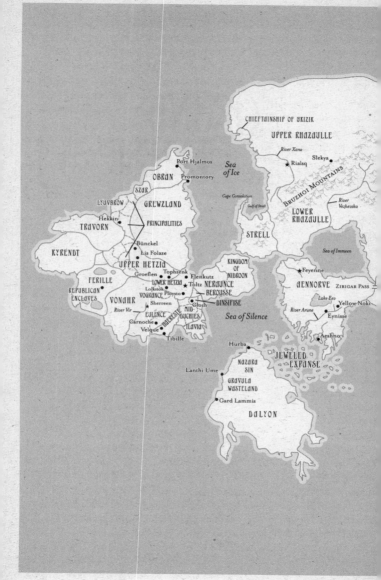

CHIEFTAINSHIP OF UKIZIK

UPPER RHAZAULLE

River Xana

Rialsq ★   Slekya

Sea
of Ice

Port Hjalmos

OBRAN

Promontory

SZAR

GREWZLAND

PRINCIPALITIES

LYUVBROW

TRAVORN

Hekkin

Cape Consolation

Gulf of Strell

BRUZHOI MOUNTAINS

*River
Vezheuska*

LOWER
RHAZAULLE

KYRENDT

Bünckel

Lis Folaze

UPPER HETZIA

STRELL

Sea of Immeen

FERILLE

Groeflen   Tophzenk

KINGDOM
OF
NIDROON

Flenkutz

LOWER HETZIA

Toltz   NERAUNCE

Feyenne ★

DENNORVE   ZIRIGAR PASS

REPUBLICAN
ENCLAVES

VONAHR

Lolkton

VOURANCE   Ploysto

Sherreen

BEROUSSE

DINSIFISE

Lake Eep

Yellow Noki

River Arune

EULENCE

Clozh

Sea of Silence

Eynisse

Carnoche

Velque

HALLREINE
MID-
DUCHIES
ILAVIA

Tibille

Hurba

Aeshno

JEWELED
EXPANSE

Lanthi Ume

NAZARA
SIN

GRAVULA
WASTELAND

Gard Lammis

DALYON

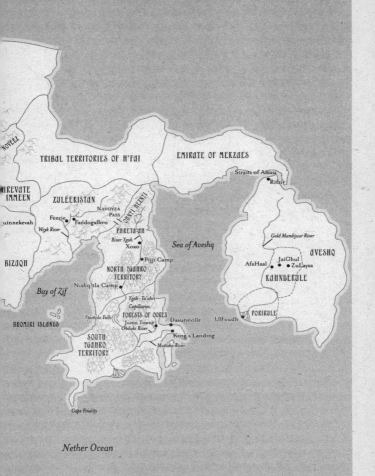

Prologue

"SHE IS INCOMPARABLE, she is exquisite, she is divine," proclaimed the king of the Low Hetz. "Have another lard-smacker, my friend, and I'll tell you about her."

"Sire, the preparations are complete," returned the adept who chose to call himself "Nevenskoi." His aspect was darkly foreign, his accent exotically flavored. "I am ready to proceed with the demonstration."

"I've never encountered so glorious a creature," the king confided. "Her smile—a tropical sunrise. Her walk—the flow of a mountain stream. Her voice—a celestial serenade."

"If Your Majesty will condescend to observe the pit-of-elements, you will view the culmination of—"

"The curve of her lips—an architect's inspiration. The texture of her skin—corporeal moonlight. The swell of her breasts—words fail me."

"The years of arcane experimentation," Nevenskoi persisted, "have borne fruit at last, sire. A discovery of considerable significance—"

"Scarcely concerns me now. There are more important things. Come, man, where's your heart, where's your imagination? Have a chili-oil eel, and try to act human."

"As Your Majesty wills." Obediently the adept styling himself "Nevenskoi" picked a morsel from the vast platter covering half the workroom table, swallowed, and felt his frustration subside. Remarkable, the heartening effect that food always exerted upon him, especially expensive food, cunningly prepared, artfully presented. And the fare at Waterwitch Palace ranged from the excellent to the sublime. The chili-oil eels, for example—moist fleshed, initially mild upon the unsuspecting tongue, then kindling to infernal heat. Extraordinary. The deep-fried lard-smackers—dense and rich beneath the airiest of batters. The caviar mille-feuilles, flecked with chives, layered with sour cream. The pickled plover's eggs. The little garlic custards in crispy shredded potato nests. The saffron barquettes, black with truffles. Delightful. No doubt about it, King Miltzin IX knew how to choose his chefs—perhaps too well, Nevenskoi reflected, conscious of the spreading middle-aged girth, so detrimental to the image that his position and profession obliged him to maintain.

Immaterial. The voluminous dark robe of a traditional savant concealed unsightly bulges, just as the thick black wig concealed his balding pate. Just as the black-dyed moustache and imperial masked his ripe jowls. Just as the affectation of an alien accent disguised the flat intonations of a Hetzian shopkeeper's son, veiling the drab truth of ordinary Nitz Neeper. Nitz the Nobody, Nitz the Nonentity, Nitz the Nothing.

Nitz no more.

"Nevenskoi" now, and self-transformed. Native son of northern Rhazaulle, scion of a noble house, mystic, medium, gifted necromancer. A man of parts. In short, a noteworthy personage, one whose abilities had won the regard of the Low Hetz's king.

Miltzin IX—dubbed "Mad Miltzin" by the irreverent— was generous to his human pets. Excessively generous, in many opinions, but the king wisely ignored such mean-spirited carping. Capable of recognizing talent, Miltzin had taken Nitz Neeper, known as Nevenskoi, into his own Waterwitch Palace; had fed and sheltered him luxuriously, paid him munificently, included him in courtly functions, shown him every mark of favor, and, most important, furnished him with the most advanced and amply equipped underground workroom that any aspiring adept had ever dreamed of. All His Majesty asked in exchange was a little occasional novelty.

These reflections enabled Nevenskoi to regard his

grasshopper-minded monarch with a kindlier eye. Mad Miltzin was still rhapsodizing.

". . . the arch of her eyebrow . . . the curve of her earlobe . . . swanlike throat . . . rounded white shoulder . . . tiny, helpless, enchanting hands, like a child's . . . adorable, irresistible . . . magical . . ."

Courtesy no less than diplomacy demanded a reply.

"The fortunate landswoman is indeed possessed of many an advantage, not the least of which is the treasure of Your Majesty's esteem," Nevenskoi hazarded in his spurious Rhazaullean accent.

Mad Miltzin halted in midpaean, and his eyes—bright, round, and protuberant as an insect's—widened.

"Who?" inquired the king.

"The Honorable Landswoman liNeuflein, Sire. The happy recipient of Your Majesty's approbation. The—"

"Oh," said Miltzin. "Her. Come, man, d'you truly imagine liNeuflein's wife worthy of such praise? You spend too much time buried alive in this workroom; it's warped your standards of judgment."

"Majesty, correct me if I am mistaken, but was it not a scant month ago that you were lauding the beauty of the honorable landswoman? Did you not at that time characterize yourself as 'the helpless slave of her matchless radiance'?"

"Perhaps; I do not recall. She's well enough, I suppose, in an overstated sort of way. But she is no longer young, and I suspect she colors her hair. Moreover, an unsightly mole disfigures her left thigh. Or was it the right? No matter. How can such overblown charms compare with the fresh young loveliness of the Regarded Madam liGrozorf?"

"Madam liGrozorf?"

"A rose, my friend, with the dew still upon her. No more than eighteen years of age, and newly come to court. Innocent, pure, impossibly unspoiled. I confess I am hopelessly smitten. Never have I known such depth of emotion—"

Miltzin was off and running again.

Once again Nevenskoi suppressed a flash of annoyance, an exercise in courtiership that he had mastered years earlier. Assuming an expression of suitably admiring encouragement, he concentrated on simulating interest in the king's latest obsession. And while he listened, he comforted himself with lard-smackers, foie gras, oil-cured olives, and fried ganzel puffs picked from the platter. Presently his innards stirred a warning, which he disregarded, for he prided himself upon his resistance to intestinal intimidation.

A slight change in the rhythm of the half-heard monologue alerted the adept's experienced ear. His sovereign's prominent eyes had lost something of their excited luster, and those expansive gestures were starting to contract. The topic was approaching exhaustion. Presently Miltzin IX paused, groping for superlatives.

Nevenskoi seized the moment. "The king wants distraction from his many cares. Allow His Majesty's servant the privilege of furnishing diversion."

"Eh? Oh, yes, you were keen on showing me something, weren't you? What was it, again?"

"The fire, Your Majesty." Nitz Neeper, alias Nevenskoi, took a deep breath. When he spoke again, his foreign accent was false as always, but his words were true, for there was nothing ersatz about his talent or his ambition. "The wonder of Sentient Fire."

"Sentient Fire. Well. A pretty title," Mad Miltzin conceded. He hesitated, apparently pondering the necessity of additional inquiry, and then demanded, "A weapon of some sort, is it?"

"Certainly, Sire, that is one of countless potential applications."

"I do not perceive the need for new and more advanced methods of destruction," the king countered at once. "We are not at war. Everybody else is, but not us. It's costly, I suppose?"

"There are certain unavoidable expenses, hardly excessive in view of the benefits. Your Majesty, my discovery is surely—"

"Ingenious no doubt, but you must understand that time has passed. I've expanded in mind and soul, I have grown beyond the need of crude weaponry. Please don't pout. I would hope to see you rejoice in my spiritual progress."

"I do," Nevenskoi returned fervently. "Indeed I do, with all my heart. And yet, with all due modesty, I am compelled to observe that my discovery of what amounts to a new element in the world may be regarded as a wondrous pathway opening to mankind—a new resource, a new direction, a fresh territory open to exploration—"

"Oh, don't get carried away, Nevenskoi," the king advised. "You're a bit full of yourself, aren't you?"

"Majesty, I intended no presumption."

"Probably not, but I must instruct you, this so-called 'wondrous pathway' of yours is very much a false lead."

"Sire?"

"Now, don't assume affronted airs. You brilliant adepts are all temperamental, scarcely fit to endure the truth. But this time you must hear it. The key to the future lies not in the exploration of fire, explosives, atmospheric ignitions, or any such commonplace incendiary effusion."

"Indeed, Sire." Dread twinged across Nevenskoi's mind. He sensed the waning of his listener's interest, and with that ebb tide went fame and glory, solvency, security. His insides commenced to knot.

"The key," Miltzin continued, blithely blind to the other's distress, "lies in the marriage of magic and science. It is this great fusion that will shape and rule the world of the future. And the nation successfully comprehending these twin forces—the nation capable of turning the new knowledge to practical use in terms of transportation and communication—will surely emerge preeminent in years to come."

Not a word about the Sentient Fire. The lard-smackers lay like stones in Nevenskoi's belly. The heat of the chili-oil eels blazed along his veins. His guts twisted and the sweat gathered on his brow, but he managed to reply, "Your Majesty limns a golden prospect. For the present, however—"

"The mechanics of transportation must be mastered," the king bounced on. "That is the first step along the path. It is my duty as a monarch to furnish guidance and encouragement. Therefore—and you are the first to know, my friend— I am planning an extraordinary event designed to focus the world's attention upon issues of truest significance."

"Admirable, Sire. But you speak of extraordinary events, and I beg leave to remind Your Majesty—"

"It will be a race," Miltzin announced. "The greatest of all time, open to all, its course describing a vast elongated circuit that I myself have plotted. I can hardly begin to express the delight I have taken in this task. Nevenskoi, it will be magnificent! The racers will travel through many lands, over sea, mountain, forest, and other such troublesome terrain, as far as Aveshq and then back again. There is no conceivable inconvenience that they won't encounter. Ha! But it will be tremendous! And that is why I have chosen to name this course I've planned—the Grand Ellipse. Well? What do you think of it?"

"Very fine, Sire."

"So I believe. I considered calling it 'the Big Oval,' but felt that designation lacked impact."

"I congratulate Your Majesty upon a wise decision." Nevenskoi strove to disregard the increasing tumult in his belly. "No doubt this proposed race will indeed serve many a noble and useful purpose."

"The mechanics of transportation, principle and application. Communication, magical and mundane. Progress!"

"Similarly useful, I believe, is the discovery that I myself have recently—"

"Oh, yes, I remember." Miltzin returned reluctantly to the present. "Some sort of fire display, wasn't it? Well, I don't know that I really have the time for such things, when there are matters of infinitely greater—oh, very well, Nevenskoi. I can't stand it when you sulk. I'll view your little pyrotechnics. Try to keep it brief."

"As you wish, Sire." He'd had a speech prepared, but he dispensed with it now, for Mad Miltzin's grasshopper eyes were wandering. Nevenskoi stepped to the pit-of-elements at the center of the room, where the prepared materials were already assembled. He wasted no time upon the theatrical posturings and declamation that ignorant spectators expected of a sorcerous adept. Rather, he used his mind as he had spent a lifetime learning to use it. He stood quite still, his eyes shut. His almost imperceptible gestures and almost inaudible utterances were the minimum required to facilitate concentration of his intellect. The coals smoldering at the pit of his stomach faded from existence. For a time he lost awareness of his immediate surroundings, for his thoughts were winging along paths unknown to all but the select sorcerous few, and his consciousness was striving toward another plane, a place intensely alien, never to be comprehended or mastered, yet familiar to him.

He had it. He was there. The mental explosion sent the arcane power surging through him. Nitz Neeper, known as Nevenskoi, opened his eyes and bent that potency upon the pit-of-elements, where the assembled preparations burst into flame that burned jealousy-green.

Heat, light, emotion, and simple awareness radiated from the fire.

Hungry. Hungry. HUNGRY!

The elemental urgency burned in Nevenskoi's brain. The innocent greed and fierce desire of his creation blended with his own thoughts; heated, colored, and all but overwhelmed them.

Food! Freedom! Now! NOW!

The psychic demands battered, but Nevenskoi stood firm and presently the fire acknowledged his mastery.

Pleasepleasepleasepleasepleaseplease!

Soon, he responded in silence. *If you are good.*

Gimmegimmegimme!

Quiet. Wait. Nevenskoi turned to his sovereign, who sat watching in tolerant silence, and announced, "Sire, the fire is conscious."

"And decidedly green," observed Mad Miltzin. "I've never seen green flames before. That's quite picturesque. Are we finished yet?"

"No. Remain seated and attentive," Nevenskoi instructed, and saw the other's brows lift at the tone of authority. Directing his thoughts inward to touch the wild, ardent consciousness impinging upon his own, he issued commands, spoken aloud for the benefit of his audience.

"Detach yourself from your present source of fuel—"

NO! NO!

"—complete a circuit of this chamber, consuming nothing, and then return."

Instantly, a whirling mass of green flame leapt from the pit-of-elements, circled the workroom at blazing speed, then rushed for the pit and the heap of chemically fortified faggots.

Nevenskoi controlled the natural rush of satisfaction that might have rocked his concentration. His eyes sought the king.

Mad Miltzin was sitting bolt upright in his chair. His forbearing expression had given way to a look of undisguised amazement.

Excellent. Again Nevenskoi addressed himself to the flames. "Nourish yourself and stand tall."

A blazing column thrust for the vaulted ceiling, high overhead.

A startled squeak escaped Miltzin IX.

"Now subside," commanded Nevenskoi. "Abandon your fuel—"

No! No! Hungry! No!

"—detach yourself momentarily and reduce yourself to the smallest spark—"

Nononopleasenopleasenononopleasenono—

Come, my darling beauty, he cajoled silently, *I will reward you.*

Promise?

Upon my hope of glory. Such concessions were unnecessary, for he was surely master, but Nevenskoi found he could not resist.

At once the great green pillar contracted, dwindling swiftly to a tiny spark, all but invisible.

"Oh," breathed Miltzin IX.

Thanks, my lovely, you will not be sorry, silently spoke Nevenskoi. Aloud, he commanded, "Resume your original stature, split yourself in equal parts, and dance a Linniana."

The green flames complied. The mutable radiant partners twirled, and the king gaped.

"And now," Nevenskoi whispered, "come to me. Come to me, my sweet one. Consume nothing, but let us be near—let us join."

The flames embraced and engulfed him. He stood at the heart of a roaring conflagration. The fire was around and within him, filling his nose and mouth, plunging down into his lungs, but it did not hurt him, never would, for its mind vibrated in tune with his own, and he could feel the furious affection, the hunger and need, that made him one with his creation. His heart throbbed and a wild joy surged through him, a lust to consume and devour—

Through the leaping curtain of green he could see Mad Miltzin rising from his chair, waving his arms and flapping his jaw, apparently shouting, but the words were unimportant. The king's pomaded curls and greying walrus moustache would ignite gorgeously. The metallic braid glinting upon His Majesty's quasi-military tunic would melt and run, a veritable river of gold. . . . And when he'd eaten the king, there remained the shelves of sorcerous supplies, the furnishings, and the hangings. Delicious.

Nevenskoi's arms, wreathed in flame, rose of their own accord. He took a single step toward Miltzin IX, and halted himself with an effort.

No. He strained his will, and his humanity reasserted itself.

"Enough," he whispered reluctantly, and the fire tingled across his moving lips. "Back to your fuel, and refresh yourself as you will."

A final painlessly fierce embrace, then the green flames roared off for the pit-of-elements. Physical separation greatly reduced the intensity of the mental connection, leaving Nevenskoi at once relieved and achingly bereft.

Beautiful, he remarked in silence. *Perfect.*

From the pit came the crackling contented reply.

EatEatEatEatEatEatEatEatEatEatEatEatEatEat.

All was well now. He could afford to relax, let the triumph flow, but not to show it. A great adept maintained his inscrutability at all times. Turning a bland professional countenance upon his monarch, Nevenskoi bowed deeply.

"Nevenskoi! Are you still *alive?*" demanded the king.

"So please Your Majesty."

"I'll summon that physician of my wife's to you. She swears by the fellow—"

"Sire, your servant is uninjured."

"How? I could feel the heat halfway across the room! Or

was it all a trick? A multisensory illusion, in the old Vonahrish style, was it? Ha, very good, very clever!"

"No illusion, but a reality easily confirmed. As I recall, Your Majesty has often expressed a pronounced dislike of Her Majesty the queen's favorite long-haired cat. Your Majesty need but order the cat consigned to the sentient flames, with results conclusively verifying the legitimacy of my demonstration."

"Tempting, but impossible. Her Majesty dotes on that purring vermin, whose incineration invites hideous consequences. Anyway, my dear fellow, I believe you. I am to understand, then, that the Sentient Fire is awake, aware, and subject to your will? You command, and the flames simply—obey?"

So obtuse an oversimplification warranted no reply. Nevenskoi permitted himself an austere smile.

"You are a talented fellow, and no mistake," Miltzin acknowledged. "I congratulate you, my friend! I confess I was quite astonished, quite stirred; and, as you know, I am not easily moved to enthusiasm! Yet despite the sprightliness of your demonstration I note that my original question remains unanswered. What is the practical use of your discovery?"

"Its uses are manifold, Sire," Nevenskoi maintained. "Urban demolition. The clearing of forested land. Increased domestic comfort and efficiency—"

"Ordinary fire is adequate to these purposes, and probably cheaper."

"The use of Sentient Fire to heat a boiler," Nevenskoi persisted, "encourages the development of the sentient steam engine—"

"Farfetched."

"Sentient illumination—"

"Unnecessary."

"There is the matter of national defense—"

"Weapons again. Barbarism. You know my convictions. It's just as I suspected. Your Sentient Fire, presently an engaging curiosity, is apt to wreak eventual havoc."

"The future cloaks itself in shadow," Nevenskoi intoned, unwilling to allow the other's resistance to solidify. "It may well be that the powers of many extraordinary minds conjoined must shape the destiny of Sentient Fire. It is for this reason that I urge you, Sire, to inform your fellow sovereigns throughout the world of the discovery nurtured and ripened in the sunlight of Your Majesty's patronage. Humanity must judge—"

"That is a wretched idea, Nevenskoi," Mad Miltzin interrupted. "You haven't the least idea what you're suggesting, for you reclusive adepts simply have no knowledge of the world. Stop and think, man! Noise your accomplishment abroad, and what is the inevitable result? Chaos. Confusion. Disaster. In short order we'd find ourselves besieged with couriers, diplomats, official and unofficial envoys thronging our capital, foreign correspondence choking our post, petitioners camping upon our threshold, and alien spies infesting our very corridors. They'd be at us night and day, Nevenskoi! They'd want that trained fire of yours for their own use, and you can imagine what *that* would be! Those Grewzians, for example—those strength-in-purity, eat-your-meat-raw, conquer-all-the-world fanatics—you can guess how they'd behave! Their imperior, my cousin Ogron, comes from the very worst branch of the family, and, believe me, he goes the limit. He'd *persecute* me! And those Vonahrish fops would be in for a wheedle, and the Strellians would be around to sermonize, and those peculiar Rhazaullean countrymen of yours would be sending me casks of that lethal vouvrak they're so unaccountably fond of, along with sea-sable coats and veiled threats. I tell you, there'd be no peace!"

"It is inevitable," Nevenskoi conceded carefully, "that the miracle of Sentient Fire will awaken foreign envy and desire—particularly now, at a time of such widespread conflict—"

"Oh, it's clear the world's gone mad, Nevenskoi, quite mad! Though my cousin Ogron's the one most at blame; he started it. He was always a bully, even as a child. Grabby, too. You got a new toy, and Ogron would take it right off you. No scruples, that one. Trinkets, tidbits, didn't matter—Ogron grabbed it all. And only look at him now—all grown up, imperior of Grewzland, and as grabby as ever. Grabbing Szar.

Grabbing Nidroon. Grabbing the Mid-Duchies, lock, stock, and barrel. Grabbing Dalyon. He's the one who touched off this appalling international uproar, and presently there won't be a peaceful acre of soil to be found from here to the antipodes!"

"May I observe," Nevenskoi essayed, "that possession of so valuable and useful a commodity as the Sentient Fire, at so critical a juncture, places Your Majesty in a most enviable position? Only consider the effect of the intelligent blaze, loosed upon an enemy army or city! The competition to secure the new knowledge will be desperate. To speak plainly, Sire, you will be able to name your price. Your Majesty, rightly called the father of the nation, may now—"

"The Low Hetzian economy," the king stated, "has always flourished in an atmosphere of perfect national neutrality."

"Sire, I only suggest—"

"Your suggestion that we involve ourselves, even indirectly, in foreign quarrels is inappropriate," Mad Miltzin sleeted. "You are a foreigner among us, and here upon our sufferance. Do not forget that, or presume too greatly upon our indulgence."

Nevenskoi started. The Hetzian monarch's mild and sunny countenance had frozen over in an instant. His eyes had emptied, and his voice had gone cold as a Rhazaullean tomb. The adept's heart began to slam, while his stomach clenched new warnings.

Soothe him. Apologize, urged the mind of the former Nitz Neeper. *Prevail. Rule,* insisted the intelligence of the sorcerer Nevenskoi.

Easier said than done. There was at least one point, it seemed, upon which the royal will caught and stuck.

"We are a neutral nation," proclaimed the king of the Low Hetz. "So we have always been, and so we shall always be. That is the decision in which we have trusted for generations. Do you, an outsider, presume to question the judgment of our fathers?"

"I place my faith in the wisdom of my sovereign," dutifully returned Nevenskoi. "I would only counsel him to consider—"

"There is nothing to consider. The neutrality of the Low

Hetz remains sacrosanct. Let the ignorant nations of the world tear one another like tigers, if they choose. Their folly does not touch or concern us. We favor neither one warrior nor another, and none of them shall receive the benefit of Sentient Fire. They will not be informed of its existence. That is my irrevocable judgment, and I will brook no contradiction. Do you understand me, Nevenskoi?"

"Perfectly, Sire."

"Very well." Mollified, the king thawed. "Don't look so glum, my dear fellow. Rest assured, you'll have the credit your very commendable work merits. Perhaps you might stage a display for all the court to witness. How entertaining that will be! That trick you do at the end, where you stand there wrapped from head to toe in green fire, is absolutely smashing! And now that I think of it, your pyrotechnics will furnish the perfect accompaniment to my public announcement of the impending race that I have christened the 'Grand Ellipse.' D'you suppose the peerless Madam liGrozorf will approve that title? I confess, my friend, the prospect enthralls me!"

Nevenskoi manufactured a faint smile. The smile remained locked in place despite the anger and disappointment simmering within, and despite the increasingly severe dyspeptic miseries racking his belly. The king noticed nothing, but another was more observant.

Pain. Trouble. Worry, crackled the radiant voice from the pit-of-elements. *Whatwhatwhatwhatwhat?*

No cause for concern, sweet one, Nevenskoi silently reassured his creation.

Pain. Sad. Mad. Pain. Whatwhatwhatwhatwhat?

This man who visits us wishes to conceal your glory from the eyes of humanity. He is beset with fears, and would therefore smother your light. His pettiness and ingratitude affront me.

Eat him? EatEatEat?

The flaming insistence pressed, and almost Nevenskoi felt himself starting to yield. Devour Mad Miltzin. Good idea. Swallow the fellow in one hugely satisfying gulp, and then move on to those luscious paper notebooks and portfolios. . . .

EATEATEATEATEAT!

Alarm bells clanged in Nevenskoi's mind. Something was

wrong. He was losing control. The physical discomfort of acute indigestion had badly shaken his concentration, blasting his focus and undermining his authority. He took a few moments to compose himself, and when he was once again confident of his dominance, he spoke inwardly:

No, loveliness, for the king is not wicked, but only small in mind. He is our benefactor, and not to be eaten lightly. However, his will shall not prevail. Already I have thwarted him.

How? How?

I have communicated with my sorcerous colleagues in every land. I have sent word to them by arcane means surpassing King Miltzin's limited understanding.

What? What?

No matter. Enough for you to know, my beauty, that we do not need the king's assistance. Let him neglect us, it doesn't matter, for now the savants and adepts throughout the world—the men of true power—are learning of your birth. These wise ones will recognize your virtue, strength, brilliance, and splendor. The word is spreading swiftly. No one can stop it now.

Now we are happy again. The green flames danced.

"What are you smiling about, Nevenskoi?" inquired Mad Miltzin.

"I rejoice in my sovereign's satisfaction."

"Good fellow; that's what I like to hear! Have another glass of champagne."

"As Your Majesty wills, now and always."

1

"AND THUS THE BHOMIRI ISLANDERS, submitting perforce to western rule, have ostensibly accepted western moral standards. They've abandoned their traditional cannibalistic practices, outlawed polygamy, and banned human sacrifice, or so they'd have us believe. Investigation, however, has revealed the falsity of this apparent transformation. Beneath the thinnest veneer of what we Vonahrish call civilization, the old culture persists. It is a culture that we can hardly afford to dismiss or despise, despite its disturbing aspects, for it is just such sources that teach us of humanity's past, of our origins, and ultimately, of ourselves." Luzelle Devaire concluded her lecture.

There was silence, and she tensed. She should never have described those Bhomiri cannibalistic feasts in such detail. She'd shocked her listeners, and it had been a mistake.

Then the audience erupted into applause, and Luzelle relaxed. Her instincts had been sound; she *was* good at her work. Sometimes she wondered, but the present response allayed all doubts.

Almost all.

Her eyes swept the ranks of enthusiasts to light upon a couple of faces in the back neither pleased nor approving.

Her father was sitting there, irate, disgruntled, affronted; her mother beside him, dutifully reflecting similar sentiments.

Why had they come today, of all days?

You invited them. You encouraged them to come.

But not today.

Questions popped at her from the audience. She answered almost automatically, while her real attention remained fixed on her parents. They were both visibly impatient. Maybe they'd get tired of waiting and go away.

No such luck.

The questions sputtered to a gradual halt. The spectators trickled from the lecture hall. Even the young would-be gallant in the front row, he of the glinting teeth and hopefully gleaming pince-nez, finally gave up and withdrew. But Master Udonse Devaire and his wife Gilinne remained.

There was no need to ask them what they had thought of her speech. Their identically pursed mouths spoke wordless volumes.

The last of the audience departed and Luzelle found herself alone in the auditorium with her parents. They were still sitting motionless in the otherwise empty back row. No way to pretend she didn't see. Drawing a deep breath, she descended from the stage and made her reluctant way up the carpeted aisle toward them.

"Father. Mother. How good of you to come. I'm so glad," Luzelle lied. She produced a suitably gracious smile.

Neither the words nor the facial contortion produced the desired effect.

"We came," Udonse Devaire informed his daughter, "because we wished to be just. I desired impartiality, and therefore chose to give you the benefit of the doubt."

"The Judge took pains, as always, to weigh all circumstances," declared Gilinne.

The Judge, she always called him. Grim, but understandable enough, for Udonse Devaire, justice of the Sherreenian Higher Court, seemed formed by nature to project grandeur. With his tall brow, aquiline nose, cold eyes, square-cut greying beard, and deliberately majestic mien, Udonse inspired awe in malefactors and family members alike—especially women. No wonder his wife, his sisters, his mother, and his various mistresses all deferred religiously to His Honor. Luzelle herself had done so, in past years.

"I have listened, I have pondered, and I have reached a verdict," announced the Judge.

Guilty. She'd thought he might reconsider, once he heard what she actually had to say, but she should have known better. Of course she couldn't have guessed that he would choose to listen today. Polygamous Bhomiri cannibals. Hardly a topic recommending itself to the Judge.

"It was repugnant, far exceeding my worst expectations," declared Udonse. "I must confess, I was appalled."

"Really, daughter, I don't wish to seem unkind, but it was disgusting," complained Gilinne. "How could you?"

"Your lecture—if so repulsive an outpouring of filth and horror may be dignified by such a term—revealed a shocking lack of taste, propriety, and above all of the general fineness of sensibility that may be termed womanly," decreed Udonse. "Your description of savage abominations plumbed the depths of lurid sensationalism, revealing a coarseness of mental fiber I should never have thought to encounter in a female bearing the family name of Devaire. Your blood is good, and you have been properly reared. Thus I can scarcely account for your mental and moral deficiencies."

"How can it be morally deficient to recount the literal truth, sir?" Luzelle inquired, and felt her lips curving in the old smile she knew would infuriate him. She had told herself she would resist the temptation, that she had grown beyond adolescent challenges and provocations, but her face automatically resumed the accustomed expressions.

"There is such a thing," Gilinne Devaire reminded her daughter, "as a lapse in taste so extreme as to rouse genuine distress in the listener. That is what the Judge means to explain to you. Do you understand, dear?"

"She should understand," remarked His Honor, "at her age."

She understood all too well. Luzelle felt her blood and breath quicken. Ridiculous. She had promised herself that she would never again allow her father's words to set her internally boiling. But now her heart was pounding and her pulses racing as if she were still sixteen years old and miserably subject to paternal autocracy.

Only she wasn't. She was an adult, and free. Time to start acting like it.

"Father and Mother, I'm sorry you were offended," she offered, carefully cleansing her face of all save courteous concern. "Another time you might be better pleased—"

"There will be no other time," His Honor informed her. "I have listened at repellent length, and now I am prepared to render judgment."

"I'm afraid it will have to wait, sir," Luzelle returned. His brows and chin rose, and once again she found herself compelled to justify, to appease. "I'm sorry, but I can't speak now. I've an appointment that I must keep."

"That is no way to speak to the Judge," Gilinne Devaire reproved. "You mustn't be disrespectful, child."

"No disrespect intended," Luzelle countered, "but the truth is—and I'm sorry—but the truth is that you've come at a very bad time. See, this will explain it all." She did not need to explain, but old habits died hard, and so she dipped into her pocket to bring forth the letter, which she extended to her father. He accepted as if granting a favor, and scanned the message frowningly. The last few words so far strained his credulity that he could not forbear reading them aloud:

"*. . . and therefore, should you prove willing to undertake the venture, we are prepared to offer full sponsorship, underwriting all legitimate expenses, including personal transportation of every necessary variety and description, both expected and unforeseen; concomitant costs of baggage transfer; room and board, to ordinary and reasonable standards of comfort throughout the course of the race; and all justifiable incidentals and emergency expenses encountered en route.*

"*We anticipate a meeting with you upon conclusion of your next scheduled lecture at University Dome, one week following the date of this correspondence. At that time we shall expect a reply, and hope for an affirmative beneficial to all parties concerned. . . .*"

"What is this new lunacy?" For a moment it seemed that

Udonse might shred the offending document, but he chose to hand it back intact.

"It is an offer of government sponsorship."

"Sponsorship. Is that what you choose to call it? Are you disingenuous, or simply gullible?"

"You note the letterhead, sir," Luzelle replied steadily. "Ministry of Foreign Affairs—"

"I note the official stationery, easily purloined or imitated. Surely you are not so simple as to accept this proposal at face value?"

"It's caught my interest, as well it might. The winner of the Hetzian king's race will receive an enormous prize—a legitimate Hetzian peerage, which carries with it ownership of some ancient manor or castle or something, somewhere in the Low Hetz—and I'd like to know—"

"It is not a legitimate offer. That is all you need to know."

"How can you be so certain?"

"The Judge knows best, dear," Gilinne interjected. "Trust in your father."

That's rich, coming from you. He's betrayed you a dozen times over, with his little seamstresses and shopgirls. And somewhere underneath all that wifely loyalty and respect, you must know it. Luzelle compressed her lips, holding the words in.

"This missive hardly carries the tone of an official communiqué," His Honor stated. "Your correspondent, this self-styled Deputy Underminister—vo Rouvignac, was it?"

Luzelle nodded.

"The fellow's connection to that famous and ancient House is very much open to question. In any event, you will note that the writer requests a meeting, but fails to specify an hour or location. If he is what he claims to be, then why has he not summoned you to the Republican Complex? The Ministry of Foreign Affairs stands close at hand, and its offices are spacious. Why do you not meet him there?"

"The hour and location have been tailored to suit my schedule. The Deputy Underminister vo Rouvignac does not summon me, but rather, waits upon my convenience," Luzelle rejoined, determined to disguise her own misgivings.

"Do not try my patience with puerile absurdity. Have you

at some point applied to the ministry for financial backing? Have you filled out the necessary forms, submitted the appropriate credentials and references, together with a written declaration of your proposed use of government funds?"

"No, I've asked for nothing."

"You have, at the very least, notified the ministry of your desire to participate in this nonsensical race, this international goose-chase, this—"

"Grand Ellipse," Luzelle supplied. "No, sir. I have expressed no such desire or intention."

"And yet, of all the doubtless eager and well-qualified male candidates, you have somehow been selected, by unknown agency, to represent the nation of Vonahr in this asinine competition, presumably at the taxpayers' expense. Tell me, daughter—does this strike you as probable?"

Luzelle was silent. Her father only voiced her own unacknowledged doubts.

"It is improbable to the verge of impossibility," the Judge instructed his listeners. "I tell you once again, this invitation you have received is a ruse, and a clumsy one at that."

"And the object of the ruse, sir?"

"Can scarcely elude the most limited understanding. Surely you will not wonder that the world questions your virtue. The immodesty and license of the life that you lead invite irregular solicitation."

Luzelle felt the angry color burn her cheeks. She managed, with effort, to keep her voice even. "The life that I lead is blameless and useful."

"The utility of pornographic public lectures is limited at best." His Honor's nostrils flared in distaste. "I regret the indelicacy of expression that your conduct obliges me to adopt."

"That's ridiculous, insulting, and completely untrue! There's nothing pornographic about my lectures. They're accurate accounts of foreign habits and customs, inoffensive to all but the hopelessly insular, as the reaction of the audience this afternoon certainly demonstrated!" She could hear her own voice rising, but found herself powerless to control it.

"I will not tolerate impertinence, daughter. You will address me with appropriate respect."

"Then don't attack my work unjustly, and don't smear my character with false accusation!"

"Your work? What need has a spinster of good family to work outside of her father's home? Are you quite blind to the embarrassment you cause your parents, or are you simply indifferent? As for your character, I should prefer to regard it as unblemished, but your actions constrain me to suspect otherwise. What unmarried female aptly described as a lady courts the attention of multitudes? Accepts financial remuneration in exchange for such public display? Lives alone in defiance of all established convention, and travels the world alone like some common adventuress? Where is your propriety, your sense of duty? Are you remotely capable of grasping such concepts? Do you dare to feign surprise that such libertines as this soi-disant deputy underminister regard you as their natural prey—an assumption no doubt reinforced by the unbecoming freedom of your manner, and the vulgarity of your appearance?"

To her horror, Luzelle felt the tears sting her eyes; tears that she would rather have died than allow him to see. She'd thought her father had long since lost the power to make her cry.

Her throat constricted. For a moment, pain and fury struck her uncharacteristically dumb.

Surprisingly, her mother came to her rescue.

"Oh, come—surely that is a little hard," Gilinne remonstrated apologetically. "Luzelle's appearance cannot rightly be termed vulgar—she is quite modestly and decently clothed."

His Honor deliberated.

"There is perhaps nothing blatantly amiss with her attire," he conceded at last. "But there is something in her air, her carriage, her general demeanor, that somehow contrives to suggest indiscretion. A thick and loosely draped shawl might improve matters, or else a capacious manteau—"

"Her figure is exceedingly well proportioned," Gilinne observed mildly. "In that our daughter is blessed."

"She need not flaunt her good fortune. Then there is the objectionable appearance of her hair—excessively abundant, ostentatiously curled—"

"The curl is natural. I remember when she was a baby, and—"

"Flamboyantly and improbably colored."

"The shade is popularly known as strawberry blond, I believe, and the fault is entirely mine, husband, for my own mother possessed locks of just such a reddish gold."

"Face swarthy as a laborer's."

"Browned by the sun of the Bhomiri Islands, but the color will fade. Perhaps nightly milk-rinses for her skin might—"

"Her facial expression is displeasing—it lacks innocence. I think the fault lies in the contour of her lips, which are too full for true refinement, and seem set in a perpetual pout."

"Your own sense of justice, sir, will hardly permit you to blame our daughter for the shape of her mouth," Gilinne suggested respectfully.

"I do not hold her culpable." The Judge favored his wife with a penetrating glance, as if suspicious of veiled levity. "But the soundness of my judgment reveals itself all too clearly in the sorry reality of her present situation. She has, through her obstinacy and imprudence, stained herself in the eyes of the world, and the results are all too apparent. She is aging, unwed, and certain to remain so. She willfully threw away her best chance, and now all chances are gone."

"But she is only twenty-five," Gilinne appealed, "and still so handsome. Perhaps it is not yet time to give up all hope? I have it upon good authority that Master Girays v'Alisante has returned to the city—"

The name shot along Luzelle's nerves like a jolt of electricity, finally breaking her paralysis.

"And the women pursue him in droves, but he remains unattached. I am convinced that our daughter's declaration of heartfelt contrition could persuade M. v'Alisante to take her back—"

"That's enough," Luzelle interrupted, pent rage and humiliation finding outlet at last. "There are a few things I wish to say to both of you, so please listen. In the first place, I'd like to point out that I've no intention whatsoever of contacting Master Girays v'Alisante. I do not care to speak to him, much less implore his forgiveness. M. v'Alisante and I are strangers. Should he presume to call on me, I will not be at home."

"Oh, but my dear——" Gilinne attempted.

"Secondly," Luzelle continued, "much as I regret the inadequacies of my face and figure, my carriage, clothing, hair color, intellect, and character, I must inform you that I am tolerably reconciled to all of them, and foresee no major alterations in the immediate future. I trust you are not unduly disappointed."

"I have prohibited insolence," Udonse reminded his daughter.

"I will try to bear that in mind, sir. And yet, with all due respect, I intend to answer certain comments you've made concerning my work——"

"As to that, I am prepared to render my decision. Understand well that this mad folly of self-sufficient self-employment ends, as of today. I have been remiss in allowing an ill-conceived and misguided experiment to continue far too long, but now I correct the error. Henceforth you will conform to normal standards of proper conduct. You will live quietly beneath your father's roof, submitting yourself to paternal authority. There will be no further appearances upon a public stage, and certainly no more of these abhorrent lectures. Should you desire an occupation, you may busy yourself with charity work, but you will accept no monetary compensation for your labors. You may still write, under a masculine nom de plume, but no manuscript will be submitted to a publisher before I have reviewed the text for suitability of subject matter and wholesomeness of content. Your infrequent excursions from the city of Sherreen will encompass the homes of those kinsmen willing to receive you, but you will not cross the borders of Vonahr—your days of unbridled vagabondage are over. Well, daughter—I trust I have made myself clear?"

"Perfectly, sir." Luzelle took a deep breath. When she spoke again, she managed to keep her voice even and her expression spuriously calm. "And I intend to follow your example. Let me make it very clear indeed to you that I do not choose to submit myself again to your authority, now or ever. I will continue to work and to live on my own, I will travel as necessity and inclination dictate, I will lecture and write as I please, and I will certainly demand fair payment for my efforts. No doubt my choices will displease you, which is regrettable, but alters nothing."

There followed a long moment of awful silence, broken at last by Gilinne Devaire's scandalized whisper, "Oh, Luzelle—to speak so to *the Judge!*"

"Do not trouble to remind her of her duty, madame—it is a useless effort," Udonse advised. "She is perverse, ungrateful, and rebellious by nature. You need only look into her eyes, to see there the pleasure she takes in defying her father."

You're quite right about that, Luzelle realized.

"But I do not think your complacency likely to prove long lived," the Judge advised his erring daughter. "Your rejection of all filial obligation frees me of paternal responsibility. Until such time as you return to my house, all ties between you and your parents are severed." His wife threw him a stricken, imploring glance, which he disregarded. "No longer a member of my family, you may expect no assistance from me, no recognition, and no support. Should you fall victim to injury or illness, do not come begging for money to pay the doctor. You'll have nothing from me, not so much as a copper biquin."

"I want nothing of yours!" Luzelle flared, her temper slipping its leash as if she were still seventeen. "I need nothing that you could possibly give."

"There you vastly flatter yourself." The Judge spoke with his habitual composure, but the icy clarity of his tone revealed the depth of his anger. "You fancy, I presume, that the monies bequeathed to you by your late maternal aunt ensure your lifelong comfort and security."

And freedom, Luzelle added silently.

"Perhaps that would be so, had you the prudence to husband your inheritance wisely. But you have squandered and continue to squander prodigal sums upon your useless, senseless international jaunts. At the rate you spend, your capital must soon exhaust itself. And when it does, you will come creeping back home, beseeching my pardon and support. Would you not prefer to spare us both that embarrassment?"

Luzelle's pulses jumped. Once again her father had demonstrated his damnable ability to verbalize her worst inner fears, but it wouldn't do to let him know that the shot had hit home. Assuming an air of indifference, she replied, "The foreign excursions are a necessity, for they furnish the material I use in the books, articles, and lectures by which I earn my living."

"I am to believe, then, that the income thus derived covers not only the cost of travel, but annual expenses as well? Shelter, food, fuel, clothing, and all the rest?"

Luzelle could feel the telltale color in her tanned cheeks deepen. Her whole face seemed to flame. The set of her father's lips communicated utter disdain. She hated that granite mask of his, but could hardly bring herself to lie to it.

"The balance sheet is not yet showing a profit," she admitted, "but my speaking fees are on the rise, my book sales are steadily increasing, and it's reasonable to expect that some day soon, possibly within the next six months"—*which is all the time I have left before my money runs out*—"my income will equal or even exceed my—"

"You waste the inheritance you are clearly unfit to control upon a foolish, futile endeavor," Udonse informed her. "You are no longer a green girl; it is time for you to recognize the reality of limited abilities and minimal talents that doom your efforts to inevitable failure. Presently bankrupt and facing eviction from your lodgings, you will admit defeat to yourself, if to nobody else. What then? Will you select a more lucrative profession, becoming in truth what so many already believe you to be?"

"Perhaps!" Luzelle fired back, and inner demons prompted her to add, "The alternative you suggest is preferable to life beneath your roof, Father!"

Gilinne Devaire began to cry, the silent tears streaming down her cheeks.

Compunction seized Luzelle. "Mother, I'm sorry," she attempted. "I never meant to grieve you—"

"You have grieved the two of us since the day you were born," the Judge declared. "And now you shame us."

Gilinne shook her head weakly, but did not venture to contradict him.

"Mother, please don't cry. It was stupid of me to lose my temper, and—"

"Leave her alone," His Honor commanded. "Have you not done enough harm? You will address your remarks to me."

"There are many remarks I might gladly address to you, but they will have to wait." Luzelle strove hard for self-control. "As I mentioned, I've an appointment, and I cannot afford to miss it. Sir, madame, I bid you good afternoon." Dropping a small, brusque curtsy, she turned and made for the exit.

"One moment," the Judge commanded.

Automatically she halted, and could have kicked herself for that unthinking obedience.

"As you choose to disassociate yourself from your family, I must require you to relinquish the surname to which you no longer possess legitimate claim," Udonse charged her. "You will understand that I cannot allow public shame or scandal to touch the name of Devaire."

Intolerable. Luzelle's self-restraint flagged for a reckless instant.

"The name of Devaire," she proclaimed, "will spread itself across the front pages of newspapers all over the world when I win the Grand Ellipse." Head held high, she turned and marched from the auditorium. Had he ordered her to stay, she was prepared this time to defy him, but he did not offer her that satisfaction.

She emerged into the foyer, empty save for a quiet figure occupying one of the spindly plush-seated chairs placed along the walls. It was a man, discreetly dark clad, unremarkable, easily overlooked. His grey-streaked head was bent over a book, but he looked up as she came through the door and Luzelle glimpsed a long-nosed, studious face, pasty indoor complexion, and a flash of light glancing off wire-rimmed spectacles. At once he slid the book into a coat pocket and rose to his feet. She saw then that he was medium sized, narrow shouldered, and skinny. More than anything else he resembled an aging academic, at home in his present surroundings. He advanced, and it occurred to her to wonder if he had overheard any or all of the wretched exchange between herself and the Judge.

"Miss Devaire." He bowed. "Allow me to express my admiration of a lecture at once eloquent, informative, and absorbing."

"You are most generous, sir." Her cheeks were still hot and her heart still hammered. Did he notice? His face was unrevealing as it was nondescript. "Deputy Underminister vo Rouvignac, is it?"

"It is. I take it you have received and reviewed my letter."

She inclined her head.

"May we discuss the contents?"

"Yes, but not here." Any moment her parents would emerge from the auditorium, and she did not want to confront them a second time. "One minute, please."

Before he could reply, she ducked into the cloakroom, found her pelisse and hat, hurriedly donned both, then paused an instant to check the result in the mirror hanging beside the door.

Bad, as usual. "*. . . the vulgarity of your appearance . . .*" Her father's words rang in her mind. He was right, of course. Her angry color was still too high, for even now, despite advancing age, she had never fully mastered that troublesome temper of hers. Her lips were too red, as if painted, and too noticeable. Her wide eyes of pale, pure aquamarine, still ablaze with emotion, glared out of her sun-bronzed face like coach lanterns. The density of long lashes and the arch of strong brows several shades darker than her hair only heightened the objectionably obvious contrast. The general effect, despite the sobriety of conservative dark-blue garments, was arguably . . . *garish*. Again she could hear her father's voice.

She didn't want to hear his voice or think of what he had to say about her. She wanted to get out of the building. She sped from the cloakroom, and there was the Deputy Underminister vo Rouvignac regarding her with an eyebrow cocked quizzically.

"Ready," she told him, and rushed for the exit. She knew without looking that he followed.

They emerged into University Square, where the grey stone architecture of the ancient lecture halls echoed the grey of an overcast sky. A fine rain, scarcely more than mist, sprinkled down to cool Luzelle's heated face. Drawing a hungry draft of chilly air, she cast her eye about the square. Thronged with students, as always during term time afternoons: unshaven youngsters, sporting their caps and long woolen scarves with native Sherreenian panache. Busy, vital. Edged with ornamental shrubs just beginning to bud. A few yards distant loomed the old Nirienne Bell Tower, originally known as the King's Tower, a title lost in the aftermath of the last century's great revolution. Likewise lost—the famous Ten Monarchs, once ranged in an arc before the entrance. Those life-sized effigies of Vonahr's greatest kings were long gone, reduced to marble gravel by a furious mob over sixty-five years ago. The space they once occupied now belonged to an uninspired bronze statue of Shorvi Nirienne, Father of the Republic, whose writings had fueled the revolutionary ardor that toppled a monarchy.

The last hereditary king of Vonahr had died at the hands of his subjects, while the aristocratic class once known as Exalted had suffered a drastic pruning. Those formerly-Exalteds so fortunate as to survive the revolution had found themselves stripped of ancient privileges, noble titles, family wealth and possessions—stripped of everything beyond inviolable arrogance. That serene assumption of innate superiority lived on, proof against every assault of reason and reality. Oddly enough, the present-day world seemed full of simpletons quite ready to furnish the deference to which so many descendants of exterminated seigneurs imagined themselves entitled.

Luzelle Devaire did not number among such simpletons. She slanted a sidelong glance at her companion. Deputy Underminister vo Rouvignac, whose name marked him as a formerly-Exalted, projected none of the traditional hauteur of his class. His aspect was professorial and unassuming. *Unlike Master Girays v'Alisante.*

The *Marquis* v'Alisante, as he would have been, but for the small matter of the Vonahrish Revolution that had deprived his grandfather of title and of life. Very much the would-be grand seigneur. Pretentious, self-important, insufferable ass. Back in town again. *The women pursue him in droves. . . .*

Let them, and welcome. She'd far more important matters to consider.

"I know a good café in Cider Alley," vo Rouvignac's voice broke in on her thoughts. "Would you like a cup of tea? Or would you rather walk?"

"The Ministry of Foreign Affairs isn't far off," she countered bluntly. "That is surely the proper place to conduct an ordinary business interview?"

"The business at hand is far from ordinary." Vo Rouvignac never blinked. "And best transacted discreetly."

"Why?" Luzelle challenged, suppressing all visible signs of uneasiness. Already the exchange showed signs of fulfilling her father's worst predictions.

"Because, Miss Devaire, should you decide to accept our offer of sponsorship, it is very much in the best interests of all concerned that your connection to the ministry remain generally unrecognized. That is for your protection as well as our own."

"Protection from what?"

"Hostile attention."

"I'm accustomed to that. Thank you for the warning, but it comes a little late. Your letter failed to request confidentiality and I've already shown it to my father, thus drawing considerable hostile attention."

"That is not quite what I meant." Vo Rouvignac smiled a little. "Throughout his life, the Judge Udonse Devaire has demonstrated consistent devotion to Vonahrish interests. His loyalty is hardly open to question. I spoke not of your family members, but—"

"You did, sir," Luzelle interrupted. "And with considerable assurance. How should you know anything of my father's attitudes or actions?"

"Surely it can't surprise you to learn that your background has been investigated."

"Investigated—I? How dare you?"

"I assure you, a standard safeguard—"

"An offensive invasion of privacy!"

"A woman so much in the public eye as yourself, Miss Devaire, may scarcely expect to enjoy the anonymity of a more commonplace individual."

Commonplace? Respectable, did he mean? No matter, Luzelle decided. She was capable of dealing with this latest critic. Her chin came up, and she drew a preparatory breath.

"Please understand," vo Rouvignac forestalled her, "that I mean no disrespect. You will perceive the necessity of our precautions, once you come to appreciate the delicacy of the situation we now confront."

"You offer to sponsor my participation in the Hetzian king's Grand Ellipse race. What's particularly delicate about that?"

"On the face of it nothing, and that is all to the good. Have you not stopped to wonder, however, why the Ministry of Foreign Affairs would choose to concern itself in this matter?"

"Vonahrish prestige," Luzelle returned at once. "The Grand Ellipse is attracting international attention. The newspapers and sporting gazettes have focused upon the competition for weeks. Speculation is intense, and I've read of enormous sums wagered upon the outcome. The victor, whoever it may be, garners great glory for his or her own country." *And a valuable piece of real estate for herself.*

"Quite true. Yet the sponsorship of a well-equipped contestant demands a considerable outlay of capital, and the endeavor itself might be termed frivolous. A large expense of such dubious necessity is particularly difficult to justify now, at a time of national crisis."

"The national crisis seems to have escaped my notice, Deputy Underminister."

"Understandable. Relatively few of our countrymen realize that invasion is imminent. In the near future—possibly a matter of weeks—Vonahr will be assaulted by forces of the Grewzian Imperium. For the present, it is best that the threat continue largely unrecognized."

Luzelle stared at him.

"The information I am about to impart is sensitive," vo Rouvignac continued. "I believe, however, that you are fit to receive it. But come, let us find someplace and go indoors. It is starting to rain in earnest."

The big drops were now pattering down fatly. Students were running for cover. Bowing her head against the onslaught, Luzelle accepted the arm her companion offered, and together they hurried across University Square into the mouth of Cider Alley, where the overhang of the old-fashioned houses afforded shelter. Presently they reached a small but very smartly painted café, and entered to find the place crowded with rain-spotted refugees. Vo Rouvignac managed to commandeer the last unoccupied table, beside the kitchen door. Seating themselves, they ordered lemon tea. For some moments neither spoke.

The steaming mugs arrived. Luzelle took a sip and set her drink aside. Meeting vo Rouvignac's eyes, she answered him at last; characteristically, with a question.

"How do you know that the Grewzians plan an invasion?"

"The independent reports of several agents confirm it," he told her. "Even were that not so, the situation is self-explanatory to those who take note of such things."

"Anyone who reads the newspapers knows that the Imperior Ogron favors expansion. He's annexed or invaded various territories to which, theoretically, Grewzland possesses legitimate claim—"

"Utterly false justifications, for the most part."

"—certain foreign allies of the ousted governments have offered active resistance, which the imperior has crushed—"

"Attacking upon the flimsiest of pretexts."

"—but the Grewzian activities have generally directed themselves eastward. Well, to the south also, these days. There's nothing I've read or heard to suggest that the imperior has any intention of shifting his attention west toward Vonahr. Certainly Grewzland possesses no reasonable claim to Vonahrish soil, and cannot pretend otherwise. We've attempted no meddling in Grewzian affairs, offered neither threat nor provocation. Furthermore, the Imperium now comprises such a vast area, it hardly seems probable that

Ogron should regard a Vonahrish conquest as necessary or even desirable—"

"Miss Devaire, you are an intelligent young person and reasonably well informed, but more than a little naive," vo Rouvignac observed, so mildly that the words lost their sting. "You argue upon the assumption that Grewzian policy is the product of rational, well-intentioned, more or less civilized intellects. In reality, nothing could be further from the truth. Grewzian policy is dictated by the will of the Imperior Ogron III. The imperior, a vainglorious mystic fancying himself a latter-day embodiment of the Gorzlaar of Grewzian folklore, is the natural scion of a culture traditionally celebrating personal courage, martial prowess, and fanatical patriotism. The Gorzlaar, if you'll recall, is a legendary warrior-king-god destined to conquer all the civilized world, thus leading the Grewzian people to their glorious collective destiny. The imperior has embarked upon this project with much élan, and assuredly will not cease either until he has accomplished his goal or until he is forcibly halted."

She believed him. Something in his dry professorial certainty convinced her, and she attempted no further denial, but instead inquired, "If that's true, why keep it a secret? Shouldn't our people be warned?"

"Such a move would only hasten the Grewzian assault."

"But Vonahr must arm herself, and quickly. The army must mobilize, the border cities strengthen their defenses, the munition factories increase production, the navy modernize its—"

"Useless," vo Rouvignac cut her off calmly. "Moments earlier you mentioned the newspapers and gazettes. If you read them, then you already know that the Imperior Ogron has spent the last half decade or so preparing his country for war. And to give credit where it's due, he has done an excellent job. Grewzland now possesses the largest, best-equipped, and best-trained army in the world; an unsurpassed navy; the most modern and efficient factories and railroads; great natural resources—its own, augmented by those seized from a growing roster of subject nations; a skilled and enthusiastic workforce; and, thanks to the great war effort, a flourishing economy. While the imperior has thus busied himself, we Vonahrish have essentially . . . fiddled. The inattention of years is not to be remedied in a matter of weeks. I assure you, we are quite unfit to resist the impending invasion."

"But we are not alone." Luzelle's mind cast swiftly about in search of salvation. "The city-states and western Republican-Enclaves must surely recognize the Grewzian threat. Kyrendt, Travorn, Ferille—clearly it would be to the advantage of all to form a defensive alliance with Vonahr."

"Not a bad thought, saving the sad reality that the condition of the nations in question hardly differs from our own. They can furnish little assistance."

"What are you saying, then?" Luzelle demanded. "That Vonahr is about to disappear down the maw of the Grewzian Imperium, and there's nothing at all we can do about it? Perhaps you advise immediate and unconditional surrender?"

"That, at least, would avert wholesale destruction."

"What sort of wretched weak-livered talk is that, coming from a Vonahrish official? Have you any *idea* how those Grewzian pigs treat their conquered territories?"

"A pretty clear one, I believe. Please calm yourself, Miss Devaire. I admire your spirit, but must advise you to rein it in until you've heard all I have to say. I do not advocate surrender at this time. There is another possibility worthy of investigation. It involves a new and potentially devastating weapon, of—er—arcane origin."

"You surprise me. I didn't think anyone in today's government would admit to a belief in the significance of arcane phenomena. A world blessed with gaslight, steam engines, and indoor plumbing has no further need of sorcery and superstition, or so I've been told." So she had indeed been told, more than once, by no less than Master Girays v'Alisante himself. And he'd dismissed her arguments to the contrary with that intolerable superior smugness of his. She only wished that he could be here now to discover how wrong he had been.

"The ancient disciplines are by no means bereft of their partisans or their practitioners," vo Rouvignac observed. "Even today there are princes and presidents aplenty known to seek counsel of sorcerous savants. One such ruler is Miltzin

IX, king of the Low Hetz. Miltzin, a collector of human odd-
ities, extends his patronage to a number of so-called magical
adepts. The favored group includes several known swindlers
and confidence men, but at least one member is widely believed to possess genuine talent of a high order. This man—
calling himself 'Nevenskoi,' and claiming unverifiable
Rhazaullean nationality—has let it be known to his sorcerous
colleagues all over the civilized world that he has succeeded in
kindling a new form of fire, a blaze imbued with rudimentary
sentience and subject to its creator's human will."

"The *fire* is supposed to be aware?" Luzelle demanded. Her
companion nodded, and she opined, "Nonsense!"

"You may well think so, but in fact the report has been
confirmed. Too many reliable correspondents have submitted
eyewitness accounts of remarkable demonstrations at King
Miltzin's Waterwitch Palace to doubt the truth of Nevenskoi's
disclosure. Clearly this Rhazaullean adept has accomplished
all that he claims. The Sentient Fire exists. It is capable of un-
supervised advance or retreat, expansion, contraction, glut-
tonous consumption or self-denial, all at the behest of its
human master. The potential military value of such a discovery at this time is incalculable, particularly to those among us
disinclined to cultivate a taste for Grewzian offal pudding and
Imperiorstein ale."

"Hard to believe, with so many so certain that the old arts
are dead," Luzelle murmured. "You're certain there's no mistake and no trickery?"

"Entirely certain."

"But how agreeable for His Majesty Miltzin. I suppose the
bidding is feverish."

"By no means. The king will have none of it. Determined
to preserve traditional Hetzian neutrality, Miltzin has declared himself unwilling to part with the secret, to anyone, at
any price. Already he has declined a bouquet of assorted offers, resisting the eloquence of the world's most persuasive
ambassadors, including our own. His Majesty displays no
sign of weakening, but perhaps the continual importuning
has begun to fray the royal nerves. As of last week, all known

foreign representatives were expelled from the Low Hetz. Requests for audiences with the king are routinely denied. Diplomatic correspondence is perused by Miltzin's personal secretaries, and no plea pertaining to the Sentient Fire is permitted to reach the king's eyes."

"Is His Majesty blessed with a singular sense of humor, or is he merely feebleminded?"

"He is an eccentric one, beyond doubt."

"Aren't there ways of circumventing eccentricity? The Low Hetz hardly qualifies as a great power. What's to prevent Vonahr from loosing a few regiments upon the city of Toltz, seizing this Nevenskoi, his records and arcana, and conveying all back home to Sherreen without further ado? And why don't we strike before the Grewzians think of doing the same? Doesn't it seem to you that every second of delay is—"

"Softly, Miss Devaire. Do you imagine that you are the first to think of that? The scheme is enterprising but impractical. You see, Miltzin IX keeps his tame sorcerer stowed away in a secret workroom hidden somewhere in the depths of the Waterwitch Palace. The workroom's location is known to few. Moreover, the Waterwitch itself—built on a small island set amid treacherous swamplands outside of Toltz—is accessible only by means of three successive drawbridges. This location and design, evidently appealing to His Majesty's sense of whimsy, in fact provide excellent defense. An assault upon the palace is sure to be a protracted affair, during the course of which Nevenskoi and his knowledge will undoubtedly vanish, perhaps forever."

"I see."

"Do you?"

"Not the whole of it." Luzelle studied her companion. "Why are you telling me all of this, Deputy Underminister? I assume it's connected in some way to the Grand Ellipse and the ministry's offer of sponsorship, but I don't see how."

"You recall the prize awaiting the winner of the race?"

"A Hetzian peerage, I believe, together with some sort of house or castle." Whose sale might keep her financially afloat, thus preserving independence, freedom, and pride.

"And one other thing—a private audience with Miltzin IX. A rare, almost unique, opportunity for a foreign emissary to catch the ear of the king."

"That's it, then?" Luzelle inquired in disbelief. "All of this elaborate, expensive strategy of sponsoring a Grand Ellipse contestant, in the faint hope that your candidate will, against all odds, not only win the race but then go on to somehow persuade the king of the Low Hetz to sell a secret that he has so far firmly refused to part with?"

"To sell the secret, or at the very least to reveal—perhaps inadvertently—the whereabouts of Master Nevenskoi."

"Rather a long shot, isn't it?"

"Better than no shot, Miss Devaire."

"Why, you people must be as loony as Mad Miltzin himself!"

"I would prefer to think otherwise. Actually, matters in Toltz have lately shown signs of change. We have it upon good authority that King Miltzin's latest enthusiasm—an investigation of the approaching Grizhni Comet's communicative properties—severely strains the depleted Hetzian treasury. The construction of the new Phoenixfire Palace at Jüschl imposes another large burden. Last summer's drought, so destructive of the Hetzian lorber crops, inflicts additional damage. In short, there's reason to hope at this juncture that a generous cash offer, appropriately presented, might find His Majesty receptive."

"Appropriately presented?"

"Set forth in the manner best calculated to touch the king's heart, as well as his mind."

"Doesn't that call for the talents of an experienced diplomat?" she inquired carefully. "Forgive my dullness, but I don't understand why you've come to me. Not that I don't appreciate the compliment, but aren't there better-qualified candidates to be found?"

"Your qualifications are most unusual, and ideally suited to the task at hand." He studied her dispassionately. "In the first place, your public reputation as an adventurous, courageous traveler justifies your participation in the race. Then, your gender masks your mission, for the enemies of Vonahr won't readily credit official reliance upon a female. And finally, your personal attributes are more than likely to impress His Majesty in your favor."

"Personal attributes? I'm not certain I understand you." She was not certain that she wanted to.

"To speak plainly, Miss Devaire, you are a woman of uncommonly striking appearance, and the king's tender susceptibility is well documented. Moreover, you are recognized as a lady of some worldly knowledge, experience, and sophistication, quite capable, should you so choose, of exploiting your many resources to best advantage in the service of your country. Thus it is much to be hoped that the charm of the messenger may greatly influence King Miltzin's response to our offer."

He spoke gracefully enough, but his meaning was clear, and not pretty. Luzelle took a thoughtful sip of tea, and briefly considered tossing the contents of the mug straight into the face of the deputy underminister. She controlled the impulse; vo Rouvignac intended no insult, after all. If he, along with the rest of the world, regarded her as a woman of questionable character, she had only herself to blame.

"The ministry's approach to the problem is novel." She let nothing show on her face. "In fact, your methods surprise me. Deputy Underminister, have you and your associates not considered the possibility of public embarrassment, should this afternoon's meeting come to light?"

"I do not believe that it will come to light." The potentially menacing observation sounded merely avuncular upon vo Rouvignac's lips. "Should I misjudge, however, whatever embarrassment or trouble that comes will be mine alone, for the minister of foreign affairs will deny all knowledge of the matter. If necessary I am prepared to assume full personal responsibility."

"I understand." She did indeed. Quite clear now why she hadn't been invited to set foot within the sacred confines of the Republican Complex.

Time now for the indignant refusal, the flash of outraged virtue, but Luzelle held her tongue, for the alternatives were bleak. She stood within six months or so of financial ruin, preceding the most humiliating imaginable return to her father's house. Once she vanished into that well-ordered limbo, she might never again emerge. On the other hand, should she compete in the Grand Ellipse at the ministry's expense, her participation alone was sure to draw public notice, boosting the sale of her books and increasing her value as a lecturer. And should she actually win the race, then her fame, fortune, and independence were assured for the rest of her life.

What then? Will you select a more lucrative profession, becoming in truth what so many already believe you to be?

I will, she silently informed her father, *if that's the only way to live free in the world. I will let nothing and nobody stop me. Whatever is necessary—*

"I will do it," she finished aloud.

"Miss Devaire?" The deputy underminister looked surprised.

"I accept your offer of sponsorship. I will run the Grand Ellipse. And make no mistake, I will win. I'll use whatever means I must, I'll do anything." Her companion was staring at her, so Luzelle added for good measure, "Anything at all."

2

EXACTLY ONE WEEK LATER she set off for the Low Hetz. The journey between Sherreen and the Hetzian capital city of Toltz demanded three days and two nights of travel by rail, but Luzelle spent the time comfortably. The cash with which the Ministry of Foreign Affairs had so amply supplied her purchased the softest lavender-scented berth in the sleeping car, the costliest of fare in the dining car, the most solicitous of porters, waiters, and conductors all along the route. It was a far cry indeed from her customarily economical mode of travel.

The unusual spectacle of a young woman traveling on her own drew the inevitable speculative attention, but those squadrons of well-paid menials furnished effective protection, and nobody harassed her.

The tracks between two such prominent capitals as Sherreen and Toltz were well maintained, and the journey northeast proceeded smoothly, through miles of rich Vonahrish farmland, over the rolling terrain of rural VoGrance Province, then down the hills and across the border into the Low Hetz, whose political neutrality immediately proclaimed itself.

The train wheezed to a halt at Lolkstok Station, and the local customs officials tramped on through the cars, demanding passports and declarations. Luzelle signed the appropriate documents, submitted her modest luggage to inspection, received the requisite stamp upon her passport, then directed her attention out the window to the platform, where, for the first time, she spied uniformed Grewzian soldiers.

They didn't look so bad—many, in fact, were distinctly handsome, with those Grewzian long-limbed frames and those Grewzian chiseled straight noses. Unjustly maligned, perhaps. The accounts of atrocities inflicted upon helpless subject populations were probably exaggerated.

Won't those clean-cut lads look just splendid, marching in triumph through the streets of Sherreen. In a matter of weeks, the deputy underminister had informed her.

The train departed Lolkstok Station, traveling north through many an improbably quaint gabled and half-timbered medieval town, over flowery meadows impossibly idyllic, to reach Toltz in the soft gloom of springtime dusk.

Luzelle alighted. A porter whisked her luggage into the station house and disappeared, reappearing moments later with a cabdriver in tow. Money changed hands, and her valise seemed to fly to the waiting vehicle, which was lower, wider, and heavier than a Sherreenian fiacre, and drawn by a correspondingly sturdy Hetzian bay. Luzelle climbed in and the door closed. The driver ascended, the whip snapped, and the cab clattered off.

She sank back into a fat upholstered seat deeper and softer than she had expected. Unlike her own countrymen, these Lower Hetzians favored comfort over elegance, and she meant to enjoy it while she could, for circumstances would alter once the race began. *Tomorrow.* The thought quickened her pulse. Only another few hours to go.

She looked out the window. The gaslight glowed through the deepening twilight, warming the pale stone faces of mansions, monuments, and ceremonial archways frilled and curlicued in the shamelessly ornate style of the previous century. Sherreen, Flugeln, Lis Folaze—virtually every capital city boasted its architectural extravaganzas, but nowhere else in all the world did the embellishment reach such heights of exuberance as here in the Low Hetz. The most elaborate structure in sight, however—the famous Aspiration Tower, a white marble effusion clothed from top to bottom in bas-relief carvings of lunatic complexity—was modern; a testament to the artistic zeal of the present king, Miltzin IX, whose heart she was required to touch.

The cab halted before the new Kingshead Hotel, a grand edifice recently replacing the King's Head Inn that had occupied the site for centuries. Many mourned the passing of the ancient inn, but undeniably the new hotel was a marvel of luxury and comfort equipped with every modern amenity, from gaslight in most chambers to an astonishing steam-powered lift. There were even private bathrooms in certain wildly extravagant suites.

The cab departed. Another porter carried her bag into a lobby ominously crowded. Taking her place in line before the registration desk, she glanced about. Was the place always so mobbed? If not, what accounted for this evening's crush?

The race, idiot.

Of course. The commencement of the Grand Ellipse *(tomorrow!)* was attracting international attention. The betting was frenetic; the gain or loss of fortunes rested upon the outcome. Sportsmen of every stripe had converged upon Toltz to see the racers off.

The Kingshead Hotel could not hold them all. Would-be guests were being turned away by the dozen. Theoretically the Ministry of Foreign Affairs had arranged her reservation, but in the event of a misunderstanding—

The line inched forward. Luzelle confronted the clerk and gave her name. No misunderstanding. Miss Devaire was expected, and her room awaited her. Miss Devaire was exceedingly welcome to the Kingshead. He was a very well schooled, discreet clerk, displaying no flicker of that impertinent curiosity she had so often encountered during the course of her travels.

He handed her a key and she followed her bag across the lobby to that incredible brand-new lift—the first she had ever seen—which bore her, to her delight, effortlessly from the ground floor all the way up to the fourth. Abandoning the lift with reluctance, she proceeded along a lushly carpeted corridor to her own room—not one of the miracle suites with a private bath, but spacious and very comfortable indeed. She tipped the bellboy generously, and the lad all but genuflected. Affluence was so enjoyable.

Alone again, she let her eyes travel the chamber. Gleaming, ponderous walnut furnishings, heavily carved in the Hetzian fashion. Tall windows along two walls, with big glass panes, obviously of modern manufacture. Thick, wine-colored carpet, matching dark-red brocade curtains and counterpane. Dark-red towels on the rack above the washstand, fresh cake of soap, generously sized pitcher and basin. Brass spittoon, polished and mercifully empty. Attractive, expensive, impersonal.

Luzelle consulted her pocket watch and her stomach, both of which told her that the dinner hour had not yet arrived. Opening her bag, she burrowed within to extract a pasteboard folder full of documents, product of anonymous bureaucratic labor. The papers included a set of maps detailing the entire curve of the Grand Ellipse; a fine assortment of tickets and tokens; a suggested itinerary; lists of hotels and inns; a fistful of railroad, stagecoach, and steamship timetables; and an international directory of commercial transport enterprises that included riverboats, livery stables, rafts, barges, the Big Wormworks, gliders, chasmistrios, hoppers, bumpers, sleighs, dogsleds, treeswingers, and more.

Her own experience in traveling had taught her the inevitability of the unexpected. Still, this pile of detailed information had to be worth something. No doubt she'd be glad she had it, someday.

And perhaps sooner than she expected. For the course of the Grand Ellipse, initially transecting the modern, comparatively civilized western nations, stretched far eastward, curving through the remote mountainous reaches of largely untamed Bizaqh and Zuleekistan, through the savage forests of Oorex, even as far as exotic Aveshq. In the weeks to come, one of those stiff little lists or maps supplied by the ministry could conceivably spell the difference between victory and defeat.

The chimes of a large clock somewhere nearby sounded the hour. Time to change for dinner, and the choice of garments was easy, for she had brought but one remotely suitable dress—a very simple, long-sleeved affair of heavy black silk twill, resistant to wrinkling, forgiving of stains, and devoid of the boning and flounces that would have devoured precious space in a suitcase. She buttoned herself into it and studied the result in the mirror above the washstand.

Sedate, almost as sedate as the Judge himself might have desired, although the indiscreet radiance of her red-gold curls would never have met with His Honor's approval. The plain, modest scoop neck of the gown screamed for decoration. Returning to her valise, she extracted the one small vanity permitted to add its weight to her luggage—a necklace and matching earrings of silver set with aquamarines the color of her eyes; pretty pieces, but not valuable enough to draw the attention of thieves. She put them on, and the image in the mirror sparkled to life. His Honor would not have been pleased.

She went down to the gently lit hotel restaurant, where an impeccably impassive headwaiter seated her alone, and not at a bad table. No doubtful or suspicious hesitation, no lifted brows, no hiding the unescorted female behind the potted palms.

A waiter took her order and retired, leaving her to wait. In earlier years she had never ventured into a public restaurant, inn, café, or cookshop without a book in hand; any random volume in which to bury her nose and her acute self-consciousness. These days, inured to the curiosity of strangers, she could afford to let her eyes range the room freely.

The place was well filled, like the hotel itself. The patrons appeared solvent, and some of them were prosperous indeed, judging by the prevalence of well-tailored jackets, ambitious gowns, and assertive jewelry. A scattering of plaid coats, diamond stickpins, and masculine pinkie rings betrayed the presence of professional sportsmen and gamblers. Their feminine companions were prone to yellow hair piled high and satin dresses cut low. There were a few men in uniforms bearing the insignia of officers, and a few others swathed in exotic robes, who might have been pleasure-jaunting eastern princelings, or perhaps simply rich eccentrics. Conversation was lively but

muted, voices pitched politely low. Therefore the two refusing
to modulate themselves were impossible to ignore.

A braying of laughter racketed through the restaurant.
Luzelle turned to look, and thought she was seeing double. A
few tables away sat a brace of young men, perhaps eighteen or
nineteen years of age. They were expensively and identically
dressed, from their wide-lapelled mauve jackets, to their
pearl-grey satin ascots, to the spray of fresh violets each wore
in his buttonhole. They were similarly identical in every detail
of prettily youthful form and feature. Twins, and apparently
rich ones. Four bottles of champagne stood open between
them—the best Vonahrish champagne, Belle of Sevagne, the
famous hexagonal gold label recognizable at a glance. Two
hundred fifty New-rekkoes per bottle, and these boys were
swigging it like cheap beer. A platter of expensive rockclingers
in blue-butter sauce sat on the table. The twins were flipping
bits of shellfish off their forks at one another, each successful
shot giving rise to uproarious laughter.

Idiots.

Luzelle's dinner arrived. For a time she applied herself to
her Consommé Dhreve Lissildt, venison medallions, beet-
and-lorber salad, braised goldtuber, and Hetzian cracklers.
But the hilarity at the twins' table never abated, and she
found herself wondering who the merry imbeciles might be,
why they were allowed to travel without a nanny, and if by
any chance they could be a couple of her fellow racers. The
restaurant might easily contain a number of Grand Ellipse
contestants. There was no way of identifying them by sight,
and her gaze wandered, only to fasten within seconds upon a
table in a corner.

Two men sat there, one approximately her own age, the
other some quarter century older. The senior member of the
pair possessed what was probably a very interesting, square-
jawed countenance, but she hardly noticed, for the other one,
the younger, was perhaps the handsomest man she had ever
seen. He had a lean, fair, clear-cut face, with beautifully
formed features; large, intelligent light eyes, whose color was
impossible to judge at the moment; and hair of the bright
golden hue that women often dyed for, but never successfully

achieved by artificial means. The really remarkable quality of
that face, Luzelle decided, lay less in its perfection of structure, noteworthy though that was, than in its individuality of
expression. Something in the eyes, the bend of the lips, the
entire cast of countenance, somehow conveyed an impression
of—what? Purity? Innate decency? Natural goodness?

Rather a lot to read into good bones and a head of yellow
hair. He was probably a vain, spoiled, womanizing fop, ad-
dicted to brandy, dicing, and his own mirror image. She
noted that he wore a military uniform. She could not make
out the nationality, but the sight rang faint bells in her memory. That handsome face, she realized, wasn't altogether unfamiliar. She had certainly never before seen it in the flesh, but
somewhere, not long ago, she'd seen a picture of it. *Newspaper? Gazette?*

He must have sensed the pressure of her regard, for he
turned his head and looked straight at her. Luzelle felt the
embarrassed color flood her face. Caught, undeniably caught
staring. Well, this particular man was surely used to being
gawked at by women. He probably imagined she was about to
swoon over him, for good-looking men were so conceited—

He smiled slightly across the room at her, as if they shared
a small joke, and it was such an engaging expression, so devoid of affectation or presumption, that her discomfort vanished at once and she smiled back at him, holding his eyes for
a moment or two before breaking the voiceless contact.

It took considerable self-control, but she did not glance in
his direction again until he and his companion paid their bill
and rose from their chairs. She risked a final covert peek then,
and saw that he was splendidly tall and broad shouldered,
with the trim, powerful build of an athlete. And she saw
something more. The stranger wore the smartly cut grey uniform and insignia of a Grewzian overcommander. He was a
servant of the Imperium, which meant that he was a pig in
human form. So much for all ridiculous thoughts of fine faces
reflecting fine character.

The blond officer and his older companion—a civilian,
clad in faultless evening wear, she dimly registered—exited
the restaurant. The remaining patrons, even the noisy twins,

faded into obscurity. Luzelle sipped a frolloberry liqueur, and considered. She was annoyed with herself. Her heart had quickened like a silly schoolgirl's when that gorgeous Grewzian swine had smiled at her; at her age she should have better sense.

She finished her drink, paid her reckoning, and walked out into the lobby, where she purchased a newspaper. For a while she entertained herself by riding the wondrous lift up and down. When the novelty began to pall, she returned to her own room, there to settle down with the *Toltziancityspeakerof.* At least that was how the nameplate literally translated into Vonahrish. She could read Hetzian, more or less. There was news of the Grand Ellipse, news of King Miltzin's activities, news of a thoroughly illegal duel in some local park, and above all, news of the Grewzian campaign. The Imperior Ogron, it seemed, had fixed his attention upon the small, essentially defenseless principality of Haereste. Which shared a border with Vonahr. Even now the imperior's troops were advancing upon the latest target, which would undoubtedly fall without a struggle. *And then?*

Luzelle tossed the newspaper aside with a scowl. She undressed, washed, donned a nightgown, climbed into bed, and occupied herself for a time with her maps, lists, and timetables, which proved dependably soporific. When her lids began to droop, she extinguished the lights, but did not fall asleep at once, for her mind was too active, too filled with anticipation of the contest that she *would* win, the competition so soon to begin—

Tomorrow.

SHE HAD TIPPED ONE OF THE CHAMBERMAIDS to knock on her door at seven in the morning, but she woke spontaneously at the break of dawn. Much too early, but she hadn't a prayer of resuming her slumbers. Luzelle rose, washed, dressed in her practical grey-green traveling suit, coiled and pinned her curls into submission, and repacked her suitcases.

Still too early.

Descending to the nearly deserted lobby, she checked out

at the desk, then repaired to the hotel restaurant, just now opening its doors for the day. There she sat for the next hour, gulping cup after cup of milky coffee, scrutinizing fellow customers, and periodically consulting her watch. She knew she ought to order a solid Hetzian breakfast, but her stomach fluttered at the notion.

Outside, the sun climbed. Inside, the seemingly petrified hands of the watch progressed a couple of degrees, liberating her at last. She carried her own bags out to the street, where the doorman summoned a cab for her. She entered, issued a command, and the vehicle set off along famous Toltzcutter Street.

The window displays in the world-renowned shops lining the avenue would ordinarily have claimed her attention, but she scarcely troubled to look at them today, nor did she cast more than a cursory glance upon any of the old city landmarks that she passed. Presently the cab entered old Irstreister Square, named after the first elected mayor of Toltz, and there along the eastern border of the square loomed the pompous city hall, her destination. And there, cramming the open space in front of the building, waited a sizable, holiday-spirited crowd. Spectators gathered to see the racers off, she decided, and it seemed odd, for there wouldn't be much to see—just a group of competitors, each sprinting for his or her conveyance of choice and pelting off down the city streets, most if not all of them headed for the train station. But the event had caught the public imagination.

The driver halted in front of city hall, as near the building as the crush of humanity permitted. On impulse Luzelle ordered him to take her around to a side entrance and to wait for her there with her luggage, then paid him generously enough to ensure his compliance. She went in, asked directions of a bent-backed sweeper, and made her way along the confusing corridors to the registrar's office, where she handed in her completed application forms, receiving in exchange a certificate of participation, together with a raised stamp upon her passport; hour, date, and location—*Toltzcityhouse, Lower Hetzia.* A second such stamp, placed at some unknown future date, would mark her completion of the Grand Ellipse.

Proceeding to the lofty foyer, official starting point of the race, she found the vast space teeming with visitors. She glanced about in momentary doubt, then noted the seething density of the crowd gathered about a gold-fringed scarlet canopy set up near the foot of the grand marble staircase upon which King Miltzin IX himself was shortly scheduled to appear. Beneath that canopy, the registrar had informed her, the Grand Ellipse contestants were to gather. She pushed her way toward it through the throng, but long before she drew near enough to glimpse the group assembled there, the crowd seemed to contract around her, and she heard her name spoken aloud, followed by a fusillade of questions chattered at her in Vonahrish, in Hetzian, and in several other languages that she did not recognize.

Luzelle halted, bewildered. The questions—those that she understood at all—made little sense. *"How do you view the competition, Miss Devaire?"* *"Luzelle, do you believe that a woman has any real chance of victory?"* *"Ca'lorphi gi nava re'flonvisse ghia, Mees D'va'r?"* *"Miss Devaire, have you consulted a prognosticator?"*

Prognosticator?

They had her closely surrounded. She couldn't move, and the din was appalling. She could barely think, much less answer. A few feet away some stranger with a notepad stood sketching her likeness, and then she understood. Journalists, dozens of them, scribbling reports for their various publications. They doubtless hoped for some sort of scandalous or at least controversial comment from her, but she was not about to oblige.

"Let me through, please," she requested politely. Nobody budged.

"What do you regard as the greatest obstacle you're likely to encounter en route?" *"Foru, Luzelle-ri, sakaito ubi Grand Ellipse-jho, chokuni okyoshin?"* *"Miss Devaire, what is your estimate of the—"* *"Tell us, Miss Devaire—"* The questions overlapped crazily. Her head was spinning.

"Please let me through," she repeated, and it still didn't work. They were crowding around her like hyenas, so close that someone's charnelhouse breath was actually stirring her hair. She was growing angry and a little afraid.

"*Mees D'va'ar*—"

Trapped. She resisted the impulse to hit or kick someone.

"*Miss Devaire*—"

"Must take her place with the other contestants," broke in a voice unmistakably Vonahrish, and impossibly familiar. "Gentlemen, if you will stand aside . . ."

She turned to the source and for a moment doubted her own eyes, for she looked up into a face that couldn't be there, a face she had excluded from her sight and her life years earlier. Excitement had surely overstimulated her imagination, for it couldn't be—

"Girays?" Her voice emerged in a small and idiotic squeak that would have embarrassed her, had not incredulity eclipsed all rival sensations. "Am I dreaming?"

"Of me? Honored indeed, Miss Devaire," replied Girays v'Alisante.

"A nightmare, then," Luzelle rejoined at once.

"Now, there we see the amiable disposition and exquisite manners I recall so well. You haven't changed in the least, Luzelle."

"You have," she returned maliciously. "You're looking older." This was somewhat true. His face—a little too long, a little too angular, a little too intellectual—with its deep-set dark eyes that missed nothing and its lines of agreeable fatigue—was a whisper wearier than she remembered. His hair, the color of unadulterated coffee, was thick and careless as ever, but a few silver threads glinted at his temples. Well, he was ten years her senior, after all. Be that as it may, he hadn't gained an ounce of weight—his frame was still elegantly lean as a dancer's. *Skinny*, she told herself. *Inconsequential*.

"Clear the way, gentlemen," Girays ordered, and that well-remembered, almost exaggeratedly upper-crust intonation of his commanded immediate respect. Which he, in the objectionable manner of his formerly-Exalted kind, accepted as his natural due.

A path opened. Girays offered his arm, which Luzelle took

reluctantly. She didn't want to accept his help, or obligate herself to him in any way. Should she refuse, however, she might never make it to the Grand Ellipse starting gate, much less the finish line. The journalists were still yammering, but at a bearable distance. Girays led her forward, and his unsettling proximity prompted her to say something, say anything.

"What in the world are you doing here?" she asked. "Have you come to see the racers off? Have you placed a wager?"

"I am a contestant like yourself," he told her. Her brows arched, and he added, "I am in earnest."

"And Belfaireau?" she inquired, still skeptical, for revolution notwithstanding, the ancestral château remained in the hands of the v'Alisante family, and its present master tended the estate with all the devotion of the ideal seigneur that he fancied himself to be. Not often or easily was Girays v'Alisante to be pried away from his beloved Belfaireau for so extended an interval as the Grand Ellipse represented.

"Safe in the hands of my capable Glimont," he told her.

Glimont? His household steward, she recalled, and her surprise deepened, impelling her to demand, "But—why?"

"A whim," he replied, to her frustration. "The race promises considerable novelty."

"Since when did you ever—"

"See, there are all the registered racers," he cut her off. "Do you not wish to inspect your rivals?"

She did indeed.

Beneath the scarlet canopy a little enclosure bounded by velvet ropes contained the Grand Ellipse contestants. There were no more than a dozen of them, herself and Girays included—fewer than she had expected in view of the prestige of the event and the magnitude of the prize, but understandable enough; for how many individuals actually possessed the time, freedom, and resources required to run King Miltzin's course?

The faces before her were interestingly varied in age, type, and expression. She spied only one other woman, which was one more than she had foreseen. Not entirely to her surprise or pleasure she recognized the youthful, noisy twins from the

Kingshead's restaurant. This morning the lads were identically turned out in sporty checked jackets and matching trousers, with red roses in their buttonholes. Neither seemed visibly the worse for recent champagne-soaked excesses. Behind the twins, his tall form towering over them by half a head, waited last night's unforgettable blond overcommander.

She shouldn't have paused to look, for the journalists were closing in again and one of them was even plucking at her sleeve. Taking note of this, Girays whisked her on to a gap in the velvet ropes, where an attendant verified the registrar's signature upon her certificate of participation before allowing her into the enclosure, beyond the reach of importunate scribblers. From her new vantage point she could see that additional velvet ropes marked out an unpeopled aisle running through the foyer, straight to the front door opening upon Irstreister Square.

"Some of these people are known to me," Girays v'Alisante observed easily. "Those twins over there, for example—Stesian and Trefian Festinette, from Travorn. Eighteen years old, and hungry for excitement. Obscenely rich. Recent coinheritors of a huge copper-mining fortune, which they are spending as hard and as fast as they can. Such is the bulk of the Festinette wealth, however, that even at the present rate of consumption the boys won't succeed in beggaring themselves for several years to come."

Luzelle glanced at him in surprise. His knowledge did not surprise her, for self-education in advance of any large endeavor was typical of this man. But she didn't understand why he should share the fruits of his research with her. They had not parted on the friendliest of terms, by any means. Certain horrid words still reverberated through her memory:

"*. . . Childish, immature, stubborn, touchy, hot-tempered, intolerant, razor-tongued little nineteen-year-old SHREW . . .*"

And her own response:

"*. . . Arrogant, overbearing, narrow, rigid, reactionary, self-important, self-satisfied, pretentious old DOLT!*"

No, not a happy division, and never a subsequent reconciliation, for she had never allowed herself—

Why should he be dispensing enlightenment now? Showing off? Demonstrating his own unfailing superiority? Probably.

"Over there." Girays pointed.

Her eyes followed his finger to a squat, well-barbered personage of conspicuous magnificence. The square face and broad torso might have belonged anywhere, but the loose, flowing garments, the high-heeled shoes, and the plenitude of pearl jewelry marked the owner as a citizen of Lanthi Ume.

"Porb Jil Liskjil," Girays announced in an undertone. "Prosperous merchant, on his way up. Climbed as high as a commoner might ordinarily hope, and now aspires to that extra social boost provided by a famous victory."

"Well, it will have to be some other famous victory."

"There." Girays's finger altered angle, directing her eyes toward a short, slim, perfectly tailored gentleman, perhaps some thirty-five years of age, but still boyish. "Mesq'r Zavune, an Aennorvi speculator. Looks as if he rides at the top of Fortune's wheel, but doesn't. Financially strapped at the moment. Should he win the Grand Ellipse, his fortunes are assured. Otherwise it's debtors' prison for him."

"Prison?" Luzelle marveled. The well-dressed Mesq'r Zavune hardly seemed a candidate for dungeon confinement. "Couldn't he just pack up and—"

"Over there." Girays's explanatory finger flicked. "That woman—"

"The one with the straggling hair and the big yellow overbite?"

"Is there any other woman in sight?"

"You are just as prickly as ever."

"That woman is particularly interesting," Girays resumed. "Her name is Szett Urrazole, and she's a Szarish inventor."

"Really? What's she invented?"

"Some sort of new conveyance that she calls '*Gorashiu qu'Osk Zenayushka.*'"

"Say that again, slowly."

"It translates to 'Miracle Self-Propelling Carriage.'"

"And is that title warranted?"

"We shall soon see. Madame Urrazole intends to demonstrate the capacities of her invention by winning the Grand Ellipse in it."

"No, she won't. Because, you see, *I'm* going to win the Grand Ellipse."

"Such resolute confidence. Formidable."

"Stop looking so amused. You don't believe I can do it? Just wait."

"Waiting is the last thing I intend. Remember, I'm competing myself, and I don't particularly relish defeat."

"Does anyone? This time, though, your vanity will have to bear it."

"Miss Devaire, you'll eat those words."

"M. v'Alisante, you are hardly the man to serve them to me. But come, let's return to your interrupted discourse. I wouldn't deny you the pleasure of parading your knowledge, so pray inform me—who is that man there?" She pointed discreetly.

"The giant with the muscles and the black beard? Bav Tchornoi. One of the greatest Ice Kings champions Rhazaulle has ever produced. All but invincible, in his day. But advancing age and cumulative injuries eventually threw his game off, and Tchornoi retired about ten years ago. Perhaps he's come to Toltz in search of his lost glory."

"And what about that fair-haired Grewzian officer over there?"

"Now, there's another interesting specimen. That is none other than the Overcommander Karsler Stornzof himself, in the celebrated flesh."

"Really?" Luzelle's eyes widened. Mere fame ordinarily awakened neither her awe nor her admiration, but this time she found herself impressed, for Karsler Stornzof was such a hero, so skilled in the arts of war, so valorous and by all accounts honorable, that even his enemies sang his praises. As for his own countrymen, they revered him to the point of idolatry, their devotion stimulated by the stream of newspaper reports and printed circulars ceaselessly lauding the exploits of Grewzland's golden son. Now she knew why that face of his had struck her as so familiar yesterday evening. She had seen drawings of it in the popular journals more than once; for even the Vonahrish press paid periodic homage to Overcommander Karsler Stornzof. "What's he doing here? I mean, he's an officer in the army of the Imperium, and there are wars all over the place. Shouldn't he be fighting at the Haerestean front or something?"

"I gather that Ogron himself has authorized—in fact, commanded—this Stornzof fellow's participation in the race, the idea being to get out there and garner glory for great Grewzland, or something along those lines. Presumably the imperior means to profit by the huge popularity of his matinée-idol emissary."

"Yes, he *is* rather good looking, isn't he?" she observed innocently.

"Perhaps, if you are partial to classical statues."

"Do I detect a note of personal dislike?"

"No. I don't know the fellow. I've no love for Grewzians, that's all."

"In that case—"

The blare of a brass band drowned her voice. Luzelle wheeled to face the musicians, whose presence she had hitherto overlooked. They were grouped near the foot of the stairs, and were now launching into the first bars of the Hetzian national anthem. The crowd in the foyer fell silent. Scores of respectful hands pressed themselves to patriotic Hetzian hearts. Foreign heads inclined politely. The anthem concluded and all eyes rose to the center of the staircase, where King Miltzin IX stood flanked by attendants.

Luzelle studied the king with more than academic interest. There was nothing particularly repulsive about Miltzin IX. His expression was brightly benign, his greying walrus moustache nicely groomed, his numerous medals and insignia lined up in neat rows across his chest. With his protuberant eyes, she thought, he resembled a giant grasshopper. Pleased with the simile, she amused herself by mentally coloring his face green and affixing imaginary antennae to his pomaded head.

Miltzin began to speak, his voice enthusiastically high pitched, his gestures distractingly expansive.

"My dear friends, this morning witnesses the commencement of a competition that is more than a sporting event, far more than a quest for personal fame or even for national glory—"

Quite right. Sentient Fire and safety for Vonahr, independence and freedom for Luzelle Devaire—these were the prizes, worth any price, *any price,* but probably that wasn't what Mad Miltzin had in mind. What was he running on about? Only then did Luzelle notice that the king of the Low Hetz was speaking in perfect Vonahrish, which wasn't surprising. His audience was polyglot, and, amid a multiplicity of differing tongues, Vonahrish was the language of diplomacy, the language comprehended by all civilized folk. *Though the head tl'gh-tiz of the Bhomiri-D'tal tribe might disagree with that assessment.*

Miltzin IX burbled on. The key to the future, he confided, lay in the marriage of magic and science, presently expressing itself in mundane practical terms of transportation and communication. Did he really think that anyone cared?

The king's address, larded with optimistic inanities, spouted forth interminably. Luzelle cast a covert glance about her, wondering how many others shared her impatience. The neighboring faces revealed nothing. Beside her Girays v'Alisante stood listening with a practiced air of respectful interest that would have convinced anybody who didn't know him. A few feet away the Rhazaullean giant Bav Tchnornoi waited, still and expressionless as a monolith. The Festinette twins were whispering to one another, grimacing and giggling. Catching her eyes upon him, one of them smirked and blew her a kiss. *Nitwits.* Her gaze returned to Mad Miltzin, whose verbal torrents were dwindling at last.

". . . to go forth, my friends, and astonish all the world!" the king concluded, and Luzelle felt her breath quicken and her stomach tighten. An attendant proffered a scarlet cushion upon which lay an ornate pistol. Miltzin accepted the weapon and raised it aloft. "In sight of the city of Toltz, the Grand Ellipse commences."

He fired, presumably a blank, and the shot blasted. Simultaneously, the velvet ropes edging the enclosure were released, and the crowd gathered in the foyer seemed to explode. A tremendous shouting arose, a roar of excitement that dwarfed the report of the gun, and a wave of humanity surged forward, overturning the flimsy barriers that marked the center aisle. As the racers sprinted for the exit, the precarious passageway vanished. An instant later the doorway was solidly choked, as racers, journalists, gamblers, and ordinary spectators struggled vigorously and vainly for egress through a portal held shut by the pressure of packed bodies.

For a moment Luzelle stood watching. She could not find Girays v'Alisante; he had already vanished into that boiling human mass. Fortunately, she herself was not obliged to do the same. Blessing the inspiration that had moved her to station her cab at the side of the building, she departed the foyer through a rear exit, threading her quick path back the way she had come along corridors relatively clear and navigable. Many a hallway loiterer stared at her in frank curiosity as she hurried by, but nobody hindered her progress. Moments later she emerged into the morning sunshine, to discover that she was not the only racer to have dodged the crush at the front of the city hall.

Her own cab still waited where she had left it, and silently she blessed the driver. Behind the cab waited a second carriage of slightly larger size and infinitely greater elegance, drawn by a pair of matched blacks built for speed. She caught a glimpse of a strong profile at the window and fancied the face familiar, but scarcely pondered the matter, for her attention anchored at once upon a third vehicle standing there, a conveyance unlike any she had ever seen in her life.

The contraption was long, low slung, silvery in color, and equipped with eight gleaming wheels. Its rear portion projected in a confusing tangle of pipes, coils, wires, tubes, flanges, cogs, vanes, and glass bulbs, while the front tapered to a featureless conical snout. Something resembling a triangular metal sail reared itself high above the roof.

No harness. Was the thing some sort of boat? *With wheels?* Trackless locomotive? Even as she paused to wonder, a gaunt figure passed her at a smart stalk, made straight for the mystery vehicle, and climbed in. Luzelle glimpsed shabby, grubby, loose-fitting garments, straggling grizzled hair, and grim jaw, which she recognized readily; Szett Urrazole, the Szarish inventor of the so-called Miracle Self-Propelling Carriage.

The door slammed shut. Seconds later the vehicle roared deafeningly to life. Luzelle flinched and clapped her hands to her ears. Pedestrians shrieked and ran for cover, horses plunged and reared. Gouts of flame spurted from its posterior orifices, and the Miracle Carriage sped off in a burst of fire and a cloud of dust, traveling at impossible speed. Luzelle gazed after the lightning Szarish carriage and wondered if the race were already lost.

Another figure hurried by her. Fair hair glinting in the morning sun, Overcommander Karsler Stornzof arrowed for the second carriage, with its splendid matched blacks and its waiting passenger, whom Luzelle now recognized as the older gentleman she had spied dining with the Grewzian hero in the Kingshead Hotel restaurant. Overcommander Stornzof cast a sidelong glance at her as he passed. Blue eyes, very blue. She wished she'd gotten a better look. Not the time to be thinking about it. Luzelle ran for her cab.

"Train station!" she commanded the driver in Vonahrish, amending in Hetzian, "Toltzcentraldepotrailwaylines!"

The Stornzof equipage had departed. Not five minutes into the race and she was already falling behind.

"Top speed!" she shouted, then realized her own folly. She already held a ticket for a seat on the southbound *Ilavian Whistler,* which wasn't scheduled to leave Toltz for another hour and a quarter. Risking life and limb to shave five minutes off the trip to the station was absurd.

The driver took her at her word, however, and the cab rattled off at a dangerous clip. Before it had advanced more than twice its own length, a series of sharp bangs, like the explosion of firecrackers, peppered the morning air. The horse snorted and shied, while the driver cursed and plied his whip.

Luzelle stuck her head out the window, craning her neck to see around the angle of the building. She beheld vast clouds of dense black smoke billowing over Irstreister Square and she heard the muffled cries of a panicked multitude. Even as she watched, a second series of sharp reports crackled and the smoke clouds darkened. Choking, soot-grimed citizens came stumbling from the square, tendrils of black vapor swirling in their wake.

"Was anyone hurt?" Luzelle called out, but received no answer, for the cab was bearing her away at top speed, as she had commanded.

Girays. Back there in the midst of that smoky chaos, perhaps injured? Probably not. M. v'Alisante, that superior person, was more than capable of looking after himself. Moreover, the smoke-bomb assault upon Irstreister Square seemed more designed to create confusion than to inflict real harm. In any case, what concern was Girays v'Alisante's safety to her? No more than hers was to him. Let him cough his smoke-filled lungs out, served him right.

She wouldn't let herself think about him; there were other matters to consider. The explosions, the smoke, the resulting tumult. What or who was the cause? She couldn't know, but one point was certain. The commotion in Irstreister Square had delayed the majority of Grand Ellipse competitors, and benefited any racer leaving the city hall by way of a side exit.

3

SHE REACHED THE STATION with time to spare, and the *Ilavian Whistler* departed on schedule. Luzelle relinquished her ticket to the conductor and settled back in her seat with a sigh. Nothing to do now but sit watching the quaint Lower Hetzian scenery roll by. She would not allow herself to worry about Girays.

It had been startling—almost shocking—to meet up with him in Toltz, and her nerves were still jangled. But it was not likely to happen again. Along with the rest of the Grand Ellipse contestants delayed in Irstreister Square, he had missed the *Ilavian Whistler*. He would have to wait at least a couple of hours for the next southeast-bound train, and by the time he boarded, he would already have missed the best connections to carry him on to the Ilavian coast. She would not see him again before the end of the race, because she'd drawn well ahead and he hadn't a prayer of overtaking her.

Resolutely she unfolded the newspaper purchased at the station, and for a while managed to distract herself with it. No mention of the smoke bombs outside city hall, of course—that news would not hit the headlines before the next edition. Plenty of front-page space devoted to the Grand Ellipse, however, and she saw her own name mentioned more than once. Lots of war news. The hurricane Grewzian conquest of Haereste was already complete. Many pages given over to accounts of local happenings uninteresting to a foreigner, but Luzelle made herself read them all, plowing laboriously through the tangled Hetzian syntax, and in this manner whiled away the hours.

The *Ilavian Whistler* chugged its way southeast, stopping at town after town. Time passed slowly until the late afternoon, when a couple of villagers clad in their relentlessly starched finest boarded Luzelle's car at Ploysto, and took the seat across the aisle from her. Their conversation caught her attention at once, for they spoke of an extraordinary occurrence unmatched in all the years of the town's history. Hours earlier an outlandish vehicle had passed straight through the center of Ploysto, traveling at fearsome speed. The conveyance, indescribably bizarre in appearance and driven by a woman of correspondingly eccentric aspect, seemed to generate its own power of movement in the manner of a locomotive, but it was no locomotive—it resembled nothing in the world that anyone had ever seen. Belching black smoke and demonic fire, the thing had roared into the market square around midmorning, to the terror of the local poultry; swerved hard, just in time to avoid collision with the town well; barely missed overturning the infirm Grandmother Deederkint, out to take the air; and sped off in a cloud of stygian vapor. One might have thought the uncanny apparition some sort of dream or delusion, had not a host of witnesses testified to its reality.

The countrified accents weren't always easy to comprehend, but Luzelle picked up enough to know that Szett Urrazole and her Miracle Self-Propelling Carriage were drawing farther ahead with every passing hour. Perhaps at some future point in the race the Miracle Carriage would break down, or better yet, run head-on into a tree.

Otherwise, she's already won.

Her fingers drummed. Deliberately, she stilled them. No point in fretting.

Luzelle's attention returned to the Hetzian newspaper, the passing scenery, the passengers boarding or departing at each stop. The hours passed, the sun set, and the scenery disappeared. At eight in the evening she sought the dining car, which was well appointed and well filled. The moment she entered, her eyes lighted upon the Overcommander Karsler Stornzof, sitting opposite his usual silver-haired, square-jawed companion. Stornzof saw her at the same time. Their eyes met, and for the longest moment she found herself unable to look away.

Idiotic. She was making a fool of herself. She could only imagine what the Judge would have to say. Tearing her eyes from his face, she seated herself, deliberately presenting her back to the Stornzof table, which removed all temptation to stare. Or so she thought until she happened to notice the high polish upon her soup spoon, whose convex bowl reflected most of the car, affording a tiny, distant image of a blond male head.

She ordered, and the prompt arrival of her soup deprived her of her mirror. Before she finished dining, Stornzof and his companion exited. Presently Luzelle returned to her seat and, not long thereafter, repaired to her berth in one of the sleeping cars.

She slumbered soundly and woke early. Around eight in the morning the *Ilavian Whistler* reached the Beroussean frontier and paused there puffing as the customs officials boarded to check passports. Luzelle's documents received the appropriate stamp. The inspectors completed their work and withdrew, and the train passed from the Low Hetz into the tiny duchy of Berousse.

Luzelle examined the customs stamp with satisfaction. A tangible sign of progress, with many more to follow. A succession of such stamps would testify to her advance along the curve of the Grand Ellipse. Her satisfaction died a quick death when the train pulled into the station at the Beroussean capital of Huizigar, where a forty-five-minute stopover afforded time to purchase a newspaper, books, a puzzle block, and lemon drops in the station. The newspaper was printed in Hetzian, official language of the duchy, and the front page proclaimed the previous evening's blazing passage through Huizigar of the eccentric Szarish inventor and Grand Ellipse contestant Szett Urrazole in her Miracle Self-Propelling Carriage.

Luzelle tossed the paper aside with a scowl.

Her dissatisfaction deepened around lunchtime, when she

lurched her way forward to the dining car and there caught
no golden glimpse of Overcommander Stornzof. She was either too early or too late. She ate slowly, dawdling over countless cups of tea, but he did not appear. At length abandoning
the vigil, she returned to her own seat, heated with annoyance
at her own folly.

Little Berousse was past in a matter of hours, and the *Ilavian Whistler* crossed the border into Dinsifise, first of the
Mid-Duchies. Another stamp upon her passport, this time
adorned with the circular Endless Fire of the Grewzian Imperium, for this was the first of the territories along the Grand
Ellipse route to acknowledge Grewzian rule. A particularly
close examination of her travel documents, an annoyingly
thorough investigation of her belongings, told her that a Vonahrish passport drew suspicious notice within the confines of
the Imperium, but nobody detained her.

The train whistled southeast through the mill towns of
Dinsifise, and the Endless Fire emblem turned up everywhere—on station platforms, on warehouses edging the
tracks, on railway overpasses, on the caps of the Grewzian soldiers now glimpsed with increasing frequency. Here upon
subject soil the demeanor of the Grewzians waxed lordly, but
Luzelle scarcely noted the alteration until the *Ilavian Whistler*
paused for half an hour in the town of Glozh, and she made
the mistake of venturing from the train.

Strolling to the end of the platform, she halted and drew a
deep breath of springtime air blighted with smoke and cinders. There was little to see from her present vantage point—
just a nondescript station house, shadowy copse behind the
station, flat-topped hills, and drab wooden houses and
shopfronts—for Glozh was neither interesting nor picturesque. Before her, however, the tracks stretched on into the
distance, curving their way southeast through the hills toward
Ilavia, with its coastline bordering the Sea of Silence, its great
port city of Ila, its merchant freighters and passenger vessels,
one of which would bear her on along the Grand Ellipse to
the great island of Dalyon.

Thanks to the minions of the Ministry of Foreign Affairs,
her passage aboard the steamer *Persistence* was already booked.

Persistence was scheduled to embark from Ila early tomorrow morning, and the timing seemed impeccable. Barring freak disaster, the *Ilavian Whistler* should be pulling into the port city around midnight. Her room at the Shipwreck Inn was reserved, and there would be time enough for several hours of sleep. All was going well; or would be, but for a certain damnably gifted Szarish inventor.

She strained her eyes southeast, as if by effort of will her vision might overtake the Miracle Self-Propelling Carriage speeding for the coast. But Szett Urrazole remained elusive and inscrutable.

Luzelle's reflections were interrupted by the creak of the platform boards behind her, the flicker of a shadow, the intrusion of a voice.

"You come with us."

The words were spoken in Grewzian, a tongue she comprehended imperfectly. Surprised, she turned to face a couple of soldiers, ordinary conscripts clad in the grey of the Imperium. One of them—short, meager, dark haired, and palely rat faced—was impossible to place. The other—tall, burly, fair, expressionless—was classically Grewzian.

Her expression must have communicated incomprehension, for the big one repeated clearly, "You come."

"We will take a walk," the white rat added. His broad gesture encompassed the shadowy copse behind the station house.

Luzelle's brows rose. In the course of her solitary travels she had often encountered just such overly hospitable young military men, and she knew how to handle them.

"No. I cannot, thank you," she replied firmly, in her awkward Grewzian. "I return to the train now." She took a step toward the *Ilavian Whistler,* and halted as a large hand closed on her arm.

"Come," commanded the big one, and she noticed then what an unusually stingy mouth he had—nothing more than a tiny, lipless slit, almost lost in the wide white-skinned wilderness of his face.

"Your hand—make it to go away!" she exclaimed, bad Grewzian deteriorating. Strange men rarely presumed to touch her, but when they did, firm measures were required. "Do not make the hands, or else difficulty! I return now train!" Her frown and the sharpness of her tone should have made her feelings clear, but the Grewzian soldiers seemed remarkably obtuse.

"Shut your trap, bitch," the short one advised. She knew just enough of the language to understand the colloquialisms he employed, and her eyes widened in amazement. "Pick up your feet."

"Go away! I will call the stationmaster!" she threatened. Both soldiers guffawed and the first twinge of fear shot through her. Still, it was broad daylight, the train waited a few yards away, and the platform was well populated. No harm could befall her here.

"Come on."

Each of them had her by one arm and they were hurrying her along the platform, their purpose all too clear, but absolutely unbelievable. Were they stupid, or mad? Did they imagine for one moment that they could get away with this?

Filling her lungs with springtime air and cinders, she yelled for the stationmaster. The cry was piercingly audible, and she expected her assailants to react, but they were stone. Her eyes raked the platform, jumping from face to alien face, and everywhere her gaze lighted, strangers looked away. She realized then that these people, townsfolk and travelers alike, were altogether cowed by the Grewzian soldiers. They might pity her, but they wouldn't dare to help. Real terror shot through her then, but the incredulity remained. She stood in Dinsifise, a civilized duchy. These were modern times. Moreover, she was no subject of the Imperium, no citizen of a conquered nation.

"I am Vonahrish!" Luzelle exclaimed. "Do you understand? Vonahrish!"

"Vonahrishwomen—whores." The white rat nodded his comprehension.

She aimed a kick at him, but her long skirts defeated the effort. A sharp twist failed to free her wrist. She pulled back, but could not slow her own swift march from the platform.

Dozens of eyes followed her reluctant progress, but nobody intervened.

Unbelievable. The persistent sense of dreamlike unreality seemed to paralyze her intellect, but instinct told her to dissemble, and breathing a sigh, she let herself go limp. Her knees buckled and her body sagged, held upright only by the force of her captors' grip.

They were not deceived.

"Get up," commanded the lipless bruiser. "Now."

"You want it here, then?" the white rat inquired.

"Around back," his companion decreed.

If she got out of this alive, she would never again travel without a loaded pistol. In the meantime, contemptuous of her feigned swoon, they were dragging her lax body toward the stairs. Raising her head, she twisted sideward to sink her teeth deep into the Grewzian hand grasping her right arm. The white rat squealed, and his grip loosened. Springing to her feet, Luzelle twisted one arm free, spun to the left, and swung a wild punch at the bruiser's lipless face. The ill-aimed blow barely grazed his cheek, and he muttered an oath as he raised a clenched fist to strike back.

"Halt." The command, spoken in Grewzian, was calm, authoritative, and instantly effective.

To Luzelle's surprise, both her assailants stiffened into immobility. She looked back over her shoulder to behold Overcommander Stornzof standing there beside his customary companion.

"Release her," Stornzof ordered.

The bruiser obeyed at once, and Luzelle stepped away from him. She was shaking, and her heart hammered.

"You two are a disgrace to the uniform you wear," Stornzof observed evenly.

"But, Overcommander," the white rat attempted, "we were only—"

"Have you received permission to speak?"

"No, Overcommander."

"Then hold your peace. Your discipline is slack as your impulses are bestial. You are unfit to call yourselves soldiers of the Imperium." He did not raise his voice, but his subordinates waxed visibly uneasy. "State your names."

The two culprits complied reluctantly.

"Report to your sergeant. Furnish an account of this incident and request appropriate punishment. Dismissed."

The two grey figures saluted and withdrew. Overcommander Stornzof turned to inquire of Luzelle in Vonahrish, "You are unhurt, Miss Devaire?"

He knew her name. A tiny current of pleasure tingled across her mind.

"Yes, only—" *Frightened almost to death,* she thought, and finished, "A little rattled, perhaps."

"I do not wonder. You have suffered an outrageous indignity." His Vonahrish was perfect, although excessively formal, and marked with a faint Grewzian accent that somehow sounded pleasant upon his lips. "Do you require the services of a physician?"

"Not at all, thank you. *And thank you* indeed, Overcommander Stornzof. I hardly know what to say. If you hadn't been here, I don't like to think what would have happened."

"It is shameful. I apologize for the actions of my countrymen." His companion flashed him a glitteringly icy glance, which Stornzof seemed not to see. "Some of these troops have been so long in the field, they have forgotten that they are civilized men."

If they ever knew it in the first place. Aloud she merely observed, "It is my very good fortune that you are here to remind them. Although I know that final command of yours must be regarded as a formality."

"Formality?"

"Well, those two won't actually go running to their sergeant in search of punishment, will they? You won't be here to see that they obey, so isn't it safe to assume that the matter will slip their minds?"

"Miss Devaire." Karsler Stornzof smiled slightly. "A direct order from a superior officer does not slip the mind of a Grewzian soldier. Such insubordination in time of war is a major offense—"

"Punishable by death." Stornzof's companion spoke up for

the first time. His voice was deep, the guttural Grewzian accent far more harshly marked than the younger man's. "They would be shot, of course."

They deserve it, Luzelle thought bravely, but could not suppress an internal chill. *Who is this walking ice-sculpture?*

"Miss Devaire, allow me to introduce the Grandlandsman Torvid Stornzof," the overcommander supplied. "My kinsman and traveling companion."

"Grandlandsman." Luzelle swept a curtsy. The title told her that the overcommander's kinsman belonged to the highest rank of Grewzian nobility. Such status, combined with his age, marked Torvid Stornzof as the head of his entire extended House. Here stood one of the greatest of Grewzians, almost certainly a relative and an intimate of the imperior, and he looked the part with his ramrod carriage and stellar tailoring, his silvery hair and heavy black brows, his arrogant impassive face and his steel-rimmed monocle that might have appeared effete on a weaker countenance, but only seemed to lend the grandlandsman an additional armoring of ice.

Torvid barely acknowledged the introduction with the smallest inclination of the head.

"You compete in the Grand Ellipse, sir?" Luzelle essayed.

His black brows lifted minutely, as if he wondered at her temerity in questioning him. For a moment he seemed to debate the necessity of reply, and at last deigned to answer, "No. I amuse myself, merely." Turning away from her, he urged his kinsman, "Come, we have dawdled long enough."

This fellow's frozen hauteur dwarfed the garden-variety insolence of the Vonahrish formerly-Exalted, Luzelle reflected. His attitude was offensive and his manners atrocious. She disliked him immediately.

"Miss Devaire, you will allow us to escort you back to the train?" Karsler Stornzof inquired.

"With pleasure, Overcommander." There was little likelihood of further unpleasantness, but she found herself disinclined to refuse his offer. Moreover, the look of disgusted impatience curdling the Grandlandsman Torvid's square-jawed visage was a spectacle of which she did not choose to deprive herself.

They walked her back to the *Ilavian Whistler,* and she boarded. Returning to her own seat, she pressed her nose to the window and watched the Stornzof kinsmen make their way along the platform to a car near the back of the train, where she lost sight of them. Luzelle turned from the window with a thoughtful frown. The overcommander certainly didn't seem to fit the stereotype of a contemporary Grewzian officer. In fact, something about him seemed quite out of place in a mundane railroad station, almost as if he were the product of some earlier era set down inappropriately in a modern world and not quite at home there.

What nonsense. Just because this renowned Grewzian overcommander looked the very image of the knightly hero, and had played that role to perfection, was no reason to let imagination run away with her. Still, he possessed a singular quality, and it wasn't simply a matter of his good looks. Perhaps it had something to do with that courteous, careful, antiquatedly correct speech of his. Or the indefinably remote expression in those blue eyes, the bluest eyes she had ever seen. Cleft chin, too.

The train coughed its way back to life and pulled away from dreary, dangerous Glozh. Extracting one of the new novels from her valise, she descended to *The Cellar of the Red Beast,* whose varied marvels were sure to divert her mind from all thought of handsome enemy officers.

Perhaps he'd be in the dining car again this evening.

But the evening hardly lived up to her hopes.

The hours passed, the sun set, the interior lamps were lit, the exterior world vanished, and the *Ilavian Whistler* took sick. Luzelle emerged from *The Cellar of the Red Beast* to find the train wheezing, shuddering, and failing. Twice the *Whistler* lost power, slowed to a crawl, and rallied. Upon the third seizure, there was no recovery. The throb of the engine ceased and the train coasted to a halt.

A buzz of speculative conversation filled the car. Setting her book aside, Luzelle peered out the window. Nothing to see but impenetrable blackness. Certainly no border had been crossed, and they remained in Grewzian-dominated Dinsifise. She frowned. Whatever the difficulty—mechanical failure, damaged rails, or stray cow blocking the tracks—it had better be resolved quickly. She counted on reaching the Shipwreck Inn in time to enjoy several hours of comfortable sleep before catching the *Persistence* in the morning.

An hour passed. The train stood motionless. Luzelle went to the dining car, where she caught no glimpse of Karsler Stornzof. She ate, returned to her seat, and submerged once more into *The Cellar of the Red Beast*. Another idle hour passed.

When a conductor ventured into the car around ten-thirty, the man was bombarded with questions, to which he responded with a vague account of "technical inexactitude," currently "in process of readjustment." When pressed for explanation, he fled and did not show his face again.

Two more hours crept by. It was well past midnight, around the time that the *Whistler* ought to be huffing into Ila Station. Instead she sat dead in the dark, somewhere short of the border. Luzelle's fingers drummed. If only it were daylight—if only they'd stopped near a town, a village, or even a farm—she might hire a carriage, a cart, a mule, anything with wheels or legs capable of carrying her on toward the coast. At night she was trapped, and there was no use in fretting about it. No use worrying about Girays v'Alisante and the others, steadily gaining on her. No use thinking of Szett Urrazole, drawing farther and farther ahead. She picked up her novel, read the same paragraph four times, and tossed the book aside.

Her joints were stiff. She was sick of sitting and sick of the ailing *Ilavian Whistler*. Rising from her seat, she paced the aisle a couple of times, made her way forward to the crowded dining car, drank a cup of tea there, and exchanged commiserations with restive fellow-travelers. Still no sign of Karsler Stornzof. Her frustration sharpened, and she realized that she had been looking for him. Ridiculous. She went back to her seat.

It was late and she was tired, but there was no berth reserved for her in the sleeping car, for by now she was supposed to be resting comfortably at the Shipwreck Inn in Ila. And no berth available, the conductor informed her. She was out of luck, then; for tired or not, she could never fall asleep sitting upright.

Her lids drooped and she dropped off to sleep at once.

The clanking vibration of machinery woke her. Luzelle opened her eyes upon morning light streaming in through the windows. Hours had passed, the night was over, and somewhere during that lost interval the *Ilavian Whistler*'s unspecified affliction had corrected itself. A sharp whistle split the air and the train resumed its interrupted advance. Luzelle yawned and consulted her watch. Her somnolence vanished. Seven o'clock. Half an hour ago the *Persistence* had embarked for Dalyon without her. Her brows drew together. She'd have to arrange alternate passage when she reached Ila, and the delay was certain to reward her rivals.

The *Ilavian Whistler* proceeded without further incident to the border, where it halted for the usual inspections. Luzelle's passport received its stamp, at which time she learned from the inspector that a second southbound passenger train, running on time, waited directly behind her own.

She could well imagine who was on it.

The *Whistler* reached Ila around noon, some twelve hours behind schedule. Exiting the train with relief, Luzelle hurried along the platform, into the station house and out the other side without a glance to spare for her surroundings. Snagging a miskin-drawn cab, she tossed her luggage in and ordered the driver to head for the docks. The man stared blankly, and she realized that he spoke no Vonahrish. She tried Hetzian without success, and then broken Grewzian, which drew results. He nodded, she entered, and off they went at a stolid miskin pace.

No use telling him to hurry—the woolly-headed double-tailed beast that he drove was not to be bullied. On they plodded through the streets of Ila, and Luzelle gazed out the open window at old wooden architecture weathered by water and salt spray to a pleasing shade of grey. The cobbles of the narrow streets echoed the muted monotone of the buildings, and the cool, tangy air spoke of fish, seaweed, salt water, and prolonged human habitation. The gulls wheeled and screeched overhead, but Luzelle hardly heard them.

Hurry, hurry, hurry.

Neither driver nor miskin complied. To the left rose the Shipwreck Inn, its timbers black with age and tar. Inside— soft feather bed, clean sheets, hot water, and soap. . . .

Not today.

On they went at the same infuriating plod through the sea-smelling streets and down to the docks, where modern steamers loomed alongside the old-fashioned sailing vessels, and the wharves were crowded with the booths of the ticketing agents and the sheds of the freight brokers. Now, if only some of them spoke Vonahrish.

Alighting from the cab, Luzelle paid the driver and turned her attention toward the agents, three of whom she tried in quick succession. All of them spoke Vonahrish, and all of them relayed identical information. The next passenger liner bound for Dalyon would not depart Ila before tomorrow morning.

With the freight brokers, she had better luck. The big steamer *Karavise* was scheduled to embark for the city-state of Lanthi Ume in just one hour's time.

"Passenger space?" Luzelle demanded.

"Some. Not what you'd call luxurious, it's a cargo ship. Not what you'd really call private, either. Four berths per slot. And no other women aboard." The broker couldn't suppress a smile. "Maybe you want to wait for the *Keldhaam Gnuxia.* Passenger liner, pleasant quarters, good chef. Leaves for Gard Lammis tomorrow morning. Now, you see that booth over there with the blue lettering on it? Just go on over there and tell the agent that you'd like a nice, clean, first-class stateroom aboard the *Keldhaam*—"

"No, I want the next ship out."

"Better think it over, little lady. It's not like you were the same as the last. At least *she* could shut herself up in that contraption of hers, for decency's sake."

"She? Contraption?"

"Turned up yesterday at the break of dawn, just in time to catch the *Rhelish Mercenary.* Perfect scarecrow of a woman— northerner, I bet—driving this outlandish fire hazard of a carriage. Wanted the carriage shipped to Dalyon, so it made sense that she'd have real need of a cargo vessel. Whereas you—"

"Whereas I am not prepared to wait." Luzelle found that her foot was tapping, her sense of urgency mounting. Szett Urrazole had come through yesterday morning, and must be over halfway to Lanthi Ume by now. *I wish I could blow that Miracle Self-Propelling Monstrosity of hers to bits. I swear I'd do it, if I could.* "May I have a slot to myself?"

"At the price of four berths."

"Agreed." *Why not? The Ministry of Foreign Affairs was paying for it.*

Money changed hands, the broker presented her with a ridiculous quartet of tickets, and Luzelle boarded the *Karavise,* a vessel clean and grimly utilitarian. One of the crew conducted her belowdecks to her slot, which proved windowless, low ceilinged, and only just large enough to accommodate a pair of narrow, steel-framed bunk beds, all hers for the duration of the trip. She might, if she chose, spend the next two nights flitting from bunk to bunk, just to make sure that the ministry got its money's worth.

The bass hoot of the whistle and the deep-throated cough of the engine recalled her to the present. *Karavise* throbbed on the verge of departure. Luzelle glanced about her. Already the walls of her slot were closing in. The space was too small for one passenger, much less four. Thrusting her bag beneath one of the beds, she made her way back to the deck, sensing the pressure of eyes on her as she went. Of course the sailors would look, no harm in that, but these fellows were decent— *at least as decent as those Grewzian soldiers back in Glozh*—and anyway, the door of her slot bolted from the inside.

The sea breeze was sharply bracing, and her spirits lifted. For a couple of minutes she strolled the deck, then went to the railing and stood there gazing down at the pier. The gangplank had not yet been removed, and a few last-minute passengers were still coming aboard. She studied them and her breath caught, for she spied a pair of youthful slim figures impossible to mistake, identically clad in cream frock coats and fawn trousers. The Festinette twins, playfully elbowing one another as they advanced, followed by porters bearing mountains of luggage. And behind the twins, a towering black-bearded man, carrying his own valise; Bav Tchornoi, the former Ice Kings champion.

Three of her competitors; and doubtless others already aboard. Luzelle expelled her breath slowly, torn between disappointment and an odd excitement. She'd thought she'd left Girays and most of the others behind in Toltz, but the *Ilavian Whistler's* protracted delay had altered matters, and the race was still very much on.

The gangplank vanished, the whistle sounded, and the *Karavise* embarked. For a time Luzelle stood watching the docks recede, the grey-blue seawater rushing beneath the hull, the raucous gulls trailing the boat, until these sights palled and she resumed her promenade along the deck. Presently she encountered Bav Tchornoi, who nodded at her with an air of guarded civility as she approached. She returned the nod but did not pause to speak, for his aspect was forbiddingly morose. His face, behind its black thatching of beard, was flushed, and he clasped a silvery flask in one huge hand. She caught a potent alcoholic reek as she passed him, and mentally registered, *vouvrak.*

On she wandered toward the bow, eyes scanning the deck as she went, lighting at length on the object of her unconscious search—a lean upright figure, dark hair, careless pose.

Luzelle stopped. Girays v'Alisante stood at the rail gazing out over the Sea of Silence, quite unaware of her presence. He had obviously escaped the smoky fracas in Irstreister Square uninjured, and the rush of relief that surged through her was followed at once by an acute sense of awkwardness. She had nothing pleasant to say to him, and no desire to quarrel, which left little room for conversation. Best to retire quietly, avoiding his notice altogether.

Then Girays turned and saw her. The smile that so enlivened his habitually weary expression glinted, and he observed, "Ah, I wondered if I should find you here."

Too late for retreat, and she wasn't about to let him see her uncertainty. Luzelle's chin came up and she advanced.

"I'm sorry I can't return the compliment," she replied. "Nor can I fathom your interest in my whereabouts."

"Then the years have surely dulled your wits. A pity," he opined in that gilt-edged, own-the-world accent of his. "The smoke assault at the start of the race furnished you a substantial lead, which I perceived as temporary. But I've overtaken you even sooner than I expected, thus affording myself the simultaneous pleasures of success and your company."

"Enjoy them both while you can," Luzelle advised. He was insufferable as ever, but he would eat dust before the end of the race. "Neither is likely to last beyond the term of this passage."

"You wrong yourself, Miss Devaire. I admire you, and truly credit your ability to keep pace with me a little while longer."

"I always thought you gifted with a sense of irony, but now perceive your sense of humor veering toward the farcical. Perhaps it is the effect of advancing age."

"Cranky little Luzelle, you are still so entertaining."

"If only the same could be said of you, how we might lighten the tedium of one another's voyage. As it is . . ." Her voice trailed sadly. She held her temper strenuously in check. "Despite the ravages of time, however, you still possess the power to satisfy my curiosity."

"I live to do so, but how shall I dare address the question to which Miss Devaire does not already possess an answer?"

"Direct observation has its advantages. Tell me what happened in Irstreister Square."

"Ah." Girays's smile faded. "Several separate small explosions, loosing quantities of smoke. Nobody burned, dismembered, or hit by flying debris that I know of. Great confusion, fear, uproar, and blind activity, though. I myself had to stumble and grope my way from the square, but managed to find my way out intact. Plenty of others, half blinded or half suffocated by the smoke, weren't so fortunate."

"What happened to them?" She wasn't sure she really wanted to know.

"Hospital in Toltz, I believe. I've heard that one of the Grand Ellipse racers—liZendorf, that Hetzian horse-breeder—was incapacitated. No fatalities, though."

"What exploded?"

"Are you requesting a recipe? You might better ask who engineered the explosions."

"Well?"

"Only a few profited by the diversion, and you are one of them."

"You think *I*—"

"Certainly not. But there are those Grewzians, and we know what they are. That flashy, synthesized hero of theirs—"

"Stornzof?"

"The demigod."

"I can't believe him responsible."

"No?" Girays's dark brows arched. "You seem certain. Do you know this Grewzian so well, then?"

"I don't know him at all, but—"

"But?"

"I've seen a bit of Stornzof since we left Toltz, and back in Glozh he did me a large favor."

"Which was?"

"Helped me out of a very sticky situation."

"Sticky? What do you mean by sticky? Are you all right? What happened?"

"Nothing came of it. But this Karsler Stornzof was more than decent, in fact he was wonderful—"

"*Wonderful,* was he?"

"And I'm not prepared to think the worst of him in the absence of proof, no matter what his nationality."

"Well, perhaps feminine eyes dazzled by all that fame and golden Grewzian radiance do not see so very clearly."

"Don't patronize me, Girays v'Alisante. You haven't even spoken to Karsler Stornzof; you don't know a thing about him."

"Ah, but I do. I know that he is *wonderful,* and that he has found a passionate defender in you. I wonder if the gallant overcommander realizes his good fortune?"

"He *is* gallant, as it happens. Believe it or not, there still is gallantry left in the world, and honor, and some chivalry—"

"To be sure, and these agreeable commodities concentrate themselves within the borders of Grewzland."

"I might have expected *M. the Marquis* to sneer. It is what he does best."

"Quite the contrary. I commend your wisdom and the soundness of your judgment. I have always admired both."

"As I have always admired your humility, your liberality of outlook, and your progressive democratic attitudes," she returned sweetly.

"That is hardly my recollection. I seem to recall your frequent criticisms of my abominable arrogance, my unspeakable conservatism, and my annoying formerly-Exalted affectations."

"Oh, but I was so childishly intolerant in those days. So immature, so very *juvenile*, as you took pains to remind me, again and again and again."

"Less juvenile, perhaps, than liberated, contemptuous of empty outmoded convention, and far too free a spirit to endure the galling restrictions of ordinary, commonplace matrimony."

"Clearly *you* did not deem me fit to endure them, as it was upon such a pretext that you chose to dissolve the betrothal."

"What remained to dissolve, following your flight from Sherreen? You were the one who left, a truth you can hardly deny, and the separation was your choice alone."

"That is neither accurate nor reasonable." An air of exaggerated patience masked her rising indignation. He was still so completely unfair, so inflexible, so unwilling to see her side! "There was no 'flight,' as you so melodramatically term it. The separation was minor and very temporary in nature—"

"Several months, was it not?"

"Six months. Six measly, insignificant little months, that's all, and they would have passed in a flash. You might have waited. In view of all your vows and declarations, I shouldn't have thought it too much to ask. But it *was* too much, and M. the Marquis's much-vaunted affections proved unequal to the challenge. So much for his constancy."

"It's a source of never-ending fascination, this ability of yours to warp and distort the past almost beyond recognition, without once letting slip your air of injured innocence. At times I believe you sincere in your delusions, and therefore now take the trouble to correct your misapprehensions. Here is the reality. Approximately one fortnight prior to the scheduled date of the wedding, you—having turned nineteen and assumed control of your inheritance—suddenly announced your intention of departing for Lakhtikhil Ice Shelf, there to remain for an indefinite period—"

"Six months!"

"In vain I entreated you to reconsider—"

"Entreated? You commanded!"

"Or even to postpone the excursion for a time—"

"I couldn't postpone. It was already autumn. Another few weeks, and the Straits of Kubringi would have frozen over, and I wouldn't have been able to reach L'mai, and the whole trip would have had to wait at least another year—"

"Would that have been such a tragedy?"

"Yes, it would! If I hadn't gone to the Shelf that year, the year the frozen mounds were discovered, then somebody else would have been there before me. Probably Fluss Ziffi, that bandit. If I hadn't published my account of the voyage before he did, then there would have been no speaking engagement at the Republican Academy. If it hadn't been for that one engagement, then I'd never—"

"Have become the personage that you are today. Yes, I understand. You got what you wanted the most. You might have become my wife and the mistress of Belfaireau, but what is that in comparison to personal glory?"

"Oh, spare me the reproaches and self-righteousness. I might have been your wife and been myself as well. You were the one to force the choice on me. If you didn't like my decision, have you anyone other than yourself to blame?"

"My wife and yourself as well? I wonder what you think you mean by that? What is your notion of marriage? Was I to sit alone at Belfaireau for months on end, awaiting my wife's occasional visitations?"

"It would only have been a few months! Then I would have been back, and we could have been married. If you'd ever cared anything about me—I mean about me myself as opposed to me as potential chatelaine of your precious estate—then you could have supported my efforts, you could have spared me those months, and afterward we might have been happy—"

"Until the next time. How long before you found yourself impelled to set forth on your travels again, for months or years on end?"

"Well, and what if that were so? Men go off all the time, and their women must wait at home. Why should the reverse not hold true? A sea captain, for example, is away for months at a time, and he expects his wife to wait patiently—"

"And perhaps she is content to do so, but I am not. I am old-fashioned, as you have so often observed, and I cherish the outmoded conviction that a wife prefers the society of her husband."

"Does that mean she's glued to his side?"

"It means that her marriage supersedes the importance of her personal ambition and her vanity."

"Vanity!"

"But your priorities are ordered otherwise, and always have been," Girays concluded dispassionately.

"Well." Drawing a deep breath, Luzelle managed to curve a condescending little smile. "I see that you are every bit as narrow, critical, and prejudiced as you ever were. It's reassuring to discover that some things never change."

"And to think I imagined you immune to the charm of tradition."

"An admission of fallibility, straight from the Marquis's own lips. The world is never devoid of marvels. M. v'Alisante, I thank you for the moral instruction, but I have drunk as much of your wisdom as my poor mind can absorb at one draft, and must now retire to contemplate the new mental treasures at leisure." Allowing him no time to reply, Luzelle turned and walked away. Her face burned and her blood raced. He had assumed his usual intolerable air of superiority, but she'd had the last word. And she would have it again, next time.

What next time?

As soon as the *Karavise* docked, she would leave Girays and the others far behind. She would not see him again, there would be no next time.

The thought was curiously deflating. Suddenly the hard salt breeze scouring the deck chilled her to the bone. It was not really that cold, but somehow seemed so.

Down she went, out of the fresh air, back to her window-less slot, where she lit the lamp and started in on another of her purchased novels, *The Shadow of the Ghoul.*

The Ghoul wasn't half bad, and she stayed with him for hours before the clang of the ship's bell recalled her to reality and summoned her to dinner. She made her way aft to the crew's mess hall, which was cramped, crowded, and moderately malodorous. The passengers aboard the *Karavise* had a table to themselves, and she saw at a glance that the ship was infested with Grand Ellipse competitors. There were the Festinette lads, exquisitely turned out in matching navy-blue jackets banded with quasi-nautical gold braid. There was Bav Tchornoi, gloomier and redder of face than ever. Girays v'Alisante, looking Exaltedly nonchalant. Mesq'r Zavune, the debt-ridden Aennorvi speculator. Porb Jil Liskjil, the rich Lanthian merchant, aglow with pearl jewelry. A few other faces she recognized from city hall, in Toltz. And there sat Overcommander Karsler Stornzof, beside his unutterably aristocratic kinsman, the Grandlandsman Torvid.

She was not surprised to encounter Karsler aboard the *Karavise,* yet her heartbeat quickened. Their eyes met and her cheeks warmed. She felt and no doubt looked like a flustered goose. Girays was watching her, and her expression must have alerted him, for his dark gaze turned from her to fix unerringly upon the overcommander's face.

The men rose briefly as she joined them. *Company manners,* she thought. *Wonder how long that will last?* With Girays the courtesy was ingrained, but the majority of the contestants were unlikely to match M. the Marquis's breeding.

There was a quick flurry of introductions, and she picked up the names of two more hitherto anonymous competitors. Founne Hay-Frinl was a tall, emaciated Kyrendtish blueblood with protruding ears and stammering speech. Dr. Phineska, a Strellian physician, boasted a rich bass voice and a suave manner.

Taking a seat between Mesq'r Zavune and Porb Jil Liskjil, she helped herself to flatbread, salt beef, fried goldtubers, boiled carrots, and sweetened stewed prunes; the same fare served to the crew—plain and dull, but decent and plentiful.

There was good ale or vile coffee to accompany the meal, and she partook sparingly of the ale. The conversation interrupted by her arrival resumed, and distinctly awkward it was, conducted in sometimes fractured Vonahrish by a polyglot group of rivals mutually wary.

But the Festinette twins weren't wary in the least, she discovered at once. Nor were they reticent. Flushed with ale and hilarity, Stesian and Trefian bombarded the table with tales of their own merry escapades—their inspired pranks, their legendary feats of drinking, their infamous nocturnal forays. There was the outrageous affair of the Ostler's Three Daughters. There was the rib-tickling Concerto of Crazed Cats. There was the immortal Two-Week Brandy Binge. There was the scandalous episode of the Beautiful Baroness's Purloined Petticoats. There was . . .

". . . And so," Stesian Festinette concluded one such narrative, "His Grace never knew how the three-legged cow found her way to the palace rooftop, and for weeks afterward kept on asking, 'D'you suppose she fell from the heavens?' And then he boarded over the skylight, to guard the stained glass against falling cows!"

The twins howled with laughter, and their listeners smiled politely, with the exception of Grandlandsman Torvid Stornzof, who appeared to have cultivated icebound deafness.

"My brother and I are mad, quite utterly mad, you see!" Trefian declared. "There's nothing we wouldn't dare, we're absolutely incorrigible! Really, the two of us should be locked up in a lunatic asylum."

"We're quite beyond redemption," Stesian concurred. "We can't help ourselves, we were simply born demented."

"Who but a pair of madmen would ever have thought of flooding the headmaster's office with eau de cologne?" Trefian demanded. "Gallons of cologne—"

"Vats of it!"

"Jasmine Seduction, was it not?"

"The place was *awash*!"

"And after that everyone *knew* we were completely crazy!"

"Sometimes we amaze even ourselves." Stesian turned to his twin. "Remember the time we got hold of the false beards, and passed ourselves off as the Demon Tax Collector, seen in two different places at once?"

"Those villagers were *panicked*!"

"They're probably still talking about us!"

Both brothers sputtered uncontrollably.

Luzelle let her eyes wander. Clearly several fellow diners shared her opinion of the Festinette conversational blockade. Girays was engaged in a quiet exchange with Bav Tchornoi, who had brought his own silvery flask with him to the table. Grandlandsman Torvid, unequivocally turning his back on the loquacious twins, was chatting in Grewzian with his famous Stornzof kinsman. She allowed her eyes to linger on Karsler's face for an instant, then turned her attention leftward to Mesq'r Zavune.

They traded a few laborious pleasantries. His Vonahrish was poor, and her Aennorvi nonexistent. Despite communicative difficulties, she formed a favorable impression of the foreign speculator. He was soft-spoken, polite, and seemingly amiable. Within the space of a few minutes she learned that he had left a wife and two children behind in Aennorve, that he wrote letters to them every day, that he was acutely homesick, and that he longed for a swift conclusion to the race.

Poor fellow, thought Luzelle, mindful of the financial disasters that mandated his participation. He ought to have been at home.

She liked Mesq'r Zavune, but was relieved when the linguistically toilsome conversation concluded. Turning to her right, she quickly discovered that the Lanthian merchant Porb Jil Liskjil spoke perfect Vonahrish, and that he was willing to demonstrate his proficiency. Too willing.

In his own relentlessly sociable way he was almost as tiresome as the Festinette boys. Apparently he knew everyone there was to know in his home city of Lanthi Ume. His intimate friends numbered in the hundreds or thousands, and he seemed determined to recite the entire list.

". . . Lord Har Fennahar, Lord and Lady Rion Vassarion, the Lord Ress Drenneress, several other great courtiers, all of us there at Parnis Lagoon to view the regatta, assembled upon the ducal float and awaiting His Grace's arrival, when some fool of a retainer—one of Fennahar's, I believe—manages to tumble overboard. He hits the water with a great splash and the spray drenches Lady Vassarion's gown, so naturally Her Ladyship screams out, 'Oh, you clumsy villain, you'll not set foot again upon this float, I forbid you to attempt it!' And when the oaf defies her, laying hands on the float and striving to pull himself from the water, Her Ladyship tears the shoe from her foot and with this makeshift weapon belabors the soggy wretch about the head, thus thwarting his efforts—you never saw so comical a sight!"

The tale lumbered to its conclusion. Other stories followed, other names and titles. Was he trying to impress her with all of this, and if so, why should he bother? Luzelle allowed her thoughts and eyes to rove. Girays was conferring with Dr. Phineska. The Festinette twins continued to hold forth loudly. The Grandlandsman Torvid still monopolized the attention of Karsler Stornzof. The food was dreary. The mess hall was airless. Bav Tchornoi was drinking himself stupid. *The Shadow of the Ghoul* could still conclude happily. The Grand Ellipse was less likely to conclude happily, unless someone did something to slow down Szett Urrazole's Miracle Self-Propelling Carriage. . . .

". . . A Cognitive feat worthy of the Select of old. . . ."

Porb Jil Liskjil's insistent voice recalled her to the present.

". . . But the concentrated power of Cognition has always distinguished the ancient and aristocratic House of Wate Basef. . . ."

The House of what? Whose name was he dropping now?

"Cognition?" Luzelle echoed.

"That is our traditional Lanthian form of magic," Jil Liskjil told her. A flush of civic pride darkened his square face, emphasizing the white luster of the pearls at his earlobes. "In years gone by, when the city-state of Lanthi Ume was a great presence in the world, the military strength of the reigning dukes was enhanced by the Cognition of the resident savants, whose magic confounded all enemies. It's even said that the talents of such men facilitated construction of the original Lanthian and Umish island-cities. The power to comprehend the very essence of reality—a power that common folk call sorcerous—has always resided within certain Lanthian minds, and its cultivation yields astonishing results. You have perhaps heard of the Select of Lanthi Ume, Miss Devaire?"

"Oh, I think so." Luzelle frowned, dredging her memory. "Some sort of ancient secret society. Mythical, wasn't it?"

"By no means, my dear lady. A very real, very exclusive organization, once wielding immense political influence. Its membership embraced the most accomplished of savants, and admission was a coveted honor. Even now the Select continue, though their current function is largely symbolic. The practice of Cognition has fallen off in modern times, and the magic of our day can't equal the Cognition of old. It survives yet, however, and even in diminished form serves to—ah—disconcert the unwary." Jil Liskjil's eyes shifted to the Stornzof kinsmen for a fraction of a second and slid away again.

Luzelle nodded discreetly. "The Lureis Lightning?" she inquired.

He inclined his head, and her brows lifted. Newspapers everywhere outside the Imperium carried accounts of conquered Lanthi Ume's resistance to her current Grewzian overlords. The historically independent city-state submitted grudgingly to alien occupation, and a number of her citizens didn't submit at all. The incidents of homegrown Lanthian defiance were numerous, colorful, and commendable. The audacious acts of sabotage, the not-so-spontaneous riots, the seditious publications, the deadly nocturnal raids upon Grewzian offices, armories, and storehouses—these happenings were reported and lauded all over the world. Only a few of the most sensational of gazettes, however, dared suggest an arcane component to the Lanthian resistance.

Such plebeian journals and their far-fetched content were scorned by the literate, but certain celebrated happenings seemed almost to demand magical explanation. One such recent episode involved an impossibly prolonged and intense barrage of lightning bolts, firing down out of a blue sky at high noon to disrupt a Grewzian awards ceremony taking place on a barge at anchor upon Lanthi Ume's famous Lureis Canal. There had been no formal accusations, and yet—

"Cognition sometimes lends its masters the ability to

create atmospheric disturbances," Jil Liskjil informed her, sotto voce. "This talent often enriches the noblest blood, the oldest Lanthian lines, and therefore it's reasonable to suppose that our city's anonymous heroes of the resistance must number among my own closest friends and associates. . . ."

"Let us pray that they remain anonymous, for now," Luzelle replied in a voice so low that only her closest neighbor could hear it, and accompanied by a warning glance across the table, where a glint of light off a monocle signaled the dangerous shift of the Grandlandsman Torvid Stornzof's attention. Porb Jil Liskjil, who had little to gain by advertising his supposed intimacy with the heroes of the Lanthian resistance to a Grewzian audience, subsided at once, while Luzelle continued smoothly and quite audibly, "You are right, Master Jil Liskjil—that Szarish woman's self-propelling carriage is sure to cause a sensation in Lanthi Ume. Has she landed yet, do you think?"

She had voiced a common concern, and all eyes turned to her.

"Szett Urrazole sailed aboard the *Rhelish Mercenary,* which is scheduled to reach Lanthi Ume at seven-fifteen tomorrow morning," announced Girays v'Alisante, characteristically well informed.

"We—we—shall be . . . hard—hard put indeed . . . to catch her," opined Founne Hay-Frinl, the effort of speech reddening his face.

"The Urrazole woman's strange vehicle gives her unfair advantage," Bav Tchornoi complained. "I think she breaks rules. She should be disqualified from competition, yes. At the very least this carriage of hers should not race."

"No rules breaked by she," Mesq'r Zavune contradicted in his lamentable Vonahrish. "What rules? Travel Grand Ellipse all ways, all good."

"Unfair," Bav Tchornoi insisted, black brows lowering. "No one else has such a carriage. It is like magic, very like. This is not fair, not sporting, this magic of hers."

"Madam Urrazole's conveyance is unusual," observed Karsler Stornzof. "But could not legitimately be termed magical, I think."

"Indeed. You are an expert in the field of arcane phenomena, Overcommander?" Girays v'Alisante inquired, a shade too courteously.

"Scarcely an expert," Karsler replied without rancor. "But in childhood I learned to detect the distinctive concentrations of controlled energy causing those disruptions of normality that are so widely and so wrongly regarded as unnatural. Such training is part of a certain traditional form of Grewzian education, and I retain the knack to this day. I viewed Madam Urrazole's carriage at close range back in Toltz, and sensed no typically 'magical' convolutions of force. Her conveyance is remarkable, but essentially mundane."

"I see." Girays inclined his head, frowning slightly.

That's one for you, M. the Marquis. Luzelle smiled internally. *You try to make him look foolish, and only succeed in revealing your own ill nature.*

"I hold the Szarish woman of little account." For the first time the Grandlandsman Torvid condescended to address his companions. "Her peculiar conveyance runs well enough on level roads, but how shall it fare on mountain pathways, in desert, in bog, fen, and forest? There the mechanism must fail, and its inventor acknowledge defeat. This foolish self-propelling carriage perhaps possesses the power to astonish ignorant minds, but nothing of lasting worth. It is a novelty, merely."

THE GRANDLANDSMAN TORVID withdrew from the mess hall as quickly as possible, for the food was execrable and the prattle of the foreigners even worse. In any case he had a task to perform.

Up to the deck he betook himself, where the night air was chilly and sharp, and the stars overhead shone with a hard radiance, remote and clean. Withdrawing a black cigarette from a platinum case, he lit up and for a brief span stood there watching the skies. Presently, eyes still fixed on the stars, he reached into the breast pocket of his tailcoat to bring forth a perforated tube. Absently unscrewing the lid, he shook the jittery tenant forth into his palm, and only then allowed his gaze to drop.

The little nightspeeder that he held lightly clasped quivered with eagerness to fly. The capsule containing a message printed in minuscule characters was well affixed to the creature's dorsal whip, and the night was providentially clear. The grandlandsman opened his hand, and ...e nightspeeder flew like shattered faith.

The resonance of a footfall upon the deck alerted Torvid, and he turned to confront a tall figure, at once alien and known to the marrow.

"I intrude, Grandlandsman," opined Karsler Stornzof.

"Not at all. I smoke, merely." A careless vaporous wave accompanied the disclaimer.

"What was it that flew from your hand, just now? I saw—"

"Nothing. A trick of the light." Torvid blew a perfect smoke ring.

There was a pause, then Karsler responded correctly, "According to your will, Grandlandsman."

Perhaps the younger Stornzof really believed him. Or else simply accepted the authority of the legitimate head of the House, which equated to belief. Either way, Karsler presented no immediate threat.

Threat. How curious to consider applying such a term to a member of the Stornzof family, an honored member at that. Karsler Stornzof was a hero and, as such, a considerable asset.

"I will leave you to your diversions, Grandlandsman," Karsler intoned irreproachably, and turned to leave.

"Stop," Torvid commanded, and the other halted at once. "One moment, Nephew. A word of advice, if I may." He did not await reply, but continued, "I did not anticipate the necessity of instructing you, but at this time find myself compelled to observe that a certain—how shall I say—careless good nature on your part is causing you to blunder."

"In what manner do you suppose me to have blundered?"

"You go out of your way to aid your rivals, at the obvious expense of Stornzof interests. You offer them assistance, you divulge personal information, you undermine your own position."

"You allude to the incident in Glozh."

"That was indeed the first of your errors. Had you not interfered upon that occasion, one of the racers would almost certainly have been eliminated from the competition then and there."

"You cannot suppose I would stand by while a woman is molested?"

"Her welfare is hardly your concern. I trust you will not wax unduly sentimental over the nonexistent virtue of some random little Vonahrish actress."

"Miss Devaire is not an actress. She is a writer and a lecturer, I believe."

"She makes a living upon the public stage, does she not? It is of no consequence. What concerns me now is the quality of your judgment. You chose unwisely to prevent an occurrence that would have benefited you. You compounded your folly by apologizing—yes, literally apologizing—to this foreign woman for the actions of your own Grewzian countrymen. We do not bow the head to inferiors and outsiders, Nephew. You understand me?"

"I understand, but I do not agree," Karsler returned. "The lady was grossly insulted, the animals assaulting her deserved court-martial, and an apology was more than indicated."

"Lady? Ah? I begin to understand. Your head has been turned by the Vonahrishwoman, then?"

"Not at all. She is very beautiful, but—"

"Her shape is quite good. So much I will grant," Torvid conceded negligently. "But she is very much the bourgeoise, conducting her small flirtations without skill or style. She plays the eyes with you continually, and there is little of subtlety in her performance."

"You are difficult to please, Grandlandsman."

"My standards are exacting."

"Miss Devaire strikes me as direct, spontaneous, and generally free of artifice. And I am accustomed to gauging character."

"Men's character, perhaps. But you know nothing of women."

"There were none at the Promontory," Karsler admitted.

"Indeed. And there you touch upon another of your own errors that duty obliges me to note. Not half an hour ago you spoke of your childhood training, informing an imbecilic foreign audience of your ability to sense arcane energy. What foolery is this? The education you received at the Promontory—the very existence of that retreat—all are private matters intended for Grewzian ears alone. The Elucidation, hallowed by time and tradition, is no fit topic for casual chat at table among strangers and enemies. This was worse than stupidity—it verged upon a betrayal of sacred trust."

Karsler Stornzof stiffened with anger, but remained punctilious as he replied, "I must respectfully disagree, Grandlandsman. I revealed nothing of the Elucidation, but only spoke briefly of my early education. I mentioned my ability to detect arcane activity, but that is a matter pertaining to myself alone, and no secret. I speak as I see fit of my own concerns, and do so with a clear conscience."

"Pah, you seek to impress the woman. Amuse yourself with her if you wish, but do not commit the *sottise* of whispering secrets in her Vonahrish ear." Irritably, Torvid flicked his cigarette over the railing into the sea. "Now listen, I speak as the head of our House. You are an officer of the Grewzian Imperium, and a Stornzof. You know well where your duty lies. You are a seasoned soldier and surely recognize the danger of divulging information to the enemy. Guard your tongue, give these fools nothing, and the battle is surely yours."

"But it is not a battle," Karsler observed with the slightest perceptible hint of dryness. "As you have noted, sir, I am a soldier, and therefore capable of distinguishing between a war and a sporting event."

"The distinction you seek to draw is one of degree, merely. A sporting event—a competition of any sort—is simply war on a small scale," Torvid stated. "The battles on the Rhazaullean front—a game of chess—the Grand Ellipse—it is all a variation upon the same theme, and the guiding principle never alters. Victory at any cost, by any available means. That is what it means to be a Stornzof and a servant of the imperior. That is your heritage, Nephew—it is in the Stornzof blood. Your years at the Promontory have served you ill if they have not taught you that."

"My years at the Promontory have taught me much,"

Karsler replied noncommittally. "Sir, I have listened to your oration, and you have made yourself quite clear."

"Well? And?"

"And, assuming there is nothing more you wish to say, I take this opportunity to bid you good evening. With all due respect, Grandlandsman." Inclining his head to the precise angle that family custom dictated, Karsler Stornzof withdrew.

Torvid resisted the impulse to order his nephew back, for there was little profit in prolonging an exchange that threatened to degenerate into a tiresome squabble. Extracting a fresh cigarette from his case, he relit and stood gazing expressionlessly out over the sea, blowing the occasional smoke ring in the wake of the vanished nightspeeder.

THE NIGHTSPEEDER ARROWED SOUTHEAST over the Sea of Silence. Guided by moon and stars, by its sense of natural forces or by unknowable internal stirrings, the creature sped on through the darkness. The hours expired. The moon conceded defeat and vanished. The stars wheeled overhead, and the messenger's speed never slackened.

The shadowed world turned invisibly on its axis, the black air gradually faded to charcoal, to slate, to steel, and down below the solid bulk of the great island-continent of Dalyon differentiated itself from the surrounding sea. The nightspeeder pressed on, the air lightened, and the Dalyonic coastline sharpened. Presently a small archipelago appeared, trailing the mainland like an afterthought. The nightspeeder descended, and the archipelago resolved itself into nine separate islands lazing in a curve around a great central harbor, all of the islands thickly bedizened with human architecture.

Lower yet, and the little lights glowing at doors and windows winked up through the fog-colored atmosphere, while the dark rifts running among the illuminated buildings looked like cracks marring ancient lacquer.

The world spun on, and now the sky was flushed with rose along the eastern horizon, and the color expanded, pumping pastel life into the morning mists that sprawled over land and water.

Lower, and the individual domes and turrets distinguished themselves. The glow along the horizon intensified, and the sun lifted over the edge of the waking world to flood the city with glory. Morning light glittered silver upon the waters of the arterial canals, dotted with countless small craft clustered along innumerable private and public moorings. The sun struck daggers off the brightly tiled towers and rooftops of the fabled palaces, flashed upon the golden crystal ornamenting bridges of green marble, washed the small alleys and market squares with matinal brilliance. Lanthi Ume woke and breathed.

The nightspeeder's instincts bade it shun the day. Fortunately, its goal and refuge lay close at hand. Beyond the prosperous region of shining palaces and monuments sped the messenger, on into the ancient inner depths of the city, skimming low over crooked streets stirring to pungent life, barely clearing the scarred wooden bridges spanning stagnant canals littered with refuse and crowded with disintegrating houseboats.

Straight to the most battered and disreputable of the houseboats flew the nightspeeder, through the open window and into the cabin, where two square-built, dark-clad proprietors sat eating fish chowder heated over a tiny alcohol stove.

Both men looked up, and one of them exclaimed with enthusiasm, in Grewzian, "Little Hilfi, back at last! Come to Papa!"

He extended his wrist, and Little Hilfi alighted at once. Papa caressed the winged creature for a moment or so, then very gently disengaged the capsule affixed to the dorsal whip. Setting Little Hilfi aside with care, he opened the capsule, extracted the message, unfolded it, and read swiftly. When he had done, he pushed the paper scrap across the table to his companion, who also read.

The two men traded glances, and Papa remarked, "Seven-fifteen."

AT EIGHT O'CLOCK the big cargo vessel *Rhelish Mercenary* steamed into the Lanthian harbor, only forty-five minutes behind schedule—an exceptionally fine run. There was a moderate delay as the Grewzian inspectors at the waterfront came aboard to check over the relevant documents, but the *Mercenary*'s paperwork was in order, and official approval quickly granted. Unloading commenced.

The ship carried but a single passenger, a female Szarish national. She was escorted at once to the customs office, where her passport, her various travel permits, and her scant personal belongings were examined with care. Thus occupied, the Szarish woman was unable to oversee the transfer of her cargo from the ship's hold to the dock.

Few workers or loiterers upon the wharves took any notice of the big, tarpaulin-wrapped bundle issuing from the depths of the *Rhelish Mercenary*. The bundle was exceptional in size and irregular in shape and yet, amid such a welter of crates, barrels, and gigantic bales, attracted no attention.

Almost no attention.

A couple of inconspicuous dark-clad masculine figures, lounging in the shadows since seven o'clock or so, had watched the ship's unloading from the start. When the outsized, oddly shaped bundle hove into view, borne on the backs of six grunting stevedores, the observers perked up.

The stevedores deposited their burden and withdrew. While his companion maintained vigil, the man calling himself Papa advanced smartly, but without conspicuous haste. When he reached his goal he halted briefly to scan his surroundings. The wharves were busy, but nobody seemed to be looking his way. Lifting a tarpaulin to reveal a section of a low-slung metallic structure, he leaned in, deposited a package beneath the driver's seat, withdrew, and allowed the canvas covering to fall back into place. Once more he cast his eyes about him, discovered nothing amiss, and calmly rejoined his comrade. Together the two men departed the spot, swiftly vanishing into the populous depths of the city.

WHEN SZETT URRAZOLE'S PASSPORT had received the requisite stamp—an embossed Lanthian civic seal, contained within the circular Endless Fire of the Grewzian Imperium—the Szarish inventor went forth from the customs office in search of her vehicle. Upon presentation of her signed and stamped bill of lading to the supercargo, she was permitted to reclaim her property.

Urrazole stripped away the canvas coverings to reveal the Miracle Self-Propelling Carriage, silvery body agleam in the morning sun. And now the loiterers indifferent to an eccentric anonymous bundle were caught by the spectacle of the outlandish conveyance and its equally uncommon inventor. Many gathered to gawk as Urrazole climbed in, hoisted the metallic sail, adjusted a couple of flanges, then settled down into the seat. Expectantly they watched on as she busied herself with unseen internal control mechanisms, and their patience did not go unrewarded.

Seconds later the vehicle came alive with a deafening roar, and then exploded with an even more deafening blast. Fire flared, smoke billowed, while chunks of metal, glass, and wood, interspersed with body parts, went flying in all directions. The explosion obliterated the Miracle Self-Propelling Carriage, tore a sizable hole in the wharf, and killed Szett Urrazole instantly, along with some twenty or so unlucky bystanders.

4

THE *KARAVISE* REACHED HARBOR around midmorning, and Luzelle was up on deck along with her fellow Ellipsoids, as the racers had taken to calling themselves, all of them itching for the first glimpse of legendary Lanthi Ume.

And there she was, dead ahead, rising from the sea like some gorgeous aging harlot of a queen from her bath. There were the shamelessly fantastical towers and jewel-hued domes, the glittering bridges and archways, the spires crowning palaces of fable, the numberless boats and barges, the general excess, the polychrome exuberance that was so hard to justify and so famously impossible to resist.

Letting her eyes drink, Luzelle drew a deep breath of the mild, humid breeze sweeping the harbor, felt her spirits soar, and remembered once again why she loved to travel, despite all discomforts and inconveniences.

A shadow touched her and she turned to find Girays at her side. He was studying the city, dark eyes filled with a pleasure that was all youth despite the whisper of grey at his temples, and she recalled then, with a pang, exactly why she had once looked forward to spending her life with him. Her hand wanted to reach out to him, and she controlled the impulse with an effort.

Almost as if he divined her thoughts, he turned to look at her, and her gaze dropped at once for fear of what he might read in her eyes. That would hardly do, so she forced herself to counter his regard squarely and to inquire with a convincing air of indifference, "Well, and what do you think of it all?"

"Marvelous sight," he answered, smiling. "A dreamer's whim caught in crystal."

Worse and worse. She'd expected some sort of formerly-Exalted superior sarcasm out of him, but his expression reflected the kind of unaffected warmth that had melted her insides at age nineteen, and now, six years later, still seemed to exert the same effect.

Remember the quarrels, she commanded herself. *Remember all the rotten things he said!*

"All the better, with you here to share it," Girays added, so lightly that he might have been joking.

We might have shared a whole world full of marvelous sights, she thought painfully, and was immediately furious with herself, because of course he was making fun of her, trying to goad her into making a fool of herself. She wasn't about to oblige. A caustic retort rose to her lips, but died unspoken, for that look in his eyes was confusing her badly.

"A fine view, alone or in company," she replied, taking refuge in quiet dignity. "But I may share it no longer, for I must go collect my luggage. The boat is about to land."

THE *KARAVISE* DOCKED and the passengers disembarked. Suitcase in hand, Luzelle made for the customs office. As she went, she noted that a wide stretch of the wharf was cordoned off, the area guarded by monolithic Grewzian soldiers. Behind the barrier gaped an impressive hole, its edges jagged and freshly charred.

She wanted to stop and ask a dozen questions, but forced herself to pass by. *No time.*

The customs office was adorned in typically exuberant Lanthian style, with paint in three different colors and a roof of glossy green tile. Luzelle went in and took her place at the end of a queue that already included several fellow Ellipsoids. No sign of Girays as yet. No Karsler. The Festinette twins were present and noisy. The line inched toward a low counter at the back of the room. Her turn came at last, and she presented her passport and luggage to the bored official seated there. Scarcely wasting a glance on the contents of her valise, he stamped her passport and motioned her on with the jerk of a thumb.

Done. Another stamp upon her passport—an emblem marred with the Imperium's Endless Fire, but a tangible milestone nonetheless. In any case, the next port of call along the Grand Ellipse lay in the land of Aennorve, where the Grewzians dared not venture. Yet.

Next order of business—book passage to Aeshno, the great port city at the southwest extremity of Aennorve. The Ministry of Foreign Affairs had reserved a stateroom for her aboard the Lanthian passenger liner *Nine Isles,* but the vessel had embarked yesterday afternoon. No great matter—she need only seek out the dockside Isle Line agent, who would certainly exchange her ticket. Or better yet, she might check the various agencies for the next eastbound steamer of any description.

Brain clicking, she exited the customs office, emerged into the sunlight, and halted to stare, for the wharf had transformed itself within the space of minutes. The broad expanse now supported a close-packed throng of restless humanity centering about the great hole that she had noted earlier. The crowd was motley, comprising old and young, male and female, rich and poor, clad in the garb of assorted nationalities. Despite the visible dissimilarities, a common sense of nerve-strung, hostile tension seemed to unite the group. The immediate source of displeasure was obvious—the area swarmed with Grewzian soldiers—but the underlying cause remained obscure.

Luzelle stretched to her best height, straining to see over hundreds of heads. No use. Some sort of suppressed commotion around the hole in the dock, a buzzing uneasiness animating the crowd, a daunting collection of Grewzian troops—that was all she could make out.

"What is this?" she demanded of her nearest neighbor, a well-dressed woman of a certain age, perhaps some captain's wife. She spoke unthinkingly in her own tongue, and was favored with a faintly startled glance. For a moment she thought her words unintelligible to the other, then the answer came in tolerably fluent but heavily Lanthian-accented Vonahrish.

"They are drowning Cezineen."

"What are cezineen?"

"His Preeminence Perif Neen Cezineen, the master of the Select. The Grewzians, they are drowning him."

"What, you mean there's to be an execution? In public? Right *now*?"

The other nodded.

"What is the crime?"

"Crime?" The Lanthian woman's mouth pursed, as if to foil the escape of indiscretions. She won the battle, and replied circumspectly, "The Grewzians, they blame the resistance for the explosion yesterday morning. They know not who makes go the bomb, but they do know that the savants of the Select support the resistance. So the Grewzians do what they can, and they drown His Preeminence Cezineen here upon the site of the crime, for warning to all, and also for revenge."

"A bomb set off by the Lanthian resistance caused the big hole in the dock?"

"So say the Grewzians. But—" The Lanthian woman cast a sharp eye about her, then lowered her voice and continued, "I say to you, I say to any and all, that this is not like the resistance. These Lanthian patriots—I mean to say, you understand me, these *criminals*—these people do not make war upon their own. This explosion that damages the wharf and kills the Szarish woman racer in her strange carriage—this same explosion also destroys good Lanthians. The men of the resistance, they do not stoop so low."

"Szett Urrazole? Killed? Are you telling me that Szett Urrazole was *killed* yesterday, and her vehicle destroyed?"

"Yes, and many others, many Lanthians. I do not think that the resistance does this. But the Grewzians, they must solve the crime and punish the guilty, for they are the rulers, all knowing, all powerful, you understand me. So now they drown Preeminence Cezineen, and surely all of us profit greatly by the lesson."

"If the Lanthian resistance didn't kill her, then who did?"

"What difference shall it make? I cannot believe it Lanthian work. Perhaps this Urrazole woman's rivals are behind it. A woman should not race. This northern Szarish creature had herself to blame, she thought herself so great, bringing her own fate upon her own hard head, and now we Lanthians must pay the price of her folly. I say she should have stayed at home, and blameless lives would have been saved, but what is that, to such a very great woman?"

"But you're quite certain that Szett Urrazole is really dead?" The query evidently merited no reply, and Luzelle continued, "What of this Preeminence Neen Cezineen? Have the Grewzians any solid proofs against him?"

"You do not understand me," the Lanthian woman answered with a hint of impatience. "The Grewzians, they do not need proofs. They do not care if Preeminence Cezineen is involved in the affair, or if he is not. That is all—how do you say—trifled? Trifling. The Grewzians, they care that all shall know that a crime against the Imperium must always bring punishment upon Lanthian heads. This is the lesson they teach."

"But the master of Lanthi Ume's Select—that's a fairly significant personage, a man of some power. The Grewzians don't fear this savant's Cognition?"

"Only watch," the other advised, "and you will see how greatly they fear."

Easier said than done. The crowd was thick, and she could not see a thing. In any case she hardly relished the spectacle of a public execution. Of all the revolting, barbaric anachronisms—so typically Grewzian. . . .

Another few weeks, and scenes like this one may be repeating themselves in Vonahr.

Luzelle made for the stand of ticketing agencies clustered at the lower end of the dock, but the jittery density of the crowd foiled her efforts. Several increasingly uncivilized attempts to force her way through failed, a couple of retaliatory elbow jabs thrust her off course, and presently she found herself, disheveled and breathing hard, wedged into a niche indenting a wall of stacked wooden crates. The way out was blocked, unless—

Her eyes rose. The great pyramid of crates, serving as makeshift bleachers, supported scores of spectators. The heap looked easy to climb. Valise in hand, she began to ascend, scrambling nimbly from box to box, careless of the flashes of petticoat and stocking glimpsed by interested strangers. By the time she reached the fourth big tier of crates, she had a clear view of her surroundings. She had not meant to linger, but paused without thought, unwillingly transfixed by the scene playing out alongside the jagged new hole in the wharf.

The Grewzians had cleared the perimeter, pushing the crowd back from the charred edges, and now the area was bare of all save grey-clad military figures and a lone prisoner, presumably the doomed Preeminence Neen Cezineen. She did not know where he had come from or when he had arrived, and the rush of shocked sympathy that filled her at sight of the elderly, silver-haired man decked in massive chains drove all such considerations from her mind. Shackles notwithstanding, Preeminence Cezineen remained an impressive figure, tall and still straight-spined, clad in the traditional black robes of a Lanthian savant. His wrists were tightly bound behind his back, and a heavy gag stopped his mouth. The facial features visible above the gag were swollen and bruised.

The crowd growled and the Grewzian soldiers tensed visibly.

They beat that old man, those Grewzian pigs. Did they have to gag him as well? What do they think he could say? Then she remembered a scrap of information culled from some long-ago text; the magical Cognition of Lanthi Ume's savants was verbal in nature, dependent upon the spoken word. The gag suppressed Preeminence Cezineen's arcane powers, such as they were.

The ranking Grewzian officer, grey uniform blazoned with the insignia of an undercommander second class, was reading the order of execution aloud in halting Lanthian. The crowd was preternaturally intent, and Luzelle told herself that she should leave this place, but found herself paralyzed, unable to tear her eyes from the condemned savant's face. All but impossible at such a distance to read Cezineen's expression above the gag, but the old man held his head high.

The undercommander concluded. Without further ado a couple of his subordinates stepped forward, seized the prisoner, and unceremoniously slung him forward into the hole in the dock. Preeminence Perif Neen Cezineen hit water with a splash easily audible in the midst of that appalled silence, and the weight of his chains dragged him under at once.

His struggles, if any, were invisible. The bright morning sunlight danced on calm waters. It looked as if nothing had happened at all.

Such casually professional efficiency seemed to gall the watching Lanthians, and a mutter of bitter indignation arose. The mutter sharpened to a snarl, hostile agitation stirred the crowd, and somebody threw a reckless insult:

"Grewzian pustules!"

A flying rock underscored the sentiment. The missile missed the undercommander second class by a hair. Instantly closing ranks, the Grewzians raised and leveled their rifles. The intensity of noise and popular fury mounted. Stones flew, along with empty bottles and bits of stink scooped up from the dock. The undercommander spoke, and his men fired into the heart of the crowd.

Luzelle felt the air sing. Her nearest neighbor—a poorly clad, pink-faced adolescent, no more than thirteen or fourteen years of age—squealed, clutched at his chest, and toppled from his place, slack body rolling down successive tiers of crates to land with a conclusive thud on the wharf below. Four or five others in her immediate vicinity likewise shrilled or grunted, grabbed at themselves, and fell.

She looked down at herself almost disbelievingly, scanning her own garments in search of spreading red stains. Nothing. She remained untouched. But for how much longer? The Grewzian soldiers, notoriously intolerant of foreign petulance, were already reloading. The crowd around her was boiling, half its members screaming for blood, the other half desperate to flee the docks. She herself belonged to the latter category.

But where to go? Her mind seemed to have slowed to a crawl.

Ticketing booths. Book passage to Aennorve. That had been her original intention.

How to get there?

The wharf swarmed with howling humanity, she could never force her way through that throng. Moreover, the Lanthians—some of them, at least—had gone quite mad, and now, instead of beating a prudent retreat while they could, were deliberately provoking the Grewzian troops, pelting them with filth and refuse, screaming obscenities, waving their furiously impotent fists in the air.

The Grewzian undercommander spoke, his soldiers fired, and fresh shrieks arose. Luzelle scrambled down from her perch, vanishing into the mob as Preeminence Neen Cezineen had vanished beneath the harbor waters. She was less of a conspicuous target now but, having abandoned her elevated vantage point, found herself packed tightly amid countless bodies, unable to move, unable to see, and all but unable to breathe. Anonymous humanity pressed her on all sides, someone's elbow was digging into her ribs, and the clamor of frantic voices was unendurable.

She heard the crack of gunfire, and then something like a whistle or a siren followed by another volley. For a few endless moments all was lunacy, pressure, and noise. At last, when she felt herself in real danger of suffocation, the dense surrounding mass rippled. The pressure eased a little, she sensed movement around her, and then she, too, was moving. A human current was carrying her along, and she could not have resisted if she had tried. She had no idea where she was going; she had lost all sense of direction, and the howling uproar had not diminished in the least.

The current quickened, the tight-packed throng loosened, and she could breathe—and even see—again. The wharf was littered with fallen Lanthians; wounded or dead, she couldn't judge their condition or their number, for the press of the crowd swept her along irresistibly. Gunfire popped, panic flared, and the mob convulsed. A violent shove from behind sent Luzelle crashing against her nearest neighbor, who thrust her violently aside. She staggered, but stayed on her feet. Should she fall in the midst of that stampede, she would not rise again.

The retreat accelerated. She glanced back over her shoulder and saw a grey-clad squadron ranged across the wharf, advancing steadily to drive the mob from the site of the execution. Those citizens unwisely attempting resistance were being shot or bayoneted by the dozen. Those so unfortunate as to lose their footing were simply trampled.

Murderers. Barbarians. Even in the thick of that chaos she did not dare so much as whisper the words aloud. How easy it was to learn fear, but then, how proficient the teachers.

The crowd was streaming along the dock, driven on by the bullets speeding inches overhead and by the staccato commands of the Grewzian shepherds. To the right, an alleyway running between two warehouses beckoned, and a human torrent poured into the opening.

She was off the wharf and running along some nameless little avenue. As she went, the way widened, divided, turned itself into a little market square, broke into crossroads, greened into a public garden, then narrowed and re-formed as a path edging one of the countless canals. At each intersection the fleeing mob split and thinned until at last there was no more mob, no more rage and terror boiling through the streets, and she found herself walking alongside the water through a world miraculously tranquil.

Luzelle paused. A few feet away a stand of flowering trees shaded a public bench, currently unoccupied. She went to the bench and let herself sink down upon it, noticing for the first time that she somehow retained her death grip upon the valise containing her passport, clothing, and money. Throughout the upheaval some unnoticed corner of her brain had apparently retained practicality. She set the valise beside her on the bench, and saw that her hands were trembling. Her heart raced and her lungs screamed, but she could hardly draw breath, for the steel stays of her corset compressed her mercilessly. Ridiculous that women should submit themselves to such torture, ridiculous and not to be borne. She herself would certainly rebel, should have done so years ago, but now was not the time to be planning sartorial revolt, not now when her head swam, her vision dimmed, and she felt herself on the verge of fainting. Absurd, she never fainted, she wasn't the type, and yet the world around her was oddly fogged and distant, and it might not be a bad idea to shut her eyes for a moment or two.

Elbow propped on the arm of the bench, she rested her head on her hand, allowed her lids to fall, and drank deeply of the springtime air. Soon her giddiness subsided, but the closed eyes were a mistake, for the images blazing through her mind sharpened. She saw the old man sink beneath the harbor waters, saw the grey soldiers firing upon the crowd, heard the Grewzian guns speak, heard the screams of pain and terror, saw the dead and wounded fall, smelled the blood and fear.

There was moisture upon her face, cold sweat and hot tears. Her shoulders shook. She would break down completely in a moment, another weakness she could not afford, so she sought refuge in anger.

Those Grewzians—the filthiest scum of the world, guilty of atrocities beside which the innocent savageries of the Bhomiri Islanders paled to insignificance. Cruel, murderous, pitiless, relentless—the very worst of humankind. Today she had learned how to hate them.

"Miss Devaire? You are ill?"

The words were spoken in Vonahrish. The voice was concerned, foreign, and familiar. She looked up and blinked, momentarily dazzled by the sunlight lancing through her tears, to behold the wavery outline of a tall figure topped with gold. Wiping her eyes with the back of her hand, she muttered in disbelief, "Karsler?"

His face changed a little, and she wondered if her free use of his first name surprised or offended him. Certainly the Judge would have deplored such impropriety, but it had slipped out and she couldn't apologize without looking worse than ever.

Perhaps the presumption failed to annoy him, for his look of concern deepened and his query transmuted to a statement. "You are ill. Allow me to assist you."

"No. Thank you," she returned, torn between gratitude at

his kindness and anger at the sight of his grey uniform. "I am quite well, truly."

"I think not." He studied her. "You will recover presently, but for now you should not be alone."

She had nothing to say to that. She did not really want to be alone, sick and faint on a park bench in a foreign city. On the other hand, she hardly relished the society of a Grewzian officer, although she found herself tempted to make an exception in his case. But the point was academic, for he clearly did not intend to leave her.

"There are smelling salts in your valise?" Karsler inquired.

"No. I never thought I'd need any. I'm not usually so wobbly."

"Wobbly? My Vonahrish is imperfect, but I believe I understand you. Today, however, you are wobbly, and surely not without cause." He was eyeing her very intently, as if to read the mind behind the face. "There was a riot breaking out upon the dock, just as the Grandlandsman and I departed. Were you caught in the midst of that disturbance? Roughly handled and alarmed, perhaps?"

"Yes." Raising her head, she met his gaze squarely. "Your countrymen were there, drowning an elderly civilian."

"A convicted saboteur, I have heard. Such terrorists murder indiscriminately, and their suppression—harsh though it may seem—ultimately saves lives."

"Perhaps. But many present believed this particular sacrificial victim innocent. When they ventured to object, the soldiers fired on the crowd."

"As I understand it, my compatriots were attacked by an armed mob. This being so, they were obliged to defend themselves. I do not mean to discount the importance of this matter, nor do I deny its tragic nature. But it is certain that the troops had no choice."

"The Lanthians were armed with pebbles and refuse, nothing more."

"It is reported that many carried firearms."

"Reported?"

"The news has spread through the city in a matter of minutes."

"But you were not there to see for yourself?"

"No. I did not see for myself."

"How did that happen, Overcommander?"

"You knew my name, a minute ago."

She repressed a smile at that. And what sort of woman would even think of smiling at such a time? No doubt the Judge could have told her. Without acknowledging his remark she continued, "I don't understand how you got away so quickly. I know I was one of the first off the *Karavise* to reach the customs office, and I didn't see you there, but you're saying that you passed through before me, and were already leaving the wharf, when—"

"No," he told her calmly, but a shadow of constraint darkened his eyes. "I was not obliged to pass through customs. In view of our nationality, the grandlandsman's title, and my own commission, the requirement was waived in our case."

"I see." She looked away. *Unfair.*

"Unfair." He nodded. "Yes, it is quite·unfair, and yet I believe that these inequities of political fortune may yet balance themselves, before the race is run."

"Are you always so telepathic?"

"I am not telepathic. Only sometimes, I can make a fairly good guess."

"Better than fairly good. How do you do that?"

"As you have asked me if I am always so telepathic, I think I may ask you if you are always so inquisitive."

"Afraid so."

"I am glad to hear it. You satisfy my hopes, along with my expectations."

Tell me your hopes, your expectations. She stifled the natural response. He was a Grewzian, after all.

"I cannot account for all of this," she compromised.

"All of—?"

"This. Such a meeting, in the middle of a great city, by mere chance. It's improbable."

"You are displeased?"

"Only surprised."

"The surprise does not appear to disagree with you. The color has come back into your face. Your eyes are clear and bright, very bright indeed, like night signals. You are looking quite wonderfully alive."

"I am?" she asked, absurdly pleased, then recollected herself. "But why are you here at all, Overcommander—Karsler? Shall I regard this meeting as coincidence alone?"

"No," he replied, to her surprise. "Not quite coincidence. I was attracted to this place, at this time, for reasons I can hardly define. Sometimes it happens that way—that is, there is the pull, the sense of nameless demand that draws me where it will, when it will. The purpose of such a summons is rarely apparent, but when it comes, it is not to be denied."

"But how extraordinary," she replied noncommittally, and sat silent for a moment, trying to decide whether or not she believed him. His remark bordered on the fantastic, yet he had no reason to lie, unless he simply sought to impress a credulous female.

"Yes, I agree—it sounds a very idle claim indeed," Karsler conceded.

Luzelle managed to repress her guilty start, but felt the telltale color heat her cheeks. He'd needed no telepathy to divine her reaction—she knew from dismal lifelong experience that she had a face all too easy to read. She forced herself to meet his eyes, and saw that he was smiling—a smile of amusement that had nothing at all of mockery or superiority about it, unlike the sneers wont to bend the formerly-Exalted lips of Master Girays v'Alisante.

"But I wouldn't presume to dismiss it," she told him, and found that she meant what she said. "However it may have happened, I'm lucky to meet you here. But now I need impose on your patience and generosity no longer, for I'm quite recovered."

"I believe that you are, or nearly so. I hope I do not presume too greatly in asking what you will do next?"

"Do?" She frowned, taken aback. "Why, I hadn't really thought about it. Go back to the waterfront, I suppose. I need to buy a steamer ticket to Aeshno, and then—"

"It is not yet safe to return to the wharf. Quite likely, all civilians have been barred from the area. In any case all commercial enterprises there, including the ticketing agencies, are certain to be shut down for the next several hours, at the very least."

"Well, then there must be someplace in town where I can book passage. Perhaps through one of the better hotels—"

"I do not think so. I have already inquired at the Prendivet Hotel, without success. May I offer a suggestion?"

"Of course."

"I left the grandlandsman in the restaurant at the Prendivet. Come back there with me now for lunch. The nourishment will do you good, I suspect. By the time you have finished eating, the wharf establishments may have reopened for business. If they have not, you may contemplate your next move at leisure, and in comfort. You lose nothing by the delay, for all the Grand Ellipse contestants present in Lanthi Ume are equally inconvenienced."

Quite right. Everyone was in the same boat, or rather, not in the boat. There was some comfort in that. And lunch in Lanthi Ume with Karsler Stornzof—not an unattractive prospect, even if he was Grewzian. But he wasn't like the rest of them, she told herself firmly. Karsler was different.

"Is the Prendivet Hotel far from here?" Luzelle inquired.

"Not at all. A hired boat could carry us there in ten minutes. Or perhaps you would prefer to walk?"

"Yes, let's walk. That's always the best way to experience a new city. You just sort of absorb it through the soles of your feet."

"I will take your word for it. I must confess, I've little experience in traveling for pleasure."

"Oh, then you find such things frivolous?"

"I find such things—astonishing."

"You sound like a visitor from some other world."

"That is not such a bad description."

"What do you mean?"

"Ah, that is a solemn subject, best left for another day. For now, let us enjoy the city and its sights, let us—absorb through the soles of our feet."

For a moment she half expected him to offer his arm, then reminded herself that the occasion was quasi-social at best.

They moved off together, and the city around them was splendid in the sunlight, despite the conspicuous presence of foreign troops. Their conversation was innocuous—for by mutual unspoken consent they avoided potentially dangerous issues—but enjoyable, easy, and, to Luzelle, distinctly novel. She had encountered a variety of celebrated men in the course of her travels, but never one so genuinely unaware of the power of his own fame and appearance as Karsler Stornzof. He didn't seem to regard himself as a hero, as a celebrity, or indeed as anything more than an ordinary officer of the Grewzian Imperium. Hard to believe, yet she could detect nothing of false modesty in his attitude. Similarly he appeared unconscious of the countless feminine eyes following him as he walked along the path.

And his effect on Luzelle Devaire?

This head is not easily turned, she assured herself. *And I have a race to win.*

They came to an intersection and he guided her to the left, along a narrow way lined with odd, old-fashioned little shops and booths. Her feet stopped of their own accord before one of them, and it took her consciousness a moment to understand why.

It was an ordinary pawnshop, small and dingy, indistinguishable from countless others of similar ilk infesting every major city. Certainly there was nothing distinctive to be glimpsed in the window display. Just the usual sad and dusty collection of other people's lost treasures; plenty of jewelry, watches, silver, china, crystal, musical instruments, expensive monogrammed shaving implements, ornaments, fancy spurs and whips, ornate ceremonial swords and daggers, a couple of big service revolvers . . .

It was the revolvers, she realized, that had halted her. Suddenly she was back again at Glozh Station, and the two Grewzian soldiers were dragging her from the platform. She could hear their voices and feel their hands on her, she could taste her own outraged fear, and she remembered her promise to herself that she would never again travel without a loaded pistol. Now was the time to fulfill that vow.

"You wish to enter?" Karsler asked.

"Yes." She turned to look up at him, and forced herself to add, "I mean to purchase a gun, for my own protection."

Now she would have to endure his disapproval, or worse, his patronage. Beyond doubt he'd inform her that possession of a lethal weapon could only maximize her own danger. She wouldn't know how to handle a gun properly, or if by any chance she managed to learn, then the knowledge would hysterically flee her mind at some critical moment. She would end up shooting herself or some innocent bystander. Or else some male aggressor far stronger, quicker, and more resolute than she would simply take the weapon away from her, snatch it right out of her hand before she could remember to squeeze the trigger, and then where would she be? She had heard the entire condescending lecture more than once, and she was not inclined to listen to it again.

Karsler surprised her.

"That is a sound thought," he observed, almost sadly. "In such a world as this you must stand prepared to defend yourself. I cannot deny the necessity. Do you know much of handguns?"

"Not a great deal," she admitted. "But I'm thinking that those two there in the window look pretty useful."

"The revolvers—yes, very useful indeed. But a little large and heavy to suit your needs, perhaps. Would you not prefer a weapon that you can carry easily and inconspicuously—in a pocket, or possibly in your reticule?"

"That's just what I need."

"Then let us see what this shop has to offer."

They entered, and found the musty dimness within inhabited by the wizened proprietress, a woman with a face seamed and shriveled as a desiccated apple. There were no other customers in evidence, and it was easy to fancy that no other customers had set foot on the premises within the past decade or so.

Luzelle stated her requirements. Following a brief, astonished glance, the pawnbroker produced a tray of assorted handguns and set it down before her.

She studied the collection with an air of businesslike competence designed to camouflage total ignorance. What was there to choose among them? They all fired bullets, didn't they?

"This one looks . . . convenient," she decided, attracted to the smallest and most decorative of the weapons. It was tiny enough to fit in the palm of her hand, very light in weight, with a mother-of-pearl grip laced with golden traceries. A woman's gun, unmistakably.

"You might carry it easily," Karsler agreed, "but you would find it effective only at the very shortest range, and then only if you hit the target in a vital area. Otherwise—a flea bite."

"I see." Luzelle returned the pretty midget to the tray and chose another, an interesting six-barreled piece with a pierced butt. "This one seems quite formidable."

"Perhaps, in some respects. But that design is awkward in its action, it is seriously muzzle-heavy, and you would find it difficult to hold an aim."

"Oh. Muzzle-heavy. Yes." She put it back.

"If you will permit me to offer a recommendation—"

"Please do!"

"The Khrennisov FK6." Noting her look of incomprehension, he pointed. "This one. An excellent short-range weapon designed for self-defense. Compact, small enough to carry in your pocket, shoots accurately, and with great force. The Khrennisov should serve your purposes admirably."

"You think?" She hefted the pocket pistol experimentally. It lay small but assertive in her hand, and it made her feel brave. She decided that she liked it. "I'll take it, then."

"You will not regret your decision."

She paid the pawnbroker's price without haggling, in appreciation whereof the old woman threw in a small box half full of ammunition, presumably furnished by the Khrennisov's former owner.

"I'll start target practice as soon as I find a spot where nobody minds flying bullets," Luzelle promised.

"It will come to feel quite natural to you much sooner than you imagine," Karsler told her.

Once more she thought to catch a hint of something like sadness or regret in his voice, but no disapproval, and she thought, *How unlike Girays he is! Girays would have pestered me to death over this, and pretended he was doing it out of concern for my welfare. It's pleasant to be regarded as a mentally sound adult.*

They exited into the sunlight, where the somber mood of the shop faded swiftly, despite the weight of the new, dense little paper-wrapped parcel that she refused to allow her companion to carry for her. On they went along the narrow street until the vista before them widened and she confronted an astonishment of palaces—high, glittering, and presumptuous, each wonderfully individual.

She had never in her life seen anything to equal the complexity of the iridescent coils coiffing the violet towers of the mansion directly before her. Another, even more imposing, sported four slim blue spires crowned with orbiting silver starbursts. Another, inconceivably vast, was clothed from ground to summit in luminous marble mosaics. Then there was the grandly peculiar conglomerate of vertical cylinders sheathed in beaten copper weathered to the color of jade. And the ambitious fantasy sprawling full length beneath nested domes, each dome elaborately pierced and sliced to reveal the complex polychrome layers beneath. And the gilded behemoth straddling no fewer than four separate quays. And the white giantess clothed in marble fretwork airy as petrified frost. And the—but no, she couldn't take them in at one glance, they were too numerous, too remarkable, and the dance of sunlight on the silver waters of the greatest of canals too distracting.

She drew a wondering breath. Karsler Stornzof turned to her and smiled.

"The Lureis Canal," he said.

The center of the city, the heart of Lanthi Ume, famed throughout the world. She had seen many colored prints and paintings of this scene, but none that did it justice. For a time they paused to marvel, then moved off along the walkway known as the Prendivet Saunter that edged the great canal. And now she noticed a displeasing multiplicity of grey-uniformed figures strolling the neighborhood, but refused to let the oppressive Grewzian presence dampen her enjoyment.

Resolutely she pushed the recurring images of the morning's horrors from her mind.

Too soon they came to the Prendivet Hotel—big and modern, but constructed in stylistic harmony with the neighboring mansions upon the site once occupied by a palace known as Vallage House. Reputedly one of the wonders of the city, Vallage House had been torn down, or burned down, or otherwise disposed of in the distant past, but for some reason popular legend had it that the glorious old structure crowning the remote extremity of Cape Consolation in the land of Strell, and likewise known as Vallage House, was an exact replica of the Lanthian original.

They went in, crossed the lobby, and passed through a tall arched doorway into the restaurant, where a solicitous headwaiter seated them at once. Luzelle glanced about uneasily. The place was handsome enough, well lit and well appointed, but disturbingly grey with Grewzian officers. She had never seen so many high-ranking enemies assembled in one room, and she hoped she never would again. Yet here she was, lunching with one of them.

She consulted the menu. Sophisticated, delicate Lanthian seafood dishes, interspersed with such red-blooded Grewzian favorites as offal pudding, deep-fried mutton gobbets, and raised venison pie.

"This place is popular among your countrymen," she observed without enthusiasm.

"That is almost inevitable," he told her. "The Prendivet Hotel is next-door neighbor to the mansion called Beffel House, in which my compatriots have established their headquarters. They find this spot most convenient for their meals."

"Most convenient," she echoed dryly, but dropped her eyes before his straight gaze, which somehow made her feel unsure, as if her implied criticism had been misplaced or even unjust.

The waiter reappeared. Luzelle requested mussels in broth, while Karsler ordered an omelet, and it crossed her mind that she had dined in his presence a couple of times aboard the

Karavise, and never yet seen him touch meat. But she gave the matter little thought, for her attention fixed almost at once on a neighboring table where a familiar well-tailored figure sat amid a gathering of very senior Grewzian officers.

"Isn't that a *general* sitting across the table from your uncle, over there?" she asked.

Karsler's eyes followed her discreetly pointing finger. "General Uhrnuss," he confirmed. "Overgeneral Brugloist beside him. There is also the Overcommander Hahltronz. The others I do not know by sight."

"Brugloist—he commands the whole Grewzian army in this part of the world, doesn't he?"

"The Southeast Expeditionary Force, yes."

"Your uncle and the overgeneral appear cordial."

"They roomed together for a couple of terms at Leistlurl, I believe," he told her, naming the oldest and most inflexibly exclusive of Grewzland's great universities.

"They seem very intent on something or other. I wonder what it could be?"

She did not have to wonder for long.

The food arrived, the conversation altered direction, and soon, to her surprise, she found herself telling him about the Judge, the hideous quarrels, and her final withdrawal from her father's house. She revealed nothing of the shattered betrothal with a fellow Ellipsoid, nothing of her own financial straits, or of her dealings with the ministry, yet her voice ran on, loosing recollections that she could never have imagined herself sharing with a near stranger, much less a Grewzian. She could hardly account for her own loquacity, but supposed that Karsler's air of intelligent interest devoid of intrusiveness invited confidences. He was remarkably easy to talk to, but the reverse did not seem to hold true, for she noticed that he spoke very little of himself or his own past. She gave him plenty of opportunity, left several conversational openings into which many men would happily have leapt, but he remained courteously reticent, and finally she began to contemplate in earnest the various means whereby she might gently and painlessly pry his mind open, at least a crack.

But she never got the chance to try, for just then the

Grandlandsman Torvid Stornzof rose from his seat and crossed to their table, where he paused, arms folded and monocle glinting.

Karsler rose dutifully, and observed in Vonahrish, "You honor me, Grandlandsman. Will you join us?"

Decline, Ice Statue, Luzelle urged silently. *Go away.*

"News, Nephew," Torvid announced in Grewzian, equally ignoring the invitation and Luzelle's presence. "I have lunched with the Overgeneral Brugloist, whose response to this morning's local impertinence is commendably decisive. The overgeneral informs me that Lanthi Ume's harbor is to be shut down until further notice. For the present, neither admission nor departure is permitted. Such firmness speaks eloquently."

"All sea trade ceases?" Karsler asked in Vonahrish. "The Lanthian economy is fueled by such commerce, is it not?"

"I am not conversant with the internal ordering of our various subject nations."

"The city is largely dependent upon imports for its ordinary foodstuffs and provisions."

"Well?"

"The harbor blockade effectively places Lanthi Ume in a state of siege, with predictable results."

"The local resistance might have considered that possibility prior to its small experiment in insolence."

"The majority of citizens, completely uninvolved in the affair, will shortly begin to starve."

"Then they will see that their own comfort dictates a repudiation of the resistance, and all concerned stand to profit by the lesson."

"Perhaps they should thank you for the instruction," Luzelle murmured, but the grandlandsman seemed not to hear her. Karsler heard her, however. She saw her own voice in his eyes.

"And if they do not repudiate the resistance?" Karsler inquired. "What then?"

"I cannot say." Torvid shrugged. "Neither of us will be here to observe."

"The race, you mean? Certainly we can proceed overland

to another point of embarkation from Dalyon, but the time involved in such an undertaking is considerable, and we must resign ourselves to a delay—"

"There will be no delay," Torvid stated. "Not for the two of us. We are Grewzian, and we may rely upon the loyalty and support of our countrymen."

"Loyalty is not the issue here and now."

"You will not acknowledge it as such, but your misconceptions scarcely alter reality. I will state the facts clearly. The harbor has been closed. For the present there will be no unauthorized entries or departures. However, the Lanthian merchant vessel *Inspiration* has received the overgeneral's personal approval, and will embark for Aennorve in approximately one hour's time. We two sail with her, the only passengers permitted aboard."

Unfair! Despite linguistic limitations, Luzelle understood Torvid's discourse clearly enough to know the worst.

"Did you arrange this, Grandlandsman?" Karsler asked.

"Permission for the *Inspiration* to sail, with the two of us aboard, yes. I cannot take credit for the closing of the harbor, however. I did not create the situation, but perceived its possibilities, merely."

"I see." Karsler eyed his uncle. "I almost wonder if it is sporting to exploit such a vast, unearned advantage."

"Pah, must you bewail your own good fortune? Should the enemy retreat before you in battle, would you hesitate to press your advantage then? And do not try my patience with artificial distinctions drawn between a battle and a race, there is no time for such foolery. Pay your reckoning, and let us be off to the docks. Or better yet, allow me." So saying, the grandlandsman produced his wallet and extracted a couple of notes, which he dropped carelessly on the table. As he did so, his eyes encountered Luzelle's, he affected to recognize her for the first time, and finally switched over to her language. "Ah, the little female traveler, the daredevil in skirts. Miss Dulaire, was it? Denaire? Contraire? Excuse me, but you must understand, I find all Vonahrish names eminently forgettable."

"But what an inconvenience, Grandlandsman," Luzelle

murmured sympathetically. "And yet I believe it quite possible, by dint of application, to overcome the handicap of a congenitally weak or defective memory."

Torvid's face congealed.

She was certain that she saw Karsler's lips quirk, but the smile was gone in an instant. His expression was once again grave as he turned to her and observed with his customary formality, "I regret that our lunch must conclude prematurely, and I hope you will pardon my discourtesy in leaving you so abruptly."

"It's no discourtesy under the circumstances," she replied. "I thank you for all of your help and kindness, as well as for your good company."

"I hope we may lunch again another day, at leisure. In the meantime, do not neglect to practice with the Khrennisov."

The grandlandsman shot his nephew a penetrating glance.

"I'll practice, I promise," vowed Luzelle. "I'll be drilling two-biquin bits at twenty paces, the next time we meet."

"In Toltz, perhaps, upon conclusion of the race," Torvid Stornzof suggested. "Surely not before."

"Oh, I shouldn't count on that, Grandlandsman," Luzelle returned. "Someone whose opinion I respect believes that these inequities of political fortune may yet balance themselves, before the race is run."

This time Karsler made no attempt to repress his smile, and the light in his blue eyes quickened her blood. She cast about for something else to say, something that would hold him a little longer, but invention failed.

"Safe voyage," she offered simply, with a smile of her own.

"I thank you. Until the next time then, Miss Devaire."

"Luzelle."

"Luzelle. Safe voyage."

The overcommander bowed deeply, while the grandlandsman inclined his head infinitesimally. Together they turned and walked out of the restaurant.

Luzelle sat watching them go, her eyes fixed on Karsler Stornzof's figure until it vanished through the tall doorway. *Gone.* She felt extraordinarily alone and let down, which was

curious, for she was used to traveling on her own and not usually troubled by solitude. She was troubled now, however;
lonely and unaccountably glum.

But there was nothing at all unaccountable about it, she reminded herself. Had it slipped her mind that she'd just received the worst possible news? The Grewzians, of all people,
the *Grewzians* were about to snatch the lead in the Grand Ellipse. This latest monstrous coup placed Karsler Stornzof and
his unlovely kinsman so far ahead of the field that they would
never be caught. She herself and her fellow disadvantaged Ellipsoids might proceed along the Dalyonic coast to some free
harbor, to Hurba or perhaps to Gard Lammis, thence em-
barking for Aennorve, but the delay was disastrous.

She could save time, money, and energy by acknowledging
defeat here and now. She could go back to Sherreen. Back to
the Judge's house.

Not yet. Not yet.

. . . *Inequities of political fortune may yet balance themselves.* . . .

They'd better balance themselves, and soon. She'd balance
them herself, if necessary.

But how?

5

"SEE, NEVENSKOI, I've brought a gift for our clever green friend," announced King Miltzin IX. Turning to the pit-of-elements, where the sentient flames crackled demurely, he tossed in a small sheaf of papers. "There you are, Master—er—Fire. Feast and be merry."

EatEatEatEatEat? queried the hot green voice from the pit.

Enjoy, Nevenskoi assented in silence, and the papery fuel vanished in a bright instant. Aloud he added, "Your Majesty is most kind, most generous. My Sentient Fire conveys its gratitude."

"Our fire might moderate his gratitude, if he knew what he consumed." Mad Miltzin smothered a chuckle. "That wad of trash we just disposed of contained no fewer than two score requests for private meetings from various ambassadors and diplomats. Have you ever heard the like? Didn't I foresee that I'd be persecuted? And so it has proved. They're like carrion flies, these foreigners. They're buzzing around everywhere, and I'm the decomposing delicacy of the day. They want our brilliant Master Fire there and they'll stop at nothing to get at him—through me, just as I expected. But they won't succeed, you see. The Low Hetz remains neutral, now and always. Eh, Nevenskoi?"

"As Your Majesty wills." Nevenskoi nodded bleakly.

"I'll speak to none of them. I'll not be sucked into the squalid whirl of foreign quarrels. They've made their own problems, and they must not look to me for rescue. I disregard both abject pleas and veiled threats. The complaints, arguments, and accusations are food for Master Fire, nothing more. Do I make myself clear?"

"Perfectly, Your Majesty." *He is suppressing the most glorious discovery of the age.* Nevenskoi bowed his head deferentially, the better to disguise the frustration burning visibly in his eyes. As always, his liege's blithe imperviousness set his teeth on edge. And as always, he concealed all external sign of disquiet. The internal signs were insistent, however. His stomach performed the flopping dance of a hooked fish, his intestines writhed and popped. The familiar twinges knifed through him, but he refused to bend. He heard the rumble of internal thunder, and prayed that the king did not. Great sorcerers transcended dyspepsia.

"Well, our flaming beauty there is likely to enjoy many a hearty meal, if these drooling foreigners continue—but really, Nevenskoi," the king interrupted himself, "this is awkward. Our fire has a mind, he must have a name as well, else we're guilty of gross discourtesy. I know, let's call him 'Matchless,' because he is surely without equal, and also because he's kindled without benefit of friction. You see the amusing double meaning there? Or wait, what about—Nonpyreil? Ha! You see—"

"Indeed, Sire." Nevenskoi winced. "But such a notably . . . witty . . . title is perhaps too sophisticated to suit my creation. I've another suggestion, simpler, yet also the product of Your Majesty's luxuriant fancy. You have already addressed the sentient flames as 'Master Fire,' and the title seems appropriate. Let it then be Masterfire."

"Masterfire." Miltzin tasted the name. "Masterfire. Plain, direct, descriptive. Excellent. I like it."

Nevenskoi did not know that he could say the same. *Master*fire? What about Mistressfire? He had no idea which gender, if either, legitimately applied. A question easily answered, however.

Do you like it, loveliness? he inquired voicelessly. *Does it suit, is it good?*

Goodgoodgood!

Calorific satisfaction danced in Nevenskoi's mind. *Master-fire. Acceptable. Welcome. A name, an identity. Goodgoodgood—*

"Good," he said.

"Well, as I was saying," Mad Miltzin continued, "Master-fire is likely to enjoy many a hearty meal in the days to come, for now your countrymen have commenced a bombardment."

"My countrymen, Sire?" Preoccupied with his creation's sensations, Nevenskoi had lost track of the conversation.

"Your compatriots, your Rhazaullean folk, man!"

"Bombardment, Majesty?"

"A merciless assault, quite merciless. Not that I actually *read* any of these melancholy missives, mind you—I believe I've already expressed myself on that topic—but I recognize that peculiar Rhazaullean script when I see it, and lately it's been coming at me in basketloads. I suppose it's not surprising, all things considered. I suppose you're concerned."

"That is so, Majesty," Nevenskoi concurred, mind working strenuously. It was not easy to tear his thoughts from the embrace of Masterfire, but necessity pressed. He found himself a little confused, a little disoriented, but knew that things would be right once he marshaled his faculties. What was Mad Miltzin chattering on about?

"Cousin Ogron's northern advance," Miltzin mused. "Predictable, of course. Inevitable, really. But who could have guessed that it would happen now?"

The king's cousin Ogron—that would be Ogron III, imperior of Grewzland. Northern advance—through the land of Rhazaulle, presumably. The Grewzian forces were pushing north toward Rialsq, the capital of Rhazaulle. The natives blocking their path were being slaughtered, and Mad Miltzin not unnaturally expected his supposedly Rhazaullean sorcerer "Nevenskoi" to display a little becoming distress.

Nitz Neeper, alias Nevenskoi, could oblige and *would* oblige shortly, only—

Big! Big! Let me be big! blazed the voice from the pit-of-elements.

Now is not the time, Nevenskoi replied.

Big! Now! Big! Pleasepleasepleasepleaseplease—

"Later. Patience," he advised aloud.

"What's that, Nevenskoi?" asked the king.

"The forces of destiny have yet to conjoin in support of Rhazaulle, Sire. The moment approaches, however. Salvation illumines the future."

"The near or distant future?"

"Later. Patience."

"Well, that's encouraging, but what of the present? You're all but buried alive down here in this workroom, but surely you've heard tales of the Grewzian atrocities. No doubt you fear for your family and friends, back in—where was it again?. You told me once, but I can't recall the name of your home village."

Nevenskoi froze. Home village? He'd cobbled a suitably colorful biography years earlier, fleshing the account with fanciful detail. He'd invented a picturesquely primitive rural point of personal origin, but what had he called the place? Usually he remembered such particulars, but just now, when he was distracted and taken so much by surprise—

His mind groped vainly, and the palms of his hands went clammy.

Trouble? Worry? Badness? asked Masterfire.

I must think of something to tell the king.

Eat him. No more worry. EatEatEatEatEat!

No!

"Chtarnavaikul, wasn't it?" recalled Miltzin. "Have I got the pronunciation right?"

"Exactly right, Sire."

Big! Big! Wannabe big!

Not now!

"Those Rhazaullean names must be invented by contortionists of the tongue," the king complained.

"Ah, Majesty, to me they seem natural as breathing," replied Nitz Neeper.

"I don't mean to disparage your native tongue, my friend. No doubt it possesses its own rough-hewn beauty. Let me hear a little, and judge. Speak to me in Rhazaullean. Say anything you like."

Nevenskoi suppressed a twitch. He spoke not a word of Rhazaullean. He had been telling himself for years that he ought to teach himself at least a few phrases of the language, just in case, but he had never found the time and now it was too late. Terror shot along his nerves and, as always, the negative emotion wreaked interior havoc. His innards knotted and the pain was fierce.

OUCH! Hurt! observed Masterfire.

"Just a few words," the king urged.

No way out of it. Nevenskoi took a deep breath.

"D'ostchenska ghoga ne voskvho." The invented syllables rolled forth fluently. "Aluskvaya troiin King Miltzin shvenskul ne Rhazaullevnyitchelska."

"Ha, but I heard my own name in there!" exclaimed the king, diverted and apparently unsuspecting.

"Indeed, Majesty." Success. Nevenskoi's alarm loosed its intestinal grip. "I just said, 'A humble expatriate's fear on behalf of his endangered Rhazaullean countrymen finds comfort in the wisdom of King Miltzin.'"

"Very prettily said, Nevenskoi. Very affecting, and very true. Comfort you will have, you deserve it. I shall personally intercede with Cousin Ogron. I'll ask him, as a favor to me, to command his Northern Expeditionary Force to spare your home village of Chtarnavaikul. Will that cheer you up? I must have my Nevenskoi in good mind and healthy spirits! Now, where is this Chtarnavaikul, exactly? Somewhere along the River Xana, I suppose?"

"Not exactly, Sire."

"Mountains? Lowlands? Near some city of note? Come, man, help me."

"The fact is, Majesty—the truth is . . ." Nevenskoi unconsciously pressed a damp palm to his unruly belly. His mind whirred. Fiction impinging upon fact was always the best. "Actually, there is no Chtarnavaikul. The village cannot be spared, for it does not exist."

"Eh?"

"Nature itself has anticipated the fury of the Grewzian invader," Nevenskoi confided sadly. "Twenty years ago it was, during the vernal thaws, a tremor of the ground—no rare phenomenon, in that part of the world—precipitated a mudslide of unparalleled severity. The vast river of mud flowing down into the valley from the surrounding hills inundated, flattened, and obliterated the village of my fathers. When all was done, it seemed that Chtarnavaikul had been swallowed whole. Survivors, their hearts and spirits broken, abandoned the site of the calamity, and now it is as if Chtarnavaikul had never been. The very name is all but forgotten." Lost in the past, Nevenskoi gazed off through the mists of time.

"Upon my word, but that is a sad tale." King Miltzin shook his curled head. "I am sorry, my friend, indeed I am." He thought a moment, and a happier notion struck him. "You mentioned survivors, however. Surely the list includes friends and family?"

He had family. A couple of Neeper siblings, many cousins, uncles, aunts, a troop of nieces and nephews, all living in or around the Low Hetzian city of Flenkutz. He had not communicated with any of them in fifteen years or more. Undoubtedly they all imagined nugatory little Nitz long dead, and he had not the slightest desire to undeceive them.

"We'll rescue them," Mad Miltzin decreed. "We'll pluck them from the path of the advancing Grewzian army and bring them back to Toltz, where you may revel in their company day and night. Eh, Nevenskoi?"

The internal uproar recommenced, infusing his voice with anguish both dramatically appropriate and perfectly genuine, as he replied, "Dead, Sire. Carried off by pestilence, famine, or misadventure. So many dead!"

"What, *all* of them?"

"Alas, Sire, your servant is alone in the world."

"Well, that is remarkable. Almost unbelievable, in fact."

Miltzin didn't believe him. An iron fist gripped his innards and twisted. A gasp escaped Nevenskoi. He doubled, and his hands clamped on the arms of his chair. An empty bowl sat on the table before him. Not an hour earlier the bowl had brimmed with chili-oil eels and spiced devilswimmers. He should have left both alone.

"What's the matter with you? Come, what is it, man?" demanded the king.

"Nothing, Sire. A momentary weakness," the stricken savant managed to answer through clenched teeth. "The recollection of the lost loved ones never fails to affect me."

"Well—er—yes. You foreigners are emotional, aren't you? Come, what will cheer you? I know. We shall seek out a few of those survivors from Chtarnavaikul, and even if they aren't your own blood, at least they'll be—"

A pang of exquisite agony tore through Nevenskoi's middle, and he could not for the life of him contain a muted moan.

Ouch! Masterfire crackled and flickered in sympathetic unrest. *What? What?*

Nothing, my beauty, Nevenskoi answered in silence. *Foolish human concerns, nothing to trouble you.*

I can help, for I am strong, I am brave, I am big, big, BIG! So saying, Masterfire arose.

A twisting column of green flame reared itself from the pit-of-elements, thrusting powerfully for the ceiling. The crackle of the little blaze deepened to the purr of a great predator, opalescent green smoke billowed, while tentacular offshoots branching from the fiery pillar snaked experimentally in all directions.

"What is our friend doing?" Mad Miltzin's eyes expanded in childlike wonder.

Exactly. *What are you doing?* Nevenskoi telepathed from a mind filled with alarmed confusion.

I am big, I am strong, I am great, I am grand, I am MASTERFIRE, I am big, bigger, BIGGEST—

No. Resume your former size.

NoNoNoNoNoNoNoNoNo—!

I do not permit you to enlarge.

Big! Strong! Hungry! Eat! I am huge, I am wonderful, I am fine and lovely, I am the winner, I am everywhere, I am MASTERFIRE!

Nevenskoi felt the savage power within himself and it was glorious, triumphant, insatiable. He was huge, he was wonderful, he was master and destroyer, emperor and hungry god, hungry, and it was goodgoodgood, and he was magnificently BIG—

But there was pain there inside him, ravening alongside

delight, and the pain weakened his will, yet anchored his awareness to reality.

No. He could hardly form the denial, even within the sanctuary of his own mind. The effort required to produce that mental syllable was inordinate. And seemingly wasted, for Masterfire ignored it.

I will make it right, I will eat this wet meat-stuff that makes badness. He is gone, EatEatEat, he is gone for good, eat.

"Splendid sight," admired His Majesty. "Our clever green friend seems so animated, so filled with enthusiasm."

His control had lapsed badly, to potentially disastrous effect, but the fear sweeping through him somehow focused Nevenskoi's intellect and his strength, superseding physical pain. He was master, he would rule. He must. He took a deep, calming breath and mutely exerted his concentrated force.

Subside. Resume your original size.

He expected instant obedience, but Masterfire resisted yet.

Big! Pleasepleasepleasepleasepleaseplease!

Small. Now. Obey.

No fun.

Shooting reluctant sparks, the great blaze grudgingly subsided, dwindling and shrinking in upon itself, relinquishing tentacles and radiant streamers, height and whirling breadth, until it crouched once again within the confines of the pit-of-elements, for all the world like a disgruntled green hearth fire.

Another day, my treasure, and you will once again stand tall, Nevenskoi vowed.

The promise seemed to produce the desired effect, for the voice from the pit resumed its accustomed tone of contentment.

EatEatEatEatEatEatEatEatEat.

The savant breathed a sigh of profound relief. His creation and his internal organs were both submissive, for the moment. He would see that they stayed that way.

"Now, what was that little effusion all about?" inquired the king.

"A simple excess of inflammable enthusiasm, Sire," Nevenskoi explained. "No doubt stimulated by the honor of Your

Majesty's presence." Determined to seize control before Mad Miltzin's capricious fancy wandered off again down undesirable paths, he added casually, "I have been meaning to ask, if I may, for the latest news of the Grand Ellipse racers."

"And well you may ask, my dear fellow! Ha, but what a surprise!" Miltzin's eyes lit up. "Which of them d'you suppose is leading the whole pack? Wouldn't you have placed your money on that Grewzian war hero fellow? If so, you'd lose your last copper! Believe it or not, there's a woman out in front. By all accounts, the Szarish scarecrow with the outlandish carriage has drawn so far ahead that the chances of overtaking her are near zero. Now that's what the mastery of technology can do! Of course," he mused, "the newspaper reports are always days behind foreign events. And in the interim I suppose there's no telling what may have happened, is there?"

DO SOMETHING. DO SOMETHING. But what? Hop across the room to the Overgeneral Brugloist's table, plop down on my knees, and beg his assistance? Weep buckets? Would it work, or would I just be thrown out of the restaurant?

Quick, before he gets away!

Even as she exhorted herself, Luzelle saw the Overgeneral Brugloist rise from his chair. His subordinates stood, and then they were all moving smartly toward the exit.

Jumping from her own chair, she scurried in pursuit, but had not advanced more than a few paces before an urgent Lanthian voice halted her.

"Madam—if you please—madam!"

She turned back reluctantly to discover a waiter holding her valise.

"I believe Madam has overlooked—"

"Oh. Thank you!" Extracting a couple of coins from the store of Lanthian currency furnished by the ministry, she tipped the waiter, took her bag, and hurried in the wake of the retreating overgeneral.

Brugloist and his officers had already exited the restaurant. Emerging into the foyer, Luzelle spotted her quarry leaving the hotel by way of the front door. She ran after him, straight out onto the spotless Prendivet moorings, and saw the over-general entering the sleek little vessel that his dignity required to carry him back to the Grewzian headquarters, all of a two minutes' walk distant.

"Overgeneral!" Luzelle let fly a shout. "Overgeneral Brugloist! Please, sir, one moment of your time!"

Certain that he'd heard her, she made for the boat at a quick trot. Long before she reached it, a couple of grey-clad soldiers intercepted her, materializing out of nowhere to block her path.

"Stay back," one of them commanded in Grewzian.

"I must with the Overgeneral Brugloist make to speak," she appealed in her own lame version of the same tongue.

"Not permitted."

"But I must—"

"He won't be interested. Maybe you'll have better luck in the alley behind the hotel."

"Please, you do not understand—"

"Yes I do, honeydugs. You think you're the first? Now run along, before you get yourself in trouble. Off with you."

A firm push punctuated the command, and Luzelle felt the alien hand close for an outrageous instant on her breast. She contained her impulse to slap the Grewzian's face. No point, no use. It would only make things worse. The Overgeneral Brugloist was already gone, and she had missed her chance.

"Do all Grewzian morons smell like goats, or is it only you?" she inquired of her molester, and backed off before he had time to formulate an answer.

Shouldn't have said that, only make him mad, if he happens to understand Vonahrish. So what? Disgusting filth.

She looked around. Behind her, the Prendivet Hotel. Ahead, the breathtaking panorama of the Lureis Canal, but she was in no fit state to appreciate the spectacle.

What now?

Railroad station? Livery stables? Train or carriage? Which best to carry her along the Dalyonic coast to some harbor free of the Grewzian stranglehold?

Railroad, most likely. And how to get to the station? Via

dombulis, one of those famous Lanthian water-taxis, always available night and day.

And today was no exception. There were scores of them out there, cruising the Lureis like hopeful sharks. She moved toward the taxi stand at the edge of the moorings. As she went, some faceless boor jostled her roughly and then, to compound the offense, grabbed her elbow as she stumbled. Angrily she pulled back, felt his clasp slide down her arm to her wrist, and then to her hand, which he squeezed firmly. Something foreign tickled her palm. She wrenched herself free and turned, ready to loose a verbal blast, but she was too late, the oaf was already gone.

Luzelle scowled, then shrugged. She noticed then that her clenched fist contained a scrap of paper, presumably pressed upon her by the anonymous lout. What now, some sort of advertisement? She was about to toss the thing aside when her eye caught the sweep of dark blue script, and she paused. The message, whatever it might be, was not printed, but handwritten. Interest snagged, she unfolded the paper and read:

> *Fastest transportation to Aennorve.*
> *Mauranyza Dome, top floor, today, three o'clock.*

What in the world? She read it over twice again without enlightenment. No salutation, no signature. But the message addressed her most immediate need, and had been placed literally in her hand. It must have been meant for her, but she had no idea who had sent it, or why, or what it might actually mean. She also did not know just what she should do about it.

Answer the mysterious summons? A waste of valuable time, most likely. Perhaps even dangerous; no telling what she might be walking into. On the other hand—fastest transportation, the note offered, if indeed it was an offer. And she had the Khrennisov to protect her, should difficulties arise. Not that she knew how to use it, but surely no one would realize that. And finally there was the matter of her own curiosity. If she failed to investigate this matter, she would probably spend the rest of her life wondering about it.

A clock atop a nearby tower chimed the hour of two, and

that decided her. It was already too late to make it by coach to the neighboring city of Hurba before sunset. She would end up spending the night at some inn along the road if she left now. The railroad might be a better bet, but not necessarily. Heavily dependent on its splendid harbor, accustomed to aqueous highways, the city of Lanthi Ume probably offered mediocre train service at best. For never in their worst dreams could the Lanthians have imagined that their access to the sea would be lost.

Nothing much to lose by gambling an hour or two on the intriguing message. She'd be positively remiss if she failed to investigate. Really, it was practically her duty.

She took a moment to strip the paper wrapping from the pistol reposing in her side pocket, then stepped to the water-taxi stand and waved. A fragile black dombulis with a high-curving prow was there in an instant. Declining the assistance of the liveried hotel attendant, she climbed in. The dombul-man shot her a questioning glance, and she commanded without hesitation, "Mauranyza Dome."

SHE ARRIVED SOME QUARTER HOUR EARLY, and thus had time to inspect the building's exterior at leisure. Very old, she saw at a glance, and wondered just how long Mauranyza Dome had stood staring at its own reflection in the waters of the surrounding canals. Centuries, most likely. And quite a reflection it was, with those rounded walls of heavy red glass and that endless spiral staircase hugging the inner curve. For a while she stood watching, but the silent structure told her nothing.

She bought a cone of ganzel puffs from a vendor and killed a few more minutes eating them. Then she heard the clock chimes tolling over the water, and knew it was time to go in. Touching her pocket to reassure herself of the loaded Khrennisov's presence, she squared her shoulders and walked into the Mauranyza Dome.

She stood in a hushed, empty foyer, which had probably once been impressive, but now seemed merely gloomy. To her right the great staircase spiraled its way along the curving glass wall. To the left stood a couple of doors, one of them ajar. She went to the open door and looked through into a big, dilapidated salon, currently unoccupied. A sad place.

She was procrastinating. She was a little uneasy, she realized; even a bit afraid. There was still time to retreat, but she did not seriously consider it. Touching her pocket once again, she began to climb the stairs.

The afternoon sun shone muted through the heavy red glass of the dome, washing the stairwell with strange light. Luzelle looked through the wall to behold Lanthi Ume spread out below, her palaces unnaturally incarnadined, her canals apparently brimming with wine.

It was a long way up. She was breathing hard by the time she reached the top floor and the door she sought. She knocked, the door opened at once, and her eyes widened.

She had harbored no definite expectations, but was nonetheless surprised to confront a grizzled, crinkle-bearded man clad in long, voluminous black robes blazoned with a double-headed dragon at the shoulder. She had seen just such a robe decorated with just such an emblem only hours earlier, clothing the person of the luckless Preeminence Perif Neen Cezineen. The man before her had to be another Lanthian savant of the Select.

"Miss Devaire. Welcome," he said in good Vonahrish. "Please come in."

She hesitated a moment, then entered cautiously, to find herself in a gigantic chamber shaped like an inverted red bowl. Great panes of colorless glass set into the walls and ceiling admitted natural light. The sole furnishings consisted of a very large circular table edged with many chairs, some of which were occupied. The familiar faces jumped at her. Girays v'Alisante, whose expression was unreadable. Bav Tchornoi. The Festinette twins, looking unwontedly subdued. Mesq'r Zavune. There were several others that she didn't know—two more black-robed savants, and a couple of youngish men clad in ordinary street garb. Her trepidation vanished.

"Who are you?" she inquired of the crinkle-bearded savant. "And why have you asked me here?"

"Please be seated, and I will tell you what I can."

She eyed him levelly and then complied, choosing the vacant chair next to Zavune.

Crinkle-beard likewise seated himself and declared, "Custom and courtesy dictate mutual introductions at this time, but the circumstances are unusual and ordinary convention must lapse."

What in the world is he talking about? Luzelle wondered.

"It is best for all," the savant continued, "that you travelers remain ignorant of our names. Enough for you to know and believe that we are Lanthian, that we oppose the Grewzian presence in our city, and that we will do all in our power to effect the restoration of Lanthian autonomy."

They were members of the resistance, Luzelle perceived; all of them subject to summary execution, should they fall into Grewzian hands. And their associates and accomplices right along with them, foreign nationality notwithstanding. They were placing lives at risk by inviting the racers to their meeting, and what could they possibly hope to gain by it?

"You doubtless question our motives in bringing you here," Crinkle-beard continued. "I will answer that our intentions are simple and straightforward—we wish to discomfort, discredit, and generally plague the Grewzian invader to the greatest extent possible. In this particular case our aims happen to coincide with your own. As of today Lanthi Ume's harbor has been shut down by order of the Overgeneral Brugloist. The overgeneral has permitted, however, the departure by steamship of the sole Grewzian competitor in the Grand Ellipse—a concession all but assuring Grewzian victory. It is our resolve that the Grewzians shall not turn the abuse of Lanthian liberties to such profitable use. Therefore we have invited you contestants here today in order to offer our assistance."

"How can you assist us?" demanded Bav Tchornoi, his eyes and voice unwontedly clear.

"Yes," chimed in Stesian Festinette. "You fellows are tremendously kind, and we appreciate the good will, but—"

"What can you actually do?" concluded his twin.

"You're not planning to sink the *Inspiration*, or anything

like that, are you?" asked Luzelle. "I mean, there are innocent people aboard—" *Karsler*.

"And there are certain fairly striking omissions," Girays observed calmly. "Porb Jil Liskjil. Founne Hay-Frinl. Dr. Phineska. They reached Lanthi Ume aboard the *Karavise* along with the rest of us, but I don't see them here this afternoon. Jil Liskjil in particular is the sole Lanthian among the racers and, as such, the obvious beneficiary of your concern. If you are all that you claim, then why have you not summoned your own compatriot?"

"Because we cannot find him or the others you speak of," one of the anonymous Lanthians clad in ordinary street wear answered in labored Vonahrish. "We search as best we may, but they are nowhere."

"It is more than probable that Master Jil Liskjil, possessing many resources here in his home city, has arranged his own affairs," suggested a hitherto silent savant.

"I see." Girays arched a skeptical brow.

"You've offered your help, and we thank you, gentlemen." Luzelle attempted diplomacy. "The note I received mentioned the fastest transportation to Aennorve. Would you please explain what that means?"

"Willingly, Miss Devaire." Crinkle-beard resumed his role as spokesman. "Your departure from Lanthi Ume by sea is prevented by the harbor blockade. You are now obliged to embark for Aennorve from an alternate port, the nearest of which is Hurba, a good two days' journey north overland from here."

"Two days!" echoed Luzelle, dismayed. She thought of the *Inspiration*, already at sea, steaming full speed toward Aeshno. "That long?"

"The roads are poor at this time of year," came the discouraging reply. "As for the railroads, their service is not reliable. Two days to Hurba by land would be good time."

"We're dead, then," shrugged Trefian Festinette, without visible concern. "Let's be good sports about it. Why don't we all repair to one of these excellent local restaurants and console ourselves with Vonahrish champagne?"

"You go drink that fizzy puppy-dog water, little boy," Bav Tchornoi advised. "I do not give up, me."

"I am go also," declared Mesq'r Zavune.

"Have you an alternative to recommend?" Girays inquired of his host.

"We do," Crinkle-beard told him. "Quite a good one, for those among you ready to avail yourselves of it."

"You sound as if you think we might not be ready," Luzelle hazarded.

"Possibly not. Hear me through, and then judge," the savant advised. "All of you are foreigners, but you probably recognize the double-headed dragon insignia that you see here today, and you know approximately what it means. You understand that my colleagues and I belong to a very old Lanthian organization devoted to the investigation of obscure phenomena. One such phenomenon encompasses the swift and precise conveyance of large objects from one point in space to another. The room in which we now gather has belonged to one member of the Select or another, as long as the Mauranyza Dome has stood. The proof of our tenancy is both tangible and relevant."

What in the world is he on about? Luzelle wondered again.

"Come, and I will show you," Crinkle-beard answered the unspoken query. "Come with me." Rising from his chair, he made for the far side of the room, where a threadbare, almost colorless circular rug of ancient workmanship drably masked a section of floor. His listeners followed and watched with interest as the savant flipped the rug aside, uncovering a hexagonal slab of black glass. Beneath the polished surface thousands of golden flecks glittered like a galaxy, seeming by some trick of design to extend an immeasurable distance.

"You see before you an ancient glass of transference known as an *ophelu,*" explained their host. "The origin and history of the device need not concern you now—suffice it to say that the Select have guarded its secret for generations. By application of the discipline that we Lanthians call 'Cognition,' the ophelu may be stimulated to induce a negative-temporal shift of cargo."

"Negative-temporal?" Girays prompted, intrigued.

"The object of transference," Crinkle-beard told him, "reaches its destination a moment or so before it sets off. This displacement is so slight and unnoticeable that it may be called negligible, but is interesting nonetheless."

"How do you know that such a displacement occurs? How have you measured its duration, and under what circumstances?" probed Girays. "What do you regard as negligible? What is the cause of this anomaly, and during its term, are we to assume that the object of transference exists simultaneously in two separate locations? Speaking of which, does the nature of the object—organic or inorganic, living or dead, insectile or human, et cetera—in any way affect the outcome, and if so—"

"Will you for once stop *pushing*?" hissed Luzelle.

"I'm not pushing. Will you for once stop and *think*—"

"Your questions might be answered, Master v'Alisante," the savant interrupted, "but only at the cost of some time, which you can ill afford. Will you consent to postpone the interrogation?"

Girays inclined his head.

"You say this send us to Hurba before we go?" inquired Mesq'r Zavune.

"Imagine—for a single shining instant—four of us!" Stesian Festinette elbowed his brother exuberantly.

"That beats the Demon Tax Collector stunt, Tref, I swear it does!"

"Not straight to Hurba, sir," Crinkle-beard answered Zavune's query. "The sundered half of this ophelu lies in a castle, well beyond the city limits of Lanthi Ume. Once you are there, one of our people will guide you across the Gravula Wasteland to a second glass, which will in turn transport you to the caverns of the Nazara Sin, whose inhabitants—traditional friends of the Select—will send you on to Hurba."

"Sounds complicated," observed Luzelle. "Are you sure it wouldn't be fastest for us simply to—"

"If all goes well, your entire group should reach your destination by sunset today."

"If?" demanded Trefian.

"We're not likely to pop up inside a cow or something, are we?" Stesian worried.

"I care nothing for the risks," Bav Tchornoi proclaimed. "I only ask—this thing, this glass here—it works?"

"It works," Crinkle-beard assured him.

"Then I will use it," Tchornoi announced. "These others may do as they please, but I will go."

"I also," said Zavune.

"Include me," requested Luzelle. Really, there was no choice. Out of the corner of her eye she saw Girays shoot her a quelling glance, but she ignored him. He ought to know by now that she was hardly one to fear unconventional methods of travel. Let him back down himself, if he thought it so dangerous.

"I'll go," said Girays without enthusiasm.

The Festinettes traded glances, and bobbed their heads in unison.

"Excellent." Crinkle-beard nodded. "The larger the illicit exodus, the greater the affront to the Grewzians. But the ophelu cannot bear all of you at once. Your group of six must split in half."

"I go first," declared Tchornoi, glaring a challenge that was superfluous, for nobody opposed him. "Who comes also I do not care, but I go first. When do you send me?"

"Now."

"Good. What do I do?"

"Step onto the glass slab."

Tchornoi complied. Smiling as if they imagined themselves about to embark on a pleasure jaunt, the Festinette twins joined him. When all three stood upon the ophelu, one of Crinkle-beard's colleagues produced a tiny jar full of white crystalline matter, depositing small heaps of the stuff at the vertices of the hexagon.

"What is this?" Tchornoi squinted suspiciously. He received no answer.

Crinkle-beard bowed his head and spoke. As the rhythmic syllables flew from his lips, the six powdery mounds ignited. Flames leapt and circled the ophelu. Ghostly vapors arose. The savant spoke on, and the vapors thickened, paled, and whirled in crazy spirals.

Cognition. The real thing. Lips parted in wonder, Luzelle watched.

Tchornoi and the Festinettes were invisible now, lost in the roiling mists; their cries, if any, drowned in the roar of a Cognitive hurricane. Luzelle pressed her hands to her ears, straining her eyes in vain to pierce the white blindness. She could see nothing, hear nothing intelligible, but sensed the psychic assault of vast forces.

And then it was over, the white hurricane abruptly stilled, the surging alien energy exhausted. The riotous mists vanished in an instant to reveal an ophelu shining and empty. Tchornoi and the Festinettes were gone.

Nobody stirred, nobody said a word.

"They are safe." Crinkle-beard finally broke the staring silence. No reaction from the stunned Ellipsoids, and he added, "They stand beneath the roof of Castle Io Wesha, some leagues beyond the city limits. Come, are you dazed? Surely you had some idea what to expect." No reply, and he inquired at last, "Are the three of you still willing to follow them?"

Wordlessly Mesq'r Zavune stepped onto the hexagonal slab. In silence Luzelle and Girays joined him. She wished that Girays would hold her hand, but would have died rather than let him know it. She stole a glance at his profile, noting the grim set of the jaw, and wondered if it would be the last look—wondered if the two of them stood within moments of uncanny annihilation.

What if we simply vanish? Forever? Her mouth was dry, which was a pity, for there were many things she wanted to say to him, she realized belatedly, and perhaps there would never be another chance.

Too late.

One of the black-robed figures was already replenishing the mounds of crystalline matter at the vertices of the slab. Crinkle-beard bowed his head and he was speaking again, chanting rhythmic syllables that she couldn't quite distinguish, but knew on instinct she would never understand.

The mounds ignited and the white vapors swirled back into being. Unthinkingly Luzelle seized Girays's arm and felt rather than saw his eyes turn toward her. Her own eyes remained fixed on Crinkle-beard, all but obscured by the mists, but still incomprehensibly audible. And now another sound was audible as well, some sort of purely mundane commotion on the landing outside the bowl-shaped chamber—a clatter of footfalls, a vocal clamor, an imperative pounding of fists on the door.

The door gave way and a squad of Grewzian soldiers burst into the room, revolvers in hand. The Lanthians shrank back and one of them, not of the Select, made a desperate dash for the exit. Three or four revolvers spoke simultaneously, and the fugitive dropped in his tracks. A couple of shots flew wide of the mark to strike the walls, marring the glass of the Mauranyza Dome with a complex network of new cracks.

All of this Luzelle glimpsed imperfectly through the thickening mists. She saw one of the black-robed savants gesture in a manner that must have struck the soldiers as threatening or annoying, for they shot him down at once. And she saw that Crinkle-beard, wholly absorbed in his Cognitive endeavor, appeared unaware of the Grewzian presence. His chanting syllables flowed forth smoothly, and the blast of gunfire never so much as shook his rhythm.

"Cognizance Oerlo Farni of the Select," the Grewzian sergeant, leader of the squadron, addressed the preoccupied Crinkle-beard, "I arrest you and your fellow enemies of the state in the name of the Grewzian Imperium."

Crinkle-beard, or Cognizance Oerlo Farni, seemed deaf. His voice flowed, and the vapors whirling about the ophelu waxed in solidity and velocity. A distant wailing of arcane winds ghosted upon the mists.

"Hands atop your head, and keep them there," commanded the sergeant. "Turn slowly and face me."

Farni spoke on. The ghostly wail drew nigh and the white mists funneled intensely above the hexagonal glass.

"Silence. Turn. Now." The sergeant cocked his gun.

If Oerlo Farni heard the command, he ignored it. The syllables gushed, the wail of the wind rose to a howl, and the sergeant fired.

Luzelle heard the report echoing under the domed ceiling

and dimly discerned the bearded victim's body falling, but the vapors veiled the scene. The mists shuddered and convulsed, for one moment fading to the verge of invisibility, and in that moment she saw the savant, prone in a puddle of blood. Her shocked eyes rose to meet those of the Grewzian sergeant.

"You three—" he began.

His words drowned in the renewed roar of the Cognitive storm. Oerlo Farni lived yet, mind and will intact for a final moment.

The room and all its furnishing seemed to shiver, and then Luzelle felt herself snatched up and hurled headlong into wild white chaos.

6

SHE WAS TUMBLING HELPLESSLY, as if caught in a breaking wave; overwhelmed and overpowered. Her white-blinded eyes snapped shut, and her cry of alarm lost itself in the roar of the supernatural gale. Then it was over, and she was set down brusquely in a different place.

Luzelle opened her eyes. She stood on a hexagonal slab of black glass set into the floor of a quiet stone chamber. A mild, fresh breeze blowing in through the open window carried the scent of open spaces. She was still clutching her valise in one hand, and Girays v'Alisante's arm in the other. She released him at once. Beside them stood Mesq'r Zavune, a little disheveled, but upright and seemingly confident as ever.

The stone room was well populated. Bav Tchornoi was there along with the Festinette boys, all manifestly whole and sound. With them stood a brace of strangers, one young and the other middle aged, both female, both arrayed in the dark robes with double-headed dragon insignia. Both appeared troubled, even alarmed.

"Something happened," the elder stated without preamble and without doubt. "What was it?"

The three on the ophelu hesitated, and the younger, almost girlish-looking savant added, "The transference was disrupted in midprocess and nearly aborted. So severe a disturbance suggests trouble, perhaps an accident or sudden illness."

"Was Cognizance—was our colleague at Mauranyza Dome injured or otherwise distracted?" the first speaker demanded.

"Shot by the Grewzians, even as he transported us. Severely wounded or dead," Girays reported. "And he wasn't the only one. I am sorry."

The shock showed on both the women's faces, but neither gave way to emotion, and the elder requested simply, "Explain."

Girays obeyed, describing the arrival of the Grewzian soldiers, the gunfire, and its consequences, in terms clear and economical. Luzelle listened in surprise, for he was not only reliably factual, as she would have expected, but diplomatic as well. The Girays she had known years ago would probably have told them exactly where their confreres back in the Mauranyza Dome had gone strategically wrong, and exactly what should be done to forestall future repetition of the disaster. Or maybe he wouldn't have really, maybe moldy indignation clouded her memory.

". . . two of your friends left alive in the hands of the Grewzians," Girays was concluding, "which I fear may jeopardize both of you Cognizances, together with other members of your organization."

"The prisoners will reveal nothing," the older woman stated. He started to protest, and she silenced him with a gesture. "It is not your concern. You have informed us, there is nothing more you can do. And we of the Select possess ample means of self-defense."

Didn't seem to work so well for the Cognizant Oerlo Farni. Or for Preeminence Cezineen, Luzelle thought, but said nothing aloud. She caught Girays's eye for an instant, and sensed that the same thought was passing through his mind. Sometimes with him, she just knew.

"Send us on our way, then, and we kick Grewzian ass around the Grand Ellipse for you," Bav Tchornoi suggested. "We make those chitterling-sucking bastards look like shit."

Tchornoi might lack a certain polish, Luzelle reflected, but he possessed a real talent for cutting straight to essentials.

Their hostesses seemed to agree.

"Come with us," the senior ordered. "Everything is prepared to speed you from this place."

Everything? What now—another white whirlwind? But Luzelle ventured no comment, following meekly as the black-robed women led the Ellipsoids from the chamber of the *ophelu,* down the stairs, and through the great hall to emerge from the castle into blinding afternoon sunlight. Standing in the courtyard was a sizable, sturdy carriage, drawn by four strong-looking horses. The driver waited in the box. The conveyance was almost disappointingly mundane.

"Are we not to carry on by way of that perfectly smashing hither-and-yon magical thingamajig that brought us here?" Stesian Festinette wanted to know.

"Seems a bit faster," Trefian opined.

"The two sundered halves of the glass that brought you are capable of transporting cargo back and forth between Mauranyza Dome and Castle Io Wesha, nothing more," the senior savant informed him.

"Cargo?" Stesian sniffed.

"Castle Io Wesha," Luzelle echoed. "I can't help but worry about the risks you run on our account. Do the Grewzians know—"

"The Grewzians know that this structure has been owned or occupied by members of my family since it was erected, over seven centuries ago," the other informed her. "They also know of my family's traditional connection to the Select of Lanthi Ume, but that is all they know, and it is not enough to do them much good."

"But it's not as if they needed actual proof to—"

"As for the risks we run," the savant cut her off, "be assured it is not on your account." She turned to the Festinettes, whose pretty brown heads were cocked at identical angles. "And you, gentlemen, take heart—your confinement to the carriage will be brief. The device that carried you here is not the only such to be found in this land."

"Oh, outstanding," Trefian comprehended. "You mean that we are being taken to—"

"I mean that it is more than time for you to go." The flick of a finger urged the Ellipsoids on toward the carriage.

Who's the driver? Luzelle wondered. *Can she be trusted? I just hate having to depend on people I don't know, and somehow it seems to happen so often!*

She entered the carriage and the other five climbed in behind her, squeezing themselves carefully into the small space. Luzelle found herself trapped between the window and Bav Tchornoi, who sat with his massive thighs spread indolently wide, forcing her to flatten herself against the carriage wall in order to avoid contact. She thought about speaking up, to order him out of her space, but could not find the nerve to do it.

Only a few hours, she assured herself. *Only a little while to put up with this gigantic, hairy, smelly, crude, rude Rhazaullean drunkard, and then it'll be over—*

Why didn't Girays have the decency to sit next to me? How could he know that I'd want him to?

She stole a glance at Girays. He had his head out the open window, and he was optimistically attempting a last exchange with the impenetrable savants.

"Cognizances, if I might request a final kindness, please tell us where we—"

"There will be guides," the older woman told him. "They are allies. Try not to fear them."

"Why would—"

The snap of the driver's whip cut the question in half. The carriage lurched to life and Girays pulled his head back in the window. Moments later the vehicle passed under Io Wesha's great arched gateway and out onto a steep hill where the fresh breezes carried the scent of wild beggarsgold, and the passengers could see for miles in every direction. Below them spread a vast expanse of rolling, uncultivated terrain. Not far to the south rose Lanthi Ume, her towers and domes shining in the sun; and beyond the city, the deep blue gleam of the sea. The road north unwound down the hill, circled the base of a great granite rise, and continued on across a wide, windswept desolation toward a misty region of distant hills.

The driver's whip sang, and the carriage thundered down the hill.

•   •   •

TIME PASSED SLOWLY. There was little conversation in the carriage, and for that Luzelle was thankful; no Festinette prattle to endure, none of Zavune's fractured syntax, no Tchornoi gloom. The Rhazaullean, in fact, occupied himself quite contentedly with his hip flask for a while before dropping off to sleep, and soon his vouvrak-perfumed snores filled the small compartment. Girays was reading something or other, she could not make out what. She herself took the opportunity to finish *The Shadow of the Ghoul.*

Some two hours into the journey, which Luzelle guessed to be about the midway point, the carriage halted beside a little stream winding among knobby hillocks crowned with tall grasses that stirred and rustled in the ceaseless winds. While the horses drank and rested, the passengers and driver alighted, scattering in all directions to lose themselves in the vegetation. Some minutes later the group returned to the carriage, where Bav Tchornoi still slumped snoring. Progress resumed, and the Rhazaullean never opened his eyes.

Luzelle stared out the window at the stark surrounding terrain swept by perpetual winds, and wondered at the nature of this empty unclaimed expanse, presumably unfit for cultivation and apparently deemed unworthy of settlement, despite obvious overcrowding within the city limits of Lanthi Ume. But the undesirability of the land itself could hardly account for the dearth of human habitation. People feared this place, and always had. The Gravula Wasteland—she dimly remembered the name from old geography lessons—was thought to be haunted. All sorts of quaint old Lanthian legends and horror stories attached themselves to the locale. Vengeful, immortal sorcerers prowling around in search of victims. Ert, the destructive divinity. White Demons—the old-time Lanthians had been very big on White Demons, with eyes of sweet death and voices of otherworldly beauty. She'd giggled over translations of those hoary Lanthian fables. Well, the Gravula didn't look particularly dangerous, only a bit forbidding.

Her eyes rose to the sky, where the position of the sun drew her brows together. *If all goes well, your entire group should reach your destination by sunset today,* Oerlo Farni had told them. But everything had not gone well, and the city of Hurba lay far to the north. At the present rate they would not arrive for another thirty-six hours or so at best. Of course, she recalled, poor Farni had spoken of a second glass.

In the middle of this place? Just lying right out in the open? Can't be.

Time passed. The sun sagged toward the horizon. The carriage jolted on, Bav Tchornoi snored on, the Gravula Wasteland rolled on. At last, when the shadows stretched to ambitious length, the daylight measured its life in minutes, and Luzelle was beginning to wonder whether their indefatigable driver meant to carry on in darkness, a landmark rose in the near distance—a sight, like the Lureis Canal, familiar through countless artistic renderings and, also like the Lureis, striking and astonishing beyond the power of any image to convey.

Directly ahead, warmly sidelit by the low red sun, a stand of huge stone blocks reared themselves skyward in mysterious symmetry. Most of them were gigantic grey prism shapes that could never have occurred in nature. These were the famous Granite Sages, unexplained in origin, ancient beyond reckoning, and said to mark an entrance to the nether regions. Entranced, Luzelle watched the Sages approaching at the stolid steady pace of the horses' progress. They were larger than she had realized, despite the accurate measurements set forth in scores of reference books—larger, and far more astonishing.

Who built that, when, and why?

Almost without thought she turned to Girays, and he glanced toward her at the same moment. Their eyes met in perfect understanding, and for a moment she was ridiculously happy.

The Granite Sages drew nigh. The world darkened as the shadow of the largest monolith—the gigantic stone known to the world as "the Master"—engulfed the carriage. Luzelle blinked in the sudden cool dimness. The vehicle halted and the driver descended from her perch.

The wordless invitation was clear, and the passengers emerged. The sharp breeze tousled Luzelle's straying curls, and she shivered a little. The Sages loomed oppressively, their

ancient vastness a voiceless commentary upon human insignificance and evanescence. The Master was the most intim-
idating of the lot, and for some reason the driver was down on
her knees before Him, scrabbling amid the weeds at His base.

The driver did something with her hands, and there followed a deep rumble of shifting stone as a hitherto invisible
door in the Master's massive flank swung open to reveal a
closet-sized interior chamber. The late sunlight slanting low
into the tiny room struck reddish glints off a black glass floor.

The second ophelu, just as Oerlo Farni had promised, but
so unexpected an apparition in that place that Luzelle could
not contain a soft, startled exclamation.

"Three of you, in," the driver spoke up for the first time
since the trip began.

Bav Tchornoi was already bulling for the entrance, as if he
imagined himself entitled to precedence by divine fiat, and she
didn't mean to let him get away with it this time. Without allowing herself time to think, Luzelle hopped in ahead of him.

Then Tchornoi was there beside her, too near, alcoholic
breath too assertive, and she hoped that Girays would be the
third, but Mesq'r Zavune slid in before him.

The cubicle was tiny, and the stone walls pressed closely on
three sides. The fourth side was open, but even so, the sense
of immeasurable solidity hemming her in chafed her nerves.

Don't get skittish.

The driver was muttering something unintelligible. No
crystalline powder around the ophelu this time. No seemingly
spontaneous combustion, no billowing smoke, and Luzelle
wondered if the Lanthian Cognition could really work without the pyrotechnical trappings. Even as she stood wondering, she was caught once again in the wild white wind, flung
through whirling icy space, spun and buffeted, and moments
later set down in a different place.

A very different place.

She tottered a little but kept her footing, and caught her
breath with a gasp. Beside her, Bav Tchornoi grunted sharply.
She looked around and felt the color drain from her face. She
stood on a hexagonal black glass slab, one of many identical
such slabs set into the stone floor of a small, plain chamber.

The place was irregularly shaped, with a vaulted stone ceiling from which the slender stalactites dripped in fragile clusters. *A cave?* Braziers placed at unpredictable intervals along the walls kept the humid air heated to an almost uncomfortable warmth. The room was windowless yet well illuminated, for the floor, ceiling, and stone walls all glowed with a mild, colorless light, apparently a natural property of the native rock. But Luzelle hardly troubled to analyze, for the chamber was far from empty, and her astounded attention focused on the occupants.

There were at least a dozen of them—slim, attenuated figures of indeterminate gender, similar to humans, yet differing in many features easily observed, for the hairless bodies before her were unclothed. Their hands, she noted, terminated in long, bonelessly tentacular digits. Their eyes were immense—palely brilliant, ringed with triple ridges of muscle that rippled and flickered ceaselessly in the otherwise still faces. Most startling of all was their flesh—white, smooth, and glowing with an endlessly variable luminosity.

The beings—she couldn't think of them as creatures, they were too near humanity, and the sentience shone in those unnerving eyes—were staring as if transfixed, as if the humans upon the ophelu were the strange and marvelous spectacle. One of them spoke up in melodious fluting tones, another answered in kind, and their speech was a kind of music, ineffably alien and beautiful.

Luzelle was trembling. *There will be guides,* the savant at Castle Io Wesha had told them. *They are allies. Try not to fear them.*

Try.

One of the luminous beings approached, gliding movements light and noiseless as smoke. Its right hand rose, boneless fingers undulating, and instinctively she shrank back until the lucent stone wall halted her retreat. Tchornoi and Zavune did likewise.

Seconds later the Cognitive storm whirled through the room, deposited Girays and the Festinette twins on the glass, and subsided. The new arrivals blinked and surveyed their surroundings. Under other circumstances their expressions of stunned incomprehension might have appeared comical. Gi-rays recovered first. His dark gaze swept the chamber, touched Luzelle, paused a heartbeat, and moved on.

The chamber was filling. The white entities—*Cave dwellers? Aborigines?*—were drifting in by silent twos and threes. A host of pale eyes glowing like lanterns veiled in lu-minous mist caught and transfixed the human invaders. Luzelle shivered. The pressure of focused inquisitive sentience was almost palpable. Those incandescent eyes, she imagined, were gazing straight into her head to read the thoughts con-cealed there, and the sensation was unnerving. Almost she sensed foreign awareness impinging upon her own, and the fancy reinforced itself when the alien flutelike voices lifted in weirdly beautiful harmony—conversation?—and the strange melody stole past all defenses, bringing the tears of grief and longing to her eyes.

Who are they? Allies, the savant of Castle Io Wesha had promised, but that explained nothing. She found the answer within her own recollections, and then those ridiculous Lan-thian fables that she had giggled at made some sense for the first time. White demons. All those legends, superstitions, and mythic accounts of the White Demons of the Caverns, lurking in their warren under the hills of the Nazara Sin. She should have known—her experience with various cultures the world over should have taught her that such legends often surrounded a kernel of truth.

The White Demons of the Caverns, she remembered, were said to feed upon unwary travelers.

Legends, born in ignorance and fear. Probably.

The room was crowded with them now, the changeable ra-diance of their flesh filling the confined space. They offered no overt threat, but there were so many of them, their atten-tion was so unnervingly concentrated, and they were staring, all of them staring with those huge, uncanny eyes.

Her heartbeat quickened, fear flooded her thoughts, and her hand slipped of its own accord into her pocket to close on the loaded pistol.

Don't touch that. Worst impulse, truly mindless. Her hand froze.

Not all of her fellow humans shared her outlook.

"They look weak, but not stupid," Bav Tchornoi decided. "We will grab one, and it will be our shield. Then we will make it show us the way out."

There was a brief, astonished pause, and then Girays advised, "Don't be such an ass, Tchornoi."

"Yes, he's right, I mean, isn't that suggestion a bit extreme, Tchornoi?" Stesian Festinette asked.

"It's not as if we're really sure they're *dangerous*, is it?" Trefian chimed in.

"We strike first, we take command," the Rhazaullean insisted.

One of the white beings stepped forward to separate itself from the bright throng. A double strand of colored pebbles draped its neck, and a large brown bat rode its shoulder. Perhaps these distinguishing features denoted rank, but there was no way to know. The tall figure advanced to confront the human knot.

It paused, and warbled incomprehensibly.

"That one," Bav Tchornoi declared. "Their leader, I would bet. We will take that one."

"You'll keep quiet and keep still," Girays told him.

"We wait for now," Mesq'r Zavune concurred.

The white being snaked its long, boneless fingers at them. The triple ridges of muscle ringing its great eyes rippled. Communication of some sort was intended, but the message was indecipherable.

"I do not need your good wishes, little lads," Tchornoi informed his critics. "And I do not need your help."

As if it understood the speaker's intent, the white being retreated, gliding its way among seemingly identical glass slabs set into the stone floor to pause before a polished hexagon gleaming near the center of the room. Turning to face the visitors, it bowed its head and fluted a plaintive cry.

"It calls to us," said Zavune.

"They mean to send us on," Girays opined.

"I do not allow these slimy overgrown *glowworms* to dispatch me where they will by magic means, no," declared Bav Tchornoi. "I walk out of this underground trap on my own two feet, and that creature there—it shows me the way out, else I rip its rickety body apart with my own two hands." His hands, huge and powerful, appeared capable of performing the feat. He took a purposeful stride toward the motionless guide.

"Stop there, you damned fool." Girays moved to block the Rhazaullean's path.

An almost negligent sweep of the former Ice Kings champion's skilled arm thrust the shorter, lighter Vonahrishman aside. The advance resumed. The White Demon, if such it was, watched inscrutably.

The only demons in sight call themselves human.

Luzelle was not entirely conscious of drawing the pistol from her pocket. She looked down to see it in her hand, aimed quite steadily at Bav Tchornoi's ample midsection, and she heard her own voice command evenly, "Stop there, Master Tchornoi. You will not lift a hand against these people."

"People? Hah! That is a joke, yes?" He wheeled to face her. "You are a blind, foolish woman. Before you make me angry, put that silly toy away."

"It is no toy, I assure you." Luzelle's tone remained deceptively assured. Out of the corner of her eye she noted the luminosity of the cave dwellers' flesh waxing and waning in rapid, erratic sequences that might or might not hold meaning, and curiosity meteored across her mind. Did they know the nature of guns? She heard the music of the alien voices, many voices, but the message was incomprehensible as ever. Her own companions' reactions, on the other hand, were clear. Consternation showed on every face.

"Have you taken leave of your senses?" Girays demanded. "Where did you get that thing?"

Ignoring the question, she addressed herself to Tchornoi. "These *people* are very generously attempting to help us"—she privately hoped she spoke the truth—"probably out of some regard for the Lanthian Select. You will not abuse that kindness, Master Tchornoi. Should you attempt violence, I will shoot you through the kneecap, and then we'll see how well you race."

"This you could not do." Tchornoi's lip curled.

"Try me. I am a dead shot, and very accustomed to handling firearms." *Does this gun have some sort of a safety lock or not?* Luzelle wondered. *If it does, is it on or off now? Should have asked Karsler when I had the chance.* She eyed Tchornoi steadily.

For a few moments he glowered at her, then muttered a few choice Rhazaullean oaths before switching to Vonahrish. "Hah, you preach against violence while waving a gun around like a drunken soldier. You should be locked in a madhouse. It is not worth my time to quarrel with a crazy woman, so for now I humor you."

"Good decision." Luzelle took care to conceal every sign of her relief. "Then humor me by stepping onto that glass there, where you will stand still and keep quiet."

Tchornoi's glare intensified, but he obeyed without argument. The Festinette twins joined him upon the polished slab, and the tall being with the pebble necklace and the brown bat on its shoulder commenced a melodic, repetitive declamation. Presently the Cognitive whirlwind screamed into existence, filled the room with fury, and departed, leaving the ophelu bare.

The Khrennisov disappeared back into Luzelle's pocket. She'd possessed it for only a few hours, and already aimed it at an unarmed man. The implications were unsettling.

High, fluting arpeggios stirred the lucent stand of spectators, and she wondered if the sound expressed wonder, or excitement, or some other emotion wholly beyond the scope of her experience. But there was no time to ponder the question, for now it was her turn to step onto the glass for another impossible transference to—she didn't know where. Then Girays was there beside her, along with Mesq'r Zavune, and this time she managed to keep herself from grabbing anybody's arm.

The tall being had already resumed its invocation, and the chanting rhythm never faltered, but the radiant gaze shifted briefly to Luzelle's face, and for a breathless instant she looked straight into the White Demon's eyes from a distance of inches. She could see the intelligence there, and a quality that she could only inadequately have described as soul, and, she would have bet money, some sort of message meant for her alone—a vital message forever beyond her comprehension.

The moment passed, and the entire scene—stone chamber, stalactites overhead, hexagonal slabs below, luminous beings, alien eyes, and all—vanished in a rush of snow-white wind. Less alarmed this time, Luzelle let herself relax a little into the storm's power, and thus found herself traveling with the wind, almost riding it, resulting in a far gentler transference.

She was deposited in a new place, and the atmosphere grew calm. She discovered herself standing with Girays and Zavune upon a glass slab set into the floor of a hexagonal closet or small room, with walls of damp old brick. *What in the world—?* Vertical slits perforating the enclosure just below ceiling level admitted thin streams of reddish light, by which she discerned an old iron ladder bolted to one wall. The ladder led to some sort of a trapdoor in the wooden ceiling, its hexagonal outline just barely visible in the ruddy gloom. Presumably Tchornoi and the Festinettes had already exited by way of the ceiling, for there was no sign of them.

Good riddance.

Valise in hand, Luzelle squirreled up the ladder. When she reached the top, she pushed at the door in the ceiling, which offered unexpected resistance. She increased the pressure, without results, and the too-familiar sensation of impending doom began to swirl at the pit of her stomach.

"Locked," she told her companions.

"Can't be. The others got out. Let me try," Girays requested.

She descended and he took her place. His own efforts to raise the trap were unsuccessful as her own, and following a few straining, quietly profane attempts, he called down, "Zavune—give me a hand."

The Aennorvi, conveniently moderate of frame, climbed the ladder and squeezed himself onto Girays's rung. Together the two men pushed at the trap above, sensed progress, increased their efforts, and were rewarded with the groan of old boards reporting the shift of a large weight above, the scrape and shout of tumbling mass, and the shriek of yielding hinges as the trapdoor opened.

Red light gushed in through the opening, along with a fish-scented puff of fresh air. Girays and Zavune stuck their heads out and looked around.

"What's out there? Where are we?" asked Luzelle.

"Garden," reported Girays.

"What do you mean, garden? *What* garden, *where* garden, *whose* garden?"

"Overgrown walled pleasure garden, somewhere near the sea, recorded deed of title currently unavailable," Girays replied, and hurried on down the ladder to claim his suitcase.

Zavune did likewise, and Luzelle seized the opportunity to race on up and out of the mildew-smelling little polyhedron of a place. Her feet clattered on old boards. Fresh air kissed her lungs, while red glory punished her eyes. She blinked, squinted against the light, and the ocular assault dwindled to a minor impertinence.

A six-sided roof peaked overhead. Carven pillars supported the roof, carven railings connected the pillars. Unregulated greenery pushed its advantage on all sides.

But what is it?

A belvedere, she realized. Onion domed, curlicued, and filigreed. A pretty little sop to the senses, set amid soft surroundings. Not the worst place in the world to conceal a sorcerous conveyance.

Who concealed it, when, and why?

She would never know. Her eyes roved. Not far away, only at the top of the garden, rose a dark house—tall, silent, and apparently lifeless. The windows were boarded, the place deserted. It looked as if it had been abandoned for the past century or more. Just the sort of place to which sensible people set torch.

The stray breeze wafted salt and fish.

But where are we?

Girays and Zavune climbed up out of the depths.

"What do it?" demanded Zavune.

"Do it?" For a moment Luzelle stared at him, then understood. Hold them prisoner down below, he meant, for it had not been an accident. Her eyes traveled and lighted upon a re-cumbent marble nymph, sprawling pinkly between the angle of the open trapdoor and the belvedere floor. The polished beauty must have equaled the weight of two full-grown men, at least.

The others followed her gaze.

"Tchornoi and the Festinettes." Girays radiated formerly-Exalted disdain. "It would have taken at least a couple of them to place that statue atop the trapdoor, and I don't think the twins could have managed it. Crooked, the lot of them."

"Murderers. We starve to death in that trap," Zavune observed somberly.

"Oh, I don't think they'd actually kill us, any more than I would actually have shot Bav Tchornoi." Luzelle realized that she was trying to convince herself. "Probably they just meant to slow us down a bit."

"Won't help them much," Girays remarked. "See, the sun's setting. Nobody will go much farther along the Grand Ellipse tonight."

A cool breeze swept the neglected garden. Luzelle's eyes went to the deserted, disintegrating mansion, with its boarded windows and its air of desolation. She shivered a little.

"Let's get out of here," she suggested. "Let's at least find out where we are."

The three of them made their way along a gravel path to a door in the high garden wall. The door hung ajar on its rusty old hinges; probably it had been used in the very recent past. They went through, transferring themselves in a disorienting moment from the forgotten rusticity of the silent garden to the bustle of a busy city street.

Luzelle stood still, trying to take it in. Tall buildings of honey-colored stone arose on all sides. Horse-drawn carriages, carts, and hansom cabs filled the wide urban avenue, and there were people, hundreds of people everywhere. The suddenness of the change was almost as startling as transference by ophelu.

"Look. Look at." Mesq'r Zavune pointed. "There is Rakstriphe's Victory Column. Very famous. We are in Hurba."

"By sunset, just as they promised," said Girays.

"Hansom. Waterfront," urged Luzelle. "Ticketing agencies. Passage to Aeshno. Come *on*, gentlemen, let's grab a cab, let's go!"

"Whew!" Zavune smiled.

"Couldn't have put it better myself," Girays agreed, entertained.

"What are you smirking about?" Luzelle asked him.

"I am not smirking. I never smirk."

"You are. You do."

"If you've detected some sign of mild amusement, it's a natural response to your rather—how shall I put it—charmingly impetuous enthusiasm."

"Girays, you know I can't stand it when you—"

"Because, you see," he continued with annoying composure, "in your eagerness you have failed to consider the lateness of the hour, and its effect. By this time the ticketing agencies are shut up for the night. There's no possibility of booking commercial passage from Dalyon before tomorrow morning."

"For now, we stuck," Zavune informed her.

"Unless, of course, you happen to enjoy access to a private yacht," Girays suggested helpfully. "Or a dependable night-flying balloon, or perhaps some really imaginative newfangled suboceanic vehicle, or a trained leviathan, or—"

"You needn't *belabor* the point." Luzelle scowled.

"The Herald Inn, not far from here," Mesq'r Zavune told them. "Very excellently clean. Good food."

Food. Luzelle's stomach rumbled responsively. She noticed herself smiling.

They took a cab to the Herald Inn, an elderly but immaculate establishment with black half-timbering and a gabled roof, where there were plenty of decent rooms available at stiff city rates.

Luzelle ate a good dinner of Hurbanese winepoachies in the Herald's old dining room, in the company of Girays and Zavune. The latter, she discovered, was almost feverishly anticipating a very temporary reunion with his wife and children in his homeland of Aennorve. The conversation scarcely touched on the Grand Ellipse, and for a short time it was possible to relax and enjoy the illusion that the three of them were ordinary dinner companions rather than rivals.

The meal ended, and camaraderie began to wane. Luzelle was already wondering if she might somehow find a way tomorrow morning of beating them both to the docks. To her surprise, Girays insisted on walking her back to her room. She suspected that he wanted some sort of private conversation, and this proved to be the case.

They paused in the empty corridor at her door, and Girays turned to face her. His angular face had lost all trace of characteristic amusement or weariness. An odd little frisson—trepidation? excitement?—ran through her at the sight, and she asked, "What is it?"

"That gun," said Girays.

"Khrennisov FK6 pocket pistol."

"So I noticed."

"Good weapon for self-defense."

"In properly trained hands. Where did it come from?"

"A pawnshop in Lanthi Ume." She paused, then added with a certain delicious enjoyment that she strove hard to disguise, "Karsler Stornzof helped me pick it out."

"But how amiable of him."

"Yes, I thought so."

"Unfortunately the gallant Grewzian seems to have overlooked a small but possibly telling detail. In his zeal to serve a lady, he has succeeded in placing a deadly weapon in the hands of one who—forgive me if I am mistaken—has not the slightest notion how to handle it."

"Oh?" She considered denial, but recognized the pointlessness. "Was it so very obvious that I don't know how to shoot?"

"It was to me, because I know your face; I know your eyes."

"Bav Tchornoi doesn't, and he was the one I needed to convince. Worked, too."

"Yes, but tell me—what would you have done if Tchornoi had called your bluff? Would you actually have fired? Do you even know how?"

"Well, it didn't go that way." Even to herself she sounded lame.

Girays smothered a curse. "That irresponsible fool of an overcommander ought to be horsewhipped. Is he trying to curry favor with you, trying to get you killed, or both?"

"Don't blame Karsler—"

"Karsler?"

"It wasn't his doing. We were walking together—"

"Indeed?"

"We met by accident, only he thinks it wasn't altogether an accident."

"Really."

"I'd been a little ill, and he'd helped me. He really was wonderful—"

"*Wonderful*, again!"

"Anyway, we passed a pawnshop, and I told him I wanted to buy a gun. He didn't suggest it, he didn't have any say in the matter. It really didn't matter whether he was with me or not, I'd have gone ahead and bought some sort of handgun in any case. Since he *was* there, he helped me pick out a good one. That's all."

"Perhaps not quite all. He encouraged you, I suppose."

"Hard though it may be for you to believe, Girays—it was my own decision."

"And then he washes his hands, he walks away, without troubling to instruct you."

"He didn't have any choice, or any time. We are in a race, after all. He told me to practice."

"Oh, well, that absolves him of all. Will you defend everything that he does?"

"This is ridiculous. I'm not obliged to defend anything or anybody, to you. Why should I?"

"Why indeed? Why should you give the slightest thought to anything in the world beyond your own determination to get whatever you want, at any cost? Only now that you have secured this damned gun, and the golden Grewzian who egged you on is nowhere to be seen, perhaps you aren't too proud to let me show you how to use it?"

"What?" For a moment she was unsure that she had heard him correctly.

"We'll probably take the same ship for Aennorve. We'll

have a few days, I can show you how to handle the Khren-nisov. If you wish."

"Oh." She drew a deep breath. He had taken her by sur-prise, and she did not know how to react. After a moment she confessed, "This isn't what I expected. I was sure you'd think it a dangerous mistake for me to carry a gun."

"I do. But I can think of an even more dangerous mis-take—for you to carry a gun that you don't know how to use. Will you let me show you?"

"Yes." The assent emerged easily, but the next words re-quired effort. "Thank you."

"Tomorrow, then." He was too well bred to display any-thing resembling triumph.

"Girays?"

"Yes?"

"What in the world possessed you to enter this race?"

"Let's talk when we have more time, aboard ship. That's what long sea voyages are good for, you know—time."

"Time and talk may be all that this one will be good for. We've fallen so far behind, we'll need a miracle or magic to catch up with the Stornzof kinsmen now."

7

THE SUN WAS HIGH IN THE SKY when the *Inspiration* embarked from Lanthi Ume, speeded on its way by the salutes of the Grewzian patrol vessels. For hours she hurried east across the Jeweled Expanse, whose blue waters echoed the color and mildness of the cloudless skies. The air was magnificent, and the scenery uncommonly noteworthy by seagoing standards, for the ship threaded a path among the countless steeply pitched, colorfully vegetated islands that lent the Jeweled Expanse its name.

Karsler Stornzof stood on the deck watching island after island go by, some so close that he needed no spyglass to distinguish the close-packed white-stuccoed houses clambering up the sharp-graded slopes. The grey-green bemubit trees with their gnarled white trunks were likewise distinguishable, along with terraced gardens dripping voluptuous cascades of the purple khilliverigia, known as Youth's-Excuse, already abloom in these sunny climes.

Not all of the islands were inhabited, or even clothed in flora. Many exposed their naked volcanic rock to the skies. Others, devoid of humankind, sheltered colonies of bright-winged liftzoomers, whose iridescent plumage decorated expensive hats all over the world.

The hours and islands passed under the sun, the memories of war receded, and earlier memories seeped to the front of Karsler Stornzof's mind; recollections of colder seas, harsher terrain, duller grey skies, and other times, better times, wherein principle and discipline supported understanding, or so he had once imagined.

But he had been a simpleton, he was starting to realize. He had been so credulous, so ignorant of reality, so unprepared. He had thought the truth of the Promontory the truth of the world, and he had been a sorry fool.

He hadn't seen that for himself, not for a while, and most of the rest of the world still didn't see it. In fact, most of the world seemed to regard him with exaggerated admiration, a phenomenon he scarcely comprehended. The troops under his command had won a few gaudy victories, the drama and significance of which had been vastly inflated by the popular press, but how many readers had ever considered the deflating reality of trained, well-equipped Grewzian strength, and enemy disadvantage?

His best Promontory teacher, the Elucidated Llakhlulz, would have had words to offer. But then, what had E. Llakhlulz himself known of the real world beyond the Promontory?

Time, salt water, and islands flowed. Karsler Stornzof watched and remembered, until a whiff of costly tobacco invaded his air. He turned to confront the Grandlandsman Torvid, and a flash of something like annoyance singed his mind before he remembered his duty.

"You dream, Nephew," Torvid observed with amusement. Sunlight glanced sharply off his coin-bright silver hair and his monocle.

"There is little else to do up here on deck, Grandlandsman." Karsler uncomfortably attempted to match the other's light tone.

"Ah, to be sure. And what could be the subject and source of your dreams? Victory, one might hope?"

"That is the goal of the race."

"Sometimes I fear you forget it. There are other dreams to fill ardent young minds."

"Or even ardent old ones."

"Oh, Nephew, you kindle my hopes. Could you be something less of a prig than I had supposed? Is it possible, Promontory notwithstanding, that you are truly a Stornzof?"

Karsler bit back an acrid reply. The anger that filled him was irrelevant and counterproductive, as E. Llakhlulz could so well have explained. He might have echoed the grandlandsman's sarcasm, but only at the expense of large values, and therefore he contented himself with the mild query, "You are a qualified judge of the breed?"

"As good as any," Torvid responded easily. "Good enough to judge the response of a healthy Stornzof male to a female in heat. Do not take my observation in the wrong way, Nephew. The little Vonahrish thing contrives to make her presence known, and it is only natural that your glands should feel the pull."

"You allude to Miss Devaire?"

"Bravo."

"You often cite our family name, Grandlandsman. Is it characteristic of a Stornzof, in your opinion, to defame respectable women?"

"Ah? It seems I was mistaken. You are indeed a prig of the first water."

"That being so, I will relieve you of the tedium of my presence."

"And an offended prig, at that. Stay where you are. I intended no affront to your well-developed sense of propriety. Quite the contrary, I compliment your taste, and I withdraw an earlier complaint. The fair Devaire is less boringly bourgeoise than I had initially supposed. She possesses a certain quality of impertinence that is not unamusing. I daresay there is entertainment to be found in bringing that one to heel."

"The point is academic, Grandlandsman." This time Karsler did not trouble to mask his disgust. "As you yourself have observed, we are unlikely to encounter Miss Devaire or any other Grand Ellipse contestant again before the conclusion of the race. Your influence with the Overgeneral Brugloist has effectively crippled the competition."

"Yes, and I do not recall receiving thanks for it."

"Your efficiency no doubt deserves credit. Nevertheless I

cannot help but wonder if an honest race, fairly run, might not have yielded a far more satisfying victory."

"You are perhaps too much the connoisseur, Nephew. Victory is victory and always sweet, particularly in light of the sole alternative. Moreover, your fine distinctions are inconsistent in their application. You never whined of inequity or dishonesty when the Szarish woman's peculiar conveyance was running us all into the ground."

"In that case the advantage stemmed legitimately from Szett Urrazole's own talents and accomplishments. And her initial lead might well have evaporated later in the race. Now we shall never know, thanks to the murderous zeal of the Lanthian resistance."

"Desperate characters." Torvid tapped a precarious cylinder of ash from the tip of his cigarette.

"I believe so, and therefore wonder at the absence of enemy action directed specifically against us. I am the only Grewzian contestant. The Overgeneral Brugloist has interceded on my behalf, all but ensuring my success; an abuse of power—that is to say, a manifestation of Grewzian solidarity—deeply offensive to rival nations."

"If Brugloist's intervention strikes you as morally objectionable, then you need scarcely have availed yourself of his assistance," Torvid observed dryly. "The *Inspiration* could and should have sailed without you, for what is worth a blot upon a sweetly pure conscience?"

"As the affair was arranged by an overgeneral of the Imperium, I scarcely enjoyed the luxury of choice."

"Well then, resign yourself to the good fortune that fate has inflicted upon you, and cease this endless complaint. You whimper like some girl who has played her virginity card, but failed to take the trick. It commences to pall."

"Then I will leave you."

"Stay where you are, we are not finished. You were suggesting, if I am not mistaken, the possibility of enemy action or reprisal. What did you mean by that? This ship and her crew are Lanthian. Do you believe it likely that any among the sailors or officers may—"

A howl of terror arising from multiple throats below truncated the grandlandsman's query. The cries repeated themselves, intensifying in volume and emotion. Moments later a trio of soot-grimed, panic-stricken sailors came bursting through the open hatch up onto the deck, where they clung cowering to the rail.

"What is it?" Torvid demanded in Grewzian of the nearest crewman. There was no reply, and he seized the other's collar in one formidable fist. "Explain."

"He is Lanthian, he doesn't understand you," Karsler remarked calmly. "And probably could not answer in any case."

Another couple of crewmen boiled up screaming through the hatch.

"Are these people mad, or idiots, merely?" Disgusted, Torvid released his hold. The liberated mariner, white beneath his tan, backed away.

"Neither, if I am not deceived. You know the nature of my training, Grandlandsman, and for the past hour or so I have sensed some echo of arcane energy infusing our atmosphere."

"And deemed it unworthy of mention?"

"I was not certain. Within the last couple of minutes the sensation has greatly intensified, and now there can be no doubt that—"

Someone below fired a gun. Three shots rang out in quick succession, followed by a full-throated scream.

"Whatever this Lanthian nonsense may be, I will settle it." Drawing a revolver from the shoulder holster perfectly concealed beneath his coat, Torvid started for the hatch.

"Do not attempt it," Karsler advised. "The force now at work upon this ship is proof against mundane weaponry. Stay away from it."

For a moment Torvid considered, then returned the gun to its holster. "I will be ruled by your superior experience in these matters, for the moment. Understand that my patience is limited, however."

"I suspect you will shortly discover that patience is not the issue."

"This deliberate obscurity of yours is—" Torvid broke off as a tentacle of midnight vapor came undulating up through the hatch into the brilliant daylight, where it paused, swaying a little, as if tasting the unfamiliar sunshine. "What is that thing?"

A couple of sailors and a junior officer on deck spied the black vapor, shouted an alarm, and ran for the stern. The dark tendril silently withdrew.

"Ah, it flees. Here is nothing to concern us." Torvid Stornzof dismissed the visitation with a shrug.

"You judge too quickly. Wait," Karsler instructed, and his tone of authority drew a narrow glance from his uncle.

"Wait while these Lanthian fools allow the ship to slow to a full stop? Wait while the fires in the boilers die because the idiot stokers have abandoned their posts? I think not." Again Torvid made for the hatch.

"Halt," Karsler spoke as if to a soldier under his command, and the tone froze the other in his tracks. "You have not the faintest idea what you are dealing with."

"Ah? I deal, it would seem, with a Stornzof who forgets that he addresses the head of his House." Torvid turned to face his nephew. "Allow me to refresh your memory. Inasmuch as excitement has clouded your judgment, however, I will indulge you so far as to hear your explanation. What, then, are we dealing with?"

"A fairly potent arcane manifestation," Karsler returned without emotion. "The product, I believe, of the traditional Lanthian Cognition. The Select of Lanthi Ume support and aid the local resistance. In this case it is safe to assume that the sorcerous support has resulted in the creation of a Cognitive shadow hidden away somewhere aboard the *Inspiration* and designed to activate itself at sea. All things considered, I cannot say I am altogether surprised."

"Are we to fear shadows?" Torvid's brushing gesture repelled imaginary gnats. "This timid rag of mist has poked itself briefly up into the light, lost its courage, and fled. It would seem the effluvium of irresolute Lanthian minds fears us."

"Do not depend upon it," Karsler advised. "And do not be too quick to dismiss Cognition. There is power in it still, and such sorcerous visitations as this are often dangerously malign."

"It would seem these little Lanthian tricksters have quite cowed you. Fortunately, I—"

"Look. Up there." Karsler pointed.

Torvid's eyes followed the other's finger to the *Inspiration*'s smokestack, whose vaporous grey plumage was swiftly changing character. Even as the Stornzof kinsmen watched, dense ropes of black insubstantiality began thrusting up from the depths of the vessel. One after another the dark tentacles shot from the smokestack, climbed for a moment or two, then curved to descend on the deck. Within seconds dozens of them tented overhead, blocking sunlight to create an eerie artificial dusk. One came down inches from the Stornzofs, its weightless touch bubbling the painted deck.

Torvid regarded the nearest writhing strand with interest. One hand reached out fearlessly.

"Do not touch that," Karsler counseled. "It is likely to burn you."

"Ah? Remarkable. Let us see." Torvid passed the tip of his index finger unhurriedly through the shadow, then drew back and watched with apparent pleasure as the skin reddened and a rash of small blisters appeared. "You are correct, Nephew. I should hardly have thought those Lanthian sheep had it in them. Here is unexpected novelty."

"There is more to come. Look."

Visible through the interstices of the shadowy Cognitive web veiling the *Inspiration,* the ship's smokestack continued to belch unnatural blackness, but again the character of the emission was changing as serpentine tentacles gave way to a larger, denser spread of midnight, swelling as it mounted skyward, darkening as it expanded.

Finally the shadow emerged in its globular entirety to hover above the smokestack, and then the features adorning the central mass revealed themselves. The wavering projection of something like a hooked beak pierced the sky, and above the beak, slightly paler than the surrounding blackness, bulged the gigantic vacuity of two dead eyes.

"I confess I am surprised," Torvid acknowledged. "Explain to me the nature of this imaginative display, Nephew."

"Cognitive in nature, moderately potent, potentially lethal." Karsler's eyes never left the empty visage looming overhead. "Make no mistake—the human bathed in that caustic shadow, or drawing the vaporous substance down into his lungs, is unlikely to survive."

"Interesting. And that appearance, somewhat reminiscent of an overgrown cephalopod—that is purely pictorial, I presume? The shadow possesses nothing resembling life?"

"It is not alive, nor does it possess true awareness," Karsler reported. "Yet it perceives, and its response to its perceptions is governed by the intention of its creator."

"And that intention?"

"To block the boat's way east to Aennorve. Perhaps nothing more. The shadow is Lanthian in origin, and the *Inspiration* is manned by Lanthians. Confronting neither resistance nor defiance, this visitant will probably cause no harm, although it possesses the power to kill."

"I see. Well, you are the supposed expert. What do you advise?"

"That we wait."

"Wait. I see. Now there's true Grewzian valor for you. Shall we then abandon ship, take to the lifeboats, and set off for the nearest island, there to loll on the beach until rescued by the next eastbound vessel? Is that your battle strategy, Nephew?"

"It is not, nor would you imagine otherwise, were you even minimally knowledgeable in this area," Karsler returned evenly. He saw the other's lips thin and, without awaiting reply, continued, "Deprived of its creator's presence and sustaining will, the shadow's term of existence is limited. Presently—within a few hours, or less, according to the skill of the originating savant—Cognitive force will flag and the shadow will cease to be."

"A few hours, to sit idle and helpless?" Torvid demanded.

"We can afford them. Barring magic and miracle, my fellow racers can hardly expect to embark from Dalyon until the day after tomorrow, at the very earliest. This Lanthian gesture amounts to nothing."

"There you mistake the matter. Passive acquiescence is not Grewzian. Nor is toleration of conspiracy and open defiance. The sooner our subjects learn that lesson, the better for all concerned."

"What remedy do you favor, Grandlandsman?"

"Cognitive sabotage or no, this ship continues on toward Aennorve. That is a simple statement of fact."

"Fact does not always lend itself to simple statements."

"Spare me the Promontory profundity, now is not the time. Observe, I will demonstrate."

The darkened deck around them boiled. Agitated sailors scurried everywhere in search of escape always blocked by snaking strands of Cognitive shadow. Torvid Stornzof reached out at random, and his estimable grip closed on a passing arm clothed in a sleeve bearing the braid and insignia of an officer.

"State your name and rank," Torvid commanded in Vonahrish, and that language was comprehended by the prisoner.

"Heek Ranzo, mate of the *Inspiration*." An unsuccessful effort to wrench free accompanied the reply.

"The ship has veered from course, and slowed almost to a halt," Torvid observed. "The crew's performance is inadequate."

"Are you mad? We're abandoning ship. Let go." Another sharp twist failed to free the trapped arm.

"You are ill informed, I think," Torvid pointed out, and a turn of his powerful wrist drew a hiss of alarmed pain from the victim. "I am a grandlandsman of Grewzland, and you will address me properly as 'Armipotence.' Is that understood, little Lanthian?"

"You Grewzian fool, turn me loose!" Ranzo snarled, then gasped as his captor calmly backhanded him across the face.

"Is that understood, little Lanthian?" Torvid repeated, without apparent rancor.

"Yes, Armipotence."

"Excellent, Mate Ranzo. Now here are your orders. You will go forward, take the helm, and steer this ship east at top speed."

"I haven't the authority, Armipotence. Now, will you let me—"

"I take responsibility," Torvid assured him. "You will carry out your orders."

"That's impossible, you—Armipotence," Ranzo recollected

himself. He pointed with his free hand toward a ladder wreathed in writhing tentacles of shadow. "Look, the way up to the bridge is blocked, and—"

"So I see," Torvid concurred serenely. "And yet I place my full trust in your resolution and competence. Surely the Mate Ranzo is not a man to be deflected by minor obstacles." He released the other's arm. "Go forward and take the helm."

"Go bugger yourself, Armipotence," Ranzo suggested, and started to turn away.

"One moment," Torvid advised, and drew his revolver.

Ranzo halted at once. He studied the gun, his expression glazed with disbelief.

"Forward to the helm," Torvid commanded calmly.

"Enough, Grandlandsman," Karsler spoke up. "This is a pointless exercise in tyranny. These men cannot hope to withstand a Cognitive—"

"Silence. You forget both soldierly and familial duty," Torvid rebuked his nephew, without letting his eyes stray from the Lanthian mariner's face.

Conflicting values waged internal war. Karsler said nothing.

"Now, Mate Ranzo, forward." Torvid took leisurely aim at the Lanthian's belly. "I will not repeat the command."

For a moment Ranzo's desperate eyes flickered between revolver and shadowy ladder, weighing the known efficacy of bullets against the unknown potency of anonymous Cognition, before opting to brave the latter.

"Bugger yourself," the mate repeated almost inaudibly, and went to the ladder.

Setting his feet to the rungs, he climbed toward the bridge, and for a moment it seemed he might reach that goal. A vaporous tentacle coiled experimentally about his leg, but the woolen fabric of his trousers seemed to ward off burns, and Ranzo shook himself free. The agile ascent continued, but the activity in the midst of its appendages must have triggered the shadow's innate defenses, for a dark throng came undulating out of nowhere to converge upon the luckless officer. Instantly Ranzo was engulfed, wrapped from head to foot in squirming Cognitive blackness. His woolen uniform gave way at once, and then his flesh began to do likewise. The flashes of white intermittently visible among shifting coils of blackness quickly darkened to red, and then the screams began, but they were brief. The strong intake of breath that his cries demanded drew the shadow deep into his lungs, and at once Ranzo tumbled headlong from the ladder. He hit the deck hard and lay still, whereupon the Cognitive strands lost interest, detached themselves, and withdrew.

Torvid Stornzof eyed the corpse in annoyance and flicked his cigarette aside. For a moment he cogitated, then concluded, "Body armor of some sort. Heavy swaddlings of fabric, perhaps. We will wrap one of these Lanthians in canvas or linen, dampen the layers, and send him to the bridge. If that proves unsuccessful, we will experiment with protective windings of rope or stout twine—"

"Your experiments are concluded for the moment," Karsler noted expressionlessly. "Look around you."

The senior Stornzof obeyed. The shadowy Cognitive net enclosing the *Inspiration* allowed a fairly clear view, and it was easy to see that the boat had come, by accident or design, to a small bay hollowed into the coastline of a steep island, one of the hundreds of such islands scattered across the broad blue reach of the Jeweled Expanse. A gap in the shadowy web had opened itself, patently inviting exit, and the crew seized upon the opportunity with enthusiasm. The anchor was lowered and the men sprinted for accessible lifeboats.

"Lanthian scum." Torvid's hand automatically sought the revolver. "We will stop them."

"We would do better to join them," Karsler told him. "Come, Grandlandsman, put that away, it is useless against Cognition. Understand that *Inspiration* fails for now, and there is nothing we can do. Console yourself with the thought that the delay is temporary."

"The delay is unacceptable. I will steer the ship myself, if all others fear to do it."

As if it comprehended the last words, the great Cognitive shadow sent a couple of midnight serpents sliding along the deck, straight for Torvid Stornzof. The grandlandsman watched them coming, and stood his ground. Stance and expression communicated nothing beyond cold contempt.

"Come, Grandlandsman," Karsler repeated. "Into the boat. That is the best course, for now. I urge you, come."

"Very well, if you are so alarmed." Torvid suffered himself to be persuaded. "This time, I will humor you."

Without further debate the Stornzof kinsmen went to the nearest boat, whose occupants admitted them reluctantly. The small vessel descended and made for the island shore.

Karsler turned to look back at the besieged ship. The *Inspiration* was lapped from stem to stern in Cognitive coils, all of which joined the huge knob of a head bulging at the summit of the tallest smokestack. As he watched, the head turned slowly, immense dead eyes aiming themselves at the trio of fleeing lifeboats. Perhaps the arcane perceptions extended beyond the confines of the ship, perhaps not. Either way, the shadow attempted no pursuit.

Minutes later the boats reached shore. Crew and passengers disembarked onto a narrow stony strand hugging the base of tall rock formations. For a while they loitered at the water's edge, watching the shadow-smothered ship in anticipation of final disaster—an explosion, or perhaps quiet disintegration—but nothing happened, and finally the bizarre but static scene began to lose interest.

The beach was bare and inhospitable. The captain issued orders, splitting the group into several reconnaissance units, dispatched separately. The sailors departed. The Stornzof kinsmen stood alone beside the water.

"Do you not wish to investigate, Grandlandsman?" Karsler asked.

"No need." Extracting a black cigarette from his platinum case, Torvid lit up. "We stand upon a rock. There is nothing to see. In any event, be assured we shall not mark time here for long. Go ahead and explore if you wish, Nephew. Amuse yourself as best you can."

"I will, Grandlandsman." Karsler inclined his head to the correct angle, and set off in the wake of the vanished sailors. Behind him lingered his faultlessly groomed uncle, an incongruously elegant figure upon that barren beach, cigarette in hand and contemplative eagle gaze trained upon the black-shrouded *Inspiration*.

Karsler turned his back and took his leave with a subtle but distinct sense of relief. He had not anticipated his own pleasure in solitude, nor had he fully recognized, until that moment, the oppressiveness of his uncle's polished iron presence. Now, for the first time in days, he could draw an unencumbered breath. He did so, pulling the clean sea air down to the bottom of his lungs, and his spirits lifted despite the misfortune that had brought him to this stark little island.

Or perhaps because of it.

He reached the level summit of a tall escarpment, where he paused to survey his surroundings. The grandlandsman had been right, there was little to see. The island—probably nameless—was small and all but devoid of vegetation. Nothing but a naked stone protrusion pushing up out of the sea, home to a colony of slovenly seabirds nesting raucously atop the rocks. No food, no fresh water. Not much space, no cover. From his present vantage point he could easily spot the separate squads of crewmen toiling antlike over the rocks, and his uncle's mannequin figure, solitary upon the strand. A bleak little sun-drenched prison, comfortless, probably frightening to the sailors confronting residency of indefinite term.

But Karsler Stornzof realized that he liked the place. A moment's reflection suggested the reason. This anonymous little crag overlooking the sea reminded him of another place, another life. There the surrounding waters and the sky were eternally grey, and here both were brilliantly blue. There the sun rarely showed its face, and here it shone unremittingly. And yet the stark pure contours of this isle recalled the granite grandeur of the Promontory, and both shared a quality of extreme isolation, a separation from the world and its frenetic concerns.

He felt at home in this unyielding place. He understood it, and vice versa, but he could not stay for long. The race called, and beyond the race, the wars that never ended. He had once regarded his withdrawal from the Promontory as very temporary, but the battles raged on, he was needed, and return waxed increasingly problematic. Of late he had begun to suspect that he would never again know the solitary tranquillity of that youthful, far-off haven. But today he caught an echo of it.

He did not know how long he sat there on the sun-washed ledge, mind lost in the past, eyes blind to the blue infinity of sea and sky. He did not sleep, yet awareness distanced itself, and when at last his sense of duty called him back, the light and colors had changed, the shadows had stretched, and the tired sun was hovering a hair above the horizon. His newly wakeful eyes shot to the *Inspiration* lying at anchor in the bay below. Tentacles of shadow clutched the ship. A well of blackness bulged above the smokestack. Vast lifeless eyes met and absorbed his gaze, returning nothing.

Hours had passed, yet the *Inspiration* remained magically immobilized, a voiceless testimony to the prowess of some unknown patriot savant. Down below, the stony beach was clotted with human figures. The Lanthian sailors, returned from their unrewarding explorations, had regrouped beside the water. Now they were sitting around in small clusters, playing at cards, playing at dice, or just staring out over the Jeweled Expanse. One ramrod figure held itself conspicuously aloof. Even at a distance it was not difficult to pick out the Grandlandsman Torvid.

Time to return. Unwillingly Karsler Stornzof abandoned his perch, making his way down from the heights to rejoin his uncle on the beach. The sun was setting and the long red rays glanced strangely off the density of the Cognitive shadow looming above the *Inspiration*. The breeze coming in off the sea sharpened, and would grow colder as dusk gave way to night, but there was little relief to be found. The island offered no fuel for fire, not so much as a handful of dry seaweed.

The three lifeboats contained lockers of foodstuffs and canisters of water, enough to sustain comfortless life for several days. No candles, lanterns, or blankets. The captain distributed provisions sparingly and equitably. Karsler Stornzof, along with everyone else, received a few swallows of stale water from a communal cup, a portion of hardtack, and a leathery strip of cured beef. The meat he offered to his nearest neighbor, a surprised sailor, and the hardtack he consumed without tasting.

The last traces of color fled the sky, the twilight deepened, the stars came out, and the moon displayed a half-averted face. Somebody's pocket yielded a stump of candle, whose light permitted continuation of the cards and dicing for a little while longer. Nobody's heart was in the game. Spirits and voices were equally low. Presently the candle guttered and expired. Conversation did likewise, and the sailors glumly composed themselves for damp and sandy slumber.

Karsler walked alone along the beach until he came to a relatively dry and rockless patch of sand mounding at the foot of a boulder, and there he reclined. For a time he lay wakeful, watching the moonlight tease the waters of the bay. The air was chill and his stomach all but empty, but he did not mind in the least, for the silence and serenity of the spot more than compensated for minor discomforts. His mind swarmed with memories, not one of them stained with the crimson of warfare. He would gladly have rested thus for hours, but his lids drooped, the moon extinguished itself, and his memories gave way to dreams.

HE WOKE AT DAWN to a sky aglow with immoderate color. For a couple of moments he lay watching the roseate clouds, then reality reclaimed him and he sat up, his glance arrowing out over the bay in search of the *Inspiration*.

The ship rode unremarkably at anchor. No sign of sorcerous shadow remained. Sometime during the night, while crew and passengers slept, the Cognition of the anonymous Lanthian savant had exhausted itself. The danger was over, the impediment gone, the way east clear again.

Karsler supposed he should have been pleased. He rose without enthusiasm and rejoined his companions, who sat grouped in a semicircle, consuming their small rations of hardtack and water.

Torvid Stornzof did not choose to seat himself among inferiors. He stood apart, inflexible posture uncorroded by the salt air, garments impossibly unrumpled, monocle firmly in place. By no sign was it evident that he had spent the night prone upon a rock-strewn beach.

But perhaps he had not slept at all, perhaps he had remained wakeful and indomitably upright throughout the hours of darkness. Perhaps he had smoked cigarette after cigarette, and walked, and plotted strategy all night long. That, Karsler reflected, would be typical of the grandlandsman, who was even now making his will known to the Lanthian sailors.

"The Cognitive inconvenience has vacated the ship. We will return now to the *Inspiration*," Torvid informed his listeners, in Vonahrish. An emphatic gesture clarified matters for the linguistically limited. "Man the boats."

They could scarcely have failed to understand him, nor could they have doubted the authority of a Grewzian noble. Yet they neither spoke nor moved, but sat still, staring.

"Man the boats," Torvid repeated slowly and clearly, as if he imagined his audience hard of hearing or deficient in intellect.

Still no response. The vertical crease between the grandlandsman's black brows deepened, and he inquired, "Are you people stupid, or cowardly, or both?"

"Neither, sir." The ship's captain spoke respectfully to a Grewzian as prudence dictated, but could not suppress every trace of anger. "The men are concerned, and I share their reservations."

"Reservations? The crew, these common seamen, harbor—reservations?"

"They do, and rightly so," the captain returned stonily. "The Cognitive shadow seems to have vanished, but who's to say that it doesn't lurk yet belowdecks? These savant-sendings do not last forever. Another few hours, and we can be certain that it's gone."

"I do not grant you hours, Captain," Torvid replied. "Our schedule admits of no such delay. One concession to your faint Lanthian heart I will allow, however. You—" He picked a sailor at random. "Take one of the boats, row out to the *Inspiration*, inspect her well, and when you have assured yourself of her safety, signal us to come aboard. You understand me?"

The question was relevant, for the Lanthian seaman displayed no sign of comprehension. He sat there blank faced, and Torvid waxed impatient. Turning to the captain, he commanded, "Instruct this animal."

The captain spoke in Lanthian, and the sailor answered in the same language. A skyward glance, together with a decided shake of the head, accompanied his reply.

"Seaman Second Class Wisfa declines," the captain reported.

"Insist," Torvid advised.

"Seaman Second Class Wisfa expresses the desire to wait until noon before approaching *Inspiration*."

"Inform Seaman Second Class Wisfa that his request is denied." Torvid drew his revolver and, for the second time within twenty-four hours, leveled it at a Lanthian stomach.

Seaman Second Class Wisfa stiffened and his eyes bulged, but he did not stir.

"Go," Torvid commanded. His victim remained motionless, and he fired.

The Lanthian sailor grunted and doubled in agony. A second shot took him between the eyes, flinging him backward onto the stones, where he twitched and died. A sharp collective intake of breath greeted the homicide. A couple of shocked imprecations made themselves heard. One of the sailors surged to his feet, found himself facing the dead-steady barrel of Torvid Stornzof's revolver, and subsided.

"Grandlandsman." Karsler scrupulously masked all visible manifestations of his disgust. "I respectfully submit that this measure of severity is unnecessary, and even—"

"Opinion noted," Torvid cut him off. "We will debate the issue another day, if the topic entertains you." Addressing himself again to the captain, he commanded, "Order your men into the boats."

"I will issue that order at noon," the Lanthian returned.

"Perhaps you fail to understand me." Torvid leveled his revolver at the other's heart.

The captain folded his arms. Meeting the grandlandsman's eyes, he permitted himself a slight, contemptuous smile.

A protest strove to escape Karsler's lips, but he managed to hold it in. Opposition would only goad his uncle. Moreover, by every ancient law of Grewzian tradition he owed the head of the House his deference, obedience, and loyalty. Beyond that stood the clear necessity of presenting a united Stornzof front to foreigners and foes. His jaw tightened and he said nothing.

"You Lanthian sailors." Torvid's strong voice was easily audible above the rush of the surf and the cries of the seabirds. "Into the boats. We return now to the *Inspiration*. Disobey, and I will execute your captain." His eyes flicked the hostage as if daring contradiction, but the captain was silent.

A muttering uneasiness ruffled the Lanthian crew. Evidently their commander was a popular man.

Only one Lanthian ventured to request, "Permission to bury Wisfa."

"Denied," Torvid replied.

Again, Karsler managed with effort to hold his peace.

The muttering Lanthian resentment darkened, but the captain's peril could not be denied. Following only a brief hesitation, the sailors manned and launched the three boats.

The voyage back to the *Inspiration* was short and silent. Once aboard, Torvid dispatched a couple of seamen to search below. Minutes later, the men returned to report the vessel clear of Cognitive visitants.

"Then weigh anchor," Torvid commanded imperturbably. "Set course for Aeshno."

The *Inspiration* steamed east.

Upon the grandlandsman's insistence the Stornzof kinsmen appropriated the captain's cabin to their own use. In the days and nights that followed, aware of the bitter resentment that surrounded them on all sides, they took to sleeping in shifts, with one or the other ever at watch beside the door. They took most of their meals in the cabin and rarely ventured out onto the deck, except in one another's company. Such enforced proximity scarcely strengthened the familial bond, but may have exerted the desired effect upon the hostile crew, for there were no incidents.

The countless islands of the Jeweled Expanse streamed by.

Around noon of the sixth day, when the Aennorvi coastline appeared on the horizon, the Stornzof kinsmen were up on deck to see it.

"You are some twenty-four hours behind schedule." Torvid's tone smacked faintly of accusation.

"That is no disaster," Karsler returned shortly.

"It is not, thanks to me. You are fortunate that I am here to protect your interests. This jaunt has taught me that you are not ruled by your head, Nephew. You are a soldier and a Stornzof, yet sometimes seem almost as silly as a woman. There is no limit to the inconveniences we should suffer, were I to indulge your childish tenderness of heart."

8

OUT! NOW! PLEASEPLEASEPLEASE!

The silent appeals blazed through Nevenskoi's mind. Masterfire's urgency pressed hard.

Soon, the adept responded in silence.

Nownownow!

Patience, loveliness. Another few moments, and you will enjoy a new experience. We are leaving the workroom.

Workroom?

The place that you know. The space enclosed by the four walls of stone. We are about to sally forth.

There is more space?

Much more. There are corridors, stairways, many great chambers, and beyond them there is the world in all its vastness.

It is big? Big? Big?

Enormous.

There is food?

More than you could consume were you to stand so tall that your tongues lick the stars.

Food! Space! Big! I will eat the world, the whole wide world! I will eat the stars, for I am grand, I am fine, I am dandy, I am hot, I am MASTERFIRE! Let us go eat all of it!

"Eat," Nevenskoi mused aloud. "All of it. Everything."

EatEatEatEatEatEatEatEatEatEatEat—

Impractical. Recalling himself with an effort, the adept

forced himself to reply, *No, my beauty must curb his enthusiasm. Today we venture only so far as the king's study.*

King? Badmeat?

Our benefactor, our royal patron. The one who visits us here, from time to time—

Badmeat.

Has summoned us to his presence.

Why?

He is king. His motives are not to be questioned. Enough to know that His Majesty Miltzin desires the company of Masterfire and Nevenskoi.

Nitz.

What? What was that?

Nitz. Neeper. NitzNeeperNitzNeeperNitzNeeperNitzNeeper—

Where did you get that name?

Inside you.

Well, keep it to yourself, sweet one.

Why?

That is a long story with which I would not weary my Masterfire. There are better things to think of. Even now Masterfire departs the workroom for the first time. There. Nevenskoi shut the door behind him. *It is done. We are out.*

Let me see! Let me see!

Not yet.

Wanna see! Let me out!

Soon, I promise. For now, repose in patience above Nevenskoi's heart. This apparently fanciful sentiment reflected literal truth. The breast pocket of the adept's voluminous robe contained and concealed the tiny shrunken spark that presently was Masterfire. Obedient to its master's commands, the flame consumed nothing. Nevenskoi experienced neither pain nor even a sense of unwonted heat upon his skin. Despite his creation's physical diminution, the mental link persisted.

Where are we? Where?

Walking along a corridor deep underground. The walls are of plain grey stone, like the walls of my workroom, and the floor is likewise stone, uncarpeted. The ceiling is low, barrel vaulted, and hung at regular intervals with iron lanterns containing lighted candles.

There are flames? Like Masterfire? Wanna see them, wanna meet them, wanna dance, dance, DANCE!

They are not like you. They are mindless, unaware, and ignorant.

Can they dance?

I suppose so.

Wanna meet them!

Not now. We go to wait upon—

Badmeat.

His Majesty.

EatEatEatEatEatEat—

Behave yourself. Now we are climbing the stairs, the secret stairs known to the favored few. Thus we ascend unobserved, and the location of my workroom remains undisclosed. Thus we ascend—

With considerable effort. Nevenskoi's lungs labored, his heart pounded, and there was a stitch in his side. Long before he reached the top of the stairs, he had to pause. Seating himself on one of the treads, he rested there, chest heaving and face sweating. No doubt about it, he was overweight and out of condition. He spent too much time in his workroom, he needed to get out and exercise. He also needed to decrease his intake of lard-smackers, deep-fried ganzels, and cracklers, or perhaps renounce them altogether. If only they weren't all so good. Just thinking of them made his stomach clench.

EatEatEatEatEatEat. Hungry! EatEatEat—

Exactly.

Where are we?

Still on the stairway, but not for long. Hauling himself to his feet, Nevenskoi resumed the ascent. Presently reaching the exit he sought, he departed the concealed stairwell, emerging into a storage closet tucked into the shadowy corner of a forgotten utility room.

The utility room opened onto a wide third-story corridor, and now his surroundings assumed a recognizably palatial aspect.

Highly polished marble underfoot, Nevenskoi reported soundlessly. *Like rose-veined ice. Tall windows, floor to ceiling, overlooking the water gardens. Gigantic mirrors in the fanciest gilt frames you ever saw, and before each mirror, the white marble statue of a two-headed, four-breasted woman. His Majesty's tastes are singularly plural.*

Let me see! Let me out!

Soon, I promise. Now we ascend three gilded steps, and pass beneath an archway covered with carven images of sharks, whales, rays, octopi, sea serpents, and other such denizens of the water—

Badwater.

And now at last we reach the entrance to the king's own apartment. Two armed sentries stand guard there, but they admit us without hesitation, for they know that His Majesty has summoned Nevenskoi.

NitzNeeperNitzNeeperNitzNeeperNitzNeeperNitzNeeper.

Please don't do that. We are passing through the door into the king's private antechamber, all hung in blue damask. The servants in their livery of blue and silver bow low before His Majesty's favorite, the famous, talented, and noble Rhazaullean mage. They respect and even fear Nevenskoi—

NitzNitzNitzNitzNitzNitzNitz.

And now they usher us through into His Majesty's study, haunt of the elite. Loveliness, we have arrived. I could almost wish those Neepers back in Flenkutz might know that little Nitz is alive and hobnobbing with royalty. Oh, if they could see me now!

Wanna see! Wanna see!

Soon. Remember your instructions. Remember—

Remember!

Nevenskoi raised an experienced hand to his black wig, which was properly positioned; ran an expert finger along his dyed moustache, which was properly groomed; squared his shoulders and marched into the king's study.

King Miltzin IX, attired in a gorgeously patterned brocade dressing gown inappropriate to the hour, sat at a desk whose surface supported a very large, beautifully crafted model comprising miniature buildings of eccentric design lining small boulevards starbursting from a central plaza. His Majesty was not alone. Beside the desk stood a stout, foreign-looking gentleman with a broad face framed in greying whiskers. It was the square cut of the beard and sideburns, Nevenskoi decided, that marked the stranger as a foreigner. That and the bristling luxuriance of the moustache, together with the sea-sable frock coat lapels so alien to Hetzian tastes.

Both men turned to the door as Nevenskoi entered.

"Ah, there you are at last, my dear fellow," observed the king.

"Sire." Nevenskoi bowed deeply.

"Come over here, my friend, you must see this, it is quite remarkable. Look at this!" Mad Miltzin's gesture encompassed the model metropolis. "Have you ever seen the like? Is it not splendid?"

"Very fine, Sire," Nevenskoi replied neutrally.

"Very fine? That's all you can find to say? Bah, you are tepid as yesterday's tea. Nevenskoi, use your eyes! Don't you see what this *is*?"

"It is an excellent model, Majesty, a miniature representation of a handsome city, no doubt a very excellent city—"

"It is not simply a city." Miltzin controlled his visible impatience. "It is *the* city, Nevenskoi—the city of the future! Only look at it. You are gazing upon the shape of things to come! The architecture, the advanced features, the design of the streets, the indescribably scientific methods of waste disposal, the inspired use of water power, steam, necromantic exploitation of ghoststrength, gaslight, rational use of vibrational vertices—it's all perfect, quite perfect, and quite killingly modern! I've never seen anything so modern in all my life. It's all *here*, Nevenskoi. The answer, the truth, right there in front of us!"

"Answer, Majesty? To what?" Nevenskoi hazarded.

"What's to become of us and our world? Where shall we go, how shall we live, what will we do? Such little questions as those, my friend! And now they're answered, our path is plain before us, impending reality sitting right there on my desk. I tell you, we are privileged! I can hardly wait to begin!"

"Begin, Sire?"

"To build, man, to build! I've already selected a site— sweetest tract of marshland you can possibly imagine, not far from Gilksborg—and I'm ready, willing, and eager to commence! When I think of the future and its wonders—when I contemplate the ideal world awaiting all mankind, the universal benefits that I shall bestow—I confess, Nevenskoi, such delight pierces my heart that I could weep with it! Ha, but it will be tremendous! Only *look* at the extraordinary details adorning my model here. Well," Mad Miltzin recalled, "to be perfectly accurate, it's actually Zelkiv's model." The king's nod recalled the existence of the silent foreigner.

"Revised to incorporate several original concepts belonging to Your Majesty, and greatly improved thereby," the stranger observed gracefully.

"That's certainly true. There's a great deal of *me* in it." The king nodded. "Nevertheless, honesty compels me to acknowledge Zelkiv here as the master architect. He is quite the clever fellow, Zelkiv is. Just like you, Nevenskoi. Moreover, he is your Rhazaullean countryman, and so I think it high time the two of you were introduced. Noble Landholder Frem Zelkiv, meet my good friend, the talented and entertaining Nevenskoi. No doubt you two northern compatriots will have much to speak of!"

The king's introduction abolished the social disparity between the noble landholder and the untitled adept. Zelkiv extended a cordial hand. A torrent of rapid Rhazaullean poured from his lips.

Nevenskoi went cold, and his mouth went dry.

Badness? asked Masterfire.

Extreme badness. I don't understand his language, to me it's all gibberish.

Gibberish bad?

Gibberish very bad, so bad that I— Nevenskoi's mind swirled, and a fresh idea shot to the surface. He took care to compose his face before remarking aloud in his accented Hetzian, "Much though the music of my native tongue delights my ear, I cannot forget that His Majesty Miltzin regards our Rhazaullean as so much northern gibberish. His Majesty is generous beyond measure, yet I would not presume too selfishly upon his patience, and must therefore express myself to the best of my limited ability in the king's own language."

"Ha! But what a pretty courtesy! Well said, Nevenskoi!" exclaimed the king.

The Noble Landholder Frem Zelkiv flushed a little at the implied rebuke and his demeanor cooled, but he conceded with apparent good nature, "Patriotic sentiment temporarily overcame my sense of perfect propriety, Sire. Fortunate am I that my countryman, burdened with no such excess warmth of feeling, stands ready to correct my error."

Nevenskoi murmured the appropriate disclaimer.

"We shall drink vouvrak and speak of Rhazaulle another day, my compatriot," Zelkiv promised frostily. "We shall share a thousand memories of our home."

Home. Shall I tell you of the flat above my father's shop in Flenkutz? Aloud Nevenskoi replied correctly, "Home is enshrined within each Rhazaullean heart, Landholder."

"Ah, my two favorite northern geniuses revel in one another's company, just as I anticipated," Miltzin misinterpreted cheerily. "But I did not bring you here to reminisce, gentlemen. That vouvrak you Rhazaulleans so unaccountably relish must wait, for there is business at hand. You are here to experience the wonder of each other's talents and accomplishments. Zelkiv, you must demonstrate the features of our marvelous model to Nevenskoi here—he's certain to appreciate our work. Go ahead, man, show him!"

For the next half hour Nevenskoi stood silently absorbed as the Noble Landholder Frem Zelkiv displayed the various futuristic features of his miniature city. There were aqueducts and fountains with real running water, tiny gaslights that glowed, moving mechanical stairways connecting the levels, glass-enclosed aerial walkways accessible by modern steam-powered lift, cleverly concealed chutes descending to the subterranean waste-disposal units, an extraordinary vibrational vertexia with moving parts, miniature boilers producing real steam, working windcatchers, an elaborate system of signal lights capable of transmitting messages clear across the city, an icehouse sheltered beneath an insulated silvery dome, and much more, all of it remarkable as the king had promised.

The demonstration concluded and Nevenskoi excreted the requisite admiration, in this instance sincere. His listeners basked briefly, and then Mad Miltzin decreed, "Your turn now, Nevenskoi. Come, astonish us, man!" His tone waxed conspiratorial. "You have brought our green friend, eh?"

The adept inclined his head.

"Ha, excellent! Then loose him at once—awaken our wonder, entertain us!"

Entertain! This is my great work, you nitwit, this is my life! Nevenskoi hid his indignation behind a deferential smile. His silent voice turned inward and elsewhere, as he inquired, *Loveliness, do you hear me?*

Hear you! returned Masterfire.

Then come forth, my beauty, to dazzle the world.

A thin, serpentine tendril of green flame slithered out of Nevenskoi's breast pocket. An audible gasp escaped the watching Noble Landholder Zelkiv.

"See? Didn't I tell you?" Mad Miltzin exulted. "But this is a trifle, this is nothing! Only wait until you see what my Masterfire can do!"

Embrace me, Nevenskoi commanded mutely, and the fiery serpent stretched, lengthening to loop itself about its master's body again and again until the adept stood lapped in endless coils of living flame that consumed nothing.

Enfold me.

The green coils swelled and merged, reared up and roared, enclosing Nevenskoi within a whirling column of flame.

The Noble Landholder Zelkiv's face was a study in disbelief. Seeing this, King Miltzin loosed a gratified giggle.

Big! declared Masterfire. *I am BIG, I am huge, I am great, I am wonderful—*

True indeed, my sweetest.

I am grand, I am glorious, I am tasty and delicious—

You are all of that and more, but now you must dwindle again. Shrink, my beauty, reduce yourself to the tiniest spark—

NONoNoNoNoNoNo!

Only for a little while, and then, I promise, you will stand taller than you have ever stood before.

Promise?

Trust me.

Goodgoodgood!

The great whirling column diminished, contracting to a single node of green fire burning harmlessly in the middle of its master's outstretched palm.

A flood of excited Rhazaullean burst from the Noble Landholder Zelkiv, and Nevenskoi took refuge in professional abstraction. Deaf to his supposed countryman's queries, he focused his intellect upon the rudimentary awareness of his creation, telepathing silent commands.

At once the sentient spark leapt from its master's hand to land at the center of Frem Zelkiv's model metropolis. An instant later Masterfire disappeared down one of the chutes leading to the underground maze of utility corridors.

"What is it doing? What is it doing?" Zelkiv demanded in alarm.

As if in reply Masterfire reappeared, his divided self spouting suddenly from the upper windows of half a dozen tall edifices ranged about the perimeter of the city.

"Call it off!" Zelkiv cried.

"Take heart, my friend," Miltzin IX counseled indulgently. "All's well. My Nevenskoi and our Masterfire know what they're about. You'll see!"

Green flame gushed from the tower windows, streamed down walls of dry thin wood textured to resemble masonry, without so much as bubbling the painted surface. Descending to ground level, the fires flashed through the miniature boulevards, hurrying from street to street, meeting at the plazas and branching out from there, until the model city burned along every artery and vein.

Masterfire destroyed nothing. Frem Zelkiv's initial alarm gave way to wonder, while Miltzin IX smiled complacently as if he imagined himself author of the marvel.

Nevenskoi enjoyed no such untroubled optimism. His psychic link with Masterfire continued, and the messages blazing in his brain invited concern.

Others! Here! Like me! Others!

Explain, Nevenskoi requested.

Others! Small ones eating gas. We meet, we dance, dance, DANCE!

The little burners beneath the tiny boilers. The gaslights.

Fires. Should such mundane flames merge with Masterfire, no predicting the result.

No dancing. Do not mingle with inferiors, never debase the purity of your substance.

DanceDanceDance!

I forbid it.

Too late. As Nevenskoi watched, the green torrents blazing through the streets of Zelkiv's model city subtly altered color and character. The wooden walls of the buildings began to darken. The paint started to blister.

"No." Nevenskoi spoke aloud. "Stop. Reduce yourself, dwindle—" Sensing no comprehension, he focused strenuously. *Shrink. Now. Obey.*

NoNoNoNoNoNo!

Obey!

No! I stand tall! You promised!

Later—

NowNowNowNowNowNowNow! So saying, the fiery rivulets filling the tiny boulevards shot clear of the model, rushed across the surface of King Miltzin's desk, cascaded down the four sides in burning streams, hit the floor, and raced off in all directions.

Come back! Resume your original size and shape! Now! There was no response, no sign that Masterfire noted or comprehended the command, and terror wrenched Nevenskoi's innards. An exquisite pang shot through him, and his jaw clenched.

"Well, this is a new one!" Mad Miltzin smiled. "Nevenskoi, my dear fellow, there is truly no end to your powers of invention! What clever feat will our Masterfire perform this time, eh?"

I have no idea! Drawing a deep breath, Nevenskoi marshaled his mental forces and exerted his will. *Obey.*

The reply came in a burst of wordless exhilaration. Roaring, Masterfire swept along the floor, up the walls, and across the ceiling. Green fire sheeted overhead. The doorway and both windows were engulfed in flame. The room remained undamaged, and its human occupants unsinged—Masterfire consumed nothing as yet—but his wild excitement was mounting, and his self-restraint probably measured itself in seconds.

"Oh, splendid." Miltzin IX's pleased eye roamed the surrounding inferno. "Nevenskoi, you have absolutely outdone yourself!"

Nevenskoi hardly heard him. Every sorcerous faculty strained. He sent his intellect questing through fiery eternity, and finally caught the echo of his creation's thoughts.

Big! Dance! Big!

Loveliness. Hear me. The adept exerted every atom of will. *Hear me.*

Hear you! I am everywhere, I am everything, I am MASTERFIRE! Dance! Big! Big! Eat! Eat! EAT!

NO.

YES! Eat!

Reduce yourself. Down, down, no higher than the hem of my robe, no wider than the tip of my finger. He had achieved nearly perfect concentration, but Masterfire resisted yet, and a hideous moment of uncertainty passed before the flame's will buckled.

Masterfire gave way suddenly and completely. Green flame flowed down the walls like water, drawing in upon itself and dwindling to a thumb-sized wisp within the space of seconds.

Nevenskoi's face was cold with sweat, and his stomach churned. It had been the contact with the mundane gas jets in Frem Zelkiv's model city, he decided. That mingling had contaminated Masterfire, blunting sentience and nearly precipitating disaster. It would never happen again. Scooping the green flame from the floor, he returned Masterfire to his breast pocket, whence emanated crackling telepathic frustration.

"Ha! Tremendous, my friend! Another delightful display!" Blind to near calamity, Miltzin IX clapped the adept's back heartily. Turning to his Rhazaullean guest, he demanded, "There, Zelkiv, did I not tell you?"

"Majesty, you did." The noble landholder ran a wondering finger along one edge of his model city, faintly scorched, but otherwise intact. "I confess myself overwhelmed."

"A convert," Miltzin triumphed.

"Indeed, Sire. My countryman," Zelkiv addressed Nevenskoi, "I offer my congratulations and my admiration."

The adept bowed modestly.

"Tell me, then," Zelkiv probed. "Could this marvelous fire of yours that dances so prettily to your tune within these four walls prove equally obliging in the outer world?"

"Beyond doubt," Nevenskoi told him.

"It expands or diminishes, consumes or abstains, as you command?"

"Invariably."

"You dispatch it where you will?"

"Effortlessly."

"Then, sir, the reports are true, and you are master of the greatest weapon the world has ever known."

"His Majesty Miltzin is master of all within Waterwitch," Nevenskoi murmured demurely.

"To be sure. Sire," Zelkiv commenced, "you realize that you hold the fate of all the world in your hand. My homeland of Rhazaulle stands in mortal peril. The Grewzian invaders lay waste to our land, our cities, and our lives. Their advance is inexorable, our defeat all but certain, unless Your Majesty prove the author of our salvation. Sire, I beseech your assistance. It cannot be an accident that Masterfire's creator is Rhazaullean. Send my compatriot Nevenskoi back home with his discovery, allow him to employ his remarkable abilities in the service of his country."

"It would seem, Landholder," King Miltzin observed with some distaste, "that you regard my Masterfire as an advanced but essentially conventional weapon of modern warfare."

"The phenomenon is anything but conventional, Majesty. It is in fact so remarkable that I—"

"You speak of loosing my Masterfire upon the Grewzian army. You speak of war and destruction. Understand clearly that this discovery—this delight, this boon to mankind—shall never be perverted to such ends. The bare suggestion offends me. We will speak of it no more."

The king's face and voice were cold as arctic midnight, but the noble landholder persevered, "Sire, you speak of this discovery as a boon to mankind, and so it may prove, according to Your Majesty's will. The Grewzian barbarians threaten to enslave the world, and in halting their depredation Masterfire surely serves all humanity."

"Wage war to serve humanity? Bah, there's warped logic for you. You have failed to comprehend our wishes, Landholder, and you presume too greatly upon our indulgence. The discussion is concluded. You may withdraw from our presence."

Zelkiv, remarkably, refused to be dismissed. Desperation must have inspired boldness, for he persisted, "Your Majesty must hear me. Sire, you *shall* hear me. For months now the rumors of an extraordinary arcane weapon capable of changing the course of the war have tantalized my ruler and his ministers. Few among us lent credence to such tales, but the nature of our plight obliged us to investigate all possibilities, and thus at last my master dispatched me to the Low Hetz. This afternoon's demonstration confirms the truth of the rumors. The weapon exists. It is all that we had heard, and more. This Masterfire discovered by a Rhazaullean will save Rhazaulle. It will—"

"Stop there." Miltzin IX folded his arms. "As I recall, your letter of introduction represented you as a private citizen—a master architect, builder, and city planner, here to observe Hetzian methods of construction."

"So I am, Sire. Yet I also serve as my sovereign's unofficial emissary—"

"You would not have secured an audience, had that been known." The king seemed almost amazed at the depth of the visitor's perfidy.

"Authorized to speak and act on the Rhazaullean ulor's behalf," Zelkiv continued. "Empowered to secure temporary use of the Sentient Fire, upon such terms as Your Majesty deems acceptable and appropriate—"

"Enough. I will hear no more. Your offers are unacceptable, and your behavior inappropriate. You have abused my hospitality, Landholder, and I must require you to depart my house at once."

"Your Majesty, in the name of justice, I ask but a quarter of an hour to state my case."

"Your case is lost, your time is up, and my patience is exhausted. Leave me," the king commanded.

"Nevenskoi, you are my countryman. Assist me," Zelkiv attempted. Hetzian vocabulary failed him, and he lapsed into impassioned Rhazaullean.

Nevenskoi's mask of polite regret hid incomprehension. Presently Miltzin IX tugged a bellpull to summon a brace of liveried attendants, who escorted the noble landholder from the study. The flood of emphatic Rhazaullean ceased.

"Well." Mad Miltzin exuded virtuous indignation. "What an unexpected unpleasantness. What was the fellow saying to you just now, when he switched over to his northern lingo?"

"Just now? Oh—he was urging me to return to Rhazaulle with him, Sire," Nevenskoi improvised. "He promised rich reward from the ulor for the use of Masterfire."

"Did he indeed? Before my very face, too! There's insolence!"

"It is of no consequence, Majesty. You will note I did not trouble to reply."

"Quite right. Good fellow! I mean to deport that countryman of yours, though. Don't try to dissuade me."

"I would not so presume, Sire."

"He's lucky I don't order him thrashed. The impudence of that northerner! The hypocrisy, the deceit! He deliberately misrepresented himself to me. In fact, he fed me a plateful of lies, and I cannot forgive that. If there's one thing I can't abide in those around me—and I'm sure you sympathize with me on this, Nevenskoi—if there's one thing I absolutely cannot tolerate, it's dishonesty!"

"BETTER HURRY," Girays v'Alisante advised.

"I'm trying to aim." Luzelle squinted along the barrel of the Khrennisov FK6. She held the pistol high, gripped firmly in both hands, as Girays had taught her.

"Try harder. You haven't much time."

"I know. Don't distract me, you're just making me nervous."

"I don't want to make you nervous, but any second now—"

"*I know!*" Luzelle set her jaw, adjusted her aim infinitesimally, held her breath, and—

The schooner-rigged paddle-and-screw steamship *Revenant* pitched, and the empty bottle set up as her target toppled from its precarious perch on the deck railing to hit the blue waters of the Jeweled Expanse.

She had been too slow again. Now he would lecture her, make her feel childish and stupid—

But he didn't.

"Try again." Drawing another empty bottle from his seemingly inexhaustible collection, Girays balanced the new target on the railing. "In light of the impossible circumstances your progress is good."

Praise from M. the Marquis? Extraordinary. She threw him a surprised glance, then refocused on her task. Taking quick aim, she squeezed the trigger, and the shot sped out over the water. An instant later the *Revenant* rocked, and the untouched bottle tumbled overboard.

"Ruination." Luzelle frowned. "I don't seem to show much talent."

"Difficult to judge, in such a place as this," Girays told her. "In any event, natural ability counts for less than persistence. Work faithfully, and you're certain to improve."

"You really think so?"

"You've mastered the essentials. Now it's simply a matter of practice, preferably conducted on solid ground."

"I'll practice until I get it right."

"And when you do get it right—practice some more."

"I promise. Girays—" She hesitated. "I want to thank you for all your help. You've spent hours instructing and encouraging me, even though you disapprove of the whole endeavor. That's above and beyond."

"Praise from Miss Devaire? Extraordinary. But you already know my reasons. I only hope you'll never need to make practical use of your new accomplishment."

"I've already needed it, and I'm not talking about the exchange with Bav Tchornoi." In answer to his look of inquiry she continued, "I've never told you why I wanted to buy a gun in the first place."

"You're not obliged to explain yourself to me. You've made that abundantly clear."

"But I want to tell you." Concisely she described the incident in Glozh—the Grewzian soldiers on the station platform, their hands on her in broad daylight, the indifference of assorted witnesses. Ordinarily reluctant to confess weakness, she now acknowledged the terror, outrage, and the nightmare sense of helplessness filling her that day, and saw Girays's face change as he listened.

"And so there's no doubt at all what would have happened if Karsler Stornzof hadn't intervened," Luzelle summed up in conclusion. "There was nothing I could do to save myself, to escape or to fight back effectively—nothing at all. It was the most hideous sensation imaginable, and I promised I'd never let it happen to me again. I needed a weapon for self-defense, and a handgun was the best choice. You can see that, can't you?"

"Six years ago I would have answered that a beautiful woman need hardly concern herself with self-defense, as she will never lack for devoted protectors, and you would have flown into a righteous rage. But then, six years ago the question wouldn't have arisen at all, because you wouldn't have deigned to justify yourself. Why do so now?"

"I suppose because I wanted you to know and believe that I haven't been indulging some idle whim."

"I don't flatter myself with the delusion that you attach much importance to my beliefs or opinions."

"Because I'm not wholly ruled by them?"

"Because you consistently ignore them."

"What an absurd exaggeration. What about the time I was thinking of buying stock in Dr. Hoonachio's Universal Panacea, Inc.? You managed to talk me out of it."

"Only because you wanted someone to talk you out of it. What about the Stubi-Grosslinger Cash Pyramid? I wasn't able to talk you out of that one, and you haven't forgotten the result."

"That was nearly seven years ago! I was a child."

"That was only one of the countless incidents. What about the excursion to v'Availleur Falls? I pleaded with you not to go, you ignored me, and that one was almost fatal."

"Well, what would you expect, when you were so overbearing about it? You spoke to me as if I were a naughty infant. If only you'd tried treating me as an intelligent adult—"

"You just finished telling me that you were a child, back then. Or did I misunderstand you?"

"I meant I was inexperienced—not stupid!"

"No one ever dreamed of calling you stupid." Without awaiting reply Girays continued, "I haven't forgotten the Mystery Valise, the Fabeque Venture, or the Green Committee, and those are only a few. Each time I ventured to voice an objection, your determination only increased. At times you seemed to take a positive delight in demonstrating your complete contempt for my judgment."

No, only my complete contempt for your authoritarian attitudes. I got enough of that at home from His Honor, and I wasn't about to take any more of it from you. But he had viewed things very differently, she inwardly conceded. Six years later she could see that he had only been trying to protect her, in classic formerly-Exalted style. His paternalistic presumption might have invited rebellion, but his intentions had surely been good. She was all grown up now, and she could afford a little tolerance. Swallowing an acid reply, she answered with unwonted mildness, "Well, it was all a long time ago, and not worth quarreling about now. Particularly when the whole conversation began with me trying to thank you."

"So it did. Let's have done with quarrels, then—they're quite pointless now."

She nodded and smiled as if pleased, but found herself oddly saddened by his remark.

"Shall I set up another target?" he asked, with no suggestion of double meaning.

"Not here—the sun's glaring into my eyes. Let's go around to the other side."

He picked up the sack of bottles, she stowed the pistol away in her pocket, and together they set off along the deck. Their conversation was carefully neutral, and when they paused beside the railing to gaze out over the water, speech suspended itself altogether for a time. The *Revenant* was passing close by Azure Tower, one of the most famous of the area's countless islands. Straight and sheer out of the water rose the celebrated mica-glittering cliffs, tier upon tier of scintillant stone thrusting ambitiously for the heavens. The mica cliffs supported luxuriant crops of the blue sea slime called false-welkin, which in turn fed vast colonies of Blue Aennorvermis, the sapphire worm of the Jeweled Expanse. The worms were out in force today, probably millions of them there gorging on slime, their bodies clothing the island from base to pinnacle in a moistly glistening mantle of blue.

Luzelle stared, caught despite her revulsion. There was something almost irresistible in the ceaseless undulation of the Aennorvermis. In its own way it was rather beautiful. She could not tear her gaze away, and did not want to. Presently her vision faltered, and the rolling blue sea and the squirming blue island seemed to merge.

Girays's voice broke her trance.

"People have been known to leap overboard and swim for that great pile of bait," he said.

Startled, she turned to find him looking insufferably amused. Her cheeks burned. Without reply she moved away from the railing, and he fell into step beside her. Soon they came upon Bav Tchornoi, sprawled in a deck chair and clutching his flask to his breast.

"So." Tchornoi glowered at her. "Here is the *dead shot*, so very accustomed to handling firearms, she brags, who practices every day but cannot hit the side of a barn at five paces."

Lifting her chin, Luzelle swept by in silence.

"I can't wait to get off of this ship and away from that Rhazaullean drunkard," she complained in an undertone, moments later. "He gives me the evil eye every time he sees me. He looks as if he'd like to break me in two."

"He probably would," Girays agreed. "Can you blame him? You pulled a gun on him, as I recall."

"He deserved it."

"Perhaps Master Tchornoi views the matter in a different light."

"Well, wouldn't you have used force to stop him that day, if you'd been armed?"

"How do you know that I wasn't—that I'm not?"

"Oh, you aren't. That wouldn't be your style."

"Still so sure that you know my style, after all these years?"

"That sounds like a challenge."

"Would you like it to be?"

"I'm up to any challenge you could possibly offer, M. v'Alisante."

"Such confidence. But do you dare put it to the test? You're certain you can read me like a book. Out of the question, in your estimate, that such a conservative, staid, thoroughly predictable character as I would ever dream of carrying a concealed weapon. Absolutely impossible. Well, would you like to place a wager?"

"A wager! I've expressed my opinion, so you wouldn't be offering a wager unless you already knew you'd won. So obviously you must have a gun. Or maybe you don't, but you've taken this approach to make me think that you do. You know I wouldn't believe that the obvious answer could be the right one, and that way you could trick me into guessing wrong. Unless you foresaw that I'd think you're trying to trick me, and—"

"Difficult, isn't it? Not quite so sure of me as you thought?"

"Bah, I'm not about to let you tie my mind into sailor knots. You're bluffing, Girays."

"I am?"

"Yes you are, but you're quite transparent."

"Call my bluff, then. Place a wager."

"Fine! How much?"

"Let's make it entertaining. Ten thousand New-rekkoes—"

"*What?*"

"Or else an honest answer to the question of my choice."

"What question?"

"Whatever I wish to ask. You hesitate. Afraid?"

"Not at all. But what of M. the Marquis? Should I win, there'll be no piddling questions—I'll want those ten thousand New-rekkoes, preferably in bills of moderate denomination. Ready to pay up?"

"Upon legitimate demand."

"Very well. The wager is in place. I say you are unarmed. If I'm wrong, prove it now."

At once he reached into his coat pocket to bring forth a pistol almost indistinguishable from her own.

"Oh. Well." So he'd gotten the better of her after all. A wave of crimson flooded her face. She felt an utter fool, but managed to ask with an air of unconcern, "Khrennisov?"

"Model FK29. A bit heavier than your FK6, somewhat greater range." Girays returned the gun to his pocket.

"Ummm. Yes. Well. You have won, then. And I'm afraid I don't have the ten thousand." Despite her genuine chagrin she was not altogether displeased. Had he lost, Girays v'Alisante could painlessly have paid off the wager, but she would not have relished divesting him of so large a sum. For reasons she could hardly fathom, it would have made her feel shabby. Now no money would change hands, she need only answer some little question, and she realized with a certain internal flutter that she hadn't the slightest idea what he would ask, any more than she'd had the slightest idea that the civilized, highly cerebral individual she thought she knew so well would actually carry a gun. Had he changed so much in recent years, or had she never really known him at all?

"Then you owe me one truthful answer."

"To what, exactly?"

"Here is the question, then." He halted, obliging her to do the same. Turning to face her, he asked, "Why did you never trouble to answer my letter, six years ago?" She was silent, and he added, "You recall the letter?"

Unwillingly she nodded. She more than recalled the letter. The missive in question still lay in the compartment at the back of her jewelry box, in her lodgings in Sherreen. The heavy stationery was creased and limp from much handling.

"My messenger assured me that he placed the envelope in your hand, the evening prior to your departure for Lakhtikhil Ice Shelf. Yet you left without so much as a word in reply. I have never understood that."

"It becomes easier to understand when I tell you I left the next morning without reading your letter."

"I see. You desired no further communication."

"It wasn't that, exactly. It was more . . ." She faltered, then forced herself to continue. She had promised honesty, after all. "I didn't open your letter the night I received it because I was afraid I'd find something there that would persuade me to change my plans—to postpone my trip, or even to cancel it altogether. I didn't want to take the chance of that happening, so I didn't let myself look. That was hard. I still remember the way my fingers itched to tear the envelope open. But I made myself place it at the bottom of my suitcase, then I piled my belongings on top, shut the suitcase, and locked it. And I didn't open that suitcase again until I was safely at sea and couldn't possibly turn back."

"Then did you read it?"

"Then I read it."

"And still didn't bother to answer."

"I couldn't answer. I should have, I wanted to, but couldn't find the words. I did try, you know."

"No. I didn't know."

"Many times, but always ended by ripping the paper to shreds. I couldn't say what I wanted to say, probably because I didn't really know what that was—I was too agitated, too confused, and too young." Almost to her own surprise, she heard herself say, "I'm sorry."

He nodded once. His dark face told her nothing. After a moment he resumed walking, and she kept pace. The silence lengthened, until at last he asked idly, "When you finally read my letter, did the contents confirm your fears?"

"Fears?"

"Was there anything there that might have caused you to alter your plans?"

"I think your victory entitled you to one question only. Now it's your turn to answer."

"My turn? Where did that come from? I recall no such obligation."

"There is no obligation." She smiled, relieved that the mood was lightening. "Think of it as formerly-Exalted largesse."

"Formerly-Exalted affectations are passé, as you've so often reminded me. What's the question?"

"Why did you decide to enter the Grand Ellipse? You promised back in Hurba that you'd tell me, aboard ship."

"I remember suggesting that we talk. The conversational topic remained unspecified."

"That's as slippery as those blue worms back there. Quite beneath Your Lordship, I'd have thought."

"Another illusion shattered."

"Oh come on, Girays, spill it!"

"Well, since you ask so prettily—"

A familiar grandly garbed, pearl-studded figure rose athwart their path. A familiar voice assaulted their ears.

"Aha—the two Vonahrish contenders, very thick. Should I worry?" inquired a ponderously jovial Porb Jil Liskjil.

"Shouldn't we all?" Luzelle rejoined gaily, masking her frustration. She had striven for days to extract an explanation from Girays, and he had repeatedly defeated her efforts. Time and again he had deflected her queries, so skillfully that the evasions seemed quite accidental. Today she had managed to lure him to the brink of revelation, only to be thwarted once more by the preternaturally ill-timed intrusion of the Lanthian merchant.

"I think we're all relatively safe from one another for the duration of this crossing," Girays reassured her. Amusement lurked in the set of his lips. "Particularly in the blessed absence of the Grewzian element. Speaking of which, Merchant Jil Liskjil, I'm eager to hear how you outwitted our offal-fed friends. I gather the harbor blockade couldn't contain you."

"Indeed it could not, sir." Porb Jil Liskjil swelled visibly. "Indeed it could not. In my own home city of Lanthi Ume, be assured I am not without some few little resources."

"I would expect no less. Yet the Lanthian resistance, eager to offer assistance to a compatriot, couldn't find you. Jil Liskjil had vanished into thin air. How was this sorcerous feat accomplished?"

"No sorcery, sir—only a little old-fashioned ingenuity, spiced with a dash of audacity," Jil Liskjil confided. "I will explain. You recall the disturbance at the wharf, the day we reached Lanthi Ume? Well, even before the *Karavise* docked, I was preparing to—"

Luzelle suppressed a sigh of boredom. She already knew the tale of Porb Jil Liskjil's adventures. Disembarking from the *Karavise,* he had passed easily through Lanthian customs, then headed straight for the worst section of town, haunt of the seediest local smugglers, one of whom had consented, upon promise of gigantic reward, to run the blockade by night. The smuggler's little bark had passed almost within hailing distance of a Grewzian patrol vessel, to slip unseen from the harbor, thence ferrying its lone passenger north along the coast to Hurba, which Porb Jil Liskjil had reached in time to book passage east aboard the *Revenant.* By now, several days into the journey, all of Jil Liskjil's fellow travelers knew all the details, and Girays v'Alisante was no exception. But there he stood, listening with that air of dedicated attentiveness that he knew so well how to assume, and no doubt inwardly laughing.

". . . Overcast skies, fog on the water, reduced our visibility, and yet the danger was immeasurable . . . remember one heart-stopping moment when the moon emerged . . . captain professed himself astonished by my daring and coolness . . ." Jil Liskjil's voice ran on and on.

It was at least the third time she had heard this story, which waxed in self-congratulation with each repetition. Luzelle's foot began to tap. Carefully she stilled it. When Porb Jil Liskjil paused briefly to draw breath, she seized the opportunity to make her excuses and her escape. Fleeing to the sanctuary of her stateroom, she started in on a new novel, *The Curse of the Witch Queen,* and remained closeted until dinner.

She did not manage to catch Girays alone again that evening, and retired for the night with her curiosity unsatisfied.

The next morning found her up on deck, ensconced in a comfortable chair. There she sat reading, or pretending to read, as fellow passengers strolled by in the sunshine. She bent her head lower over her book, feigning absorption, as Stesian and Trefian Festinette giggled their way aft. But she looked up with a smile as Mesq'r Zavune drew nigh, and seeing this, he paused to chat, more or less intelligibly.

Zavune, she soon discerned, simmered with excitement at

the imminence of the Aennorvi sojourn. He spoke at length of contacting his family, of somehow arranging a short reunion, even at the expense of time that an Ellipsoid could ill afford. Luzelle smiled and nodded as she listened, but inwardly thought, for the hundredth time, *That man should be at home.*

Mesq'r Zavune moved on. Time passed, salt water and numberless islands flowed by. The Witch Queen eventually tasted her just deserts, but Girays v'Alisante never showed himself. Luzelle did not glimpse him again until noon, when the materialization of the Aennorvi coastline upon the horizon drew all passengers to the deck. And there he was among the others at the railing, hands buried in his pockets, dark hair stirring in the breeze. She might accost him if she chose, but now she no longer cared. Another hour or more would pass before the *Revenant* reached the port of Aeshno, but her thoughts were already winging ahead to the docks in search of advantage. This time, she resolved, she would definitely be first off the boat, first in line at the customs office—

And maybe she could find out how long ago Karsler Stornzof had passed through.

Frowning, she turned away from the railing, and a pair of identical mauve-clad figures caught her attention. Not far away the Festinette boys stood conferring with the *Revenant*'s captain. The pretty twin faces were uncharacteristically intent, and Luzelle caught the flash of gold changing hands, a sight to set internal alarm bells clanging.

9

THE *REVENANT* DOCKED and her engines fell silent. The gangplank was lowered, but the three crewmen stationed before it blocked disembarkation. In response to countless queries regarding the delay, the sailors vaguely cited bureaucratic confusion revolving about the vessel's collection of international commercial permits. Assorted travelers complained and the crewmen, bored with argument, went mute.

Shortly thereafter the captain, followed by a brace of identically youthful, mauve-clad companions, descended to the wharf and vanished from sight. Luzelle observed the retreat, and her suspicions crystallized to certainty. The slimy little Travornish cheats had bribed the captain. They had managed to trap their rivals on board the *Revenant* while they continued along the Grand Ellipse, and *they were getting away with it*. Outrage all but choked her.

Four agonizing hours passed, and the afternoon shadows crept. The frustrated passengers loitered, sipped iced drinks, and grumbled. At length the captain reboarded alone. Minutes later the prisoners were liberated.

Angry and worried, Luzelle made her way down the gangplank and along the wharf as far as the customhouse, above which flew the violet-and-black banner of Aennorve. She had waited on deck for half the day, resisting the lure of the saloon's conviviality, and her self-denial had yielded reward. She was first off the *Revenant* and first in line to present her passport to the local officials.

But Aennorvi bureaucrats displayed a curious blend of indifference and exaggerated zeal. Forty minutes at least passed before the importantly preoccupied individual behind the desk deigned to acknowledge her existence. When he finally did, her belongings were subjected to the most rigorous, prolonged examination ever devised. There was no item too humdrum or too intimate to escape microscopic inspection, and when at last her passport received the requisite stamp and her tormentor waved her on toward the exit, Luzelle was inwardly boiling.

She cast a hostile glance back over her shoulder to witness the Aennorvi official subjecting the next traveler in line to exactly the same invasive scrutiny that she herself had endured. Comprehension dawned. The twins, and their damnable money, again. *Cheats.* At this rate the last of the *Revenant* passengers wouldn't be through customs before nightfall.

Not entirely bad. Perhaps one or two of her rivals might be eliminated from the competition here and now. Her eye traveled the queue to light on Girays v'Alisante. No stopping M. the Marquis, but the present delay granted her a slight advantage that she did not mean to waste.

Train station. Ticket. Next stop—Bizaqh. Hurryhurryhurry.

Valise in hand, she exited the customhouse, making her way from the wharf to the nearest street, where she might ordinarily expect to find a squadron of hansom cabs. Today there were none. Puzzled, she cast her eyes up and down the warm, sunlit street. She saw white stuccoed buildings and terra-cotta tiled roofs adorned with elaborate wrought-iron grillwork. She saw fanciful aerial walkways linking the taller structures. She saw hordes of sun-browned pedestrians clad in the light, brightly hued Aennorvi mode that would have appeared so frivolous in chillier climes. She saw pushcart vendors, handwagoneers, roller-boarders, a flamboyant unicyclist. But nowhere did she spot a hansom, a private carriage, a donkey cart, or indeed, any serviceable vehicle other than a single slow and old-fashioned miskin-master.

Odd. Aeshno was a thriving port city. Travelers swarmed across these docks every day and they needed transportation, of which there seemed to be none. The twins again? Impossible. Even the Festinette resources were unequal to such a feat.

Luzelle approached the nearest pushcart vendor, a cerise-clad peacock with glossy dark curls, dark eyes, and an extravagant moustache. The avid black eyes lit up as she drew near. "Where can I find a cab?" she asked in Vonahrish. He stared at her, and she repeated the query. He displayed no sign of comprehension, and she tried Kyrendtish, then Hetzian, and then broken Grewzian. The vendor replied in Aennorvi, which she did not understand. His excited gestures directed her attention to the cheap leather wares filling his cart.

No good. She walked away and tried another vendor, this one a seller of repulsive brass and glass jewelry. The vendor chattered Aennorvi and rattled loathsome trinkets at her. Luzelle retreated, frowning.

Nobody seemed to speak Vonahrish. She might have expected such ignorance of the Bhomiri Islanders, but Aennorve was supposedly civilized. She walked on along the street, and still there were no cabs. An expensive-looking little pumpkin-colored barouche drawn by a pair of matched bays passed at a smart clip, and she caught a brief glimpse of the passenger within; female, oval white face smooth as a polished pebble, opaque shark's eyes. For a moment she thought of calling out to the white shark, but embarrassment stilled her tongue. Annoyed with herself, she walked on, valise now weighing on her arm. Five minutes later, when she spied a mule-drawn cart heaped with cabbages and carrots, she did not hesitate, but hurried straight to the slow-moving vehicle, waving her arm vigorously.

The driver pulled up and sat gazing down at her in surprise. A stoop-shouldered, lank, and grizzled individual, face seamed and wrinkled beneath a plain workman's cap. He looked poor and harmless enough, both qualities recommending him to her attention. Now, if only she could communicate with the fellow.

She tried Vonahrish, and he stared. Her secondary languages proved equally useless, and at last she resorted to Lanthian, of which she possessed a sorry smattering.

"Carriage? Aeshno-town? Go. Streets. Go. Money." Feeling like an idiot, she produced a New-rekko note and pantomimed payment, then arched her brows interrogatively.

"Fiacre?" the carter inquired in Lanthian.

She understood him at once, for the word was a Vonahrish cognate, oddly accented but easily recognizable. For a moment she was surprised, then recalled that Lanthian travelers shuttled endlessly between Dalyon and Aennorve, bringing heavy trade along with them. Many Aennorvis inhabiting the coastal port cities spoke some Lanthian.

He repeated the query, and she nodded emphatically.

"Yes. Fiacre," she agreed, adding for good measure, "Yes. Yes."

"No," he told her clearly. "Fiacres gone. All gone."

"Gone?" she echoed. "All? Where?"

The carter launched a volley of Lanthian sentences, poorly pronounced and largely unintelligible.

"Again, please. Slow, please," Luzelle requested.

He complied, and this time she caught more of it.

"*Hours ago . . . two—*" Word unknown. "*From the Hurbanese boat, and*" —gabble, gabble, gabble— "*brothers . . . alike . . . same face, same clothes . . . money . . . Travornish—*" Phrase unknown, definitely uncomplimentary. "*Fiacres at the dock . . . few there because of the* strevvio—" Meaning of *strevvio* unknown. "*Horses scarce . . .* strevvio"—gabble, gabble— "*owners . . . high prices . . . Travornish brothers pay . . . fiacres go. . . .*"

"Wait." Luzelle reviewed Lanthian vocabulary, then inquired laboriously, "Travornish brothers paying all fiacres to go away dock?"

"Yes. All fiacres," the carter confirmed her latest suspicions.

"That's the filthiest trick I've ever heard of! Those sneaking little twin ferrets ought to be disqualified!" she exclaimed in outraged Vonahrish. Unbelievable. How had they managed it? "They won't get away with this! I'm going to complain!"

Right. To whom, exactly?

No point in fuming, there were better ways to spend her time. What next? *Think.* The carter was watching in frank curiosity. Switching back to her feeble Lanthian, she suggested, "You move me inside wagon to—" What was the word for train station? She had no idea. Another cognate, perhaps? "Railroad," she concluded in Vonahrish. Her listener's face remained blank. "Depot. Railway lines. Tracks. Station house," she attempted. He shrugged and she tried alternate languages, without success. At last, in desperation, she chugged in locomotive rhythm, climaxing the performance with a discreet double hoot reminiscent of a train whistle.

The carter burst out laughing, and she felt her face go red. But he was welcome to laugh all he liked, provided he understood her.

"Ferignello?" he asked.

She hoped that was Lanthian for *train station.* "You move me inside wagon," she urged. "I pay money."

He did not seem favorably disposed. A spate of negative Lanthian flew at her, and several times she caught the mysterious term *strevvio,* which seemed to denote some sort of difficulty or obstacle. An individual? Tyrannical bureaucrat? Atmospheric disturbance? Flood? Fog? Whoever or whatever, she was not about to let any *strevvio* stop her.

"Money. I pay. Money. Money." She flapped an alluring fistful of New-rekko notes at him.

He seemed to expostulate.

"Money. Money."

He nodded in resignation, accepted the cash, and she scrambled up onto the seat beside him. *"Ferignello?"* she asked brightly.

"Ferignello." He exhorted the mules, and the vehicle moved off.

Success. She had overcome the language barrier and she was on her way. Luzelle congratulated herself. She had doubtless pulled ahead of every fellow Ellipsoid traveling aboard the *Revenant,* with the exception of those pestilential Festinette boys, who in turn trailed the Grewzian kinsmen.

Karsler Stornzof and his ice-statue uncle. Unjustly favored, and by this time doubtless far ahead along the Grand Ellipse.

She could not afford to let herself think about it. The Grewzians were not going to win. Their luck would run out, and she would surely catch them—one day.

KARSLER STORNZOF AND HIS UNCLE faced one another like duelists. Mutually unacknowledged antipathy charged the air between them. Their eyes locked, momentarily excluding the dockside tumult.

"It is a disaster," Torvid Stornzof opined. "An unmitigated disaster."

"Scarcely such a dire matter, Grandlandsman," Karsler suggested.

"Ah? I stand corrected. The Hurbanese vessel carrying a veritable mob of your rivals has matched the *Inspiration*'s speed to Aeshno, but what of that? I have spied more than one of those foreigners blundering about the wharf, but this is no source of concern."

"It is rather a source of wonder. How did the Vonahrish and the others transfer themselves so rapidly from Lanthi Ume to Hurba? What means of transport could they possibly have used? The feat defies understanding."

"The mechanics are irrelevant. What signifies is that you have sacrificed your former advantage."

"I do not mourn its loss, Grandlandsman."

"Then you are a fool. But the state of your intellect is hardly an issue of paramount importance; there are more pressing concerns. You are aware that the railroad laborers in this anarchic sinkhole have launched a full-scale revolt."

"I speak no Aennorvi," Karsler returned. "I gather from your translations that the workers are on strike."

"The local authorities inexplicably fail to crush the rebellion."

"It is possible they favor subtler methods."

"Subtlety is the first refuge of the weak. You are also aware," Torvid continued, "that the antics of those Travornish twin cretins have delayed you by hours or days."

"They seem remarkably inventive, as cretins go."

"When you have finished amusing yourself, perhaps you

will be so good as to state your immediate plan of action, if in fact you have one."

"I will use whatever means available to travel from Aeshno to the town of Eynisse, on the River Arune," Karsler replied without hesitation. "There it is possible to book barge passage east to Yellow Noki, where I will pick up the eastbound coach headed for Quinnekevah, in Bizaqh. Once over the Bizaqhi border, and train service will resume."

"You have toiled like some little clerk over your maps and timetables, and you have formulated a strategy worthy of a clerk—meticulous and pedestrian. You will keep in mind, I trust, as you laze along some river on a mule-drawn barge, that those Travornish buffoons will increase their lead with every passing hour."

"For now there is little to be done." Karsler's impassive courtesy never wavered. "We can only proceed in the hope that an opportunity to regain lost time will eventually present itself."

"You may do so if you wish, Nephew. As for me, I am not in the habit of awaiting opportunity—I prefer to make my own."

"So I have observed. As you are not a Grand Ellipse contestant, however, the point is academic."

"Exactly so. My agreeable state of uninvolvement frees me of countless tiresome obligations. Just now, for example, I escape the necessity of enduring purgatorial progress across Aennorve, a land whose climate, customs, and population I despise. These Aennorvi peasants are animals, little better."

Philanthropy hardly informed his uncle's judgment, yet the complaint was not altogether unfounded. The crowd milling about them on the wharf was surly beyond normal expectation. Several times he was roughly jostled, not by accident, and once some urchin actually dared to spit, missing his boot by inches. He had often known foreign enmity, but never before so intensely immediate, and never so fearlessly expressed. His blood quickened a little, but no sign of perturbation touched his face as he observed, "These Aennorvis are no friends of the Imperium. Perhaps the sight of my uniform offends them."

"Bah, they want the lash, that is all. Happily I need not concern myself, as I intend to abandon this dismal little olive-oil slick of a nation within the hour. Assuming that those idiots in the customhouse have not misinformed me, there remain staterooms available aboard the next ship out."

"Indeed." Karsler suppressed every outward sign of pleasant surprise. "Your plans have altered, and you are homeward bound, Grandlandsman?"

"Not at all. I do not desert the Grand Ellipse, but shorten its tedium, merely. The prospect of protracted Aennorvi junketing succeeded by the archaic discomforts of Bizaqh and Zuleekistan appalls me, and therefore I have chosen to proceed directly to Jumo, there to await your coming."

"According to your will, Grandlandsman."

"The separation should serve us well," Torvid added unexpectedly. "We are too much in each other's way, Nephew—like two wolves locked in a small cage. We chafe one another, we are always annoyed, and it is so foolish, when we are natural allies linked by blood and Destiny. It is my hope that a time apart will restore proper perspective."

"My hope as well, Grandlandsman." Karsler's concealed surprise deepened.

"A point of accord at last. Upon that happy note I will take my leave. Nephew, I wish you a journey swift and untroubled—in assurance whereof, you would do well to observe your fellow racers closely. It is more than probable that some serve in agency of their respective governments, and in such cases a preemptive strike may best serve your purposes. As far as that goes, I leave the matter in your hands. You will report your actions when we meet again in Jumo."

"Understood. Farewell, Grandlandsman."

Torvid turned and marched away, straight-spined figure swiftly vanishing from view. Karsler Stornzof stood motionless, bemused by the speed and suddenness of his kinsman's disappearance. For the first time since the race began he was fully free of Torvid's pervasive presence, and certain to remain so for days or weeks to come. It was as if an invisible band of steel encircling his temples had fallen away. An odd sense of almost forgotten freedom dawned within him; a new buoyancy, and a contentment unknown since his Promontory days. Someone elbowed him aggressively, and he caught a snarling burst of Aennorvi, unintelligible but unmistakably imprecatory. He hardly heard it. Drawing a deep breath of sea-smelling fresh air down to the bottom of his lungs, he savored the moment, despite the nearly tangible hatred simmering all around him.

THE MULES PLODDED. The cart seemed scarcely to move. Nothing much to be done about it, either, given the nature of mules. She would have traded kingdoms for a proper hansom. Luzelle shifted her weight and flashed an impatient glance around her. Pedestrians, donkey carts, and miskin wagons clogged the street, but nowhere did she spy a horse-drawn vehicle. The Festinette boys couldn't have banished all of them. The *"strevvio"* that her carter had mentioned—a disease of horses, perhaps?

The cart plowed on through dusty streets filled with light, noise, and a rich swirl of rival odors ruled by the garlic-powered fragrance of hroviapoul, the famous Aennorvi stew of squid, silverdarts, and assorted native mollusks. Luzelle's nostrils flared and her stomach growled. She had not eaten since early morning and she badly wanted a meal, but it would wait. Soon she would be on a train speeding east toward Bizaqh, and the train would include a restaurant car, a lounge, and presumably plush sleeping compartments as well, as the Aennorvi folk were famously devoted to their personal comforts.

Should the train schedules favor her, she might expect to gain several hours of advantage over her competitors.

Except for the Stornzofs. And the Festinettes.

The streets lagged by at the stolid mules' pace, and her eagerness grew along with her impatience and hunger. Had she spoken his language, she might have urged the carter to ply his whip; not that it would have done much good. As it was, she sat wordlessly fidgeting.

The avenue terminated at the verge of a broad plaza. Straight ahead rose a massive structure of white stone roofed in rich red-brown tile. The carter pointed.

"Ferignello," he announced.

The train station, as she had hoped, but who were those men assembled before it? There must have been at least two hundred of them blocking the entrance, and certainly it was no random, spontaneous gathering. The men—ordinary, respectable workers, by the look of them—stood ranged in neat, quasi-military ranks stretching the entire width of the big building. Many of them carried signs, large placards hand lettered in Aennorvi, which she could not read. They were singing or chanting something in unison, the words incomprehensible, but suggestive of infinite determination.

"What?" Luzelle inquired concisely.

"Ferignello," the carter explained.

"The men. There. Men. They doing?"

"Strevvio."

"What is *strevvio*?"

He chattered bad Lanthian at her, and she understood next to nothing. She held up one hand, and the verbal current slackened.

"Train men stop work. Want money. Bigger money, or trains no go. *Strevvio.*"

"You're telling me that the Aennorvi railroad workers have called a strike?" Luzelle comprehended. "Can they do that? Won't the government intervene?" The other's eyes went blank, and she knew that she must have spoken Vonahrish. *"Strevvio*—trains no go?" she amended in the appropriate tongue.

"Trains no go," he agreed.

"Voyagers do what?"

The carter shrugged. *"Ferignello,"* he declared conclusively, and his meaning was clear. He had fulfilled his commission, his task was done, and he wanted to be on his way.

She resisted the impulse to grab him and shake him. For a moment she was unreasonably angry, then perceived her own folly. It certainly wasn't the driver's fault, he had even tried to warn her. Climbing down from the seat, she dismissed him with an adequately civil nod, and the cart lumbered on its way.

Now what? A couple of hundred resolute workers stood

between herself and the station. Bigger money, or trains no go. But perhaps service hadn't entirely halted yet? If anything was moving east along those tracks, she would brave a thousand striking workers to reach it.

Chin up, she advanced on the picket line as if expecting a path to open itself for her.

The human barrier stood firm. She confronted closed ranks and closed faces. She aimed herself at one such face. Its owner was male, young, and possibly susceptible.

"Do you speak Vonahrish, sir?" she inquired melodiously.

He shook his head, uncomprehending but interested.

"Speak Lanthian?" she essayed in that tongue.

"Like a native," he returned enthusiastically. "I could probably pass myself off as a Dalyonic noble, if I wanted. I know how to assume the grand manner to perfection. Would you like to see?"

His accent and pronunciation were far superior to the carter's, and she understood him surprisingly well.

"Other time, perhaps." An admiring smile softened the refusal.

"Oh. You sure? Well, what can I do for you, then?"

"*Strevvio* stop all trains?"

"Absolutely. Nothing moves until we get that salary increase, and that could take days or weeks. If only they'd listen to me, I know how we could get it before midnight, though. I've come up with a plan, you see. Guaranteed success. Would you like to hear about it?"

"Other time. Nothing go east? To Bizaqh?"

"Not since three o'clock this afternoon. That was the last train out."

Three o'clock. Plenty of time for the Festinette boys to secure seats. *Damn them.*

"What travelers east doing, then?"

"Waiting, I suppose. But cheer up, it's not so bad. Aeshno is a fine city, with plenty to see and do. I know every street by heart, I know all the best places. Would you like me to show them to you?"

"Other time."

"You sure? No one knows his way around the Sailors' Cemetery the way I do. Then there's Feyp's Windmill, that dates back all the way to—"

"Other ways go east Bizaqh?"

"Why go there? Bizaqh's a dump. Take it from me, you're better off here. There's nothing can match Aeshno for excitement. Have you ever heard of Youpi's Bog? No? Where have you been living? Well, just outside the city limits, there's—"

"Horses go east?"

"Oh, you won't have any luck there. Mule cart, now, or maybe a miskin—"

"Too slow. *Horses.*"

"Gone, sold at inflated prices days ago, as soon as it was known that we meant business about the strike. There may still be a few fiacres hanging about the waterfront, but they're doing such business, they'll never sell out. No horses."

"Yes. Some. Saw them." She frowned, reviewed vocabulary, and continued, "Horses with carriage of—of—fruit."

"Horse-drawn fruit cart? I don't think so, not these days."

"Carriage. Color of fruit."

"Apple? Soapfruit? Grape? Kiwi?"

Pumpkin. What was the Lanthian word for pumpkin? She could not remember, or else she had never known.

"Red-yellow," she compromised. "Yellow-red."

"Orange? Tangerine? Sweetspitter?"

"Yes. Yes."

"You want some really ripe sweetspitters? I know all the best fruit stalls at North Market. Best produce, best prices. Want me to show you?"

"Today no, thank you. You know sweetspitter carriage?"

"Who doesn't? That flashy eyesore belongs to Madame Phingria Tastriune, wife of none other than Gleftus Tastriune himself." He eyed her expectantly, as if awaiting a reaction. "That's *the* Gleftus Tastriune, otherwise known as Mr. Moneybags, chief stockholder and president of the Feyenne-Aeshno Railroad. If the Moneybags could only bring himself to loosen those purse strings just a trifle, let me tell you, this strike would be over before nightfall."

It would only be another hour or so before nightfall, Luzelle realized. The sun was dipping below the city skyline, and the long rays were tinting the white stuccoed buildings with pink. Soon the color would fade, the shops would close, and presumably the picketers would retire for the night. Should she fail to secure transportation, she would find herself obliged to seek the nearest decent hotel, there to sit cooling her heels for the next twelve hours or more, during which time the Festinettes would increase their ill-gotten lead, and farther yet along the Grand Ellipse the Stornzof kinsmen would doubtless be doing the same. . . .

"Madame Tastriune sell horse?" she inquired.

"What, and abandon her pleasure? Not for a million."

"Pleasure?"

"The rich lady trots those nags of hers all over town, just to make mouths water. People swarm around begging to buy, and she toys with them for a while, then enjoys the satisfaction of turning them down and tossing 'em out. If the customers hang around her door after that, she's been known to set the dogs on them. Oh, she's the proper consort to Mr. Moneybags, all right. They were made for each other!"

I believe it. Pebble face, shark eyes.

"Madame Tastriune live where?" Luzelle inquired.

"New brick mansion the color of raw meat in Old Knightly Crescent," he told her. "But you're not thinking of going there, are you?"

"Ummm—"

"Don't even consider it; she'll only sic the mastiffs on you. I've got a better idea. Why don't you plan on spending a few days or a few weeks here in Aeshno? Don't worry about the expense. My sister-in-law's second cousin once removed has a room with an extra cot, and if I put in the word, she'll let you sleep there for free. Free porridge in the morning too. You can't do better than that."

"I cannot stay, thank you."

"You don't really mean to leave without seeing Youpi's Bog, do you?"

"Madame Tastriune in Old Knightly Crescent?"

"Fancy section of town. Lots of big new houses. Would you like to see them?"

"Yes, I go there."

"If you'll just wait for another hour, the picket line folds up for the night, and then I—"

"I cannot wait. Thank you for help. Good luck with *strevvio*." She turned and walked away. As she went, she heard his voice behind her.

"I know the best route to Old Knightly Crescent—wouldn't you like me to show you?"

. . . The Honorable Flen Oshune, together with his family members, staff, retainers, and all other Aennorvi nationals expelled from the Governor's Mansion and the neighboring residences, are currently upon the high seas, en route for Feyenne. The many Aennorvi citizens slain during the final defense of Jumo Towne remain incompletely accounted for, their bodies awaiting final disposition dependent upon the approval of the Overcommander Kilke Ghonauer, current leader of the Grewzian occupying force. To date Overcommander Ghonauer has declined to issue a list of Aennorvi dead. As for the courageous and loyal South Ygahri natives offering up their lives in defense of the Aennorvi Empire, no estimate of their number has yet been made available. . . .

Girays v'Alisante tossed the newspaper aside without finishing the lead article, whose content and style equally annoyed him. So the Grewzians had grabbed Jumo, site of those famous diamond mines, longtime source of Aennorvi prosperity. Kicked out the colonial governor and his flunkies, wiped out squadrons of doubtless bewildered Ygahri natives, and declared themselves new administrators of the entire South Ygahro Territory. The repercussions of the loss would soon be making themselves felt throughout Aennorve and beyond. No wonder the prevailing mood in Aeshno was sour.

The plate on the table before him bore a pair of the famous

Aennorvi giant black olives, each the size of a duck's egg, each stuffed with a mixture of ground lamb, onion, shredded seaweed, and herbs. Beside the plate stood a mug of iced citruswater. Girays applied himself to the snack, while letting his eyes wander. He sat beneath a broad canvas awning shading one of Aeshno's countless outdoor *akrobatterías,* where the little wrought-iron tables edged the perimeter of a circular space left clear for the use of the professional acrobats so beloved of the locals.

A performance was presently in progress. At the center of the open area a muscular woman clad in silver-spangled tights and leotard balanced on the shaky back of a two-legged chair, her whole weight supported on one lean arm, her body twisting itself into astonishing knots. At the moment, both glittering legs arched backward over an impossibly flexible spine, while two satin-slippered feet framed an insouciant dark face.

The contortionist was remarkable, but Girays scarcely glanced at her. His searching gaze swept the surrounding streets, but nowhere did he spy a hansom or a horse-drawn vehicle of any description. He had not caught sight of one since quitting the *Revenant,* hours earlier. With his excellent knowledge of the Aennorvi language, it had not taken him long to discover the Travornish co-optation of the dockside cabs, a coup initially perceived as a minor annoyance. Suitcase in hand, he had set forth from the wharf on foot, confident of securing commercial transportation long before reaching his destination, on the far side of Aeshno.

He had found none, however; a state of affairs less influenced by the Festinettes than by the railroad strike. He had walked the afternoon away through Aeshno's sun-glaring white streets, walked until his mouth was parched and his arm ached with the weight of the suitcase, and only then had he stopped at the *akrobattería* for rest and refreshment.

No time for much of either. Still no sign of a hansom anywhere, and he had tarried long enough. He signaled, and his waiter was instantly present.

The newspaper lay on the table. Noting the front-page banner, GREWZIAN ATROCITIES IN JUMO, the waiter observed,

"Next thing you know, those offal-rooting swine will be setting their sights on Feyenne."

"Sherreen, more likely," Girays opined, his perfect Aennorvi belied by a very Vonahrish shrug.

"They are nothing but a gang of overgrown hooligans, these Grewzians. Their imperior is the worst of the lot. Someone should teach this Ogron ruffian of theirs a lesson. I wish we had this Ogron right here in Aeshno, this very moment. I'd like to turn the kitchen lads loose on him with their spits and ladles. Ho, but a good basting would teach the mighty imperior a thing or two."

Perhaps, but the entire Aennorvi and Vonahrish armies combined hadn't strength enough to accomplish that feat, Girays reflected. Aloud he merely replied, "Fine spirit, my friend."

"We Aennorvis burn with spirit, sir," the waiter declared. "Only some fools don't know what to do with it. The railroad workers, for instance. The Grewzians rob and flout us, we should unite against the foreigners, but these workers think only of their own pockets, and so they stop the trains. At such a time, this is almost like treason."

"Worse, an inconvenience," Girays murmured. "No horses to be purchased or rented, I presume?"

"Not at any price, sir. Where are you bound for?"

"Willune's Wheels, in Wheeler Street." The name and address had been supplied by an amiable vendor at the wharf.

"Isn't that way 'cross town? Hope you're a good walker."

"I will be, before this is finished. Can you give me directions?"

"Sorry, I don't know that section."

"Neither does anyone else in the world. Never mind, I'll find it eventually." So saying, Girays paid his bill, reluctantly picked up his suitcase, and departed.

The brief rest had served him well. His thirst was quenched, his aches had subsided, and he could observe his surroundings with renewed interest. The elongated shadows of late afternoon relieved the glare of sunlight on white buildings and palely dusty pavement. A salt-sharp breeze cut the heavy warmth of southern springtime. The long midday break had concluded, the shops and booths along the avenue were reopening for business, and the citizens were venturing from their shady shuttered refuges as the town of Aeshno woke from its afternoon nap.

By his reckoning another half hour of walking would bring him to Wheeler Street. Girays loosened his cravat, shifted his grip on the suitcase, and marched on. The strong colors of the crowd filled his eyes, the voices swirled about him, and the atmosphere seemed festive, as if the Aennorvis generated celebration out of daily routine. But as he went, the quality of sound and movement altered. The voices rang with new emotion and the human currents pressed with feverish intensity. He hurried on, and now he heard shouting, and the moving stream coagulated into a dense but highly animated human mass packed around some central object invisible from his present vantage point. The clamor swelled, and mass fury scorched the air. In the midst of that uproar individual vituperation perished, but one word bursting from multiple angry mouths distinguished itself: *Butcher.*

Butcher?

Grewzian butcher.

Curious, Girays advanced through the crowd, elbowing his way forward until he glimpsed the object of popular wrath, at sight of which he checked in amazement. For there stood none other than the Overcommander Karsler Stornzof, the glorious golden Grewzian demigod himself, backed up against a wall and hemmed in by enraged Aennorvis. Stornzof—sole Ellipsoid permitted to sail freely from occupied Lanthi Ume by order of his anthropoid Grewzian countrymen, whose notions of sportsmanship were rudimentary at best. Stornzof, whose unearned advantage should have placed him at the front of the race, hundreds of miles ahead of his closest rival. Stornzof, unaccountably here.

And hardly thriving.

The demigod had suffered some damage. His grey uniform was torn and muddied, his damnable golden hair disheveled. A gash along his brow was bleeding freely.

An officer of the Imperium tasting a little of his own medicine? Difficult to work up much sympathy. In fact, rather an agreeable sight.

The probable source of the demigod's injury soon revealed itself. Somebody in the crowd threw a fist-sized rock. Stornzof ducked and the missile whizzed by, missing his head by inches.

The overcommander raised one hand in a universally recognizable request for attention that his tormentors refused to grant. The noise did not abate in the least, and Stornzof was obliged to shout.

"Citizens of Aeshno—Aennorvis—I am not here as your enemy—"

Much chance a uniformed Grewzian had of convincing them of that, particularly when he wasn't even speaking their language. Presumably Stornzof knew no Aennorvi, for he was yelling in Vonahrish, which his listeners did not understand, or else chose to ignore.

"My presence is unwelcome, and I will depart your city at once, if—"

Another rock flew, and Stornzof managed to dodge it. The next grazed his left hand. Blood welled from a fresh cut, and the mob whooped joyously.

Girays felt his initial mean satisfaction ebbing fast. This Aennorvi crowd seemed quite ready to stone the Grewzian to death right here in the street for the crime of his nationality, much as v'Alisante family members at the time of the revolution had been slaughtered in the streets of Sherreen for the crime of their Exalted birth. Nobody merited such treatment.

But why didn't the fellow use his revolver? He was armed, and knew enough about guns *to persuade certain credulous, dangerously reckless females to arm themselves unnecessarily. . . .* A couple of warning shots—

Would only incense the mob. And if he killed one or two rabid Aennorvis? Worse yet. The survivors would tear him limb from limb. The Grewzian had sense and self-control enough to keep his hands off the gun.

Sense and self-control notwithstanding, Stornzof's chances of survival appeared slight, for the rocks were flying and the avenues of escape solidly blocked.

Girays intended no intervention, for a Grewzian rival's troubles were no concern of his. In fact, the overcommander's permanent removal offered pure advantage. It was quite to his own surprise that he found himself pushing forward, pistol in hand, to take a place at Stornzof's side. He hardly noted the other's astonished glance. Aiming skyward, he squeezed the trigger and the Khrennisov in his hand popped sharply. The crowd squalled, then drew in its breath. Into the ensuing lull Girays tossed his fluent Aennorvi.

"Citizens, calm yourselves," he enjoined. "This Grewzian officer comes among you not as a soldier of the Imperium, but rather as a contestant in the Grand Ellipse race—as I do."

"Vonahrishman?" someone demanded.

"Yes."

"What Vonahrishman in his right mind takes up for an offal chomper?"

"One who recognizes the truce existing among sportsmen. This Grewzian racer means no harm, and desires nothing more than leave to pass across Aennorvi territory as speedily as possible."

"Shoot 'im out of a cannon, then," some anonymous wit offered helpfully. "Now, there's speedy travel."

Affirmative hoots from his listeners.

"The Grand Ellipse is open to all nations," Girays continued, ignoring both the suggestion and the response. "One of your own Aennorvi countrymen competes. What sort of treatment may Mesq'r Zavune expect to encounter on foreign soil? Perhaps his reception abroad will be influenced by the handling that aliens receive here in Aennorve. The injury or murder of a Grand Ellipse contestant in the streets of Aeshno will stain Aennorvi honor in the eyes of all the world. It will also," he added clearly, "arouse the extreme wrath of the Grewzian Imperium, and understandably so. There will be consequences." This point appeared to register with the listeners, and Girays swiftly followed through with another, of a more face-saving character. "And what if your Master Zavune should win the race? Slaughter his rivals to ensure his success, and this Aennorvi victory is defiled and devalued. You do your own compatriot no service."

Perhaps his arguments carried some weight, or perhaps the popular rage was simply starting to flag. Whatever the reason, the vocal volume was subsiding and the shouts diminishing to a muted condemnatory mutter. For a few moments longer the crowd retained its cohesion, then began to erode as individual members wandered off. A pathway opened and Girays made for it. Stornzof fell into step beside him, and the two retreated smartly. The citizens jeered, but let them go. Somebody flung a final rock, but the missile fell short of its target. The angry voices faded behind them.

"What did you say to them?" Stornzof asked, some minutes later. Producing a handkerchief, he pressed the linen to his gashed forehead.

"I cannot recall the entire harangue," Girays returned carelessly. "Largely an appeal to their sense of justice, I believe."

"I am much in your debt."

"Not at all. I was concerned for the welfare of these Aennorvi citizens, who seemed too ready to compromise their national neutrality, thus furnishing your imperior with an excuse for reprisal."

"Nevertheless"—Stornzof courteously disregarded the barb—"your intervention surely preserved me from serious injury or death. You have my gratitude, together with my promise to return the favor, should the opportunity arise."

The formal, old-fashioned phrasing that should have sounded pompous or quaint somehow possessed a curious dignity upon this man's lips, Girays noted with annoyance. Grewzians were barbarous boors, dangerous but distinctly absurd, fit butt of formerly-Exalted scorn, but this one managed to defy mockery.

"I scarcely seek recompense, Overcommander," he heard himself say, and knew even as he spoke that his aim was off and that he sounded merely churlish. He met the other's clear, grave gaze, and remembered then that he had read or heard somewhere that the troops under Karsler Stornzof's command idolized their leader as a being set above the general run of mankind. For a moment Girays could almost see how simple souls might think so. Ridiculous, of course; a fallacy largely based on the fellow's appearance, reinforced by a few effective little tricks of speech and manner. Nothing substantive; well, perhaps the famous victory at Düschlekl had been extraordinary, but certainly great good luck had blessed the Grewzian forces upon that occasion. The overcommander was undeniably capable and courageous, but his divinity remained unverified. He was only another Grewzian, rather more palatable than some, but still a minion of the Imperium. There was neither point nor profit in prolonging the exchange, and thus it was almost to his own surprise that Girays found himself asking, "Do you need stitches for that cut?"

"Not at all."

"Best take care—this uniformed Grewzian progress through the streets of Aeshno draws attention, and the blood on your face doesn't help matters. Where are you going?"

"Wheeler Street," Stornzof replied.

"Willune's Wheels?"

"The velocipedia, yes. And you?"

"The same, if I can find it. I've been misdirected half a dozen times this afternoon, and the map I bought is useless."

"Mine is quite good. It is printed in Grewzian." Stornzof proffered a folded paper sheet. "You are welcome to make use of it."

Girays suppressed the instinctive refusal. The Grewzian was doing him no favor, but only repaying a legitimate debt. Moreover, the arrangement equally benefited both parties. The overcommander whose uniform proclaimed his detestable nationality might well require further assistance before departing Aennorve.

"I'll take a look at the map," he conceded.

Stornzof handed it over, and the two men paused.

"This way, I think." The overcommander's finger was tracing a route before his companion had even begun to decipher the Grewzian print.

"Agreed." Girays returned the map to its owner. Progress resumed, and a thought struck him. "But what of your kinsman, the grandlandsman? I suppose he's somewhere about."

"The grandlandsman and I have parted company for the time being," Stornzof told him.

Girays caught a fleeting hint of contentment in the other's eyes and voice. Interesting. Perhaps the Stornzof family ties were raveling?

They pushed on through the streets of Aeshno, where the Grewzian officer's uniform drew many a hostile glare. The insults crackled in their wake, but nobody raised a hand against them. The taunts and obscenities flew unaccompanied by stones. The dusty white avenues narrowed as they went, the architecture aged and dwindled in height, the stuccoed walls cracked and coated themselves in grime. Presently they passed beneath a heavy old archway into a breathless alley indented with deeply recessed doorways designed to collect shadows. The incised lettering upon the archway identified Wheeler Street. And there, straight ahead, a faded old sign bearing the image of a velocipede proclaimed the presence of Willune's Wheels.

They went in to discover a seen-better-days old shop presided over by a pockmarked paragon of adolescent insolence, presumably the owner's son and heir. There were no single-seat velocipedes left in stock, the youth announced without apology. The last of them had been snapped up days ago, their value boosted by the *strevvio*. Really it was a joke, people would pay any price. Now the vehicles were gone, and there would be no more until the *strevvio* concluded. In the meantime all that remained was a rusty double-seater, heavy as a dreadnought, its mass beyond the power of any lone rider to balance and propel. Twin pilots were required.

Girays and the Grewzian regarded the double-seater in silence for a gloomy span, then turned to inspect one another. Stornzof finally voiced the melancholy inevitable.

"We will share."

THE SKIES WERE DIMMING and her stomach was growling. A nearby restaurant was already lighted for the evening. Its sign, shaped in the likeness of a scallop shell, suggested seafood. Luzelle went in and waited for fifteen minutes to be shown to a bad table, where she sat and consulted the menu. It was handwritten in Aennorvi, and she did not recognize a single word. Even the numbers in the price column were oddly formed and difficult to read. A manifestly disapproving waiter approached. Disinclined to beg his assistance, she chose a dish at random, indicating her selection with a tap of her forefinger.

Jerking a curt nod, the waiter withdrew. Luzelle looked around her. The dining room was small and undistinguished, its décor vaguely nautical. Several patrons sat watching the unescorted female customer in undisguised curiosity. She met one such pair of speculative eyes coolly, and its owner did not trouble to lower his gaze. Provincial oaf. She glowered briefly and looked away. Inevitable, of course, that she would encounter such rudeness somewhere or other along the Grand Ellipse. The wonder was that it hadn't happened sooner.

Her eyes traveled on. The neighboring table belonged to a lone diner occupied with a newspaper whose front-page headline, printed in very large Lanthian, she could make out even at a distance.

GREWZIAN TROOPS ENTER JUMO

Jumo Towne, capital of the South Ygahro Territory, an Aennorvi possession and site of the famous diamond mines, annexed by Grewzland. An open invitation to war. But surely Aennorve, justifiable fury notwithstanding, would never dare accept.

Her meal arrived, and Luzelle studied the plate before her in dismay. She beheld a tall mound of plump blue strands, supple as noodles but distinctively striated and segmented, glistening with a tavril-scented blue dressing. *What in the world?* Then her questing fork turned up a tiny triangular head marked with sapphire sensory organs, and she knew what she confronted. Blue Aennorvermis in Sauce Feyennaise, a famous local delicacy.

Poached sea worms.

Dinner.

She twisted a worm around her fork, raised it to her lips, and took a wary nibble. Overly soft consistency for her taste, but not as bad as she had feared. No discernible flavor to the worm—the taste of the dish resided in the sauce, which blended tavril, juniper, and mountain thyme in a manner unexpectedly pleasing.

She finished her meal down to the last blue squirmer, paid her bill, and walked out into the lamplit street. The sky was rich with stars and the air had cooled, but she scarcely noticed.

Old Knightly Crescent, home of Madame Moneybags, proprietress of at least two highly desirable horses. How to find it, without a map and without knowledge of the Aennorvi language?

The problem resolved itself with unexpected ease. One of the precious rare hansoms of Aeshno appeared as if by divine intervention. Luzelle hailed the cabman, who halted at once. She issued her commands in Lanthian, and he appeared to understand. Climbing in, she shut the door, and the hansom clattered off into the night.

Aeshno went by her, street by lamplit street. When she reached Old Knightly Crescent, the affluence and extreme modernity of the neighborhood proclaimed itself in the glow of the gaslights flanking the portals of certain morning-new mansions designed to resemble the castles and temples of old.

Incongruous, she thought.

Her goal was easy to spot. *New brick mansion the color of raw meat in Old Knightly Crescent,* her picketer informant had told her, and there it was, a turreted architectural offense, ridiculously equipped with crenellations and machicolations worthy of a medieval stronghold. Any lingering doubts vanished when she spied the signpost topped with the three-dimensional model railway car, cast in bronze and monogrammed with an ornate capital *T.*

T for Tastriune, chief stockholder and president of the Feyenne-Aeshno Railroad.

Luzelle rapped the roof and the cab halted. She hopped out, paid the driver, and he departed, leaving her alone on an alien night-mantled street. It did not occur to her to worry.

Horses. How to get them?

No point in trying to buy them, her picketer had explained, and he had seemed knowledgeable. If Madame Moneybags wouldn't sell at any price, then she wasn't likely to rent either. What remained? A plea to her sisterly sympathies? The sympathies of a woman fond of setting her dogs on the overly importunate? An appeal to her sporting instincts, then? Probably Tastriune's wife had never even heard of the Grand Ellipse. And if by chance she had heard of it, wouldn't she, as an Aennorvi, naturally favor the sole Aennorvi contender, Mesq'r Zavune? Of course she would. No good. What else? Chicanery of some sort? Find a way of convincing the owner that the horses were about to be appropriated by the local authorities, and that a quick sale would forestall major loss? Too elaborate, too improbable, and she couldn't even speak the language. She would never pull it off. What else? What else?

And the thought surfaced effortlessly: *Oh, leave off the silly fluttering. If you want a horse, just get in there and grab one.*

The idea amazed her. Steal a horse? Not only morally wrong, but a serious criminal offense, carrying a jail sentence or worse. She did not know the local laws, but in some places they hanged horse thieves. One hand rose unconsciously to her throat. Anyway, the point was academic; she was Luzelle Devaire, and she didn't steal.

You won't be stealing if you leave a fair price behind.

Madame Tastriune had at least two horses, maybe more. She could easily afford to let one go.

Luzelle could imagine what the Judge would have to say. She could hear his voice too clearly in her mind. *Your blood is good, and you have been properly reared. Thus I can scarcely account for your mental and moral deficiencies.* Should she lose the Grand Ellipse, of course, she would not need to imagine or remember—his perfectly real voice would reverberate in her ears, perhaps for decades to come.

But she would not lose the Grand Ellipse. She had promised vo Rouvignac and herself a victory at any cost, any cost at all.

She realized that her feet were carrying her along the tradesmen's alley that led to the back of the mansion, where she might reasonably expect to discover a stable. *They'll have the place well protected. I can't be the first one to think of snatching one of Madame's precious horses.*

The carriage house rose before her, a miniature castle in its own right, connected to the main house by a long colonnade. Faint light shone yellow at the windows. The great front door, tall and broad enough to accommodate the largest coach, was shut. No servants visible roaming the grounds. No watchdogs in evidence. Approaching with caution, she peeped in a window to behold a cavernous space, its gloom relieved by the glow of two or three ordinary lanterns. No ultramodern gaslight here.

A couple of sturdy, plainly clad young men sat playing cards at a small deal table beside the window. Grooms, stable-boys, coachmen, groundskeepers—she did not know which, but certainly servants of some sort, stationed there to guard the premises. She ducked back quickly. Her luck held; neither of the men had noticed her. And if they did? Her hand strayed to the pistol in her pocket and she paused momentarily, once again astonished at herself.

Horses. Focus.

She circled the building in the dark, passing a couple of small side doors and a larger back door, none of which she dared to touch. Along the southern wall a row of big, heavily shuttered square windows almost certainly marked the location of the stalls. She tried one at random, very quietly. Locked, as she had expected. Pressing her ear to the shutter, she listened intently and caught the ghost of a muted equine snort.

A horse, inches away. She wanted to tear straight through the wall.

Have to find a way in, have to, have to, have to. . . .

Bribe the guards? Never. There was no amount she could offer large enough to tempt the two of them to risk losing their comfortable posts in the rich Tastriune household. Wait until they fall asleep? No, they probably slept in alternating shifts.

Resuming her circuit of the building, she soon found herself prowling a secluded back corner of the Tastriune property. Here the moonlight played on trees and ornamental shrubbery, and behind them something else, something solid. Brick or stone walls, she thought, and stole forward to investigate.

Behind the stand of greenery, discreetly veiled from casual view, she found a small brick structure with a peaked wooden roof and a door of painted planking. Surely not an outhouse, not for modern Madame Moneybags. Something utilitarian, though. Toolshed? Potting shed? Cautiously she opened the door, which swung on its well-oiled hinges without a squeak. Darkness smothered the interior.

Her valise contained a box of matches, an item that experience had taught her never to travel without. Now she extracted the box and struck a light, with which she jabbed the black space. The darkness flinched and she saw a closet-sized compartment, empty but for a big cylindrical metal tank standing solidly upright on its flat base. The tank's domed summit sported something resembling a spigot connected by a short length of heavy hose to a metal pipe rising out of the clay floor. Alongside the spigot glinted a glass-faced round device with a needle and a calibrated dial. A gauge of some sort?

Luzelle stared. The flame nipped her fingers, she dropped the match, and the darkness jumped back into place. For a moment she stood wondering, and then comprehension dawned. Of course. She was looking at the Tastriunes' gas tank, containing the fuel that fed those newfangled lamps of theirs. Someday, probably quite soon, the gas would be produced and piped commercially, in quantities sufficient to light entire streets, even entire cities. Or so the optimistic theory ran. She'd believe that when she saw it. In the meantime rich arrivistes ambitious of distinction, like the Tastriunes, were still obliged to install and maintain their own fuel tanks, safely removed from the house itself, for fear of fire or explosion.

Fire? Explosion?

What are you thinking? Her capacity to astonish herself was not yet exhausted. *Have you gone mad?*

But the cold, clear section of her mind, the part unreservedly dedicated to victory, seemed to have assumed control. And that part, deaf to remonstrance and awesomely efficient, was thrusting her hands into her valise to bring forth useless timetables and reservations furnished by the Ministry of Foreign Affairs; crumpling those documents and piling them in a corner; lighting a match, and setting the paper ablaze.

The small flames jumped, their flickery light suffusing the small space. Luzelle plucked her clasp knife from the side pocket of her valise and then, as if from a distance, watched her own hands unfolding the blade and driving the steel point into the hose connecting the tank and pipeline. A faint hiss of escaping gas rewarded her efforts, and a new odor added itself to the atmosphere. Grabbing up her valise, she jumped for the exit, slammed the door shut behind her, and ran for cover.

Rounding the corner of the carriage house, she pressed her back hard to the wall, let herself sink down behind the bushes masking the foundation, and there rested in shadow. She had no idea how long she waited, heart racing and palms sweating. The seconds or minutes or hours stretched into centuries, and presently she began to imagine herself trapped in a dream, for Luzelle Devaire was no arsonist, and surely the scene in the outbuilding could not have been quite real.

The deep, almost muffled boom of an explosion drove such fancies from her mind. The brick walls of the outbuilding withstood the force of the blast, but the wooden door went flying, and the roof sundered with a shout. A great blossom of fire unfurled, lit the night for a spectacular moment, and wilted.

I did that? Half disbelievingly she studied the wreckage; brick walls singed but still standing, shattered remains of the wooden roof blazing fiercely.

A door opened nearby, and weak light spilled from the carriage house. The two guards emerged and made for the fire at a run. Seconds later the lights in the mansion windows dimmed out of existence. A distant gabble of excited Aennorvi arose. Another door banged open, and shadowy figures burst from the Tastriunes' house.

She did not pause to observe their actions. The carriage house stood unguarded, but would not remain so for long. She stood. Hugging the shadows, she skulked her way to the open door, where she hesitated only an instant before slipping through.

She cast a quick look about her. The place was big, high

ceilinged, and elaborately equipped. Dimly she noted the
presence of two bloated carriages, several smaller but no less
obviously costly vehicles, a commonplace wagon, an antique
sedan chair, and someone's rusty velocipede.

She hurried on toward the rear, passing a couple of anonymous closed doors, and then she spied the row of big box
stalls, six of them, all occupied.

Nobody needs six horses, no one ought to have that many, she
told herself, and made herself believe it.

The animals were awake, no doubt roused by unaccus-
tomed sounds and sights. A well-shaped chestnut head poked
inquiringly from the nearest stall, whose door bore a small
brass plate engraved with a name: *Ballerina.*

She clucked, and the horse whickered softly.

You, she thought. *I'll just lead you right out of here, and
then—*

And then? She could ride, but not without a bridle and
saddle. She did know how to saddle a horse, she had acquired
that skill as a girl, without His Honor's knowledge or consent.
It had been a long time ago, but she would still remember—
she must.

Tack room? Behind one of those two closed doors she had
just passed. Dropping her valise, she hurried back to the first
door, opened it, and looked into the feed room, then opened
the second to discover an impressive collection of leather
equipment. She went in and stepped to the wall, where a
score of circular brackets supported an assortment of spotless
bridles. Each bracket carried a nameplate, just barely legible
in the low light pushing through the open door. Well-organ-
ized place. Her eyes hurried. She found the nameplate she
sought: *Ballerina.* She plucked a bridle furnished with a simple snaffle from its bracket, and turned away from the wall.
Her eyes jumped to the dustcloth shrouding the nearest
stand. She yanked the cloth aside to uncover a scrupulously
polished hacking saddle, its girth detached and lying across
the seat, its stirrup irons pulled up. She lifted the saddle from
its stand, and draped it over her arm. Saddle pads? Where
were they?

No time!

The chestnut would have to do without. *Sorry, Ballerina.*

Exiting the tack room, she hurried back to the stall, murmured a few theoretically reassuring words to its occupant, and slipped in. The horse, an elegantly formed mare, displayed neither alarm nor hostility. An even-tempered animal, a prize. Luzelle set the saddle carefully aside, and took the bridle into her hand. No time to warm the bit in her palm, but the springtime temperatures were mild, and the metal tolerable to the touch. Approaching diagonally, she slipped the reins over the pretty red head, then unbuckled and removed the stable halter. Her left thumb pressed unnecessarily; the mare's mouth opened at once, and the bit slipped effortlessly into place, while the crownpiece slid smoothly over the ears. *Oh, you red darling.* Her fingers flew; buckling, checking. Everything correctly in place.

The not-so-distant clamor of Aennorvi voices reached her ears. A sizable crowd must have gathered around that ruined outbuilding. For a while the fire there would anchor collective attention, but how long could that last? *Hurry, hurry, hurry.*

She ran a quick hand along the mare's back, dislodging a stray wisp of straw. Not good enough, but no time for more brushing, no time. Lifting the saddle, she laid it a few inches before the withers, then slid it backward into place. The animal shifted restlessly, sensing strangeness.

"Easy," Luzelle muttered, to the horse and to herself. "Easy."

Her own deftness in attaching the girth almost surprised her. No time to fool with the stirrups, they would have to do for now. She turned the mare gently toward the stall door, and led her through without difficulty. The sight of her valise on the floor beside the door recalled her to certain unpleasant realities. Most of her money reposed within the bag, and she remembered that she had vowed to leave a fair price in exchange for the horse she was stealing—*purchasing*—not to mention the property she had destroyed. A pretty piece of futility, of course. She might leave cash enough to pay for twenty chestnut mares, but the Tastriunes would never see a single New-rekko of it. The entire sum would disappear into the pocket of the first stableboy lucky enough to find it.

Am I responsible for the dishonesty of the servants? inquired the wholly committed portion of her mind.

Then there was the matter of the valise itself—a roomy, hard-sided container, difficult to carry on horseback.

Impossible to carry. She would have to leave the valise.

My clothes! My sewing kit and nail file! My clean underwear! All replaceable.

Already she was down on her knees, rooting through the contents of her bag. The passport and well-lined wallet slid into the inner pocket of her broadcloth jacket. A generous fistful of New-rekko notes remained in the valise, but the surviving maps and documents furnished by the ministry, together with the little box of ammunition, dropped into the pockets already containing the Khrennisov, the clasp knife, and the matches. Nothing remained to reveal her identity. Another moment or two of searching, and she would probably lay hands on the miniature sewing kit—

No time!

Which way out? The exit farthest from the site of the explosion. Rising, she tightened the girth, then led the chestnut through the carriage house to the huge front door, where she shoved the bar aside and pushed. One of the great wooden halves swung wide, and she coaxed the mare on through.

Heavy smoke weighted the cool night breeze. Ballerina snorted and tossed her head.

"Quiet," Luzelle begged in a whisper. *Just another minute, and I'll have us out of here, with nobody the wiser—*

That minute was not to be hers. The light glowing through the open door caught her squarely, and she was spotted at once. Somebody nearby started yelling. No chance now of an inconspicuous exit.

As a young girl she had learned to ride decorously sidesaddle, in accordance with His Honor's dictates. She might never have known any other way, had not the first matriarch of the Uiiviisian plainswomen taken pity and taught her to ride astride. Now she hiked her long skirts and petticoat high, indifferent to the indecent display of lace-trimmed muslin drawers. Tossing the mass of fabric over one arm, she grabbed the pommel, swung herself up into the saddle, clapped her heels to the mare's flanks, and sped off at a gallop.

The yelling furor behind her intensified, and she heard the deep-throated baying of dogs, but these sounds were receding, and soon they were gone, lost in the steady rhythm of hoof-beats. Luzelle slowed her stolen mount to a walk. Her heart was pounding—with exhilaration, she realized. What would His Honor have said? A shameless laugh broke from her.

And what would Karsler say? For some reason the thought popped into her head, and the laughter died on her lips. She did not know why she should think of him at such a time, but she could see his face very clearly in her mind, and there was no condemnation there, but something in the steady clarity of his eyes reproached her.

A ridiculous fancy. As if a Grewzian overcommander, of all people, would presume to pose as some sort of moral arbiter. Comical, really. But she was not smiling.

She noticed then that she was tired. The rush of excitement sustaining her throughout the last half hour or so had ebbed, and now she wanted a clean feather bed and deep sleep. But she would have neither for some time to come.

She needed to leave Aeshno at once—both for the sake of the Grand Ellipse and her own safety. Madame Tastriune's elegant chestnut mare was quite recognizable, its present rider not unnoticeable, and the authorities would be looking for her now.

East to Bizaqh, next designated stop along the Grand Ellipse. East, beyond the reach of the *strevvio,* the trains that did not run, the horses that could not be bought, the decent transportation that did not exist.

Her sense of direction, always solid, told her that the waterfront from which she had come lay to her left. Lifting her face to the night, she studied the skies. There above, to her right, to the east, shone the constellation known in Vonahr as the Princess; demoted during the revolution to the Laundress, but lately restored to her original rank.

Turning her mount toward the Princess, she rode east. Time passed, and Aeshno fell away behind her. She was out on the dusty highway under the stars and the moon, the road clear before her, and pursuit before morning unlikely. She was tired, but not to the point of exhaustion, and she knew she could ride on for hours if necessary. With any luck she would happen upon a roadside inn well before midnight.

The moon inched across the sky and her vision turned inward to focus upon assorted faces. Karsler's with its unexpressed reproach. Madame Tastriune's, with more of the same. Szett Urrazole, killed in an explosion, another explosion, nothing to do with gas tanks. Girays v'Alisante, and his questions. The Festinette twins, somewhere far ahead, giggling in triumph. Grandlandsman Torvid Stornzof, monocle flashing like sunlit ice. Others, many others, coming and going, but Girays and Karsler always hovered near, linked in her imagination despite their dissimilarities, and often she found herself thinking of them both at once, wondering where they were and how they fared.

10

". . . THUS THE INTERVENTION of the Lanthian resistance delayed our arrival by many hours," Karsler Stornzof concluded his explanation. "The inconvenience was considerable, but I must admire the ingenuity of our enemies."

Perfectly in chivalrous character. Girays v'Alisante bent a sour smile. Twenty-four hours in Karsler Stornzof's company, and he had yet to detect a crack in the knightly façade. Nor had he caught the faintest whiff of conscious hypocrisy, and his nose for that scent was keen. It seemed that the Grewzian took his heroic role quite to heart. Perhaps he had read too many sugared articles about himself in those fool gazettes.

A pity the Lanthian ingenuity the overcommander so admired hadn't succeeded in prolonging that island interlude another day or two. On the other hand, Stornzof's assistance with the two-seater had proved invaluable; essential, in fact. He could never have managed the mechanical monstrosity on his own, Girays inwardly admitted. Even powered by two riders, the contraption generated endless grief. Reluctant locomotion. Clanking, screeching, squealing protest. Poor balance. Unreliable steering. Nonexistent braking. And unremitting obstinacy, as if this man-made conglomerate of iron, wood, and leather housed the soul of a malevolent mule.

The present instance was a perfect case in point. The miserably rutted, muddy Aeshno-Eynisse Road that wound its way among countless rock-strewn hills now ascended a sharp grade, and the two-seater was fighting every inch of the way. In such a place, an old-fashioned velocipede propelled by the thrust of its rider's foot against the ground would have been more practical. But the two-seater was equipped with the supposed advantage of pedals, and modernity was exacting its toll.

The afternoon sun blazed sturdily overhead. The sweat was dripping into his eyes, and Girays raised a hand to his face. No sooner had he relinquished his hold on one of the leather handlebar grips than the big front wheel hit soft mud, twisted sharply on its pivot, and the two-seater lurched for the side of the road. With a muttered oath he reclaimed the grip, yanked the iron tire around, overcompensated, and sent the vehicle lumbering off at a new angle. He pulled again, managed to straighten the tire, but could not control the violent shuddering of the heavy frame. The two-seater shook, bucked, and screeched. Despite all such metallic protest, uphill progress scarcely slackened.

It was the force from the rear, Girays realized. He alone could never have pedaled up the slope. If left to his own devices, he would have dismounted and walked the two-seater gradually to the summit or, more likely, left the hunk of junk lying at the side of the road. Under the eyes of a Grewzian rival he could do neither, and now found himself obliged to acknowledge what he had already suspected—that Stornzof's efforts were keeping them on course, and that Stornzof was carrying a good deal more than half the burden.

He might have consoled himself with the theory that the rear position offered a mechanical advantage, perhaps a more efficient exploitation of applied force, had personal experience not taught him otherwise. The rider in front controlled the steering, thus claiming dominant status, and it was presumably for this reason that the Overcommander Stornzof had suggested early on that the two riders periodically alternate seats. It was just such conspicuous, subtly self-laudatory fair-mindedness that doubtless struck certain impressionable observers as *wonderful*. Girays had now ridden both front and back, and knew for a fact that the two positions were equally demanding. And no imaginary mechanical advantage could be used to explain away the superior performance of a Grewzian athlete considerably larger, some ten years younger, and just plain stronger than himself.

Actually the front seat was better. There, Stornzof wasn't in his line of sight.

Girays pedaled on grimly. Presently the two-seater crested the rise, leveled briefly, then commenced a teeth-rattling descent. It was much easier now. In fact the vehicle was coasting along effortlessly, picking up speed as it went. There was a sharp clank as the front tire dipped into a hole in the road. The wheel twisted, and Girays reflexively twitched it back into line. He was getting better at steering, he decided. He would be an expert before the trip was over. The two-seater's uncontrollable acceleration, which would have alarmed him a scant twenty-four hours earlier, now struck him as exhilarating. The breeze cooling his moist face was agreeable. For the first time he began to see the potential pleasure in this sport. With a decent velocipede perhaps, definitely a mono-seater, on a properly maintained road—

The two-seater neared the bottom of the slope, and now it was practically flying, squealing along so rapidly that the broad wet patch overspreading the roadway was under the iron tires almost before Girays had noted its existence. A massive spray of mud flew, spattering his face and filling his eyes. He felt the handlebar jerk beneath his hands, the front wheel swiveled, and the two-seater skidded, careering across the roadway at a wild diagonal until a plangent clang proclaimed the impact of metal on stone.

The front tire had struck a large rock. The two-seater overturned and Girays fell, hitting the soft mud with an ignominious plop. For a moment he sprawled prone where he had landed, the breath knocked out of him. Then labored respiration and thought resumed. Some sort of weight was pressing his back and squeezing his lungs. Raising his head, he glanced about to discover that he had fallen beneath the two-seater, whose rusty bulk pinned him where he lay. The contraption was heavy, but he could surely wriggle his way out from under it, provided he had broken no major bones—

The thought had barely resolved itself before he felt the

pressure on his back ease, and he looked around again to see Karsler Stornzof lifting the two-seater and moving it aside. But for the muddy splotches on his boots and the dirty speckling across his uniform, the overcommander remained unsullied. When the two-seater overturned, he must have managed to land on his feet.

"Thank you," said Girays, and the words all but stuck in his throat.

"You are injured?" Stornzof inquired.

"I think not." Girays sat up carefully. He was sore in places, but everything seemed to work. "A few bruises, nothing more."

This was not entirely true, for his pride had suffered some laceration. He had been steering the two-seater, he should have avoided the mud; he was responsible for the accident. He met the Grewzian's eyes, expecting to encounter accusation or resentment, but found nothing there beyond a certain thoughtful, oddly impenetrable composure.

"I believe you are correct. I shall see to the machine, then." Stornzof turned away.

Girays hauled himself to his feet. The overcommander, he noted with grudging approval, had the tact to withhold offers of assistance neither wanted nor required. He seemed, in fact, generally devoid of Grewzian boorishness. Indeed, but for the slightly stilted speech, the fellow might almost have been Vonahrish.

Brushing a few clots of mud from his coat, Girays inquired, "Ready to continue?"

"On foot, I fear," the other informed him. "Come, see here."

Girays approached with reluctance, and spotted the trouble at once. It would have been hard to miss—the collision had damaged the front tire severely, indenting a section of the iron circle and mangling several spokes.

So his incompetence had disabled their vehicle. Under the eyes of a Grewzian overcommander described as *wonderful*.

Stornzof, however, displayed no sign of rancor, remarking only, "I am certain this could be hammered back into shape quite easily."

"Do you have a hammer?"

"It is not a thing I ordinarily carry."

"Strangely enough, neither do I."

"Should we encounter a coach along this road, the driver may well possess a toolbox."

"Perhaps, but we can hardly afford to sit and wait for a coach. Is it possible to walk the two-seater?"

"Let us put it to the test." So saying, Stornzof effortlessly righted the fallen vehicle, grasped the handlebar, and advanced. The front tire clanked woefully. A grating protest underscored each revolution, until Stornzof paused to alter the position of a bent wire spoke. The second big tire and the little flying balance-wheel at the back were undamaged. The two suitcases remained securely strapped to the rear carrier.

"Some effort is required, but this can be done," Stornzof reported. "We need not abandon the machine."

"I'll push it along for now," Girays stated. He was prepared to push the wretched heap of scrap to Aveshq and back, if that could redeem his blundering.

"As you wish."

The Grewzian stepped aside and Girays took his place. He discovered at once that Stornzof had been right. The damaged two-seater, unwieldy at best, was now a misery to handle, but it could be done.

He pushed and the two-seater moved. The Grewzian walked beside him. The road before them wound southeast.

THE HOURS PASSED and the scenery altered. The hills sharpened, the bare granite blushed pink, the gnarl-limbed shrubs gave way to blue-grey conifers, and the first creeping daggers appeared. The creeping dagger vine—infamous for its hardihood, its uncanny rapidity of growth, and the murderous keenness of its countless thorns—figured prominently in Aennorvi history. According to popular belief, the plant had been created by the legendary sorcerer Aekropi at the behest of a local prince bent on punishing the infidelity of his beautiful but excessively vivacious young wife. Confining his princess and her lover to a small stone cottage somewhere in the heart of the forested hills, the prince had summoned Aekropi, who had loosed the creeping daggers. The vines had grown at magical speed, blanketing the cottage within the space of a single night, imprisoning the occupants and condemning them to uninterrupted togetherness for the term of their unnaturally prolonged lives. The cottage had long since lost itself amid the spreading vines, but locals swore that travelers in the hills could still sometimes catch the echo of screaming mutual recrimination.

The truth of this tale was perhaps open to question. There could be no doubt, however, that the Aennorvi general Ulyune had used creeping dagger plants to choke the Zirigar Pass, thus blocking the advance of the invading Bizaqhi army less than two hundred years earlier, for this was a matter of historical record. Nor could there be any doubt that the nearly indestructible vines were more than a minor nuisance, for the finger-length thorns were indeed sharp as poniards, and the crimson fluid they exuded was toxic.

"Let us halt for a time," Stornzof suggested.

"Very well." Girays let nothing show on his face. His arms, shoulders, and back ached with the effort of wheeling the crippled two-seater over the hills, but he would never have permitted himself to beg a respite.

They moved to the side of the road, where Girays muted a groan of relief as he laid his burden down. He seated himself in the grass beside the two-seater, and Stornzof did likewise. Both carried water flasks purchased in Aeshno, and both drank from them now.

Drawing a handkerchief from his pocket, Girays mopped the dirt and sweat from his face, then let his eyes wander. The blue-grey conifers loomed about him, and now he saw that the trunks were wound with creeping daggers. The boughs were likewise encumbered, and everywhere the vigorous vines looped through the air from tree to tree, enclosing the forest in a living net. The ground was carpeted with blue-grey needles, many of them darkly beaded. At first he took the sticky beading for resin from the trees, but closer inspection revealed the presence of the mildly venomous scarlet secretions of countless thorns.

He felt a slight vibration through the ground beneath him, and there could be but one explanation.

"Coach coming," said Girays.

His companion nodded. They stood. Moments later the Aruneside District No. 3 mail coach rounded a bend in the road and came hurrying into view. Both men hailed it urgently.

The driver saw them. His eyes fastened on the Grewzian overcommander, his teeth showed, and he flashed the obscene Feyennese Four Fingers. The mail coach sped by without slackening its speed, and soon disappeared.

"It is the uniform," Stornzof observed quietly. "It is a liability here in Aennorve. Had I been wiser, I should have stood out of sight."

He was right about that. So the golden Grewzian demigod was capable of error. Girays regarded his companion with a kindlier eye.

"We'd best move on," he said. He would have preferred to rest a while longer. His strained muscles complained.

Stornzof inclined his head. "I will wheel the machine now."

"If you insist," Girays yielded, disguising his elation. The fellow was remarkably decent, for a Grewzian. "But at this point I think we'd best consider leaving the two-seater. It's become clear we'll find no means of repairing the wheel out here in the middle of nowhere. If we can't fix it, then we're better off without it."

"That is true enough. But I am not yet ready to give up hope of salvaging the machine. I believe that the opportunity will soon arise. I think it is close at hand." His listener's expression must have communicated incomprehension, for Stornzof added, "It is a feeling that I have."

"I see. A feeling."

"Let us gamble a little more time and strength upon the two-seater."

"Your decision." Girays's own private decision classified the Grewzian as peculiar, perhaps a trifle unbalanced.

The trek resumed. Another half hour passed, and the creeping daggers were thicker than ever, strangling the trees and clogging the clearings. The road cut its way between sharp, sheer granite cliffs, and the rock faces were invisible behind leafy green curtains pocked with scarlet.

Girays's stomach rumbled audibly. It was sudden and unaccountable, for he had lunched adequately, and not so long ago. Nevertheless, his belly was making its wishes known, and it seemed to him then that he caught the faint fragrance of grilling meat carried on the spring breeze. The breeze shifted, and the scent was gone. Imagination? His stomach did not seem to think so. On they trudged, the two-seater clanking between them, until Stornzof halted, freezing into abrupt immobility in the middle of the road.

Peculiar.

"Shall I take over the two-seater for a while?" Girays offered.

No answer.

Beyond peculiar.

"Are you ill, Stornzof?"

Still no answer, and the overcommander wore an oddly distant look, as if he listened to voices from another world. Perhaps he did. Controlling his impatience, Girays waited, and presently the other's trance broke.

"There is something here," Stornzof announced.

He spoke with such conviction that Girays cast an involuntary glance around him. He saw muddy, empty road, rocky outcroppings, and an endless, impenetrable tangle of creeping daggers. Nothing more.

"I sense an influence at work," Stornzof continued.

"What influence?" Girays could not forbear asking.

"That which is often termed 'magical,' or 'sorcerous.' It is quite unmistakable."

"Indeed. Sorcerous." Girays's brows rose. "But how colorful."

"Ah, you are skeptical. That is to be expected. Perhaps I can convince you."

"Scarcely necessary. Do not trouble yourself. Let us say you are correct. I am willing to concede the possibility. May we move on now?"

"Not yet. The matter demands investigation. Perhaps this is what we seek. I suspect that it is."

"Really. Another feeling that you have?"

"Sometimes they are difficult to ignore. If you would be so good as to take the machine—"

Girays grasped the handlebar, and Stornzof moved at once to the base of the nearest cliff. He advanced several paces, paused to stretch forth a hand to the creeping daggers, and promptly drew the hand back.

"Real," he reported.

"Real what? What are you doing?" Ridiculous to humor this Grewzian eccentric's fancies, but Girays found that he could not repress the queries. "What are you looking for?"

"We are very near it, I am certain," Stornzof insisted.

"Near what? If you'd tell me what you're looking for, perhaps I could—"

"Silence, if you please," the Grewzian enjoined absently.

Girays swallowed a disgusted retort. The fellow was definitely unbalanced.

Stornzof, lost in his delusions, wandered alongside the creeping daggers, now pausing to finger the thorns, now to consult inner voices. Girays trailed irritably, and as he went, the idea took hold that he might free himself at one stroke of ruined two-seater and crackbrained Grewzian demigod alike. He could strike out on his own and probably do better. He was hovering on the verge of certainty when his companion halted with an air of finality.

"Here," Stornzof declared. He stood before an expanse of vine-covered granite cliff, indistinguishable from any other section of the cliffs lining this stretch of the Aeshno-Eynisse Road.

Girays wheeled the two-seater forward for a better look. Proximity failed to improve the prospect. He saw granite, vines, and scarlet-tipped thorns. For a moment the smell of grilling meat filled his nostrils. He wondered where it came from, and then it was gone again.

"Well?" he asked.

"Here," Stornzof repeated. "Here is the site of the disruption."

"Disruption. Quite. Listen, Stornzof, I've given this matter a good deal of thought, and it seems to me that it might be better if the two of us were to go our sep—"

"The energetic concentrations are quite distinct, and unmistakable," Stornzof continued. "The source is near at hand."

"What are you talking about? Never mind, it doesn't matter. I was saying that I think the time has come for the two of us to—"

"Now is not the time to suggest a separation. Not now, when we are likely to have the machine repaired within the half hour."

"What makes you think so? Don't tell me it's a feeling that you have."

"I believe I mentioned once that I learned long ago to detect the convolutions of force regarded as 'magical.' No doubt you discounted the claim, but I did not exaggerate. I sense the magical distortion of normality here, now, and it is visual in nature—that is to say, an adept of some sort has created an illusion."

Purest gobbledygook, but Girays's interest sparked nonetheless, for the power of illusion resonated within Vonahrish minds, particularly those of formerly-Exalted configuration. Family legends extolled the so-called magical prowess of his own v'Alisante ancestors, and he had never really believed such tales, but they caught his imagination all the same.

"Improbable," he murmured with a shrug, but could not resist asking, "You search in hope that the author of this supposed illusion possesses not only magic, but a hammer as well?"

"It is not an impossibility. I ask another moment only of your patience."

"Certainly." Girays's courteous air masked irritation, incredulity, and hopping curiosity. It was absurd, but he found himself hooked.

Stornzof was at it again, fingering those vicious thorns, prodding at the vines and cliffs, squandering time with such an air of grave diligence that his folly somehow assumed an air of intelligent purpose.

Ridiculous. Girays smiled slightly, amused at his own puerility. For a moment he had actually expected to witness

something extraordinary, something—for lack of a better
word—magical. At his age.

"Ah. I have found it. Here." Karsler Stornzof's right hand,
wrist, and forearm up to the elbow disappeared into the mass
of creeping daggers.

The Grewzian was mad. Those thorns would pierce him to
the bone.

The arm withdrew unscathed. There was no mark on the
bare hand, no trace of blood. Girays stared.

"Come. Here is the way," Stornzof directed. His companion said nothing, and he added without condescension, "The
barrier is quite unreal."

The creeping daggers, the granite ramparts—unreal? It was
like something out of an old Vonahrish tale spun for children,
but he would keep an open mind. Girays wheeled the two-
seater forward, and soon the front tire bumped vine-covered
rock.

"Unreal?" he inquired.

"Ah, your mind fulfills its own expectations. In truth, however, the way is clear. I shall prove it." So saying, Stornzof
took the handlebar, assuming control of the two-seater.

He advanced the vehicle unhesitatingly, and the front tire
appeared to sink into solid stone, followed by the handlebar
and the hands gripping it, then by the tall grey-clad figure of
the overcommander. Girays drew in his breath sharply as the
Grewzian vanished, along with the second tire and rear seat,
the carrier and suitcases, and the flying-wheel. Nothing remained to be seen but vine-veiled cliff face, seemingly solid
and undisturbed.

"Stornzof—are you there?" Girays demanded. "Can you
hear me?"

"I hear you plainly." The Grewzian's voice was close and
unobstructed. "I see you as well. The illusion is single direc-
tional, and you are clearly visible to me."

"What else is visible on your side?"

"Come through and see for yourself. Walk straight forward. There is nothing in your path. You must believe this."

Girays hesitated only a moment, then advanced steadily,

with arms outstretched. He knew he must resemble a resolute sleepwalker, but could not bring himself to walk face-first into the creeping daggers. Which were not real, he assured himself. If a demonstrably corporeal Grewzian demigod could walk straight through, then a Vonahrish formerly-Exalted could do at least as well.

His arms plunged shoulder deep into the tangle of vines. For a moment he thought he sensed resistance, he even thought he felt the stab of the thorns, but mastered the instinctive shrinking of his flesh and marched on. The illusory sensations subsided, he seemed to pass through a region of fog or shadow, then the world sharpened into focus and he found himself face-to-face with Karsler Stornzof. Steep rocky walls hemmed them closely on two sides. The illusory granite and vines masked the opening of a narrow defile, which extended only a few yards before opening onto a bare, shallow slope.

At the juncture of defile and slope stood a twin pair of horse-drawn caravans, whose exuberant ornamentation and distinctive boatlike design marked them as the property of wandering Turos. The owners were gathered about a small campfire, where skewers of spiced meat cooked on a makeshift grill. Girays quickly counted some two dozen people, more or less—it was hard to be certain, for the gang of swarthy, elf-locked children orbiting the fire in perpetual motion defied quantification. There were at least half a dozen women, ranging in age from ripening adolescent to decayed beldam. Of these half dozen, two clasped infants to their brown breasts, and another was visibly pregnant. The men were similarly diverse in age, if similar in type—all bronzed, slant eyed, and plump lipped, with agile bodies and quick gestures. Four of them now produced fowling pieces, seemingly out of nowhere. As the intruders approached, the four stood as one, leveled their weapons, and took aim.

The Ellipsoids halted at once.

"Hold your fire, we are not enemies," Girays advised in Vonahrish, without hesitation or reflection. But his instincts were good, for the Turos, citizens of the world and of nowhere, knew the predominant international tongue.

"Grewzians enemies of everyone," replied a Turo man of middle years and unusual breadth of shoulder, probably a leader. "Your national talent."

"I am Vonahrish, and enemy of no one."

"You keep bad company, then." The Turo favored the uniformed overcommander with a brief, hostile glance. "These Grewzian assassins hunt our kind through Neraunce and Nidroon, this is their idea of sport. They slaughter us like hogs in the Mid-Duchies."

"Not this one. He competes in the Grand Ellipse race."

"Today his race is run."

"I am sorry to hear it, for your sake." Girays assumed an air of sympathy. "Should this overcommander vanish from the competition, his Grewzian countrymen will make their displeasure known, and the sufferings that your people have already endured will be as nothing compared to what must follow. And that does not even begin to address the issue of my own removal—an unavoidable necessity in the event of my companion's murder—and the consequences thereof. I am a v'Alisante, and not exactly invisible," he observed mildly.

Unease clouded the faces of his Turo listeners.

"How do you find your way in here?" The Turo spokesman scowled.

"Easily," Stornzof informed him. "The image concealing your campsite is sound but rudimentary, its nature obvious to the trained observer. You've an illusionist in your company?" There was no response, and he concluded, "You may hardly rely upon so weak a defense."

The Turo uneasiness deepened.

"What do you want here?" The Turo leader's black eyes glittered.

"Assistance. The benefit of your skill," Girays returned casually, as if unaware of guns trained upon his heart. "Our vehicle is damaged. Hammer the dented tire back into shape, and I'll pay you ten New-rekkoes."

The Turo reflected. At last he countered grudgingly, "Fifteen."

"Agreed."

"You pay now."

Girays did so.

The other signaled his followers, and the fowling pieces vanished as magically as they had appeared.

"You wait now." The Turo took the two-seater from Stornzof. "Over here. You want some of our meat, that is another twelve New-rekkoes."

Girays wavered, tempted by the aroma, but Stornzof replied without hesitation, courteously as if answering a gracious invitation, "Thank you, I will decline the meat."

For the next half hour they waited there, seated on the ground in the defile, listening to the clang of hammer on iron and the low murmur of Turo conversation. At the end of that time, one of the women wheeled the repaired two-seater smoothly back to them. Both men stood, and Stornzof stepped forward to take the vehicle.

She halted him with a gesture. Her nostrils flared at sight of his Grewzian uniform, but her eyes widened with interest as they rose to his face.

"Machine oiled," the woman announced. "One New-rekko extra."

Stornzof paid her and took the two-seater. The Turo woman withdrew, casting a long glance back over her shoulder at him as she went.

His own existence, Girays observed with amused chagrin, seemed to go unnoticed.

They mounted the two-seater, with Stornzof in front, and pedaled out of the defile. The fog obscured Girays's vision for a few seconds, then they were back on the Aeshno-Eynisse Road, and the expanse of vine-draped granite lining the way before and behind them appeared unbroken. The riders exerted themselves, and the two-seater gathered speed.

The breeze of passage was cooling his face again, it felt fine, and they were pelting along northeast toward Eynisse at a much better speed than he could have achieved by any other currently available means. The Grewzian overcommander had made good on all claims and promises, Girays was forced to concede. Even that apparently fantastic boast about his ability to detect the magical "convolutions of force," the "disruptions of normality"—he had proved that he could do it.

"Stornzof," he said aloud.

"Yes?" The Grewzian's eyes remained fixed on the road before him.

"I admit to an error."

"Error?"

"I questioned your claims."

"Do you imagine that an unusual occurrence?"

"I wouldn't know. I do know that I was mistaken, because you've proved it." Girays forced himself to add, "I won't doubt your word again."

"Do not make rash promises," the Grewzian advised with a hint of dryness. "In any case you owe nothing to me, whose life you have saved twice within the space of two days."

That was almost certainly true, Girays reflected, and felt better.

The road before them ran downhill at a gentle grade. Pedaling was easy, and the newly oiled two-seater sped like a racehorse. Girays's spirits rose, and he observed, "At this rate we should reach Eynisse by noon tomorrow."

"We might do better yet," Stornzof suggested.

"Ah, ride on straight through the night, you mean?"

"Short rest stops as required. Catch up on sleep later, aboard barge on the Arune."

"Excellent. Then we'll hit Eynisse around dawn." Provided his own strength held out, Girays reflected, but kept the misgiving to himself, for there was only so much humility he could swallow at one draft. "I doubt that many of the others will do as well. In fact, I suspect the railroad strike will have knocked more than a few clean out of the race."

"Perhaps, but many will persevere. Mesq'r Zavune, for example, may expect assistance from his own countrymen."

"Then there's Porb Jil Liskjil, with his bottomless pockets, who can buy his way out of any difficulty. And Bav Tchornoi could bully his way through stone walls."

"And Miss Devaire?" Stornzof inquired. "She is resourceful, but now perhaps she must admit defeat?"

"Never," Girays responded with absolute conviction. "She will not give up. Not while she breathes."

Stornzof cast a clear glance back over his shoulder. "I see," he said.

SHE HAD STOLEN HERSELF a lovely horse, Luzelle reflected. *Purchased.*

Ballerina was fleet and sweet, well bred and well trained. She had carried her abductor—*new owner*—lightly through the night, her smooth stride devouring miles, until the flush of rose in the east had colored the white stucco walls of a roadside inn, and Luzelle had judged it safe to pause for a few hours of sleep. The city of Aeshno lay far behind her. Even had her escape route been noted, nobody would have pursued her over so great a distance; not for the sake of a stolen mare, not even for the sake of vandalized property. Or so she assured herself.

Relinquishing Ballerina to the charge of a sleepy ostler, Luzelle walked into the inn to confront a night clerk whose surprise showed on his face. She could scarcely blame him. A young foreign woman, traveling alone by night, without a single piece of luggage to her name—naturally he was taken aback. His surprise sharpened to open curiosity when she asked in Vonahrish to be wakened with a knock on her door in exactly six hours. She could see the questions struggling to emerge, but he managed to contain them. And when she produced a roll of good Vonahrish New-rekkoes, he retained sufficient presence of mind to assume the air of respect that every solvent guest merited. She paid in advance without demur, he handed her a key, and she felt his speculative gaze press her back as she walked away.

Luzelle climbed two flights of stairs, remembering with regret the wondrous lift in the Kingshead Hotel in Toltz. Locating her assigned room, she let herself in and locked the door. She hardly noted the character of her surroundings, which were plain, old-fashioned, and decent enough. She saw only the bed. She was tired, very tired. She had managed to ignore, evade, or resist fatigue for hours, but it had caught up with her now. She felt she could not stand upright another minute.

The southern springtime air was sultry. She stripped off her clothes and let them drop to the floor. Why not? They were already sweat stained and grimy from hours of riding. She herself was similarly grimy, but had not bothered to ask for a bath. What point, when she had no clean clothes, no change of underwear, no means at present of preserving personal decency, and above all, no energy? She did not want to wash her clothes, or even herself. She wanted nothing but sleep.

The sheets were clean, she was not, and she did not care. She tumbled into bed, her head hit the pillow, and she was immediately unconscious, or rather her consciousness changed. The dreams came, full of fire, smoke, noise; and those were the mild ones. Far more frightening were the visions of herself back in the neat, modestly appointed little bedroom she had occupied as a child in her father's house. She was looking at herself in the small mirror that hung above the washstand, and the face that gazed back from the glass was the wondering unmarked face of a child. But as she watched, the face altered and aged, shifting through the phases of adolescence, early and full maturity, middle age, and thence to sallow old age. And throughout all successive transformations, the chamber in which her mirrored image stood immured never changed at all.

A knock on the door banished such visions. Luzelle opened her eyes. She was still tired, but less so. Her eyes traveled about a plain, unfamiliar chamber. She remembered where she was, and how she had come. She did not want to get up yet, but the race was very much on. Yawning, she arose, noticed her own condition, and blinked. Her garments, visibly the worse for wear, lay scattered about the floor. Oh yes, she had dropped them there.

She ran her tongue across teeth that seemed slicked with rancid lard. Stumbling to the washstand, she rinsed her mouth out, then made the best possible use of water, soap, and towel before resuming yesterday's grubby garments. No comb, no hairbrush. Readjusting half a dozen pins, she anchored the riotous mass of red-gold curls as best she could, then hurried on down to the old-fashioned common room, where she breakfasted, or lunched, on skewered lamb and lentils, indifferent to the scrutiny of her fellow guests, some of them obviously hostile.

Too bad.

She looked up quickly from her plate to meet a pair of yellow eyes lancing out of a swarthy face, and felt her own color rise against the silent condemnation. She had seen it before, many times. She should be used to it by now, but somehow her nerves, blood, and stomach never inured themselves.

She chanced another look. Her silent critic flaunted saffron robes, black finger sheaths, looped linen streamers with black-edged cutwork. An orthodox Iyecktori, committed to the Gifted Iyecktor's vision of a stable, well-structured universe. Such a vision left no room for random peripatetic females, free to spread disorder throughout the world. The anger in the eyes of the watching Iyecktori confirmed her moral failing. She curbed the impulse to flash the Feyennese Four Fingers, for this was only the beginning. Heading east into the homeland of the Gifted Iyecktor, she was bound to encounter much more of the same, and she had better start learning to ignore insults.

Her eyes dropped to her plate. She ate quickly, without tasting, paid her bill, returned to the foyer, and asked the clerk on duty for her horse. Minutes later the ostler led Ballerina to the front. Luzelle tipped the ostler, mounted the stolen mare without assistance, and headed east.

For hours she rode hard under the strong Aennorvi sun, which was stooping westward by the time she came to a bone-white village, bleached and crumbling in the midst of the stony hills. She paused at the public trough in the middle of a plaza pale with ashen dust and black with intense southern shadow. She dismounted. While her horse drank, Luzelle studied the area. At first she thought the place dead, but presently discerned movement under the purple-diapered awning at the far end of the square, where the tradesmen were emerging from their midday coma. Pausing long enough to wrap Ballerina's reins around one of the public rails beside the trough, she hurried to the wakening shop, and entered a small-town general mart designed to meet modest needs.

The proprietor sported finger sheaths and linen streamers. His wife wore thumbless black gloves and a black cap with linen lappets. Orthodox Iyecktories beyond doubt, and the undisguised animosity hardening both bronzed faces momentarily gave her pause.

She rallied quickly. Advancing as if confident of her welcome, she asked in Vonahrish, "Do you sell women's clothing? Linen?"

The shopkeeper answered in curt Aennorvi.

"Clothing." Luzelle fingered the folds of her skirt illustratively.

Her female listener chattered shrilly.

Several bolts of fabric lay on a table at the center of the room. Luzelle turned to investigate, and the chattering rose in volume. The shopkeeper lifted a hand, rigid outstretched finger pointing the way to the exit. Luzelle displayed a fistful of New-rekkoes, and the irritable Aennorvi voices fell silent.

The cloth awaited the scissors and needles of industrious local housewives. No ready-made garments were offered for sale, with the exception of big, geometrically patterned scarves that could double as shawls, and genderless hooded rainwear of olive-drab oilcloth. She chose a handsome scarf and an ugly poncho. She also picked up needles, thread, soap, nail file, toothbrush, comb, hairbrush, handkerchiefs, a basket of apples, raisins, crackers, a canteen, a carpetbag to hold it all, and a couple of buckled straps with which to fasten the carpetbag to Ballerina's saddle cantle.

No fresh clothing. No change of linen. Not today.

Selections complete, she returned to the counter to confront the proprietor, who thrust three upright fingers forward, almost into her face. For a moment she imagined a local variant of the Feyennese Four, then realized that he was specifying a price of three hundred New-rekkoes. A wholly outrageous price, of course. She supposed she was expected to bargain, but she hadn't the time, the inclination, or the knowledge of the language. Swallowing outrage, she laid the money out on the counter, swept her purchases into the carpetbag, and turned to go.

A high-pitched verbal fusillade halted her. She turned back to confront the shopkeeper's wife, who was yelling, gesticulating, pointing at the carpetbag with one hand, and shaking four stiffened fingers at the ceiling with the other. This time the line between financial negotiation and deliberate insult was unclear. Luzelle curled her lip and made for the door. A geyser of unintelligible abuse sprayed behind her. A volley of tiny missiles struck her back, and there was no pain, but the surprise momentarily froze her. Little pellets were hitting the plank floor all around her, and it took her a moment to realize that the shopkeeper or his consort had flung a handful of dried white beans.

Savages. Spinning on her heel, she flashed four fingers at her tormentors and flounced from the shop, leaving the door wide open to the flies.

Idiots. Ranting fanatics. Yes, and how many more of the same between herself and the border? And after the border, farther east, deep in the stronghold of the Gifted Iyecktor, how much the worse?

For a moment she was almost glad that she spoke no Aennorvi; otherwise she would have wanted to stay and argue.

Hurrying across the square to her horse, she filled the new canteen with water from the pump beside the trough, and slung the strap over her shoulder. She fastened the carpetbag to the cantle, then loosed the reins from the rail, mounted, and turned Ballerina east. She departed the village without regret, but not without incident. As she passed the ripe garbage heap wreathed in creeping daggers that marked the end of what passed for a main street, a gang of local yellow-eyed urchins leapt forth yelling and flinging clods. The soft dirt balls broke against her skirts. Her horse snorted and shied. A nauseous stench arose, a buzzing fog darkened the air, and Luzelle felt the sting of countless fiery darts. Her face and neck prickled and burned. A cry escaped her, and she beat at the seething air with her hands. Dimly she noted the taunting yelps of the victorious youngsters. A brittle dirt ball shattered against her hair, the buzzing intensified, and the small darts stabbed her ears and the sensitive skin around her mouth. Even as her hands flew protectively to her eyes, the thought registered, *clay nesters*. The village children must have stockpiled scores of the delicate spheres, home to countless stinging winged arachnids, and now the intrusion of a lone female, odd and foreign, offered a welcome opportunity to launch the entire arsenal.

Ballerina plunged, and Luzelle barely kept her seat. The spectacle pleased the audience. A fairy chorus of excited juvenile laughter arose, and somebody threw a clay nest at the horse, then somebody else hurled a rock.

Little monsters. Their orthodox parents would probably be proud. She curbed the impulse to turn and yell at them; they would only take it as encouragement. Clapping her heels hard to the red mare's sides, she galloped east, and the laughing taunts and swarming clay nesters fell away behind her.

Once safely clear of the village, she let Ballerina slow to a walk. She was breathing hard and her heart was pounding. Her eyes burned and watered. Emotion? She thought not. Lifting a hand to her face, she found that the skin stung, as if with a sunburn. The hand itself was covered with a rash of tiny red pinpricks.

The clay-nester venom was not strong enough to cause serious illness. Except in unusual cases. The rash on her face and hands would vanish within hours. Probably.

The southern sun beat down on her. Her skin stung and itched. Opening the canteen, she swallowed a little water, then splashed coolness on her face. It helped. She took the big new scarf, wrapped it around her head Aennorvi style, and that helped too, but not enough. *Too bad*. Nothing more to be done about it at present.

Luzelle scowled, and pushed east. She rode at a moderate pace, but her imagination raced, flashing along the curve of the Grand Ellipse to overtake and surpass every rival. The Festinette twins. The Grewzians. Anyone else who might have pulled ahead while she had been delayed in Aeshno.

Glumly she wondered if a single one of them was a fraction as uncomfortable as she.

.   .   .

"THE ANGLE OF THE LIGHT annoys me. Change it," Torvid Stornzof commanded. Settling himself back among fat cushions, he added irritably, "A well-trained attendant requires no reminder. Your masters are remiss. Well, they are Zuleeki."

His listener, evincing neither guilt nor resentment—in fact, communicating nothing at all through the big ocher cloak and hood that contained his or her identity—bowed deeply and tweaked the strings that angled the wooden slats admitting sunlight to the hired chasmistrio. A gloved hand was visible for a moment.

The light altered nicely. The objectionable heat and glare abated, and a cool shadow kissed the grandlandsman's brow. At least these idiots could do something right, when properly instructed.

He caught a glimpse of a hairy, broad-snouted, yellow-tusked countenance and then it was gone, swallowed in the shadow of the hood, and none too soon. He did not wish to trouble his vision with excessive ugliness. There were better things to do with his eyes.

Torvid gazed down through the wooden slats and glass walls upon a vista of sheer cliffs edging ax-stroke gorges, rising above a wrathful river and its tributaries. Typical scenery of half-tamed Zuleekistan, very stirring, very picturesque, and he could appreciate its charm while holding himself aloof from its dangers.

The pagoda-roofed glass-and-steel chasmistrio hung suspended like some piece of jewelry upon the great aerial cable bridging the clouds a thousand feet above the Wzykii Cleft, and connecting the formerly great trading center of Feezie with the string of villages littering the cliff top on the far side of the white-fanged Wzyk River.

Feezie. A deplorable backwater midden. The grandlandsman's lip curled at the recollection. No comforts, no amenities, no entertainment. A dreary, tannery-stinking blight upon the face of the world, a testimony to the inferiority of its inhabitants. If only the tale he had told his shining star of a Promontory nephew had been true—if only he had traveled straight to civilized, amusing Jumo Towne, then life would have been far more pleasant. But duty called, his obligation to the imperior commanded, and thus he found himself reluctantly rusticated.

At least he had skipped over the dusty grime of Aennorve and the primitive rigors of Bizaqh. That was one consolation. And his sojourn in goat-and-bandit-infested Zuleekistan was likely to prove brief. That was another.

Torvid exhaled an impatient cloud of cigarette smoke, and saw his attendant turn away. No refuge, no pure mountain air to be found within the glass walls of the chasmistrio, and the other knew it but presumably wished to register his—her—its objection to the atmospheric pollution. Insolent freak of nature. A crease deepened between the grandlandsman's brows.

"You—here," he commanded. He tapped the low inlaid table before him sharply. "My glass." He was prepared to punish the slightest hesitation with a blow, but his companion bent at once to refill the depleted flute with Vonahrish champagne, and no disciplinary opportunity presented itself. The silent other's hirsute face was level with his own for a moment. He caught the feral gleam of red eyes under the shadow of the hood, and the itch in his palm vanished magically.

For a time there was silence broken only by the rush of the mountain winds and the grumble of metal on metal as the chasmistrio ascended, its swaying weight dragged along the cable by the power of unseen hands upon the great winch anchored to the cliff above the Wzyk.

Torvid Stornzof sipped champagne, studied the scenery, and smoked. Presently the chasmistrio attained a region of low-lying cloud, and ghost-grey mists obscured the world below. Grey smoke correspondingly hazed the car's interior, visibility dwindled to nothing, and the ocher-robed menial began to gurgle. A low, hoarse, bubbling vocalization issued from under the hood. *Urghurrhurgahrurrgh* . . . The creature was simulating pulmonary distress, presumably to score some reproachful little point, but Torvid Stornzof did not number susceptibility among his failings. Calmly exhaling a warm grey fog, he commanded, "Silence."

Uuurghhhurgurhurgh—iiYUHHK, iiYUHHK, iiYUHHK—
Ridiculous hiccups underscored the gurgles. Purple mucus dripped from the broad nostrils. The impertinence was

beneath notice, and ordinarily Torvid would have ignored it. But the close confines of the chasmistrio precluded indulgence, and he found himself obliged to address the other's failing.

"Silence," he repeated.

Uuurghhhurgurhur—iiYUHHK, iiYARGHKKK—

This was as deliberately defiant as it was irritating, and corporal chastisement was more than warranted. Rising from the divan, Torvid took a step forward, lifted his hand, and struck the hairy face beneath the hood. The other's head snapped aside and then thrust forward, eyes redly ablaze, yellow tusks bared an inch from his throat. Torvid drew back a step, pulled the pistol from his breast pocket, and fired without hesitation. The shot blasted, a third red eye appeared in the middle of the other's forehead, and the creature fell dead.

Awkward. He had acted in self-defense, yet his reception at the far side of the Wzykii Cleft now waxed problematical. Torvid scowled and poured himself another glass of champagne.

A stench arose to fill the glass compartment. The dead body was venting assorted vapors. Torvid set his glass aside.

The chasmistrio inched along the cable. Eventually the mists thinned and the surrounding crags distinguished themselves. A bump, scrape, and conclusive thud announced the end of the journey. Forced to attend to himself, Torvid unlatched and opened the steel-barred door with his own hand, stepping forth from his conveyance to confront a quartet of cloaked and hooded ocher figures stationed about the winch. With them stood a flint-eyed overseer clad in the Zuleeki peasant garb of full-sleeved blouse, loose vest, and short homespun kilt.

Ignoring the ocher menials, Torvid addressed himself to the overseer.

"The Mongrel awaits me?"

"You will find him at the lightning-blasted pine below the village of Faddogalbro," the native replied in tolerable Grewzian.

"You will guide me there." Money changed hands.

Pungent gases wafted from the open chasmistrio. The

ocher quartet snorted, whined, clicked their teeth, and shifted uneasily beneath their robes. Observing this, the overseer frowned.

"There has been a mishap." Torvid pulled a few bills from his wallet. "To cover your loss."

The other took the cash, counted it, shrugged, and nodded. "Come, then. This way."

Together they set off along the narrow cliff-top path. Behind them four inhuman voices rose in mournful howls.

The hike was silent and uneventful. The Mongrel waited at the fallen pine, as promised. With their chief stood three mustachioed and hawk-nosed subordinates, their heads wrapped in the traditional streaming kerchiefs, their carbines slung across their backs. Not far away grazed four smallish, shaggy horses of the hardy local breed.

Torvid gestured imperatively, and his companion fell back. The grandlandsman went on alone, and the Mongrel advanced to meet him. Presently they halted face-to-face, and something in the famous brigand's fearless, almost haughty demeanor prompted the grandlandsman to draw forth the platinum case, snap it open, and proffer the contents with unwonted civility.

"Smoke?" he invited simply.

Accepting a black cigarette, the Mongrel inclined his head without servility. The two men lit up and puffed in silence.

"You will accept the commission?" Torvid asked at last, in Vonahrish.

The Mongrel's eagle eyes narrowed, and he exhaled a thoughtful grey cloud.

"I will accept it," he replied at last.

Torvid handed over a wad of New-rekkoes, which the other pocketed without counting. Terse conversation ensued, peppered with many references to "the Travornish twin brothers," to "the Navoyza Pass," and to "*Een Djasseen.*"

The interview concluded, and the two men shook hands, almost as equals. The Mongrel and his followers remounted and rode away. Torvid Stornzof rejoined the overseer, and they made their way back along the trail to the chasmistrio, where the four unclassifiable ocher attendants awaited.

Torvid felt the hot red glare of their eyes upon him as he drew near, and caught the muted rumble of low growls, but ignored such impertinences. He entered the glass-and-steel car, whose dead tenant had been removed during his absence. The enclosed atmosphere stank of lavender cologne, presumably intended to mask less palatable odors. A fresh bottle of champagne stood in the silver cooler on the low table, but there was no attendant there to pour it out for him. Evidently he was to make the return journey alone, a state that suited him well enough, for he far preferred self-sufficiency to the vexation of sullen or clumsy service.

The Zuleeki overseer set off his signal flare, which must have been glimpsed on the far side of the Wzykii Cleft, for scant minutes later the slack in the endless lines was taken up and the car began to move along the cable, commencing its slow return to Feezie.

Torvid sipped champagne and considered. His impressions of the Mongrel had been favorable, and he believed the brigand capable of fulfilling his commission. This being so, Nephew Karsler's path to victory lay clear before him, the Stornzof triumph was assured, and the day's work rewarding, even though—the grandlandsman's black brows drew together—even though his own personal intervention should have been unnecessary. Karsler should and could have concluded the affair unassisted, but for the handicap of an absurdly antiquated honorable code—product, no doubt, of a curious education—that often seemed self-defeating, even self-indulgent. For at times it was only too clear that the younger Stornzof placed certain foolish concerns above and beyond his duty to his imperior and to his own House. And if he did so, then he was unworthy of the family name he bore.

A weakling, an irresolute dreamer—and a Stornzof?

But no. The famous overcommander's martial triumphs proved otherwise. His blood was of the best, and the crippling effect of his education an inconvenience, merely.

The champagne was execrable, Torvid decided. And he could not abide the stench of lavender. Travel by chasmistrio was fit for dogs and Zuleekis.

No matter. Another couple of hours and he would be back in

Feezie, whose best inn was almost tolerable. He had already booked passage aboard the eastbound steamer *Diamond Solitaire.* Before tomorrow's sun cleared the horizon, he would be at sea, heading for Jumo Towne and the blessings of civilization.

THE HILLS ROSE STEEP and jagged above the Navoyza Pass. The vegetation at such altitudes was low and hardy, the springtime wildflowers dotting the defile with fuchsia and intense purple, the broad fields of sinquerriva spreading watercolor washes of pale gold along the slopes. The air was clear, pure, and cool to the verge of discomfort. The sky was ridiculously blue—an artist reproducing the shade on canvas would have been mocked by the critics—and streaked with trailing, traveling clouds. High overhead a hawk glided on stationary wing, and down closer to the ground a flying weasel launched itself at a rock sweeper foraging on the far side of the pass.

A caravan of six camels followed the ancient trail flanked by lofty cliffs. Three of the camels were cream-colored, long-haired, double-humped *jehdavis,* a breed prized for its strength and endurance. The first of these valuable creatures, striding at the head of the party, belonged to a grizzled Zuleeki clad in battered leathers—evidently the leader and guide. The other two were ridden by a pair of youthful foreign patrons, prettily identical in face and form, identical in every detail of dandified Vonahrish-cut costume. The remaining three camels were noticeably inferior in quality. Two of them were ridden by flat-faced local laborers taken on as temporary servants, and the third, serving as a pack animal, carried a mountain of expensive matched leather luggage.

The clean winds sang through the Navoyza Pass, the picture-perfect clouds sailed across the improbable sky, and one of the young travelers turned to inform the other, "I think I'm going to throw up again."

"Fight it, Tref," Stesian Festinette advised. "Set your mind on something else."

"I can't. It's the way this infernal creature *sways* when it moves. It's worse than a sailboat in a hurricane."

"Well, it doesn't seem all that bad to *me*."

"Well, *you* didn't eat any of those grilled rock sweepers. Those miserable little mouse things aren't fit for human consumption. They did not agree with me."

"Then why did you go and pop a whole bowlful of 'em?"

"They tasted all right. How was I to know they were *poisonous*? Now I'm extremely ill, ready to fall right off this disgusting camel, and a fat lot of sympathy I get from *you*."

"I'm sympathetic, Tref. I'm so sympathetic that I'm starting to get queasy just listening to you. You know what happens to me when you get sick—"

"Well, that works both ways!"

"So would you please stop *dwelling* on it? Just try to concentrate on something else, something *cheerful*. Think of—oh, think of the time we spiked the punch bowl at the headmaster's retirement party with that Strellian emetic—"

"You're not helping, Stes!"

"Sorry. All right, then think about—well, think about fame. Think about prestige. Think about blazing, radiant, unspeakable glory. Think about winning the Grand Ellipse. I tell you, Tref, it'll be our best stunt yet—the three-legged cow was nothing compared to this! And we *are* going to win, don't you know. We've drawn so far ahead of the pack, there's no one can catch us now!"

"Don't forget the offal chompers."

"I haven't forgotten. But where are they now? There's been no news. If they're ahead of us and we're following in their footsteps, don't you think we'd run into someone who's seen 'em? But nobody's sighted the wandering Grewzians—not in Aennorve, or Bizaqh, or Zuleekistan. You know what I'm starting to suspect? Something's happened. Something's held them up, they've fallen behind, and this race is *ours*."

"I guess that's worth a nauseating camel ride or two." Trefian brightened. "You know what we should do after we've won? Once we're back in Toltz, we rent a hall and throw a huge victory celebration, I mean a full-scale rip-roaring bash, with champagne, food, entertainment, all of that. We'll invite everyone, absolutely everyone. Then, when the party's at its peak, we have someone outside the hall set off some firecrackers—you know, the big ones that boom like cannons. Then we have someone come running in to announce that the Grewzians have invaded, and that the city is under attack. I tell you, Stes, the place will *explode,* everyone there will go mad, utterly *mad*! What a spectacle!"

"Outstanding! Now there's something to look forward to!"

Both brothers burst into uncontrollable giggles.

As the caravan rounded a bend in the trail, the abrupt materialization of a mounted band cut the laughter short. They seemed to come out of nowhere—a dozen hawk-faced riders, picturesquely garbed, and armed with serviceable-looking carbines. Their leader, an individual of coolly authoritative aspect, called out some comment or command in the local dialect, and the caravan halted at once. The hired guide inclined his head with an air of extreme respect.

"What did he say?" Trefian Festinette inquired.

"What in the world is going on?" Stesian demanded.

"Silence," their guide instructed quietly, in Vonahrish. "It is the Mongrel."

"Who or what is—"

"Silence."

The guide and the Mongrel conversed briefly in dialect, the tenor of their discourse unintelligible to their Travornish listeners. The guide appeared to remonstrate. The Mongrel shrugged and replied firmly. The guide nodded a regretful acquiescence, whereupon the Mongrel gestured, and a couple of his followers advanced to clip lead lines to the halters of the Festinettes' *jehdavis.*

"What do you think you're doing there, my man?" Trefian Festinette demanded.

"Is this some sort of native custom?" inquired his twin.

There was no reply.

The Mongrel lifted his hand and the horsemen sped off along the trail, drawing the Festinettes in their wake. A spate of alarmed inquiries went unanswered.

For the next two hours the band rode hard, through the Navoyza Pass and along the winding mountain trails. At last

they paused to water the horses. Trefian and Stesian slid from
their camels with small moans of relief. One of the Zuleekis
loitered nearby, and the twins accosted him at once.

"See here, I wonder if you wouldn't mind telling us—"
Trefian began.

"You mustn't think we don't appreciate your lively attentions, but we should very much like to know—" Stesian sec-
onded his brother.

The Zuleeki responded curtly in dialect, and turned away.

"What curious manners these people have," Trefian murmured.

"I don't think he understood us, Tref. They're not terrifi-
cally civilized, these Zuleekis. Or civil, for that matter."

"Maybe we'll have better luck with—" Trefian pointed,
and his brother's eyes followed.

Not far away the Mongrel leaned stilly against a rock,
piercing gaze aimed at the jagged horizon. The twins hurried
to his side.

"Master—er—Mongrel, do you happen to speak Vonahrish?" Stesian essayed.

The Mongrel turned to inspect them at leisure. At last he
answered, "Some."

"Oh, outstanding. Then perhaps you would be so good as
to tell us, sir, what this is all about? Not that it hasn't all been
a tremendous lark, you understand, but the fact is, my
brother and I compete in the Grand Ellipse, which, in case
you didn't know, is this whacking great race around—"

"I know the Grand Ellipse," said the Mongrel.

"Excellent. Then you'll surely understand that—genuinely
interesting an interlude though this has been—my brother
and I must really be on our way."

"Yes."

Something in the Mongrel's quiet tone prompted an exchange of uneasy glances between the twins, and Stesian
prompted dubiously, "To—?"

"To *Een Djasseen*."

·   ·   ·

THE JOURNEY RESUMED and there followed another two hours of riding over wild terrain, along the smallest and stoniest of mountain trails. At the end of that time they came to a sharp grade rising to a small plateau edged with a high wall of reddish stone. Up the path to the great iron portcullis guarding the gateway rode the Mongrel and his followers. The guards on duty raised the portcullis at once, and the party passed into the courtyard of a red fortress topped with a dozen twisted lead-roofed turrets. Each turret carried an iron spike crowned with a human skull.

"What place is *this*?" asked Trefian Festinette.

There was no answer.

The riders halted with a jingle of bits and spurs. An enormously tall and broad Zuleeki with a glossy bald head emerged from the building to meet them. A brief colloquy between the Mongrel and the bald man ensued, at the conclusion of which the Mongrel accepted a softly clinking leather pouch, and the lead lines of the Festinettes' camels were placed in the bald man's hand.

The Mongrel and his followers galloped from the courtyard.

The twins and their host surveyed one another in silence for a moment. The Zuleeki barked a sharp command in dialect, accompanied by a peculiar tongue click recognizable to the camels, both of which instantly knelt.

"Dismount," the bald man commanded in Vonahrish.

The twins, obedient as the camels, did as they were bid.

"You come," the bald man informed them.

Trefian Festinette found his wits and his voice. "Who are *you*?" he asked.

"I am Ilciu. I serve," their host announced.

"Serve what, serve whom?"

"My master. The lord of this place and the lands that surround it."

"And your master is—"

"*Een Djasseen.*"

· · ·

ILCIU LED THEM INTO THE FORTRESS, along dim and grim echoing corridors, past niches housing suits of antique armor, past wall displays of monstrous swords, pikes, and battle-axes, through chambers hung with threadbare tapestries ancient beyond reckoning, until at last they passed through a great double doorway into what seemed another world.

The twins gazed about them in wonder. They stood in a vast vaulted chamber with billowy hangings of lilac silk and mauve gauze, crystal chandeliers with rose-colored shades, spraying perfumed fountains, and tall marble statues of gods and athletes, painted in lifelike colors. Here the air was soft, warm, and humid. Strains of music delicate as drifting petals sweetened the atmosphere, and the fragrance of violets hung like a pall over all.

The chamber was well populated. A floor of gleaming rose and lilac marble tile supported countless polychrome rugs and fringed cushions, upon which sat or reclined no fewer than half a hundred young males, ranging in age from earliest adolescence to full maturity. All of them were well proportioned, all fit and firm—these attributes easily judged, for all were similarly clothed in abbreviated silken breechclouts and nothing more. All had handsome faces—most of the olive-skinned, hawk-featured Zuleeki type, but some fair northerners among them, and one calf-eyed, full-lipped adolescent cherub who might have been Aveshquian. The young faces were painted, the eyes lined and exaggerated with kohl, the lids brightened with metallic color, the cheeks and lips deeply reddened. Fingernails and toenails were varnished in tones of coral and poppy. The carefully pomaded curls were often highlighted with streaks of gold, white, or blue.

"What an outlandish crew," Stesian observed, sotto voce. "D'you suppose they're *actors* or something?"

"Don't gawk," advised his brother. "Remember, we're cosmopolitan."

A low murmur of speculative interest greeted the entrance of the Travornish twins. A couple of youths rose from their cushions, stretching for a better look. Ignoring the spectators, Ilciu clapped his hands smartly. A quartet of white-haired, toothless, stooped but spry crones answered the summons at once. Ilciu issued orders in dialect. The crones bowed low, then turned and seized the astonished brothers, hurried them across the great chamber, under an alabaster archway, and into an adjoining room, where twilight filtering through a stained-glass skylight played upon a great, turquoise-tiled bath.

The crones stripped them expertly and pushed them into the bath. The water was warm, scented, and pleasantly peppered with floating blossoms; the ministrations of the crones agreeable, if almost too thorough. Presently, well scrubbed and tingling, the brothers were plucked from their bath, toweled until they glowed, anointed with perfumed oils, and wrapped in identical embroidered silken breechclouts. Next their faces were carefully painted, their eyebrows plucked and shaped, their fingernails lacquered, their brown curls pomaded and styled. As a finishing touch, each brother was adorned with a pair of dangling jeweled earrings.

"I don't know, Tref." Stesian Festinette shook his head, and the long earrings jingled. "I'm not so sure about all this. Especially the blue fingernails."

"Local customs," his brother reminded him. "Exotic Zuleeki hospitality, that's all. Isn't travel supposed to be a broadening experience?"

The question went unanswered. Ilciu reappeared, and the four crones sank to their creaky knees. The bald-headed man inspected their handiwork at length, then nodded and addressed them in dialect. The old ladies rose, bowed, and departed cackling.

"I tell them it is good," Ilciu informed the twins. "You will please him."

"Oh—" Trefian's look of confusion cleared. "Do we finally get to meet our host, then?"

"Yes. Now you go to *Een Djasseen*."

Ilciu clapped his hands. A brace of menials fully as large and broad as himself appeared, bearing a litter. The twins were placed upon the litter, artistically positioned back-to-back, and violet petals scattered over their bare shoulders.

Ilciu flicked a finger. The bearers took up the litter and carried it from the room.

"Most peculiar customs," Stesian murmured to his twin as they went.

"Entertaining, I call it," Trefian rejoined. "I'm quite looking forward to meeting this *Een Djasseen* fellow. No doubt he's an odd figure."

"I wonder what in the world he'll want to talk about?"

11

"GOOD-BYE, BALLERINA. I'll miss you," said Luzelle.

"Aihee treat dees lovely one lakka daughter," the new owner vowed in execrable Vonahrish.

"She likes to have her nose stroked."

"Aihee stroke nose, feed oats, polish feet. She ees star een sky."

She is stolen property, and you probably guess as much. Luzelle smiled, nodded, and said nothing.

"Come, then, red beauty." The fortunate Bizaqhi buyer led the chestnut mare away.

Luzelle sighed. Her eyes stung. Ballerina would surely receive kind treatment, but she hated herself anyway. Her glance dropped to the sheaf of Bizaqhi currency—a ridiculously low price for the stolen horse—still clasped in her right hand. Her wrist twitched, and she came within a nerve of throwing the money to the winds. A stupid impulse. There were better uses for those Bizaqhi notes.

Her eyes ranged the dusty plaza, fly-ridden heart of ancient Quinnekevah. Not much to see. A big stone spire at the center, theoretically marking the site of the Gifted Iyecktor's vision of the Three Fires, and indisputably marking the site of the annual Goat Fair held for the past five hundred years and more. A few old wooden buildings of indeterminate function, distinguished by their domed roofs and windows of golden-tinted glass. A few small, unpainted booths housing vendors

and their wares. A few wandering ring-tailed dogs, a few donkey carts, and more than a few pedestrians; the men in their
huge baggy breeches, the women all wearing black caps with
linen lappets, the children in sleeveless knee-length tunics or
in nothing at all. A bustling, oddly timeless scene that had
probably changed little since Iyecktor's day.

There was at least one change, however. On the far side of
the plaza the recently constructed but already outdated-
looking Quinnekevah train station rose in all its dun-colored
brick glory. Here in Bizaqh the trains were running, but one
of her timetables told her that the next one heading east toward Zuleekistan was not scheduled to arrive for another
hour, which left a little time to dispose of her local currency.
What to buy? Food? Trinkets? A ring-tailed dog?

Fresh clothes.

She looked down at herself. After days of hard riding
across Aennorve she was just barely respectable, or perhaps
not quite. Her sober dark-blue skirts were muddied about the
hem, her jacket was dusty and travel stained. As for her
linen—she did not want to think about it.

One of the booths displayed Bizaqhi garments, and she
hurried straight to it. The proprietress was a strapping young
woman who spoke no Vonahrish, no Grewzian, no Lanthian,
no comprehensible western tongue.

Luzelle scanned the exotic wares, and she pointed. The
merchant nodded vigorously and handed her a long skirt of
thin, crinkly black cotton with a drawstring waist. Upon
closer inspection she found the apparently feminine skirt divided to form a pair of vastly voluminous trousers. What a
clever idea. She smiled and pointed again, this time choosing
a loose emerald-green tunic with bands of black embroidery
about the hem and along the wide sleeves. Experimentally she
held the garment up against herself. The vendor grinned
broadly, rubbed her hands together in what seemed a local
gesture of approval or encouragement, and offered a wide
black sash with fringed ends and green embroidery. Luzelle
took the sash, along with a second tunic of mulberry cotton, a
matching sash, a quilted surcoat, and several linen undergarments whose design was foreign but perfectly comprehensi-

ble. Selections complete, she handed a fistful of money to the vendor, who looked surprised, counted the cash, and actually handed back a couple of notes. Remarkable.

She stowed her purchases away in the carpetbag, then marched across the plaza into the lofty dim coolness of the train station, where she paused to consult her watch. Another twenty minutes to wait. Plenty of time. A discreet trio of concentric circles carved into a door panel identified the women's rest room. She went in and found the place unusually modern by Bizaqhi standards, with wooden partitions separating the half-dozen holes in the wooden latrine bench, and plentiful ventilation. She changed quickly into the black divided skirt, the green tunic and sash, while her grubby Vonahrish garments went into the carpetbag to rest atop the corset that she had left off wearing days earlier but somehow did not quite dare to discard. Perhaps before the trip was over she would find the time to wash them. The new clothes were light and loose, offering miraculous comfort and freedom. These Bizaqhis weren't so backward as many westerners imagined.

There was no mirror and she had no idea how she looked clad in exotic peasant gear. Probably absurd, but what did it matter? She felt marvelous.

She smiled and drew a deep breath; this last a mistake, for she gagged on the latrine atmosphere. Exiting quickly, she hurried to the ticket window, where her expressive finger-jabbing at the map on the wall wordlessly communicated her needs. Money and a crudely printed ticket traded hands. A spate of unintelligible Bizaqhi dialect followed. Luzelle smiled, shrugged, and spread uncomprehending hands. The man behind the window pointed at the great clock on the wall behind her, waggled his fingers, shook his head, and chattered earnestly. She turned to glance at the clock, then looked back at him. He was still talking.

She wished she understood him. Beaming a final friendly, puzzled smile, she turned away and went to claim a seat on the wooden bench closest to the departure gate. To do so she was obliged to wiggle her way into a narrow space between two broad Bizaqhi wives, each encumbered with husband, children, black cap, and linen lappets, each displeased at the intrusion. Angry eyes fastened upon her uncovered, unruly red-gold hair. Indignant female voices muttered at her.

Sh'tishkur.

Fa kuta.

She did not know the words, and did not want to know. She fixed her eyes on the dun-colored tile floor. The voices subsided. An aggressive elbow pressed her arm, and she ignored it. Time passed, and her thoughts drifted.

The chimes of the big clock recalled her to reality. The eastbound train should be pulling into Quinnekevah Station about now. Exactly now.

There was no announcement. Her mind wandered off in pursuit of blue worms and red mares. It seemed hardly more than a moment before the clock chimed again. An hour had passed. The train had not arrived.

She lifted her head and looked around her. The waiting room was quite full, most of the benches lined with ordinary Bizaqhi travelers, the majority of them carting suitcases, bags, knapsacks, head trays; a few carrying cages of chickens or pigeons, one leading a white goat. Women were knitting and chatting, men smoking, children romping, babies squalling. There was much audible consumption of fruit, nuts, and various salted treats, a sight that set her stomach rumbling. The scene was unremarkable, but something about it troubled her. A moment's consideration pinpointed the source of her unease: the collective air of nonchalance, the absence of expectancy. Her fellow travelers hardly seemed poised on the verge of departure; rather they looked ready to take up permanent residence in the waiting room.

Eastern fatalism. Good for the digestion. Profit by their example. She closed her eyes. She willed herself to relax. It worked, and she fell asleep.

The chimes of the clock woke her two hours later. Still no sign of the train, and now it was very late indeed. But definitely running, she assured herself. There was no *strevvio* here in Bizaqh, nothing seriously amiss. And perhaps this delay that seemed so excessive to her was ordinary by local standards. Certainly her fellow travelers appeared untroubled. Reaching into her carpetbag, she brought forth a packet of raisins and commenced nibbling. Her movements jogged the alien elbow lodged against her right arm, and there was a prompt retaliatory poke, followed by an angry feminine hiss.

"*Sh'tishkur.*"

Turning to face her critic, she glowered and pushed the intrusive elbow away, requesting coldly, "Please don't touch me."

The words were spoken in Vonahrish, but the sentiment was doubtless comprehensible to her listener, who responded with a torrent of high-pitched Bizaqhi abuse. The term *fa kuta* recurred many times, a clenched fist waved suggestively, and the outraged local concluded with an expressive blast of saliva, aimed at the floor.

Disgusted, Luzelle rose from the bench and her neighbors instantly shifted position, wide hips converging to eliminate the space she had vacated. She flashed them the Feyennese Four, which elicited no reaction; that incomparably useful gesture seemed to carry no meaning in this part of the world. Sticking her tongue out as far as it would go, she turned her back on her tormentors. Vituperation fountained in her wake.

She was tired of sitting, anyway. It would be good to stretch her legs. Carpetbag in hand, she strolled along the perimeter of the big waiting room. She had not advanced more than a few yards before a dapper figure rose from one of the benches to accost her.

"Miss D'vaire?"

"Mesq'r Zavune!" Surprise, pleasure at sight of an amiable familiar face, frustration at sight of a rival she had thought outdistanced, all mingled in her mind. She liked Zavune, but wished him a hundred miles behind her. Producing a genuine if half-unwilling smile, she noted that the Aennorvi speculator's expression reflected sentiments similar to her own. He was looking well, she thought. Rested, clear eyed, fit, and content. However had he managed it? He was newly minted immaculate, freshly laundered, barbered, and manicured, his well-tailored linen garments impossibly unwrinkled. By contrast she knew she presented a ridiculous spectacle, with her flimsy native fripperies and her straggling curls. She wasn't even properly clean.

He looked her up and down, and his smile seemed devoid of mockery as he observed, "These Bizaqhi clothings—very pretty for you."

"I had to get hold of some clean things, I was desperate," she told him. "You see, I went and lost almost everything I had back in Aeshno. I didn't want to leave my valise, but there wasn't any choice at the time—"

"Your valise is stealed in Aeshno?"

"Not exactly. But it's gone, and so I've been traveling for days without a change and I suppose, all things considered, that it pretty well serves me right, but it's getting pretty noisome, and I just couldn't stand it any longer, so I was ready to grab anything I could find, so long as it was *clean*—" She broke off, aware that she was babbling.

Probably Mesq'r Zavune understood no more than half of what she had said, for his brow was clouded as he repeated reassuringly, "Very pretty for you."

"Thank you." She drew a breath and collected herself. "And you are looking very well, Master Zavune. You've made good time, since we disembarked in Aeshno."

"Ah. Time. Yes." He nodded. "In Aennorve I am home, I am among many friends. Much they help me. I am given use of carriage, good horses, to carry me comfortable to Quinnekevah. I am having easy time of it in Aennorve."

"You must have enjoyed that."

"Muchly. Truth, so muchly that I myself make difficult to fly along."

"You mean, you were so happy to be home in Aennorve that it was hard for you to move on?" she translated.

"You have striked the nail. There in Aeshno I am with the Madame Zavune, the sons and small daughter Zavune. It is good but brief, so brief, and when do I see them all again?"

"Not so very long from now, I think. The race goes quickly."

"Today it does not. I am here in station this morning, six o'clock sharp, for eastbound train Number 344, the *Flying Goatherd,* and it does not come. I wait. No train. I wait. Still no train, somebody clips that goatherd's wings. I wait past noon, and now I am waiting for next scheduled train, Number 682, *Bizaqhi Bullet*, scheduled depart one P.M."

"Yes, I'm waiting for the *Bizaqhi Bullet* too."

"And waiting. And waiting. No train."

So much the better, Luzelle thought. *Had you caught that morning train, you'd be miles ahead of me now.* Aloud she said only, "There is no help for it, unless you want to look for some other means of transportation."

"No, no. Train is best, when it come. If it come."

"It will. All of these people"—her gesture encompassed the populous waiting room—"can't be wrong."

"I hope it. I hope too for something to eat, before long. I am not eating since dawn, but I dare not go from here in search of food. What if *Bizaqhi Bullet* hits station while I am gone?"

"I've got raisins. Would you like some?"

"Miss D'vaire, you are goddess of mercy."

They walked on together. As they went, he consumed two packets of her raisins and a handful of blifilnuts. Conversation was agreeable, if labored, centering largely upon amusing or appalling recent experiences. She told him about the claynester ambush in the Iyecktori village, he told her of the outrageously crooked innkeeper along the Eastwest High Road. She had grown used to his thick accent, his fractured syntax, and his speech was increasingly comprehensible. The better she understood, the more clearly she perceived his longing for home, and once again she thought, *Poor fellow, he shouldn't be here.*

They walked on through clouds of somebody's foul cigar smoke, and she wondered if they might step outdoors into comparatively fresh air, if only for a moment. Her eyes jumped to the main doorway, and her breath caught.

Mesq'r Zavune followed her gaze. "Ah," he murmured sadly. "Surprise."

Two fellow Ellipsoids had caught up with them. Girays v'Alisante and Karsler Stornzof walked into Quinnekevah Station together. Side by side, in fact.

Karsler? Here? He should have been miles ahead by now,

half a world ahead. What could have delayed him, how could
he be here now? And with Girays v'Alisante, of all people?

They couldn't have been traveling in company. Girays,
who disliked Grewzians, would never voluntarily spend time
or share space with Karsler Stornzof. Their simultaneous arrival was surely coincidental.

It did not look coincidental. They were hurrying straight
for the ticket window, and they were talking as they went. She
could not begin to imagine the conversational topic, but Girays said something to which Karsler responded with a nod
and a smile, and it all seemed very sociable indeed.

They were, she mused inconsequentially, dissimilar in almost every way; externally, at least. She willed herself not to
stare.

"We give greeting?" Zavune inquired.

"What? Oh—later, perhaps," she replied. She found herself curiously uncertain. She would not have hesitated to approach either Karsler or Girays individually—in fact, she
would have welcomed the chance—but confronting both at
once seemed indefinably awkward. "I've walked enough,
haven't you? Let's sit down."

He nodded, and they found space on one of the benches at
the rear of the room. She risked a covert glance at the ticket
window, where Girays and Karsler stood engaged in some sort
of exchange with the cashier. He was probably telling them in
Bizaqhi that the trains were running endless hours behind
schedule, and they did not understand him, but they would
figure it out soon enough. They had not yet noticed her presence, and she was content to remain invisible for the moment.

Mesq'r Zavune was saying something or other, and she
would never understand if she didn't concentrate. She turned
back to him with a smile, waited while he laboriously constructed some polite query about her last series of lectures,
and replied graciously. Innocuous conversation ensued. Out
of the corner of her eye she saw Girays and Karsler seat themselves. Together. Very strange.

The skies visible through the dusty station window darkened, and the stars appeared. The lamps in the waiting room

were lit, and presently the big clock on the wall chimed the hour of eight. Dinnertime, and she was more than ready. Reaching into her carpetbag, she groped in vain for a packet of raisins, a handful of nuts, or an apple. Not an edible morsel remained.

"I eat all your foods?" Zavune correctly interpreted her look of regret. "This is bad of me."

"Not at all. I'm not really hungry," she lied. Her stomach growled a contradiction.

"This is bad of me," Zavune repeated. "I must to try to repair."

"No, really—"

"Wait, please." He turned away to face his left-hand neighbor, another of those large, linen-capped Iyecktori women.

Luzelle could not make out what he was saying to the Iyecktori. Probably he did not speak her language, but Zavune was not letting that stop him, and the exchange appeared animated. No scowling disapproval or insults directed at *him,* she noticed. A man was allowed to travel alone, without compromise of respectability. Nobody minded *his* uncovered hair. In fact, the Iyecktori was beaming a soupy, maternal, gap-toothed smile, the kind of expression usually directed at adorable urchins or gamboling puppies. Now she was reaching into the wicker hamper on the floor before her to bring forth a couple of napkin-wrapped bundles, which she pressed upon him. And when he attempted to give her money, she shook her head, handed him another little bundle, and actually patted his cheek. It was revolting, really.

But she changed her mind when Zavune turned back to face her, unknotted the napkins, and invited her to share the contents, which included stuffed grape leaves, an herb loaf, and dried apricots. She ate, and her mood improved.

Thereafter conversation lagged and time stretched. She would have given worlds for a book or newspaper, but there was none. Finally—bored with waiting, tired of sitting, and sick to death of Quinnekevah Station—she closed her eyes against surrounding sights and promptly fell asleep, sitting there upright on the hard wooden bench.

A hum of voices and a stir of movement woke her. Luzelle

opened her eyes. Her head was resting against Mesq'r Zavune's shoulder. He was asleep, his cheek pressing her hair. She drew back, and the disengagement awakened him. All around them people were rising from the benches and moving toward the departure gate. Evidently the train had arrived. Her eyes sought the clock. She blinked. The time was 2:11 A.M. Disgraceful.

Stifling a yawn, she stood. Zavune did likewise. She scanned the room, and was instantly wide awake. For there, not forty feet distant, dark-bearded head towering above the crowd, Bav Tchornoi was pushing aggressively for the exit. He must have entered the station while she slept. Her eyes wandered on almost unwillingly, to light too soon upon the insistently splendiferous figure of Porb Jil Liskjil, whose jewelry caught and bounced the lamplight. And not only Jil Liskjil. For there was the Strellian physician, Dr. Phineska, one of the Grand Ellipse racers whose chances of victory she had dismissed at the start. And there was that Kyrendtish blueblood, the one with the protruding ears and the stammer—Founne Hay-Frinl. She had not caught sight of Hay-Frinl since Lanthi Ume, and had thought him eliminated from the competition long ago. Yet here he was. The night was full of unwelcome surprises.

Sighing, she picked up her carpetbag and made for the exit. Zavune walked beside her. They went out onto the platform, and there was the train, venting steam, and there were the scores of long-delayed travelers scrambling to climb aboard. The competition was intense, and many ticket holders were actually shoving or elbowing one another.

Wretched manners, thought Luzelle, and quickly remembered to amend, *Different customs, different outlook. Not necessarily inferior, just different.* But it didn't mean she had to like them.

She and Zavune went politely to the end of the amorphous line, there to wait their turn in decent western fashion. They boarded at last, and the source of passenger rivalry revealed itself. The train was full to bursting, and all the seats were taken. Along the aisles they stumbled, encumbered with their luggage, through car after car, and everywhere they went the seats were occupied, sometimes doubly so, with children sleeping across their parents' laps, and cages of live birds wedged in between seated bodies.

As they neared the back of the train, the aisles clogged up with the displaced unfortunates, forced to sit or recline atop their own baggage. A whistle screeched, the train pulled out of Quinnekevah Station, and progress waxed problematic. The third time she tripped over some anonymous recumbent form, Luzelle balked.

"Enough," she said.

"Of—?" Zavune prompted.

"Staggering around. There are no seats left. I'm staying here." She let fall her carpetbag.

"You give up, then?"

"I certainly do. On finding a vacant seat, that is."

"I am still look."

"Good luck, Master Zavune. And thanks for dinner."

"My pleasure, Miss D'vaire. And you good luck also." Suitcase in hand, Zavune lurched off.

She watched until he disappeared from view. Placing her carpetbag between her spine and the wall, she settled back against it with a sigh. Despite the makeshift cushion she felt the vibration of the train through every bone. The floor she sat on was filthy; fortunately, her Bizaqhi divided skirt was black. The car was dimly lit and quiet save for the luxurious snores of assorted sleepers. They were lucky, she reflected. She could never sleep in such a place. She dozed off quickly, and woke to the sound of the conductor's voice. His words were unintelligible but his meaning was clear, and she handed him her ticket at once. He clipped the pasteboard, gave her a stub, and moved on. She sank back against the carpetbag and let her eyes close. Her thoughts drifted, slowed, and smudged into dreams.

The train wheezed east through the night toward Zuleekistan.

She woke again at dawn. The lamps had burned out. Cool morning light flowed in through the windows. A few passengers were already yawning, stretching, coughing, and cracking their joints. Luzelle was stiff and aching. Her eyes were scratchy-dry, and she was lightly powdered with cinders. She knuckled her eyes, brushed herself off as best she could, and rose. Stumbling three cars forward, she paused briefly to avail herself of a genderless convenience, blessedly unoccupied at such an hour. She finger-combed her ..air, rinsed out her mouth with water from her own canteen, splashed more of the water across her face, then continued on, scrupulously overstepping inert bodies, to work her way toward the front in hope of finding the dining car open for business.

It was. A faint mew of relief escaped her. She wanted strong coffee to burn off the mental mists, and she wanted it at once. A few crescent rolls with fresh butter wouldn't hurt either. She entered to find the car all but deserted. Only two of the tables were occupied, one of them by a pair of familiar figures: Girays and Karsler. Together.

She halted. For a moment she even contemplated retreat, but then Girays spotted her there in the doorway, and the opportunity was gone. He looked her up and down, taking in her disheveled curls and Bizaqhi costume, and his lips quirked infinitesimally. Then Karsler glanced back over his shoulder—she had almost forgotten how blue his eyes were—and smiled at her. Her sense of awkwardness subsided a little. No choice now but to join them, but at least she would find out how the younger Stornzof had lost the lead procured by the intervention of his ice-statue uncle, who was presently . . . where? Returning the smile, she went straight to their table, exchanged greetings, and seated herself. A waiter approached and poured her a cup of coffee. The distraction was welcome, for she found herself oddly at a loss for words.

"Does anyone know why the train was so late?" was all she could think of to say.

"Bizaqhi version of normality, I suspect," returned Girays.

"Whatever the reason, v'Alisante and I are fortunate in the delay," observed Karsler. "Had the train run on schedule, we should not have reached the station in time to catch it."

"We might have found another two-seater," Girays suggested.

We? wondered Luzelle.

"Ah, you jest, and yet you must concede—the two-seater was not so bad as the rotting barge on the River Arune," Karsler replied.

"What will it take to convince you that stink didn't come from the barge, it came from the mules?"

"I believe you are in error. Your view is not unbiased. You developed a pronounced antipathy toward the mules after you were bitten."

"No, I'd developed it before I was bitten, but that alters nothing. My nose was keen enough, you must admit, to scent out the swindling ticket agent in Yellow Noki."

"Your perspicacity was commendable, but I do not think your olfactory sense was involved."

"I was speaking figuratively."

"I see. Shall I regard your comments concerning mules as similarly figurative?"

"Literal as a laundry list."

They seemed quite in tune, practically—chummy, Luzelle thought, and found the notion displeasing. She could hardly have said why. Her lips were compressed, and she conscientiously stretched them into a smile. Letting her eyes dwell on the robust scenery rolling by outside the window, she took a sip of coffee and remarked, "This is so very pleasant."

TAKE ME WITH YOU, Masterfire begged.

"Not this time, my beauty," Nevenskoi replied aloud. "You haven't been summoned."

Pleasepleasepleasepleasepleasepleaseplease!

"Not today. You wouldn't enjoy it anyway. I go to attend His Majesty, and you don't relish his society."

Want OUT, out NOW, more SPACE, bigger PLACE! Out-outout! PLEASEpleaseplease!

"I don't really think—"

PLEASEPLEASEPLEASE! Masterfire leapt frantically up and down.

"Oh, all right," Nevenskoi surrendered.

AAAhhh—I am big, I am huge, I am vast—

"No. You may come with me, but only on one condition," Nevenskoi decreed. "You are small, no more than a tiny spark hiding in my pocket. No one may know you are there."

Nononono. I am bigbigbig!

"You are smallsmallsmall. Else you do not leave this workroom today. The choice is yours."

I am small. So saying, Masterfire dwindled, shrinking within seconds to the dimension dictated by his creator. Hopping flealike from the pit-of-elements, the bright spark hurried across the floor to Nevenskoi's foot, jumped to the hem of the adept's sweeping robe, thence ascending to the breast pocket, into which Masterfire vanished smokelessly.

"You are well?" asked Nevenskoi.

I am excellent, I am wonderful, I am Masterfire. Let us go now into bigger space.

"Remember to stay out of sight."

Fervent telepathic confirmation.

Exiting the workroom, Nevenskoi made his practiced way along the subterranean corridor, up the secret staircase, through the storage closet and utility room, along the polished corridor to the king's own apartment, past the sentries and through the blue damask antechamber into the private study.

Miltzin IX, attired in a splendid dressing gown of midnight-blue silk embroidered with golden constellations, sat at the desk whose surface had not long ago supported the model of a futuristic city. The model was gone now, its place usurped by maps, charts, and intricate diagrams. Amid the parchment scrolls sat a platter containing the remains of His Majesty's lunch; pigeons stuffed with plums stuffed with truffled pâté, Nevenskoi's eyes registered; potato-beet-turnip triple-helixes, butterflied greens, red-cream ramekins, a bottle of Grand Zorlhov '39. His stomach stirred at the sight.

Hungry, came the soundless voice from his breast pocket. *Eateateat.*

Not now, he answered in silence, simultaneously mastering his creation and himself.

The king's curled head was bent over one of the charts, but he glanced up as his favorite human oddity entered.

"Ah, my dear fellow!" exclaimed Miltzin IX. "Come in and look at this. You will be amazed. It is a marvel. *She* is a marvel."

"It? She?" echoed Nevenskoi.

"Her talents are truly remarkable, her natural gifts matched only by her cultivated intellect. Never have I encountered such an extraordinary being. She is my equal, Nevenskoi, I do not blush to own it—she is quite my equal. You will see for yourself when you meet her."

"Majesty, I require no persuasion," Nevenskoi rejoined suavely. "I am the lady's humble servant."

"If you think so now, just wait until you hear her speak!"

"Sire?" Nevenskoi took care to conceal his puzzled impatience. "If you will recall, I have been privileged to enjoy the young lady's discourse upon many a happy occasion."

"What, you knew her in Neraunce, then?"

"Neraunce?"

"Well, that's where she's spent the last two years, although she is of course Strellian by birth. Her history is quite astonishing, you know. You must entreat her to relate the whole of it when you meet."

"The Regarded Madam liGrozorf is Strellian by birth?" Nevenskoi was confused.

"Who?" Miltzin frowned, then his face cleared. "But you imagined I was speaking of little Ibbie liGrozorf?"

"Sire, mindful of your warm friendship with the lady, I naturally assumed—"

"Hah! But what a notion! Oh, not that the liGrozorf isn't a pretty, sweet little creature, really quite dear. But she is only a young girl, scarcely more than a child, and of mediocre intelligence at that. Perhaps my head was turned briefly, but the recent arrival of the Countess Larishka has opened my eyes to higher possibilities."

"Countess Larishka?"

"Indeed. A woman, my friend. Do you appreciate the significance? No green girl, but a *woman*—mature in judgment, sophisticated, fascinating, a citizen of the world. And intellectual, don't you know, outstandingly brilliant, in fact. You cannot imagine the delight I find in conversing with a female quite on my own level. Her learning, Nevenskoi! The depth and breadth of her knowledge would astound you! The acuity of her perceptions, the delicacy of her sensibilities, the scope of her vision! She has taught me what it is to meet a woman upon a higher plane, a mental and spiritual plane, if you will. It is there alone that meaningful union is possible. It exists solely in the marriage of true minds. Pretty faces and supple bodies are nothing. It's only the mind that matters, my friend—the mind is everything!"

"Quite."

"*Her* mind is like a great and glorious banquet—"

Nevenskoi's eyes jumped involuntarily to the platter on the desk. One of the pigeons remained untouched, its skin gorgeously golden. He swallowed.

Eateateateateateat—

"Its bounty never exhausted or depleted," Miltzin concluded. "Already her wisdom has nourished me, and I hope to see your own understanding similarly enriched."

"Enriched? Sire?" Nevenskoi channeled his attention.

"Here. Look at this." Miltzin's forefinger tapped one of the charts on the desk. "Feast your eyes. You have never beheld the like."

Nevenskoi advanced a couple of paces to examine the designated parchment. He saw interlocking circles, dotted lines describing complex arches, signs, symbols, constellations, projected planetary paths, intersections and vortices, divisions and conjunctions.

"It is an astrological propheticus," he said.

"It is the past, present, and future, set forth in terms clear and comprehensible to the educated eye. This is a scientific fact that has been scientifically proved. It is all here, Nevenskoi! Everything we could ever need to know, all secrets of the universe revealed to those who read the language of the stars! The Countess Larishka has cast this propheticus with her own hand. Magnificent, is it not?"

"Most impressive, Sire."

"Words are inadequate. She has created this, it is the product of that superb mind. She is going to teach me to read the charts. Only imagine!"

"Very fine, Majesty."

"Oh, Nevenskoi, when I think of the years I've squandered, I could weep. When I consider the wasted endeavors, the misguided efforts—and all the time the truth was plain before me, had I but lifted my eyes to the stars! But now I know, thanks to her, and it is not too late to change direction. Nor is it too late for you, my friend, for I mean to share the new treasures, they are meant for all! Come, look here, right here at this stellar vortex—" Miltzin's plump finger jabbed a diagram.

"I see it, Sire." Nevenskoi suppressed a sigh.

"It is only now achieving existence, and its significance is—" The king broke off with a gasp. His hands clenched, and he doubled, then dropped to his knees. A soprano squeal tore from him.

"Majesty, what is it?" cried Nevenskoi.

Miltzin IX toppled to the carpeted floor, where he lay writhing. His knees were drawn up, both arms locked around his middle, face violently contorted.

For a moment Nevenskoi stood staring, then ran to the bellpull and yanked it.

"I've summoned assistance, Sire." He was not certain that the other heard him. Kneeling at his monarch's side, he promised, "Help is on the way."

A sweating royal hand shot out to grasp the adept's wrist.

"Magic," whispered the agonized king. A spasm shook him. "Help me, man. Your magic."

His particular species of magic had nothing whatever to do with healing. He was utterly unqualified to deal with the king's dyspepsia, or indeed with bodily ills of any sort but one. He had a recipe for a poultice handed down from Grandmother Neeper, known to relieve the itch of certain genital rashes, and that was the full extent of his medical expertise, but there was no point in disillusioning his patron.

"Tut, Sire." Nevenskoi attempted an easy smile. "A touch of indigestion—"

"Poison," gasped the king.

"Impossible." But was it really? A glance down into the stricken man's greenish countenance failed to reassure him. Miltzin IX's lips were lightly coated with bile-colored froth.

His facial muscles were twitching, and his limbs were jerking. He did look as if he might have been poisoned; in fact, he looked moribund. And if he should actually die? The dire prospect flashed across Nevenskoi's imagination. His royal patron, protector, and supporter gone. An unsympathetic successor to the throne; expulsion from the Waterwitch Palace, loss of position, prestige, stipend, loss of his incomparable workroom . . . disaster.

"Majesty!" exclaimed Nevenskoi. "You must live!"

Miltzin IX turned his head away and vomited. His ejecta were streaked with blood.

Where were the servants?

"Help!" The former Nitz Neeper screamed at the top of his lungs.

What? What? asked Masterfire.

Trouble, Nevenskoi responded in his thoughts.

I will eat all trouble, eat.

You cannot.

I can eat anything. Let me show you. Badmeat gone, trouble gone. Let me.

Let him. Nevenskoi wavered, tempted. Trouble gone. Eateateat. A good solution.

A discreet tap intruded upon his inner debate.

"Come!" he shouted.

The study door opened. A deferential head poked in.

"Fetch a physician! Quickly!" Nevenskoi commanded, and the head withdrew.

Alone again with the suffering king, and now Mad Miltzin was convulsing, blood-flecked foam spraying from his mouth and nose.

Nitz Neeper, alias Nevenskoi, hadn't the slightest idea what to do. All his years of arcane research had never prepared him for this. Patting the king's icy hand, he murmured soothing homilies.

The door opened again. The king's personal physician, the omniscient Dr. Arnheltz, entered in haste, attended by a trio of lackeys. Waving Nevenskoi aside, Arnheltz knelt beside his master, performed a lightning examination that included a scrutiny of the sick man's vomit, then snapped his fingers.

One of the lackeys instantly proffered a leather medical bag, from which the doctor extracted a glass-stoppered bottle, whose contents he poured down Miltzin's throat.

The king gagged and vomited extravagantly; rested a moment, vomited again, and lay panting.

Withdrawing two new bottles from his bag, Arnheltz frowningly measured their contents into a small graduate cylinder, stirred the mixture, and lifted his patient's head. Miltzin whimpered and grimaced. Not troubling to argue, the doctor firmly pinched the other's nostrils, and the royal mouth opened. Arnheltz administered his potion, and Miltzin groaned deeply. His muscles relaxed, his eyes closed, and he lay still.

Rising to his feet, Dr. Arnheltz gestured in regal silence. Miltzin IX was placed upon a stretcher and borne from the study by two lackeys. The physician scanned the chamber, and his eye lighted upon the remnants of the king's most recent meal. He snapped his fingers, and the remaining servant appropriated the platter. Physician and servant made for the exit.

"Wait." Nevenskoi intercepted the retreating pair. "How would you describe His Majesty's condition?"

"No time now." Arnheltz's pace did not slacken.

"Will he recover?"

"If properly treated."

"Was he poisoned?"

"Quite thoroughly."

"Was it—"

"A report will be issued."

Physician and lackey departed, and the door closed behind them. Nevenskoi stood bewildered.

What? What? What? A tongue of Masterfire's substance snaked inquiringly from the adept's breast pocket.

"Someone has tried to murder the king, my lovely," Nevenskoi explained. "Kill him with poison."

What is poison?

"A substance that is harmful. Think of somebody feeding you large quantities of water."

Badbadbadbadbadbadbadbadbadbadbadbadbad!

"Exactly. Well, that's more or less what somebody has tried to do to His Majesty. The king has been saved, though. Because of me," Nevenskoi realized. "Because *I* was present, and I had presence of mind to summon help, he received the prompt treatment that preserved his life. I have saved him, sweet one. I am not quite a hero, perhaps, but surely deserving of gratitude. Although," he recalled, "that physician person seemed hardly to think so. He was brusque to the point of discourtesy, was he not?"

Physician person badness?

"He was probably preoccupied. He meant no offense, it was nothing personal, unless"—a terrible thought surfaced—"unless he had some idea that I might be responsible for the attempt upon King Miltzin's life. Unless that curtness I took for impatience in fact revealed hostile suspicion. But no. Impossible. His Majesty Miltzin has honored me with every mark of favor. Who could think that I would plot against so generous a patron? Who could doubt the loyalty of Nevenskoi?"

Nitz. Nitz. NitzNeeperNitzNeeperNitzNeeperNitzNeeper—

"Please stop that. But I do see what you mean," the adept confessed. "In respect of my identity, I have misrepresented myself. I have been less than truthful about my name, and thus my honesty in general is compromised, or so they will claim. But it isn't true, it isn't fair! The question of my name is a separate issue, unrelated to any other, it is *absolutely immaterial*—!"

Badness? Masterfire inquired.

"Nobody could know, anyway," Nevenskoi insisted. "There's no way that anybody could possibly know, or even begin to guess."

The thunderbolt of pain transfixing his belly shattered his precarious equanimity. Nevenskoi clutched himself, and the sweat started out on his brow.

Whatwhatwhat? Masterfire demanded.

"I'm poisoned!" The reply burst from him, but even as he spoke, he recognized the improbability. He had touched none of the king's meal, he had no enemies, there was nothing amiss with him beyond the usual nervous inner turmoil, and there was no reason to fear—

"No reason at all," he muttered. He forced himself to take a deep breath. And another. His insides gradually calmed themselves. His thoughts did likewise. The king would recover. The real culprit would be discovered. And no unjust suspicion would fall upon Nitz Neeper.

ALL THREE PREDICTIONS proved accurate. King Miltzin remained bedridden for the next seven days, during which time reports of his progress were issued at regular intervals. At the end of the week the king was pronounced well, and that evening saw him at the gaming tables, pale and visibly thinner, but jovial, neatly curled, and plentifully pomaded.

Throughout the term of the king's convalescence the appointed investigators labored, and their efforts yielded qualified success. Experimentation with the remains of Miltzin's lunch proved fatal to a couple of luckless dogs, both of which died foamingly following ingestion of the pâté-stuffed plums that filled the untouched pigeon. Identification of the poisonous source led detectives to the Waterwitch kitchens, whose staff endured prolonged interrogation. The king's personal chef, entrusted with the planning and preparation of His Majesty's daily meals, had not personally overseen the preparation of the plums. That task had fallen to a recently hired sous-chef possessed of awesome credentials.

Forged, as it happened. The dispatch of two lightning messengers quickly confirmed the falsity of the sous-chef's references, but already it was too late to act upon the new information. A descent upon the closet shared by the suspect and two other sous-chefs discovered the bird already flown. He had departed under cover of darkness and the chance to wring the truth from him was gone, but a questioning of the roommates limned the portrait of a solitary young man, filled with angry sympathy for the inoffensive folk of Rhazaulle threatened by the Grewzian invasion, and resolved to aid the innocent at any cost.

The ulor's agents knew how to use such a tool. Those aware of Masterfire's existence recognized the potential consequence of Miltzin IX's removal in favor of a successor less inflexibly neutral, and perhaps more willing to sell the secret of Sentient Fire to beleaguered Rhazaulle.

The erring sous-chef was promptly replaced by a staid Hetzian bourgeois of sterling character, a peerless artist in appetizers, and life resumed its accustomed course in the Waterwitch kitchens.

King Miltzin IX seemed remarkably undismayed by his brush with death, for he had now learned how to protect himself. The astrological propheticus cast by the Countess Larishka contained clear warning of every future danger destined to assail him. It was all there, embedded in the signs and symbols. Forewarned was forearmed, and disaster easily avoided by the astrologically literate.

12

"LOOK. LOOK OVER THERE." Luzelle pointed. Far to the south the glint of sun on seawater was discernible.

"The Bay of Zif," Girays informed her unnecessarily.

"I know that," she snapped. His brows rose at her tone, but she hardly cared, for irritability helped to mask sickening apprehension. Better that he take her for a shrew than a miserable little coward, scared to death of flying. "I'm not exactly unfamiliar with the local geography, you know. I *have* visited the Bhomiri Islands."

"Cannibalistic natives, I've heard." He smiled annoyingly. "Anyone try to stick you in a pot?"

"They were more inclined to stick me in a hut. Their chief offered to accept me on a trial basis as junior wife number thirteen."

"Really. I suppose you told him that he'd have to allow you freedom to fly the hut for six-month excursions, from time to time."

"He probably wouldn't have objected. He was a lot more liberal minded and tolerant than certain supposedly civilized westerners I could name."

"Ah, the perfect man for you."

The incursion of another voice spared her the necessity of caustic reply.

"We are losing altitude," observed Karsler Stornzof.

Luzelle's eyes shifted to Karsler's face for a surprised instant, then dropped to the ground below, not very far below, not far enough, and drawing closer by the second. The jagged, snow-capped peaks of the Ohnyi Heznyi, the Ramparts of Forever—or, as western cartographers had it, the Lesser Crescent Range—were wheeling toward her at terrible speed. But even now there was no sense of movement; even now, the balloon and its passengers seemed suspended, weightless and motionless, above a revolving array of ice-clad granite fangs.

We're going to crash; we're going to die. Fear choked her, and her hands clamped on the edge of the basket. Her gaze anchored on the spinning rocks, and she did not want to look, but seemed somehow powerless to turn away or to shut her eyes. She was cold, dreadfully cold despite the layers of clothing and the extra blanket in which she had wrapped herself to ward off the bitter chill of the upper air; despite even the proximity of the fire that heated the atmosphere filling the great, gaily colored envelope of waterproofed linen. Curious that she could think of nothing more important at such a moment, but she was cold to the core.

"There is no cause for alarm, I think," said Karsler.

His voice cracked the spell, and she was able to turn her head and look up at him, but still she could not speak. He smiled almost imperceptibly at her, more a smile of the eyes than the lips, but his look was so reassuring, so serenely certain, that her terror subsided and she found her voice.

"I'm not afraid," she said, and the lie was suddenly the truth, because of him.

He reached out as if unconsciously to press her hand briefly, and his own hand was warm enough to set the vital currents pulsing through her again.

His hand withdrew too soon. She tore her eyes from his face, and saw Girays v'Alisante expostulating with their pilot, the Traveler Meemo Echmeemi, owner-operator of The Traveler Echmeemi's Astonishing Flights, whose task it was to carry the three racers east out of Zuleekistan, over the Ramparts of Forever and down into the North Ygahro Territory, next designated stop along the Grand Ellipse. Girays was speaking emphatically, but she did not really note his words, and probably neither did the pilot, for the Traveler Ech-meemi's Vonahrish was rudimentary at best. A blindingly white smile split the balloonist's bearded brown face. He shrugged, responded in blithely unintelligible Zuleeki dialect, and tossed a couple of sandbags out of the basket.

Instantly the teeth of Ohnyi Heznyi receded. The view altered, and the broad yellow-brown plain lying southeast of the mountains swung into sight.

She was not about to die quite yet. Her breathing eased by degrees. And only to think, she had imagined this aerial hop over the Lesser Crescent Range a splendid shortcut, likely to place her hours or days ahead of rival racers electing to sail east from Zuleekistan across the Bay of Zif. The discovery among her few surviving maps and timetables of a brief reference to the independent commercial balloonists of eastern Zuleekistan, an area swept in springtime by consistently northwesterly winds, had caught her interest and fired her hopes of finally taking the lead over all competitors other than the Festinettes. (And where in the world were the twins?) Of course she had meant to keep the scheme to herself, and would have managed it, had she not committed the error of questioning that Vonahrish-speaking native guide at the Navoyza Pass. The guide must have reported the conversation back to Girays, Karsler had presumably overheard, and after that all hope of aeronautical exclusivity died. The two of them, as taken with the idea as she, had insisted on accompanying her to Echmeemi's and she had been unable to elude them, despite considerable effort. She supposed she ought to be glad that Tchornoi, Jil Liskjil, Zavune, and the others had not caught wind of the plan as well, but gratitude was hard to muster in the face of cosmic injustice. It was so unfair—the balloon idea had been hers.

Strange to find herself so glad of their company now, Luzelle reflected. She had not anticipated her own fear of hitherto unimaginable heights. She simply had not expected the icy qualms, the cold sweats, the inner tremors. Had she traveled alone, she would have fled at first sight of the vast crimson-and-yellow inflated sack looming above the mountain shack that housed The Traveler Echmeemi's Astonishing Flights. Fortunately for her hope of future victory, shame had triumphed over terror, and in the presence of two male observers she had suppressed all outward manifestations of alarm, or at least she had tried. She had forced herself to climb into the rickety, pitifully flimsy excuse for a basket. She had endured the ghastly swift ascent, she had suppressed all shrieks, squeaks, and gasps, she had controlled her inclination to vomit, she had even contrived to engage in conversation of sorts. In short, she had carried on as a reasonable, competent adult.

Girays had been taken in. He might view her as short tempered and sharp tongued, but probably did not recognize the underlying incipient panic. Karsler Stornzof was another matter, however. Perhaps his observation of soldiers on the eve of battle had heightened his perceptions. Whatever the reason, she knew beyond question that he saw her weakness, but neither pitied nor despised it.

Yes, all things considered, she was very happy to have them with her. And she would leave them both behind at the very first opportunity.

The hours passed, the mountains spun by, and her fears subsided. Her belly gradually unclenched itself, and around noon, when the Traveler Echmeemi opened up his sack of provisions, she was able to lunch on bread, goat cheese, and rough red wine without ill effect. Presently she even found herself awakening to the wonders of the scenery below. The Lesser Crescents deserved attention, for they were spectacular, with their glassy ice caps flashing in the sun, their chiseled crags, their knife-edged gorges and ravines filled with violet shadow. The air at these altitudes was clear as it was cold, and every detail of the landscape retained a sharpness that permitted the eye no rest. Luzelle found herself blinking, half dazzled by the sunlight glancing off the icy peaks, but reluctant to look away for fear of missing some marvel. Her persistence was rewarded when she glimpsed a soaring, pure white, broad-winged form that she recognized as a snow eagle.

She was almost tranquil by the time the Lesser Crescents had dwindled to rugged foothills sparsely studded with villages and lush with high pastures roamed by curly-horned goats pied red and black.

The foothills gave way to the wide expanse known as the Phreta'ah that rolled in featureless yellow-brown waves between the Ramparts of Forever and the Forests of Oorex.

But the Phreta'ah was not truly featureless. An aerial view revealed the plenitude of streams and rivulets rushing down from the mountains and across the wide grasslands, converging south of the Lesser Crescent Range to form the headwaters of the immense River Ygah that flowed thirty-five hundred miles south to the Nether Ocean. The river, fed by countless tributaries, widened as it went, curving its leisurely way through a vast depression shaped like a shallow salad bowl filled with greenery—the legendary Forests of Oorex, largely unexplored and untamed to this very day. She could just make out the great smudge of dark green in the far distance. With any luck the winds would bear them toward it.

For some hours the winds obliged. Endless yellow-brown billows rolled by below, their monotony relieved only by the glint of sun on silvery running water, the narrow dark ribbon of a dirt road, the occasional rounded protuberance of a thatch-roofed roadside prayer-hut. Once Luzelle spotted a cart drawn by oxen trudging toward the Ohnyi Heznyi, and the air was still so limpid that she could make out the details of the driver's costume—loose white tunic, green neckerchief, broad hat. His face was upturned to the sky, and as the balloon passed over, he stood up in the cart, waving both arms with abandon. Luzelle returned the salute, but already the cart, oxen, and driver were behind her and receding.

The balloon sailed on, and the Forests of Oorex expanded greenly before it, while the undulations of the Phreta'ah below changed character at last, the long yellow-brown waves darkening with new and richer vegetation watered by the burgeoning River Ygah.

The river was an assertive presence now, its great serpent length winding on forever, its shadowy mane of forest dominating the landscape. At the edge of the jungle, at a wide and tranquil bend in the river, rose the town of Xoxo, capital of the North Ygahro Territory and next stop along the Grand Ellipse.

Luzelle could make out low buildings of brown brick with brown tile roofs, wooden leaf-thatched houses built on piles, and crooked unpaved streets. Not an impressive sight. Of greater interest were the sizable ships of modern design moored at the Xoxo wharfs. Grewzian, she realized. That infamous Grewzian advance upon Jumo had launched itself from the North Ygahro Territory.

Involuntarily she glanced over at Karsler. He was studying the scene and his profile told her nothing, but the strong light emphasized the contrast between the red mark on his forehead and the surrounding fair skin; that mark a souvenir, he had explained without visible concern, of an encounter with a group of citizens in Aeshno. The mental image of an enraged Aennorvi mob stoning this man to death in the streets made her shudder, and for a moment she felt the cold again as she hadn't in hours. Girays v'Alisante's intervention upon that occasion had at the very least spared him serious injury and quite probably saved his life, Karsler had also informed her; a detail that Girays himself had neglected to mention.

Her regard shifted to her countryman. The unforgiving sunlight picked out the threads of grey at his temples, and the faint lines etching the skin around his eyes. He looked dark and small beside the Grewzian overcommander, but who wouldn't?

Xoxo was drawing closer by the moment. The Traveler Echmeemi twitched the valve line, releasing heated atmosphere, and the ground appeared to rise. Now Luzelle could distinguish the wagons in the narrow dirt streets, the native pedestrians in their outsized hats, the wandering dogs, and the numerous grey figures recognizable as Grewzian soldiers.

Back in the Imperium, again. Her gorge rose.

Perhaps before long the Imperium would be everywhere.

The wind veered and the town of Xoxo wheeled westward. At once the Traveler Echmeemi plied the valve line, and the balloon descended swiftly, too swiftly. It seemed to be dropping freely out of the sky, and all of Luzelle's fears reawakened. Her stomach lurched. One hand flew to her mouth to contain a scream.

The Traveler Echmeemi was not dismayed. Nonchalantly

he loosed one of the sandbags dangling from the rail of the basket, and the precipitous descent slowed. Another bag went and the balloon sank smoothly, struck the ground without violence, bounced and struck again, scraped along for several yards, then came to rest. The Traveler Echmeemi pulled wide the rip panel, and the great linen envelope began to deflate. The passengers debarked.

They stood ankle deep in vigorous coarse grass cropped by fat dekwoaties, the potbellied striped ruminant of the region. A skinny little Ygahri boy clad in a large hat and nothing else sat watching the animals. A few hundred yards behind him squatted a low farmhouse with awnings of woven grasses. As the balloon came down, the dekwoaties scattered, while the native boy leapt to his feet and fled shrieking for the house.

"He think he see evil spirit," the Traveler Echmeemi explained, and roared with laughter.

It was midafternoon, and the shadows were pointing the way east toward Xoxo. The town, some five or six miles distant, squatted mud-brown and drab before the intense green backdrop of the jungle. A haze of smoke and heat hovered above the rooftops. The air was very warm, Luzelle noticed for the first time; humid, heavy, and uncomfortable. Already her forehead was moist with sweat. At once she rid herself of the blanket, but remained too heavily wrapped in multiple Bizaqhi layers.

"Xoxo." The Traveler Echmeemi extended a triumphant finger, then proceeded to explain in his execrable Vonahrish that the respectable Ygahro businessman Grh'fixi, his brother-in-soul, a most excellent fellow with whom he shared a pleasant and mutually convenient little arrangement, would soon arrive in a splendid buffalo-drawn cart equipped to bear passengers in reasonably priced luxury all the way to Xoxo. And if by chance the admirable Grh'fixi should fail to appear before sunset, then the nearby farmhouse would doubtless offer comfortable overnight shelter.

Luzelle studied the landscape and reported, "I see no cart. No buffaloes, either."

"It come, it come," the Traveler Echmeemi insisted.

"When?"

"Soon."

"How soon?"

"Maybe half hour. Two, three hour, no more. Grh'fixi come before dark, for sure. Or tomorrow morning early, this is certain. You wait here."

"I do not wait here. I haven't the time."

"What, then?" The Traveler Echmeémi permitted himself an indulgent smile. "You walk whole way Xoxo?"

"That's right."

"No. Too dirty. Dekwoati crap all over. And big hairy spiders. They eat you."

"I don't care about the dirt, and I'm not afraid of spiders."

"Scorpions too. Poison."

"I don't believe that."

The Traveler Echmeemi turned to the men and appealed, "You tell your woman she must wait for Grh'fixi."

"She won't obey," Girays explained, straight-faced. "The jade's ill trained."

"Then you should beat her."

"You are probably right, my friend."

Venting a disgusted snort, Luzelle snatched up her carpetbag and marched off across the fields. Loud Zuleeki remonstration erupted in her wake, but she did not trouble to turn her head. On she went and soon heard the thud of quick footsteps behind her, but still did not deign to look back. A moment later they caught up with her.

"It is not a place for you to walk unaccompanied," observed Karsler.

"Nor would I wish to allow a rival Ellipsoid to leave me behind," Girays declared.

"You'd better prepare yourself; it's only a matter of time," she warned Girays tartly, then turned to offer Karsler a warm smile. She would never have confessed to either of them, particularly not to Girays, how relieved she was that they had not allowed her to face the terrors of spiders, scorpions, and dekwoati droppings all alone.

For the next two hours or more they hiked across fields heavily blanketed with coarse, damp, yellow-green grasses that sometimes grew waist high. Most of the time Karsler led

the way, the passage of his tall form forcing a path for his followers through the vegetation. Luzelle perceived that she
could not have managed on her own, at least not without sacrifice of the carpetbag. Even as it was, the burden dragged on
her arm, its weight increasing with every hard-won quarter
mile. The humid air pressed with a weight all its own, and the
sweat was streaming down her face. Clouds of gnats hovered
about her head, and slapping at them simply wasted energy.

From time to time they came upon wide, clear expanses
where the grazing dekwoaties had cropped the grass down to
the ground, and there the droppings were all that the Traveler
Echmeemi had promised, and more. Ripe yellow mounds
alive with flies clustered underfoot, and there was no avoiding
them. Luzelle's feet sank deep with every step. A stench filled
the air, and she gagged on it. Pinching her nostrils between
two fingers, she breathed through her mouth and her nausea
receded. Her shoes would have to be discarded, after this. The
wide legs of her divided skirt were plastered with filth, but the
gauzy fabric would wash well and dry quickly. She pictured
herself attempting such a trek in conventional western garb—
voluminous long skirts, petticoats, whalebone stays, and all
the rest—and smiled at the ludicrous image.

She saw no scorpions, but several times spied saucer-sized
plots of short, yellow-green grass that seemed indefinably
anomalous, and once she thought that one of them moved. A
trick of the light, she supposed, but closer inspection revealed
the presence of a gigantic spider soft with yellow-green fur.
Big hairy spiders, just as the Traveler Echmeemi had promised; but none of them tried to eat her.

At the end of a strenuous and sweaty span, they stumbled
forth from the high grasses to find themselves at the side of
the rutted dirt road that carried on into the town of Xoxo,
now some three miles distant and imperfectly visible through
the trees that grew along the river. Here they rested for a while
upon a flat rock free of droppings, but slimy with green mold
or moss of some sort. The vegetation flourished everywhere;
eager weeds thrust up in the middle of the road, algae coated
the puddles filling ruts worn by wagon wheels, and the
wooden ruins of a public prayer-hut were smothered in white

fungi. There was something distasteful in such immoderate vitality; something almost threatening.

They could not afford to linger there, were they to reach Xoxo before dark. It was late afternoon, and the sun was well past its zenith. The trek resumed and soon they were slogging along a roadway deep in mud and droppings. Luzelle's filthy wet skirts slapped at her ankles with every step. She was soaked in sweat, the gnats were everywhere, and the carpetbag was heavy as an anvil. Both Girays and Karsler had volunteered more than once to carry the bag for her, and it had taken all the willpower she possessed to decline such offers. Decline them she had, however; pride no less than a simple sense of justice demanded as much.

Perhaps she should have waited for Grh'fixi.

But no. She thought of the Festinette twins, somewhere up ahead along the Grand Ellipse. She thought of Jil Liskjil, Tchornoi, Zavune, Phineska, Hay-Frinl, and the others, so determined and resourceful, so close upon her heels. No, she couldn't possibly have waited.

The sun, now startlingly red, was stooping to the horizon by the time they reached Xoxo. An unappetizing place, Luzelle decided at once, with its dreary mud-colored buildings, its narrow streets that served as public sewers, its wandering packs of gaunt stray dogs, its rat-riddled refuse heaps, its stink of rancid oil and ordure, its unsmiling copper-faced citizens, and its large population of Grewzian soldiers. The spruce grey figures were much in evidence, knots of them loitering about the new watch-stations marked with the symbol of the Endless Fire, bands of them striding the streets with an air of ownership. Where the Grewzians walked, the native Ygahris gave way with a kind of whipped servility that was sickening to behold. Luzelle boiled inwardly, but dared no criticism.

Welcome to the Imperium, she thought.

Had she found herself alone, with the recollection of the attack in Glozh still fresh in her mind, she would have been afraid. But now she walked beside a Grewzian officer whose uniform and insignia, travel stained though they were, garnered instant respect that extended to his companions. Karsler Stornzof's compatriots saluted smartly as he passed, and there were several courteous inclinations of the head in Luzelle's direction. Some of the grey soldiers, she fancied, recognized the celebrated overcommander by sight and wanted to say so, but Grewzian military discipline precluded such familiarity. Karsler himself only once availed himself of his officer's privilege of initiating conversation, and that was to ask the way to the city hall.

An impeccably blond undercommander furnished directions, and the three of them walked on along crooked malodorous lanes now sinking into humid twilight. As the light waned, the gnats retired and the mosquitoes emerged in force. A high-pitched humming filled the air, and the blood feast began. Luzelle slapped, batted, and flapped her free arm in vain. Her Bizaqhi garments covered her body and limbs, and one of the long sashes draped across the lower portion of her face furnished additional protection. But her hands were bare, and within minutes they were spotted with itchy red lumps. Uncomfortable and annoying, but nothing to worry about. There were certain modern scientific cranks who actually imagined the obnoxious little insects responsible for the transmission of deadly diseases, but Luzelle's common sense rejected such farfetched notions.

The dim avenue terminated at the verge of a paved plaza, large and imposing by local standards, edged with lanterns just now being lit for the evening. The buildings here were the largest Luzelle had seen so far in Xoxo, graceless constructions of the native drab brick perched above flood level upon massive stone supports, and incongruously adorned with whitewashed wooden columns of classical design.

They had reached Xoxo's western enclave, site of the administrative offices employed by successive contingents of the North Ygahro Territory's colonial overlords. Here rose the city hall, the archives, the governor's residence, the countinghouse, the offices, and an assortment of private dwellings occupied by western-born officials, lower-level bureaucrats, their families, pets, and servants. A variety of flags had flown above these buildings. At the moment the flags were Grewzian.

Luzelle scarcely noticed the architecture. Her attention fastened on a makeshift wooden platform set up in the middle of the square and she gasped, then whispered without thought, "Oh, what is that?"

A superfluous question, really; the spectacle was self-explanatory. The platform bore an apparatus reminiscent of an old-fashioned pillory, with strong upright posts supporting a wide horizontal board furnished with apertures that confined the necks and wrists of four prisoners. The victims were Ygahri natives, male, naked save for abbreviated loincloths. All four were small, thin, bowlegged, and black haired, their elaborately coiled braids threaded with beads and rings. Their faces and bodies were either painted or tattooed with intricate swirling designs in blue and green punctuated with symmetrical raised scars, but the ornamentation did not disguise the bruises, welts, and bloody cuts marking the coppery flesh. The partially dried blood attracted a host of voracious insects. Clouds of winged forms hovered about the immobilized bodies; multilegged legions crawled freely over and into the exposed wounds. The buzzing and humming were audible throughout the square. The stooped, cramped posture imposed by the pillory must have been almost as torturous in itself as the combined miseries of a recent beating, insects, and thirst. But no sign of perturbation touched the faces of the four prisoners, whose stoicism was well illumined by the lanterns placed about the platform. Clearly the spectacle of punishment was meant to edify the public.

This is something out of another century, thought Luzelle.

A patrol of Grewzian soldiers was passing. Karsler halted the men with a word, jerked a nod at the platform, and demanded, "What is the meaning of this?"

The patrol's leader, a pug-nosed sergeant, answered, "Discipline of refractory natives, sir."

"Upon whose authority?"

"Standing orders of the Undergeneral Ermendtrof, sir."

"The Undergeneral Ermendtrof sanctions this particular form of punishment?"

"Yes, sir. As indicated, sir."

"And in this case?"

"Very much indicated, sir."

"Explain."

"Sir, those four natives there aren't townsmen. You can see by the scars and tattoos that they're jungle scum of the Nine Blessed Tribes. In fact, they're elders of the Aocreotalexi tribe. These forest savages are always troublesome. Disobedient. Underhanded. They're not civilized, sir, and they have no idea how to behave. They're more like apes than men, and a good whipping is the only kind of language they understand."

"What was their offense?" Karsler inquired expressionlessly.

"They were insolent, sir."

"Specify."

"They accosted the Undergeneral Ermendtrof himself in the street, blocked his way, and stood there yapping complaints. Something about the men of the Forty-seventh Squadron digging latrines into some old native burial ground near the edge of the forest. Wanted the latrines relocated, and the profaned site ritually purified. As if a good Grewzian contribution wouldn't enrich their ancestors' sorry bones! I say we were doing the apes a favor, but they don't know how to be grateful. When those four troublemakers there were ordered from the undergeneral's path, they wouldn't budge, and that kind of disobedience can't be tolerated. An example was made."

"When are they scheduled for release?"

"Tomorrow afternoon."

"Then see to it that they are given water at regular intervals until that time."

"Sir, the Undergeneral Ermendtrof's orders do not mention—"

"You comprehend my instructions, Sergeant?"

"Yes, Overcommander."

"Dismissed."

The sergeant saluted smartly, and the patrol withdrew. As soon as the soldiers were out of earshot, Luzelle turned on Karsler to demand, "Won't you *do* something?"

"I have done what I could." His somber gaze was fixed on the pilloried natives.

"But why didn't you order those men released?"

"I have not the authority to countermand the orders of the Undergeneral Ermendtrof."

"Hang the Undergeneral Ermendtrof! This is no way to

treat human beings—it's barbaric, it's monstrous. You know that."

"I am a soldier, and my duty as such prohibits insubordination. My personal convictions do not signify."

"How can you say that? A soldier isn't an automaton. He has a mind and a conscience. Can yours allow you to condone this?" Her condemnatory gesture encompassed the platform. "You can do something about it, if you choose."

"What I might choose as an individual is irrelevant. As an officer of the Imperium I recognize the necessities and realities of war."

"The torture of four Ygahri tribesmen who committed the terrible crime of complaining about their graveyard's desecration—that is a necessity? Do you really believe—"

"Luzelle. Leave him alone." Girays finally entered the discussion.

Her eyes widened in surprise. "But—"

"You've overlooked or else you don't know the rigor of Grewzian military discipline. The sort of righteous mutiny that you recommend would probably get Stornzof shot."

"But I never—"

"Before you next presume to judge and demand, perhaps you might take a moment to consider possible consequences," Girays concluded.

Luzelle said nothing. Her face burned.

In comfortless silence the three of them crossed the square to the ugly city hall, with its registrar's office manned by some petty official authorized to stamp their passports. A Grewzian sentry at the front door barred the way.

"Closed for the night," the sentry announced. "Come back tomorrow morning, eight o'clock."

"We require a clerk," Karsler informed his countryman. "It is not late, there will still be a few about. Stand aside."

The sentry straightened smartly. "You'll find someone up on the second floor, Overcommander," he answered with respect. "But I can't admit these civilians, sir."

Unfair, Luzelle thought, not for the first time.

"They are with me," Karsler said.

Perhaps he was reading her mind again. Certainly it seemed that his reluctance to exploit yet another unearned advantage was undermining his will to win. Much as she admired such nobility, she had no intention of emulating it.

"Sorry, sir," the sentry returned. "Orders of the Undergeneral Ermendtrof. No civilians after hours."

"Very well." Turning to his companions/competitors, Karsler spoke with some regret. "It seems that we must part."

"Don't exult too soon, Stornzof," Girays advised with a smile. "We shall probably find ourselves passengers on the same steamboat heading downriver tomorrow morning."

Unless I'm trapped here half the day tomorrow waiting to get my passport stamped, thought Luzelle. *If so, I might not be able to get out of this town until the day after. This may be a disaster. Oh, curse those Grewzians!* Aloud, she remarked with such good grace as she could muster, "Good-bye for now, Karsler. Good luck."

"Good luck to you as well. Until next time, then." Karsler walked into the building, and the door shut behind him.

"Well." Luzelle turned to face Girays. She had not quite forgiven him for the recent, stinging rebuke. "This seems somehow—strange. That he's gone, I mean."

"Yes." Girays looked bemused. "I discover I've grown accustomed to Stornzof's company."

"Evidently. The way you *leaped* to his defense when I ventured to voice an opinion—"

"When you tried to take his head off."

"Well, your loyalty was touching. Really. Touching."

"Oh, I experience a kind of spontaneous fraternal sympathy for all fellow victims of the Devaire verbal stiletto."

"Thank you. Better take care, or you'll end up best friends with a Grewzian."

"I hardly think so. I'll acknowledge Stornzof as less of a boor than the majority of his countrymen—in fact, he's actually quite decent in his own peculiar way—"

"M. the Marquis waxes lyrical."

"But we are rivals, our association was a matter of expediency, and it is finished now."

"You and I are rivals too. What about our association?"

"Good for another few hours, at least," Girays told her. "Long enough to dine together, if you'll join me."

"Gladly." She hadn't meant to say that. She was still angry, she should have turned him down, but the assent had slipped out easily and naturally. "Where shall we go?"

"I don't suppose a place like Xoxo has any restaurants or cafés, but maybe there's a cookshop somewhere. Let's look."

They walked away from the city hall, across the lamplit square, by tacit agreement circling wide of the platform and pillory, but Luzelle could not help glancing at the prisoners as she passed, and she caught too clear a glimpse of oozing wounds, busy insects, and bruised impassive faces. She looked away quickly, but could not banish the picture from her mind. She wondered if Girays was as revolted as she. His face told her little, but he was unusually silent.

They found neither restaurant nor cookshop, but a small western-style travelers' inn stood at the darker and dirtier end of the plaza, and the establishment boasted an old-fashioned common room whose hand-lettered sign promised Vonahrish cuisine. They studied the bill of fare tacked up below the sign, and everything listed was purely Grewzian, with the exception of *potage Ygahroisse*, the Vonahrish version of a native soup incorporating local tubers seasoned with the astringent bark of the native shrink-tree, and enriched with condensed buffalo milk.

The common room contained too many Grewzian soldiers for comfort, but there was nowhere else to go. They seated themselves, and both ordered the soup. Luzelle wanted nothing more; the sight of the battered prisoners exposed to public view had killed her appetite.

The soup arrived, accompanied by a small loaf of dense Grewzian-style bread. Luzelle ate without tasting. Her eyes traveled the dingy common room, encountered nothing agreeable, and returned to her bowl.

"I suppose we can stay here tonight," she said at last. "There must be vacancies."

"No doubt. Xoxo is hardly teeming with travelers. The real question is, what do we do tomorrow once we've had our passports stamped? Have you made any plans?"

"Well, there's not much choice, is there? Steamboat down-river, south through the Forests of Oorex. No other practical means of transportation."

"If we don't make it to the wharves by eight-thirty A.M., we don't get out of town tomorrow."

"Why not?"

"Because that's the only scheduled southbound departure for the day. I've a timetable. See for yourself." He placed a creased paper sheet on the table before her.

She scanned the schedule, saw that he was right, and lost what little was left of her appetite. "We're ruined, Girays! The city hall doesn't open until eight. We can't get our passports stamped there and then reach the wharves by eight-thirty. It's impossible. We're dead!"

"Not necessarily. I think we might manage, provided we plan well."

"Oh, what good will that do? Planning can't slow the clock. Karsler's going to pull ahead, it isn't fair, and there's nothing we can do about it. Oh, confound these Grewzians!"

"Luzelle. Calm yourself. Focus."

"I am perfectly calm!" she exclaimed.

"And watch what you say about Grewzians around here," he advised quietly.

"I don't care if they hear me!" Thinking better of it, she lowered her voice. "Maybe they don't understand Vonahrish, anyway."

"Don't bank on it. Look here." He produced another paper sheet. "It's a map of Xoxo."

"Where in the world did you get that?"

"Some street vendor, somewhere or other. See"—his fore-finger tapped the map—"we're sitting here at the southeast corner of the town square. Tomorrow morning at eight we cross the square to the city hall—"

"Let's get there earlier."

"If you think it will do any good. But when a Grewzian tells you the place opens at eight, he doesn't mean seven fifty-nine. In any case, we'll have our passports stamped as quickly as pos-sible, and then we head for the wharves. The distance between the town square and the waterfront is a little over a mile. There are no cabs available, no carriages for hire, no livery stable—we'll have to walk. Here's the most direct route." Girays's finger traced a line across the street map. "If we hurry, we might cover the distance in about fifteen minutes, reaching the wharves in time to board the"—he consulted the timetable—"the *Water Sprite.*"

"We'd better. Maybe we should hire someone to carry our luggage."

"No time. If the bags slow us down, we'll have to discard them. Are you ready to do that?"

"Certainly, if necessary. I've done it once already, back in Aeshno."

"I had wondered about that new carpetbag. What happened?"

She hesitated. She did not particularly care to confess her experiment in larceny to Girays v'Alisante. She had only done what she needed to do in order to stay in the race. There had really been no choice, she reminded herself, and yet she was ashamed. She should have kept her big mouth shut about it, but now she was obliged to answer him. "I rode horseback from Aeshno to Quinnekevah, and couldn't carry the valise."

"No way of strapping it to the saddle?"

"No time for that."

"Curious. All it would have taken would have been a simple—"

"I was in a hurry."

"I see." He considered. "How did you manage to secure a horse in Aeshno? Neither Stornzof nor I could find one. We were both informed that horses were absolutely unobtainable. Where did you—"

"Oh, really, what does it matter?" She could feel the telltale heat in her cheeks. "I found a way, that's all."

"I see," Girays repeated dryly. "My compliments, Miss Devaire."

He looked as if he could see straight through her, and her discomfort deepened. Guilty conscience, nothing more. M. the Marquis wasn't about to throw her off balance as easily as that, she wouldn't give him the satisfaction. Lifting her chin, she met his eyes squarely, and murmured with apparent nonchalance, "The *Water Sprite,* eh? Let us hope she doesn't live up to her name and disappear on us."

FINISHING THEIR MODEST DINNER, they left the common room and went to the desk, where the concierge entered their names in his ledger, then issued them separate room numbers and keys. Together they climbed to the second story, where they paused briefly at the head of the stairs.

"Seven-forty, front door," Girays enjoined.

"Seven-forty," Luzelle agreed, and they parted. Proceeding alone to her assigned chamber, she let herself in and froze on the threshold, unpleasantly surprised.

The inn—even more antiquated than she had first supposed—still employed the old-fashioned system of communal sleeping quarters. A small oil lamp hanging from the ceiling illumined a sizable dormitory containing ten narrow beds, each eerily misted with mosquito netting. Four of the beds were occupied. Two of the tenants were wide awake and sitting up. Luzelle glimpsed blond heads and solid buxom forms clothed in chaste white nightgowns. The features swam behind plentiful netting.

"Close the door, if you please," one of the blondes requested in Grewzian.

"You will let in the unwholesome night air," the other observed in the same language.

The place could use a little unwholesome night air, Luzelle noticed. The windows were closed, the mildew-edged atmosphere heavy and humming with insect life. Nevertheless she shut the door, and the noise woke a third tenant, who stirred and inquired in sleepy Grewzian, "What is that?"

"Someone new has come in."

"Forty-seventh?"

"Are you?" the first blonde demanded of Luzelle.

"Am I what?"

"Visiting a soldier of the Forty-seventh Squadron?"

"No, I—"

"Kreinzaufer's Eagle Battalion, then. What rank? *My* husband is the Captain Hefhohn, a hero of the Ygahri campaign.

Twice he has been decorated, and once commended for decisive action. What rank is yours?"

"I am not come here as a visitor of soldiers," Luzelle replied in her awkward Grewzian. "I make the fast trip through."

"You are not a woman of Grewzland," the captain's wife accused. She looked the new arrival up and down, taking in the bedraggled Bizaqhi costume. "What are you, some native? You cannot stay here."

"I am a native of Vonahr," Luzelle explained politely. "And I will certainly stay here tonight." So saying, she marched to the bed at the far end of the room and set her carpetbag firmly down beside it. The whispers sizzled behind her.

"She is Vonahrish, she says."

"Well, that is not so bad. At least her skin is white."

"Yes, but is it *clean*? The Vonahrish are a dirty people. Everyone knows it."

"They do not wash, but cover themselves with perfume."

"Look at the clothes. They are unseemly, and very dirty."

"Disgustingly dirty. I would die of shame to let myself be seen so."

"Ah, but the Vonahrish have no pride."

I'd like to see how you'd look after hiking through acres of dek-woati droppings, you witless Grewzian cows, Luzelle thought. Stripping to her linen, she stalked to the washstand and cleaned herself with ostentatious thoroughness, but this demonstration failed to satisfy her critics. The whispering commentary continued.

"Look, she parades about in her underwear."

"The Vonahrishwoman has no modesty."

"Will she sleep so?"

"This is not like a respectable woman."

"I think that one is no better than she should be."

Reining in her temper, Luzelle maintained silence. There was no point in picking a quarrel with these people. Moreover, what they said of her clothing was only the simple truth. Retrieving the garments, she washed them quickly in the basin, wrung them well, then draped them over a couple of pegs affixed to the wall near her bed. The gauzy, almost weightless fabric would probably dry before morning.

"Remove those wet things, if you please," the captain's wife requested from her bed. "It is not the proper place for them. You must know this is not a laundry."

Another truth. Jaw set, Luzelle took down the tunic and divided skirt, and spread them out over the wooden railing at the foot of her bed. A pleasant thought struck her. Stepping to the nearest window, she pushed the casement wide open. The dead air stirred to life. Now her clothes would surely dry.

"You will shut the window at once, if you please," directed one of the recumbent blondes. "The night air enters."

"Yes. Is it not refreshing?" Luzelle smiled guilelessly. "So clean."

"It is unhealthy. It is damp and full of jungle rot. You will shut the window now."

"I prefer it open. If you please." Luzelle's rock-candy smile did not waver. For a few moments she waited to see if anyone would dare attempt to close the window, but nobody moved. Climbing into bed, she pulled the mosquito netting into place around her, drew the sheet up, and turned her face to the wall. Behind her the whispering feminine colloquy resumed.

"This Vonahrishwoman does not know how to behave."

"Her whims threaten our health."

"And I think she must be a hussy."

"She should not be allowed to stay here. It is not right."

"Tomorrow morning I will speak to my husband, the Captain Hefhohn. My husband is not without influence. Something will surely be done."

Meaningless noise, no more significant than the hum of the insects, or the periodic slap of the giant winged cockroaches flying from wall to wall. Luzelle shut her eyes, and the noises distanced themselves. She was deeply tired and sleep claimed her almost before she found time to wonder how Girays v'Alisante happened to be carrying two such unlikely items as a street map of Xoxo and a printed schedule of Ygahri riverboat departures.

HAD THE WINDOW REMAINED CLOSED against the unwholesome night air, the voices outside might not have

disturbed her. As it was, the sound came pushing into the
dormitory and into her dreams, whence it woke her.

Luzelle opened her eyes. She had no idea what time it was,
but sensed that she had slept for some hours. The oil lamp
still glowed above, its diffuse light upon her bed mottled with
the shadows of the giant winged roaches clinging to the netting. A muffled exclamation escaped her. She slapped at the
netting, and the roaches whirred off. Gingerly she parted the
draperies and poked her head out.

Her Grewzian roommates slept on, their dreams proof
against the chanting assault of native voices. Wide awake now,
she sat listening for a moment. A small group, she estimated,
perhaps half a dozen of them; men and women together, or
possibly men and boys. Their rhythmic vocalization—half
chant, half song—was not unpleasant, but something about it
stirred the hairs at the back of her neck. Her mouth was dry.
She was profoundly uneasy, even afraid, and at the same time
blazing with curiosity. If they were performing some sort of
native ritual, she could watch, she could write a monograph
and submit it to the Republican Academy—

No time!

Time enough for a short investigation, though. That much
she would not deny herself. Rising from the bed, she made for
the window, where the kiss of the night air on her bare skin
recalled her state of undress. *Look, she parades about in her underwear.* Not such a bad idea in this climate, but likely to attract attention.

Snatching up her clothes, she dressed quickly. The Bizaqhi
tunic and divided skirt, still damp, clung indecently. Fortunate that the Grewzian officers' wives weren't awake to observe and comment.

Slipping noiselessly from the dormitory chamber, Luzelle
hurried along the corridor, down the stairs, and out the front
door into Xoxo's town square.

The night was warm and heavy as blood. The insects
shrilled feverishly. Southern constellations never glimpsed in
Vonahr glittered overhead, looking impossibly close. The
moon had set but the streetlamps still glowed, their light
washing the broad paved expanse of the square. Her eyes flew

instinctively to the platform and the pillory at its center. The four prisoners stood there motionless in their bonds, stoic as ever, deaf or else indifferent to the voices of their compatriots. Less impassive were the two Grewzian sentries stationed before the platform. Visibly uneasy, they were scanning the square on all sides in search of the unseen vocalists.

If they spied her, they would doubtless detain her for questioning or worse. Holding her breath, Luzelle shrank back into the shadows, and the Grewzian gazes passed over without pausing.

She resumed breathing. The voices she sought rose near at hand. She heard them clearly, but could not pinpoint their location. Behind her? Inside the darkened mouth of the alley? For a mad moment she thought she heard them in the air above her, and then they seemed to come from underground. Her nerves tingled and the gooseflesh rose along her arms, despite the heat of the night.

Ridiculous. She shook her head, half amused and half annoyed with herself, then stood still and listened intently. This time there could be no doubt. The invisible natives hid themselves in the darkness somewhere to her left, probably not more than a few dozen yards distant. Her eyes traveled and soon lighted upon a constricted pathway lying between a pair of the anonymous brick buildings edging the square. In there, beyond question.

Hugging the shadows, she stole forward on tiptoe. She reached the mouth of the passageway, and the chanting was strong in her ears. Her heart hurried and her spine tingled. There was something uncanny about those voices, something almost inhuman in the crystalline soprano notes. She forced herself to peek around the corner, and confronted nothing but darkness.

The voices were not quite as near as she had thought, or perhaps their owners had retreated. Luzelle inched on. Her eyes adjusted and she descried the brick walls rising on either side, but saw no sign of the native singers. She could still hear them clearly somewhere up ahead, not far away. On she went to the end of the passage, stepping out onto an anonymous narrow street lined with wooden houses on stilts, their lightless windows blindfolded with mats of woven rushes. The singers remained invisible, but their voices were still audible, still near, somewhere to the right.

She followed the sound down the street, around a bend, and along another walkway without catching sight of her quarry, then passed through a darkened grove of massive stone pilings to find herself back in the town square, a few buildings down from her starting point. The native voices rose and fell—somewhere behind her.

Lunacy. She had made some sort of mistake, probably somewhere among those pilings. She had better listen, really listen. Drawing a deep breath, she held it and shut her eyes.

Someone's hand touched her shoulder lightly. Stifling a cry, she whirled to face a tall figure clothed in a grey uniform. Grewzian. Loathsome. Alarm and hostility gave way to astonishment as recognition dawned.

"Karsler! Where did you come from?" In his company she did not need to fear the notice of the Grewzian sentries or of anyone else, but nonetheless she pitched her voice low, hardly above a whisper.

"From the house of the Acting Governor Janztoph, who heard that I was in town and offered me hospitality for the night." He too almost whispered. "How is it that I am not surprised to meet you here?"

"I have a way of turning up."

"Indeed. It cannot be an accident."

He was eyeing her very intently, and his gaze was fixed on her face, yet all at once she was acutely conscious of the damp garments molding every curve of her body.

"You have felt it too, have you not?" Karsler asked.

She stared at him, momentarily tongue-tied.

"You heard the voices, they called to you," he prompted. "You felt the power."

"I felt . . . something. I don't know quite what," she answered slowly. "I thought perhaps it was a native ceremony that I might watch."

"It is more than that. Do not attempt rational analysis, it will not serve you now. Listen now to your blood and nerves. What do they tell you?"

"Nothing. Nothing. I don't understand what you're talking about. I think I'd best go back to my room now."

"I do not mean to alarm you."

"You haven't—you couldn't. It's just this place—those voices—there's something strange and disturbing about them. They've confused and unnerved me—" She realized that she was prattling, and concluded quickly, "I'm perhaps not quite myself."

"You are entirely yourself, and your fear is based on sound instinct," he told her. "But I must ask you not to go back to your room quite yet. It is not safe. Something is going to happen here."

"What do you mean?"

"I sense a force at work around us, and I sense also the imminence of violent consummation."

"Violent! What's going to happen?"

"I have not the ability to predict. And yet I know that it is upon us, that we stand at the nexus of arcane forces, born of conjoined minds."

"Those voices out there—"

"Yes, that is the source."

"Who are they? What are they?"

"Tribesmen of the jungle, I think. Their shamans are reputedly accomplished. I do not know if you believe, probably you do not, and so I ask it as a personal favor. Humor my fancy, and come away from this spot. Will you?"

"Yes, if you wish," she replied without hesitation. His claims were fantastic, yet here and now she believed him completely. "Where shall we go?"

"It is localized. We need not go far, I think."

He extended his hand, and she took it. It seemed to her that a spark jumped between them, and she wondered if he felt anything of the sort. She looked up into his eyes and forgot about arcane forces, forgot imminent violence, forgot for an instant even the Grand Ellipse; forgot everything beyond the warmth of the current passing from his hand to hers.

She did not want to think or to move, but he was drawing her along a dim little avenue, and she went unresistingly. They had not advanced a half-dozen paces before she heard a muffled boom like subterranean thunder, and the ground beneath her shivered. Luzelle gasped and staggered, but stayed on her feet.

"Oh—it's true!" she cried.

"Come. A little farther," Karsler urged, his calm tones oddly underscoring the chant of native voices.

The ground groaned and shuddered again. Luzelle lost her balance, pitched forward, and would have fallen had not Karsler caught her and held her upright. For a moment she clung, then relaxed her grip and let him lead her on along the street, up a sloping incline to a solid, motionless summit from which they could view the town square.

The night was tranquil no longer. Lights had appeared at the windows of several of the buildings overlooking the square, and by their glow Luzelle could see the jagged new fissures sundering the pavement. Men, women, and children in nightshirts and nightgowns were spilling from the inn, from the governor's mansion, and from the neighboring houses. Frightened voices rose in confusion, then the hubbub splintered to shrieks as the thunder underfoot boomed again and the ground quaked. White-clad figures fell sprawling, and the small cupola surmounting the governor's residence tumbled from its perch to hit the pavement below with a crash. At the same time the streetlamps bordering the square began to topple in quick succession, each extinguishing itself as it fell. Darkness encroached upon the square, then retreated as the flame from an overturned lantern caught the dry matting at someone's window and fire spouted from the second story. The screaming panic below intensified.

Girays. Almost certainly somewhere in the midst of it all. Luzelle's jaw tightened.

"He will be all right," Karsler told her.

"What?"

"V'Alisante will not be injured. No one will, I think, for that is not the intent of this demonstration."

"How could you know the intent?"

"It is a feeling that I have. You need not fear for your friend."

"I wish I could share your confidence. But let me assure you, M. v'Alisante's welfare is no particular concern of mine."

"It is possible that you mistake yourself."

"No I don't." She hesitated. "What makes you think so?"

"Perhaps it has something to do with your present effort to squeeze my hand to a pulp."

"Oh! Sorry." She released his hand, and at once regretted the lost contact.

"See," Karsler observed quietly, "someone has already doused the fire. The quakes have ceased. There will be no further damage, the exercise is concluded."

"Another feeling?"

"Yes, but that is not the only guide. Listen. What do you hear? Or rather, what do you not hear?"

"The chanting, the voices—they've stopped."

"Their purpose is accomplished."

"What purpose? The ruin of their own town?"

"That square and its architecture are western in nature, designed to suit the needs of colonial administrators. They do not truly belong to this place, and I do not believe that the Ygahri natives would mourn their loss."

"But your own Undergeneral Ermendtrof—and your Acting Governor Janztoph—may view the matter in a different light. They won't hesitate to make their displeasure known, and the locals are likely to pay the price. Won't there be reprisals?"

"Perhaps."

Grewzian reprisals were notorious. Xoxo faced a sizable reduction in population.

"But it is not probable," Karsler answered her thought, or else continued his own. "Grewzland does not officially recognize the reality of arcane force. To punish the natives is to hold them accountable for the ground tremors that damaged the square. But how could such backward people control a natural phenomenon? Ygahri guilt confirms Ygahri sorcerous power, and that is something my countrymen will not openly acknowledge. Hence there was no crime, there is no guilt, and there can be no punishment."

"Very neat. I only hope that you're right. Certainly you were right about—how did you put it? 'The imminence of violent consummation.' "

"It is not difficult to detect."

"For you, perhaps. I remember what you said that night aboard the *Karavise*—that you learned in childhood to sense the working of arcane energy. I didn't altogether believe you then, but I do now. I'm sorry that I doubted."

"What intelligent individual would not question such a claim?"

"Didn't you say at the time that the training was part of some traditional form of Grewzian education?"

"Yes."

"If Grewzian tradition includes the study of arcane energy, then how can the Imperium refuse to acknowledge it?"

"The current administration values modern rationality, or at least the general appearance thereof. The Promontory, whose existence links the presence to the past, cleaves yet to the old ways and the old wisdom. But that is a matter rarely discussed with foreigners."

"I see," she murmured. Disappointment filled her, for she suspected that an explanation might furnish some key to the enigma of his character.

"It is not a topic of casual conversation," Karsler continued. "I will tell you something of the Promontory, however, because you seek knowledge, because it pleases me to remember, and because somehow I would find pleasure in sharing those memories with you. This is no violation of trust, but only a departure from convention, an indulgence that I will permit myself tonight."

"Don't tell me anything that you'll regret."

"I will regret nothing." Karsler reflected a moment, then commenced, "The Promontory is a granite fortress, austere in aspect, ancient beyond memory, enthroned upon a high crag overlooking grey seas at the northern extremity of Grewzland. This structure is the stronghold, training ground, and—I believe the Vonahrish term would be 'retreat'—of the group known in my country as 'Laagstraften.' In Vonahrish, that is 'the Confraternity.' You have heard of this?"

Luzelle shook her head.

"I am not surprised. The order of the Confraternity, though greatly revered, so consistently shuns public attention that its very existence is hardly noted beyond the borders of our homeland. And even there the order contrives to efface itself. Yet this group has figured prominently in Grewzian affairs. Its influence has altered the course of war, guided the destinies of princes, shaped national history.

"The membership comprises the sons of the noblest and oldest of our Houses, relinquished in early childhood by their families and raised in seclusion within the confines of the Promontory. There the young aspirants are subjected to the most rigorous discipline; enrolled in a program of training designed to strengthen and purify them in body, mind, and character; schooled in varied arts and sciences, some of them all but forgotten elsewhere; fortified against the power of magic; taught the secrets of totality and transcendence; in short, required to fulfill the highest potential of their own talents and abilities. Such a difficult and prolonged regimen hardly suits all natures, and the attrition rate is high. But those remaining to complete the program are tested upon conclusion, and those successfully meeting all such challenges win the title of Elucidated, which grants them full privileges of membership. In Grewzland this is regarded as a great honor."

"And you have won this title?" asked Luzelle.

"Yes. I entered the Promontory at the age of four, and never set foot without its walls for the next seventeen years. At the end of that time I am Elucidated, and my blood is declared *aflegrenskuldt*."

"Declared what?"

"*Aflegrenskuldt*—that is, either 'virtuous' or 'battle worthy,' depending upon the context. It is a tradition of my country that the heart's blood of the Elucidated must quench the steel composing the weapons and armor of Grewzian royalty, in this manner imparting battle worthiness to the finished products. Originally, the blood was obtained by means of human sacrifice—"

"But that was in the distant past, surely."

"The custom continued unchanged up until the end of the last century. Perhaps that sounds barbaric to foreign ears, and yet you must understand that the heart's-gift is the ultimate and highest act of patriotism, and the donors regard themselves as privileged. Within the past fifty years, however, matters have altered and the Elucidated are more often than not accorded the luxury of natural death."

"More often than not?"

"I had thought to remain immured within the Confraternity's stronghold for the whole of my life," Karsler continued. "I expected to study, to teach, to administer, or to contribute my blood gladly, should that have been asked. I knew no other way of life, and desired none. My reading and my conversations with those more knowledgeable than myself woke in me no desire to explore the mad world beyond the Promontory's walls. Quite the contrary, I learned to prize the order and tranquillity of my existence.

"It was not to continue, however," Karsler observed with regret that contained no hint of self-pity. "The wars commenced, and my services were required. We Stornzofs must take up arms, you see, in times of conflict—it is the way of our House, and so it has always been. Nor does such labor in the service of Grewzland violate the principles of the Confraternity. Thus I exchanged the Promontory for the army, where my family name alone instantly won me an officer's commission. I had not earned it and did not deserve it, but that is the way of this world. Fortunately for all concerned, I displayed some aptitude for the work—it is in the Stornzof blood, after all. I proved useful in certain capacities, promotions followed, there was constant activity to keep me occupied, and I grew as accustomed to the military life as ever I had been to the contemplative life that preceded it. So I have passed the last five years, and they have not been unhappy. And yet it is curious—there has never been a single day in all those years that I have not thought of the Promontory, never a day that I have not heard its call."

"Will you ever go back?" asked Luzelle.

"For a very long time after leaving, there was no question in my mind that I should return at the first opportunity. But the wars continue, the years accumulate, time and distance alter all things. When the fighting ends at last and I am finally free, I think that I shall find myself so greatly changed that I will not belong to the Promontory. There will be no place for me there."

"Perhaps that won't be true. But if it is?"

"Then I will look back no longer, but content myself with present reality, which offers its own considerable rewards," he told her. Before she could analyze the remark, he added, "Your patience in listening is one such reward. I hope this monologue has not too greatly wearied you."

"Anything but that. I'm glad that you've told me these things, answering questions that I wouldn't have presumed to ask. Now I begin to know you a little."

"We began to know one another long before tonight, and not through words," he said deliberately.

"You feel that?" Her breath caught.

"Yes. Am I mistaken?"

"No," she whispered. He was standing very near her. Their eyes met and merged, her pulses throbbed, and she wondered confusedly whether he would try to kiss her, and even more confusedly whether she would let him. Of course she shouldn't, no respectable woman would allow it outside of marriage, not even with her own betrothed, much less a near stranger, a rival, a Grewzian. But the magnetism was powerful, the starlight compelling, and her own impulses chaotic. If he took her in his arms and kissed her now, she would not resist him, she would not even try.

His hands closed on her shoulders, and her blood sang. Letting her eyes close, she swayed toward him. For a moment the hands remained, then he released her and stepped back. Bewildered and suddenly chilled, Luzelle opened her eyes to stare up at him.

"Forgive me. I take advantage," Karsler told her. "This is reprehensible."

"What do you mean, take advantage?" She frowned, scenting condescension. "Take advantage of what?"

"Your warm heart and your generous nature. I realize now that I exploit them, although without design."

"You exploit nothing, Karsler. Do you think so little of me? I am neither a fool nor a child, and I am not so easily manipulated as that." She spoke a trifle tartly, as pride dictated, but inwardly she glowed. He'd said she had a warm heart and a generous nature.

"I stand corrected. You are right, you are neither gull nor victim. You may perhaps concede that you are somewhat reckless, and disinclined to consider possible complications. We both compete in the same race. Tomorrow morning I must be ready to leave you behind without hesitation and without a backward glance. You must be prepared to do the same to me, should the opportunity arise. Neither of us may pause to offer the other help in time of trouble or care in time of illness. How difficult does this become when a friendship or connection between the two of us forges invisible chains?"

"Difficult, but not impossible," Luzelle returned. "I mean to win, and friendship or no, I'll do whatever I must."

"You think so now, but somewhere along the way you may find the price higher than you expect."

"I will pay it nonetheless."

"It may be that you cannot. There are some compromises too degrading for self-respect to sustain."

"My self-respect will thrive, provided I win."

"I wonder. You cannot truly know what you will do until the moment of choice arrives, and then you may surprise yourself."

"We'll see." There would be no kissing now, the moment had definitely passed. Relief and disappointment swirled through her.

A moment's silence followed, and Karsler observed, "It is quiet down there now. I believe it is safe to return."

He escorted her down the slope and back to Xoxo's town square, where a few lights glowing from neighboring windows illuminated broken pavement, fallen lampposts, and scattered wreckage. A number of shaken citizens tarried there, conversing in hushed tones, but most had already returned to their homes or lodgings.

At the door of the inn they paused, and Luzelle remarked, "Time for another farewell. They seem so frequent."

"For now. But there is life after the Grand Ellipse, is there not?"

Yes, and by that time Vonahr and Grewzland will probably be at war, she thought.

"And even war is finite, although often it seems otherwise," he said.

"Telepathy again?" She smiled. "Well, that insight of yours saved me from a good shaking or worse tonight. Now I'll know to run for the hills if I hear those voices again before morning."

"You will not hear them. They have achieved their objective. Look there." Karsler pointed.

Her eyes followed his finger to the center of the town square, where the pillory stood empty and abandoned. The four prisoners were gone.

13

"WHAT BECAME OF YOU LAST NIGHT?" asked Girays. "When that ground tremor shook me out of bed, I went down the hall to your room, there to confront a gaggle of hysterical Grewzian women. No sign of you among them, so I thought you must already have left the building. I went out into the square, but didn't see you."

"Oh, I was about," Luzelle replied vaguely.

"I quartered that square like a bird dog. I don't understand how I could have missed you."

"Well, it was dark, and there was a lot of confusion," she evaded, unwilling to reveal the circumstances of her encounter with Karsler Stornzof. "I'm just glad you weren't hurt."

"Judging by what I've heard, nobody was. It's quite remarkable."

"Almost magical."

"And providential for those poor wretches in the pillory. Somehow in the midst of the confusion they escaped, or else someone released them. In any case, the four of them are gone. Had you noticed?"

"Yes. That empty platform was a welcome sight. But perhaps this isn't the best place to speak of it." She glanced toward the Grewzian sentry stationed a few feet away at the entrance to the city hall.

"Whom do we offend in discussing a natural phenomenon? But the timing was extraordinary, wasn't it? Seismic activity is unusual in this part of the world, yet that quake occurred at exactly the right moment to assist the escape of—"

"An extraordinary coincidence." Anxious to change the subject, Luzelle climbed the brick steps to address the sentry in Grewzian. "It is now please the time to admit us."

"City hall opens at eight o'clock." The sentry consulted his watch. "It is now seven fifty-eight."

Breathing a sigh, Luzelle returned to Girays. "His watch is slow, I just know it," she complained. "I hate this waiting, there's nothing worse."

"I can think of a few things."

"Have your map ready?"

"Yes, but we won't need it. I've got our route memorized."

"You sure? I mean, this town has streets with as many twists and turns as—as a plateful of Blue Aennorvermis."

"Don't worry."

She did worry, but there was no point in harping on it. She let her eyes wander the square, where the native workmen, directed by Grewzian overseers, were at work removing wreckage and righting fallen lampposts. Several Ygahris loitered inquisitively about the empty pillory, and an angry grey-clad soldier chased them away. In front of the countinghouse a gang of naked copper-skinned children skipped and hopped in intricate sequences over the new cracks in the pavement.

Her eyes returned to Girays. For almost the first time since she had known him, he was less than flawlessly groomed. His dark hair, in need of a trim, had grown appealingly shaggy. His khaki garments were clean but heavily wrinkled, and a button was missing from his shirt. But none of these small imperfections could truly impair his bred-in-the-bone Vonahrish elegance. Girays v'Alisante might dive headfirst into a heap of manure, and somehow he would still be M. the Marquis. The shadows under his eyes were darker than usual, the lines in his face deeper—he could not have had much sleep last night—but he was looking alert, confident, downright cheerful.

"Girays," she ventured, "you really don't mind all this, do you?"

"Mind?" He considered. "You know, these past weeks I've experienced more discomfort, annoyance, tedium, inconvenience, and frustration than I've known in all my lifetime. There's also been more novelty, diversion, and discovery than I've ever known. There's a great deal that I mind, but I wouldn't have missed it for the world."

"That doesn't sound like M. the Marquis, who once wanted nothing more than to shuttle endlessly between Sherreen and Belfaireau."

"He may have changed a little, or perhaps you didn't know him quite as well as you thought."

"Well—which is it?"

"Why not both?"

"You're teasing me."

He never replied, for at that moment the sentry stood aside from the entrance and motioned them into the city hall.

Up the stairs they sped together, through the door and into the drably utilitarian vestibule, where a bored guard directed them to the underclerk of the Municipal Authority on the second floor. Up more stairs, past smart grey-uniformed figures, past fair westerners in civilian dress who turned to stare as they hurried by, down a featureless corridor to a door with a frosted-glass pane and a neatly painted Grewzian sign: MUNICIPAL AUTHORITY.

Girays knocked, and did not wait for a response before trying the door. It was unlocked. He opened it, and they went in.

The room beyond was plain, functional, and scrupulously ordered. Tall file cabinets lined the walls. There was an old wooden desk, two chairs, a bookcase behind the desk, and no other furniture. A baby-faced bald clerk in wire-rimmed spectacles and civilian garb sat at the desk. He looked up as they entered, and his brows rose.

"You are the underclerk of the Municipal Authority, yes?" inquired Girays.

His Grewzian, Luzelle noted, was not much better than her own.

"That is correct," the underclerk replied in precise, high-pitched tones.

"We must the passports make to be stamped with the official seal."

"Official Xoxo city seal," Luzelle added helpfully. With a melting smile, she produced her passport and placed it on the desk. "You make to stamp, if you please."

Girays placed his own passport beside hers.

The underclerk of the Municipal Authority glanced at the documents, observing, "Vonahrish, yes?"

"That is correct, Master Underclerk," Luzelle fluttered prettily.

He looked her up and down, taking in the Bizaqhi gauze tunic and divided skirt, the riotous red-gold curls hastily gathered at the nape of her neck and streaming down her back. His brows elevated another fraction of an inch toward his distant hairline.

Luzelle felt her color rise. *Grewzian snot,* she thought. She met his gaze limpidly.

The underclerk's regard shifted to Girays, shaggy and wrinkled, and he said, "You race in the Grand Ellipse, perhaps?"

"That is correct, Master Underclerk," Girays replied.

"You are the most clever to guess this, Master Underclerk," Luzelle admired.

"Our Grewzian contender, the Overcommander Stornzof, will whip your Vonahrish backsides," the underclerk opined. There was no immediate reply, and he added, "Our Stornzof has already passed through. He is ahead, you will not catch him, you may as well give up now."

"That is as may be, Master Underclerk," Girays answered, "but we must continue. If you would please to stamp our passports—"

"I myself have wagered on the Grand Ellipse," the underclerk confided. "Twenty silver grewzauslins I have placed upon the victory of our Overcommander Stornzof."

"This is fine sporting spirit." Luzelle nodded.

"So you see," the underclerk confessed pensively, "a Grewzian triumph is more than a matter of patriotic pride to me—it is a great personal concern as well. I am sure you understand."

Luzelle and Girays traded uneasy looks.

"Now, as to these Vonahrish passports of yours," the underclerk continued, "they require close inspection. It is necessary to make certain that all is in order."

"I assure you—" Girays began.

"You will wait in silence now, if you please," the underclerk instructed. "You may sit if you wish. Some time may be required."

"But we do not have time!" Luzelle objected. "And—"

"Silence, now. I must verify the authenticity of the various stamps and seals that you present to me. The task demands my full attention."

"But—" Luzelle began. A warning look from Girays quelled her.

The underclerk opened one of the passports, studied the first page at length, then rose unhurriedly from his desk, went to the bookcase, withdrew a massive volume, and returned to his seat. Opening the book, he scanned the index and turned to a page bearing an elaborate civic stamp, which he compared painstakingly to the mark on the passport page. Satisfied at last, he nodded, shifted his regard to the next stamp on the passport, inspected it, then rose to fetch another volume.

Luzelle watched and fidgeted. The underclerk studied on, and the minutes ticked by. At this rate he would never be done, and she could stand it no longer. She coughed a little, but he did not raise his head.

"Master Underclerk—" she implored.

He looked up.

"Master Underclerk, we are greatly wanting to make the big speed, and our documents official are truly in perfect order—"

"That remains to be seen," the underclerk informed her. "The verification has scarcely commenced. Perhaps you would like to go away and come back again at the end of the day. The processing may perhaps be completed by then."

"Sir, you do not understand! We cannot wait! We—" Girays caught her eye, shook his head infinitesimally, and Luzelle cut herself off.

"Master Underclerk," Girays interjected respectfully, and

the Grewzian eyes behind the wire-rimmed spectacles turned to him. "Permit me if you please to offer a suggestion. You are the busy official of the Imperium, your time is too valuable to waste upon such small matters. Perhaps a gift to the office of the Municipal Authority will serve to demonstrate our good faith, allowing you in turn to dispense with certain formalities." Drawing several notes from his wallet, he placed them on the desk.

"Ah? What is this?" The underclerk studied the offering. "Vonahrish New-rekkoes?"

"Good throughout the world," Girays declared. "The New-rekkoes I give are equal to forty grewzauslins. To prove our good faith."

"This gift speaks well for you," the underclerk decided. "You prove yourself a friend of the Imperium, and therefore I will accept your travel documentation, which appears perfectly in order, at face value."

A small thud of inked rubber on paper signaled the official confirmation of Girays v'Alisante's presence in the town of Xoxo.

"Here." The underclerk returned the passport to its owner. "You have prevailed upon my good nature. But you will understand, I am sure, that the gesture of confidence can hardly embrace this woman here, whose papers demand scrupulous inspection."

Expectantly Luzelle awaited M. the Marquis's offer of a bribe and guarantees on her behalf.

"I understand, Master Underclerk," Girays murmured gravely. "You are an official of the Imperium, and you must perform your duty. I leave her with you, then." Apparently blind to the Grewzian's look of surprise, he turned toward the door.

"Don't you dare, you snake," Luzelle muttered. Producing a fistful of New-rekkoes, she slapped the notes down on the desk. "Here! They must be worth fifty grewzauslins or more, probably more. To prove my good faith. Master Underclerk, sir."

"Ah." The underclerk counted. "Good. I am convinced of your honesty. And your documents appear valid." With an air of generosity he stamped and returned her passport.

"Thank you, Master Underclerk," Luzelle forced herself to reply. "We will be on our way now."

"As you wish. Your efforts are useless, however. You will never overtake our Overcommander Stornzof, he is destined for victory. He is Grewzian, you see."

"Watch the gazettes," Luzelle advised. Together she and Girays departed the office of the Municipal Authority.

Moments later they hurried out the front door, past the sentry, and down the steps to the sunlit town square, where Luzelle consulted her pocket watch.

"Eight-seventeen," she reported grimly, as they trotted along. "That little brute of an underclerk deliberately delayed us. Those Grewzians have no notion of fair play." She thought of Karsler Stornzof and the look in his eyes. "Most of them, at least. And it would have been a lot worse if you hadn't thought to bribe him. That was brilliant. But would you really have left me there just now?"

"We're in a race, aren't we?"

"But—"

"Faster." Girays quickened his pace. "Move faster."

"Can't," she huffed. "It's this carpetbag, it's clumsy—"

"Throw it away, then. I won't slow down for you."

"Nobody's asking you to." She wouldn't discard her bag, she resolved. Not again. A labored spurt brought her to his side. Her breath was coming hard. "How—much—farther?"

Without troubling to answer, he altered direction, leading her off along some anonymous little lane terminating in a makeshift bridge of slime-slicked planks spanning a runnel thick with raw sewage. The neighboring dwellings were small and dirty, their leaf-thatched roofs blotched with black mold.

He knew where he was going, Luzelle assured herself. He'd said that he had memorized the best route, and Girays v'Alisante was not given to idle claims.

On he led across the bridge, along another garbage-strewn lane, and then the scene was improving, the lane widening, the neglected wooden houses giving way to larger structures, low slung, stoutly built, spotlessly clean, with long window-less walls. Grewzian, beyond question. Warehouses? If so, a good sign, for the wharves must be near at hand.

Another turn into a tight walkway squeezed between warehouses, and suddenly the way was blocked by the wall of an enclosed passage linking two of the buildings. They halted.

"This is wrong." Girays frowned. "It's not on the map, it shouldn't be here."

"Could you have taken a wrong turn?" Luzelle took the opportunity to set her carpetbag down for a moment.

He did not deign to acknowledge the suggestion. "New construction," he decided. "The waterfront should be just on the other side. We'll have to go around."

"Is there any point?" She could not resist another glance at her watch. "It's eight thirty-two. We've missed it, Girays. That swine of an underclerk has scuttled us."

"Only if the *Water Sprite* embarked exactly on time. But how likely is that?"

"Is the crew Grewzian?"

"If she's just five or ten minutes behind schedule, we can still make it. So pick up your bag and come along, or else I'll leave you here."

"I really hate it when you *threaten* me." She picked up her bag.

He led her back the way they had come, out of the walkway and into the street, along the street to an intersection where they turned left to weave a path among the warehouses. The buildings all looked exactly alike, and presently she began to suspect that they were traveling in circles. She was on the verge of telling him so when they emerged from the warehouse wilderness to find themselves on Wharf No. 1, with the wide mud-colored Ygah rippling before them, the waterbirds swooping and screeching overhead, and a dizzying variety of boats moored at the dock. The crafts ranged in size from tiny native square-sail to modern transport vessel, and in shape from streamlined Grewzian patrol boat to squat Ygahri riverhouse, but nowhere among them did Luzelle spy anything resembling a commercial steamer. The *Water Sprite,* she recalled, was scheduled to depart from Wharf No. 12, several hundred yards downriver.

"This way." Girays was already moving.

She had to scramble to catch up with him. True to his

threats, he was making no allowances for her, and now the bag she refused to relinquish was dragging like an anchor, but she managed to keep pace.

Wharf No. 4. She saw the sign, freshly painted in neat Grewzian characters, out of the corner of her eye as she passed. She also noted an assortment of curious heads turning to watch the jogging progress of the breathless western couple, but there was no time for embarrassment.

Wharf No. 7. Wharf No. 8. There was a stitch in her side, and her arm muscles were in rebellion. The carpetbag began to slide from her sweaty hand, and she tightened her grasp almost spasmodically.

Wharf No. 10, and her spirits were rising, for she felt that they were going to make it. Girays had been right, as he so often was.

Wharf No. 11, and then there was No. 12 at last. And there was the *Water Sprite,* a serviceable-looking side-wheeler with a shallow bargelike hull, pulling away from the dock. The deep hoot of her whistle announced triumphant departure, very nearly on time.

A yowl of grief and fury escaped Luzelle. Sprinting to the edge of the pier, she stood there waving her free arm and shouting. She could see passengers and crew on the deck watching and pointing at her, but the *Water Sprite* did not reverse course. Several inarticulate exclamations shot out of her mouth.

Girays had followed, and now he stood beside her. Turning to face him, she demanded, "Make them come back!"

"How, exactly?" he inquired politely. "What do you expect me to do?"

"I don't know! Think of something! You're formerly-Exalted, you're used to ordering people around. It's in your blood—your grandfather had *serfs,* didn't he?"

"Yes, but I didn't inherit any of them. Luzelle, calm down and face facts. We missed the boat, it won't come back, and there's nothing we can do about it."

"We have to think of something. Karsler Stornzof is certainly aboard that thing, and if we're ever to—"

"Stornzof isn't the only problem," Girays interrupted.

His flat tone warned her, and she unwillingly followed his gaze to the deck of the side-wheeler. One of the figures standing at the rail looked familiar. Not Karsler. Somebody shorter, darker, bulkier, dressed in florid foreign style. The passenger's voluminously cut, full-sleeved maroon shirt was unmistakable even at a distance.

"Porb Jil Liskjil!" she exclaimed. "I thought we'd left him behind in Zuleekistan. How could he have managed this?"

"Money," Girays replied succinctly.

"D'you think he bribed that sentry at the city hall? Or the underclerk?"

"It's a safe bet that he bribed somebody."

"It isn't fair." She resisted the impulse to shake her fist after the receding *Water Sprite*. Jil Liskjil would only enjoy the gesture. "Not fair at all."

"Perhaps not, but there's no point in agonizing over it. The next boat south leaves tomorrow morning, and we'll be aboard. Until then we're stuck here in Xoxo, which is not, contrary to all appearances, the end of the world. The race is far from over, and somewhere along the way the chance may come to catch up with—"

"No," she told him firmly. "No. Not good enough. I don't accept it."

"Fine spirit, but I'm afraid you haven't much choice."

"Yes I do."

"Really. Planning to swim downstream to Jumo?"

"If necessary, but I think there are better ways of getting there, which might have occurred to you if only you weren't quite so ready to *give up* and *give in*—"

"I'm ready to accept reality, a concept that sometimes eludes you," he snapped. "And if you've got some wild notion of traveling on foot through the jungle, then I can only conclude that your mental grasp is slackening by the moment."

"My mental grasp is just fine, but I wonder if the same can be said of your imagination," she suggested. "If you had any, you might have noticed that there are boats all over the place, most of them privately owned. And somewhere among those owners, there's someone we can hire to carry us downriver."

The moment the words left her mouth she was furious

with herself, for Girays was regarding her with an expression of faintly surprised interest, and she could see that he thought her idea viable, in which case she should certainly have kept it to herself. She had just sacrificed a potential Elliptical advantage, and once again she had her quick temper and her loose tongue to thank for the loss.

"Private transport," Girays mused. "Not a bad idea. You are right, Luzelle—my imagination was asleep. I apologize for the way I spoke to you just now."

Almost worth the blunder just to hear him say so.

"Quite all right," she replied, suppressing every outward sign of satisfaction. She looked around. Boats everywhere. "Well—where should we start?"

"Which one takes your fancy?"

"I see any number of likely possibilities. This should be easy," opined Luzelle.

But it was not quite as easy as she expected.

So many of them moored and presently vacant. Others hopelessly unsuitable—too large for private hire, too tiny for passengers, too alarmingly decrepit. They went first to a clean, freshly painted, beautifully maintained little packet, whose spit-and-polish westernized native skipper expressed perfect willingness to carry them as far as Nishq'tla Camp, the last port of call along his usual route—but not a mile farther.

"Too far to Jumo," the skipper explained in excellent Vonahrish. "Too dangerous for small boats, and the large merchant steamers aren't available for private hire, unless you can afford a price of thirty thousand New-rekkoes or so."

Luzelle and Girays looked at each other. Both had money, but not that much.

"Passenger boat stops at Xoxo Wharf Number Twelve tomorrow morning," the skipper informed them. "But no, now that I think of it, I heard today that the *Waterweed* ran aground north of Flewn's Bend. Day after tomorrow, you should be able to book passage."

"We can't wait that long," Girays told him, and they walked on along the dock.

The next four captain-owners they approached proved

similarly negative. A fifth, speaking only Ygahri dialect, looked eager and interested until they succeeded in communicating their needs.

"Jumo," Luzelle directed distinctly. She pointed south. "JUMO TOWNE."

He understood her. He grunted, shook his head, and turned away. They moved on.

Lowering their sights, they tried a couple of the smaller boats, whose owners refused the commission at any price. Overhearing this, the native owner of a dugout canoe sidled near, proposing to paddle them all the way down the Ygah to the Nether Ocean and beyond in peace and safety, should the gods bless the venture.

"The gods willing, I shall paddle you to the stars," he promised with a demented grin.

"We will consider your offer," Luzelle told him, and realized that she meant it. They moved on.

Another three refusals in a row, and her initial assurance waned. She was feeling the weight of the carpetbag again, and discouragement was heavier yet.

"Maybe we should think about that dugout," she said.

"No we shouldn't," Girays returned. "Impractical. Also I didn't like the look of the owner. I think he may be deranged."

"He is," rumbled a bass voice behind them, in Vonahrish. "Mad as a firestinker in springtime, that one. Wrecked as a rabid rodent, loony as a purple-pissing prince. But Jhiv-Huze is not."

They turned to confront the speaker, a tall, massive figure that seemed at first glance an overgrown native attired in the baggy trousers, loose tunic, and thong sandals typical of the Ygahri townsman. His long, elaborately plaited locks were threaded with glass beads and wooden rings, his face blue with intricate designs. Closer inspection discovered pale freckled skin behind the tattoos, grey eyes glittering in the shade of deep sockets, and grey-streaked carrot-colored hair winding among the countless ornaments. A westerner, unmistakably.

"You are in luck today," the stranger continued, his fluent Vonahrish laced with flat Kyrendtish vowels. "Jhiv-Huze has overheard your conversation, he understands your problem, and it is your good fortune that he is here to solve it. Roupe Jhiv-Huze, at your service, is an experienced river pilot, owner and captain of a spanking little steamer available to carry you south to Jumo Towne for the trifling sum of one thousand New-rekkoes. Sir and Madame, be content. Your troubles are at an end."

"Indeed." Luzelle eyed the stranger narrowly. She noted pinpoint pupils, telltale yellow stains about the lips, and an air of manic buoyancy; all classic signs of maruki influence. The natives of the region, she recalled from her reading, were widely devoted to the use of *marukiñutu,* a beverage infused from the podlike fruit of the maruki tree. In its milder forms the drink exerted a pleasantly tonic effect. Stronger infusions produced assorted symptoms ranging from exhilaration to euphoria, while protracted use of the infamous, highly addictive version known as *maru-tcho* induced eventual madness. She glanced at Girays and saw her own reservations mirrored in his eyes.

"Mmm, yes." Captain Jhiv-Huze rumbled a chuckle. "Private transport downriver is not so easily obtained, as you have no doubt discovered. But Roupe Jhiv-Huze is in an expansive mood, brimming with philanthropy and eager to share in his contentment. Today he is disposed to generosity. Therefore he places himself and his vessel at your disposal. He is ready to leave at once. This very moment. He trusts you will not delay. Come, let us be off."

"We thank you, Captain, but your services will not be required," decreed Girays.

"Wait, I'm not so sure—" Luzelle began.

"Jhiv-Huze understands. You have made other arrangements." The captain nodded benevolently. "No doubt you embark within the hour."

"We are investigating the possibilities."

"They are myriad, sir."

"Girays, may I have a word with you? In private?" Luzelle

requested sweetly. Grabbing his arm, she dragged him off a few yards along the dock, then turned on him to demand in a heated undertone, "What do you think you're doing?"

"Forestalling disaster," he replied. "That fellow is unreliable. I will not place our lives in his hands."

"We haven't any choice."

"You don't understand. There's a local stimulant that affects the intellect and powers of judgment—"

"Yes, I know all about the *marukiñutu*, and *you're* the one who doesn't understand. We have to get out of this place, Girays! At least I do. Right away, right *now*, at any cost, and I can't afford to pick and choose. If this Jhiv-Huze person has a boat capable of carrying me to Jumo, then I don't care what he's been drinking."

"You'll care when that drug-addled loon wrecks his boat on the rocks and spills you out into a beetle-infested river. The local aquatic beetles are carnivorous, you know. They swim in schools like fish, and they can strip a body down to the bone in a matter of minutes."

"Killer beetles? That's picturesque. I've underestimated your powers of invention."

"Invention has nothing to do with it; I'm stating literal fact. That tattoo-riddled Kyrendtish inebriate over there isn't fit to pilot a rowboat, and I won't allow you to—"

"Allow. Now there speaks the old Girays that I remember so well. I wondered how long it would take him to show his face."

"This is hardly the time or place to resume old quarrels. If I've offended you, that's regrettable, but you must understand that I speak out of genuine concern for your wel—"

"Yes, that was always your justification for every sort of domineering presumption—that it was all for my own good. Well, I thank you for your 'genuine concern,' but I'm quite capable of making my own decisions. My decision now is to book passage aboard this Kyrendtish fellow's boat. If you want to accompany me, then pick up your bag and come along, or else I'll leave you here. Sound familiar?" Feeling triumphant, she turned and flounced away. She heard him mutter a curse, but no sound of his footsteps on the wooden wharf behind her, and doubt invaded her mind. Maybe he really *would* let her go off alone, maybe he would stay behind to continue the search for another and possibly superior conveyance. Well, let him. So much the better, she assured herself. He might search until sunset for another boat without finding one. He might end up waiting another two days for the next available commercial steamer. Yes, he was welcome to stay behind, quite welcome.

She halted before the massive tattooed figure. "Captain Jhiv-Huze—" she began.

"Ah, you are ready to embark!" The yellow-stained grin flashed amid blue tattoos. "A very wise decision, Madame. Mmm, yes. Very wise."

"You are really prepared to undertake such a long trip on such short notice?"

"For a thousand New-rekkoes, all things are possible."

"Your boat is well fueled and provisioned?"

"We acquire all necessities en route. The jungle, Madame, may be viewed as the wise man's treasure trove."

"What about the boat herself? Recently inspected? In good repair? Sound and riverworthy?"

"As worthy as a pious widow struggling to support her eight hungry children. As worthy as an itinerant holy man washing the feet of the poor. As worthy as—"

"And the crew?"

"Consists of the captain and a stoker."

"That's all? You have no mate? No other assistance?"

"And require none, Jhiv-Huze is proud to say. Look on the bright side, Madame—he always does. In the absence of a crew, your privacy is assured. May he assume that you have elected to travel downriver alone?"

"Alone?" She hesitated. His pinpoint pupils dotted richly bloodshot eyes whose brilliant vitreous sheen suddenly unnerved her. She pictured herself aboard a boat on the wide Ygah at night, alone with this outlandish character, a stoker, and a hold full of *marukiñutu*. Every instinct screamed a warning. She couldn't afford cowardice, not if she wanted to win, and she did carry the pocket pistol, but nevertheless—

"Madame travels in my company," announced the voice of Girays v'Alisante.

She turned to find him right behind her, and the rush of relief actually brought a couple of tears to her eyes. She blinked them away and prayed that he had not seen. He would have every right to mock her without mercy. On the other hand, she reminded herself stoutly, she *would* have gone ahead and traveled alone if necessary. She would have slept fully dressed, with the Khrennisov under her pillow—assuming that she had a pillow—but she would indeed have gone ahead, alone.

"Decided to come along, then?" she inquired with a creditable affectation of nonchalance.

"I've had enough of wandering the wharf," he told her easily. "And so I've decided to take a chance on Jhiv-Huze here."

"Excellent." The captain nodded. "Excellent. Jhiv-Huze congratulates you, sir. You and Madame may anticipate a memorable journey."

"No doubt. Then lead us to your vessel, Captain."

"With the greatest of pride and pleasure. You will be astonished. This way."

He led them along the wharf to a stand of worm-eaten pilings, blue-green with algae, home to an assortment of disintegrating derelicts seemingly abandoned to rot in peace.

"There she is. Jhiv-Huze's pride, his beauty, his delight." The captain's broad gesture encompassed a filthy, rusty, antiquated tub with peeling paint and a dented smokestack. A tattered tricolored banner, denoting an independent operator, drooped from the staff. Faded lettering along the bow spelled out the vessel's name: *Blind Cripple*.

Luzelle's jaw dropped. She did not dare to meet Girays's eyes.

"She doesn't go in much for paint and pennants," Jhiv-Huze confessed sentimentally. "She isn't quite the fashionable belle. But she has the heart of a champion, the *Cripple* has, and she'll burst her sweet boiler to carry you safe to Jumo."

"But how long will she take to do it? Can we hope to overtake the *Water Sprite*?"

"Overtake her? Rest assured, we'll leave that overblown,

overloaded, glorified scow wallowing in our wake within the space of hours. Depend on it."

Luzelle drew a deep breath and compelled herself to request, "Then allow us to board, Captain."

"Mmm, yes. Madame will recall . . ." He rubbed his thumb and two fingers together expressively.

"Oh, certainly." Her wallet produced five hundred Newrekkoes, which she handed over with a false air of confidence. Girays did likewise, and Captain Jhiv-Huze grandly motioned them on to the slippery, creaky gangplank.

The *Blind Cripple* stank of rancid cooking oil, cheap cigars, old fish, and fresh excrement. A single whiff served notice that a slop bucket or chamber pot located somewhere below was emptied on an irregular basis at best. Luzelle's nose wrinkled. Courtesy just barely prevented her from pinching her nostrils. Her eyes encountered Girays's. One of his dark brows rose. Suddenly she discovered giggles bubbling at the back of her throat, and she suppressed them with an effort. There was nothing to laugh about, she told herself sternly. The *Blind Cripple* was disgusting and doubtless unhealthy—

A sputter escaped her, and she turned it into a cough.

She would probably contract some dreadful disease aboard this floating pesthouse. The air alone would be enough to poison her over the course of—of—

"How many days to Jumo?" Luzelle inquired.

"From five to twelve, depending upon the weather, the condition of the river, and the disposition of the Nine Blessed Tribes," Jhiv-Huze returned serenely.

"Oh." Her merriment evaporated. Five days aboard the *Blind Cripple* constituted serious hardship. Twice that was unthinkable.

"Considerable variation there," Girays observed without visible concern. "How would you evaluate the current condition of weather, river, and Blessed Tribesmen, Captain?"

"Weather favorable," the other declared. "Spring rains all but over, summer heat not yet set in. Prime flesh-borer season, but that shouldn't trouble us much aboard the *Cripple*. The river is high and swift, the shoals well submerged. It isn't easy to run aground at this time of the year, and thus the *Waterweed*'s recent encounter with a sandbar above Flewn's Bend marks a rare triumph for her pilot—he's accomplished the nearly impossible. As for the disposition of the Blessed Tribesmen, that's not so easily gauged. Beyond question they're angered by recent events and, given the opportunity, won't hesitate to express their dissatisfaction. But opportunities are few between here and Ygah-Ta'ahri, thanks to the Grewzian presence. The offal-chomping gut-gobblers—that is to say, the stalwart sons of the Imperium—swarm like busy little grey bees along that stretch of the river, and to give them their due, they maintain good order. Below Ygah-Ta'ahri the Ypsiñolo Falls force all vessels into the detour of the Ta'ahri Capillaries, whose complexity defies even Grewzian efficiency. There, where the channels are narrow and the jungle dense, the Blessed Tribesmen remain a force to be reckoned with. But Roupe Jhiv-Huze is ready to face them. His fortunes are fair, his star in the ascendant. Sir and Madame, you are privileged to enjoy his protection."

"That was a most informative evaluation, Captain," Girays remarked with apparent appreciation. He glanced at Luzelle, and his eyes spoke. *Still time to back out.*

Never, she replied in silence. Aloud she requested, "Will you show us to our quarters, Captain?"

"Below," Jhiv-Huze directed amiably. "Easily located. Madame need only follow her nose."

"We want separate staterooms," she announced.

"Staterooms?" He pondered. "Madame will soon discover that we aboard the *Cripple* lead lives of extreme simplicity. The captain alone enjoys private quarters. Passengers and crew sling hammocks where they find space."

"But surely you can't expect me to share accommodations with—I mean, you must see that it's quite impossible—"

"Madame may come to appreciate the spacious airy comfort of the deck in the evening. Moonlight upon the river, the glory of the stars overhead, the kiss of the forest breezes upon your brow—"

"The kiss of countless mosquitoes upon every inch of

exposed skin, the caress of torrential downpours—no, Captain." Luzelle folded her arms. "The deck won't do, and—"

"And Madame will doubtless wish to investigate alternatives," the captain observed cheerily. "The engine room, the bilge, the galley—the possibilities are manifold. Perhaps Madame will seek the advice of Oonuvu, who knows every inch of the *Blind Cripple*."

"Oonuvu?"

"The stoker. A splendid lad."

"But—"

"And now Jhiv-Huze must set to work. Sir and Madame, you will find all that you require below. Come, let us cast off!" So saying, the captain paused above an open hatch to shout orders in Ygahri dialect down to an invisible subordinate, then turned away to begin wrestling with the gangplank.

"Do you mean to follow his suggestion?" Girays did not trouble to hide his amusement. "If not, better decide quickly."

"Nothing to decide," she declared, and slipped neatly by him to descend the companionway to a verminous galley, which she passed through without letting her eyes linger. Beyond the galley lay the blistering engine room, with its primitive boiler presided over by a muscular, sweat-gleaming Ygahri youth, perhaps fifteen years of age, clad in an abbreviated loincloth. He turned as she entered, and she caught the flash of slanted black eyes burning beneath a long fringe of tangled black hair. Oonuvu, without doubt. Luzelle essayed a polite tepid smile, which was not returned. The young stoker's devouring eyes narrowed. Setting his shovel aside, he squatted down on his haunches and studied her at expressionless length. Presently his hands began to slide back and forth along his thighs, streaking the coppery flesh with dark coal dust. Uneasiness stirred at the pit of her stomach. She should not have left Girays up on deck. Mistake. *Bother Girays. I can look after myself.* She turned and walked away.

Behind her she heard Oonuvu's voice, whispering in Ygahri. She did not understand a single word, and somehow felt that she did not want to.

The next door she opened disclosed a tiny closet containing a hammock, a padlocked oaken chest, a padlocked locker, and a table supporting an alcohol burner. The enclosed space reeked of *marukiñutu*. These were manifestly the captain's quarters, and she shut the door at once.

Proceeding forward to the main cabin, she discovered dirt, evil odors, and half a dozen filthy hammocks. No washstand. No pillows, no sheets. No privacy. No feasible alternative. She set her bag down on the floor.

A creak alerted her, and she turned to find Oonuvu framed in the narrow doorway. He was leaning against the jamb, compact body motionless, coppery face still as a mask, unwinking slanted eyes fixed upon her.

"What is the matter?" she inquired with a distant courtesy designed to mask her apprehension. His face did not change, and she wondered if he understood any language other than his own native dialect.

She repeated the query in Grewzian. Still no response, not a flicker, not a twitch. His inscrutable immobility was beginning to wear on her nerves, but she hardly ventured to complain, for the boy had done nothing wrong.

Marukiñutu? she wondered, but could not judge by his eyes, for the black of his pupils merged indistinguishably with the black of the surrounding irises.

"Go away," she commanded sharply. "Go back to your work."

He did not react, and her hand automatically sought the Khrennisov in her pocket. The touch of steel gave her pause. Draw a loaded gun on an adolescent who offered no overt threat? A ridiculous, hysterical notion. Or was it? She looked into his obsidian eyes and wondered.

The hoot of a whistle resolved the dilemma. The *Blind Cripple* pulled away from the dock.

"Back to your work." Luzelle emphasized the command with a gesture. Oonuvu studied her another endless moment, then withdrew as silently as he had come.

She expelled a relieved breath. For a moment she stood still, then stepped to the porthole and looked out without seeing. Her thoughts jumped to the immediate future; sleeping, eating, washing, dressing, and undressing aboard the *Blind*

Cripple for the next five days and more. Uncomfortable. Embarrassing. Unsafe. Intolerable.

But not so intolerable as defeat. And not nearly so intolerable as the snide remarks that Girays would produce should she try to back out now. She had made her own hammock, and now she would lie in it.

14

XOXO RECEDED INTO THE DISTANCE. Dense forest crowded the banks of the Ygah. Luzelle returned to the deck and stationed herself at the rail, eager for the sight of untrammeled greenery, exotic blossoms of violent color, and highly improbable birds. They were all there, as gorgeous as ever she had imagined, but she could not enjoy the spectacle. The atmosphere—sweltering, saturated, and weighted with the stench of decay—lay inert in her lungs. She was languid with the heat, her head heavy, her body bathed in sweat. No corresponding torpor assailed the countless airborne insects buzzing about the boat. Bees. Horseflies. Green-headed scarlet-winged things that peeped sweetly and bit torturously. Flying legions of them, invincible and insatiable.

The little monsters didn't seem to bother the captain, she noted with some resentment. There was Jhiv-Huze up on the bridge—bareheaded, sleeves and loose trousers rolled—happily immune to assault. And that stoker, the eerie Oonuvu, skulked around almost naked without ill effect. And Girays v'Alisante, briar pipe in hand, wreathed himself in clouds of expensive tobacco smoke that repelled the insects, and seemed happy enough. Whereas she, female and fair skinned—

Another of the scarlet-winged creatures bit, and she slapped uselessly. It wasn't fair. Perhaps she should ask Girays for the loan of a pipe. She could smoke it while polishing her gun. Cigarettes, perhaps? She could probably purchase or trade for a supply the first time the *Blind Cripple* docked at some camp along the river. Some women did smoke—a few eccentric socialites too rich and powerful to care for public opinion; certain actresses, artists' models, bohemians, demi-mondaines, and the like. Into her mind popped the picture of the Grandlandsman Torvid Stornzof and his signature black cigarettes. No, she would not smoke.

Her chin itched. Her hand rose to the freshly swollen bump there and she rubbed it, sorely tempted.

"Don't scratch," advised a voice behind her.

The sharp scent of *marukiñutu* filled her nostrils. She turned to confront Jhiv-Huze.

"Activates the insect venom, spreads it around, intensifies the irritation. Quite soon the bite festers. In this climate, a serious matter. Sometimes fatal. Mmm, yes. Roupe Jhiv-Huze has seen it more than once," the captain continued with relish. "The afflicted visage, discolored and distorted almost beyond recognition, pocked with clustering suppurations. Each sore swollen to the size of a grape, the skin stretched tight and shiny, the surrounding flesh intensely livid. Then—the pustules rupture, their contents spurting forth in corrosive streams. The pain of this process is excruciating, the sight appalling, the stench unspeakable. Many victims succumb, and those that survive are disfigured, their faces marked forever with jagged craters and raised scars. Jhiv-Huze would hate to see such a fate befall a face so charming as Madame's, and therefore he most earnestly enjoins her not to scratch."

"She won't." Suddenly queasy, Luzelle turned away and made for the companionway.

"*Marukiñutu*," the captain recommended. "The fragrance of strongly infused *marukiñutu* repels all manner of winged pests. They cannot abide it. Jhiv-Huze can hardly imagine why, but knows how to profit by their ignorance, and he advises his passengers to do the same. Dose yourself well, Madame. The alternative—torment, infection, oozing pus, welling blood, facial necrosis, the nauseous reek of mortifying flesh, the inevitable maggots—"

One hand pressed to her mouth, Luzelle fled. Behind her rumbled volcanic eructations of laughter.

Son of a sow did that on purpose, she thought. Girays was right again. *I just hate it when he's right.*

Reaching the inadequate sanctuary of the main cabin, she let herself sink gingerly into a dirty hammock, and there remained until her qualms subsided. The place stank like an outhouse, but offered limited refuge from the insects. There was one significant advantage to a hammock, even a filthy one, she reflected—no possibility of bedbugs. It was not a great comfort, but it was something.

She sat up. Drawing her bag near, she opened it to discover that her belongings had been disarranged, and none too subtly. The small bundle of raisins purchased in Zuleekistan gaped wide, and she had left it securely tied. Several of her linen undergarments were blackly streaked with coal dust. Indignation, embarrassment, and uneasiness fluttered her insides. Her hand automatically sought the Khrennisov. The weapon was safe in her pocket, along with her money and passport, which she always kept with her.

Instinct pulled her gaze to the doorway, where the young stoker Oonuvu stood silently watching her. Their eyes met, and his did not waver. After a moment his hands began to slide slowly up and down along his thighs.

Her own hands tightened, along with her jaw. She wanted to get away, but he was blocking the exit. Of course he would stand aside if she made for the door, he would not dare hesitate. And if she was wrong about that, she really did not want to know, so she stayed where she was.

He's only a boy, she reminded herself. *Scarcely more than a child. Harmless.*

But he looked neither childish nor harmless. His body was compact but powerful, the muscles bulging beneath the skin. Beyond question he was stronger than she.

She glanced down at her open bag, with its violated contents, and anger stiffened her spine. Rising to her feet and confronting him squarely, she demanded, "Did you touch my belongings?"

There was no response, no indication that he had heard much less understood her. She repeated the query sharply, without result. His blank, hot gaze rattled her, and her cheeks flushed. Carefully maintaining a firm but calm tone, she told him, "This bag and everything in it are mine. You are not to touch them. Do you understand?" No reply, and she mouthed very distinctly, "Mine. Do not touch."

His slanting eyes flickered, and she resisted the impulse to step backward.

He whispered something in Ygahri.

"Get out of here." She heard herself snap out the command like a Grewzian overseer. "Go back to the engine room. Get out."

He was still staring fathomlessly at her, and might have stood there in the doorway for the rest of the day had the imperative call of the captain not rung through the boat. Oonuvu unhurriedly licked the palm of his hand—another obscure gesture—and retired, leaving her alone.

Luzelle expelled a prolonged, slow breath. Stepping to the porthole, she gazed out at the opaque yellow-brown waters of the Ygah. For a long time she stood there without moving.

UNCOMFORTABLE AND BORED, she lurked in the cabin until the sun's decline in the early evening promised relief from steamy heat and voracious insects. Then at last she returned to the deck where Girays, comfortable in the shade of a tropical straw hat, sat poring over a battered copy of v'Ierre's *History of the Jurlian-Zenki Wars*.

"Lost in the past?" she asked, smiling.

"It is less puzzling than the future and less humid than the present." He returned her smile. "Where have you been all afternoon? Napping?"

"I wish. Sewing, actually. I'm starting to resemble a Bizaqhi beggar, so I thought I'd best use the spare time to mend some of my disintegrating clothes."

"Sewing. Hard to imagine. I never pictured the dashing Miss Devaire as a repository of domestic virtues."

"I don't think you ever pictured the dashing Miss Devaire as a repository of any virtues."

"Ah, you impugn my good judgment."

"No, only your good nature. But you can prove me wrong by diverting me with your conversation for a few minutes."

"Good to know that it qualifies as diverting."

"Come, set that old book aside for now. I'll bet it's dry as last week's bread, anyway."

"Don't you believe it. In this climate nothing's dry for long."

As if in confirmation, a brief shower of raindrops spattered out of the dimming sky. It was over in a minute or two, leaving the damp world marginally cooler.

"That felt wonderful." Luzelle shook her wet hair, and the water droplets flew in all directions. "Is it my imagination, or do I actually feel something like a feeble breeze?"

"Impossible. Well"—he reconsidered—"maybe the mournful ghost of a breeze."

"Or the vague premonition." She moved to the railing, and he rose from his chair to follow. "The rain seems to have chased most of the bugs away, for now. There are moments here and there when this place almost verges on bearable." A glow of light caught her eye and she blinked, then pointed. "Look, Girays—look over there."

A pale submerged luminescence was moving along the Ygah, making its way north against the current. The radiant cloud wavered beneath the water, its pure light dulled and colored by the muddy ripples of the river.

"It looks like a ghost," she marveled.

"It is, of sorts. That's the River Phantom." In answer to her mute inquiry he explained, "A school of zephusa fish, native to the Ygah and seen nowhere else in the world. I've read of such fish and their ghostly light in the water, but never imagined that I'd actually see it."

He was smiling, much the same sort of smile that had marked his first glimpse of Lanthi Ume rising out of the sea. She was smiling herself, and the thought came unbidden, *If only it could always be like this.*

A tiny pinprick broke the trance. A high-pitched humming filled her ears. She slapped reflexively, squashed the target, and saw her own blood mingled with insect remains smear across her wrist. A grunt of disgust escaped her.

Twilight. The Hour of the Mosquitoes.

"They're eating me alive!" she complained. "Why do they seem to single me out?"

"Discriminating palates," Girays approved heartlessly.

"Oh, laugh all you please, but you wouldn't find it quite so funny if you were the one covered with itchy red lumps that you didn't dare scratch. The captain recommended dosing myself with *marukiñutu*. I'm almost desperate enough to try it. What do you think?"

"Let me be certain that I understand you. You are asking for my advice?"

"I don't promise to follow it."

"Good, that reassures me that I am confronting the real Luzelle, and no substitute. Here's my opinion, then. Stay away from the *marukiñutu*. It's addictive, and its efficacy as an insect repellent remains unproved. I wouldn't be inclined to accept Jhiv-Huze's word on the subject—in all probability he's simply seeking a companion in debauchery."

"Sometimes you sound very like my father."

"Who could not have been wrong one hundred percent of the time, but that's another day's debate. I've a vial of Urq's Universal Unguent in my valise. Take it, apply some to the bug bites, and see if it helps. I believe Jhiv-Huze intends to dock briefly tomorrow at Pijji Camp, and you may find that the Ygahris there can furnish native concoctions far more effective than anything offered elsewhere."

"All right, I'll try it."

"Did I hear you correctly? Where did all this sweet complaisance spring from? You detest my suggestions. You enjoy nothing more than the satisfaction of rejecting them."

"No, not at all. Well—" She thought a moment and amended, "Maybe that was somewhat true when I was nineteen. A *little* true. But years have passed since then, and some things do change. I'll prove it. Have you any more advice to offer, if I ask?"

"The fund is inexhaustible. What's the subject?"

"An awkward one. Tonight, you see . . ." She stirred uncomfortably and forced herself to continue. "Everyone other than the captain sleeps in the main cabin. I suppose I could manage that, if only it weren't for that boy, that Oonuvu—"

"What, the little Ygahri stoker? A trifle. He won't be there. For that matter, neither will I. You shall not lack privacy."

"Girays, I couldn't turn you out of the cabin to sleep on deck, it wouldn't be fair. I appreciate the gallantry, but—"

"The matter is not open to discussion. I'll do well enough, never fear. As for the stoker, do you imagine that I—or any other Vonahrishman of honor—could actually permit you to share sleeping accommodations with a male native? The notion is absurd."

"Permit?"

"Oh, I know the word annoys you, and perhaps it was ill chosen. But I trust that your modern passion for independence doesn't blind you to the simple reality of the matter. I would not allow the Ygahri boy to intrude upon any Vonahrishwoman, much less you."

"Perhaps M. the Marquis would be so good as to explain the relevance of nationality?"

"The explanation is self-evident. Will you pretend otherwise?"

"But we poor mortals do not all share in His Lordship's ability to simplify. His judgments are based upon the broadest possible generalizations, the creakiest prejudices, and these suffice. Vonahrishwoman. Ygahri boy. That's all he needs to know."

"Self-righteousness hardly becomes you. Bare moments ago, you yourself were complaining of this troublesome native."

"You didn't think to ask why. It never even occurred to you that I might have some specific objection beyond the mere fact of his race."

"You need none."

"That's unfair, that's narrow, that's"—she groped for an adjective likely to dent his complacency and found one—"irrational."

"Instruct me, then. Describe the countless virtues and achievements of the Nine Blessed Tribes. Remind me of the great Ygahri contributions to art, literature, architecture, science, law, and philosophy. Somehow they have slipped my mind."

"Oh, sometimes there's no talking to you!"

"Your speech seems unimpaired, but I'll try to make it easier. Explain the stoker's offense, if you will."

"Well, he rifled my belongings."

"Little brute steal anything?"

"I believe not, but the bare thought of him touching my things—" She grimaced.

"Inquisitive as monkeys, some of these natives."

"Girays—!"

"No disrespect intended. Monkeys are very engaging creatures. Has he done anything else?"

"Not exactly. He stares at me—"

"Understandable. Can't really blame him for that."

"I don't like the look in his eyes, or the way he uses his hands."

"Has he touched you?" Girays's face hardened.

"No, he only touches himself. Not what you're thinking, nothing so obvious. And once he licked—well, never mind. The point is, I can't abide him."

"You won't need to. I've already promised that you'll have the cabin to yourself. I'll make my wishes known to little Oonuvu, and if he proves uncooperative, I'll whip him bloody."

"You wouldn't. You're too civilized and too decent."

"You didn't think it was in me to carry a gun, as I recall."

"Well then, how do you plan to make your wishes known to little Oonuvu, unless you happen to speak Ygahri? Anyway, better take care. Damage his stoker, and the captain is likely to put us both off his boat."

"Then I'll pay the captain to keep Oonuvu out of the cabin. Better?"

"Much. But if anyone pays Jhiv-Huze, it ought to be me."

"Let us balance accounts some other time. For the present I prefer to watch the sunset and swat mosquitoes."

THE *BLIND CRIPPLE* DROPPED ANCHOR for the night. Dinner, prepared by the captain himself, followed shortly thereafter. A tiny drop-leaf table, hinged to the galley wall and supported by a rickety gateleg, barely accommodated the four diners. The lamplight was feeble and shaky, the atmosphere motionless and malodorous. Winged things flitted about the closet-sized space, while the occasional nimble dark form scuttled across the floor.

Luzelle studied the green mold growing in the cracks between the boards of the tabletop for a few moments, then averted her eyes. A bowl of food was placed before her—a stew of some sort, dense and oily. And venerable, she noted at first bite; probably heated and reheated half a dozen times. She ate mechanically, without allowing herself to taste. No water to rinse her mouth clean—the local water was lethal to foreigners. There was weak beer and potent greenish xussi, the locally distilled liquor. She drank sparingly of the former.

At least she did not have to manufacture conversation, and neither did Girays, for Captain Jhiv-Huze's store of river anecdotes was limitless and his willingness to relate them equally so. The bass voice boomed interminably, the flow of words interrupting itself periodically as the speaker paused to refresh himself with drafts of xussi. Time passed, the greenish spirits flowed, and the voice slurred but never ceased. At first the tales possessed a certain freshness, but as the alcohol took hold, Jhiv-Huze waxed vague, digressive, and repetitive.

Luzelle's attention wandered. She tried not to think about the food before her, the way it looked or smelled or tasted. She tried not to think about Oonuvu, whose black eyes glittered through the curtain of his black hair, as he matched his captain draft for greenish draft. She tried not to think about five days or more of the same. Far better to think of Jumo Towne, where civilization and its amenities resumed. Decent hotels. A bath. Good food. Clean clothes. *Dry* clothes. Her own garments were still damp from the rain, and likely to remain so, for nothing ever dried thoroughly in this climate. Her sturdy walking shoes were wet, and so were her feet inside them. She would have to switch over to sandals before her well-soaked flesh began to soften, allowing potentially disastrous sores to open.

Beside her Girays sat enviably cool and at ease in his light khakis. And he, known to rebuke his own chef at Belfaireau for the sin of overcooking a fresh brook trout by the space of ninety seconds, now spooned his questionably edible stew without visible reluctance. How did he do it? The captain's voice ran on, and her thoughts ranged.

Dinner concluded when Jhiv-Huze pushed his bowl aside, laid his head down on the table before him, and went to sleep. Oonuvu rose and slid noiselessly from the galley.

Luzelle shot a dubious glance at Girays. He shrugged. Together they rose and returned to the deck, where they lingered for a time watching the stars. Moonlight glanced tremulously off the ripples of the river, but the forests crowding the banks drowned in deepest shadow. Out of the blackness issued a cry, a stabbing wail of ultimate grief.

"What was that?" Luzelle felt the hairs stir at the back of her neck.

"Hunter or hunted." Girays spoke almost in a whisper.

They stood listening, but the cry was not repeated. Eventually suspense dwindled and Luzelle realized that she was tired. Perhaps the suffocating atmosphere sapped energy, or maybe dinner had poisoned her. Whatever the reason, it was early but she wanted to sleep.

"I'm going below now," she announced, adding uncomfortably, "Did you ever have a word with Jhiv-Huze about—"

"All difficulties resolved," Girays assured her. "The stoker has been instructed, the captain has the matter well in hand."

"The captain, if I'm not mistaken, is thoroughly drunk and dead to the world until morning."

"The affair has been settled. Don't worry, you'll not be disturbed."

"But what about you?"

"I'm wondering if I might not commandeer the captain's quarters for tonight. Jhiv-Huze, as you've observed, is unlikely to notice."

"You wouldn't dare!" She could not help laughing.

"Well, it's something to consider. In the meantime, you go get some sleep."

"I will—and thank you." For once it was easy to thank him. Making her way down the companion and forward to the main cabin, she opened the door and stuck her head in cautiously. Moonlight washing through the porthole illumined an empty compartment, and she released a relieved breath. She stepped in and shut the door behind her. No lock, she observed with regret. Not so much as a chair to brace beneath the latch. Well, she didn't need one. She was quite unnecessarily skittish.

Nevertheless she hesitated to undress, but the dank state of her garments decided her. Pulling a pair of knee-length muslin drawers and one of the long, loose Bizaqhi tunics from her bag, she cast a wary glance about and then, crouched on the floor with her back to the door, hurriedly and furtively changed her wet clothes for the dry ones. Relatively dry; the sodden air seemed to have permeated everything she owned. The pocket pistol went into the bag to lie atop the contents, in easy reach should she need it.

She spread her damp garments out across one of the vacant hammocks, and spread herself out in another. The canvas beneath her was moist and it smelled of mildew. There was no pillow, no sheet, and no need of the latter, for the atmosphere lay heavy as a soggy woolen blanket. But the slight rocking motion of the ship at anchor was curiously soothing, and she was genuinely tired. Presently her thoughts slowed, her eyes closed, and she slept.

SHE HAD NO IDEA what minute sound or acute instinct woke her. Luzelle opened her eyes. She could not have slumbered very long, for the moonlight streaming into the cabin had scarcely altered. By that pale glow she discerned the form of the stoker Oonuvu squatting close beside her hammock. He was staring down at her where she lay, his hands sliding slowly back and forth along his bare thighs. His face was in shadow, but she caught the gleam of melted-pitch eyes. A cry too spontaneous for prudence or dignity to contain escaped her. Rolling from the hammock, she hit the floor on all fours and scrambled to her feet.

He whispered something in Ygahri.

She did not pause to interpret or analyze, but sprang for

the door. She was through it in a flash, stumbling aft through
the dark in search of the companionway. She did not know if
Oonuvu followed, did not even know for certain that she had
anything to fear from him, but she did belatedly realize that
she had left herself defenseless. The Khrennisov still lay where
she had so carefully placed it in her bag.

She was up on deck again, the night air soft and thick
around her, the moonlight serviceably bright. A shadow slid
along the edge of her vision, and she whirled to confront Girays, who had sprung out of nowhere.

He took one look and asked, "What's happened?"

"That boy—" Her voice came out a frightened, ridiculous
squeak, and she took care to lower it. "In the cabin—"

"Did he lay a hand on you?"

"No, no he didn't. But I woke up, and he was just *there*,
right beside me, staring down—"

"That does it. The little animal's off this boat, right now.
I'm going to dump him over the side, and he can swim for the
bank."

"Girays, you can't do that!"

"Better than killing him outright, isn't it?" He made for the
companionway.

His expression astonished her. Gone were all traces of characteristic weariness and amusement. He looked composed,
purposeful, and dangerous. She had never seen him look like
that, had never guessed that he could look like that. For a moment he seemed almost a stranger.

"Wait." She dragged vainly at his arm. "Stop. Please listen.
That boy surprised me, but he didn't actually do anything
wrong. Girays, do you hear me? I said he didn't *do* anything—"

"He broke into your room, didn't he?"

"Not exactly. It wasn't locked and it isn't really my room.
Remember, he normally sleeps there—"

"Not tonight."

"Maybe he didn't know that. You spoke with the captain,
who might easily have neglected to pass the word to the
stoker. Remember how drunk he was."

"You mean, you think this incident accidental? You believe
the boy ignorant and innocent?"

"Well—" She pictured Oonuvu squatting beside the hammock, she remembered his eyes in the moonlight. No, she didn't believe him innocent for one moment, but— "I don't really know," she confessed aloud. "We can't even speak his language, and I suppose we can't just assume the worst for no better reason than—than the look in his eyes. . . ."

"Luzelle." Girays finally halted and turned to face her. "What are you trying to say? That you don't need or want my assistance? There is nothing new in that. I should have remembered."

"That isn't what I meant. Don't you know how glad I am that you're here? I don't think I could stand it if you weren't." She hesitated, embarrassed, and concluded lamely, "I just don't want you to do anything rash."

"Then our accustomed roles are reversed tonight. Very well." The grim set of his jaw relaxed a little. "I promise to permit Oonuvu full opportunity to explain himself before I throw him overboard. What could be more fair? Now let us go track down the little beast."

He advanced and she followed. Soon they reached the main cabin, whose door stood wide open. Her carpetbag, likewise open, lay on the floor where she had left it. Hurrying to the bag, Luzelle knelt and quickly checked the contents.

"Nothing missing," she reported.

"Except the stoker, but there aren't many places he can hide. Come, we'll check the engine room."

"Girays, no. Just let it go. *Please*."

He hesitated so long that she thought he was going to refuse, but at last he conceded, "If that is what you truly prefer."

"You sound disappointed. You really *want* to throw him overboard, don't you?"

"I want matters clearly resolved."

"Maybe we can sic the captain on Oonuvu tomorrow."

"Perhaps. In the meantime there's no lock on your door, and he could come back."

"I don't think he will." Even to herself she sounded feeble. "Anyway, I'll be all right, I still have the pistol."

"I will sleep in the corridor before your door," he announced as if she had not spoken.

"Please don't. It's unnecessary, and too formerly-Exalted for human tolerance."

"Wholly selfish, I assure you. I wish only to set my own mind at rest."

"What about my mind? How do you think I'll feel, knowing that you're so uncomfortable because of me?"

"Our respective discomforts should balance nicely, then, thus satisfying your keen appetite for equality."

"I've a better idea. Take one of the empty hammocks, and sleep in here." His brows arched, and she added, "It's the most practical and sensible thing to do."

"Wonder if your father would agree."

"He'd probably fear for your reputation." She saw him waver, and added, "I'll feel safer if you're in here." This was both truthful and effective. He nodded and, without further argument, stretched himself out in the hammock nearest the door.

Luzelle returned to her own interrupted repose, or tried to. For what seemed an eternity she lay with her eyes closed, her muscles conscientiously relaxed. But she was thoroughly wakeful and likely to remain so; attuned to the motion of the ship at anchor, alert to every creak and rustle, and above all aware of Girays's nearness. Not that he was making any noise. No coughing or snoring, certainly no attempted conversation. Eyes still closed, she listened intently, but caught no sound of his breathing, whose quality might have told her if he slept. For some reason it seemed immensely important to know whether he shared her insomnia.

The minutes passed. She opened her eyes, watched the ceiling, and listened to the *Blind Cripple*. At last, very slowly, she turned her head to risk a surreptitious peek over the edge of her hammock.

Girays lay with his face turned away from her. She could see a patch of his dark hair, the pale angle of his cheekbone, and a portion of a khaki-clad shoulder; the curve of the canvas sling in which he lay obscured the rest. If his eyes were open, he would be gazing straight out the porthole at the night sky. She had only to whisper his name to find out, but somehow could not. Nor could she seem to turn away from him, but lay there wide awake, silently watching and wondering.

MORNING CAME and the *Blind Cripple* resumed progress. For hours Luzelle sat up on deck watching the ferociously green, orchid-spangled Forests of Oorex glide by. The heat and humidity were oppressive as ever, but Urq's Universal Unguent furnished some relief from the insects. There was no sign of Oonuvu—perhaps he had received orders to stay out of sight, or else he was busy below—and she did not try to analyze, but simply enjoyed his invisibility. She had a book that Girays had lent her, one of his historical treatises—not what she would have chosen, yet unexpectedly palatable. The time passed slowly, but it passed.

Shortly before noon the *Blind Cripple* docked at Pijji Camp, and all aboard were freed for the space of an hour. No use complaining about the loss of time. Captain Jhiv-Huze was jovial but adamant; certain supplies were required, and the delay was necessary.

Luzelle went ashore to explore the primitive little makeshift quasi-village where, as Girays had predicted, she found Ygahris willing to sell or barter ointments guaranteed to repel the most voracious of insects. She was surprised and a little uneasy to discover how easy it was to communicate with the natives in broken Grewzian. Most of them knew at least several phrases and some were decidedly fluent. The Grewzian presence, so prevalent along this stretch of the river, was much in evidence at Pijji Camp, whose inhabitants flaunted Grewzian cigarettes, jewelry incorporating the amber glass fragments of Grewzian ale bottles, and small medals stamped with the likeness of the Grewzian imperior.

Her bag of raisins, an exotic rarity to the locals, purchased her a supply of evil-smelling ointment wrapped in the leathery leaves of some nameless native shrub. Mission accomplished, she reboarded the *Blind Cripple* and soon Captain Jhiv-Huze did likewise. The alteration in his demeanor caught her attention at once. Gone was the joviality. The captain's footsteps dragged. The set of jaw and shoulders communicated resentful despondency. He glanced at her briefly in passing, but did not trouble to acknowledge her existence. She gazed after him with a frown.

The *Blind Cripple* departed Pijji Camp. Luzelle smeared Ygahri ointment over her face, neck, hands, wrists, and exposed forearms, then returned to her reading. The hours passed. The ointment fulfilled all promises, and the insects left her alone.

Twice Girays approached to converse with her briefly, and she found herself curiously self-conscious in his presence. He was altogether amiable—he even affected a polite unawareness of her assertively scented native salve—but she was uneasy all the same. It had started last night, she realized, and it was absurd, but she could not banish the memory of lying wide awake in the moonlit cabin, watching him as he slept or pretended to sleep.

And what of the night to come? And the night after that?

She let nothing show on her face. She chatted brightly and lightly. After a while he went away.

In the midafternoon the *Blind Cripple* docked again at a bend in the river where the jungle growths gave way to a sorry little collection of leaf-thatched huts that reeked of impermanence.

Another delay. Why? Scowling, Luzelle set her book aside and watched as Captain Jhiv-Huze disembarked alone. He hurried toward the huts, and soon the flimsy walls hid him from view. Rising from her chair, she paced to and fro. Forty endless minutes elapsed before he reappeared. Head and shoulders adroop, he shuffled back aboard. The gangplank rose and the *Blind Cripple* steamed off.

At this rate they would never overtake the *Water Sprite.* Luzelle fumed helplessly. Girays's book no longer held her attention.

Four hours later when the *Blind Cripple* paused once again, this time at a tiny village with an unpronounceable name, her temper flared. Confronting the captain, she complained bitterly.

He did not bother to answer. Plodding by as if blind and deaf to her presence, he made his way ashore. Luzelle glared after him, but her indignation veiled rising trepidation. There was something disquieting in his expression, something wrong about the eyes; a glazed, empty, almost lifeless look. She had seen such eyes staring down at her from stuffed animal heads mounted on walls.

Was Jhiv-Huze sick? Fever, perhaps? If so, could he pilot the *Blind Cripple* on toward Jumo? A thoroughly selfish concern, she knew. Once she would have been ashamed of herself, but not now.

An hour passed and the captain returned, dully morose as ever. The *Blind Cripple* steamed south for a few scant miles, then dropped anchor at sunset. Jhiv-Huze retired to his own quarters. The engine fell silent. Sultry darkness descended.

"I wonder if we'll eat tonight," Luzelle worried aloud.

"Can't face the captain's cooking?" Girays inquired.

"It's just barely preferable to starvation. But he's been so—what should I call it—distracted today that I think he may forget to feed us."

The two of them stood at the rail watching the moon rise over the Forests of Oorex. A thin mist diffused the pallid light. The night birds hooted, the insects hummed, the frogs sang, and Luzelle's stomach rumbled emphatically. She colored and wondered if he had heard.

"I am ready to dine, and not disposed to wait upon this Jhiv-Huze fellow's eccentric whims," Girays announced.

Yes, he had heard all right, and now he was being diplomatic.

"I suggest we ransack the galley," he continued. "Perhaps we'll find something more or less edible."

She nodded and they went below, where the sound of choking grunts lured them to the captain's quarters. The door stood open. Luzelle looked in and saw Jhiv-Huze huddled on the floor, face buried in his hands, shoulders shaking. If she had paused to think, she might have elected to withdraw in silence. She did not pause, but asked in some concern, "Captain, what is it? Are you ill?"

He looked up, and she saw that his eyes were swollen and his tattooed face streaked with tears. His mouth worked and then he managed to tell her, "There is none to be had."

"What?"

"Jhiv-Huze has offered money, trinkets, tobacco, xussi, transportation. He's volunteered Oonuvu's services. He's offered all that he possesses, and it's made no difference. There is none to be had."

"Captain, you're not well. You'd best lie down. I could bring you a cool wet cloth to lay across your—"

"Useless. It is his special draft that Jhiv-Huze wants and needs, the dear elixir that is his peace and joy. And he tells you there is none! Three times today he's paused along the river to inquire, and always it is the same. The blight has withered the leaves, supplies are exhausted, it's not to be had at any price!"

"Unlucky. But never mind, we'll improvise." She thought quickly. This tearful quivering wretch needed some sort of tonic to restore his nautical competence, and a tonic he would have. "There must be plenty of ingredients in the galley. We'll concoct some sort of substitute—"

"You driveling female idiot, there is no substitute!" the captain cried. "Are you blind, are you stupid? There is one, only one, exquisite and without equal. One queen, one empress, one goddess, one—"

"*Marukiñutu?*" Girays suggested easily. "You've consumed your entire store of *marukiñutu*, Captain?"

"A glimmer of intelligence at last." Jhiv-Huze nodded. The fresh tears welled. "As you have surmised, sir. Jhiv-Huze's solace is gone. How shall he endure the night to come? How shall he endure the morning? He must replenish depleted supplies. There are half a dozen camps to be found between here and Ygah-Ta'ahri. He will try them all."

"No!" Luzelle exclaimed, unable to contain her dismay. "We can't afford the time. No more unscheduled stops. Absolutely not."

"Haste must defer to the greater necessity." A small muscle in his cheek jerked spasmodically, yanking Jhiv-Huze's lips into a fleeting lopsided smile.

"Out of the question. No more stops, I won't stand for it!"

"Roupe Jhiv-Huze commands the *Blind Cripple*. He is captain here, and he advises Madame to remember it."

"An honest captain with any sense of responsibility—" Luzelle began, and managed to squelch herself. Carefully moderating her tone, she enticed, "We might renegotiate our fare, Captain. Perhaps an additional consideration—"

"There is no sum sufficient to turn Jhiv-Huze from his present purpose."

Her indignation rekindled, and she commenced hotly, "I seem to recall that Jhiv-Huze promised to carry us posthaste to Jumo—"

"A course that best serves his own interests, as well as ours," Girays cut her off smoothly. The captain turned blank wet eyes upon him, and he explained, "You've tried three settlements today without success. Your luck tomorrow will be as bad. These unscheduled stops waste time, the local settlements are useless. But Jumo Towne is a well that never runs dry. There, Jhiv-Huze's beloved *marukiñutu* flows on everlastingly as the Ygah itself. Hasten straight to Jumo, Captain. There you will find your happiness promptly restored."

The captain seemed struck by this suggestion. For some moments he pondered in silence. At last he answered, "Sir, Jhiv-Huze believes you have hit upon something. You are in the right, and he concedes it. He will follow your recommendation. Help him to his feet, if you will."

Girays complied.

"Ah, that is better." The captain tottered a little and regained his balance. "Jhiv-Huze is himself again, master of his own destiny, aflame with new resolve. His salvation lies in Jumo Towne. We have dawdled too long. We will squander no more time, but push on south at top speed this very hour, this very moment."

"Good!" Luzelle exclaimed.

"Ah, Madame has regained her good humor. Jhiv-Huze understands that many of her earlier remarks were rooted in ignorance rather than malice, and he is willing to overlook them."

"Ready to weigh anchor, then?"

"Jhiv-Huze is ready to set the river on fire."

"Inadvisable," Girays opined. Ignoring her shocked, accusatory stare, he added, "You cannot pilot the boat by night, Captain."

"Yes he can," Luzelle fired back. "Jhiv-Huze is up to the challenge. Isn't he, Captain?"

"Madame, he is—"

"Only mortal, and thus unable to read the river in the dark," Girays pointed out imperturbably. "Unable to spy the eddies, the fallen trees, the half-submerged obstacles; unable to descry the landmarks—"

"Doesn't matter," Luzelle insisted. "The water's deep at this time of year, the hazards minimal. Didn't you say so yourself, Captain? Come, let's go! Let's go!"

"A single error, and the *Blind Cripple* runs aground, leaving us stranded far from Jumo and its blessings, perhaps for days," Girays continued inexorably. "Will the captain give way to reckless impulse?"

"He will not," Jhiv-Huze decided.

"Oh, you men!" Luzelle exclaimed in frustration. "Where's your courage?"

"Jhiv-Huze admires Madame's spirit, but counsels her to temper enthusiasm with prudence." The captain's own spirit seemed to have mended itself. His tears had evaporated and his eyes had returned to life. He even produced the ghost of a chuckle. "Trust in Jhiv-Huze's renewed resolution. At the first sign of morning light the *Cripple* flies! But for now, good friends, let us be sociable, let us dine. Tonight Jhiv-Huze is pleased to announce that he can offer you stew."

THE NIGHT WAS STICKY, sweaty, and endless. Luzelle slept fitfully, the insomniac interludes merging so seamlessly with uneasy dreams that she was uncertain whether the scratching at the cabin door was real or imaginary. Had she traveled alone, alarm would have jolted her wide awake. But Girays was there and she was unafraid.

The blast of the ship's whistle woke her at dawn. The weak grey light of near morning barely pushed in through the porthole, but the engine was already throbbing. Girays's hammock was empty. He had gone off somewhere, leaving her to the tender mercies of Oonuvu. But no, with the *Blind Cripple* in motion, the stoker was all but chained to the boiler. Nothing to fear from him, for now.

She got up, refreshed her appearance as best she could, then made her way aft to the galley, where she paused to breakfast vilely on a few mouthfuls of yesterday's stew before ascending to the deck.

The damp air was fresh, by local standards. Ghost-white mists lay thick upon the river, and the tall trees crowding the banks loomed indistinct and insubstantial. The ceaseless shrilling of countless invisible insects filled the fog.

Within an hour or so the rising sun would burn the morning mists away. But Roupe Jhiv-Huze, she noted with approval, disdained to wait upon nature. The captain stood at the helm. Jaw outthrust, literally blind to possible dangers, he steered the *Blind Cripple* south toward Jumo at not inconsiderable full speed.

The breeze of their passage stirred her hair and pleasantly cooled her perspiring flesh. To maintain such velocity the boiler had to be operating at full capacity; down below, the stoker was presently toiling like a slave. Excellent.

For a time she stood there enjoying the sense of swift motion, and then the rain came. The skies darkened until it seemed that night had reclaimed the world, the Forests of Oorex faded from view, and the rain fell in sheets. She could barely discern her immediate surroundings, and knew that the captain must be similarly handicapped, but the *Blind Cripple* never slackened speed. Such recklessness was deplorable or else superb, she was not sure which.

It was too late to avoid a drenching. Her clothes were already soaked through. She went below to change and found the folded garments in her bag furred with luxuriant white mold. She rubbed a patch of mold with one finger, and an acrid odor released itself. A grunt of disgust escaped her. For now, there would be no change of clothes.

She spent the next hour washing her moldy garments and

spreading them out over the hammock ropes. Not that they were likely to air-dry; she would probably end up toasting the moisture out over the stove in the galley.

When she had finished the washing she returned to Girays's book, which held her attention throughout the morning. Around noon the rain abated, along with the *Blind Cripple*'s speed. The grumble of the engine altered, the boat decelerated noticeably, and then she heard the captain's voice, loud and angry. Interested, Luzelle returned to a deck now washed with tentative sunshine, where a single glance answered most of her questions.

Oonuvu the stoker squatted there wolfing down a double portion of doubtless soggy hardtack. His body was sweat drenched and black with coal dust. His chest rose and fell rapidly, the obvious effect of recent exertion. Evidently he had paused in his labors for a little rest and refreshment. The boy had every natural right to eat his lunch in peace, Luzelle would have imagined, but the captain did not seem to see it that way.

Roupe Jhiv-Huze, his customary joviality transformed, was barely recognizable. His contorted face was purple behind the tattoos, and he was spewing Ygahri dialect at the top of his lungs. Luzelle did not understand a word, but the captain's furious gestures spoke for themselves. The stoker was being ordered back to his post.

Oonuvu shrugged and muttered something with his mouth full. The captain barked a command. Oonuvu stared straight ahead and chewed on. Bending down, Jhiv-Huze snatched the hardtack from the other's grasp and flung it over the rail. Oonuvu hissed, and his teeth showed. Jhiv-Huze roared and brandished a fist.

Luzelle's breath caught. Her eyes flew to Girays, who stood not far away observing the scene. She must unconsciously have transmitted some question or appeal, which he answered with a brief, unequivocal shake of the head. *Stay out of it,* he was telling her in silence. *Don't interfere.*

She could hardly have expected anything more of a formerly-Exalted v'Alisante, a hereditary seigneur at that. He had, after all, been raised in the firm conviction that his social inferiors were his inferiors in every sense. Intractable servants, lazy or refractory menials, rebellious peasants and laborers were unlikely to win the sympathies of M. the Marquis. Probably he believed that a sound hiding was just what the impudent Ygahri deserved.

But Luzelle Devaire carried not a drop of formerly-Exalted blood in her veins, and she was not about to stand idly by while a large Kyrendtish captain brutalized his native underling. If Jhiv-Huze actually struck the lad, she would—she would—

What? Complain? Protest?

She did neither, for at that moment Oonuvu himself resolved her dilemma by rising unhurriedly to his feet. He yawned elaborately and slouched off toward the companionway. Jhiv-Huze jabbered angry dialect. The stoker cast an indolent glance back over his bare shoulder. His black eyes touched Luzelle in passing, and he ran a slow tongue along his lower lip. Her sympathy for him instantly died.

Oonuvu disappeared below. The smokestack belched and the voice of the engine deepened. Roupe Jhiv-Huze loosed a grunt of satisfaction and resumed the helm. The *Blind Cripple* picked up speed and Luzelle returned to her interrupted reading.

In the late afternoon a second vocal explosion drew her back to the deck. This time Girays was not in evidence. But there sat Oonuvu—sweatier and filthier than ever—with a jug of xussi cradled in his lap. Above him loomed the noisily irate Jhiv-Huze. While his captain fumed and blustered, the stoker raised the jug to his lips and swallowed a leisurely draft. Setting the xussi aside, he turned his face to the sky, furrowed his brow in concentration, and spat Ygahri-style, launching a fat dollop of alcoholic saliva high into the air. The flying globule described a steep arc and splashed the deck inches from Roupe Jhiv-Huze's sandaled foot. That same foot promptly lashed forward to strike Oonuvu's ribs with a solid thud, flinging the stoker sideways. The xussi jug jumped, fell, and broke into pieces, spilling liquor across the deck. Snarling,

Oonuvu grabbed a dagger-pointed pottery shard and sprang to his feet. A knife materialized in the hand of the captain. The two faced one another in chest-heaving silence.

Luzelle watched disbelievingly. Her mind seemed to have frozen. They were about to kill each other, this addled captain and his delinquent stoker, and there was nothing she could say or do to stop them. Their idiotic violence was certain to slow her down, perhaps ruining her chances, and she was powerless to prevent it.

No matter, the recently emerged, wholly purposeful portion of her intellect reassured her. *With one or even both of them gone, Girays and I could still find a way to pilot this tub downriver.*

The cold clarity of the thought surprised her. For a fleeting instant she wondered at herself.

Finding her voice, she commenced urgently, "Stop, stop right now. Captain, please—"

Jhiv-Huze ignored her. A fusillade of Kyrendtish curses drowned her entreaties.

Oonuvu's black eyes glittered. He whispered something.

Jhiv-Huze flicked an expressive steel blade.

The stoker looked the other up and down, then carelessly tossed the pottery shard away. Oozing contempt, he turned and sauntered off. A violent kick from behind accelerated his departure. Oonuvu staggered, whirled, and regarded his captain with an expression that chilled Luzelle's blood. Then he whispered something with a smile, which was worse yet. After a moment he glided noiselessly down the companion and disappeared from view.

Good humor instantly restored, Roupe Jhiv-Huze pocketed his knife. Turning to encounter Luzelle's alarmed gaze, he advised with an air of whimsy, "Do not trouble yourself, Madame. Jhiv-Huze has educated his subordinate, that is all. Sometimes a small touch of kindly firmness is indicated."

EARLY THAT EVENING, not long before sunset, the *Blind Cripple* entered the narrow, convoluted Ta'ahri Capillaries. The Forests of Oorex, hitherto distanced by the broad expanse of the Ygah, now crowded close, almost ominously immediate.

Luzelle and Girays were on deck. She had already described the second confrontation between Jhiv-Huze and Oonuvu, and he had pronounced the captain a sodden swine and the stoker a perverted urchin. Thereafter conversation paused while they stood watching the jungle flow by.

The forests were different when viewed at such intimate range. Bigger. Darker. More powerful. The channel just barely accommodating the *Blind Cripple* was so constricted that the arching branches of the tall trees that lined the banks met above the water to roof a shadowy tunnel. The dim air was very still, very dank, and unpleasantly redolent of fungus. Luzelle could imagine drawing assorted airborne spores down into her lungs and, in the rampant fertility of the jungle, picture them taking hold there, spreading and expanding throughout her body to cram every organ with triumphant mold. She shuddered.

"What's wrong?" asked Girays.

"Nothing beyond an overactive imagination. I don't like this place, that's all," she confided. "It may be exotic and wonderful in its own way, but I just don't like it. I feel as if I'm being watched."

"You very probably are," he concurred unnervingly. "Here in the Ta'ahri Capillaries the Grewzian presence is almost negligible. Here the Blessed Tribesmen reign yet, and it's more than likely that they keep close watch over the strangers in their midst."

"They're really out there, then?" Her searching gaze strained to pierce shadows, but the dark forest kept its secrets. Another thought struck her. "Do those Blessed Tribesmen ever attack travelers? Are they dangerous?"

"Partial to blowguns and poisoned darts, I'm told," returned Girays, and very soon thereafter the two of them sought sanctuary belowdecks.

THE *BLIND CRIPPLE* DROPPED ANCHOR as the surrounding grey atmosphere deepened to the black of the darkest imaginable night. No straying beam of moonlight, nor the faintest glimmer of starlight, filtered down through the branches overhead. The waters of the Capillaries lapping against the hull could be heard but not seen.

They made a late dinner of stew that evening, and Oonuvu was not present to share it. Luzelle assumed that the stoker must be either exiled or sulking. She did not care enough to ask which. Roupe Jhiv-Huze partook hugely of xussi, regaled his audience with repetitive reminiscences, and presently fell asleep at the table. His snores filled the tiny galley, all but excluding the incessant hum of insects, the amphibious croaks, the avian hoots and bestial roars from the depths of the forest, the elusive trilling of flutes—

Flutes?

Thin, high notes tripping along the edge of her consciousness; audible for some time before she had quite noticed them, and now impossible to ignore. The music, if such it was, struck her as intensely alien, the fruit of unknowable minds presumably belonging to the Blessed Tribesmen. She glanced across the table at Girays and saw that he heard it too. Their eyes met and he shrugged, minutely but with eloquence.

Leaving Captain Jhiv-Huze unconscious in his chair, they made their way back to the main cabin, where Luzelle composed herself for slumber in utter darkness. At length she climbed into her hammock and heard the ropes creak on the opposite side of the room as Girays did the same.

For a while she lay with her eyes wide open and sightless, her ears alert to the uncanny chorus of the jungle flutes. The sound was intermittent, unpredictable, and oddly compelling. Each time it paused she found herself waiting, breath bated in comfortless suspense.

Ridiculous. A little night music was nothing to fear.

Blowguns and poisoned darts, Girays had said. Had he really needed to mention that? And having destroyed her repose, was he now comfortably sleeping? She lay there wondering. The flutes wailed and the darkness pressed with a weight all its own. At last she could bear it no longer, and whispered very softly, "Girays?"

"Yes?" he answered at once.

"Did I wake you?"

"No. Are you all right?"

"Yes, of course. I'm sorry, I shouldn't have disturbed you."

"You haven't. What's the matter?"

"Nothing. It's only that it's so dark in here, and I just wanted to check—wanted to be sure—"

"Of what?"

"That you're still here."

"I'm here."

She could not see a thing, but knew that he smiled. An answering smile curved her lips invisibly in the dark. After that she dropped off to sleep almost at once.

15

THE BANG OF THE CABIN DOOR flinging wide woke her at the crack of dawn. Luzelle's eyes snapped open and she sat up. Anemic grey light trickled into the little room. She saw that Girays was already on his feet and facing Roupe Jhiv-Huze, who stood in the doorway.

Jhiv-Huze—blear eyed, puffy faced, and still reeking of xussi—radiated intense agitation. His hands were jerking and his bloodshot eyes darted everywhere as he announced without preamble, "Passengers, we are in a state of emergency! Your services are required!"

"What emergency?" Wide awake, Luzelle scrambled from her hammock. "What services?"

"He is gone!" Jhiv-Huze declared. "The ungrateful little deserter has jumped ship. In a less indulgent age his captain would order him hanged!"

"His captain would have to catch him first," Girays suggested. "You allude to the stoker, I presume."

"Disappeared during the night, without a thought to spare for loyalty or duty. Over the side to join his fellow savages of the jungle, no doubt."

"I cannot imagine what possessed him," Girays murmured.

"Sir, your levity is misplaced," the captain complained. "Allow Jhiv-Huze to remind you that laughter hardly fuels the boiler. Oonuvu's desertion leaves us stranded here in the Capillaries perhaps for days to come. Laugh at that if you can."

"Surely the Ygahri boy can be replaced," Girays opined.

"But at what cost of time?" Jhiv-Huze gnawed his lower lip. "How many hours, how many days, do we languish here, far from Jumo and all civilized amenities?"

The captain, Luzelle suspected, was starving for his *marukiñutu*. Good. His desperation served her purposes admirably. Once again she was surprised and a little disturbed by the workings of her own mind, but there was no time to worry about it, for Jhiv-Huze was still talking.

"We can't spare the time, we've no leisure to search the forests for a healthy and tractable native. At this juncture one remedy alone presents itself. It is you, my friend. You are our hope and our salvation. Master v'Alisante, you are the *Blind Cripple*'s new stoker. I trust you will serve well."

Had the man lost his wits? Luzelle wondered. Did he not understand that he addressed a formerly-Exalted v'Alisante, master of Belfaireau, and possessor of several quarts of Vonahr's bluest blood? Did he actually imagine it possible that M. the Marquis could or would stoop to *shoveling coal*?

"Right," Girays returned without the slightest flicker of affront and Luzelle stared at him in amazement. "Fire survive the night?"

"Just barely," the captain told him. "A few small embers glow yet, and Jhiv-Huze has already fed them."

"Good. Let's move, then."

"Jhiv-Huze admires your spirit, sir."

"Wait." Luzelle found her voice, and both men turned to look at her. "Girays shouldn't have to do all the work. I'll help."

Girays and the captain traded brief glances of unendurable amusement.

"Thank you, Luzelle. That's kind, but I don't think I'll require assistance," Girays replied with a courteous gravity that would have deceived anyone who did not know him well.

"Don't you think I'm capable of lifting a few shovelfuls of coal?" she inquired, carefully suppressing any note of belligerence.

"I'm sure that you are, but it's simply unnecessary."

"But heavy exertion in these temperatures will take its toll, and you'll need relief from time to time. While you rest, I can—"

"Madame's womanly concern is charming, quite charming." Jhiv-Huze beamed tolerance. "Alas that we have not the leisure to lavish upon her the admiration that her generosity merits."

Condescending crackpot, thought Luzelle, and cast about for a politely annihilating reply.

"No more delay." Girays's decree cut her cogitations short. "Let's go."

The two men exited. Scowling after them, she thought, *Very well, M. the Marquis, treat me like some foolish child if you will. You are welcome to your masculine pride and you are also welcome to drown in your own sweat.*

She washed, breakfasted on cold stew, and ascended to the deck. The air was almost cool by local standards, but would not remain so for long. The sun was up, its low rays slanting through the leafy branches overhead to dapple the boat and water with quivery sunlight and shadow. Soon the humid atmosphere would heat to steambath temperatures, but for now she could stroll the deck in relative comfort. And why not? That was all her traveling companions deemed her fit for.

She made her slow way aft, pausing often to study the intensely hued flora glowing amid the deep jungle shadows, the jumping play of the morning sun on the ripples of the Ygah, the aerial acrobatics of the indigenous diurnal bats. A moist breeze cooled her face. The *Blind Cripple* had picked up considerable speed; down below Girays must be toiling devotedly. And he wasn't used to such labor, he wasn't born to it or for it, and it would be just like him to drive himself to the point of collapse. . . .

No he wouldn't; he was smarter than that. She contained the impulse to rush down to the engine room. He had made it clear that he didn't need or want her help; he would hardly relish her intrusion. Let him work himself sick, then, it was his own choice.

Frowning, she continued her promenade. Her mind's eye focused on coal, shovels, flames, and steam; she no longer heeded her actual surroundings, until she rounded the stern to the starboard side of the boat and there found a couple of small foreign objects protruding from the rail. They did not belong there, and they caught her attention at once. She took a closer look and discovered a pair of delicate feathered darts with needle points well sunk in the wood. They were beautifully made, and must have been launched with a certain force.

Blowguns and poisoned darts, Girays had said.

Her eyes jumped to the forest, but failed to penetrate the green gloom. She saw nobody there, and it occurred to her then that she herself stood completely exposed and vulnerable to attack. A little late to be thinking of that. Anyone so inclined might easily have picked her off at any time during the past quarter hour or so. Just as anyone might easily pick off the captain, who stood on the bridge, protected from rain or killing sun by an awning of ragged canvas, but otherwise fully exposed. Jhiv-Huze wasn't worrying, however, and neither should she. There was no reason to expect hostility from the natives, she assured herself. On the other hand, the arrival of the darts should be directed to the captain's attention.

Gingerly she plucked the two little missiles from the rail and, holding both at arm's length, advanced along the main deck as far as the bridge.

"Captain," she called, and he looked down at her. She held the darts aloft for his inspection. "Found these stuck to the railing."

"Very fine." Jhiv-Huze nodded equably. "A delightful souvenir of Madame's voyage."

"But what do you suppose they mean?" She let her arm sink.

"The Blessed Tribesmen remind us of their presence."

"Yes, but why? What's the message? Is it a warning? A threat? A challenge?"

"Who can say? Jhiv-Huze has piloted his vessel along this river for twenty-five years and more, and even he cannot claim perfect comprehension of the Ygahri mind. It is useless to speculate."

"But don't you think you ought to take some sort of precautions?"

"What sort?"

Good question. Her brow wrinkled. No practical solution came to mind.

Noting her expression, the captain rumbled a benign chuckle. "Madame need not concern herself," he advised. "The natives are friendly, the weather is fine, and Jhiv-Huze is at the helm." His gaze returned to the river.

She had patently been dismissed. For a moment longer she stood looking up at him, then shrugged and moved away. The two darts remained clasped in her right hand, and she wondered what to do with them. Dump them overboard, she supposed. They were probably poisoned, and quite dangerous. Still, they were so well crafted that it seemed a shame to throw them away. She studied them closely, noting for the first time the tiny designs incised into the polished shaft of each dart. Exquisite work, and curiously familiar. Something about the symbols, something she had seen somewhere, sometime.

She squinted. A magnifying glass would have helped, but her eyes were good and she was able to make out minuscule sets of parallel wavy lines, elaborate intersecting polygons, clustering dots, leaf shapes, boat shapes, stylized birds, and much more.

It was the leaf shapes that jogged her memory. Distinctively palmate, they were impossible to mistake, and now she remembered just where she had once seen them—on the ancient carven plaques decorating the hut of the head *tl'gh-tiz* of the Bhomiri-D'tal tribe; the same *tl'gh-tiz* who had once offered to accept her on a trial basis as junior wife number thirteen. She squinted harder; yes, the same symbol, beyond doubt. But how? The Bhomiri Islands rose near the center of the Bay of Zif, hundreds of miles to the west. How could the Bhomiri-D'tals share symbols with the Blessed Tribesmen of the Ygahro Territories? Coincidentally similar stylized renderings of the same plant? No. For the highly recognizable palmately compound leaves of the symbol abounded in the Forests of Oorex. She did not know the name of the shrub, but she saw it all around her, flourishing along the banks of the Ta'ahri Capillaries. No such shrub, however, graced the Bhomiri Islands. The head *tl'gh-tiz* had characterized the leaf as *uxe hoivo-Tl'ghurhi*—belonging to Paradise—and she had deemed the description purely fanciful. But now she recalled that the Bhomiri-D'tal term for Paradise translated with equal facility to "Land of the Blessed," or "Land of the Ancestors." She remembered also that Bhomiri-D'tal oral history included tales of the first Bhomiri ancestors sailing unimaginable distances from their homeland far beyond the rising sun.

Had some ancient party of Blessed Tribesmen sailed west from the mouth of the Ygah, following the warm fish-hospitable currents over the Nether Ocean and northwest into the Bay of Zif, there to settle upon the Bhomiri Islands? If such a connection existed and she could prove it, then she could write a book, an important book certain to attract notice. There would be speaking engagements—healthy lecture fees—a comfortable independent living, even if she failed to win the Grand Ellipse.

But she would not fail to win the Grand Ellipse.

Still, the thought of a respectable alternative—

She was hurrying along at an excited trot, her lips curved in an unconscious smile, the two darts tightly gripped in her hand. And to think, but moments earlier she had actually considered throwing such treasures away. She would preserve them at all costs now.

Returning to the main cabin, she wrapped the darts with care and stowed them at the bottom of her carpetbag. This done, she raced to the engine room.

The place was infernal. The heat was unbearable, the atmosphere all but unbreathable, and the sole occupant barely recognizable. Girays v'Alisante, ordinarily so impeccable, was sweat soaked, disheveled, and coal blackened. He had removed his shirt, a sensible move under the circumstances, but she had never seen him without it before, and now all thoughts of decorated darts and seafaring tribesmen fled her mind. She had never quite realized that his lean frame was so well muscled. She was trying hard not to stare at his bare chest, shoulders, and arms, so she anchored her eyes steadfastly on his face and felt an utter fool. She realized that she was blushing like a schoolgirl, and her discomfort deepened.

She asked if she could bring him a drink, and he assented readily. She went to the galley, filled a dented tin cup with beer, carried it back to the engine room, and watched in some wonder as he gulped it down. She had not hitherto imagined M. the Marquis capable of gulping, or indeed of anything less than perfect deportment. He wiped his mouth with the back of his hand, and her wonder increased. She noticed that his unwontedly long hair was straggling across his wet forehead, and she curbed the impulse to brush the stray locks away from his eyes. He ought to have some sort of scarf or rag tied across his forehead to absorb the sweat. She pictured a red bandanna accenting that angular, sun-browned, dark-eyed face; added a gold earring for emphasis, and found the resulting image so incongruously piratical that she burst into laughter. When he asked her why she was laughing, she refused to tell him, but spoke instead of the Ygahri darts she had discovered stuck in the starboard railing, and of the captain's lackadaisical reaction. She wanted to tell him of the leaf symbol and its possible significance, but the fire under the boiler demanded replenishment, and Girays was obliged to apply himself to his shovel.

She fetched him another cup of beer and a bowl of cold stew, watching bemusedly as he gulped the one and wolfed the other. When she offered once more to take a turn at shoveling coal, his instant refusal fulfilled her expectations.

"You must think me quite useless," she accused.

"Far from it. But I couldn't stand by watching while you break your back over the coal bin."

"I'm not made of porcelain, Girays."

"I've sometimes wondered if you aren't made of steel, but that's beside the point. You're young and strong, and I freely concede that a few minutes of physical labor are unlikely to injure your health, but my own peace of mind would suffer. It is the fault of my upbringing, I suppose. Try not to take it as a personal insult, but I'm not letting go of this shovel."

She had to laugh at that, but departed the engine room incompletely mollified. Despite his humor and diplomacy it was plain that he viewed her as useless. Or else she would always think that he did, no matter how often he denied it. . . .

The *Blind Cripple* maintained good speed throughout the day, perhaps too good for safety. Luzelle worried at the jovial abandon with which Jhiv-Huze hurled his craft through the narrow, shallow channels of the Ta'ahri Capillaries, around the treacherous sharp bends, straight through the blinding veils of leafy low-hanging boughs and vines. A single fallen tree in the water or the slightest misjudgment of a channel's navigable curve might have proved disastrous, but the captain possessed either preternatural skill or luck. The *Blind Cripple* rushed through unscathed, and Luzelle's uneasiness subsided. She might simply have relished the sensation of swift progress, but for the increasingly noticeable presence of the Blessed Tribesmen.

She caught the thin high notes of their flutes trailing through the forests around noon, and her heart jumped. Stepping to the rail, she peered off into the shadows, but saw nothing. The sound faded, and her knotted muscles relaxed; too soon, for minutes later it was back, faint and intermittent at first, then waxing in authority as the day wore on. She could neither ignore it nor make any sense of it, for there was nothing resembling a recognizable tune, a rhythm, or even a consistent pattern, but she could not stop trying to find one.

The sound broke off around midafternoon, and that was when she caught her first glimpse of the Blessed Tribesmen. A couple of compact tattooed figures lingered in the deep shade near the bank, watching in still silence as the *Blind Cripple* steamed by. So motionless were they, so much a part of their surroundings, although they made no effort at concealment, that she might easily have overlooked them had not a glancing ray of sunlight struck fire off the glass beads woven into their braided hair. She caught her breath and stared. They looked straight back at her, and their faces told her nothing at all. Both tribesmen carried slim tubes in their hands. Flutes? Or blowguns? In such uncertain light, impossible to judge.

The *Blind Cripple* sped on. The statuelike tribesmen were behind her, then they were gone. The flutes resumed, along with Luzelle's breathing.

After that, throughout the rest of the afternoon, she glimpsed them sporadically; sometimes poised in the shadows under the trees, sometimes squatting on the flat mossy rocks along the bank, sometimes crouched in the branches overhanging the water. They offered no overt hostility. There were no taunts or flying darts, but Luzelle sensed an animosity so dark and profound that the responsive prickling of her flesh eventually drove her belowdecks, where she kept herself occupied with one of Girays's histories for hours.

That night, as she lay in the moonless starless dark of the cabin, she did not need to wonder whether Girays slept or not. He had plunged into deep slumber the moment he reclined in his hammock. Now the sound of his deep, regular breathing blended with the endless vocalization of the jungle and the wailing of the flutes. She expected protracted insomnia, but fell asleep almost at once.

She woke to the green dimness typical of the region. Girays's hammock was empty. The engine was pulsing, and the *Blind Cripple* was already under way. The captain's efficiency was commendable. The scent of *marukiñutu* must be strong in his nostrils.

She washed, ate, and returned to a scene grown too familiar. Captain on the bridge, speeding his vessel through the tortuous tunnels of the Ta'ahri Capillaries; Blessed Tribesmen slipping through the dark of the undergrowth along both banks; alien music and menace weighting the air.

Somehow it seemed worse this morning, the hostility stronger and darker. Probably her imagination, she told herself.

But today no borrowed book could hold her attention.

She visited with Girays in the engine room for a while, but found him immersed in his labors and insensitive to atmospheric inhospitality. His shirt was off again. She watched as he shoveled and for a while the play of his muscles kept her diverted, but eventually the forebodings resurfaced and she went away, more restless than ever.

Morning crawled toward noon, and she saw a party of six Blessed Tribesmen keeping pace with the boat. One of the copper-skinned figures looked familiar, and for a moment she thought she recognized the face and form of the erstwhile stoker Oonuvu, but the light was low, the tribesmen some yards distant, and she only caught a fleeting glimpse. Then the forest swallowed them and she was left to wonder.

Half an hour later the quality of the flutes changed; assuming a new urgency, and for the first time the voices of the Blessed Tribesmen could be heard, uplifted in high-pitched, wolfish yelps. Soon a strong new voice rose to challenge the Ygahri chorus. Luzelle's eyes swung to the bridge, where Roupe Jhiv-Huze stood bellowing out the Kyrendtish national anthem. The captain's head was thrown back, his tattooed face alight with exultation. When he had roared through the anthem twice, his aggressive baritone eclipsing the Ygahri yelps, he switched over to a Kyrendtish drinking song, and after that belted out an obscene Nidroonish jingle. Quavering, uncanny ululation answered from the forest.

Throughout the morning the *Blind Cripple* had traveled one of the skinniest and crookedest of the Ta'ahri Capillaries. Now she rounded the sharpest bend along that constricted channel, a tight bend defining the contour of a narrow projecting finger of forest, and Roupe Jhiv-Huze never faltered, but steered his craft full speed ahead, with fire in his eye and a loud song on his lips.

As the *Blind Cripple* cleared the tip of the forested spit, Luzelle saw for the first time that the channel on the far side was blocked. Three great fallen trees, their trunks marked with recent ax strokes, lay spanning the water from bank to bank. Along this makeshift bridge prowled Blessed Tribesmen armed with blowguns. Before the barrier waited the commercial steamer *Water Sprite,* her deck dotted with passengers.

Jhiv-Huze's song cut off and he twisted the wheel hard, but the boat had scarcely begun to alter course before one of the natives patrolling the starboard shore—an agile young figure clearly recognizable as the former crewman Oonuvu—lifted a blowgun to his lips and launched a tiny feathered shaft. The dart flew straight and true to bury itself in the captain's throat. Jhiv-Huze gurgled and fell. Oonuvu watched expressionlessly. The *Blind Cripple* rushed on toward the trapped *Water Sprite,* whose passengers shrieked and scattered.

Luzelle stood staring for an eternal paralyzed instant, then unfroze and sprinted for the ladder to the bridge. Instinct bade her seize the wheel, much as she might have grabbed the reins from the stricken driver of a runaway carriage. If she had stopped to think, she would have known that instinct played her false, for there could be no turning the steamboat in the time and space available. She was up the ladder in a flash, checked briefly at the top by the sight of Roupe Jhiv-Huze's wide-open sightless gaze, and then she was running for the wheel. Before she reached it, the violent impact of the *Blind Cripple*'s bow ramming the *Water Sprite*'s port quarter threw her to her knees. She was back on her feet at once, watching in fascinated horror as some half-dozen luckless passengers slid through a gap in the *Water Sprite*'s shattered railing to plunge headlong into the waters of the Ta'ahri Capillaries.

Ropes and a lone life preserver flew from the deck of the packet, and three of the fallen passengers were quickly lifted to safety. The remaining three were less fortunate.

A great uneasiness seized the channel. The waters trembled, frothed, and seemed to boil. A gorgeous iridescence blanketed the surface, a wondrous changeable blend of a hundred jewel colors, radiant even in the shade of the jungle canopy. Luzelle watched and marveled, momentarily uncomprehending.

The iridescence engulfed the three men in the water, all of whom began to thrash and scream. A curious vibration rose to envelop the shrieks. The amorphous jeweled colors resolved into countless polished wings beating too fast for the eye to follow, and whirring as they moved.

Beetles, Luzelle realized. A vast swarm or school of aquatic beetles.

The bare flesh of the fallen passengers was encrusted with gleaming insect forms. The faces were obscured and unrecognizable, but Luzelle glimpsed a voluminously cut maroon shirt that she knew. A gap appeared in its owner's polished polychrome mask and a scream emerged, to choke off abruptly as a stream of beetles flowed into the open mouth. The man in the water clawed wildly at his own face, briefly clearing an expanse of bloody flesh. The savaged features of Porb Jil Liskjil were visible for an instant before the beetles returned to their voracious work. Another moment and Jil Liskjil, his struggles already diminishing, sank out of sight beneath the water. His two fellow victims soon followed. For several minutes the water in that spot seethed and roiled, while the insectile iridescence ebbed and flowed in glowing tides, but at last the feast concluded, and the beetle horde flowed away.

Luzelle became aware that she was clinging to the useless helm. Her head swam and her stomach churned. She took a few deep breaths, and the qualm subsided. She heard a footstep behind her and turned her head to look at Girays.

"Porb Jil Liskjil," she said dully.

"I know. I saw."

"There were two others in the water with him. I couldn't see them. Karsler—"

"Wasn't there. Depend on it."

"And Jhiv-Huze. Oonuvu shot him."

"Are you sure?"

"Yes."

"Are you all right?"

"Yes. You?"

"Yes."

"What happens now?" She looked around her. The *Blind Cripple* and the *Water Sprite* were firmly engaged and fully immobilized. Neither seemed to be taking on water, but the passengers aboard each were stranded, or perhaps imprisoned. Unlike the *Blind Cripple,* the *Water Sprite* carried a lifeboat capable of ferrying successive groups of passengers and crew to shore. But the Blessed Tribesmen with their blowguns stalked the barrier blocking the channel, dozens more patrolled the banks, and Ygahri intentions as yet remained unclear. Even now one of the officers stood at the bow of the packet, calling down in dialect to the tribesmen below, but the natives appeared deaf.

"We wait, I believe," Girays told her. "For now, there's nothing else."

But they did not have to wait for long.

Presently a muttering of Ygahri voices rose from below as a sizable raft came alongside. A grappling hook caught the *Blind Cripple*'s railing, and four nearly naked figures swarmed up the rope and onto the main deck. The smallest and youngest of the newcomers glanced up at the bridge, and

Luzelle looked into the eyes of Oonuvu. A blowgun hung on a leather thong suspended about his neck. A leather band encircling his waist supported a tiny quiver full of darts, a broad-bladed knife, and a stout short-handled ax. His companions were similarly armed.

Luzelle thought of the Khrennisov FK6 lying at the bottom of her carpetbag on the floor in the main cabin. It might just as well be lying at the bottom of the sea.

The Ygahri quartet ascended to the bridge, and Luzelle resisted the impulse to back away. Jaw clenched, she stood still. Girays, standing beside her, slid a protective arm around her shoulders. Six years earlier she might have resented the presumption, but now she welcomed the reassuring contact.

Gliding forward to the fallen captain's side, Oonuvu stooped and plucked his dart from the corpse's neck. He wiped the point clean, returned the dart to his quiver, and stood up. For a moment he eyed his victim without a flicker of expression, then lifted his loincloth and carefully urinated into Jhiv-Huze's face.

Luzelle could not suppress a gasp, and Oonuvu's eyes turned to her. He whispered in Ygahri and smiled. She felt Girays's hand tighten on her shoulder. Lifting her chin a fraction, she met the obsidian gaze.

An incomprehensible colloquy among the four natives followed. Oonuvu jabbered insistently and his senior colleagues responded without enthusiasm. At length there was a nodding of heads suggestive of general accord, whereupon Oonuvu turned to his Vonahrish audience and gestured curtly toward the ladder. His meaning was clear. They were to descend.

Luzelle glanced at Girays. His bare shoulders sketched a shrug. The two of them climbed down to the main deck, and the Ygahris followed. One of the natives stepped to the railing, grasped the rope, swung himself over the side, and descended to the waiting raft. Oonuvu gestured. Again his meaning was clear. They were to follow.

"What do you want with us, Oonuvu?" Girays asked quietly.

No reply, no sign of comprehension.

"You understand me, I think," Girays persisted.

Silence. Oonuvu gestured again. When the objects of his attention failed to respond, he drew a dart from his quiver and slid it into the blowgun. The two prisoners, as they now perceived themselves to be, moved reluctantly to the rail.

Luzelle looked down. The distance to the raft was not great, and the rope was knotted at regular intervals. Descent appeared neither dangerous nor difficult. And then?

She hesitated and heard Girays say in a low tone, "I'll go before you. If you slip, I'll be there." Classic formerly-Exalted gallantry, and once again she found herself appreciating it, paternalism and all. Without awaiting reply he grasped the rope, swung himself over the rail, and descended ably. An alien hand pressing the small of her back urged her on, and she followed Girays. The Bizaqhi divided skirt simplified matters. She climbed down easily, sliding from knot to knot until her feet hit the logs of the roughly constructed Ygahri raft. Oonuvu and his companions came after. The flick of a tattooed wrist sent a wave along the rope, and the grappling hook tumbled from the rail. One of the tribesmen took up a great staff and poled for the shore.

Luzelle's eyes rose to the *Water Sprite,* whose crew and passengers clustered at the stern. They were watching intently, doubtless alarmed and mystified as she. It crossed her mind then that she and Girays might leap from the raft to swim for the packet, there to find sanctuary and relative safety in numbers. Then she thought of Porb Jil Liskjil and his armor plating of beetles in the water, and the impulse died.

The raft bumped land, and the natives herded their captives ashore. A gap in the undergrowth offered access to a narrow trail leading off into the forest. The tribesmen made for the gap and Luzelle balked. Oonuvu drew his knife, and her feet began to move again. She cast one longing glance back over her shoulder at the stationary *Water Sprite,* then the river was gone and the jungle was all around her.

They walked in single file, Ygahris at the front and rear, Vonahrish prisoners sandwiched in between. Lush high greenery enclosed the trail, crowding in so hard and close that Luzelle could not avoid brushing gigantic, saw-edged leaves as she passed. Each time she touched one, the clinging water spattered off in showers and soon she was dampened from head to foot. But the native tribesmen somehow managed to advance without dislodging a single drop, and without ever stumbling over the innumerable creepers and exposed roots snaking across their path. The dark soil underfoot was soft with moss and perennially moist. The air smelled of astringent leaves and excessively sweet flowers, exotic fungi and water scum, burgeoning life and decay. They marched for an hour and a half or more along the trail, and a new odor weighted the dense atmosphere—smoke. Cooking fires? On they went, the smoke scent sharpening in their nostrils, until the trail abruptly concluded and the world expanded around them.

They had come to a clearing containing a collection of frame huts with walls of woven branches and thatching of palm leaves. The corner posts of each hut were carved and painted in a style familiar to Luzelle, who had seen such posts supporting the dwellings of the Bhomiri Islanders. An emblem of serpentine intertwining human spinal columns crowned the entrance to the largest hut. A somewhat similar emblem decorated the lodge of the *tl'gh-tiz* of the Bhomiri-D'tals. Had she accepted the position of junior wife number thirteen, she would have been expected to wash and polish the bones every day. At the center of the clearing yawned a great fire pit. An immense iron spit rested upon twin cleft posts above the pit. The cannibalistic Bhomiri-D'tals possessed and greatly prized just such a spit.

A number of women and girl-children sat before their huts, grating edible roots or pounding out fibrous stalks on flat stones. Small naked boys romped and wrestled about the fire pit. There were not many men in evidence, and the few present were bent and wrinkled with age. Probably most of the younger ones were off gloating over the trapped *Water Sprite*.

As the four Ygahris and the two foreigners walked into the clearing, the attention of the residents instantly focused. The children came racing for a closer look, followed at a more dignified pace by their elders. Within seconds the new arrivals were heavily surrounded.

The tattooed faces revealed nothing. The slanting black eyes were opaque. Even the children were unfathomable, Luzelle decided. Well, perhaps not entirely. Some of the youngest ones projected a certain pleased excitement, together with a curiosity that seemed to fasten with particular intensity upon her red-gold curls. Probably they had never seen a western woman before. More than one small copper hand reached out to touch her, and Oonuvu, who walked too close upon her heels, slapped the straying hands aside with a proprietary air that boded ill.

Straight across the clearing they marched to the dwelling marked with the spinal emblem, where they ranged themselves before the doorway, foreigners flanked by natives. One of the Blessed Tribesmen called out something that might have been a name or a title. A moment later a grizzled Ygahri of middle years emerged from the hut. Like the others of his tribe, both male and female, he wore no clothing beyond an abbreviated loincloth of woven fiber cloth. His body was heavily adorned with tattoos and raised scars, his hair elaborately braided and beaded, and he wore a large medallion of carven onyx that might or might not have indicated rank. A certain air of lofty dignity suggested high status.

A hush fell over the gathering. The headman spoke, his voice rising interrogatively. The largest member of Oonuvu's party, presumably its leader, stepped forward and performed a gesture that lifted Luzelle's eyebrows, for she recognized the hand-over-heart inclination of the head with which the Bhomiri-D'tals were wont to express respect.

The Blessed Tribesman spoke at some length. His words were unintelligible, but sometimes he pointed off in the direction of the river, sometimes his gestures encompassed the Vonahrish captives, and once or twice the twitch of a thumb seemed to single Oonuvu out for special recognition. Clearly a report or explanation was being offered.

The headman addressed Oonuvu, who responded with a spate of rapid commentary. His head was high and his chest

swelled victoriously as he spoke. At the close of his oration he
lifted a strand of Luzelle's streaming hair and laid his free
hand on his groin. Releasing the hair, he jerked his head at
Girays, then turned and pointed across the clearing at the
great iron spit spanning the fire pit.

Not a muscle in Girays's face moved, but Luzelle stood
close beside him and saw that he had gone white under his
tan. She noted the headman's attitude of grave deliberation,
and her own flesh went cold. She glanced down and saw that
her hands were shaking shamefully, which she could not allow
because she intended to emulate Girays, who scorned to display fear before these people. She wondered what to do about
her hands, and the answer was unexpectedly clear in her
mind.

Stepping forward, she pressed her right palm firmly to her
heart and bowed her head in the Bhomiri-D'tal gesture of respect that seemed to serve a corresponding function among
the Blessed Tribesmen. The headman studied her inscrutably.
Oonuvu grasped her arm and yanked peremptorily. Girays
immediately leveled a blow that sent the Ygahri boy sprawling. Oonuvu bounded to his feet, knife in hand and white
teeth bared.

A sharp hiss from the headman halted the fight. He spoke,
and Oonuvu reluctantly sheathed his knife.

Luzelle repeated the gesture of respect, recapturing the
headman's attention. Looking straight into his eyes, she
spread her empty hands, palms upturned, touched the finger-
tips of both hands to her heart, her lips, and her forehead,
then ceremoniously allowed her hands to sink back to her
sides. She could only hope that this ancient salute, imbued
with an almost sacred force among the Bhomiri D'tals, possessed some similar significance among the Ygahris, but it was
impossible to judge, for the headman's face was utterly expressionless. Perhaps he had no idea what she was doing, perhaps
he took her for a madwoman given to senseless gesticulation.
He was staring at her, and so was everyone else present, but
the faces and eyes communicated nothing.

She repeated the salute, and this time spoke the time-
honored phrase that always accompanied the gestures. The

Bhomiri words could mean nothing to the Blessed Tribesmen, but they were traditional, and she could not omit them.

"I am a stranger come in friendship," Luzelle intoned, stumbling only slightly over the spiky Bhomiri syllables. "In the name of the gods and by Their will, I claim your hospitality."

Still no reaction from the headman, only blank-faced silence, but a low muttering simmered among the observers, and her hands, which had steadied briefly, recommenced trembling. She clasped them firmly and waited with an appearance of composure, her eyes fixed on the headman's face.

For an endless interval he studied her, and impassive though he was, she thought to glimpse something like astonishment in his eyes. At last he uttered some command that sent one of the women hurrying across the clearing to a hut whose ornate corner posts were studded with human and animal skulls painted with geometric designs in red and ocher. The messenger disappeared into the hut, then emerged moments later followed by a trio of white-haired shamans tattooed head to foot in red and ocher, masked in snakeskin, and crowned with towering headdresses built of human ribs.

The crowd parted deferentially, and the shamans advanced to take their place beside the headman, who pressed a hand to his heart and bowed his head in respect. Three sets of black eyes scrutinized Luzelle through the apertures in the snakeskin masks. One of the shamans addressed her and she could not understand the words, but guessed their purport.

Slowly and deliberately she performed the ancient gestures, and spoke aloud the ritual Bhomiri formula. "I am a stranger come in friendship. In the name of the gods and by Their will, I claim your hospitality."

The three shamans whispered among themselves, then one said something to her. This time she had no idea at all what was meant or required, and she let her incomprehension show on her face. They whispered again, and one of them spoke up haltingly in Bhomiri dialect. His accent and pronunciation differed considerably from those of the island folk, yet the words were intelligible enough as he asked, "How do you know the Old Tongue?"

She stiffened, momentarily doubting her own senses. But there had been no mistake, the fantastic figure before her had uttered Bhomiri syllables. Concealing her astonishment, she replied in her own laborious version of the language, "I am friend of the People who talk this tongue all days."

"What people?"

Luzelle frowned. The Bhomiri-D'tals' name for themselves simply translated as "the People," by which title they distinguished themselves from the various extratribal biped beasts and demons, deceptively humanoid in appearance but devoid of soul and therefore less than true men. But an answer was essential, and she essayed, "They are masters of great islands in the salt sea, far beyond the forests, in the west."

"How do they know the Old Tongue?"

"Some say their fathers' fathers set forth from the Forests of Oorex on rafts to follow the great River Ygah south to the salt sea." Luzelle shrugged. "Or else it may be that the gods taught them."

"They speak with the gods?"

"Their wise men are like the dutiful sons of the gods."

"Their wise men teach you the will of the gods?"

"Yes. They teach that the gods punish those who break the sacred law of hospitality."

The shamans conferred briefly in their own dialect, then one of the masked figures observed, "This man with you does not claim hospitality."

"I claim for him. I have that right, I am his senior wife number one."

"This man permits his wife to speak for him?"

"This day he must. He speaks many tongues, but knows not the Old Tongue."

"What do you seek of the Blessed?"

"We ask the Blessed to help us on through the forests toward Jumo Towne. We must run fast."

Following another whispered consultation with his confreres, one of the shamans spoke aloud and at some length in Ygahri. He addressed the headman, but his words were audible to all. Presumably he furnished explanation, but before he had finished speaking, Oonuvu raised an angry voice. The shaman listened, then informed Luzelle in Bhomiri, "The young Oonuvu, who is now a man, claims ownership of the two captives. He reminds us that they are property, unable to claim hospitality."

"This is not so." Luzelle contrived to appear mildly taken aback at the egregious unsoundness of the other's reasoning. "If we are prisoners, there is no justice. We do not war with the Blessed Tribesmen, we are not enemies. We are not thieves, or murderers, or defilers of sacred things. We are peaceful travelers and we claim your hospitality in the name of the gods."

Oonuvu spoke again, and the shaman translated, "It is said that you are friends of our foes, the grey Grewzians."

"This is not so." Luzelle shook her head firmly. "The grey Grewzians are enemies of our tribe, enemies of all tribes."

The black eyes appraised her at length, then turned away. The whispering conference resumed. At its conclusion one of the shamans addressed the headman, who nodded once, and then the same masked figure translated for Luzelle, "The truth is unclear. We will ponder. You will wait."

Luzelle wanted to argue and plead, but contained the impulse. Pressing one hand to her heart, she inclined her head. The headman issued an order and a gang of Blessed Tribesmen shepherded the captives across the clearing to an empty hut, pushed them inside, and shut the door.

The interior was dim and smoky. A hole in the roof admitted a little light. The small space was empty save for a fire-blackened circle of stones at the center and a couple of woven mats spread out on the packed dirt floor.

No sooner had the door closed behind them than Girays turned to her and asked, "What happened? What did you say to them? I thought you didn't speak Ygahri."

"I don't." She related the entire exchange with the shamans, not excluding her claim to the position of senior wife number one, to which he only remarked that it had very nearly been true. She then explained the nature and origin of her ability to converse with the tribal wise men who preserved knowledge of the Old Tongue, obsolete among the Blessed Tribesmen but still current among their distant cousins of the Bhomiri Islands.

Girays listened attentively until she had finished, and then said, "You seem to have some understanding of these people—what are they likely to do with us?"

"Well, if they're like the Bhomiri-D'tals—and they do seem very like, in many ways—and they decide that we have a legitimate right to their hospitality, then they'll do all in their power to help us. They'll spare no effort or resource—if we are their guests."

"And if we aren't?"

She said nothing, and Girays nodded. For a while neither spoke, and during that time the murmur of Ygahri voices penetrating the flimsy walls told them that the hut was surrounded. Luzelle applied her eye to a small gap in one of the walls, and spied the muscular back of one of the armed tribesmen from the *Blind Cripple* boarding party standing before the door. Another was stationed nearby.

"I don't suppose you have that gun of yours handy?" she asked without shifting her gaze.

"If I did, I'd have used it long ago."

She turned away from the wall. Girays had seated himself on one of the woven mats. She went and sat down beside him.

"Have you any idea how long they'll take?" he asked.

"No."

They looked at each other, and for the second time that day he slid an arm around her shoulders. When he drew her near she did not resist, but let herself relax against him, her head resting on his shoulder, her eyes shut. She felt inappropriately contented and safe. Her fears subsided as if quenched by drugs or sorcery, which was absurd, for the danger was close and real, but somehow did not seem so. She might almost have thought herself happy, and for a moment that happiness blended oddly with a pang of regret for all that might have been.

She lost track of time sitting there so close to him. She had no idea if they waited for minutes or for hours. She did not stir until she heard the door open and felt the influx of fresh air.

Luzelle opened her eyes. The three masked shamans stood before her. One of them bore a pair of identical covered baskets. Extending the baskets, he declared in Bhomiri, "The man will choose."

Luzelle and Girays stood up, and the shaman repeated the command, adding, "The gods rule his hand."

"What does he say?" Girays asked steadily.

"He wants you to choose one of the baskets," Luzelle answered. "I don't know why."

Girays pointed.

"Take it," the shaman directed.

Luzelle translated, and Girays accepted one of the containers.

"He will draw forth the contents."

Luzelle relayed the message. Lifting the cover, Girays reached into the basket to remove a fist-sized stone. The polished surface was black as despair, sparked with flecks of an almost incandescent crimson. Girays studied the sinister object for a moment, then politely returned it to its owner.

"The gods have spoken," declared the shaman. Turning briefly to face the attentive Blessed Tribesmen gathered outside the hut, he held the stone aloft and spoke Ygahri in a carrying voice, then informed his Vonahrish listeners, "Their will is known. You are our guests."

"Even so." Luzelle bowed her head gravely. Catching Girays's eye, she mouthed in silence, *Guests.*

"Lucky," he replied aloud. "And if I'd chosen the other basket?"

The shaman seemed to understand the query. Lifting the cover, he tilted the rejected container a little to display the contents. Coiled at the bottom of the basket lay a bright turquoise snake with a triangular head and emerald markings.

"Wonderful color," admired Luzelle.

"Isn't it, though?" Girays studied the serpent with interest. "If I'm not mistaken, that's an uaxhui—quite a rare and remarkable specimen. It's one of the most poisonous creatures known to science. A single drop of its venom can kill a grown man within seconds. There is no known antidote."

"Oh!" said Luzelle. She backed away.

"Come." The shaman replaced the basket's cover, hiding the uaxhui from view. "The gods favor you, but you do not belong to the forests, you are not meant to be here." His companions murmured affirmatively. "We will give you food and speed you on your way."

"We thank you in the name of the gods," Luzelle returned. "You will guide us back to our boat?"

"No, for we have closed the river passages to the vessels of the accursed. The arms of the forest will carry you."

She had no idea what he meant, but judged it best to conceal her ignorance, and nodded solemnly.

"Come."

The three masked figures led the way from the hut, through the staring ranks of the Blessed, across the clearing, and into the jungle beyond. Once again the boughs roofed overhead, and the world sank into green shade.

Girays shot her a questioning glance, and Luzelle advised him discreetly, "They say that the arms of the forest will carry us."

He did not appear enlightened.

On they went until they came to a small grove of dead trees, still upright, their gaunt trunks and branches wrapped with flourishing parasitic vines. Here the group paused, and one of the shamans informed Luzelle, "You stay. We go on."

"You leave us?" she inquired, confused.

"It is not for eyes unblessed to behold the secrets of the wise." He placed a sack on the ground before her. "You are guests, here is food for the journey."

"Thank you. We go on alone, then."

"No. Stay. Wait."

The three shamans melted noiselessly into the jungle, leaving Luzelle and Girays alone among the dead trees.

"We are free, I take it," Girays observed. "We'll have to find our own way back to the boats. We could certainly have used a guide, but I suppose we should be thankful. This way, I believe." He pointed.

"No. Stay. Wait," she said. His brows rose, and she explained, "That's what he told me, that's what they want us to do."

"Why? Wait for what?"

"I don't know."

"How long?"

"I've no idea."

"What did they tell you just now?"

"Virtually nothing."

"We can't wait indefinitely. Do you want to be standing around this place after dark?"

"No, but I believe the wise men have some plan in mind for us. Don't you think we should follow their instructions and wait, for at least a little while?"

"How long? It must be late, the sun will be setting soon, and then what? If we start now, we might still be able to find our way back to the *Water Sprite* before the light gives out."

"That makes sense, but—"

The sound of native voices uplifted not far away interrupted her. They—presumably the three Blessed shamans—were half chanting, half singing, their tones impossibly high and pure. The sudden eeriness of the sound prickled the gooseflesh along her forearms and also stirred her memory. She had heard just such chants preceding the ground tremor that had rocked Xoxo's main square, and having heard, she could never forget.

A similar ground tremor here in this place could send the dead trees crashing down on herself and Girays, but somehow she did not believe that it would happen. She was frightened of the strange force expressing itself through those voices, frightened of a great power that she did not understand, but sensed no malign intent. For a moment she wondered at her own optimism, or trust, then recalled Karsler Stornzof's advice that night in Xoxo: *Listen now to your blood and nerves.* She had been doing that, she realized, and her instincts offered reassurance.

She glanced at Girays. He was frowning. Their eyes met, and he began, "We'd better—"

The comment went unfinished, for at that moment the air tingled and the surrounding vegetation awoke. With a loosening and shifting of great serpentine coils, the parasitic vines untwined from the surrounding trees. Long runners snaked

down from the dead branches overhead to wrap themselves
tenderly about the astounded travelers. Luzelle had only time
to grab the sack of provisions before she felt herself raised
gently from the ground and lifted high, alarmingly high, and
unbelievably higher yet, up above the bare dead branches and
higher, up to the level of the leafy spreading boughs of the
great live trees. Greenery slapped lightly at her face as she ascended, elastic thin branches whipped her limbs, but they did
not hurt her, for the vines that bore her aloft knew how to tilt
and guide her around obstacles, knew how to keep her from
harm, and the only ill that need presently concern her was the
churning seasick protest of a stomach outraged at such irregular locomotion.

She curbed the natural impulse to struggle, for the vines
that wound about her body clasped her kindly, yet she felt the
vast mindless life force capable of driving roots through inhospitable soil, the relentless slow strength able to break
through granite walls. No opposing such power, and potentially suicidal to attempt it at such heights, so she lay quies-
cent in the close green embrace. Turning her face to the side,
she saw Girays, bound like a python's prey in looping coils,
rising toward the treetops. She caught a flashing glimpse of
his face, frozen with astonishment, and then the leaves were
back in the way blocking her view, and she saw nothing but
greenery for a while.

Up, higher yet, through a region of thin young branches
supporting clusters of huge glossy leaves extravagantly bathed
in light, home to colonies of pygmy marmosets that watched
and chittered in wonder as she passed. Up higher, and suddenly she burst through the top of the forest canopy into the
full glare of the westering sun. She blinked and squinted
against the dazzle, but soon her eyes adjusted and she could
look out for miles over the treetops, all the way to the vast
glinting brown bend of the River Ygah. A warm perfumed
wind blew in her face, and she was filled with a kind of awed
joy. She wondered if Girays felt the same; she hoped he did.

What happens now?

She felt herself placed gently among branches strong
enough to bear her weight. Her vine released its hold and left

her there. For a moment terror chilled her, and then she felt the quiver of arcane vitality in the branches. They curved to enfold her, the tree arched its trunk and transferred her delicately to the branches of another tree, which in turn passed her painlessly and efficiently on to another.

Presently she heard a rustling of leaves and branches too rhythmic for the wind's work, and an immense vine reared up before her, swaying like a serpent before its charmer. The vine took her from the tree, bore her on for some distance, then relinquished her to the care of some creepers.

Throughout the rest of the afternoon the wakeful vegetation passed her on from one plant to another like a parcel. At sunset, however, their energy ebbed. There was only just time for a pair of trees to weave their topmost branches into a shallow, resilient nest and deposit her therein before darkness fell and the plants sank into immobile unconsciousness.

"Girays?" Suddenly afraid, she called out to him, and he answered at once. She peered through the deepening gloom, and spied him leaning out over the edge of a nest similar to her own, no more than a few yards distant. "Are you all right?"

"Yes. Thirsty, though. Have you still got that sack?"

"Yes, just a second." She checked. The sack donated by the Blessed Tribesmen contained two bundles of food and two corked water gourds. She took one of each, then called out, "Girays, I'm going to throw this to you. Ready?"

"Ready."

He sounded so trusting, as if it never crossed his mind that her aim might be off, and that the sole nourishment available to him for hours to come might easily fly off into the shadows to land on the forest floor hundreds of feet below. His face was a pale blur. Praying for accuracy, she tossed the sack.

"Got it. Thanks."

The voice was clear, but the speaker was now all but invisible. Darkness enveloped the Forests of Oorex. Luzelle ate and drank, then composed herself for unlikely slumber high above the jungle. A few yards away, Girays would be doing the same. He was certainly still awake.

It's his turn to talk.

She strained her ears. Nothing from Girays, but the jungle sang, and its melody lulled her to sleep.

At sunrise the vegetation awoke and the journey resumed. Luzelle was shaken from sleep by the sensation of a great vine coiling about her body. She was lifted from the nest. The two trees supporting her through the night disengaged, and the nest was no more. Startled and confused, she cast her eyes around but did not see Girays. She called out his name and heard an answering shout. The vine thrust her up above the canopy into the glory of the morning sun and she saw him. Her alarm subsided.

The vine transferred her neatly to the grasp of a neighboring epiphyte, which in turn presented her to a slithery hydra tree. The hours passed and the jungle bore her south toward Jumo Towne.

16

"I THINK COUSIN OGRON means to invade Vonahr. Perhaps within weeks," opined King Miltzin. He picked a morsel from the kaleidoscopic platter of appetizers sitting on the desk before him and nibbled appreciatively. "You must try one of these little marinated shrimp-scallop-mushroom brochette things, Nevenskoi. They're marvelous. Come, no ceremony. Help yourself."

"I thank you, Sire." Nevenskoi took a brochette, which proved excellent as the king had promised. The deep-fried serpent's knot that followed was just as good, and the cold sliced galantine of duckling was downright exquisite. His pleasure, although keen, was offset by the spectacle of Masterfire reduced to dwarfish proportions and squatting humbly beneath a chafing dish. The most extraordinary, awesome discovery of the age employed to warm the king's spiced dipping sauce! It was demeaning and offensive, but Mad Miltzin deemed the spectacle delightful. Nevenskoi stifled his outrage as best he could, but his creation caught it.

Badness? the small voice crackled under the chafing dish.

We are denied our just due, sweet one, Nevenskoi responded in silence. *We are robbed of the greatness that is ours by right. The king does not appreciate us.*

Badness? Eat king?

Not today.

Pleasepleaseplease?

No. Dangerous thoughts. Nevenskoi deliberately shifted mental gears. "Your Majesty has received communication from the Grewzian imperior?"

"Gad no, Cousin Ogron doesn't believe in writing. But the recent convergence of additional Grewzian troops on occupied Haereste means something, wouldn't you say? I think Vonahr's in for it. The Zoketsa thinks so too, and she should know. She's psychic, you see."

"The Zoketsa, Sire? The opera singer?"

"Reigning soprano of sopranos, a goddess among us. Have you heard her *sing,* man? Have you experienced her performance in the role of Queen Phantina? Such majesty and grandeur—such heights of glorious exultation, such depths of noble grief! You must see it, Nevenskoi—it will transform your existence as it has transformed mine!"

"I believe her reviews are generally favorable." For the first time since he had entered the king's study, Nevenskoi noticed that the astrological charts lately covering the desktop had given way to leather-bound musical scores.

"Reviews—bah! Her performance is sublime, an education and an inspiration. It has revealed the wonder of a life given over to art and beauty. Her art is her passion, Nevenskoi—she lives for it, the creative urge blazes at the center of her being. There is something in such fiery intensity that I find wonderfully stimulating."

"I do not doubt it for a moment, Sire."

"She is so *alive,* Nevenskoi! She lives every moment to the fullest! Each hour is *crammed* with color and meaning! She allows free rein to her emotions, she is guided by her instincts. She lives in harmony with the cosmos, which perhaps accounts for her psychic powers."

"Very likely, Sire."

"She senses things, she feels them in her soul."

"She senses and feels in her soul that Grewzland will shortly attack Vonahr?"

"She does, and such is my faith in her abilities that I should believe her even without the supporting evidence of the recent Vonahrish diplomatic antics. Have one of the creamed snail-asparagus tartlets, my friend. They're superb."

"Indeed, Sire." Nevenskoi tasted, and concurred with the king's judgment. "Majesty, I must confess my ignorance of current diplomatic events."

"That's no wonder, you're buried alive in your workroom most of the time. I'll tell you what it is, Nevenskoi. The Vonahrish president and his congressional flunkies have been pestering me for weeks now. It's the usual plea. They've heard of Masterfire, they see our green friend there as the ultimate weapon of war, and they want him. They're absolutely relentless, and you'd scarcely credit the underhanded methods they employ to advance their cause! They've contrived to slip their wheedling letters into my newspapers, in among the cushions of my carriage—I even found one tucked into the pocket of my dressing gown. Perhaps I'd pity their desperation, had they confined themselves to written importunities, but they've gone much further. They have actually attempted to smuggle their agents into the Waterwitch itself. Three times within the past month Vonahrish trespassers have been discovered sneaking about the palace grounds. It's outrageous. Oh, but I am persecuted!"

"Truly, Sire." Nevenskoi nodded gravely. He swallowed a bone-marrow fritter, noted the silky texture and inspired seasoning, but did not pause to savor, for his thoughts ran on another track. After a moment he continued, "Your Majesty is indeed abused, but perhaps I can offer a solution. I think the time has come for the king of the Low Hetz to assert his august will. A small display of royal resolution will surely serve to curb foreign presumption."

"Royal resolution. The term pleases me."

"Set Masterfire to ring the Waterwitch Palace with a wall of green flame," Nevenskoi urged softly. "Your Majesty's persecutors, recognizing the power and greatness of the Hetzian monarch, will venture no further impertinence." *And the world will behold my creation at last, and all mankind will marvel,* he added silently. Visions of lofty flaming ramparts filled his mind.

Big! I am BIG, I am VAST, I am HUGE, I am EVERYWHERE—

Masterfire had caught his creator's thought. Taken off

guard, Nevenskoi hesitated a startled instant, then tightened his mental grip.

Too late.

The green fire blossomed, expanding in an instant to cover the desktop, thence streaming down the sides to hit the floor and shoot off in all directions. Momentarily helpless to halt the spreading blaze, Nevenskoi could only enjoin mentally, *Consume nothing! Hear me, sweet one—consume nothing!*

Dancedancedance! replied Masterfire.

"Well—another demonstration?" the king inquired without interest. "Haven't you already done this one?"

Demonstration. Yes, that was what it could be, a demonstration to camouflage his temporary lapse. Masterfire, though imperfectly controlled, remained subject to his creator's influence. So far he had consumed nothing. A little additional guidance might constructively channel all of that burning exuberance. Nevenskoi spoke in his mind. *Loveliness, hear me. You are bigbigbig—*

Big! Bigger! Biggest!

You are great and grand—

Great! Grand! Greatgrand!

Now show the king how clever you are. Cover the study walls from floor to ceiling. Consume nothing. Do not touch the door or windows, leave them clear. Go now, frolic.

Wheeeeee!

Masterfire followed instructions precisely. A moment later the study was evenly lined with green fire that did not destroy. Assuming an expression of modest satisfaction, Nevenskoi murmured, "If Your Majesty would but deign to visualize just such a wall as this enclosing all of Waterwitch Palace."

"Impressive, I grant." Frowning, Miltzin bit into a miniature frog leg glossed with sauce Jerundière. "But rather a warlike display, is it not?"

"Purely a defensive measure, Sire."

"And I will not countenance perversion of our Masterfire to such barbaric ends. No, I will find some other way of repelling pertinacious diplomats."

"As Your Majesty wills." Jaw set behind the black-dyed imperial, Nevenskoi bowed his head. Frustration smoldered within him, and the green flames blanketing the study walls crackled in fierce sympathy.

"And yet our Masterfire *is* extraordinary," Miltzin mused. "How might his talents best impress and educate my subjects? Ah, I've a thought. The Zoketsa sings Queen Phantina again tomorrow evening. You recall the famous Mad Scene, in which Phantina sets torch to the palace? Only think what it would be to see vast torrents of green flame engulfing all the stage! Yes! That's how it should be, and the verisimilitude will inspire the diva to scale new artistic heights. Ah, she will be so happy!"

"Let me assure myself that I understand Your Majesty. You wish to use Masterfire as a theatrical property?"

"The spectacle will be magnificent."

"I see." *Frivolous, trivial, insulting.* An angry retort rose to Nevenskoi's lips, and he suppressed it with the self-control born of practice. He filled his mouth with an anchovy barquette, the better to obstruct the escape of rash words, and while he chewed, he considered. A night at the opera for Masterfire. An absurd indignity on the face of it, and yet undoubtedly a step up from the king's chafing dish. The Toltz Opera House, at least, was public and urban. Masterfire would be seen. . . . *Vast torrents of green flame engulfing all the stage.* . . . Mad Miltzin was right, the spectacle would overwhelm the audience. Masterfire's fame would spread, along with the fame of his creator. Great things might eventually come of it. It was, at least, a start.

His spirits rose. The anchovy barquette, he noticed, was delightfully piquant.

Now we are happy again. Masterfire flowed like water over the study walls.

"An inspired suggestion, Majesty," Nevenskoi murmured suavely.

"Yes, my friend, I am inspired, for I am touched by the fire of the Zoketsa's genius. She and I are psychically linked. I have never known such intense closeness with a woman, it is a marriage of souls." Lost in golden dreams, Miltzin took an allumette garnished with truffles and crayfish tails, ate it, and broke from his trance to observe, "Gad, but that new sous-chef is a wonder! In his own way he possesses a kind of genius that rivals the Zoketsa's own. Or yours, for that matter."

"It is true, Sire," Nevenskoi conceded without reservation. The cook in question, hired weeks earlier to fill the vacancy left by the flight of the king's poisoner, had lost no time in establishing indispensability. He was an artist almost glaringly marked for greatness.

"Such talent and diligence merit reward. The fellow must receive a royal commendation. What's his name again?"

"Majesty, I've no idea."

"Oh, vexation." Miltzin yanked a bellpull.

Moments later a footman answered the summons. The servant took one look at the study walls swimming in green flame and flinched.

"That new sous-chef, hired a few weeks ago—d'you know his name?" the king demanded, cheerfully blind to the other's distress.

"Sire, I do." The footman took a breath and reclaimed his professional impassivity. "The cook in question, a native of Your Majesty's city of Flenkutz, is named Giggy Neeper."

Cousin Giggy. Always liked to putter with pastry and pâtés, even as a boy. Hadn't seen his kinsman Nitz in fifteen years, but surely would not have forgotten. Cousin Giggy—here in the Waterwitch Palace.

Nevenskoi's intestines writhed, and a pang of exquisite agony shot through him.

THE GREAT VINE LOWERED LUZELLE to the ground and released her so gently and smoothly that she staggered a little but never lost her footing. The next moment Girays was set down beside her. The vines withdrew, retracting into the jungle. The arms of the forest stilled themselves.

She caught her breath and surveyed her surroundings. Behind her the green wild terminated abruptly. Before her rose small wooden shacks bordering scraggly vegetable gardens, a cluster of small market stalls, and a public prayer hut. Beyond them loomed the high and handsome white architecture of Jumo Towne, arch-windowed and adorned in fanciful Aennorvi style with wrought-iron grillwork and rooftop gardens. Her eyes widened, for the spectacle of that pristine, thoroughly westernized city set in the midst of the jungle was startling despite the many descriptions of this place she had read or heard. The descriptions had not prepared her for the almost unsettling contrast between sophistication and surrounding untamed nature, between upstart civilization and the ancient savagery poised to obliterate it. Jumo Towne, for all its elegance or because of it, appeared distinctly precarious.

But civilization and comfort would endure so long as the diamond mines continued to generate wealth. The huge profits from the mines, which had transformed an obscure Aennorvi colonial outpost into a city as luxurious as any to be found in the world, ensured protection and survival. So long as the great pits yielded bits of crystal, the theaters and casinos would flourish, the grand hotels would offer the finest cuisine, the shops would stock the costliest wares, the streets and mansions would shine, and the jungle would be held at bay. But even the richest of mines were not inexhaustible, and the jungle knew how to wait.

Luzelle slanted a look at Girays. He seemed hardly aware of the white city ahead. His eyes anchored on the jungle. He looked as if he wanted to run back in, track down the tribal shamans, and milk them of magical secrets. She could understand that particular mental itch, which she shared, but it was not something she would have expected of M. the Marquis. Girays v'Alisante, however, was no longer recognizable as a hereditary seigneur, a formerly-Exalted, or even as a moderately respectable member of society. Shirtless, ragged, filthy, unshorn, and unshaven, his chin black with disreputable stubble, M. the Marquis looked like a vagrant, or worse.

She herself was almost as bad, with her dirty sap-sticky clothing, her dirty curls and dirty face, but at least she was fully covered. No matter. Jumo Towne offered every conceivable amenity at a price, and she retained a full wallet. Within a matter of hours she and Girays would revert to their former selves, unless he had lost all his belongings, in which case his antiquated formerly-Exalted code would probably deny her permission to pay his bills.

"Girays." She jogged his arm, and his dark eyes tore themselves from the forest. "Have you still got your passport and money?"

He slid a hand into a pocket, verified the contents, and nodded.

"Good. Let's go spend some, then." She began to walk on into the city, and he fell into step beside her.

"On what?" he asked as they went.

"I want a bath, a long, perfumed bath. I want new clothes and travel gear. I want some decent food, preferably expensive. I want a *plush* hotel room, or better yet, a suite. I want—"

"I get your general drift, but may I offer a practical suggestion?"

"I'm not in the mood for practical suggestions."

"This one is small and fairly painless. Before we do anything else, I propose that we find our way to the city hall before it closes for the day, and have our passports stamped. Once that's accomplished, we can afford to relax a little. What do you think?"

We, he kept saying, as if he had forgotten that they were rivals. It would be so easy and natural to let herself forget as well. The so-easy-and-natural road to defeat, and she would not take that road. She would maintain her detachment, and she would leave him behind at the first opportunity.

"You're right, of course," she murmured submissively, and he darted a sharp glance at her. "We'd better get it done. I just hope it won't take long. Remember the underclerk in Xoxo?"

"Too well. 'Our Grewzian contender, the Overcommander Stornzof, will whip your Vonahrish backsides.' "

"Karsler." Luzelle's forehead creased. "What do you think has happened to him? If he was aboard the *Water Sprite,* he might still be trapped in the Ta'ahri Capillaries. The Blessed Tribesmen may have killed him, or he could starve in the jungle."

"Possible, but I doubt it. Stornzof's a singular character of unusual abilities—"

"Oh, you admit it?"

"I admit it. He's likely to prevail on his own merits. But if you're worried, here's what we can do. Remember, the South Ygahro Territory's part of the Imperium now. When we get to the city hall, we can tell the Grewzian authorities what happened to the *Water Sprite*. When they hear what the natives have been up to, they'll probably send troops to the rescue."

"Seems like a terrible thing to do to the Blessed Tribesmen, after they helped us."

"Yes, but it's not every stranded traveler who happens to know how to claim Ygahri hospitality. Those tribesmen are violent, they should be controlled."

"But they're only acting in self-defense, aren't they?"

"The death of Jhiv-Huze—self-defense?"

"The tribesmen might maintain that Oonuvu acted in defense of his honor. Besides, they must regard all westerners as invaders, which we are, and naturally they defend their own homeland. Can you really blame them for that?"

"Yes, when they attack and murder harmless civilian travelers."

"But are those civilian travelers really harmless? Only consider—"

They continued arguing the point as they advanced into Jumo Towne. Absorbed though she was in the debate, Luzelle did not fail to note the little native shacks and hovels that cluttered the outskirts of the city giving way to spotless white town houses lining wonderfully clean paved avenues. Everything was perfectly maintained, and no wonder. All around her she saw native menials gathering litter and animal droppings, raking gravel, scrubbing stucco, polishing glass and brass. The lawns bordering the houses were beautifully groomed, and the remarkable gardens combined jungle vitality and tropical color with rigorous westernized order.

On they marched along streets filled with the smartest carriages drawn by horses that would have shone anywhere in the world, pausing once for Girays to ask a random pedestrian for directions to the city hall. The pedestrian averted his eyes, quickened his pace, and hurried by without reply. Probably he thought that the foreign scarecrow was trying to ask for money.

Luzelle felt her face go red. Both of them looked wretched, but Girays was conspicuously half naked. The guards at the entrance would never admit him to the city hall in such a state. When she spied a pushcart vendor of oddments at the side of the road, she halted to observe, "Look, he's got a shirt for sale. Better take it."

"It's purple, Luzelle."

"I'd call it more of an aubergine."

"It resembles a giant bruise."

"It will keep you from being arrested for indecent exposure."

"My exposure is not indecent, only indecorous."

"Semantics. Just veil your charms for now, the world isn't ready."

He bought the shirt and put it on. Luzelle looked at him and felt the giggles rising. Girays was not a large man, but the shirt—clearly intended for a compact Ygahri wearer—was far too small for him. The sleeves ended inches short of his wrists, and there was not enough fabric to tuck into his waistband. The color was execrable.

"You're enjoying this, aren't you?" Girays was watching her face.

"I wish I had one of those new light-sensitive glass plate things to capture the image for posterity. What is that shirt made of?"

"Tissue paper, I believe. Come on, let's get this over with."

The vendor furnished directions, and they moved on toward the city hall. The buildings grew taller and grander around them as they went, and they passed a splendid white hotel on which Luzelle cast a longing eye. QUEEN OF DIAMONDS, the sign above the entrance proclaimed in Vonahrish, and the place looked as if it might live up to its name. But they would never let her cross the threshold in her present condition, and she found herself wondering whether Jumo Towne harbored an old-fashioned public bathhouse of which she and Girays might avail themselves before purchasing decent clothes, before checking into that beautiful hotel. And then, dinner. . . . But somewhere in the midst of all that pleasant activity, perhaps during the shopping phase, she would have to slip away on her own to investigate available travel options, for she needed to reach the port of Dasuneville, there to book passage for Aveshq, exotic eastern extremity of the

Grand Ellipse. And best to do it without Girays's knowledge, for the chance might arise to pull ahead. . . .

What an underhanded notion. A slight sense of shame or guilt burned her. She could only hope that Girays would not read her mind, and sometimes M. the Marquis seemed almost as telepathic as Karsler Stornzof. But then, she reminded herself, she had nothing to be ashamed of. Girays had been willing to abandon her in Xoxo. He would leave her behind in Jumo, if possible. As he himself had observed, they were in a race.

The city hall rose before them, a handsome Aennorvi-style edifice topped with the Grewzian flag. They approached, and a grey-uniformed sentry demanded their business and their credentials. They explained one and produced the other, and the sentry let them in. They found their way to the registrar's office without difficulty, there to discover an elderly Aennorvi bureaucrat too insignificant to merit a Grewzian replacement. Girays addressed the registrar in his excellent fluent Aennorvi, and drew a strongly positive response. Both Vonahrish passports immediately received stamps. Girays described the plight of the *Water Sprite,* and the registrar promised to relay the information to the appropriate authorities. The two travelers departed.

Done, easily and efficiently. Another official mark of progress along the Grand Ellipse. And now for a little well-deserved self-indulgence.

Luzelle was smiling as they emerged into the steamy sunlit glare of the tropical afternoon. "Have you realized," she asked, "that we've probably now pulled ahead of everyone else in the race, with the possible exception of the Festinette twins? Where d'you suppose those two are, anyway?"

"Haven't heard anything about them in weeks. Can't speak for Tchornoi, Zavune, or a couple of the others, either, for that matter."

"When last seen, those others were behind us. The Festinettes drew ahead long ago, then vanished. If they'd been through Xoxo before us, surely we would have heard. Think they might have had some sort of accident?"

"No way of knowing, no point in speculating."

"That's so phlegmatic."

"I'd call it logical."

"No it isn't, because you're wrong, there's plenty of point in speculating. Speculation raises questions, stimulates the intellect—" She chattered on as they walked, enjoying the mental exercise.

They drew level with the mouth of a small alley, and the sound of angry voices pulled her eyes into the passageway, where she saw two khaki-uniformed Jumo Towne constables beating a native. The Ygahri—nearly naked, covered with bruises and cuts—offered no resistance. Arms raised to shield his head, he crouched whimpering on the ground. Deaf or indifferent to all pleas, the constables methodically plied their truncheons.

"Here—stop that!" Luzelle did not pause to think. Already she was running down the alley, shouting as she went. "You're killing him, stop!"

The constables looked up from their work, and one of them snarled something in Aennorvi. His words were meaningless to her, but the gesture that accompanied them was perfectly intelligible. She herself had addressed them in Vonahrish, which the officers might or might not know, but surely she could make herself understood. Halting, she moderated her tone, appealing quietly, "Please stop. He is not resisting you. Stop."

The constables stared at her. The native crouched on the ground did likewise. One of the khaki officers snapped an angry command.

"He's telling you to keep out of it," Girays translated. He had advanced to stand beside her.

"You can talk to them. Tell them to stop before they kill that man."

"I don't think it will do any good."

"Please try."

"Very well." Girays addressed the constables in their own language. He spoke calmly, reasonably, and they listened for a few moments, then fired a burst of irritable Aennorvi at him. "They say that this man is a fugitive worker from the diamond mines," he translated. "They say that the native miners are forbidden by law to abandon their labors—"

"That's outrageous, that's serfdom!"

"And that recaptured escapees are always soundly thrashed, at the very least, as a matter of policy. Sets an example for the other native malcontents."

"They're disgusting. I might have expected this of the Grewzians, but these people are Aennorvis, aren't they?" She addressed herself to the constables, this time speaking in Grewzian, which they might well comprehend. "Very well, you have the prisoner made secured, and you have punished well and truly. Now why, if you please, cannot you merely—"

The hostile eyes were turned in her direction. Seizing the providential opportunity, the battered Ygahri sprang to his feet and streaked for the mouth of the alley. Yelling, the constables gave chase.

"Wait!" Instinctively Luzelle moved to block their path. One of the officers collided with her, and she sat down hard. From her new position on the ground, she had a clear view of Girays's foot discreetly positioning itself to intercept the second Aennorvi, who tripped and fell full length. His partner paused at the intersection, glancing right and left. Evidently the quarry had already vanished, for he turned away with a curse.

The fallen constable arose to spew infuriated Aennorvi at Girays, who murmured a bland, meek apology that failed to turn aside wrath. The angry tirade continued. Luzelle stood up, and the second constable opened verbal fire in Aennorvi. She shrugged her incomprehension, and he switched to Grewzian.

"You have aided and abetted a fugitive. You have hindered city officers in the performance of their duty. These are serious felonies."

"Accidents, sir. I am the most clumsy," Luzelle confessed remorsefully, taking her cue from Girays's demeanor. "I regret all trouble, but truly, made only the unfortunate accidents."

"You blocked my path and delayed me, while this clown in the purple shirt tripped my partner. The fugitive native has escaped justice for now, thanks to your meddling. You claim all this was accidental?"

"Truly, Constable, the most unfortunate—"

"Silence, you are both under arrest. You are in Jumo Towne, a city of the Imperium now, and our laws are not to be mocked by foreign beggars, vagabonds, and vagrants."

Why you miserable spineless little collaborators, I'll wager most of your fellow Aennorvis would like to tear you apart, Luzelle thought. She clamped her jaw to keep the words in.

"Officers, gentlemen, we are neither beggars nor vagabonds." Girays spoke up politely. "We are two respectable Vonahrish travelers. We compete in the Grand Ellipse race. You have heard of the Grand Ellipse, yes?"

"Enough foolery, these lies make things worse for you," a constable advised.

"No lies," Girays maintained. "See, I will show you my passport." His hand approached his pocket.

"Halt."

Service revolvers materialized in the hands of both officers. Luzelle gasped. Girays froze.

"Hands up. Both of you."

The prisoners obeyed. One of the constables searched them brusquely, removing passports and wallets.

"Blue ground," the investigator reported with a low whistle. "Take a look at this." He displayed the contents of the confiscated wallets. "Vonahrish New-rekkoes. Thousands."

"So." His partner nodded with an air of confirmed expectation, then demanded of Girays, "Where did you steal this?"

"I did not steal it," Girays returned. "The passports and wallets belong to me and to this lady."

"Do yourself a favor, don't make us angry."

"But he does truly indeed speak the truth," Luzelle insisted, bad Grewzian deteriorating under stress. "This is all our own property that belongs to us, if you please."

"No doubt. And the two of you are really rich travelers, disguising yourselves as dirty tramps for the sheer novelty of it all. You go to a masquerade, perhaps?"

"No, no—we are in accident, all of our clothing is lost—"

"Better and better." The officer holding the two passports

checked each. "Girays v'Alisante, Luzelle Devaire, Vonahrish citizens."

"We are," Girays concurred.

"The real v'Alisante and Devaire will soon report the theft of their property to the authorities. Perhaps the report has already been filed."

"Constable, sir, how shall I prove I am myself?" Luzelle implored.

"That is assuming the owners remain alive," the officer continued as if he had not heard her. "We have here a large sum of money, worth killing for. Perhaps you found it necessary to dispose of the real v'Alisante and Devaire, yes?"

"The constable concocts fairy tales." Girays could not repress a slight curl of the lip.

"We'll see soon enough. Hands behind your back."

Girays obeyed and the constable snapped manacles on him.

"You too," the second officer informed Luzelle.

She dared not argue. The irons closed about her wrists. She jingled the short length of chain disbelievingly. One of the officers was holding her left arm above the elbow, and he pulled imperatively.

"Where do you take us?" she asked.

"West Street Station. Move," he commanded.

They marched straight through the heart of Jumo Towne, and everywhere the citizens paused to stare at the khaki officers with their outlandishly garbed, fettered captives. Luzelle's cheeks burned. Longing for invisibility, she kept her eyes fixed on the ground at first, but soon self-respect or vanity came to her rescue, and she raised her head to advance with the remote dignity of some formerly-Exalted en route to execution in the days of the revolution.

They entered the station house, its front door bearing the emblem of the Endless Fire, and the pressure of glaring sunlight and staring humanity vanished. The front office was dim, airless, and quiet. A desk clerk and a couple of guards on duty there greeted the arrival of constables and prisoners with mild interest.

"A pair of undesirable aliens," one of the arresting officers announced in Grewzian. "Caught assisting a fugitive native. Obstructed justice and assaulted two officers of the law. Suspected of grand larceny or worse. Stolen property found in their possession." He slapped the confiscated wallets and passports down on the desk.

The clerk checked the contents of the wallets and his look of boredom vanished. Carefully he entered a notation in one of his ledgers, then locked the money and documents away in the top drawer of the desk.

"Any reports on that yet?"

"Not yet."

"Keep an eye open. This may be a big one."

"We are not thieves! This is not stolen property!" Luzelle burst out. "We have done nothing wrong!"

"Name?" the clerk demanded, pen poised above a notebook.

"Luzelle Devaire. I am Vonahrish. I compete in the Grand Ellipse. So also does M. v'Alisante. We did not mean to obstruct justice. It was an accident, and we are sorry. We—"

"Enter her as 'Anonymous female, nonresponsive,'" directed a constable. The clerk complied.

"This is not true! I am not nonresponsive. My name truly is Luzelle Devaire. I—"

"Name?" the clerk inquired of the male prisoner.

"Girays v'Alisante. Vonahrish traveler. Before you enter me as 'Anonymous, nonresponsive,' let me suggest that you allow me to speak with the captain, or whoever is in charge here. Only permit this, and all confusion will soon correct itself—"

"The confusion is yours alone, if you imagine that these lies will help you. As for the captain, rest assured that you will answer to him when he returns."

"When will that be?"

"Two days from today, at which time you will almost certainly be transferred to Central Station jail."

"Two days!" Luzelle exclaimed. "We compete in the Grand Ellipse, we cannot sit around this place for two days!"

"If you are simply thieves, you will sit around the South Ygahro Territory House of Corrections for some years to come, or else you will be assigned to the road gangs, and our station house will seem a pleasure garden by comparison," an officer informed her. "If we discover that you have murdered the legitimate owners of these wallets, you will be shot. Decapitation used to be our favored local form of execution, but we are in the Imperium now, and our methods have improved. Lock them up," he instructed the guards.

Luzelle protested in vain as she and Girays were herded through a stout wooden door at the rear of the office and into the reeking lockup beyond. The place contained some half-dozen cells, one of them larger than the other five combined. The large cell alone was occupied, confining seven men, five native Ygahris and two westerners, all stinking of xussi, filth, and vomit. The ennui of the West Street Station staff now explained itself; official activity in this particular neighborhood focused largely upon the control of public inebriation.

A couple of the caged drunks eyed Luzelle with interest as she came in. One smiled and waved amiably, but most remained glazedly inert.

The manacles were removed. Luzelle and Girays were placed in adjoining unoccupied cells. The doors clanged shut, the locks snapped, and the guards exited.

Luzelle's closet-sized cell contained a pallet bolted to the wall, a slop bucket, a rusted water pannikin, many buzzing flies, and nothing else. The compartment backed against one of the supporting stone walls of the station house. The other three cell walls consisted of floor-to-ceiling iron bars that left her entirely exposed to view. Should she need to use that slop bucket, there would be an audience.

As if he could read her mind, one of the drunks in the big cell smacked his lips to draw her attention, then cheerfully began to unbutton himself. She looked away.

Girays caught her eye. He extended his hand through the bars that separated them, and she took it. For a while they stood silently attached, until she asked, "How long do you suppose it will take these imbecilic policemen to figure out that we're not thieves and murderers?"

"Eventually it will dawn on them that no one is reporting any pertinent crimes, and then they'll reconsider. We might find help sooner if we could get word to the Vonahrish legation here in Jumo, but I'm not certain it remains open in the wake of the Grewzian invasion."

"Grewzians, again. Always the Grewzians."

"This time the offenders are colonial Aennorvis."

"Collaborators, though."

"Can't altogether fault their suspicions, in view of our present appearance."

"Well *I* can fault them easily enough, and I do. Nitwits. Oh, I suppose we'll laugh about all of this someday—"

"Assuming they don't shoot or decapitate us."

"But I can't laugh now. All I can think about is the time this is costing us. Every minute we spend locked up here is undermining our chances, eating away at our lead." *Our chances . . . our lead.* She caught the slip and frowned at herself. She was forgetting their rivalry as he had forgotten it not long ago. She would not let it happen again. Aloud she continued without a break, "Tchornoi, Zavune, or a couple of the others might still catch up." One name was omitted. Suddenly self-conscious, she drew her hand from his.

Girays looked at her and said flatly, "Stornzof."

17

THE SKIES WERE DARK and the lamps alight all over Jumo Towne as Karsler Stornzof made his way along a richly carpeted corridor to Suite 303 of the Queen of Diamonds Hotel. He knocked with reluctance but without hesitation, heard a familiar voice bid him enter, opened the door, and went into a luxuriously appointed sitting room hazed with smoke.

The Grandlandsman Torvid Stornzof, attired in irreproachable evening wear, occupied a brocade couch. A low table before him supported a crystal ashtray, enameled cigarette box, a couple of glasses, and a silver ice bucket containing a slim black bottle. Pressed into a corner at the far side of the room cowered a radiantly blond, saucer-eyed girl, some eleven or twelve years of age.

"Ah, Nephew." Torvid nodded with measured cordiality. "You are here at last. I have been expecting your arrival this past week."

"I have encountered delays en route, Grandlandsman," Karsler reported. "The most recent involved an artificial blockage of the Ta'ahri Capillaries. The private vessel lent me by Janztoph in Xoxo was halted, and I was obliged to hire a *hrukiku-tcho* and driver to carry me through the Forests of Oorex."

"*Hrukiku-tcho*—an indigenous beast reminiscent of an overgrown rat, is it not?"

"Not a bad description."

"But what an imaginative solution to the problem. A lesser strategist might have compelled the local natives to open the channels, but you have scorned the obvious and opted for the large rat. I must commend your originality."

He had all but forgotten the pleasures of intrafamilial conversation. Karsler said nothing.

"I trust the rewards of the journey will justify your efforts." Torvid glinted an icebound smile. "Jumo Towne is not altogether backward. There is entertainment to be found here." As if recalling her existence, he glanced at the child in the corner and informed her, "That will be all for today. You may go."

She exited at a run.

"The casinos are not half bad," the grandlandsman continued, "and one or two of the actresses at the Crown Theater are worth a glance. We will dine, Nephew—it is possible to find a perfectly adequate veal cutlet imperior-style here in town— and then we shall amuse ourselves."

"With your permission I will dine and retire early," Karsler returned. "I must rise at dawn to secure transportation to Dasuneville. I do not know what is locally available, and will allow time to compare options."

"No need to trouble yourself. The matter has already been arranged. The best mount at Lunune's Livery in Orchid Street has been set aside for your use. You will ride the animal to the inn halfway along the Jumo-Dasune Passage, where a fresh horse of equal quality awaits you. Make a moderately early start in the morning, and you will reach Dasuneville before nightfall, the day after tomorrow. This is the fastest means of travel available. Your belated arrival has left me ample time to, as you put it, compare options."

"I see. I am obliged, Grandlandsman."

"A trifle, Nephew. When you arrive in Dasuneville, you will proceed to the Portside Inn, where a room has been reserved for you. The following morning you will embark for Aveshq aboard the Grewzian transport vessel *Triumphant*, whose captain has awaited your coming with an impatience equaling my own. This little affair has been arranged courtesy of the Overcommander Ghonauer, leader of the occupying force, whose father, fortunately for all concerned, happens to be an old schoolfellow of mine."

"You have been thorough."

"That is my habit. Rest assured, Nephew, I am willing to exert myself on your behalf, a necessity in view of your obvious reluctance to meet all requirements of your position."

"I will not pretend to misunderstand you." The recollections of his early training enabled Karsler Stornzof to will an unexpectedly powerful rush of anger out of existence. "Our perceptions of necessity differ greatly, yet I believe we will agree that debate is pointless. Therefore, having reported my arrival in accordance with your request, I will bid you good evening."

"One moment. Be so good as to favor me with your company a little while longer."

"According to your will, Grandlandsman."

"Sit down, then."

Karsler obeyed.

Torvid poured out a couple of drinks from the black bottle and handed one to his visitor. "This is caschia, a locally produced aperitif, surprisingly decent. I trust your Promontory principles do not limit you to cold water?"

"Not at all."

"Then you will consider it no violation of conscience to drink the imperior's health?"

"His health." Calmly refusing the bait, Karsler clinked glasses with his uncle and drank.

Torvid set his glass aside. "And now I will require a full accounting of your activities since Aeshno."

Karsler concisely obliged, omitting those details most likely to draw his listener's complaint.

Torvid listened in meditative silence, observing only at the close of the narration, "It would seem that you spend a disproportionate quantity of your time in the company of the two Vonahrish racers."

"Happenstance, Grandlandsman."

"Is it? Are you quite certain? I do not discount the attractions of that shapely little actress—lecturer—ballet girl—whatever you insist is her profession. What is her name, again—La Faire?"

"Devaire," Karsler corrected shortly.

"Of course. Prominent though her bourgeois charms may be, her importance is negligible, and I cannot help but suspect the influence of a more significant force at work. I refer of course to the other Vonahrish traveler."

"V'Alisante—what of him?"

"A formerly-Exalted of the best and oldest blood, a titled seigneur but for the current regrettable ascendancy of democrats and peasants in his land. Wealthy, cultivated, well connected. All in all a personage of some consequence, a man with a personal stake in the protection of the national status quo. Just the sort of character most likely at this time to draw the desperate attention of the Vonahrish Ministry of Foreign Affairs. You recall I advised you in Aeshno to observe your fellow racers closely, as it is almost certain that some serve as agents of their respective governments. You would do well to consider M. v'Alisante in such a light, and thus as a potential threat to Grewzian interests in the Low Hetz."

"There is little evidence to support your suspicions," Karsler observed. "I have spent considerable time in this Vonahrishman's company, and never at any time has he attempted to hinder, much less arrest, my progress. Quite the contrary, in fact—he has more than once offered me literally life-saving assistance."

"He has slipped within your guard, that's all too clear."

"To what purpose? I would almost certainly have been eliminated from the race, if not the world, back in Aeshno, but for v'Alisante's intervention."

"The Vonahrish are not unsubtle, Nephew. Nor, I think, do they care to brave the Imperium's wrath any sooner than they must, although their respite is brief at best. It is not essential to his purposes that M. v'Alisante eliminate you from the competition—he need only defeat you, and if this can be accomplished by means that appear aboveboard, all the better. For now, he simply keeps you in his sights and bides his time."

"Speculation, Grandlandsman."

"Intelligent foresight, Nephew. I believe I have already directed your attention to the advantages of a preemptive strike."

"You have."

"And?"

"I am sensible of your opinion and will take your advice into consideration. Duty demands no less."

"Duty demands considerably more, a truth you seem inclined to ignore."

"Let me assure myself that I understand you correctly. You are urging me to launch a preemptive strike—in other words, to remove or incapacitate a fellow sportsman, Girays v'Alisante, to whom I am personally indebted?"

"Come, this schoolboy chatter of fellow sportsmen and personal debt begins to weary me. You are a soldier confronting the enemy. It is as simple as that. Are you a Grewzian? A Stornzof? If so, you will do what must be done to serve the Imperium."

"To serve the Imperium." Karsler reflected briefly, and then remarked with apparent irrelevance, "Grandlandsman, I will describe an incident I witnessed en route to this hotel and this meeting. It was late afternoon, and the streets of the city were steaming. I walked along, thinking of little beyond the heat and discomfort, until I came to a plaza at the bottom of Eev Street, where a considerable crowd had gathered. The buildings lining the square were fire blackened and bullet scarred, for this was the site of the great massacre of the last Aennorvi and native defenders of Jumo Towne, some weeks past. At the center of the square rose a rough scaffold equipped with a post and a block. A squad of Grewzian troops surrounded the scaffold."

Torvid took a cigarette from the enameled box. Lighting it, he listened in silence.

"Something was about to happen there," Karsler continued, "and so I paused to watch. Presently a cart containing several uniformed constables of the local police force arrived at the foot of the scaffold. The constables escorted a prisoner, a naked Ygahri male, who was removed from the cart and transferred to the custody of our countrymen. At this juncture a warrant was read aloud, and the crimes of the prisoner were made known to the public. It seems he was a fugitive native laborer guilty of fleeing the diamond mines, an illegality under the old Aennorvi law, which as yet remains active under the Grewzian administration. Moreover, it was the second such offense of which this Ygahri had been adjudged guilty. The punishment, fixed by statute, involved both corporal discipline and mutilation.

"The sentence was carried out by our Grewzian soldiers in full view of the assembled citizens," Karsler reported expressionlessly. "The native was bound to the post and whipped until his back streamed with blood. He was then taken down and conveyed to the block, where a Grewzian sergeant equipped with an ax amputated the anterior portion of the culprit's right foot, an operation certain to discourage future excursions. The wound was cauterized with a heated iron, and the prisoner—now unconscious—was returned to the cart and removed. The constables and troops withdrew, the crowd dispersed, and I continued on to the Queen of Diamonds Hotel." Karsler fell silent.

"Well?" Torvid prompted at last. "Your point?"

"Is it not self-evident?"

"You are about to plunge, I suspect, neck deep into some morass of sentimental guilt, and you hope to drag me down into the sweet muck to wallow alongside you."

"You have spoken of serving the Imperium." Karsler chose his words with care. "That is the first duty of our House, and so it has always been. Does that duty demand blind obedience and unquestioning loyalty? If so, we Stornzofs have willingly enslaved ourselves."

"What is this?" Frowning, Torvid extinguished his cigarette.

"Our system is deeply flawed," Karsler returned deliberately. "This is a fact I failed to recognize during my Promontory years of seclusion, and one I could overlook as a soldier at war. In recent weeks, however, I have been out in the world, where certain truths are impossible to ignore. The imperfections in the Imperium's structure are so obvious and marked that only a fool could fail to perceive them, and only a hypocrite or a coward could refuse to acknowledge them. I am a Stornzof as well as an Elucidated, and I believe as deeply as you do in serving our nation. But I ask you now, as your nephew and kinsman, to consider the possibility that we most truly serve Grewzland in striving to correct the Imperium's greatest defects."

"I see." Torvid appeared to consider his reply at some length. When finally he spoke, his tone was unwontedly forbearing. "You have appealed to me as a kinsman, and I will answer you as such. Indeed, it seems I can hardly do otherwise, which may be a weakness. But you are my oldest sister's son by our second cousin, thus doubly a Stornzof, your blood a distillate of Grewzland's finest, and I cannot forget that. Therefore I will tell you this. Your questions and misgivings are the product of youthful indecision, merely. I will go so far as to confess that such qualms sometimes clouded my own vision and judgment when I was a boy. I, too, pondered issues of conscience. Irresolution all but paralyzed my will. Almost perversely I undermined my own value to country and imperior. But then, before it was too late, I recognized my error. My eyes opened, and I realized that a man cannot serve his country with a divided heart and mind. He must commit himself fully, without reservation, or else he is worse than useless—he becomes a liability. Recognizing the dangerous arrogance of my doubts, I chose of my own volition to abandon them. I, a Stornzof, submitted to something that I could recognize as greater and more important than myself and my personal concerns, greater even than all my House—that is, the might and glory of the Grewzian Imperium. I did this because Grewzland required it, and in that yielding discovered the strength that is unconquerable. It is more than time for you to do the same."

Karsler recalled the grey seas and grey skies of the past. They seemed far distant. He said nothing.

"You are silent." Torvid studied his nephew. "Be aware that I have spoken to you of inward things, as I would to few others, because you are of my blood and we are linked by the strongest bonds, despite all differences. It is no small thing for me to hold out the hand, and it is not a gesture to be ignored. You understand me?"

"Yes, Grandlandsman," Karsler replied. "Now as never before, I understand you."

"PLEASE, SIR, WHAT IS THE HOUR?" Luzelle appealed in Grewzian.

Ignoring her query, the guard propelled a new drunk into the communal cage, locked the door, and turned away.

"Please, sir," she persisted, "will you not, if you please, tell us how long we are here? There is no clock, no window to see the sun, and—"

The guard exited the lockup in silence, and the door closed behind him.

"Oh, why don't they ever answer?" she exclaimed in frustration. "I only ask the time of day, would it kill them to tell me?"

"Ah, but an insect tyrant must take his pleasure where he finds it," Girays suggested.

"I hate them. They're malevolent morons."

"I quite agree, but outrage won't mend matters. You'll only make yourself ill."

"Thank you, Doctor v'Alisante. How long do you think we've been here?"

"I don't know, but I believe we're well into the afternoon, which would make it about twenty-four hours."

"A whole day lost—we can't afford it, I can't stand it! These rotten little Aennorvi nincompoops are ruining us, over nothing! We're going to lose, and it's all their fault! Oh, I'd like to throttle somebody!"

A couple of listening drunks whistled and whooped.

"Please, Luzelle, calm yourself," Girays enjoined wearily. "If you've no concern for your own health, then spare a thought for mine. You are giving me a headache."

"Oh—sorry." She considered. "I really am sorry. I must be making life miserable for you."

"Don't take credit for Aennorvi work."

"Well, I'm not helping much. I'll try to be more patient, I'll try to be quiet and calm. It won't be easy, but I will try."

"Interesting."

"What is?"

"You. I've never heard you express such sentiments, wouldn't have thought you had it in you. You've changed a bit, these past few years."

"Not for the worse, I hope."

"Far from it."

"Well. I suppose I must have been something of a brat in those days."

"You were indeed. A very charming brat."

"Oh." She was not certain whether she had been complimented or insulted. "Well, you know, you've changed too. The Girays v'Alisante I knew six years ago wouldn't have exerted himself, much less risked his own freedom, in defense of some nameless fugitive native laborer."

"Exerted? I served as your translator, nothing more."

"A little more." She lowered her voice discreetly. "You saved that poor native. He'd never have escaped, but for you. I saw you trip the constable and I know you did it on purpose."

"The constable?" Girays shrugged. "A very clumsy fellow, a most unlucky chance. I am a conservative traditionalist, as you know, and could never knowingly violate the law."

"Quite so. As time goes by, I am coming to realize just how truly conservative Your Lordship really is."

SHE KEPT HER WORD. She strove for patience, she tried to be quiet and calm. The miserable hours crawled by. The sweltering air pressed, the drunks vocalized and vomited, the flies swarmed by the hundreds, but she stifled all complaint. Eyes shut, she lay for a while upon her pallet in the hope that sleep might offer relief, but the flies buzzed and lighted on her damp flesh, the nameless wingless insects feasted on her blood, the agitated thoughts swirled through her head, and sleep eluded her. Rising to her feet, she paced the tiny confines of her cell, but activity only inflamed the mental fever. She envisioned her rivals, pressing on toward Aveshq. She contemplated the injustice of it all. Indignation, frustration, and mounting desperation scorched her brain.

The counsel of Girays might have helped to cool and clear her head, but he had somehow managed to fall asleep, and she would not disturb him. The counsel of the drunks she did not desire.

Time seemed to have suspended itself, and yet in the real world outside the West Street Station the hours must have been passing—in fact, evening must have arrived, for presently a khaki guard entered with a supper of bread and water for the prisoners. Attending first to the men, he came at last to Luzelle's little cage, where he paused to scrutinize her at unhurried length.

He was medium sized and nondescript, with a round tanned face and bushy black hair that sprang from his head in wiry ringlets. Evidently he did not believe in bathing. Even in the fetid atmosphere of the station lockup, the rank odor of his body was noticeable.

"Please, sir," Luzelle essayed in Grewzian, without much hope of success, "would you if you please tell me what is now the hour?"

"Six," he answered, to her surprise.

"May we if you please speak with the captain?"

"Captain will be back the day after tomorrow. Or else the day after that."

His breath fanned her face foully, and she resisted the impulse to step back. "This day has brought no report of stolen money?" she inquired.

"Not yet."

"There will come none, for the money and passports are truly ours. We are innocent, we have done nothing." His face did not change, and she added urgently, "We are held wrongly. We ask for the chance to prove this."

He shrugged, tossed a hunk of bread through the bars, and commanded, "Pannikin."

She stooped to retrieve the tin vessel, and his eyes followed every move. She held the pannikin out, and he filled it from his long-spouted water can. This done; he stood stilly staring at her.

"We are not thieves, for nothing has been stolen from any person," she insisted. "We ask for justice, merely."

He studied her a while longer, then departed without reply.

Luzelle took a small sip of water, which was warm and no doubt poisonously dirty. She was probably condemning herself to severe diarrhea at the very least, but simple thirst triumphed over caution. She wet her mouth sparingly, then set the pannikin aside and picked the bread up off the filthy floor. The crust was damp and patched with green mold. Her nose wrinkled. She came within a twitch of flinging the loaf from her cell, but managed to contain the impulse. When she grew hungry enough, she would consume her soggy supper, mold and all.

She placed the bread beside the water, then stretched herself out again upon the pallet. Her hopes of slumber were slight. The insects were as offensive and her mind as busy as ever. Her thoughts hopped chaotically, the vermin did likewise, her misery intensified, and soon, to her disgust, she felt the hot tears scalding her eyes. Not here, not now, when she lay exposed to the view of guards, random drunks, and worst of all, Girays. She did not want him to see her weeping like an idiot infant, she did not want anyone to see, but particularly not him. But the tears were welling uncontrollably, streaming down her temples into her hair. Her face contorted, and the sharp, involuntary intake of her breath signaled an impending explosion of sobs.

Rolling over onto her side to face the stone wall, she buried her face in the crook of her arm. The tears gushed and her shoulders shook, but no sound escaped her. At last the storm abated, leaving her with a stuffed nose and an aching head. A little ashamed of herself, she snuffled and surreptitiously wiped her nose on her sleeve. She risked no glance back over her shoulder. If her lapse had drawn attention, if anyone was watching, she did not want to know.

Her head was hot and seemed too heavy to lift. The intense noiseless weeping had exhausted her. She let her swollen eyelids drop, and soon, despite the heat, the stench, and bugs, she fell asleep.

SHE NEVER KNEW EXACTLY what woke her—perhaps the tap of a footstep outside her cell, perhaps the pressure of alien regard. Her eyes flew open. She knew where she was, and she knew upon instinct that she had slept for several hours. She also knew without turning her head that someone stood at her cell door looking in, and the pungent unwashed odor told her who it was. She lay quietly, studying the wall before her. The stones were bathed in weak yellowish light, by which she inferred that a lone ceiling lamp illuminated the lockup. She could hear the buzz of nocturnal insects, the honking snores of assorted neighboring drunks, and little else. The smelly night guard stood not more than five or six feet behind her, his silent gaze pressing her back. Perhaps, if he thought her unconscious, he would grow bored with watching and go away.

He did not.

She heard the jingle of keys, the snap of a lock, and the squeal of hinges as the barred door opened. He stepped into the cell, closed and relocked the door. No further point in playing dead. She rose from the pallet and faced him squarely.

An unremarkable, ordinary-looking man, her mind registered inconsequentially. Nothing to distinguish him, apart from his odor; almost invisibly anonymous.

For a couple of seconds he stood eyeing her expectantly, as if he anticipated questions, pleas, or even attempted flight. She neither moved nor spoke, and at last he muttered in Grewzian, "You were not properly searched for weapons upon arrest. They did not follow procedure. You must be searched."

"I am unarmed," she told him.

"You must be searched," he repeated doggedly. "There could be thin blades, or steel bands, or wires, hidden anywhere about you, under your clothes. You will take off your clothes."

"No," she answered with spurious calmness. Her heart slammed, her mouth went dry, and the sudden fear flashed along every nerve.

"Do it," he advised. "Or I will strip you."

"Touch me and I will scream for help," she warned.

"Scream all you want, there is nobody to hear. I am on duty alone here, and I am in full charge until the morning. I am in command. Now you will obey me."

She shook her head, and he lunged at her with unexpected speed. There was neither time nor room to evade him. One of his hands closed on her wrist, immobilizing her right arm, and the other flew to the neck of her Bizaqhi tunic. He pulled hard, and the gauzy fabric tore from neck to waist, exposing her linen chemise. An involuntary scream escaped her, which woke every prisoner in the lockup. The drunks, now comparatively sober, stirred and mumbled. Girays sat up, looked into the adjoining cell, and was instantly on his feet.

The night guard's fingers hooked in the bodice of her chemise. He yanked, but the linen held. Doubling her left fist, Luzelle swung wildly and hit the side of his head a glancing blow. He muttered something in Aennorvi and struck back. Instinctively she ducked, and his flying fist grazed her jaw. She staggered, and he pulled her to him. His hand thrust into her bodice to close on one of her breasts, which he squeezed viciously. A high cry of pain tore from her. She clawed at his face with her free hand, then stiffened her fingers and jabbed at his eyes. His breath hissed and he jerked his head back. Twisting her wrist sharply, she broke his grip and sprang for the barred door, which she pulled at and rattled in vain. She was yelling at the top of her lungs, screaming for help, dimly aware that Girays was yelling as well, and there was some excited vociferation from the drunks, but the lockup door remained firmly closed. Either the office beyond was indeed empty, or else its tenants were ignoring the uproar.

Looping an arm around her waist, the night guard dragged her backward from the door. Her elbow hammered his ribs, then she twisted to face him and drove a knee at his groin. Releasing his hold, he dodged and threw a punch that caught her cheek. The pain exploded in her head, her vision swam, and she tottered. Shoving her down on the pallet, he flung himself atop her and pried her legs apart. His hand, fumbling at her crotch, discovered the unexpected impediment of the Bizaqhi divided skirt, and he spat an Aennorvi expletive. The hand shifted to her waist and tugged at the drawstring. His other hand, with most of his weight behind it, clutched her throat.

She was suffocating, the red lights flaring behind her

closed lids, her lungs on fire, and even so the reek of his flesh and the stench of his breath seemed to fill the universe. There was a curious roaring in her ears, and somewhere she thought she could still hear Girays's voice, as if at a great distance.

The drawstring at her waist was stubbornly knotted, and the crushing pressure on her neck ceased as the guard began pulling at her skirt with two hands. He was kneeling above her, his weight pinning her thighs. She could breathe again, and her hands were free. Reaching up with both arms, she grabbed his head, pulled him down, sank her teeth into the side of his neck, and felt his blood fill her mouth.

Loosing a howl of astonished pain, he recoiled, and she scrambled from the pallet. He recovered in an instant, his nondescript face twisted with rage, and he sprang at her. She tried to duck out of reach, but there was no room. He grabbed her, and she struggled violently. Locked together, they reeled across the cell to crash against the wall of bars separating Luzelle's cage from its neighbor.

At once a purple-clad arm snaked through the bars to lock from behind around the night guard's neck. Girays tightened his hold, pressing hard on his captive's windpipe, and the guard began to gasp for breath. His grip on Luzelle weakened. She tore herself free and backed away.

The guard's hands rose to pull vainly at the wiry purple arm that was choking him. His mouth gaped, his eyes bulged, and his face darkened.

The spectacle was not unsatisfying, but she did not want to turn her defender into a murderer.

"Girays—" she began, uncertain whether he could hear her voice above the yammering of the drunks.

The night guard's eyes turned up, his struggles ceased, he slumped unconscious, and Girays relaxed the pressure, but maintained his grip.

"Luzelle. The keys," he directed, his voice impossibly calm, even nonchalant.

She threw him an amazed glance, then hastened to obey. Overcoming vast repugnance, she approached the guard and started patting his pockets. His odor filled her nostrils sickeningly. Holding her breath, she persevered and soon discovered a steel ring jangling with at least a dozen keys.

She rose, stepped to the door, and began trying the keys one after another. Her hands were shaky, too eager, and clumsy. She had trouble inserting the keys into the lock, and once she dropped the entire ring. Stooping to retrieve it, she was hardly aware that she whispered aloud, "Sorry, I'm sorry."

"You're doing well," Girays reassured her in the same astonishingly easy, tranquil tone.

Quietly though they spoke, their voices prodded the awareness of the guard, who groaned and stirred. Seizing a handful of bushy black hair, Girays rapped the captive head sharply against the iron bars, and the guard relapsed into unconsciousness.

She found the right key at last. The door screeched open. Stepping from the cell, Luzelle shut and relocked the door behind her. Girays released the guard, who slid to the floor with a small, affronted moan. She went to his cage and unlocked it with the same key she had used on her own.

He emerged, and they hurried to the exit. The drunks yelped, and Luzelle glanced back over her shoulder at them. Her questioning eyes shifted to Girays's face, and he shook his head. He was right, she realized. A bevy of liberated prisoners wandering the neighborhood was more than likely to attract undesirable notice.

The front office was empty, it had to be. Luzelle's heart was pounding as she silently lifted the latch, cracked open the door, and applied her eye to the fissure. She spied a section of quiet unoccupied chamber; bare wooden floor, a desk, a chair. No khaki guards, no constables. She opened the door fully and they slipped through.

"Desk," said Girays.

"Windows," she replied.

While he adjusted the wooden slats of the window blinds to shut the lamplit office off from the view of the darkened world, she sought and found the key to the locked desk drawer. The drawer opened, and there lay the confiscated passports and wallets, the contents of the latter intact. She handed his property over to Girays, and hurriedly stuffed her own belongings into her hip pocket. As she did so she looked down and saw her tunic, rent from neck to waist, gaping wide to expose her underwear. The display was dangerously conspicuous, but for now there was little to be done about it. Hurriedly she tucked the dangling end of torn fabric into the neckline of her chemise; a slight improvement.

Girays peered out through the chinks in the closed blinds. "All clear," he reported.

Opening the front door with care, they quietly exited the West Street Station house.

The air outside, although close and sultry, seemed marvelously fresh to Luzelle. She drew hungry drafts deep into her lungs. West Street was quiet and deserted, the shopfronts closed, the windows dark. A stray cat slunk from shadow to shadow, the atmosphere vibrated with the song of countless insects, but these were the sole signs of life.

For some silent minutes they hurried through the maze of foreign streets, and only when they had placed a long stretch of darkness between themselves and the jail did they dare to slacken their pace and exchange whispered words.

"What time d'you think it is?" asked Luzelle.

"Dead of night. Perhaps another couple of hours until dawn."

"When the station guard changes and they discover us gone, do you think they'll hunt us?"

"Under the circumstances, yes. I don't want to alarm you, but it's best to face facts."

"Yes." Fact—she had landed him in this mess. Fact—if it hadn't been for her impulsiveness, he would have spent the night in some opulent hotel. Fact—if he ended up facing an Aennorvi firing squad, it would be on her account alone. Aloud she observed, "And we won't be hard to spot, either. A scruffy, unshaven Vonahrishman in a miniature purple shirt, a reddish-haired Vonahrishwoman with a battered face and visible underwear."

"Battered face? Did that swine—"

"He landed a couple of good ones," she informed him unemotionally. "But I'm all right, and you paid him back with interest."

"Let me see." Halting in the light of a streetlamp, he examined her face. "My poor Luzelle. He's given you a black eye. Bruises. A split lip. I should have killed him when I had the chance."

"No you shouldn't."

"We'll find a doctor for you."

"No need. A few bruises won't kill me. They're trivial compared to what would have happened if you hadn't been there." She hesitated, and continued with difficulty, "I like to think that I can take care of myself. Usually I can. But not always, and not this time. This time I needed help and I needed it badly. You saved me, and telling you that I am grateful hardly seems adequate."

"It's more than adequate, since it evens the score between us," he returned lightly. "Have you any idea how irksome it was to realize that I owed my life to your knowledge and resourcefulness alone when we came among the Blessed Tribesmen? You saved me then and it was almost intolerable, but now I've bandaged my wounded vanity."

She smiled unwillingly. Trust M. the Marquis to say the right thing. Trust M. the Marquis, period. But his loyalty was liable to cost him dearly. If she allowed it.

"Time for a few decisions," Girays announced. "We'll have to go without sleep for the rest of the night and make it up when we can. As soon as it's light, we'll see about coach transportation to Dasuneville. If nothing's immediately available, we'll check the livery stables. But it might be wise, before we begin, to alter our appearance. If we simply revert to decent western clothing, and I shave off the beard, we'll be almost unrecogni—"

"We'll be entirely recognizable," she told him calmly, "and you know it. Either one of us alone is noticeable enough. Together, we're impossible to overlook." He was silent, and she continued, "The police will be searching for the two of us, and they'll probably pick us up within hours unless we separate, which is what we must do now."

"Absolutely not. Do you think I'd leave you alone at night on some street corner in a foreign city, with the local constabulary on your trail?"

"Yes, because the alternative is even more dangerous for both of us. After what we did to the night guard, the police aren't about to treat us gently when they find us. And they *will* find us if we stick together, and you know it; I can see by your face."

"That's speculation, and the most pessimistic speculation at that. Come, where's your spirit? We're Vonahrish, and together we'll outwit these Aennorvi colonial clods."

"They're not such fools as you seem to imagine. Listen, I know you're trying to protect me, but this isn't the way. This is only increasing the risk for each of us, and I don't want to be the cause of your—"

"In any case the matter is not open to discussion," he interrupted. "I can't allow you to go gadding off on your own, and there's an end to it."

"Allow? You can't *allow*?"

"Correct, and I'm in no humor to argue the point; we've no time now for emancipated nonsense. You'll behave prudently for once, you'll stay with me for now, and I don't want to hear another word on the subject."

"Very well, you won't." Turning on her heel, she jumped for the darkness of the nearest alley.

She heard him call her name once, and then he cut himself off. He could not afford to disturb the peace of sleeping Jumo Towne, he would not dare shout through the streets after her, but he was not giving up. He was following, she could hear his quick footsteps, and if he caught her she would have to submit quietly, for resistance would invite disastrous public attention.

She quickened her pace, and it flashed through her mind how incongruous it was, how madly awry, that she should find herself obliged to run and hide from Girays v'Alisante, of all people in the world. Well, it was for his own good as well as hers, and somewhere underneath all that formerly-Exalted domineering gallantry he must know it. She hoped he wasn't too furious with her.

The alley terminated and she emerged into a star-shaped intersection. Four new paths offered themselves. She chose one at random, ran a few feet, then paused in the shadow of a recessed doorway. She had a clear view of the intersection, but she herself was invisible.

Girays came out of the alley and halted, listening intently. There were no footsteps for him to hear. His eyes scanned the streets before him. He hesitated, then chose one; the wrong one.

She listened to his footfalls receding. Soon they were gone. She was alone, truly alone for the first time in weeks, and the tropical night suddenly seemed darker and heavier than any she had ever known.

It was not too late to change her mind, she could still go after him.

No.

Stepping forth from the shadows, she sent a mental message flying in his wake. *Good luck. Be careful. I owe you an apology the next time we meet.*

Whenever and wherever that might be.

18

A FAINT FLUSH stained the eastern skies. Dawn was breaking, and Jumo Towne was stirring to life. A few pedestrians were out and about, a few carts rumbled along the streets. Perhaps the morning guards had already reported to West Street Station, there to discover the escape of the Vonahrish prisoners. If so, the hunt had commenced.

Luzelle's eyes ranged. No constables in sight, but how much longer could it be before she tripped over one? And then, what constable on the lookout could possibly fail to recognize her? She needed to disguise herself, and quickly. But how to do it? A half-dozen far-fetched schemes zipped through her mind, each to be rejected in turn. Her thoughts whirled, but one fact stood clear and firm: in the shabbier sections of Jumo Towne, her present disreputable appearance would attract less attention.

She walked on, holding herself to a moderate pace, and as she went the skies lightened and the streets filled. A few carriages began to mingle with the utilitarian wagons passing by, and once she spied a youth on a red velocipede, its brilliant enamel flashing in the light of the rising sun. Caught by the scarlet glitter, she turned her head to watch for a moment, then turned back to confront the straightforward curiosity of an early-morning flower vendor. The vendor was staring at her face, no doubt intrigued by the fresh bruises and lacerations. Ducking her head a little, Luzelle hurried on. The incident was bound to repeat itself, probably with increasing frequency as the sun climbed.

She needed quite literally to hide her face. A pity that vizard masks had gone out of style. Contemporary actresses painted their faces with oily substances guaranteed to conceal the most glaring imperfections of complexion, but where in Jumo Towne would she find theatrical cosmetics? Or the equally concealing widow's weeds, for that matter? Her wallet was stuffed with cash, Jumo Towne overflowed with merchandise, there had to be a way. Her mind spun, and she hurried on.

The white marble town houses of the wealthy diamond merchants rose about her. The natives toiling in the gardens eyed her askance as she passed, and understandably so.

She pushed on along beautiful broad boulevards lined with mansions of ever-increasing grandeur, and at length began to wonder if the unwelcome magnificence would ever end. But then she came to a slightly humbler avenue where white marble yielded to handsome white stucco, and after that there were comparatively modest dwellings and shops of whitewashed brick. The streets were not quite so clean anymore. There was litter strewn about, heaps of refuse presided over by stilt-legged scavenger birds, animal droppings, and swarms of golden phoenix flies. Encouraged, she trudged on, and now the fine buildings and carriages were finally gone, and the heavy air carried the nauseous sweetness of decaying garbage, while the western faces mingled with copper Ygahri visages in equal proportion along the termite-plagued elevated wooden sidewalks. The down-at-heels little shopfronts bore signs written in Aennorvi, for here it seemed that the Grewzians had not as yet troubled to leave their visible mark.

She could not read a word of Aennorvi, but many of the signs bore pictorial devices designed to advertise the wares or services offered within, and in quick succession she spotted a wineshop, a locksmith, a tobacconist, and a shoemaker. Then she came to a small draper's shop, with the painted Eye of the Gifted Iyecktor staring down from the sign, and her mind winged back to the village store in the south of Aennorve with its hostile Iyecktori proprietors. She remembered the shopkeeper's indignant wife, who had shrilled insults and flung a

handful of dried white beans at her. A typical Iyecktori matron, clad in shapeless saffron robes, thumbless black gloves,
and a black cap with linen lappets concealing every strand of
hair. Nothing of the woman's body beyond her thumbs and
her blunt-featured face had shown. And, Luzelle recalled, orthodox Iyecktori women mourning male family members
were wont to veil even the face. . . .

Especially the face.

She went into the draper's shop. The place was small and
old but immaculate, offering a limited selection of fabrics and
ready-made Iyecktori accoutrements. The proprietor, an aged
grey wisp of a man garbed in the traditional costume of his
sect, sported looped linen streamers trimmed with the finest
black-edged cutwork. His eyes widened in simple surprise as
she entered. He took in the bruises marking her face, and his
expression changed to one of sadness perhaps mixed with
pity. He addressed her gently in Aennorvi.

Expecting animosity and disapproval, Luzelle was taken by
surprise. Her eyes stung, and she blinked back a couple of
sudden silly tears. She answered the shopkeeper in Vonahrish,
and deep gratitude filled her when he displayed perfect comprehension.

She stated her needs and he asked no questions, but simply
furnished her with a loose traditional robe, thumbless gloves,
black cap with lappets, a black veil of mourning, and a pair of
faquerishi, the tiny matched brooches used to pin the veil in
place. He also offered a leather wallet-belt, worn around the
waist beneath the robe, and accessible through a discreet gap
in a side seam.

She purchased the Iyecktori gear without haggling, then
retired to a tiny curtained alcove at the rear of the shop to don
the new garments. Designed for practicality and modesty,
they were easily managed, comfortable, and no doubt unbecoming. All to the good; a striking appearance was the last
thing she wanted at the moment. A tiny wall mirror of polished tin reflected her face, primly framed in linen, every single flamboyantly hued hair hidden. She dropped the veil over
her head and pinned it. The filmy gauze permitted almost

unimpaired vision, but effectively obscured her face. A dark ghost gazed back from the mirror. She smiled invisibly.

Her Bizaqhi clothing, filthy and torn, was fit only for disposal. Emerging from the alcove, she deposited the ruined garments in the shopkeeper's rag bin, not without regret, for the divided skirt had served her well indeed. She bade the proprietor farewell, and left.

The sun was bright and the streets were teeming, but she was no longer so afraid. It would take an uncommonly sharp official eye to penetrate her new disguise.

She walked along the elevated sidewalk, and nobody paid her much heed; evidently a veiled Iyecktori woman was a commonplace sight. Her confidence and spirits mounted, and when she came upon a public banesman swabbing the wooden sidewalk with an insecticidal wash, she dared to ask directions in halting Grewzian.

The banesman displayed no sign of suspicion as he described the best route to Jumo-Dasune Circle, site of the posting house where travelers boarded the Dasuneville coach. The distance was not inconsiderable, and the bereaved Respected Matron might wish to consider the benefits of a hansom. Such vehicles rarely entered this particular neighborhood, but the Respected Matron might walk on as far as Orchid Street, where public transportation was usually available.

She thanked him and moved on. Fifteen minutes of walking brought her to the Orchid Street intersection, where a couple of hansoms waited for customers. She chose one, instructed the driver, and climbed in. The vehicle sped off, and Luzelle settled back in her seat with a sigh. *Safe*. Comparatively.

The minutes passed and the white streets rattled by. The hansom came at last to Jumo-Dasune Circle, mouth of the busy Jumo-Dasune Passage. The circle was edged with commercial enterprise and filled with traffic. Straight ahead was the posting house, its façade newly graced with the symbol of the Endless Fire. Pedestrians crowded the walkways, and among them she spied many a trim grey-uniformed figure, no source of immediate alarm. Far worse were the khaki constables patrolling the area, a pair of them stationed before the front entrance of the posting house. Perhaps their presence meant nothing, perhaps they were always there. Perhaps not.

The hansom halted. Luzelle alighted and paid the driver. The vehicle departed. For a moment she stood watching it go, then bowed her head in pious grief, let her shoulders sag, and made for the posting house.

The constables on guard barely glanced at her as she slipped past them into the small waiting room, where a trio of travelers perched on uncomfortable wooden benches. A timetable chalked on a slate affixed to the wall furnished information. A coach was scheduled to leave for Dasuneville in ten minutes' time. It would be the final departure of the day.

Just in time. Another quarter of an hour in finding her way to this place, and she might have been trapped in Jumo Towne for an extra day and a night. Seating herself at the end of an empty bench, she clasped her hands in an attitude of glum reverence, and waited.

Three quarters of an hour passed, and her foot began to tap beneath the long robe. The Grewzians now controlled the South Ygahro Territory and would no doubt soon have the stagecoaches running on time, but they had not managed it yet. The Dasuneville coach might be hours late. It might not come at all. . . .

Just as her stomach was starting to tighten, the coach—drawn by a quartet of the locally bred thick-legged horses—pulled up at the side door. The passengers rose and filed from the waiting room, passing beneath the bored gaze of a constable stationed at the exit. Luzelle, greatly daring, inclined a courteous veiled head at him as she went by, and he returned the gesture affably enough.

Assorted bags and boxes were handed up to the roof of the coach and tied in place. The bereaved Iyecktori matron's lack of luggage could hardly have gone unnoticed, but no inquiries were voiced. The passengers paid the driver, and the Iyecktori's Vonahrish New-rekkoes were accepted without demur. They entered the coach, the door closed, the driver ascended, the whip snapped, and the big vehicle began to move.

Muscles tensed beneath her voluminous robes, Luzelle

awaited the inevitable blast of a constable's whistle. Nothing happened, and gradually she began to relax as the coach swung around the curve of the circle to enter the Jumo-Dasune Passage. The pavement under the wheels was clean and smooth. The clatter and vibration of the coach subsided as the thick-legged horses settled into a steady pace.

Leaning back against the lumpy upholstery, she covertly studied her three fellow passengers, all of them male western-ers. A couple of pale and sedentary-looking youngish men, brown hair slicked down with pomade, cheaply clad in ready-made seersucker suits. Highly polished, inexpensive shoes. Nondescript, anxiously respectable. Neophyte commercial travelers, perhaps. And the third man—older, threadbare, big restless hands, sour expression. Tradesman or artisan, down on his luck, she guessed. Nothing remarkable or even interest-ing enough to hold her attention. The neighboring faces faded from her consciousness, and she found herself dwelling on another face, dark and slightly worn.

Girays. Free and safe? Or recaptured and returned to the city jail? He had nearly strangled one of the guards, on her ac-count. If he fell into their hands again, they would probably kill him. And she had abandoned him.

The coach rumbled on along the road. The buildings of Jumo Towne were already thinning out of existence, but Luzelle never noticed. She stared out the window and saw nothing.

UNTIL COMPARATIVELY RECENT TIMES, travelers toiling be-tween Jumo Towne and the eastern coastal port of Da-suneville had endured a circuitous slow voyage down the tributary Obiluki River to the great Ygah, down the Ygah to the Muñako River, and upstream along the Muñako as far as King's Landing, where muleteers could be hired to navigate the final overland portion of the journey.

The creation of the Jumo-Dasune Passage had changed all of that. A scant twenty years earlier, the will of an Aennorvi monarch eager to facilitate the swiftest possible transfer of di-amonds from the mines of the South Ygahro Territory to the tables of the master cutters in Feyenne had mandated construction of a roadway slicing straight through the seventy-odd miles of deep jungle that separated Jumo Towne from the coast. The task—over three years in completion, and beset with every possible difficulty—had claimed the lives of several hundred native laborers, but eventually the great work had drawn to its conclusion and the wheeled traffic had commenced flowing between Jumo Towne and Dasuneville.

Within weeks of completion, however, it had become apparent that certain difficulties persisted. The jungle—slashed, burned, hacked, chopped, and paved over with stone—remained invincibly vital. The greenery so murderously pruned required no encouragement to regenerate, and every spattering of warm rain prompted wild vegetative incursion. The Jumo-Dasune Passage demanded continual maintenance, and to this end the colonial authorities legislated the formation of road gangs composed of convicted felons sentenced to hard labor.

There was no dearth of manpower. Criminals of the legally disenfranchised native Ygahri stripe abounded. Those legions succumbing to malnutrition, heat, disease, exhaustion, and abuse were easily replaced. The road gangs slaved almost unnoticed from dawn until dark every day of the year, and the diamonds streamed on toward Aennorve.

Toward Grewzland, now. The crystalline flow had recently altered course.

The coach rumbled by a chained gang engaged in tearing weeds from the cracks in the pavement, and Luzelle caught a clear glimpse of fettered wrists, scarred naked backs, and empty ageless faces. They were gone within seconds, but their image lingered, a voiceless reproach.

She breathed a small sigh. Leaning her head back, she let her eyes close. She discovered that she was deeply tired; not surprising, for she had scarcely rested within the past twenty-four hours. She could afford sleep now, and she drifted off within seconds.

She woke around noon, when the coach halted at the side of the road. While the horses rested, the passengers vanished briefly into the bush, then reappeared to stride vigorously back and forth, stretching cramped muscles.

Some twenty minutes later the journey resumed, and now her fellow travelers produced small sacks containing provisions for the midday meal. Simple-enough fare—bread, cheese, dried fruit, sweet biscuits—but her stomach clenched at the sight of it. She had tasted no food since yesterday's jail-house supper, and she had brought nothing with her.

Nothing but money.

Slipping a surreptitious hand through the aperture in her robe, she drew a couple of coins from her wallet-belt. Proffering the silver to her nearest neighbor, one of the slicked-down young men, she suggested in halting Grewzian, "You sell some bread?" He stared at her blankly, and she added for good measure, "I am hungry."

He took the coins, handed her a substantial chunk of bread, and added a fistful of dried fruit for good measure. Seeing this, the sour-faced threadbare fellow passed her a couple of hard-cooked eggs and a sugar biscuit. When she attempted to pay him, he shook his head gruffly.

"Thank you," she murmured, and looked down shyly, terminating the exchange.

Head bent modestly over her lap, she lifted the veil of mourning and proceeded to eat her lunch. Without looking up she knew that her companions were watching for a glimpse of her face, but they weren't about to get one. The dangling lappets of her cap hid her profile, obscuring western complexion, fresh bruises, split lip, and all. When she finished eating, she carefully lowered the veil back into place before lifting her head. The desultory curiosity surrounding her promptly expired.

The two young men began playing cards. The generous sour-faced fellow cogitated frowningly. Luzelle went back to sleep. She was dimly aware, a couple of hours later, that the coach halted again beside the road, but she did not trouble to emerge.

Progress resumed. The vehicle passed another fettered road gang, and paused once more for a half hour in the late afternoon. It did not stop again until early evening, at which time the driver pulled up at the entrance to the Halfway Inn, whose location marked the halfway point between Jumo Towne and Dasuneville.

The passengers disembarked and the driver handed down their luggage. Having no suitcase to wait for, Luzelle preceded her companions into the building—a curious hybrid structure, long and low-slung in the native style, with walls of whitewashed western brick and a roof of curved red-brown tile.

She registered under a false name, and once again her lack of luggage went unquestioned, while her New-rekkoes were accepted without hesitation.

Her room was clean, spacious, and equipped with a private bath, which she promptly used. Only when she had scoured herself pink and the water was starting to cool did she emerge, feeling thoroughly and marvelously clean for the first time in days.

She toweled herself dry, then went to the mirror hanging above the washstand, wiped the moisture away, and checked her face. The bruises were still fresh and dark, but most of the swelling had subsided. Encouraging, but she would need to remain covered for another few days to come.

Resuming the Iyecktori garb, she ventured forth as far as the common room, where the lamplight shone on a sizable gathering of travelers. She spotted the passengers and driver from her own coach at once, but made no move to join them. Presumably an orthodox Iyecktori matron in mourning would minimize contact with infidels.

She ate alone, head bowed and lappets dangling. Afterward she paused briefly at the desk to order a boxed lunch for tomorrow's journey before returning to the pleasant chamber altogether devoid of books, newspapers, or any other source of entertainment.

There was really nothing to do but sleep. Extinguishing all the lamps, she climbed without undressing into a soft bed furnished with clean lemon-scented sheets. She was comfortable there, but she had slumbered through most of the afternoon, and she was thoroughly wakeful now. She lay motionlessly alert, uneasy, ears straining to catch the sound of—what? Flutes in the jungle? The roar of some forest man-eater? The shriek of a constable's whistle?

What she actually heard was the whir and hum of the airborne creatures inhabiting her room in defiance of all window screens. The mosquito netting guarded her space, they could not get at her flesh, but they could sting and goad her imagination, filling her head with visions of Girays v'Alisante in manacles, behind bars, in trouble and even in danger because of her. She pictured him slaving in a chained road gang somewhere along the Jumo-Dasune Passage, and her eyes tingled behind their tightly closed lids. Absurd, of course. Such things did not happen to men of means. M. the Marquis possessed money, rank, connections, influence—

Thousands of miles away.

More important, he owned a sharp mind and a cool head. The police wouldn't catch him, they wouldn't even come close.

Perhaps.

She lay wide awake for hours. At last she slid into restless sleep poisoned with bad dreams, only to waken before dawn. Rising from bed, she stepped to one of the windows, opened the louvers, and stood staring up at the southern stars.

The skies lightened gradually. The insect chorus diminished, the night birds muted themselves, the stars faded away, color bloomed in the east, and a rim of sun rose into view above the Forests of Oorex.

She washed, finger-combed her clean hair, then resumed her cap, veil, and thumbless gloves. After breakfasting in the common room she returned to a busy lobby, stood in line to pay her reckoning at the desk, collected the boxed lunch she had ordered, then walked out the front door to find the stagecoach waiting amid a clutter of assorted commercial and private conveyances. The driver greeted her as she drew near, and she muttered a modest muffled courtesy in reply before taking her seat.

Fifteen minutes passed before the two slicked-down young men handed their luggage up to the roof and boarded. There was no sign of yesterday's sour-faced passenger. Another ten minutes passed, and he did not appear. The driver snapped his whip, and the coach rattled away from the inn.

The second day's travel along the Jumo-Dasune Passage was a repetition of the first; a tedious long span, its hot monotony broken only by periodic rest stops and by periodic glimpses of convict-slaves tending the roadway. This time, when her companions invited her to join their card game, Luzelle accepted. Probably the choice compromised her orthodox disguise, but she was almost beyond caring, so thoroughly had boredom corroded caution.

The afternoon wore on to its finish, and so at last did the journey. The sun was hovering above the horizon as the coach lumbered up to the posting house in the old port town of Dasuneville. A busy place, she saw at a glance; rough-hewn and utilitarian, coarse by comparison with Jumo Towne's studied elegance, but attractive nonetheless, thanks to its air. Fresh sea air, very warm but braced with a salty tang, rushing through the streets to sweep Dasuneville clear of jungle miasma. She drew a deep breath that seemed to clean her lungs out for the first time in days. New vigor filled her, and her spirits rose.

The passengers disembarked and went their separate ways. Unencumbered with personal belongings, Luzelle strolled the old brick-paved avenues until, with the aid of directions gleaned from random citizens, she found her way to the waterfront.

The ticketing agencies had already closed for the evening, but timetables posted on wooden walls offered unwelcome information. The next steamship bound northeast for Aveshq was not scheduled to depart until the day after tomorrow. There were no alternatives. No possibility of engaging private transport across the wide Sea of Aveshq. No balloons, no revolutionary subaqueous vessels, no convenient magic. Nothing to do but hang around town for the next thirty-six hours.

During which time, Girays might turn up. For all she knew, he had reached Dasuneville ahead of her. He could be holed up in some nearby inn or hotel, he might be eating an early dinner, he might be wandering the streets or the waterfront. She cast a glance around her, half expecting to spot him, but the faces she confronted belonged to strangers. A pang of disappointment twinged through her.

Inappropriate. She'd been waiting for weeks for a chance to leave him behind, hadn't she?

Departing the wharves in dissatisfaction, she wandered the darkening streets until she happened upon a clean old rooming house, where she engaged lodgings for two nights. She ate a forgettable meal in her own room, and then, thoroughly bored, retired early.

The sun was high in the sky when she awoke. For once she could afford the luxury of late slumber, one of the few advantages of the present situation. She could also afford to devote the day to the replacement of her lost belongings.

She sponge-bathed unhurriedly, and the mirror above the washstand reflected a face whose bruises had faded to greenish-yellow. Another day or so, and she would be able to discard the veil. But then, another day or so and she would be clear of the South Ygahro Territory, and it would no longer matter if her face drew notice.

Resuming her orthodox disguise, she marched forth into bustling streets plentifully greyed with uniformed Grewzians. No sign of Karsler Stornzof among them, and she realized that she had been looking for him.

She breakfasted on fried pastries purchased of a sidewalk vendor, then hurried back to the waterfront to book passage aboard the steamer *Talghya Jeria*, sailing east under the neutral Strellian flag. Money changed hands and she received her ticket, which vanished into her wallet-belt. Thereafter she was free to explore the shops and booths of the town.

It wasn't Jumo Towne. Dasuneville offered no rich profusion of luxury goods, but the old port was moderately prosperous, and a couple of the local tradesmen stocked ready-made garments of decent quality.

Her purchases were massive. Within the space of a few hours she acquired two new and reasonably well-fitting western dresses, two skirts and blouses, a soft shawl, a couple of muslin nightgowns, shoes, stockings, and linen. There was a hooded rain cloak and umbrella, a miraculously compressible wide-brimmed straw hat, a drawstring reticule, handkerchiefs, assorted toiletries, a new valise, matches and penknife, a supply of new books printed in Vonahrish, even a tiny jar of rice powder to disguise her bruises.

Only one necessity of civilized life was absent—a corset. She might have purchased one easily enough. She *should* have purchased one; it was hardly respectable to go without. Having enjoyed weeks of freedom and comfort, however, she could not quite bring herself to submit once again to the tyranny of steel stays.

Later, she thought. *In Immeen. Or Rhazaulle. Later.*

A native porter carried her boxes and bundles all the way back to the rooming house. And if the citizens of Dasuneville thought it strange to see an orthodox Iyecktori woman, veiled in mourning and supposedly indifferent to material luxuries, trailed through the streets by a walking mountain of parcels— well, they were free to wonder.

The porter deposited her packages on the floor. She paid him and he left. No sooner had the door closed behind him than she was down on her knees, tearing the wrappings away from half a dozen pasteboard boxes. The contents were hardly remarkable—just a few fresh garments of unexceptional quality, and a collection of ordinary personal items. But they were new, and she had done without for so long that the most commonplace necessities now sparkled like treasures.

When she had done gloating over clothes and toiletries, she turned her attention to the books. One of them, a collection of essays by one of the Exalted wits of prerevolutionary Vonahr, held her attention through the rest of the afternoon.

That evening she dined in her room, read for a while, packed the new valise with care, retired early, and slept soundly.

She woke, rested and genuinely refreshed, in the humid warmth of the dawn. Rising without reluctance, she washed, and studied her face in the mirror. Not too bad. The bruises had paled to faint lemon smudges. When she patted rice powder across her nose and cheeks, the yellow splotches disappeared. She coiled and anchored her hair into a proper chignon, clothed herself in one of the new dresses—serviceable grey broadcloth softened with wine trim—and, for the first time in days, beheld the reflection of a respectable and recognizable self.

Departing her lodgings, she emerged into sea-scented streets already bustling. Even at that early hour it was easy to secure a porter to carry her new valise to the wharves, where the *Talghya Jeria* awaited. The Strellian vessel, carrying both passengers and cargo east from the Bay of Zif around the tip of Cape Finality, was large, modern, and clean-looking. Luzelle boarded, and a steward conducted her to the best stateroom she had encountered since the journey began. Ninety minutes later the *Talghya Jeria* steamed out of the harbor, continuing its course toward fabled Aveshq and the eastern extremity of the Grand Ellipse.

THIS TIME SHE ACTUALLY ENJOYED the crossing. The ship was well appointed and well managed, the food was good, the accommodations agreeable, the passengers and crew congenial. Even the elements cooperated, offering a succession of warm, bright, breezy days and mild moonlit nights. Luzelle spent her time reading, strolling the decks, and playing cards with fellow travelers. She was relaxed, comfortable, and in good spirits. Saving her concern for the safety of Girays and Karsler, she was content.

The first three sunny days of the voyage were nearly identical, but the fourth witnessed a change. The day dawned grey and dull, and stayed that way. The morning advanced, the wind strengthened, and the skies darkened. By the time a rim of dark coastline appeared on the horizon dead ahead, a light rain had begun to fall.

It was, Luzelle recalled, monsoon season in Aveshq.

The rain continued throughout the following hours, intensifying as the ship neared land. In the early afternoon the *Talghya Jeria* docked at the ancient port of UlFoudh in the princely state of Poriule, where the sacred Gold Mandijhuur emptied into the Sea of Aveshq. Those passengers displaying valid passports were permitted to disembark in the midst of a downpour.

Blessing the inspiration that had purchased her a rain cloak and umbrella back in Dasuneville, Luzelle stood on the wharf and surveyed her surroundings through curtains of rain. The buildings lining the waterfront were predictably utilitarian, and largely western in style. The signs and placards, she noted with a lift of her heart, were printed in Vonahrish, and the flag of her country dangled wetly above the most imposing edifice in sight, probably the customhouse.

For the state of Poriule, ostensibly ruled by a hereditary ghochallon, was, like so many other native states of Aveshq, a Vonahrish protectorate, tightly controlled by western authorities. The figurehead ghochallon might lament his lot to the skies, the disenfranchised natives might grumble in secret and threaten revolt—perhaps something would come of all that grumbling one day—but for now Vonahrish power remained absolute, unshaken even in these days of Vonahr's imperiled autonomy. The wars engulfing so much of the world had not as yet reached Aveshq.

The wharf teemed with fair westerners and golden-skinned Aveshquians alike, most of them all but lost in the shade of their umbrellas and rain hoods. But she spied not a single grey uniform in the crowd. No Grewzian soldiers. No Endless Fire. No Imperium. Not here. The rain was pelting down in torrents, but suddenly it seemed as if the sun shone. She was smiling as she splashed her way through the puddles lying between herself and the big building she took for the customhouse, where her passport might receive the civic stamp of UlFoudh required by the rules of the Grand Ellipse.

It was the customhouse, the Vonahrish lettering above the entrance identified it as such. She went in and found the clerks surprisingly busy. At least a couple of ships must have reached the port almost simultaneously. A polyglot babble assaulted her ears, a crush of miscellaneously garbed humanity confused her vision, and she hesitated, momentarily bewildered, then spied a placard announcing, or enjoining, VONAHRISH NATIONALS, and launched herself at it.

The desk below the sign was occupied by a young clerk whom she took for a half-caste by reason of his blue-black Aveshquian hair and eyes, his western nose and lips, and his light skin faintly warmed with gold. He looked bored, and justifiably so, for he was glaringly underemployed. The floor space before his desk was clear.

The room was filled with men who looked as if they might have been queuing there for hours, and Luzelle marched past them all to be served without an instant's delay. She was, after all, a Vonahrish national in Aveshq. This was the sort of privileged treatment that Karsler Stornzof routinely received throughout the Imperium, but now at last her turn had come to reap the benefits of injustice, and she was enjoying it.

The clerk's look of boredom vanished in the presence of a Vonahrishwoman, and he sat up straight.

"May I assist you, Esteemed Madame?" he inquired with extreme courtesy verging on servility. The singsong accent of an Aveshquian native colored his perfect diction.

She stated her need, and he stamped her passport without question or hesitation, then looked up to inquire with an air of dedication, "Is there anything more that the Esteemed Madame requires?"

"Why yes," she replied, welcoming the opening. "I could do with a little information, if you would be so kind."

"I am honored to serve Madame."

"I need to catch a train north to ZuLaysa, in the state of Kahnderule. Could you tell me the fastest way to get to the railroad station?"

"Ah, Esteemed Madame." The clerk shook his head sadly. "I regret to inform you that most of the trains throughout Poriule are presently out of service, and likely to remain so for some days or weeks to come."

"Don't tell me that the railroad workers are on strike here too!"

"They would not so presume, Esteemed Madame. It is the rain, you see. The rains are exceptional this year. The Gold Mandijhuur has risen vastly, there is much flooding, and long stretches of track are properly submerged."

"I must reach ZuLaysa as quickly as possible. What's the best means of travel?"

"The best means of travel, Esteemed Madame, is currently the only means of travel. A yahdeen-drawn barge will carry

Madame up the Gold Mandijhuur into the Ghochallate of Kahnderule, as far as the town of AfaHaal. Soon the railroad will reach AfaHaal—already construction is under way—but that happy day has not yet arrived. In the meantime Madame must make her way east across the plains from AfaHaal to Zu-Laysa by hired conveyance."

"Hired conveyance of what sort?"

"That is as fate may decree, Esteemed Madame."

"I see. Where shall I go for a yahdeen-drawn barge?"

"The Khad-ji, Esteemed Madame."

"The what?"

"Khad-ji, Madame. It is the river pier at the north end of the city. There you may strike a bargain with a yahdeeneer, whose beasts will pull your barge through the delta channels into the Gold Mandijhuur River."

"That sounds easy enough. And this Khad-ji place—accessible by fiacre?"

"No fiacres here in UlFoudh, Esteemed Madame," the clerk confessed. "Alas, we enjoy no such advanced western marvels. Here Madame must go by fhozhee. You will find the hurriers waiting beneath the awning at the south corner of the customhouse."

"I'll go there at once. Allow me to thank you for your help and kindness."

"It is my very great pleasure and privilege to serve the Esteemed Madame." A deferential inclination of his head accompanied the declaration.

A little too deferential, Luzelle decided. She was not used to such subservience, which, luscious though it seemed at first bite, would very soon cloy. Nodding a farewell, she turned and made for the exit. Long before she reached it, a familiar voice halted her in her tracks.

"Miss D'vaire! Over here—over here!"

She turned and spotted him at once—a short, damp, but dapper figure clad in an expensive raincoat, standing near the front of one of the longest queues.

Mesq'r Zavune. Here in UlFoudh, running neck and neck with her, when she had thought him far behind. Why couldn't the ship bearing him east from the South Ygahro Territory just have been struck by lightning or something?

What an unsporting, unworthy thought. She genuinely liked Zavune. And genuinely wished him out of the race; nothing fatal, a temporary incapacitation would do.

Producing a smile of adequate warmth, she detoured to greet him. He was looking well, she noted sourly. Rested, alert, and fit. How did he do it?

"How do you do this?" he echoed her thought. "All this long way we travel, and you are looking like Sherreen fashion."

"Scarcely. It's good of you to say so, and it's also good to see that you made it safe and sound through the Forests of Oorex. Not everyone did."

"This is a trueness. Once, I think I am dead in there. These jungles wilds are filled with beasts, Ygahri savages, and Grewzians. I do not know which is worst of lot."

"I do."

"Ah, yes." Zavune smiled. "Here the Imperium rules not, here the tongue is free to move! These Grewzians it is who flame up anger of the Blessed Tribesmen. Before Grewzians, I am telled, the tribesmen are not so bad."

"It wouldn't surprise me."

"I am glad you come through jungles safe, Miss D'vair. We compete, but I see you are a fine person, and I am wishing you only good fortunes."

"Thank you." And she had wished *him* incapacitated, moments earlier. Suddenly ashamed of her mental meanness, she added with sincerity, "The best of luck to you too, Master Zavune."

"I am needing it."

"Well, I'd like to hear what happened to you in the jungles when you thought you were dead, but right now—"

"We race, I know. You must make the fly along."

"Exactly. Until next time, then."

"Next time, Miss D'vaire."

She left him standing in line. Unfurling her umbrella as she exited the customhouse, she turned to the left and made for the south corner of the building. A pair of two-wheeled fhozhees waited there, their brightly colored cushions and pennants sodden in the rain. Two native hurriers huddled for shelter beneath a nearby awning, and she compared them swiftly. One was short, scrawny, grizzled, and damply decrepit. The other was young, muscular, and eagle eyed. She went straight to the prize specimen, who bowed with profound respect.

"The Khad-ji, please," she directed. "At your best speed."

"Alas, Esteemed Madame," replied the hurrier, his singsong Aveshquian accent far more pronounced than the clerk's. "It cannot be. This humble one is already bespoken."

"What do you mean?"

"Not long ago, an Esteemed—not of Vonahr, but Esteemed nonetheless—paid me well, bade me await his return, and vanished into the customhouse. He is in there yet."

"Perhaps he will never emerge," Luzelle suggested creatively. "Surely he has changed his mind. I will double his offer, whatever it may be. Now, are we agreed?"

"Here is a puzzle." Enticed, the hurrier wavered. "Do the gods will me great good fortune? Or do They try my honesty with temptation? Either way it is clearly written that I shall tread the Khad-ji this day, for this is likewise the destination of the Esteemed within the customhouse."

"Really." A horrid suspicion invaded Luzelle's mind. "The man you speak of—is he quite short and slim? Is he wearing a beige raincoat? Does he speak Vonahrish in a way that's difficult to understand?"

"Before the gods, this is the very man."

"I know this man. He is inconstant as a feather in the breeze, he has forgotten you. Think no more of him. I will triple his offer. Now, let us be off."

"Triple?"

"Yes. I'm in a hurry, a great hurry." This was an understatement, for beating Mesq'r Zavune to the river pier at this particular juncture could prove critical, but the hurrier seemed unable to appreciate the urgency of the matter.

"Triple. Aeh, but what do I hear?" He thumbed his jaw. "It is too much, there is mischief afoot. I am number-one champion hurrier of southside UlFoudh, two years in a row. Perhaps the gods suspect that it has made me proud. If such an offer is real—"

"It is real, I assure you. May we go now?"

"Then truly They put me to the test. I will not fail." The hurrier straightened. "Madame, I will honor my word, I will await the raincoat Esteemed until the crack of doom, if need be. There, it is done, this one has met the test."

"Listen," Luzelle began, "this is not some test, I'm telling you in all honesty—"

"Madame? Esteemed Madame?" A reedy new voice intruded upon the dialogue. It was the other hurrier, the rickety oldster whose existence she had all but ignored. "Permit this humble one the honor of serving Madame. *I* will hurry you on to the Khad-ji in comfort and style, at a pace that none shall match."

"You?" Luzelle surveyed the speaker. He was shorter than Mesq'r Zavune, he looked as if a breeze might knock him over, and she doubted his ability to draw a loaded fhozhee half the length of a city block.

"Truly, Esteemed Madame." The greying native bobbed a surprisingly agile bow. "I am NaiZind, of the Order of Flow, and at Madame's service."

"Thank you, no." She smiled kindly to soften the refusal. "I will make other arrangements." Turning back to the strong young hurrier, she persisted, "If you doubt my good faith, I'm prepared to pay you half in advance, and the balance upon—"

"No, Madame." The other shook his head vehemently. "I have pledged my word to the raincoat, I have accepted his coin, and I will not break faith. The Esteemed Madame must find another to hurry her. That old one NaiZind will serve her, or else there are others, over there." He pointed.

"Others?" Her eyes followed his finger several hundred yards along the dockside to another building, another awning. If hurriers waited there, she could not see them, but she would have to take his word for it. "Very well, if you really won't change your mind."

She started for the designated awning. Before she had covered a quarter of the distance, the plash of sandaled feet

scampering through puddles caught her ear, and then
NaiZind was beside her, gaunt old face alive with enthusiasm.

"Madame—Esteemed Madame—one word, if I may."

"I'm sorry, but I haven't the time." She did not slacken her
pace.

"Truly, the business of the gods and of the Vonahrish admits of no delay, and yet this humble one begs but an instant.
Esteemed Madame, for your own greatest good, allow
NaiZind to persuade you that he is the man for the job, the
best man, the only man, devoted, dependable, fearless, resourceful, indomitable—"

"All of that?" She could not repress a smile, despite her impatience. "Listen, NaiZind, I'm afraid you don't understand.
You see, I need to reach the Khad-ji ahead of the raincoat who
hired that big young hurrier back there. I'm sure you're very
good, but I require speed, and I fear—"

"Fear that NaiZind cannot outpace and outdo that overgrown *boy*, that shambling heap of fresh warm goat droppings, that mewling, milk-sucking *babe* with a head of lard
and feet of lead—Madame does not believe that I can truly
do this thing? Aeh! In my sleep, Madame. Believe it. Believe
that youth and strength are no match for wisdom and daring.
There are ways of ensuring the Esteemed Madame's success.
See"—his reedy voice dropped to a whisper—"I will show
you."

Luzelle realized that she had come to a full stop. Somehow
NaiZind was squarely in front of her, blocking her path, and
now he was displacing a fold of his oilcloth rain cloak to reveal an implement of some sort gripped in one skinny hand.
A hatchet, she perceived; short handled and sturdy.

"A few swift strokes—" NaiZind gestured discreetly and let
his cloak fall back into place. "Only pay me what you would
give that *boy*, and Madame's triumph is certain."

"You're not suggesting—you don't imagine I'd hire you to
attack someone—"

"The gods forbid! Rather should this one lose his last remaining tooth than shed a single drop of human blood. I
contemplate but a few short strokes of steel upon wood—"

"Wood?"

"The axle, Esteemed Madame. The axle of the raincoat's fhozhee. A few blows, the axle breaks, and the tale is ended."

"I see." *Madame's triumph is certain.* It would be an underhanded trick to play on Mesq'r Zavune, not to mention the young hurrier. Downright unscrupulous, in fact. *Madame's triumph is certain.* Of course, nobody would be harmed, but it was wrong, it was contemptible. *Madame's triumph—*

"Well, you couldn't manage it anyway," Luzelle objected slowly. "The *boy,* as you call him, would certainly see what you were up to, and—"

"Aeh, he sees nothing, if the Esteemed Madame but fill his eyes and his ears. Go back and speak to him once more, Madame. Wave money before his face, and he will look nowhere else."

NaiZind was probably right about that. The plan was distasteful, but not infeasible. And she couldn't very well allow a rival Ellipsoid to enjoy the services of southside UlFoudh's number-one champion hurrier; not if she meant to win. Luzelle hesitated no longer.

"Do what you must," she instructed. Turning from him, she went back to accost the number-one champion a second time.

She was hardly aware of what she said to him. She argued loudly, she gestured broadly, she waved fistfuls of Newrekkoes under his nose. She did everything short of handsprings to keep his attention fixed on her, and all the while, out of the corner of her eye, she watched the fhozhees standing in the rain. She saw old NaiZind's spry, drably draped figure steal near one of the vehicles and disappear beneath. After that she kept an ear cocked for the thud of hatchet strokes, but the heavy pounding of the rain together with her own extravagant vociferation covered the sound, if such there was. Through it all the southside champion stood steadfastly virtuous. Presently NaiZind emerged into view and slunk away. Whatever he had done was done.

She could stop now. Luzelle let herself fall silent. Affecting an air of reluctant resignation, she took her leave of the undefeated champion. Feeling shabby, she walked away, and NaiZind was beside her at once.

"Allow this humble one the honor of bearing the Esteemed Madame's burdens," he suggested, and she let him take her valise. The bag went into the fhozhee's box and Luzelle boarded the vehicle, settling herself uncomfortably upon the sopping seat.

As NaiZind placed himself between the shafts, Mesq'r Zavune exited the customhouse. Carpetbag in one hand, umbrella in the other, he hastened straight to the southside champion.

"Go—go!" Luzelle commanded her own hurrier.

"Madame need fear no rival," NaiZind tossed back over his shoulder, and set off at an indifferent trot, probably his best speed.

She could hardly share his confidence. Luzelle looked back to behold the southside champion solidly positioned between the shafts and galloping like a racehorse. Mesq'r Zavune's fhozhee drew level with her own within a matter of seconds, and then it was past, the distance between the two vehicles lengthening by the moment. She suppressed an angry exclamation. It was happening just as she had feared. Mesq'r Zavune was taking the lead. He would beat her to the Khad-ji, he would secure the best yahdeeneer as he had already secured the best hurrier, he would be first into the city of ZuLaysa, and things would only get worse after that. She should, she realized belatedly, have investigated the alternate hurriers, but she had never even reached them, because the unspeakable NaiZind had managed to intercept, delay, and dupe her, and she had *let* him.

"If that raincoat beats us to the Khad-ji"—Luzelle raised her voice to make herself heard above the pounding of the rain, the creak of wooden wheels, and the general hubbub of a crowded Aveshquian city—"you shall not have your ten Newrekkoes."

"Aeh, but they are surely mine," NaiZind returned cheerfully. "This is written in the stars. Madame need not fear."

"Madame wishes she'd never laid eyes on you," Luzelle muttered under her breath. The old fraud had probably never so much as touched the rival vehicle's axle.

"Now, see—look there, Madame, look there!" NaiZind directed with an air of happy excitement.

Not far ahead the narrow street took a sharp bend. As the southside champion rounded the curve at a run, the sabotaged axle gave way. The fhozhee shuddered, the two big wheels tilted at crazy angles, then one of them released itself and spun away. The vehicle overturned, and Mesq'r Zavune was thrown from his seat.

Remarkable how slowly his body seemed to fly through the air. Luzelle had an unobstructed view, and there was more than ample opportunity to study Zavune's arm-flailing trajectory. For one impossible moment he seemed to hang motionless in midair, his face frozen in an open-mouthed, wide-eyed gape of astonishment. Then he crashed to the ground and lay still. Pedestrians instantly converged on the spot.

"Aeh! So much for the famous southside champion!" crowed NaiZind.

"Stop—stop where you are!" Luzelle exclaimed.

"But Esteemed Madame—"

"I said stop!"

NaiZind obeyed. The fhozhee halted a few feet from the site of the accident, and Luzelle stood up on the seat for a better look. She could see that the southside champion hurrier was quite unharmed. But Mesq'r Zavune lay motionless in the churned-up mud of the roadway, and there was blood on his face, blood that renewed itself as fast as the rain washed it away. His stillness was dreadful. If he was dead, then she was his murderess.

She stood there watching as the crowd gathered and the rain poured down, and minutes passed, centuries passed. Eternity expired and Zavune stirred but did not open his eyes. He was still alive, at least for now. Luzelle closed her own eyes, but saw him clearly as ever. A singsong voice impinged on her remorse.

"Esteemed Madame—if you would be pleased to seat yourself, Madame—I shall hurry you now to the Khad-ji, as promised and agreed upon. Madame's triumph is certain."

"Hold your tongue." She glared down at him, hating him

for what he had caused her to do, fully aware that the responsibility was her own. "This is my fault, do you suppose I'll leave him lying there in the street?"

"What else is there for Madame to do?"

Good question. She thought. "I can see to it that he's carried to the nearest doctor—"

"Aeh, but the Stick-fellows of the city watch will do that. They will be here within minutes."

"Then I can at least remain to learn if he'll live."

"And if he does not?"

No satisfactory answer presented itself.

"The Esteemed Madame must know that the fate of the raincoat lies in the hands of the gods," NaiZind observed matter-of-factly. "He lives or dies according to Their will. Should he perish this day, it is only because his appointed hour has come. There is nothing Madame or I can do to hasten or delay that hour by so much as a single second."

She stifled a bitter contradiction. No point in arguing philosophy with a devout fatalist.

"I want you to hurry that man to the nearest doctor—" she began, but even as she spoke, a trio of uniformed natives arrived, bearing a stretcher. Their identical rain cloaks displayed the insignia of the UlFoudh city watch, and the crowd made way for them at once.

"Stick-fellows," NaiZind explained.

Hurrying straight to the injured man's side, the Stick-fellows knelt, performed a swift examination, then transferred Mesq'r Zavune to the stretcher. While two of them carried him off, the third remained to question the witnesses, commencing with the southside champion. Who might have guessed by now that his fhozhee had been tampered with. Who might have a pretty good idea who had done it.

"There, you see?" NaiZind's good cheer never faltered. "Everything all right now."

"Is it?"

"The gods have smiled upon the Esteemed Madame, her troubles are ended. The Khad-ji and victory await."

A word from her would set the fhozhee in motion. Luzelle hesitated. Her conscience ached like a wound. She should follow Mesq'r Zavune; see to it that he received the best care, pay his medical bills or his funeral expenses as the case might be, pen a letter to his wife back in Aennorve, do what she could to help, inadequate though her efforts might be. On the other hand, she could not afford to linger in UlFoudh—not if she wanted to win the Grand Ellipse. She could not afford the luxury of rectitude, it was bound to slow her down, and she most assuredly could not afford a touchy conscience. She had known from the start that certain sacrifices would be necessary.

Luzelle sat down.

"The Khad-ji," she commanded. "Go."

19

"THE BEST, ESTEEMED MADAME," promised the yahdee-neer. "The best in UlFoudh, the best in all of Aveshq. The finest barge, the most scientifically advanced luxurious accommodations. Would Madame care to inspect the cabin? It is bone dry, Madame, it is most perfectly waterproof."

"That's very nice, but it's the quality of the beasts that concerns me," Luzelle told him. "I need the fastest possible transportation, and—"

"Look upon my beautiful BuBuuj," the yahdeeneer invited. "Feast your eyes upon my magnificent MoomYahl. Have you ever seen the like? Esteemed Madame, these are princesses among yahdeeni, they are without equal for loveliness, strength, endurance, swiftness, intelligence, and sweetness."

"Well—" Luzelle surveyed the princesses in question. She could credit the claims for strength and endurance, as the two yahdeeni floating half submerged beside the river pier were indeed enormous, well fed, and powerfully muscled creatures, built like living fortresses. But loveliness? In the fond eye of their master, perhaps, but she herself could see little beauty in the massive ungainly forms colored yellow-brown as the river water, and even less in the broad-snouted visages. As for intelligence—that was difficult to gauge. And sweetness? She gazed down into a pair of porcine yahdeeni eyes and saw no sweetness there. The small yellow orbs seemed to reflect a certain sullen malevolence, but perhaps it was her imagination. In any case she was clearly no judge of yahdeeni-flesh. This was the third team she had inspected, and they all seemed much the same to her. But the afternoon was advancing, she needed to make a quick decision if she hoped for significant upstream progress before nightfall, and this lot seemed as good as any.

"How much?" she asked.

The yahdeeneer named a figure. It was high, but did not seem unreasonably so.

"Agreed," she returned, and the flame of incredulous joy briefly lighting the other's dark Aveshquian eyes told her at once that she should have haggled, that she had probably just consented to pay three or four times the appropriate fare. Well, she didn't have time to haggle. And it wasn't her money, anyway. Let the ministry worry about it.

Assisting her aboard, the yahdeeneer placed her valise in the tiny cabin, which was horribly daubed in magenta and gold, but well caulked and dry as promised. He then set about fastening and adjusting the huge harnesses, while Luzelle watched from the shelter of the painted awning overhanging the cabin door. For a while all went well until one of the princesses, patience overtaxed, gave a pettish shake of her huge head and turned within the traces to face her keeper. The yahdeen's cavernous jaws gaped. Luzelle caught a glimpse of big yellow teeth and a blast of foul fishy breath. The yahdeeneer, accustomed to his charges' idiosyncrasies, stepped back just in time to avoid a powerfully projected vomitous stream stinking of fish and decayed vegetation. The hot green tide surged across the deck, missing her new shoes by inches. Luzelle gagged and turned her face away, while the yahdeen loosed a hoarse cry of triumph blending the bray of a jackass with the scream of an eagle.

"MoomYahl—MoomYahl!" A burst of reproachful Aveshquian dialect followed.

MoomYahl subsided, grumbling passionately, and her master resumed his labors.

The stench of yahdeen vomit hung in the air. Grimacing, Luzelle applied one of the new handkerchiefs to her nose. The yahdeeneer paused to slosh a bucket of water across the deck, and the diluted green pool spread. Luzelle stepped back into her cabin and shut the door.

Some half hour later a torrent of rousing Aveshquian rhetoric lured her forth. The rain had washed the deck clean, and the smell was gone. The yahdeeneer had completed his preparations, and now he was plying his pole, his spiked goader, and his tongue to set his team in motion.

The princesses were disinclined to abandon the pier. While MoomYahl shook her great head, wheezed, and groaned, BuBuuj presented a wrinkled tan posterior briefly to the grey skies and dived for the bottom. The water roiled violently and a shuddering shock rocked the barge. Luzelle tottered and grabbed the doorjamb. Cursing in Vonahrish, remonstrating in Aveshquian, the yahdeeneer sawed the reins and worked his goader. At last his ministrations, combined with the buoyancy of the many inflated floaters attached to the harness, forced BuBuuj back to the surface. Her master greeted her with rapture. The yahdeen groaned and spat. The yahdeeneer lilted a musical call, and the princesses commenced swimming.

CONTRARY TO LUZELLE'S INITIAL IMPRESSION, the rains were not ceaseless. From time to time they paused, often for minutes at a stretch, and during these lulls she could emerge from the cabin and survey the slowly passing landscape. For the first six hours or so of the journey, while the barge navigated the narrow delta channels, she saw small flooded farms with fields entirely submerged and opaque yellow-brown water lapping at the very windows of the ruined wooden houses. She saw innumerable floating animal carcasses, household furnishings, wreckage, and debris, along with many small rowboats and rafts loaded with entire families, their belongings, and sometimes their livestock as well. She wondered where they were going. Where, indeed, could they go?

MoomYahl and BuBuuj were tireless if grudging swimmers, and in the evening, as the wet skies deepened from lead to slate, the barge attained Yeybeh Passage, one of the four great arms of the Gold Mandijhuur, and there dropped anchor for the night.

While the yahdeeni dived for aquatic weeds and fish, their master cooked dinner over a tiny charcoal grill set up on deck beneath a canvas lean-to. Despite all disadvantages he managed to produce a surprisingly palatable mess of rice and the native green spikkij seasoned with morsels of smoked meat— the meat of the wild dog, he cheerily announced.

After dinner Luzelle read in her cabin by the light of a single candle. When the candle was guttering and the print swimming, she extinguished the light and climbed into a narrow bed whose sheets, although clean, smelled strongly of Aveshquian spices. For a while she lay there listening to the rain beating the roof, the river slapping the hull, and the yahdeeni complaining in their sleep. From time to time the recollection of Mesq'r Zavune stretched bloodstained and senseless in the mud of the roadway flashed before her mind's eye, and then she would thrust the picture away, deliberately substituting the image of His Honor's granite face and recalling all that she had to look forward to should she fail to win the race. This technique was effective, and Zavune retreated.

He had been unlucky, she told herself. He must have known that the Grand Ellipse was risky business. She regretted any part that she might have played in his misfortune, but could not take full blame for it. She had only done what was necessary.

THE TINY IMPACT OF A WATER DROPLET hitting her face woke her early in the morning. Luzelle wiped the moisture away and opened her eyes. Another drop splashed her forehead, and she looked up to behold the magenta ceiling beaded with water. It seemed that the most perfectly waterproof cabin had sprung a leak. The yahdeeneer would have to fix it at once. Or more likely, the realistic portion of her mind recognized, she would have to move the bed. . . .

The rains poured down throughout the day. MoomYahl and

BuBuuj surged resentfully upstream, drawing the barge north through the Yeybeh Passage and into the Gold Mandijhuur, which seemed less a river than an inland sea, its far bank lost in the distance, its surface chopped with foamy tumult. The near bank was lined with the great estates of the wealthy Vonahrish planters. The valuable fields of tavril, the spice famed throughout the world for its pungent flavor and blue color, now lay submerged beneath yellow-brown floodwaters. The big plantation houses, most of them built in classically western style, were veiled in mist and all but hidden from view. The private riverfront piers were under water, and the river itself almost bare of traffic.

Exotic, colorful, legendary Aveshq. Land of mystery and fable, unknowable and eternal. The reality was dismal, disappointing, and far too wet. Retreating into her leaky cabin, Luzelle shut the door and immersed herself in a new novel. Hours later the call of the yahdeeneer lured her forth.

"Madame, Esteemed Madame—"

Opening the door, she stuck her head out. "What is it?"

"See there!" He pointed in triumph.

"What?" She stepped out under the awning for a better look. Following the other's extended finger, she peered through curtains of rain at a tall stone post or marker of some kind rising above the floodwaters. An emblem painted in purple, black, and gold surmounted the marker. "What is that?"

"The border, Madame," declared the yahdeeneer. "We now leave the state of Poriule behind, and we enter the Ghochallate of Kahnderule."

Progress. Encouraged, Luzelle smiled. "When do you suppose we'll reach—"

A hoarse bellow of protest drowned her voice. The princesses, evidently loath to depart their homeland, were making their displeasure known. Turning within their double harness, the two yahdeeni simultaneously vomited onto the barge, then dived for the bottom of the river with the coordinated precision of professional acrobats.

The reeking green tide swept the deck, spattering the hem of Luzelle's new grey dress and thoroughly fouling her shoes. She loosed a squawk of disgust. The barge rocked, the river roiled, and a rushing influx of water spread the vomit far and wide.

"MoomYah!—BuBuuj!" The yahdeeneer pleaded and plied his pole. "Ladies! Beauties! Queens! I command you, I *entreat* you, return to the light!"

Stepping back into the cabin, Luzelle slammed the door shut. Quickly she changed her clothes and shoes, then found a rag, moistened it, and cleaned her soiled garments as best she could. No telling when, if ever, they would dry. While she was thus engaged, the conflict between yahdeeneer and princesses continued. The barge pitched, dirty water flowed in under the cabin door, and at last a succession of protesting moans announced the resurfacing of the two great beasts. The yahdeeneer warbled a command, upstream progress resumed, and the vessel crossed the border into Kahnderule.

There was, Luzelle soon decided, no discernible difference between the states of Poriule and Kahnderule. Each seemed to comprise an endless succession of big, Vonahrish-owned tavril plantations lining the banks of the Gold Mandijhuur, each seemed equally drowned and drab. But the yahdeeneer, a citizen of UlFoudh and proud of it, insisted otherwise.

"Most truly there is a great difference," he assured her that evening, as they ate their dinner of rice and stewed pijhallies on deck in the shelter of the lean-to. "For look you, Esteemed Madame—the men of Poriule and Kahnderule come of two different tribes, and thus we speak two different tongues. The Kahnderulese deem their own language the greater—the 'Queen Tongue,' they call it, and think themselves most highly prized of the gods. They are vainglorious, boastful, and full of insolence, while we of Poriule are modest and courteous. They are closemouthed and secret, while we are honest and open. They are coldhearted and grasping, while we are warm, friendly, and generous. They will not eat the meat of the wild dog, and sneer at us for doing so. And yet they do not ritually purify their own food, and thus they are themselves little better than scavengers. Esteemed Madame, we are nothing like them."

"I see," Luzelle murmured gravely. "I see."

. . .

THE JOURNEY RESUMED in the rainswept dawn. The rain was still falling seven hours later, when the barge docked at AfaHaal. Luzelle paid the yahdeeneer the balance of her fare, and he assisted her to disembark, then handed her valise up onto the wharf.

"Madame travels on to ZuLaysa?" he inquired with a bow.

"As soon as I can find some sort of transportation."

"I pray that Madame will not tarry in AfaHaal. The river has thrust its way into the town, and I have heard that crocodiles walk the main streets."

"Crocodiles! Can that really be true?"

"So this one has heard. As for the little hyuuls, of course it is known they are everywhere."

"The little what?"

"Hyuuls, Esteemed Madame. Small, poison-toothed water snakes that swim in tribes. A bite or two will not kill a man, but only make him long for death. But three or four bites—aeh!" He shrugged expressively. "What once was dry land now stands inches deep in water, and the little hyuuls have found their worldly paradise. Their numbers increase by the hour, and so it will be until the rains abate. Madame must take care where she treads."

"I will." Luzelle cast an uneasy glance around her, but spied no snakes underfoot.

"The perils of Kahnderule are great," the yahdeeneer observed. "It is not too late for Madame to reconsider. I am willing to carry her all the way back downriver to the safety and comfort of UlFoudh, at a mere half the cost of her original passage."

"No, I do not go back."

"Alas. I make this offer only in respect of my very great regard for Madame, and because I sense that MoomYahl and BuBuuj have come to love her."

"Indeed." Luzelle eyed the yahdeeni. One of them, resenting the inspection, muttered and spat at her.

"And perhaps, if she will confess it, Madame has come to return the affections of my princesses?"

"Rest assured Madame will never forget them."

WHAT NEXT? Beyond the docks the town spread out before her—a wide tangle of streets and buildings, several of them fairly imposing; for AfaHaal was a river port of some importance, arrival site of goods bound for markets scattered throughout western Kahnderule, including the ancient capital city of ZuLaysa. Many of the private and public edifices flaunted the polychrome wooden fretwork characteristic of the region, and everywhere rose the tall carven staffs designed to display rows of colored pennants whose sequence constituted a kind of local language. Today the fretwork was spattered and dulled with mud, and the carven staffs stood empty in the rain. The citizens of the town were out in force, but their brightly hued garments hid beneath dull oilcloth rain cloaks, hoods, and black umbrellas. AfaHaal, a kaleidoscopic spectacle in the sun, now crouched sodden and colorless.

The street underfoot streamed with water to the depth of an inch or more. A few enterprising souls were striding about on short stilts, some wore heavily greased boots, but the majority of native pedestrians teetered atop tall chopines. Luzelle possessed neither stilts nor specialized footwear, and her long western skirts and walking shoes were soaked within seconds. Breathing a sigh, she splashed her way past noisy beggars, importunate jukkha vendors, eerie snake-shimmies, and other such denizens of the gutter whose pleas might ordinarily have caught her attention, but not today. Mindful of the yahdeeneer's possibly mendacious warnings, her eyes ranged in search of strolling crocodiles and small aquatic snakes. She discovered neither, but soon fixed on a far more agreeable sight—a westerner clad in the buff-and-brown uniform of a lieutenant of the Eighteenth Aveshquian Division. She hurried to him at once.

"Lieutenant?"

He turned at the sound of her voice to present a face that would have looked at home on any Sherreenian street corner. It was the most typically Vonahrish face she had encountered in weeks, and she could not help smiling at the sight of it.

"Yes, Madame?" He returned the smile.

"Could you please advise me? I need to reach ZuLaysa as quickly as possible. What's the best way to do it?"

"You are traveling alone, Madame?"

She nodded. His accent was northern and slightly countrified, she noted. Fabeque Province, beyond doubt. A real Vonahrishman.

"Then my best advice to you is to wait here in AfaHaal for another week or two until the worst of the rains are over before attempting to move east," he told her. "There's considerable flooding between here and ZuLaysa. The stage has suspended operation until further notice, and there's no alternate means of travel that I might in good conscience suggest to a lady."

"I appreciate your concern, sir, but I can't wait, my business is urgent. Is it possible to hire private transportation?"

"If it is possible," he warned, "I wouldn't recommend it. You must understand that these yellow-fellows—that is, these Aveshquian natives—are an oddly mixed lot. Some are loyal and dependable as guard dogs—the most faithful and devoted of servants. Others are treacherous, malicious, and cunning beyond western ken. It's the divided nature of the eastern mind, I suppose."

That sounds like something a Grewzian would say, thought Luzelle, amazed.

"You might find yourself a yellow with a wagon willing to carry you east, at a price," the lieutenant continued. "And he might bring you safe and sound into ZuLaysa—or else he might take it into his head to rob and murder you, or worse. I do not mean to alarm you, Madame, but with these natives, one never knows. I strongly advise you to await the resumption of regular coach service."

"Thank you, Lieutenant." She marched away, head and umbrella held high.

Find yourself a yellow with a wagon, he had said. Where in the whole dripping town of AfaHaal would she look for such a thing? She had no idea; she would have to start asking anyone and everyone, if need be.

Spying a stout covered wagon drawn by a pair of bullocks, she hurried on over to accost the owner, a burly character swathed in oilcloth rain gear. Like most natives he spoke fluent Vonahrish, and his reply was enlightening.

"The Esteemed Madame asks the impossible," he declared.

"Impossible?" She scowled.

"Truly. The land between AfaHaal and the city of ZuLaysa is presently an impassable bog, treacherous underfoot, soft with hungry mud, and spotted with standing pools. My wheels would sink in the mire straightaway. Or if they did not, then the little hyuuls swarming in the water would torment and perhaps kill the bullocks with their venom. It cannot be."

"It must be. It shall be. Somehow. Come," she coaxed, "you are a big, strong fellow. Surely you do not *fear* a bit of water and a few paltry snakes? I'll pay you well for your trouble. I will pay you"—she hesitated for effect—"twenty-five New-rekkoes."

His eyes widened. The munificence of the offer amazed him, as she had intended that it should, but he did not waver.

"No, Esteemed Madame." He shook his head. "Not even for twenty-five *hundred* would I attempt this thing. Nor would any other mortal of sound reason."

"You do not understand," she persisted grimly. "It is necessary that I proceed to ZuLaysa without delay. I must go, I *will* go."

"Not in my wagon, lady," he replied, and must have recalled that so flat a contradiction of an Esteemed Vonahrishwoman's assertion was unseemly as it was unsafe, for he continued almost without pause, "If Madame is truly set upon this course, then she might seek the counsel of Heesh-Nuri, who performs great wonders and marvels."

"HeeshNuri? Does he own a good covered wagon and a strong team of bullocks—mules—whatever? Or is he a hurrier with a fhozhee?"

"No, Madame. HeeshNuri is HeeshNuri-in-Wings, greatest astromage in all the western counties of Kahnderule. He reads the Script, that one, as if it were his gazette!"

A mumbo-jumbo *fortune-teller*? Luzelle bottled the impatient query. Native astromages—regarded as gifted individuals empowered to decipher the stellar configurations known as the Script of the Gods, wherein divine will is revealed unto humankind—were deeply revered throughout Aveshq. An open display of disrespect could only offend her listener, and so she replied politely, "No doubt your astromage possesses great wisdom, but I seek ordinary transportation, nothing more."

"HeeshNuri-in-Wings is more than an astromage, Esteemed Madame," insisted the other. "He is a master of magic, a conduit of that mystic power flowing into our world from the land of the gods. HeeshNuri directs this power where he will, and behold! Costly miracles occur. And the Esteemed Madame appears to seek a miracle."

"A good wagon would do," Luzelle replied, and took her leave, resolved to hunt down a driver of bolder spirit.

But the quarry proved elusive. Half a dozen times within the next hour she approached likely-looking natives attached to likely-looking wagons, and half a dozen times her offers, pleas, and arguments were turned down, always for the same reasons. *Giant swamp . . . great quagmire . . . seas of sucking mud . . . the little hyuuls . . . dangerous . . . madness . . . impossible.* She soon grew sick of hearing it. These Aveshquian natives, she decided, were a pitiful lot, deficient in courage and imagination alike. Their responses were drearily repetitive, right down to the recurring recommendations that she seek the aid of their local witch-doctor, this HeeshNuri-in-Wings character.

"Where would I find him?" she asked at last, without much interest.

"The house of HeeshNuri stands atop the highest of the hills overlooking this town," the latest of her reluctant wagoners explained. "Give me five zinnus, Esteemed Madame, and I will drive you there."

"I will give you five *hundred* zinnus, if you will drive me to ZuLaysa." She saw his eyes light, and her own did likewise.

"Truly it is a great sum, a princely sum."

"Indeed. It is not often that such an opportunity arises."

"Aeh." He shook his head, and the light in his eyes extinguished itself. "Here is only an opportunity to watch my wagon and bullocks sink in the mud. Keep the five hundred, I will satisfy myself with the five."

"You will satisfy yourself with none," she told him irritably, and splashed off down the twisty little rivulet of a street.

The clock was ticking and she was squandering time. The pusillanimous locals seemed uniformly unwilling to drive her to ZuLaysa. Alternatives? Buy a wagon and team outright, and drive herself? Possible, but how practical would that be? She had no experience in driving a wagon, managing a team of bullocks, or finding her way across flooded, snake-infested terrain. Purchase a horse and ride east? Purchase a horse where? She had not caught sight of a single horse since reaching AfaHaal. Mule? Slow and difficult to manage. Well, she'd do it somehow, if necessary. In the meantime the hire of a competent driver was still her best possibility, and she was not quite ready to give up on it yet.

The next three natives she approached refused her in quick succession. When the last offered to drive her to the house of HeeshNuri-in-Wings for the sum of six zinnus, she broke down and consented. Perhaps this fortune-teller that people spoke so highly of might offer some useful advice or suggestions. Perhaps he would sell her a wagon. It could not hurt to ask.

The ride was consistently uphill, and problematic in the rain. Water rushing down the slopes had turned the unpaved road to chocolate pudding. The bullock was up to his pasterns in mud, the wagon wheels sank and dragged, progress was slow and halting. And for the first time Luzelle began to appreciate the magnitude of the task she confronted. If a native driver, skilled and practiced, could barely manage to cover the two miles or less separating HeeshNuri's house from the town of AfaHaal, then how should she, alone and wholly inexperienced, hope to drive a wagon east through the floods, all the way to ZuLaysa?

Never mind, she thought, *I'll do it if I must.*

The covered wagon halted, and she heard the driver calling her.

"What is it?" Luzelle stuck her head out.

"Esteemed Madame, we have arrived. Here is the house of HeeshNuri."

"Good. Your payment." She gave him a ten-zinnu piece that she had picked up somewhere en route. "Now I want you to wait for me here. I'll give you another ten zinnus plus a bonus for carrying me back down into town. Will you wait?"

"Until the end of time, Esteemed Madame."

"Very well." She eyed him narrowly, wondering if she dared leave her valise with him. She decided against it. Valise in one hand, umbrella in the other, she alighted from the wagon and advanced along an immaculate white gravel walk edged with scrupulously tended shrubbery.

The house of HeeshNuri-in-Wings did not at all meet her expectations. A provincial native fortune-teller, she had assumed, would inhabit some dirtily bedizened little shack somewhere on the outskirts of town. HeeshNuri's dwelling, built of rose-veined dove-colored stone, bespoke wealth and settled solidity. The design recalled the perfectly proportioned elegance of the best Sherreenian town houses, but the tall oval windows with their elaborate surrounds and the small dome surmounting the portico were distinctly Aveshquian in style.

Marching straight to the front door, she let fall the gilded knocker, and a houseboy answered at once. He was garbed in spotless white linen, crisp and perfect, and even though he was only a servant and a native at that, she was suddenly aware of her wet, filthy skirt hem, her muddy shoes, and her escaped tendrils of hair curling uncontrollably in the humid air.

"Madame?" the houseboy inquired.

"I am Luzelle Devaire, a Vonahrish traveler, here to see HeeshNuri-in-Wings upon a matter of business. Is he at home?"

"Enter, Madame." He ushered her in with a bow.

Lowering her umbrella and pushing back her hood, she stepped over the threshold into a gleaming marble vestibule. Slender columns two stories high supported a dark-blue vaulted ceiling punctuated with golden constellations. She stood in the home of an astromage, after all.

"I will relay Madame's message." The houseboy's air was solicitous. "Would Madame care to add anything more?"

State your business, he was suggesting with an exquisite tact that somehow implied the unhappy consequences of refusal.

"I need transportation to ZuLaysa," she explained shortly. "I've been told that HeeshNuri may be able to assist me."

"I will relay the message," the houseboy repeated. "If the Esteemed Madame would be pleased to wait."

She wasn't particularly pleased—time pressed—but she inclined her head with such graciousness as she could muster, and the servant retired, leaving her alone. Seating herself gingerly on the edge of a western-style brocaded settee more than likely to suffer by contact with her soiled skirts, she waited. The minutes passed and she lost herself in contemplation of the tessellated marble floor, until a flash of motion at the edge of her vision caught her attention, and she raised her head. She looked out through one of the big oval windows to behold the wagon in which she had arrived departing the property of HeeshNuri-in-Wings. The driver—bored with waiting, or else worried about the steadily deteriorating condition of the steep road—was heading back toward AfaHaal.

Luzelle jumped up, ran to the door, and struggled with the unfamiliar latch. By the time she got it open, the wagon was almost out of sight. She shouted at the driver, who did not turn his head. If he heard her voice above the rain, he chose to ignore it. The wagon rounded a bend in the road and disappeared from view. She suppressed the impulse to chase after it.

Mouthing a silent imprecation, she slammed the door shut and returned to the settee, where she sat fidgeting for another five minutes. Wasted minutes, no doubt. Wasted hours, priceless time squandered. This stupid excursion to the home of some jerkwater would-be wizard had been a mistake from the start.

The houseboy reappeared to announce, "The master invites Madame to join him and his guests in the salon. This way, if you please."

His guests? She had come at a bad time.

"May I take Madame's valise and umbrella?" the houseboy ventured as if asking a favor.

She relinquished both articles, and he led her along a carpeted corridor past a succession of lavishly appointed rooms, one of which contained a figure that caught her eye. It was someone quite tall and heavy, powerful looking, clothed in the conventional Aveshquian costume of baggy trousers and voluminous tunic, with a sash knotted at the waist. Less conventional were the deep hood, leather mask, and leather gloves concealing every trace of identity. Height, bulk, and breadth of shoulder marked the individual as a man. He stood in a shadowy corner, and something in his utter immobility struck Luzelle as peculiar, even disquieting. For a moment she was unsure whether she looked upon a human being or a mannequin.

Her doubt must have shown on her face, for the houseboy reassured her, "Madame need not concern herself, it is only one of the master's Quiet-fellows."

His what? She said nothing. Moments later she spied another figure of similar type, masked and muffled, impersonating a statue at the far end of the hall. She tried not to stare.

The houseboy led her to a double set of polished ebony doors inlaid with countless tiny ivory lozenges. He knocked, and a resonant voice speaking in lightly accented Vonahrish bade him enter. Opening the door, he announced, "Esteemed Miss Devaire."

Luzelle walked into an opulent salon. The door closed behind her and the houseboy withdrew, but she hardly noticed, for the occupants of the room claimed her full attention. Three men rose from their chairs as she entered. One of them—Aveshquian, tall, imposing, handsomely gowned in robes of damson silk embroidered with gold and jet—had to be the astromage. Beside him stood Girays v'Alisante and Karsler Stornzof. Together. Both apparently unharmed. And here in this place ahead of her. *How?*

Did it really matter how, so long as they were both safe? No road-gang labor for M. the Marquis. No envenomed Ygahri darts for Karsler. An almost painful gratitude filled her.

Girays was himself again; clean shaven, hair trimmed, dressed in well-cut khakis suitable to the climate. She had almost begun to forget how he looked without a scruffy beard and dark locks straggling over his brow. He was regarding her with a smile, probably amused at her expression of transparent astonishment; or perhaps simply relieved to see her whole and healthy as she was relieved to see him. And Karsler . . . his impact was still startling. Her mind had not properly retained the remarkable blue of his eyes, or their indefinable remoteness.

"Miss Devaire. My house is honored by your presence," the tall Aveshquian intoned ceremoniously, but without a trace of the servility that she had already come to expect from the natives. But this was clearly no ordinary native. The golden insignia attached to the fringed sash wrapping his waist proclaimed his membership in the Order of Wings, one of the highest of the ancient Aveshquian social divisions. His speech was that of an educated man, his manner faultless, his bearing regal. She judged his years to be something over sixty, by reason of his plentiful silver hair, the lines grooving his high forehead and lean cheeks, and the pigmented spots spattering his long-fingered hands. But his eyes—uncommonly large, deep set, and blackly brilliant—were ageless. "I am HeeshNuri-in-Wings. I believe my guests are already known to you."

"They are, and I am glad to see them well. I greet Heesh-Nuri-in-Wings, most famed and gracious of astromages," she responded musically. "His wisdom is celebrated and his arcane skills deemed incomparable. I come in hope that he will assist a lone, unprotected woman in her hour of distress." She saw Girays's lips turn down at the corners, and Karsler blinked.

"Such talents and resources as I possess are at Miss Devaire's command."

"HeeshNuri-in-Wings is generous."

"I am unworthy of praise. Will it please you to sit, Miss Devaire?"

"Thank you." She seated herself, and the men resumed their chairs.

"May I offer you refreshment? Tea, perhaps?"

"You are most kind, but I think not." Actually she would have liked some tea, but did not care to linger over the rituals of hospitality.

"Ah, I understand. You are pressed for time and filled with urgent purpose." HeeshNuri nodded paternally. "It is often so with my visitors, many of whom live as if striving to outpace fate itself. The three of you, however—all contestants in the famous Grand Ellipse—simply strive to outpace one another, and to this end you seek my assistance. You see, Miss Devaire, your rivals M. v'Alisante and the Overcommander Stornzof have already explained matters."

"But how convenient," she murmured, still wondering how the two of them had managed to reach this place ahead of her.

"You require transportation east to ZuLaysa," HeeshNuri continued. "Or rather, east as far as the village of JaiGhul, where railroad service resumes. I am capable of furnishing such transportation."

"Indeed?" Luzelle brightened. "You offer a wagon—a carriage—a fhozhee?"

"None of these would serve your needs," HeeshNuri observed. "No ordinary wheeled vehicle will navigate the seas of mud that presently bar your way east. For that you must avail yourselves of my Quiet-fellows."

"Quiet-fellows?"

"Servants of a specialized nature, possessed of certain unusual attributes."

"What unusual attributes?"

"They are complex and manifold. Suffice it to say, my servants are fully capable of bearing occupied palanquins across the flooded plains to the village of JaiGhul, a journey of some forty-eight hours' duration."

"Forty-eight hours?" Luzelle's brows rose, for the estimate struck her as more than a little optimistic. "Pardon me, Heesh-Nuri-in-Wings, but I have studied the map, and I do not see how this can be. The distance is considerable, and if one assumes that progress is restricted to the daylight hours—"

"No such restriction exists," the astromage informed her. "My Quiet-fellows travel by night or day."

"They'll need to sleep, though."

"They are beyond that."

"Rest? Eat?"

"No."

"And all those little poisonous snakes—?"

"Will not trouble my Quiet-fellows."

"I see." Luzelle wondered if Girays and Karsler believed all or any of this. She shot a dubious glance at them, but their faces, ordinarily so dissimilar, were now identically inscrutable.

"Perhaps," she essayed, "you could summon one or two of your Quiet-fellows, and we might have a word with them."

"Impossible, Miss Devaire." HeeshNuri shook his head. "They do not speak Vonahrish. In fact, they do not speak at all."

Or sleep? Or eat? Madness. She should slog back on down the hill to AfaHaal, she was wasting her time here. Or was she? What if the astromage's offer turned out to be legitimate? If so, she could hardly afford to retreat, leaving the field clear to Girays and Karsler. Neither of *them,* she noticed, seemed disposed to withdraw. Did they know something she didn't? Luzelle gnawed her lower lip.

"Forgive me, HeeshNuri-in-Wings, but I do not understand," she confessed.

"Ah, the rational western mind craves the unreliable crutch of logic. But you are in Aveshq, Miss Devaire, and the forces at work in this land may perhaps exceed your experience. I might describe the nature of my Quiet-fellows to you, but the explanation would surely strain your credulity."

"My credulity might surprise you."

"Perhaps." HeeshNuri allowed himself a small smile. "But time presses, does it not? Please accept the word of one whose stars have led him down many a curious path—the Quiet-fellows may be relied upon to serve your needs. M. v'Alisante and the Overcommander Stornzof have chosen to believe this. Their questions, so like your own, were answered prior to your arrival, and that, no doubt, is why they sit so quietly now."

"Quite right," interjected Girays. "The options are limited, and I've decided to take a chance on your Quiet-fellows. Since I'm eager to be off, I'd like to conclude our transaction quickly." He reached into a pocket to bring forth his wallet.

Luzelle was taken aback. When last she had seen him, Girays v'Alisante had spoken and acted as her companion and ally. Now he was unmistakably her competitor. He was not even looking at her. He had hardly acknowledged her. He must still be angry at the way she'd run off and left him, back in Jumo Towne. Well, let him sulk.

Her surprise deepened when Karsler concurred quietly, "I too will hire a palanquin."

The two of them seemed quite certain, and that was good enough for her. She would trust their judgment.

"I too," declared Luzelle. "Oh, but what about food and water? For a two-day journey, we'll need—"

"You are unanimous, then," HeeshNuri interrupted, so gently that his courtliness seemed uncompromised. "Such perfect accord is rare and precious as the tears of a god. It is, however, my unhappy task at this time to acknowledge a minor obstacle. I see before me three travelers. I have at my disposal but two palanquins, and four Quiet-fellows to bear them. You perceive the difficulty."

She perceived it perfectly, and she also perceived the remedy. "HeeshNuri-in-Wings, I will pay you well for the use of a palanquin and bearers. What price do you ask?"

"Price? Ah." The astromage sighed. "I hardly know how to reply; such matters sadden me. I will rely upon Miss Devaire's good sense and good conscience. What does she offer?"

"Oh. Well." She thought about it. She had no idea what constituted a fair price, but amid such surroundings did not wish to appear stingy. "One hundred New-rekkoes?" she suggested. That was certainly more than generous.

"A handsome sum," HeeshNuri murmured.

"I will match it," Karsler Stornzof offered promptly. "I will pay seventy-five grewzauslins, which is the equivalent of Miss Devaire's hundred New-rekkoes."

Two palanquins taken, none left for Girays, Luzelle reflected. Bad luck for M. the Marquis. Now he would have to seek alternate transportation, else hang around AfaHaal until the rains ended. A pity. He really should have spoken up faster.

"One hundred fifty New-rekkoes for a palanquin and bearers," Girays offered.

He wasn't playing fair. Luzelle frowned at him. He was too late, the palanquins were both spoken for. He ought to accept defeat gracefully. No doubt their host would reject the inappropriate offer out of hand.

"One hundred fifty. It is considerable," mused HeeshNuri-in-Wings.

She wasn't about to let Girays get away with it. "One hundred seventy-five," she snapped.

To her unpleasant surprise Karsler instantly countered, "One hundred fifty grewzauslins."

She would never have expected it of him. Where had all his chivalry gone? And what would it take to beat his offer? She had never liked mathematics, she could not easily do numbers in her head, she just needed to bid enough to knock one of these men out of the competition.

"Three hundred New-rekkoes!" she exclaimed recklessly. That should certainly do it. Extravagant, but worth the price.

"Four hundred," said Girays.

Outrageous. M. the Marquis used that money of his like a club, he thought it would win him anything. But not this time. She would show him.

"Four-fifty," said Luzelle.

"Three hundred seventy-five grewzauslins," Karsler offered.

Did that beat her last bid? She supposed it must, else he would not have bothered, but how could he be so ruthless? She darted a reproachful glance at him, and his face told her nothing, but she saw Girays smiling with that insufferable amusement of his, and the sight was so infuriating that she heard herself exclaim, "Six hundred New-rekkoes! Heesh-Nuri-in-Wings, I'll pay you six hundred!"

"Six hundred," echoed the astromage. "Truly, I am bewildered."

"Eight hundred," Girays offered with alarming nonchalance.

He was trying to intimidate her. It wasn't going to work.

"Six hundred grewzauslins," said Karsler.

Her head for numbers was not so poor that she failed to note that he had simply matched the highest bid without exceeding it. That, of course, was all he needed to do, but Karsler's sudden access of caution suggested dwindling means. He probably wanted to conserve his resources, at least until he was back in the Imperium. It occurred to her then for the first time that her own funds were not unlimited, although they had seemed so at the start of the race. Her hoard of cash, diminishing over the course of weeks, was now seriously depleted, not that it really mattered. The letter of credit furnished by the Ministry of Foreign Affairs would open vaults all over the world. She need only present it at the Vonahrish Residency in ZuLaysa. But she had to get to ZuLaysa first.

"Eight hundred twenty-five New-rekkoes." Luzelle could hear the first quaver of uncertainty in her own voice.

Girays v'Alisante instantly offered a thousand, and she shot him a look of appalled wonder. No use trying to outbid M. the Marquis with his bottomless pockets; she hadn't a chance. But she might defeat Karsler Stornzof. She did not know how much cash he carried with him, but surely she held the heavier wallet.

Or perhaps not.

The bidding continued, and the fare to ZuLaysa shot up to eighteen hundred New-rekkoes. It was impossible, unreal. Her blood ran cold when Girays serenely offered two thousand, and Karsler at once followed with a bid of fourteen hundred fifty grewzauslins. Fourteen fifty. That would be— she figured feverishly—something over nineteen hundred New-rekkoes. Nineteen hundred and—and—thirty—whatever. She needed to beat that in order to stay in the race, and she was not certain that she could.

"One moment," she requested, and produced her wallet. She counted the contents quickly. Nineteen hundred twelve New-rekkoes. In addition, a small assortment of international notes and coins, acquired en route and amounting to little. Not enough. *Not enough.*

"HeeshNuri-in-Wings." She spoke very calmly. "I am prepared to exceed the highest bid, whatever it may be, by the sum of one hundred New-rekkoes, provided you are willing to accept my promissory note."

"I fear that is out of the question," the astromage returned gently.

"But I am entirely good for the debt. I carry a letter of credit from the Vonahrish Ministry of Foreign Affairs. Look, I will show you—" She worked hard to keep the desperation out of her voice.

"That is quite unnecessary, Miss Devaire. I am certain your credit is excellent."

"It is, and the moment I reach ZuLaysa, I can—"

"I am truly sorry," he cut her off mellifluously. "But I cannot accept a note. The oldest and simplest ways are the best, I have found, and therefore my dealings include neither borrowing nor lending."

"I suggest neither. I only ask a little time to secure the cash. I would, of course, leave a deposit of eighteen hundred New-rekkoes with you, and post the balance just as soon as I—"

"I must decline. Let us speak of it no more."

"But—" She cast agonized eyes around her. Karsler looked a little perturbed, but Girays was observing the exchange with that odious amusement of his. He was *enjoying* her misery, and she hated him thoroughly; she would find a way of wiping that unbearable superior little smirk right off his face.

"HeeshNuri-in-Wings, I appeal to your chivalry. You belong to a high and noble Order. Surely you will pity the plight of a woman in distress—alone, unprotected, helpless, stranded in a strange land," she wheedled shamelessly. A few tears might have helped, but she could not produce them at will. She was able, however, to achieve an effectively piteous vocal tremor. "Help me, HeeshNuri-in-Wings, else I am surely lost."

She saw Girays roll his eyes, but would not let him distract her. She concentrated her imploring attention upon her host, who seemed to display some signs of compunction.

"You move me, Miss Devaire. Truly, you have touched my heart." HeeshNuri bowed his head and sighed. "You will understand that I cannot alter the principles of a lifetime to satisfy your need. And yet I am greatly disposed to assist you, and I believe that there may be a way. Yes—it is perhaps irregular—but I feel I can offer a solution."

"I am certain you can, if only you will, HeeshNuri-in-Wings."

"Here is my decision, then," the astromage proclaimed with an air of generosity. "My two palanquins and four Quiet-fellows shall be hired out as a team. The rental price of this team is thirty-eight hundred New-rekkoes plus fourteen hundred fifty grewzauslins."

This bandit is skinning us alive, thought Luzelle. But the bandit was doing her as well as himself a large favor. Smiling in pretty gratitude, she replied, "You have resolved all difficulties, HeeshNuri-in-Wings."

"I think not," Girays objected instantly. "Two palanquins cannot accommodate three travelers."

The smirk was gone, Luzelle observed with satisfaction.

"The litters are commodious, Master v'Alisante," soothed HeeshNuri. "No doubt you will make do through so short a span as forty-eight hours."

"The arrangement you propose is unacceptable. I have offered two thousand New-rekkoes—rather a substantial sum—for the private use of a palanquin and bearers."

"That is a matter to be decided among you and your companions."

"I am traveling alone," Girays informed him.

"In that case, perhaps M. v'Alisante alone would prefer to assume the entire cost of the team's hire?" the astromage suggested.

Luzelle's breath caught. She had not thought of that. If he could afford it, M. the Marquis held the power to trap two of his rivals here in soggy AfaHaal for days to come.

Girays said nothing. Perhaps his pockets were not quite bottomless after all.

"No? Then I shall assume that my three guests embark upon a joint venture." The astromage nodded benignly. "No doubt you are eager to set forth, and I shall do all in my poor power to speed your departure. Even as we speak, my servants ready the palanquins for your use. I go now to instruct the Quiet-fellows. During my brief absence, I entreat you to regard my home as your own." Silk robes royally sweeping, HeeshNuri-in-Wings strode from the salon.

"We've good reason to regard his home as our own," Girays observed sourly. "The price that extortionist is wringing out of us would purchase the entire property. He's made fools of us all."

"His strategy is admirable," Karsler approved. "He uses our rivalry to excellent advantage, and we do not recognize the ploy until it is too late."

"You recognized it," Luzelle realized. "You were trying to hold the bidding within reasonable bounds, weren't you?"

"I was unable to do so," Karsler acknowledged.

Because Girays and I were going at it, she thought. *Well, he started it.* She glanced at Girays, wondering just how annoyed with her he was, but his face told her nothing. He was not even looking at her.

"I wish I'd stopped to think," she told Karsler. "If we'd all cooperated, we might have saved a fortune. I'm sorry I didn't use my head." Curious how easily she could admit an error to him. Probably because he never seemed to find her foolish or juvenile, she could tell him things that she could hardly reveal to M. the Marquis.

Perhaps the same thought struck Girays, for now he did glance at her very briefly, no more than a quick flick of expressionless dark eyes, then looked away again.

"We race, we strive to exceed one another," Karsler returned. "We do not ordinarily attempt cooperation or combined effort—it is not the first thought."

"Yes, you once warned me about something like that." She met his eyes. "You recall?"

"Clearly."

Her peripheral vision encompassed Girays's face. It did not alter in the slightest; in fact, he appeared inattentive. Something like disappointment flashed through her too swiftly to analyze.

"I lost track of you after that," she continued without a

pause. "I thought you must have left Xoxo before me, and wondered if the Blessed Tribesmen of the jungles hadn't eaten you alive. Literally."

"I survived the Forests of Oorex and reached Jumo Towne intact," Karsler told her. "I rode horseback from Jumo Towne to Dasuneville, whence I sailed for Aveshq aboard the Grewzian transport vessel *Triumphant.* Halfway through the passage the ship's engine malfunctioned, and the pause for repairs delayed my arrival by some twenty-four hours. In UlFoudh I made my way to the river pier known as the Khad-ji, where I encountered v'Alisante. Together we traveled by barge up the Gold Mandijhuur to AfaHaal."

"The two of you reached UlFoudh ahead of me, then," Luzelle observed. She still did not see how it was possible. Turning to Girays, she inquired uncomfortably, "And what did you do, after—we last saw each other?"

"Hired a horse in the early morning, the moment the livery stable opened its doors," he replied shortly. "Rode hard and reached Dasuneville the next day just in time to catch the last scheduled eastbound steamer."

"Which I missed. Now I understand. Except"—Luzelle frowned—"did you ride all night along the Jumo-Dasune Passage?"

"No, I stopped at the Halfway Inn."

"But I was there too. You mean we spent the night at the same inn, and never even knew it?"

"I knew it." He shrugged. "I spotted you in the dining room. You were bundled up in Iyecktori mourning."

"You saw me? You knew I was there, and you never even spoke to me?"

"I did not wish to compromise your disguise," he returned coldly.

"I see." He was trying to punish her, but she wasn't about to flatter him with pained reproaches. She manufactured a cool smile. "That was considerate."

Turning back to Karsler, she urged him to recount his experiences in the Forests of Oorex. He obliged, and she learned for the first time that he had not traveled aboard the ill-starred *Water Sprite*. He knew, however, of Porb Jil Liskjil's death, of the kidnapping by the Blessed Tribesmen and the subsequent magical cradling in the arms of the forest, for Girays had described all of it during their shared barge trip up the Gold Mandijhuur.

And had Girays likewise described the ugly, degrading encounter with the Jumo Towne constabulary? She threw him a questioning glance, which he ignored.

Karsler asked nothing about Jumo Towne and she volunteered nothing, but spoke instead of yahdeeni and their deplorable eccentricities. They were still talking when their host returned.

"It is done," HeeshNuri-in-Wings announced. "The palanquins await. Your baggage has been loaded, there is food and drink, the Quiet-fellows have been instructed." He paused.

Money changed hands. Wallets shrank.

"Come, then."

They followed him from the salon, along a corridor and through a short covered walkway connecting the house and a small outbuilding, the Aveshquian equivalent of a carriage house. But Aveshquian natives rarely if ever kept western-style carriages. The outbuilding sheltered two very fine fhozhees, one sturdy wagon, a wheelbarrow, and two large palanquins on which her eyes fastened appraisingly. Wooden construction, strong looking, stout poles, fresh caulking. Shuttered windows on two sides. Good. And stationed beside each palanquin, a brace of Quiet-fellow bearers, each hooded, gloved, masked, shod in outlandishly broad-soled sandals, and heavily cloaked in waterproof oilcloth. She studied the still figures curiously. She could not see much—the clothing masked all details of face and form—and thus could hardly account for her own powerful sense of their strangeness. She could only guess that it had something to do with their preternatural immobility. None of the four so much as twitched, and she detected no evidence of respiration.

"I assume that the gentlemen will occupy one palanquin, Miss Devaire the other, and the baggage has been disposed accordingly," HeeshNuri reported. "Correct me if I am mistaken."

Girays assured him that he was not.

"Very well. Know this, then," their host advised. "The Quiet-fellows will carry you east across the plains by the shortest and most direct route to the outskirts of JaiGhul, where they will leave you. No detour or alteration in course is possible, nor will your bearers remain with you once their task is complete. There are only two commands you may issue to which they will respond. One is 'Go,' the other is 'Halt.' Thus you may pause as often and as long as you wish. A word of caution, however. Should difficulty arise along the way—illness, accident, an emergency of any kind—the Quiet-fellows will furnish no assistance. They cannot. You understand this?"

Why not? Are they mentally defective? Luzelle wondered, but nodded dutifully.

"And if a Quiet-fellow is ill, or hurts himself, what then?" she wanted to know.

"This is not a concern."

Why not? she wondered again, but the astromage's smooth gesture invited them to board, and it seemed the wrong time to press for an explanation.

As she approached her palanquin, she passed close by one of the Quiet-fellows and her nostrils flared. A powerful fragrance of aromatic spices wafted from his garments, and underlying the spice was something rank and repellent. Not like the body odor of the night guard in Jumo Towne; more like rancid food, bad meat. She slanted a very quick glance up into his face, and caught the milky sheen of pale eyes glinting through the holes in the mask; not typically Aveshquian eyes at all. A faint qualm chilled her, and she hesitated.

Bad time to be losing her nerve. Karsler and Girays were guilty of no such weakness, they had already boarded. She took a deep breath, climbed into the palanquin, and closed the door firmly behind her. Dark as a closet. She groped at the nearest set of shutters, found the catch, and opened a window. Weak light straggled in, and she saw her valise and umbrella on the floor, and beside them a wicker hamper, presumably filled with provisions. She stuck her head out in time to see HeeshNuri-in-Wings throw wide a pair of big wooden doors. Wind and water swept into the carriage house, and Luzelle pulled her head in. The astromage clapped his hands sharply, rapped out an unintelligible Aveshquian command, and the Quiet-fellows took up their burdens.

HeeshNuri spoke again and the Quiet-fellows strode forth into the rain, their pace an unvarying mechanical plod.

Rain drummed the palanquin roof. Droplets sprayed in through the window, and Luzelle closed the shutters again, leaving only a crack to peep through. For a while she surveyed the dim and drowning landscape on one side, then switched to the opposite window, from which she could see the other palanquin moving along at a pace that matched her own. One of its windows was ajar, and she glimpsed Girays's face at the opening. She waved to him once, but he did not acknowledge the gesture. Either he had not seen it, or else he was ignoring her. She closed the shutters with an irritable bang. The rain poured down and the Quiet-fellows marched on.

HOURS PASSED, the miles swam by, and presently the dull grey skies darkened. There came a rare lull in the rain, and when her bearers attained the relatively mud-free summit of a stony rise, Luzelle took the opportunity to order a necessary rest stop.

The Quiet-fellows stopped dead on command. They set their load down brusquely. Luzelle looked out one window, and then the other. Mist and gathering darkness obscured her vision. There was no sign of the other palanquin. She scanned the ground, but spied no snakes. Alighting gingerly, she set her foot on solid ground and advanced a few paces, then glanced back at the bearers to see if they were watching, or perhaps even following her.

Nothing of the sort. The two cloaked figures stood motionless and seemingly blind to her existence, masked faces aimed straight ahead. She retired briefly behind a cluster of rocks, then came back and, as she drew near, saw a brown worm crawling across the lead Quiet-fellow's foot. She squinted. Not a worm; a small snake, almost certainly one of the venomous hyuuls of which she had been warned. A spontaneous cry of alarm escaped her; not the best response, she realized too late. The noise would startle the native bearer, he would jerk or jump, and the frightened snake would strike. The man would sicken or even die, and it would be her own stupid fault.

She might have spared herself the worry. The Quiet-fellow neither jerked nor jumped. Nor did he look down at the creature slithering across his sandaled foot. He never stirred at all.

His self-control was almost superhuman. Of course he was right in standing perfectly still, but how did he endure it? She held her breath, held her peace, and watched. Seconds later the snake crawled away and the spell broke.

"Are you all right?" She hurried straight to him. He remained motionless, masked gaze fixed on the mists, and she remembered that he spoke no Vonahrish; neither bearer did, but surely she could make herself understood. She pointed at his foot. "The snake did not bite? You are not hurt?"

No sign of awareness, much less comprehension. She looked down at his foot, which displayed no puncture wounds, but the mud-caked flesh visible between the straps of his sandals was puffy and livid, almost green in color. So he had been bitten, then. But no, the other foot was exactly the same, and surely the hyuul could not have struck both, and they would not have puffed up and turned green so quickly, anyway. They probably weren't even really green, it was just a trick of the failing light.

Then she caught another whiff of that putrid meat stench coming off the Quiet-fellow, and an unreasoning sort of fear boiled up inside her. Quite irrational, and she was not about to let it show. The bearer was uninjured, the incident was closed. She reentered the palanquin and shut the door behind her.

"Go," she commanded, and the journey continued.

She ate cold rice salad and drank fruit juice from one of the bottles in the wicker hamper while enough light remained to distinguish the contents. Then the rain started up again, and the light failed altogether. The Quiet-fellows bore their burden east through intense darkness, and never for a moment did their pace falter.

There was no lamp or candle. When she peered out through the window she could see nothing, and so she listened intently, but heard only the rain, the wind, the creak of wooden joints, and the squelch of the Quiet-fellows' feet in the mud. The other palanquin could not have been far off, but the blackness had swallowed it whole; the blackness had swallowed all the world.

The squelching was rhythmic and almost soporific; the patter of the rain on the roof insidiously relaxing. The dank darkness pressed her eyelids shut, and she slept.

IT WAS STILL DARK AND RAINY when she awoke. Neither the rhythm nor tempo of squelching had altered perceptibly. She opened one of the windows, and leaden light pushed in. Morning, then. Yawning, she knuckled her eyes, and stuck her head out to let the rain wash her face. When she was thoroughly awake, she surveyed her surroundings.

Not much to see. An endless plain, probably a desert of dust in the dry weather, presently a sea of yellowish mud. Mist and cloud veiled the landscape, but she could discern the clustering low rooftops of some small village squatting in the middle distance. Not JaiGhul, not yet. She drew back inside and checked the view through the other window. More mud, and, not far away, the other palanquin following a course parallel to her own.

She drank a little fruit juice, ate some flatbread, and settled back with a book. When she judged the terrain favorable she ordered another rest stop, with reluctance; for the thought of the rival palanquin taking the lead, even by a matter of yards, was intolerable.

Lifting her skirts immodestly high to clear the muck, she slogged on back to her conveyance, but paused before entering to check the bearers' feet for snakes. She saw none, but noted for the first time that the rear Quiet-fellow's right foot lacked its large toe. His left foot was missing its large and small toes. Both feet were caked with mud, and it was impossible to judge the age or recency of the amputations. The front Quiet-fellow's left foot was also four toed. Curious that she had not noticed it yesterday. The presence of a venomous snake must have blinded her to all else. Unfortunate for the bearers, but at least their losses were not slowing them down.

The journey continued and the wet, dull day wore on. The Quiet-fellows never rested, never ate, never slept, never slackened, never faltered. Obviously their master had fortified them in some arcane way, but she could not fathom how he had done it, and something told her that she did not really want to know.

In the late afternoon they came to a region of gently rolling hillocks and hollows, through which flowed some nameless stream fringed with heavy growths of waist-high reeds. Undeterred, the Quiet-fellows plowed their way through the vegetation and marched straight on into the water, which quickly rose to chest level.

Luzelle looked out the window to see the turbulent tan waters almost lapping the bottom of the palanquin. She could reach down and touch them, and did so in the idle manner of a picnicker in a rowboat upon a quiet Vonahrish pond. The sensation was agreeable, and she allowed her hand to trail along until she saw an elongated snout cleaving a swift approach and glimpsed a pair of lidless reptilian eyes coming toward her. Then she snatched her hand away and shouted an urgent warning to the bearers, who did not alter their pace.

The snout and eyes preceded a long form that she recognized too readily. As she drew her hand from the water, the crocodile changed course, veering for the front Quiet-fellow. Leaning out the window, she yelled at the bearer, "Come inside—get out of the water!"

He did not so much as glance in her direction. She waved her arm frantically and screamed, but he seemed deaf. The crocodile submerged, disappearing from view, and then the Quiet-fellow appeared to rock under the impact of some giant invisible blow. He teetered and the palanquin tipped, throwing Luzelle heavily against the door. The latch gave way, the door swung wide, and she slid out into the stream.

For a moment she splashed and sputtered, then her feet found soft bottom and she righted herself. She stood neck deep in muddy, moderately warm water, and even as she shook the sopping hair out of her eyes, she saw a second crocodile emerge from the shelter of the reeds to slip into the water and launch itself at her.

The Quiet-fellows righted the palanquin and trudged on without her.

"Halt!" she yelled wildly, and they stopped. "Wait for me, wait for me," she muttered as she floundered toward them. They stood motionless, staring straight ahead.

She reached the palanquin. Grasping the door frame, she jumped up, struggled desperately, and managed to drag herself aboard. The door gaped. As she leaned forward to grab it, a crocodile surfaced, its jaws yawning inches below her outstretched arm. She slammed the door in the reptile's face, latched it securely, and likewise fastened both sets of window shutters.

"Go," she croaked.

The Quiet-fellows strode imperturbably on. Moments later they reached the far bank and emerged from the stream.

For a time Luzelle sat trembling and dripping in the darkness. When her tremors subsided, she took a deep breath, changed her wet garments for dry ones, then cracked the shutters open and warily peeked out.

She saw muddy plains, dim grey skies, and falling rain. When she looked down at the ground, she saw that the big puddles filling every dip and hollow swarmed with little brown snakes, through which the Quiet-fellows walked without hesitation or mishap.

They had displayed a similar indifference to the crocodiles, and that confidence had justified itself. Following the initial assault on the front bearer, the crocodiles had left the Quiet-fellows alone.

When next she ventured to order a brief rest stop, Luzelle took the opportunity to scrutinize her companions. The right leg of the front bearer's baggy trousers had been shredded from knee to ankle, baring a length of livid shank. The flesh bore deep puncture marks. A chunk of meat had been ripped out of the calf, and Luzelle glimpsed a white flash of bone. But the

wound that should have crippled the victim seemed to go unnoticed. The Quiet-fellow displayed neither pain nor awareness. And there was not a single drop of blood to be seen.

She did not let herself think about it.

RAINY GREY DAY DARKENED to rainy black night. The muffled tread of marching feet lulled Luzelle to sleep, and was
with her when she woke in the morning. The rain had ceased,
no doubt temporarily, and for once she could afford to open
both windows. She checked the vistas right and left. More
mud, more puddles and snakes, but the terrain was no longer
quite so flat. An expanse of shallow, rolling hills relieved the
monotony. Off to the left, not far away, the other palanquin
kept pace with her own. Evidently Girays and Karsler had
won safely past the crocodiles.

Time passed, the rain resumed, they bypassed another village, and Luzelle's spirits began to rise, for the journey was
surely nearing its end. Forty-eight hours, HeeshNuri-in-
Wings had promised, and those two days were almost spent.
Heedless of the rain, she stuck her head out the window,
straining her eyes for a glimpse of JaiGhul, where the railroad
service resumed, but saw only mud and mist. She drew back
with a sigh.

Railroad. Normal conveyance, filled with normal human
beings. Modern transportation into the city of ZuLaysa,
where her depleted wallet would receive a transfusion, and
then north to the port city of Rifzir, where she could book
normal ferry passage across the Straits of Aisuu to the Emirate
of Mekzaes. Railroad. Normality. Soon.

The palanquin wobbled. One of the Quiet-fellows, unbelievably, had missed a step. The march regained its rhythm
briefly, then the palanquin lurched again and its rear end
dropped abruptly, tipping Luzelle backward against the cushions. The poles hit the ground, and the impact jarred through
her. For some reason the back bearer had lost or relinquished
his burden, but the lead Quiet-fellow tramped on, indifferent
or unaware. The palanquin, inclined at a sharp angle, scraped
and dragged along at a teeth-rattling crawl.

Righting herself with an effort, Luzelle poked her head out and looked back to behold the rear Quiet-fellow knee-deep in mud, immobilized, and unconscious of his own plight. While his trapped legs strained to move, his torso swung forward, precipitating the overbalanced figure face-first into the mire. Even then his efforts to advance continued until Luzelle thought to order a halt. The front bearer stopped on command. The mired figure lay still.

Now what? She needed both bearers. She would have to lift the fallen Quiet-fellow and steer him back to his post, but he was larger than she, and it was not certain that she possessed the strength. Perhaps she could find a way, but she needed to reach him first, and a single glance told her that the wet ground lying between herself and the bearer swarmed with little brown snakes. Hundreds of hyuuls, perhaps thousands, and every one of them poisonous. She glanced from the snakes to the Quiet-fellow and back again. Her mind spun. Seat cushions? Improvise a movable elevated path? Tie them to her feet?

A flash of motion caught her eye. She looked up and saw the rival palanquin drawing level with her own. The shutters stood ajar. Girays's face appeared at the window, and she waved urgently.

He saw her, there could be no doubt, and her predicament was self-explanatory. M. the Marquis would know what to do.

He did indeed. The shutters closed and Girays's face vanished. The palanquin moved on and she stared after it, open-mouthed.

How could he? Did he want her to die out here in the middle of muddy nowhere? The tears rose to her eyes and she dashed them away. That self-satisfied, supercilious swine wasn't about to make her cry. He wouldn't get the better of her, either. She would show him. She would show them all.

Back to practical matters. She willed her mind into action. Cushions. They would lift and support her safely above the mud and the serpents. Clumsy but probably effective, if only she could find a way of attaching them to her feet. Tie them in place with strips of cloth torn from one of her new muslin nightgowns? Not impossible. Nightgowns and penknife lay in her valise. She retrieved both and went to work.

The strips she tore off were long but flimsy. She tried twisting a couple together to form a cord, but they would not stay twisted, not even when she wet them. Braiding worked better, but took some time. For the next several minutes her fingers flew.

When the braids were done, she tried tying the cushions to her feet. The task was trickier than she expected, and several efforts failed, but soon she hit upon a winding configuration of braids that seemed to hold the cushions securely. They had better be secure, at least secure enough to carry her across several yards of snake-infested mud. How many yards? She glanced back to gauge the distance and, through the pouring rain, discerned a tall grey figure dragging the fallen Quiet-fellow free of the mire.

"Karsler?" she breathed, entranced. His high boots, she noted at once, were certainly serpentproof.

The trapped feet emerged with an audible plop, and Karsler hauled the Quiet-fellow upright. The bearer swayed dangerously, then regained his balance and stood motionless. Karsler issued a quiet command and together they advanced. As they drew near, Luzelle saw before she could look away that the Quiet-fellow's mask had slipped, revealing most of a milky-eyed, greenly distended countenance. She thought she glimpsed a jagged palisade of rotting teeth, but only upper teeth, for the lower jaw was entirely gone. But the rain might have confused her sight, and in any case, she promptly pushed the vision from her mind.

They reached the palanquin, and the bearer took up the rear poles. Karsler stepped around to the window.

"Luzelle, you are unhurt?" he inquired.

"Yes, I'm fine." She opened the door. "Please, come on in out of the rain."

He complied and she shut the door behind him. He was soaked, his uniform plastered to him, the water dripping from his hat, and Luzelle thought she had never seen anyone more beautiful.

"Thank you—oh, thank you, Karsler!" she exclaimed. "If you hadn't helped me, I don't know what I would have done."

"I think I can see what you would have done." His eyes

dropped to the cushions tied to her feet, and he smiled slightly. "This is most imaginative. I do not know that it is quite practical, but I must commend your ingenuity."

"Yes, you're right, it's ridiculous."

"I do not say so. Comical appearance notwithstanding, this unorthodox method you have devised might perhaps have proved successful."

"And might not. I'm glad I needn't put it to the test, thanks to you. You're extraordinarily generous to stop for me this way. I'm surprised you got Girays to agree to it."

"He did not agree. He did not see the necessity, but professed great confidence in your ability to overcome all obstacles. Perhaps he was right about that, but I did not wish to take the chance. Therefore v'Alisante and I have parted company, and he has continued on his way."

"What, you mean he just took the palanquin you'd both paid for and abandoned you here? He had no right to do that."

"I hope I do not presume too greatly in hoping you will allow me to share your conveyance."

"I'll very much enjoy your company. And I think Girays v'Alisante ought to be ashamed. He's played you a miserable trick."

"I do not see it that way. We race, and he is not obligated to pause for anyone. It is something I may choose for myself, but cannot expect of another."

"Neither can I," she returned. "This isn't right, you shouldn't damage your chances of winning on my account."

"Ah, almost you speak like the grandlandsman."

"That is not my ambition. Where is your uncle, anyway? I haven't seen him in a long time."

"He has gone on ahead. Preferring to shorten the tedium of the journey, he has proceeded directly to Lis Folaze, where I shall meet him next."

"Somehow I suspect you aren't so very eager to overtake him."

"I am far more eager to overtake v'Alisante," Karsler parried. "His lead increases by the minute."

Quite right.

"*Go!*" Luzelle commanded sharply, and the Quiet-fellows marched.

Karsler smiled at her, and she remembered the sun.

"That is better," he said.

"Much better," she replied, and smiled back at him.

20

"MAJESTY, I AM PLEASED to announce an accomplishment. Our Masterfire has attained new levels of dexterity and control," proclaimed Nevenskoi.

"Has he?" King Miltzin appeared to suppress a yawn.

"Indeed." Resolved to overcome his monarch's obvious ennui, the adept adopted an air of dignified enthusiasm. "We have prepared a demonstration, a new marvel to stimulate Your Majesty's sense of wonder."

"Another of the fire things? How many of those have I seen? Really, Nevenskoi, hasn't it occurred to you that this is all becoming a trifle repetitive? Isn't it about time for you to expand your horizons a bit?"

"But, Sire—" The adept's intestines stirred uneasily. "The Sentient Fire is a discovery of enormous significance, one whose potential has scarcely begun to be explored—"

"To my mind it's been explored to the limit and beyond, these past few months. Can't you come up with anything *new*?"

New? One of the great arcane advances in history at his disposal, and this royal retardate was already bored with it? Nevenskoi's innards began to churn.

"Sire—" The adept moistened his lips and spoke with exquisite restraint. "I beg leave to observe that Masterfire's talent to amuse remains very much intact. Your Majesty need only recall the enthusiasm of the audience at the opera house—"

"Yes, that *was* a triumph, wasn't it?" Miltzin's eyes kindled briefly. "The spectacle was astounding! Even the Zoketsa professed herself amazed. But there is all the trouble, you see. The triumph was a disaster in disguise. Ever since that night I've been pelted with pleas and demands, most of them originating among my own subjects. I should never have whetted the public appetite. It was a splendid show, but I know now that it was a mistake, exposing our green friend to the view of the vulgar—a mistake that I shall not repeat."

"I see." Another hope dashed. Nevenskoi strove to contain his resentment, but his creation, presently stationed beneath the king's chafing dish, caught the emotional emanation. The fire leapt responsively, and green tongues licked out across the desk.

Down. Small, my beauty, small, Nevenskoi soundlessly enjoined, and Masterfire subsided without argument.

"Hereafter Masterfire must limit his activities to the confines of the Waterwitch," the king decreed. Frowning, he selected a deep-fried oyster puff from the inevitable platter of appetizers. "And that being so, it's only too clear that the novelty of the various little demonstrations and displays has quite exhausted itself."

"Majesty, allow your servant the honor of proving you wrong," Nevenskoi suggested.

"Ha! Wrong! You are very blunt. Never mind, I take no offense. Well, then, my friend, prove me wrong by all means. I shall be pleasantly surprised if you can do it."

"Sire, I do not boast when I assure you that Masterfire has achieved new heights of proficiency."

"Proficiency in what?"

"In molding and shaping his own substance. He has developed a remarkable degree of control and precision, combined with infinite versatility. In short, Your Majesty, Masterfire is capable of assuming virtually any shape imaginable. I will show you."

Loveliness. Having caught his creation's attention, Nevenskoi issued silent commands.

At once Masterfire shot out from under the chafing dish,

sprang from the desktop, raced to the center of the room, and reached for the ceiling. A column of green flame roared into being. For a few moments the column whirled wildly, its light almost unendurable to the eye, then gradually the revolutions decelerated, the fierce radiance palpitated like a stricken heart, and the shape of the fiery mass began to change.

Branches of flame snaked out from the trunk, twigs sprouted from the branches, the twigs divided, and broad green leaves of fire extruded themselves. The small whorls crowning the twigs gave birth to buds that quickly opened to blazing blossoms, distinct down to the smallest detail of pistil and stamen.

"Well. It's a tree," said the king.

"Perfect in every part." Nevenskoi's eyes feasted. "Majesty, observe the astonishing accuracy—the texture of the bark, the curve of each individual petal, the fiery knots along the bole, the precise fashioning of every part—"

"It's very nice. It looks just like a tree. What does it do?"

"Do?"

"Does it just stand there like a tame forest fire, or does it *do* anything?"

"What, if I may be so bold as to inquire, does Your Majesty expect it to *do*?"

"How should I know? Some sort of trick, I suppose, something entertaining. That's your concern, isn't it? Really, Nevenskoi, do you expect me to do your work for you? Use your imagination, man!"

"Sire, you see before you a fire that is sentient and aware, the first of its kind, capable of altering its own shape at will, capable of assuming to perfection an infinite variety of forms, and you complain that it is not sufficiently entertaining? Your Majesty, I should like to point out—" Nevenskoi caught himself up with an effort. There was no good at all in pointing out the king's pathetic paucity of vision; quite the contrary, in fact. Biting back his contempt, he continued quite smoothly, "I should like to point out that Masterfire's abilities have barely begun to express themselves. Only watch, Sire."

What shape, what form, was likely to capture Mad Miltzin's

capricious fancy? *Use your imagination, man!* Nevenskoi opened his mind to the universe, and inspiration accordingly found entrance.

He spoke again in his thoughts, fashioning his instructions with care, and Masterfire instantly responded. The flowering tree whirled out of existence. The column of flame reappeared, spun briefly on its axis, then shrank and dwindled, molded and reshaped itself, sculpting a richly curved naked female form, slender shapely limbs, and the radiant face of a debauched fairy. The green siren that was Masterfire smiled and shook back her blazing cloud of hair.

"Oh," breathed Mad Miltzin. His grasshopper eyes bulged expressively. "Oh."

"You see, Sire." Nevenskoi noted his monarch's reaction with satisfaction. "Masterfire's potential remains largely untapped. Will you not concede as much?"

"Magnificent," whispered the king. "Spectacular. She is so very beautiful!"

"Your Majesty's pleasure is my greatest reward."

"She is the most glorious creature I have ever beheld," opined His Majesty. "Flawless. Peerless. Never have I encountered such intensity, such unabashed ardor!"

"It is but one form among countless possibilities, each more wondrous than the last," Nevenskoi suggested with a significant smile.

"To think how we've misjudged!" marveled the king. "This entity that we've known as Masterfire should by rights bear the title of—Mistressfire. Yes, it is perfect—*she* is perfect. The very essence of true femininity—and we did not perceive it, until now! How could we have been so blind?"

"Majesty, all mortals err."

"Nevenskoi, I must touch her! It's possible, is it not? Do not deny me, my friend, do not deny *her*—for I sense her longing, it burns in those incomparable eyes!"

"I believe that a certain limited contact may be possible," Nevenskoi consented cautiously. He considered. He controlled Masterfire, he could trust Masterfire, up to a point. "Yes. You may hold her hand. Briefly."

"It is a start." Miltzin's eyes traveled the undulant green form. "The start of a journey, I am certain."

"One moment, Sire." Nevenskoi concentrated his thoughts and spoke with his mind. *Loveliness. You have done well, I am proud of you. Now hear me. It is important, very important.*

Whatwhatwhat? asked Masterfire.

The king desires to touch you.

Eateateateateateat—

None of that. You will suffer his touch, and you will consume nothing.

Badmeat touches me, I eat.

No! You will not eat. Not a morsel. You will not so much as frizzle a hair on his head. Do you understand me?

NoNoNo.

Yes you do.

Who is badmeat to touch Masterfire?

Our sovereign, our ruler.

Not mine.

No more argument. Nevenskoi focused his will. *You hear my commands. You will obey.*

No fun.

Offer your hand to the king.

Not a real hand, anyway. Complaints notwithstanding, the blazing beauty extended a graceful green arm.

Miltzin hesitantly accepted the proffered member. The slim hand of fire lay harmlessly across his open palm, and an entranced smile overspread his face. Very gently he closed his fingers to clasp the hand of Masterfire, and for some moments stood savoring the contact.

"I sense the wild flare of her emotions," the king proclaimed at length. "And I believe that Mistressfire likewise senses mine. We are kindred spirits, she and I. We have bonded." Lightly he stroked the long green fingers, which flickered at his touch. "Ah, she is exquisitely responsive."

EAT! Masterfire shivered with eagerness, and for a split second the human guise wavered. *Pleasepleaseplease!*

No. I absolutely forbid it.

WHY?

"She is passion personified," observed the king. "She is divine. I must know her fully, Nevenskoi—I must experience her totality. You will find a way of effecting our union. I am relying on you, my friend."

"I—well. Union. Your Majesty has taken me by surprise," Nevenskoi answered with perfect truth.

Eateateateateateateateateat—

"But it is not so amazing," Miltzin IX observed reasonably. "You are the creator of Mistressfire, her father and teacher. Surely you, who know her so well, must have perceived that she and your monarch possess twin souls of fire. What could be more natural than the longing of two such spirits to merge? For I trust I do not flatter myself in assuming that Mistressfire shares my desires."

Eateateateateateateateateat—

"I can safely report that she is not indifferent, Sire. Still—"

A sharp knock at the study door spared Nevenskoi the necessity of further invention.

"Ah, I had quite forgotten." Miltzin shook his head. "But then, my attention has been fully occupied!" He raised his voice. "Come!"

The door opened. A footman hovered at the threshold. He took in the naked green flaming female handfasted to the king, and his eyes rounded. His jaw dropped, but no words emerged.

"Send him in, send him in," Miltzin commanded, amused.

The footman bowed deeply and retired mutely.

"It quite slipped my mind, I've sent for that marvelous new sous-chef," the king explained blithely. "That talented fellow shall have a royal commendation, and perhaps a little pourboire to go with it. I'm sure you'll agree, my friend, that he deserves both."

"The sous-chef?" Nevenskoi froze, paralyzed as if some blood vessel in his brain had burst, and he could only repeat helplessly, "The sous-chef?"

"The new sous-chef, man! The genius, the rising star, the Architect of Appetizers. The gifted—what was his name, again? Oh, yes—the gifted Master Giggy Neeper!"

A new figure appeared in the doorway.

"You may approach," Miltzin invited graciously.

The newcomer bowed low, entered, and there was Cousin Giggy, much as Nitz Neeper remembered. Fifteen years older, of course. The snub-nosed, freckled, skinny adolescent of yore had thickened around the middle and his sandy hair was receding, but Giggy remained entirely recognizable.

Terror welled within Nevenskoi, and he cast desperate eyes around him. Trapped.

Giggy Neeper's astounded eyes fastened on Masterfire. For a moment or two he saw nothing else. Recollecting the presence of his sovereign, he tore his eyes from the green woman, fixed them on the king, and held them there with obvious effort.

"Master Neeper, I have summoned you to my presence in order to commend the excellence of your work," the king announced. "I have been most favorably impressed—indeed, I've been delighted—by your manifestations of skill, imagination, and virtuosity. Your ganzel puffs are the lightest in the world. Your truffled tartlets beggar description."

"I am greatly honored, Sire." A flush of pleasure suffused the sous-chef's face.

"Truly, my dear fellow, you are an artist marked for greatness in your chosen field. It gives me pleasure to surround myself with men of talent, I revel in the juxtaposition of masterly minds. Thus I'm doubly pleased to present you to a fellow admirer of your work, the ingenious adept Nevenskoi, creator of this gorgeous fiery stunner here, whose presence I think you haven't overlooked. Nevenskoi can't resist your brandied dormice. Eh, Nevenskoi?"

The adept inclined his head in wordless assent.

"I am most grateful, Majesty. Your praise overwhelms me," Giggy declared with becoming modesty. He turned to Nevenskoi. "And I thank you, too, sir. Maybe it would interest you to know that the brandied dormice recipe is a refinement of a dish that my grandmother used to prepare for special family gatherings. I can still remember sitting at her big polished table as a boy, feasting on her soused dormice. Everyone loved them, and I had one cousin in particular who used to gobble them by the handful—" He stopped. He stared. His eyes rounded and his voice rose an incredulous octave. "Nitz? Nitz Neeper, is it *you?*"

"I do not understand you." Nevenskoi's Rhazaullean accent was more than ordinarily pronounced. Behind the façade of polite incomprehension his heart hammered and his guts twisted.

Badness? asked Masterfire.

"It *is* you!" Giggy decided. "I can hardly believe it! Nitz, we all thought you were dead!"

"You jest, Master Neeper?" Nevenskoi frowned, mildly puzzled. Out of the corner of his eye he noted the king observing the scene with interest, and his alarm approached panic.

Whatwhatwhat? Masterfire demanded.

"Wait until Dosie and Jilfur hear that you're alive! They'll be absolutely bowled over! They speak of you often, you know. Why in the world haven't you been in touch all these years?"

"And what is all this, my dear fellow?" inquired the king. "You and my Nevenskoi know each other?"

"Know each other! Sire, this is my dear cousin Nitz Neeper, missing these fifteen years. It's like a miracle, finding him here like this!"

"Majesty—" Attempting a faintly bemused smile, Nevenskoi produced a pained facial contortion. "This kitchen person makes a joke or else a mistake. I have never seen him before in my life, nor have I encountered any member of his family."

"Nitz, how can you say that?" Giggy Neeper reproached. "What's the matter with you? You can't have forgotten your own kin!"

"Master Neeper, I believe you commit an honest error," Nevenskoi returned generously. "This I can understand. Perhaps I bear some resemblance to this long-lost cousin of yours. Such things happen. But please understand, we have never met before this day."

"Nitz, that's plain ridiculous. Do you think your own first cousin won't know you, just because you've gone and colored your hair? I don't remember you ever having that much hair, though. Oh, I see. It's a wig."

"You are very much mistaken. You—"

"Gad, *is* it a wig?" demanded the king. He stared. "He's right, isn't he? I never noticed that!"

"No, Sire, this is a great misunderstanding—"

"Give it a tug, then. A good, firm tug."

"Majesty, I take exception. This is most demeaning, most distasteful—"

"Give it a tug, Nevenskoi, or I'll call in one of the footmen to do it for you."

"That will not be necessary." Nevenskoi's innards were up in rebellion. Ignoring the internal tumult, he drew a deep breath and met his sovereign's eyes squarely. "I confess it is true, Sire. I wear a wig. A small vanity, harmless and quite meaningless. I hope you will not think too ill of your servant."

"And what of your name, man? Is that likewise a small vanity?"

"Never, Sire. I am born of an ancient and noble Rhazaullean line."

"Oh, come off it, Nitz," Giggy Neeper advised. "You ought to be ashamed, spinning such tales. Your father was Klisp Neeper, shopkeeper of Flenkutz, and a very good man too. What do you think he'd say if he could hear you now?"

"My family's estate stood above the village of Chtarnavaikul, as Your Majesty already knows." Nevenskoi's eyes watered with desperate sincerity. "Then came the deadly mudslide—"

"You and your whoppers." Giggy Neeper shook his head. "I'd almost forgotten those incredible lies, but now it all comes back to me. All right, Nitz. If we've never met before, then how is it I know about that scar on your right wrist? You were about seventeen years old, and you were fooling around at Granny's hearth—you had some wild notion that you could make the fire do some sort of trick, I forget what, and it didn't work anyway—you only managed to give yourself a beauty of a burn, which left the scar. What about it?"

"Yes, what about it?" echoed the king. "Is your wrist really scarred, Nevenskoi? Push back your sleeve, let's have a look."

"Majesty, this is absurd."

"You refuse?" Miltzin IX's smile vanished.

"Sire, what signifies a scar? It means nothing and proves nothing. I—I do not deserve this." *Not after all my hard work,* he wanted to say. *Not after I've come so far and accomplished so much. I am creator of Masterfire, a great marvel. What does it matter where I came from, or who my father was, why should anyone care?* All of this and more he wanted to say, but the words caught in his throat, the familiar nervous pangs lanced his belly, and he clutched his middle with a gasp.

Owww! A cry of silent sympathetic pain burst from the mind of Masterfire.

Nevenskoi scarcely noticed. Preoccupied with miseries both physical and mental, he allowed his link with the sentient flame to falter, along with his control.

"Owww!" This time the yelp of pain came from Miltzin IX. Abruptly dropping the green woman's hand, he inspected his own palm, which was deeply reddened and no doubt destined to blister.

The woman of flame suddenly roared into greatness, stretching to a height of some twelve feet. For a moment or two she stood there fully intact, wild cloud of hair scorching and blackening the ceiling, intense heat radiating from her body. Then the limbs flickered and twisted, the sculpted curves of the torso gave way to glaring chaos, the head appeared to explode, and a formless mass of ungoverned fire blazed at the center of the king's study.

Miltzin squawked and backed away, both arms up to shield his face. Giggy Neeper screamed, dashed for the exit, was through it and gone in an instant.

The carpet beneath and around Masterfire blackened. The brocade window curtains vanished in a green flash, and the polished wood of the desk began to char.

"Stop!" Nevenskoi was not aware that he spoke aloud. There was no reply, no intimation that he had been heard, and it took all the experience and expertise at his command to force himself to pause, to order his thoughts and collect his faculties, before addressing Masterfire again. *Stop.*

EAT! The green flame sent excited experimental tentacles snaking toward the bookcases. *DANCE! BIG! EAT!*

Stop. Pain and alarm still rocked his concentration, and Nevenskoi forcibly suppressed both. *Stop. Now. Obey.*

DANCEDANCEDANCE! I am Masterfire, and I am feeling FINE! I am glorious, I am gorgeous, I am me. The musical scores littering the desktop went up in flames.

Stop. Consume nothing more. Dwindle. Small. Small.

Don't wanna. A stack of unopened correspondence vanished.

Stop that. Soon I will be angry. Obey. Now.

Nevenskoi strained his will to the uttermost, and his creation, struck by the desperate force of the assault, submitted without further resistance. In an instant Masterfire shrank, great mass dwindling to a fist-sized ball of flame. Nevenskoi's shoulders sagged and a long sigh gusted from the depths of his lungs. After a moment he ventured a glance at the king.

Miltzin IX stood poised for flight. His face was white and the palm of his right hand was red. He was staring at Masterfire, his expression shocked as he observed, "She attacked me."

"An overspill of youthful high spirits, Majesty," Nevenskoi soothed. "Unsuitable perhaps, but essentially innocent."

"She would have killed me. I was unprepared for the violence, the treachery."

"Sire, there was no malice in this. It was an accident. Masterfire is like a child, unruly and impetuous at times, but—"

"A child full of cunning and duplicity," the king interrupted. "And where did she learn them, I wonder? Who was her master? It is not a difficult puzzle. Who is the habitual liar, the cheat, the impostor? Push back your sleeve, Nevenskoi, or whatever your name is. I want to see your wrist."

"No need, Sire," Nevenskoi returned. He stood up straight and spoke without a trace of Rhazaullean accent. "It is scarred, as Giggy described."

"You do know him, then? You admit it?"

Nevenskoi nodded, almost with a sense of relief.

"And everything he said was true? You admit that too?"

Another mute confirmation.

"I see." For an instant Miltzin looked childishly disappointed, but rallied quickly to accuse, "Then you have lied to me from the start. You've always lied."

"About the small things, Sire. Not the large ones."

"You dare to qualify your guilt? You're a charlatan, a common fraud."

"But there is nothing common or fraudulent about Masterfire. The Sentient Fire is all that I have promised, and more."

"You've betrayed the trust of a king. That's more than a personal insult, it's a criminal act."

"Punish me as you see fit, Sire. Banish or imprison me, but don't extinguish Masterfire's light. A discovery of such importance—"

"Hold your tongue. I don't want to hear your voice. I don't want to see your face, either, so take yourself out of my sight. I'll decide presently how to deal with you. In the meantime, just get out." King Miltzin's eye fell on the ball of fire squatting tamely at its master's feet. "And take that green harlot with you!"

"COME, DECIDE QUICKLY," the pilot commanded in tolerable if impatient Vonahrish. "Which of you two is it to be?"

"I will go first," Karsler informed Luzelle. "If the machine supports my weight safely, then it will easily support yours."

She nodded reluctant agreement and watched as he ascended to take his seat. She would gladly have gone with him despite the horrifying fragility of the conveyance, but the gorgeflier was built to carry no more than one passenger at a time. The launching mechanism, reminiscent of a gigantic crossbow, had been readied by the pilot's trio of assistants; its two huge arms—each powered by the tension of a twisted fiber skein—pulled back by means of a cord attached to a windlass, its great stock angled to loft the glider high.

There was not much time to worry about it. Karsler settled into his seat, the pilot signaled, and one of the assistants released the trigger. The bow responded too quickly for the eye to follow, and the glider shot out into the air above the Gorge of Vezhevska.

There was nothing holding the thing up. No balloon, no giant mythic bird, no magic. And yet it was not dropping straight out of the sky, as Luzelle had half expected. The pilot, through inspired manipulation of rudder and movable bits on the featherweight wings, was somehow holding his craft aloft and riding the air currents toward Rhazaulle. For now, at least.

She watched without blinking, almost without breathing, for another thirty seconds or so, after which the glider disappeared into the mists. She strained her eyes after it, but saw nothing. Karsler was gone, and a sense of uneasy gloom filled her. It was, she realized, one of the few times they had been truly separated since the afternoon he had dragged her fallen Quiet-fellow free of the mud, back in Aveshq. Her palanquin had carried them both on as far as the town of JaiGhul that day, and they had traveled more or less together ever since. Not that either had intended to do so, she reminded herself. Things had simply turned out that way.

Unlike Girays v'Alisante, they had not reached the tiny train station in time to catch the only train of the day. JaiGhul possessed nothing resembling an inn, so they had spent the night dozing fitfully on the hard wooden benches in the waiting room. The next day, reaching rain-drenched ZuLaysa, they had taken separate rooms at the same hotel in the thoroughly westernized section of town known as Little Sherreen. They had boarded the same train departing Central Station for the port of Rifzir, sailed the same ferry across the Straits of Aisuu, run consistently neck and neck northwest through the Emirate of Mekzaes by oxcart and canoe, and shared the services of the same native guide across the grassy Tribal Territories of H'fai.

Through it all they had never quite caught up with Girays, who never seemed to increase his twenty-four-hour lead, but did not lose it either. Likewise they had never quite returned to the moonlit moment of near intimacy that they had shared in Xoxo. Luzelle often thought of it. She would have let him kiss her that night and he had wanted to, she was sure of it, but he had declined to exploit her momentary weakness. Her lapse was unlikely to repeat itself; she was now quite prepared to rebuff indecorous advances with an ironclad propriety that would have won the Judge's wholehearted approval. But the opportunity to flaunt her virtue never arose. Karsler Stornzof did not try to kiss her; he did not even try to hold her hand.

At first she thought him high minded, and admired the strength of his principles, but later on the doubts began to infiltrate her mind. What if she had simply been wrong about that moonlit exchange? What if he had held back not through principle, but rather through preference? Perhaps he found those pouty red lips of hers gross and repellent. Nonsense, he had explained himself clearly that night. But what if he had simply been trying to spare her feelings?

The doubts persisted and pestered. Often when he looked at her they subsided, but never for long, and presently she began to wonder if she could make him try to kiss her if she worked at it. She wouldn't actually let him, of course; it would not do to cheapen herself. She only wanted a little reassurance. But not at Karsler Stornzof's expense. It wasn't fair or even decent to mislead him, so perhaps she should just let him kiss her. That might be the truly right thing to do. . . .

But she never found the right moment to perform the experiment, for the guide was with them night and day every step of the way through the Tribal Territories, and she did not relish an audience. And when they crossed the border into the Dhrevate of Immeen matters worsened, for Immeen was one of the great bastions of Iyecktori purity, a land wherein women adjudged guilty of immodesty—a term open to broad interpretation—were publicly stripped and whipped. And therefore, as they made their way north into chillier climes over increasingly rugged terrain, she attempted no flirtation.

Now, however, they were leaving Immeen for the colder, harsher, but legally looser land of Rhazaulle, where the Gifted Iyecktor wielded little official influence. The River Vezhevska marked the border between the two nations, and the newfangled gorgeflier carrying them across eliminated a two-day journey to the nearest accessible fording place at the base of the cliffs. The gorgeflier offered tremendous advantages, offset by the possibility of sudden death.

The duration of the flight itself, she had been told, was something under ten minutes, depending on the whim of the winds. Ten minutes across, ten minutes back, a few extra minutes thrown in for positioning of the glider for relaunch on the far side, and the little craft should reemerge from those mists within the half hour, assuming that all had gone well—a considerable assumption.

Luzelle scanned the skies. No sign of the gorgeflier, and surely the half hour had elapsed. She glanced at the pilot's assistants, who, having rewound the cord to re-flex the two great arms of the vast crossbow, now lounged around smoking their wide-mouthed wooden pipes. They displayed no uneasiness, so everything must be all right, probably, but she could not banish the mental image of the tiny glider suddenly losing altitude, plunging from great heights to dash itself to pieces on the rocks below.

She shivered a little, cold despite the protection of the heavy, musty-smelling parka and fur-lined gloves that she had acquired from a tribesman of H'fai in exchange for her penknife and a box of matches. She had hated to let the knife and matches go, but would have hated even more doing without an overcoat, for the air at these high altitudes was pure but perennially bitter, even in the long-delayed springtime. Back in Vonahr the freshness of spring would by now have given way to the languor of early summer, but here in this scoliotic spine of northern mountains known in Immeen as "Hul Noveez" and called the "Bruzhois" in Rhazaulle, winter had scarcely loosened its grip. The jagged peaks were armored in ice and likely to remain so.

Her breath misted before her face, and she hugged herself, rubbing her arms and stamping her feet. The native Immeenis, she noted with envy, went gloveless and wore their long vests unbuttoned over homespun shirts, evidently deeming the weather balmy. They seemed very much at ease, and she heard them laughing among themselves over some incomprehensible joke or other. For a moment she wondered if they

were laughing at her obvious discomfort, but quickly dismissed the notion. They could not be laughing at her because
they were scarcely aware of her. To them she was simply a
piece of luggage belonging to a Grewzian overcommander.
This perception, demeaning though it was, actually worked
to her advantage. Had she traveled on her own, a woman un-
veiled and unattached in Iyecktori Immeen, the natives would
have taken her for a prostitute and regarded her as fair game,
natural target of insult, abuse, and worse. But the property of
a foreign officer was another matter altogether, and nobody
had offered so much as an unpleasant word. She did not
much care to think what might have befallen her in Immeen,
but for the presence of Karsler Stornzof.

Where was that glider? It should certainly have returned by
now. She paced back and forth, worrying. The men ignored
her. Just as she was steeling herself to attempt an interrogation, the gorgeflier emerged from the mists, glided smoothly
down onto the snowy flat expanse topping the cliff, slid a distance on its runners, and eventually slowed to a stop. The pilot got out.

Long before the glider halted, the assistants were on their feet
and plowing toward it through the snow. Running ropes
through a couple of lugs attached to the light body, they hauled
the craft back to the launching device and positioned it with
care. The pilot reboarded, then looked at Luzelle and beckoned.

"You come now," he commanded.

She hesitated. The glider perched atop the crossbow was
pale and fragile as a giant dead moth, and probably just about
as reliable. She wanted nothing to do with it.

"Now," he insisted. "Come, it is safe."

She was not aware that she shook her head.

"You do what you like, then," he told her. "But either way,
I keep the money. It is mine now."

Out of the corner of her eye she noted the assistants watching and grinning, and that decided her. Her chin came up
and she advanced with an air of grim resolution that only
broadened their smiles. Somebody helped her to board and
she settled into the passenger seat, hoping they would launch
the gorgeflier before she could change her mind.

They obliged.

The trigger snapped, the windlass claws released their grasp, the cord blurred, and the glider shot sickeningly into space, the force of its sudden ascent pressing Luzelle back hard against the seat. Her humiliating squeal was drowned in the rush of the wind. Eyes screwed shut, she clung to the horribly flimsy body of the craft.

For the better part of two minutes she remained paralyzed, conscious of little beyond the blast of the freezing wind in her face and the nauseating sudden dips, tilts, and accelerations of the gorgeflier. Presently curiosity overcame terror, and she opened her eyes to gaze down through mists at the River Vezhevska, rushing along the bottom of its rocky gorge hundreds of feet below. The snow-clad mountains rose all around her, their grim grandeur a sight to remember for a lifetime. Soon she began to admire the skill with which the pilot tweaked the movable bits of his craft to exploit every current of air. A new and tentative exhilaration stirred to life within her, and by the time the glider started its descent toward the snowfield on the far side of the river, she was almost sorry to see the trip end.

The glider's belly bumped snow. The white scenery flashed by, and then the craft gradually slowed to a stop. Within moments a couple of bearded laborers were there to haul the glider back to a stretch of flat clifftop space, site of a great crossbow identical to its counterpart on the Immeeni side, and of three very stoutly constructed wooden buildings. As she drew near, Luzelle saw that one of the buildings sported the big painted sign of a commercial establishment, but she could not read the Rhazaullean print. A livery stable of some sort, she hoped.

The glider stopped again. Pilot and passenger alighted onto slick, hard-packed snow. Luzelle saw Karsler coming toward her, and the exhilaration born of the recent flight heightened. He had waited for her. He had sacrificed the chance of a half-hour lead—not much, but conceivably significant—and he had waited. He was smiling at her, and she had to suppress the unsuitable impulse to run to him.

"I am gratified to see you safe and well," Karsler declared.

She had grown accustomed to that formality, which no longer struck her as quaint or cold.

"I was concerned for you," he added.

"And I for you," she returned, resisting the urge to reach out a hand and touch him. "I still am. I'm very glad to see you, but you shouldn't have waited. We're competing in a race. Remember what you said—"

"I have not forgotten," he assured her. "Nor have my convictions altered. In this case, however, I was obliged to wait. It seems that the proprietor of this establishment here"—his gesture encompassed the building with the incomprehensible sign—"has at this time but a single sleigh available for hire. Aware of your approach, he refused to rent the sleigh to me alone, but insisted upon awaiting your arrival in order to collect a double fare."

"I see." She nodded, a little disappointed, but then the thought struck, *And how did he know of my approach?* Of course, the pilot might have blabbed. That probably explained it. She chanced a look into Karsler's eyes, which revealed nothing beyond the glory of their color.

"We must share the sleigh," he continued. "It is the only arrangement the owner is willing to consider."

"Then we must," she murmured philosophically.

"He will furnish us with a driver."

"Oh." She still would not be alone with him.

The proprietor approached. He was a burly, bearded mountaineer, barbarically clad in leathers trimmed with some sort of shaggy fur, and speaking a very little broken Vonahrish. The transaction was quickly concluded, money moved, sleigh and driver appeared. The vehicle was old and battered, but the runners were sharp and gleaming. The two horses that drew it were likewise old and battered. The driver, squat and hirsute, eyed Karsler inscrutably, and Luzelle recalled with a slight shock of alarm that Grewzland and Rhazaulle were presently at war. According to the latest newspaper reports she had been able to get her hands on, the Grewzian Northern Expeditionary Force was marching north on the Rhazaullean capital of Rialsq, pushing hard to beat the spring thaws that would soon transform the land into an unnavigable bog persisting for weeks to come. This local entrepreneur's willingness to trade with a uniformed Grewzian officer implied certain possibilities: that the Rhazaullean was utterly venal, or else that this section of the Bruzhoi Mountains was already subjugated and occupied by Grewzian forces. Or very likely both. The gorgeflier's landing field lay within a day's journey of the TransBruzh, the ancient road winding its way through the mountains to link the southern lowlands and northern highlands of Rhazaulle. Not at all unlikely that the invaders would have moved at once to seize that vital artery.

She would know soon enough. She was about to descend the Bruzhois by way of the TransBruzh, provided the road remained open to civilian travelers. Thereafter the course curved northwest toward the Chieftainship of Ukizik, the next designated stop along the Grand Ellipse. Ukizik, a tiny independent tribal territory of northern aborigines occupying a section of Upper Rhazaulle's northwestern coastline, maintained a strict neutrality acknowledged by all civilized nations, even Grewzland. The requirements of the race included no Rhazaullean passport stamp—this omission representing Mad Miltzin's rare concession to the realities of war. The shortest route to Ukizik, however, cut straight through the combat zone.

The passengers climbed in, and Luzelle snuggled down under a couple of ratty but warm fur lap robes. The driver plied his whip, and the sleigh swung off smoothly over the snow. Luzelle twisted around in her seat to cast one last look back at the gorgeflier. She wanted another flight, she realized to her own surprise. Maybe someday the chance would come to do it again.

The Vezhevska Gorge receded into the distance. The sleigh slid on along a steeply pitched path too narrow to qualify as a road. Black-green conifers, their branches freighted with snow, loomed on both sides, walling the world from view. A little mist smudged the cold air, and the light filtered down from a softly somber sky.

They traveled the tree-lined passage throughout the rest of the day, and in the early evening reached the TransBruzh—a winding, ancient way, white with compressed snow that would not completely melt away until the end of summer. They traveled easily along the road for another three hours or more. Although the snow still lay everywhere, the days had already grown long in these northern latitudes. When the skies were beginning to darken at last, they paused for the night at a cone-shaped warmstop, one of the countless tiny emergency shelters scattered across the length and breadth of Rhazaulle. The warmstop, bare of all save firepit and fuel, offered neither comfort nor privacy, but it was free. The departing tenant's sole responsibility was replenishment of the woodpile, but that obligation was sacred.

They spent a cramped and smoky night sleeping on a floor of packed dirt covered with such few blankets, lap robes, and heavy garments as they had brought with them. Luzelle lay with her head pillowed on her leather valise. Despite all discomfort she slept soundly. Karsler and the driver chopped wood at dawn, and the journey resumed. The TransBruzh descended at a sharp grade, snaking its way down the northern slopes of the mountains into a region of gentler foothills. As the day advanced the sleigh hastened north, until it came in the late afternoon to the summit of a sharp rise overlooking a shallow valley blessed with a small jewel of a lake, and there it stopped abruptly.

Jolted from light slumber by the sudden halt, Luzelle opened her eyes and looked around her. A pale weak sun hung low in the western sky. The steepest peaks of the Bruzhois rose at her back. Around and before her rolled gentler forested hills. The frozen lake in the valley below was peppered with the symmetrical round holes cut by anglers, but nobody was out there fishing now. Beside the lake stood a village straight out of some old Rhazaullean fairy tale, complete with gabled roofs and fanciful wooden gingerbread. She would have liked to examine the village at closer range, but the opportunity to do so was unlikely to arise. The road down into the valley was blocked by a squad of Grewzian soldiers.

21

ONE OF THE SOLDIERS barked out something in authoritative Rhazaullean. The driver answered at conciliatory length. Before he completed his explanation, if such it was, Karsler calmly cut in to inquire in Grewzian, "What is the meaning of this, Lieutenant?"

Taking in the speaker's grey uniform and overcommander's insignia, the lieutenant stiffened to attention, saluted, and replied in a noticeably altered tone, "Orders, sir. These hills are full of Rhazaullean terrorists, and the villagers down there shelter them. We've orders to halt all traffic."

"I see. You will allow me to pass, however."

"Yes, Overcommander. Sir, if you go to join the General Froschl, you will find the Thirteenth Division presently camped southwest of—"

"I do not seek the Thirteenth," Karsler stated. "I travel north toward Ukizik. I trust our troops have suppressed local resistance between this point and the River Xana?"

"For the most part, sir. Forgive me, sir, I do not understand. Ukizik, did you say? The main body of the Rhazaullean force stands between ourselves and—" The lieutenant broke off as comprehension dawned. He stared. "You are the Overcommander Stornzof."

Karsler inclined his head.

"The great race takes you to Ukizik. I myself have wagered upon your victory," the lieutenant confided, enthusiasm overcoming iron military decorum. "Many of us here have so wagered, sir."

A subdued mutter of agreement arose among his followers. None of the soldiers ventured to speak aloud, but their faces shone with excitement.

They looked so young, Luzelle noted with surprise. Many of these Grewzian infantrymen could not have been above eighteen or nineteen years of age. Boys, really. And they looked so wholesome with their smooth well-scrubbed faces, their neatly trimmed fair hair, and their eyes alight with admiration for the famous Overcommander Stornzof. Exemplary sons, brothers, sweethearts of girls back in Grewzland. Hard to believe that they could be dangerous.

"Men, I will try to justify your confidence," Karsler promised. "You may help me to do so by clearing my path."

"We'll do all we can to assist you, Overcommander. An armed detachment will escort you to the Xana. You will make it to the far side of the valley before sundown." The lieutenant paused, then added with visible discomfort, "But the two civilians—the driver and the lady—I'm afraid we can't allow them to pass."

"I will vouch for them personally."

"No exceptions. Sorry, Overcommander. Orders, sir."

"I cannot deprive these two of transportation."

"No need, sir. Leave the sleigh. We've a few first-rate horses."

It was happening again, Luzelle realized. Once again Karsler Stornzof was receiving preferential treatment because of his nationality, and it was grossly unfair, but there wasn't a thing she could do other than try to counterfeit good sportsmanship. He was looking at her, concern and compunction clear in his eyes, and she could only shrug with spurious unconcern.

"Fortunes of war," she remarked lightly. "My turn for good luck, next time around."

"I should like to think so," he returned.

She did not doubt that he meant it. He was looking at her as if he wanted to say more, but she did not wish to prolong the scene, and so she told him with a smile, "On your way, then. Don't worry, I'll catch up with you sooner than you expect. And then, before you know what's hit you, I'll pull ahead."

"There is the spirit I admire." He did not return her smile. He hesitated briefly and then continued, "But I must ask you to listen to me now. You will not want to hear what I have to say, but I must speak."

"What is it?" she asked uneasily.

"This obstacle that confronts you now is like no other that you have yet encountered. It is not to be conquered or circumvented. My countrymen will permit no civilian traffic to pass along this road until such time as the region has been restored to order. Should you attempt to bypass the roadblock by way of the woods, and a patrol discovers you, you will be executed as a spy. I should not be there to intercede in your behalf, and nothing would save you. You are an intrepid, resourceful woman, but you cannot overcome the Grewzian army. The Grand Ellipse race means much to you, but it is not worth dying for."

"I've no intention of dying just yet."

"I am certain you do not intend it, but the danger is very real, and it is for that reason that I urge you at this time to consider the possibility of retreat."

"Retreat?"

"Your driver would willingly carry you back the way you came. I would suggest a return to Immeen, which is neutral, there to await the cessation of hostilities. Or if you will not wait, at least you might chart an alternative route that does not intersect our army's advance."

Luzelle sat silent for a thoughtful moment, and finally answered, "Karsler, if anyone but you offered such advice, I'd be angry and suspicious of his motives. But I know your concern is genuine, and I'm not so blind that I can't see the truth in what you say. I won't believe that it's the whole truth or the only truth, though. You said just now that the road will reopen when the region has been restored to order. How long will that take?"

"I am in no position to judge."

"Well—could it happen in the next twenty-four hours?"

"That is not entirely impossible. Nor is it impossible that it will not happen in the next twenty-four days."

"Oh, I can't let myself believe that. I'm going to wait here, for a while at least. Something will happen, something will change, it has to. Because I am going to get past your Grewzian army. I'll find a way. I am going on to Ukizik, and then Obran, and I am going to win the Grand Ellipse."

"Seeing and hearing you now, I could almost believe it. Yes—I can believe. Good luck, Luzelle. Be careful, and please consider my advice."

"I will consider it. Until next time, Karsler—and there *will* be a next time."

"Until then." Once again Karsler looked as if he wanted to say more. Instead he stepped out of the sleigh and addressed the lieutenant, switching back to the Grewzian language. "Have someone escort this lady to a safe location. And make it clear to the driver that he is not to abandon her."

"Yes, sir." The lieutenant loosed a harsh stream of patently menacing Rhazaullean.

Literally cringing, the driver nodded and muttered.

The lieutenant spoke again, and one of his men stepped forward. Men? A boy, this one, surely no more than eighteen, and looking years younger than that, with his peach-bloom skin and gilt curls.

"Just a little way back along the road, Madame. A few travelers like yourself elect to wait," the young soldier explained very courteously in careful Vonahrish. "I will lead the way, if you please."

The companion of the famous Overcommander Stornzof merited some respect, it seemed, or at least the appearance thereof. She looked back once to see Karsler already retreating, enveloped in a grey cloud of his admiring compatriots, and then she turned her eyes resolutely forward as her guide conducted her back the way she had come along the Trans-Bruzh for a few hundred yards to a break in the trees and a narrow offshoot cutting through the woods to a roughly circular clearing. Two sleighs and a heavy wagon stood there. No telling how long they had waited in that place. Long enough to build a big, smoky bonfire around which passengers and drivers huddled.

"Here, Madame," the soldier declared. "Here you are out of harm's way. But I cannot say how long before the road opens, and it will be cold here, very cold, come nightspill."

"Nightfall?"

"Yes. Pardon me, Madame, my Vonahrish is very poor."

"No, it's excellent."

"I thank you for your kind words. I offer you best wishes, together with this assurance. You may rely on the men of my squadron, there is nothing we would not do for a friend of the Overcommander Stornzof. If this driver of yours attempts to flee, let us know, and we shall bring him back to you. If anyone in this place troubles you, call on us. We are at Madame's service."

Grewzians at her service. What a thought. This boy and his comrades misconstrued her connection to Karsler, but their mistake only worked to her advantage. And the gallantry of the offer was practically Vonahrish.

"Thank you." She flashed her best smile. "I'll remember."

He departed, and she alighted from the sleigh to approach the fire. Four men sat there on logs, and her eyes went straight to the face of Girays v'Alisante, whose expression reflected chagrin. Understandably so—he must have thought that he had left her safely behind, and now she had caught up with him. Her sense of satisfaction was short lived. Next to Girays sat a squat, wide-faced frog of a fellow, probably his driver. And next to the driver, a shaggy, roughly garbed peasant farmer, presumably the owner of the wagon. But it was the fourth figure, big and muscular and black bearded, on whom she gazed with a shock of unpleasant recognition. Bav Tchornoi. She had not caught sight of him since Quinneke-vah Station. She had imagined and hoped that he had fallen somewhere by the wayside, and here he was, gigantic and morose-looking as ever.

And evidently here ahead of her. How in the world?

Four sets of eyes followed her as she seated herself upon a log. She felt her color rise. Her driver planted himself nearby, momentarily drawing collective attention, and then the eyes returned to Luzelle. The silence pressed, and at last she remarked civilly, "Girays, Master Tchornoi, I hope you are both well."

"Quite well," Girays returned with equal civility.

"Well—hah!" Bav Tchornoi exclaimed explosively. "And how shall we be well when these Grewzian piss lickers keep us cooling our heels in the snow until the crack of doom? Cooling our heels—that is funny, yes."

"How long have you been here?" asked Luzelle.

"Since yesterday afternoon," Girays told her. "Spent last night in a warmstop a couple of miles back along the road."

"I remember passing that."

"And I arrive this morning," Tchornoi proclaimed. "Only to find these Grewzians telling me where I can go, where I cannot go, in my own land. I am Rhazaullean, this is my place. That village down below beside the lake—that is Slekya, the village of my mother, where I have people. And these Grewzians puff out their little chests and wave their little guns, and tell me I cannot go there, the road is closed. Closed, by their order! I would like to get my hands on one or two of these fine blond boys, yes." Pulling a flask from his pocket, he pulled the stopper and downed an irritable draft.

"Yes, it would make me angry too," Luzelle told him truthfully.

"It would, eh? Maybe so. You have got some backbone, you have proved that. Here, you have some vouvrak." Tchornoi proffered his flask.

Evidently he had decided to forgive her for drawing a gun on him in the caves of the Nazara Sin. Fine, she had no desire to quarrel with anyone, and she would not reject an obvious peace offering. Luzelle accepted the flask. Eye-watering alcoholic fumes wafted from the interior, and she blinked. Taking a cautious swallow, she felt the liquid fire burn its way down her throat. The heat reached her stomach and spread out from there. Carefully she contained all coughs and sputters.

"Good, eh?" Tchornoi nodded almost affably.

She bobbed her head.

"You have some more, then. Go on, you help yourself."

In the interests of amity she forced down another mouthful, and handed the flask back to its owner, who thereafter lapsed into thirsty silence. Minutes later, when he had drained the contents, Tchornoi surged to his feet, stalked across the clearing to his sleigh, rummaged therein for a fresh bottle, and returned to his place by the fire.

Time passed slowly. Conversation was sporadic. Eventually the anonymous farmer glanced up at the weak sun, now hovering just above the treetops, shook his head glumly, rose, and went to his wagon. Climbing in, he shook the reins and departed the clearing without a word.

Observing this, Girays's driver spoke up in Rhazaullean.

"I do not understand you," said Girays.

"He says he goes now," Bav Tchornoi translated, emerging from an apparent stupor for the first time in an hour or more.

"He can't go, I've need of his services," declared M. the Marquis. He pulled out his wallet.

Typical, thought Luzelle.

Tchornoi shrugged his big shoulders.

"How much to stay?" Girays v'Alisante's dexterous manipulation of paper currency transcended all language barriers.

The driver mumbled.

"He says he does not spend another night in this place for any amount of money. He says he goes home now," Tchornoi reported.

"Then tell him I'll buy his sleigh and horses."

Tchornoi translated and the driver shook his head.

"Tell him I'll pay—" Girays named an improbable figure.

"Hah! You are crazy, Vonahrishman. This is like a comedy."

Bav Tchornoi relayed the message, and the driver's eyes rounded. He nodded. Presently he departed on foot, clutching a wad of cash.

Luzelle's driver observed the retreat wistfully. He leaned his chin on his hand. He said nothing.

Retrieving books from their respective vehicles, Luzelle and Girays sat reading in silence. The driver watched the fire and sang to himself, while Bav Tchornoi drank.

When the atmosphere began to dim, Luzelle looked up

from her book to inquire hopefully, "Anyone want to go ask the soldiers if we can get through yet?"

Nobody troubled to reply, and she began to wonder seriously, for the first time, if Karsler had not been right. Perhaps she needed to plot an alternative route north. And if so, she should do it quickly, before all hope of victory froze to death in icebound Rhazaulle.

The small pangs of hunger recalled the passage of time. The sleigh carried some provisions, assorted foodstuffs that required no cooking. Luzelle fetched bread, cheese, potted meat, pickled onions, and shelled almonds for herself and the driver. Girays went to his own vehicle and brought similar supplies back to the fire. Bav Tchornoi did not bother with food.

They ate in reasonably companionable silence as the sun went down. The air darkened, a new chill descended upon the clearing, and Luzelle's driver threw a couple of logs on the fire. Sparks flew, the flames jumped, and the long shadows stretching out behind them writhed. Luzelle returned to her reading, but looked up in surprise when Bav Tchornoi spoke, his voice slow and slurred.

"These Grewzian cockroaches think their campaign is all but won. They think we Rhazaulleans are all finished, beaten, ready to take it up the ass. Hah. They are fools," opined Tchornoi. "They know nothing. They forget our great resources."

"You mean the Rhazaullean climate?" asked Girays.

"Yes, that is one. Spring has come, the weather is warm and mild. Pleasant, yes?"

No, thought Luzelle. Snow lay everywhere, and the evening breezes knifed through her parka.

"Very nice, very comfortable, but what do you suppose happens next?" Tchornoi demanded. "The sun shines, the ice melts. The little blond boys trundle their guns north along the frozen River Xana, and one sweet, bright afternoon— *crack!* The ice gives way beneath their feet, and then *splash!* The big guns, the caissons, the wagons and horses, and all the little golden lads—down they go into the water. They do not last long there, I think. Or let us say they are not quite that stupid, and they stay off the ice. Then what? They march north toward Rialsq, and the ground softens beneath them as they go, and soon they sink in mud that sucks like quicksand. And as they wallow there, along come our men on *grushtyevniks*—that is, what you would call mudskidders— and where are the Grewzians then?"

"I think there may be some truth to that," Girays conceded, interested.

"You think, eh? Well, there is more." Tchornoi gulped vouvrak and continued, "My country is a stern land. Many within our borders have died by violence, and the site of such death is often haunted by the ghosts of the slain. Our necromancers rule these ghosts, use them against the enemies of Rhazaulle. How do the Grewzians fight a gathering of ghosts? Hah? Shoot guns at them?"

"I don't quite understand you." Girays spoke with an air of polite forbearance.

"I've read about it," Luzelle volunteered. "Rhazaulle has a tradition of necromancy dating back hundreds of years. It was said that the sorcerous masters wielded absolute power over the ghosts they summoned. But the drugs and poisons used in the rituals induced violent insanity, so the practice was outlawed centuries ago. I daresay it secretly survives to this day, though."

"The woman knows more than you do, v'Alisante," Tchornoi chaffed. "She has got it right."

"So necromancy is still secretly practiced in Rhazaulle." Girays shrugged. "What of it? You think some magical gibberish muttered at the dark of the moon will impede the Grewzian advance? You think the ghosts will start popping up like flowers in springtime?"

"I think you do not know much of Rhazaulle," Tchornoi returned. "I think you do not know that that village of Slekya down there is a place of power, center of many forces. My mother grows up in this place, she often tells me. There are secret things there. These Grewzians do not know what they deal with in Slekya."

"Possibly not," Girays conceded wearily.

"Nor do they know what they deal with in *me*." Tchornoi

drained the last of the latest bottle. "I am Bav Tchornoi, and it is not for the likes of the Grewzians to tell me where I go, where I do not go. No. Tonight it pleases me to visit the village of my mother and drink in the tavern there. Let no man hinder me." So saying, he drew a revolver from his pocket and laid it across his knees.

Luzelle and Girays traded consternated glances. Out of the corner of her eye she noted the similarly alarmed expression of the driver.

"Hah, your faces. So shocked, so scared." Tchornoi chuckled. Meeting Luzelle's eyes, he inquired jovially, "You think you are the only one to carry a gun? You are good teacher, little woman. I pick up revolver in Bizaqh for a song. Now I use it on anyone blocking my way."

Drunk, stinking drunk and belligerent, thought Luzelle. *The miserable fool will get himself killed, and the rest of us along with him.* Aloud she appealed gently, "Master Tchornoi, you won't defy an entire squadron of Grewzian soldiers, will you? You're very courageous, but you've no hope of defeating so many."

"You are right. There are too many blond cockroaches on the road; I cannot squash them all. No, I will cut through the woods on foot."

"Don't try it," Girays advised. "The woods are full of patrols. You can't get through."

"Patrols? You think I fear patrols? Listen, I know these woods. Often I am here as a boy—I learn to play Ice Kings on that lake down below. I have not forgotten the paths. The offal chompers, they know nothing. I flip them the Feyennese Four as I go by, they do not see."

The driver pointed at the gun and loosed a brief spate of frightened Rhazaullean. Nobody heeded him.

"Please don't do it, Bav Tchornoi," Luzelle frankly begged. "At least, not tonight. Visit Slekya some other time, when it's safer. Tomorrow, perhaps. There's no sense in risking your life over nothing."

"I do not risk my life over nothing. If I risk my life, it is over something big—my right to come and go as I please in my own land. Who will deny me?" He rose to his full height, casting an immense shadow across the snow.

Despite the quarts of vouvrak and the slurred speech, Luzelle suspected that it was not alcohol alone talking. She had no answer.

Girays did. "Forget yourself and your precious rights for now," he snapped. "You're putting the rest of us at risk. You can't do it."

"Can't? You say so?" The revolver leveled itself at Girays's chest. "You think you stop me? Hah, don't worry, you and the woman are safe. Nobody sees me, I slide right on by under their Grewzian noses."

"Put that gun away, you'll get us all killed." Girays drew a deep breath. "Listen, Tchornoi, stop and think. If you'll just wait—"

"I have waited long enough. I have waited all through the day, and now I wait no longer. Now I go to Slekya. Out of my way." So saying, Bav Tchornoi lurched from the circle of firelight into the shadow of the trees. The darkness swallowed him.

They gazed after him. No one attempted pursuit.

"Think he'll make it?" asked Luzelle.

"In his present state, I'd say he hasn't a chance," Girays told her. "He'll probably be nailed within minutes, and I don't want the Grewzians thinking we're in league with that idiot. We'd best get out of here."

"Warmstop?"

"Yes."

She communicated her intentions to the driver by means of pantomime. He nodded, lit the sleigh lanterns, and resumed his seat. She climbed in behind him and they set off, closely followed by Girays's vehicle. The white road and black trees streamed by. Presently the crackle of not-so-distant gunfire broke the silence of the night. Luzelle stiffened at the sound, and her gloved fists clenched beneath the lap robe. She listened and heard it again—two isolated pops, followed by the quick rataplan of a barrage. Her breath quickened, steaming on the cold air.

"Faster," she whispered. "Faster."

In the unlikely event that he heard her, the driver would not have understood her language, yet he clearly shared her sentiments, for he snapped his whip and the horses broke into a trot.

The conical warmstop rose before them. The two sleighs arrived almost simultaneously. While the men tended the horses, Luzelle carried lap robes and fur throws into the little shelter, dumped her burden on the floor, and kindled the fire. By the time Girays and the driver came in, the smoke was rising through the hole in the roof and the interior was starting to warm.

Girays dropped the heavy bar across the door; no protection against Grewzian soldiery, but it made Luzelle feel safer all the same. For a time they sat mutely around the fire, the three of them listening for the sound of gunfire—footsteps—voices—fists pounding the door—anything. Silence reigned.

The air grew heavy with warmth and smoke. Girays banked the fire and the three composed themselves for slumber. For a while Luzelle lay wide awake, the musty smell of the old fur robe in her nostrils, ears and mind straining for the sounds that never came, but finally her lids drooped and the world slid away.

SHE WOKE AT DAWN. The atmosphere of the warmstop was cold but still smoky. Girays lay deeply sleeping. The driver was absent. He had probably stepped outside to relieve himself. His nest of robes and rugs was gone; he must already have returned them to the sleigh. Very efficient. She would give him a nice little bonus when they parted company, the poor fellow deserved it.

Luzelle yawned, rubbed the sleep from her eyes, and stepped to the door, unbarred as the driver had left it. She listened, heard nothing sinister, and opened the door to look out at the empty patch of trampled snow where her sleigh had stopped last night. Girays's sleigh stood a few feet from the shelter, and his horse was tethered to a nearby tree. Her own vehicle, horse, and driver were gone. Her valise sat beside the door. Her driver, a sneak and a coward, at least was no thief.

For a moment she gazed about almost without comprehension. Then reality sank in, dismay flooded her mind, and anger erupted. He had simply abandoned her to starve or freeze in the middle of nowhere. The slimy little Rhazaullean poltroon wasn't going to get away with it. Those friendly Grewzian soldiers had promised to retrieve her driver in the event of desertion, and she now intended to accept that offer. She would have to walk two miles or so along the snowy TransBruzh, carrying her valise, or—

Her eyes jumped to Girays's sleigh, and then to the tethered horse. She could probably manage to harness the animal, it couldn't be that complicated, and she could certainly manage the short drive. She could be gone before Girays awoke to stop her, she could hurry to the Grewzians, sic them on her fugitive driver, then return the sleigh to its owner, with no harm done. Or—the darkly brilliant thought was suddenly whole—she might expedite matters by simply neglecting to return Girays's sleigh. By stealing it. Perhaps by now the TransBruzh was open, and she could drive on toward Rialsq, or if necessary acquire a new driver somewhere along the way. And it wasn't as if Girays would be endangered. The warmstop stood within a few miles of Slekya, where he would find shelter, food, and alternative transportation. He wouldn't be harmed, merely inconvenienced. And she would gain a potentially vital lead.

Not for the first time since the race began, the workings of her own intellect disturbed her. Steal from Girays? Cheat Girays? An extraordinarily ugly notion. Where had it sprung from?

From necessity. The demands of the race. Moreover— should she fail to grab the one sleigh now, while she had the chance, Girays would shortly awake, and then *she* might be the one left behind. Perhaps he would be generous and let her ride with him, perhaps not. He certainly had every right to leave her. They were in a race, and the sleigh belonged to him. And then? The Grewzian soldiers might fail to recapture her own driver, or they might be too busy to bother, gallant assurances notwithstanding. At the very least she was likely to fall behind, far behind, unless she seized opportunity now.

She would do what was necessary.

But steal—from Girays? She turned and looked at him.

His hair was growing shaggy again. He looked younger asleep, his face relaxed, bronzed by the sun of Mekzaes and the Tribal Territories. He looked peaceful and totally unsuspecting. Guilt froze her, exigency pushed, and even as she stood vacillating, Girays opened his eyes and sat up. Frustration, anger at her own irresolution, and deep relief mingled confusedly within her.

He took one look at her and said, "Something's happened. Tchornoi turn up?"

"No. My driver has made off with the sleigh."

"Did he? Did he really do that to you? Astonishing that the villain would dare." Girays shook his head. "But what a misfortune."

He was laughing at her, and she wanted to throw something at him. She should have taken the sleigh when she had the chance. She should have left him here to rot, and serve him right. She had blundered badly.

"And what will you do now?" he inquired kindly. "Any plans?"

"Yes, as a matter of fact," she replied with an air of confidence that she hoped would disappoint him. "I'll ask the help of those Grewzian soldiers down the road."

"The Grewzian soldiers. They'll be eager to assist you, they are philanthropy personified."

"They *are* eager to assist me, as it happens." She smiled guilelessly. "There's nothing they won't do, they assured me, for a friend of the Overcommander Stornzof."

"Stornzof. I see."

"Yes, we'd been traveling together," she confided, noting with grim satisfaction that his amusement had evaporated. "But when we reached the roadblock, he passed through while I could not, and the soldiers urged me to call on them for help, should I need it. Well, it seems that I need it now."

"I see," Girays repeated. He considered. "You'd really do it, wouldn't you?"

"Ask the Grewzians for help, you mean? They offered, and I haven't much choice. I can't walk to Ukizik."

"The theatrics are unnecessary. You know that I won't leave

you stranded here, and you also know that I wouldn't care to see you trade for advantage upon some fictional status as the 'little friend' of a Grewzian officer."

"Oh, is that what they'd think I am?" she murmured, gently amazed, and before he could reply, inquired, "You're offering me a ride in your sleigh, then?"

"At least until we're clear of the Grewzian army."

"I accept," she replied, adding with real feeling, "Thank you, Girays. You're kinder than I deserve."

"Someday, when you least expect it, I'll remind you that you said so."

"Think the road's open yet?"

"That's the first thing we'll check," he told her. "If it's still closed, we'll have to choose. Stay or go? Wait around another day, or retreat and rethink our route?"

"I can't stand any more waiting. Karsler's pulling farther ahead every minute. And Tchornoi too, for all I know."

"Tchornoi's probably passed out cold on the floor of that tavern down in Slekya."

"I hope so. More for his sake than for ours, I sincerely hope so."

They prepared for departure as quickly as possible, eating a hurried cold breakfast, then stuffing their belongings any which way into the sleigh. While Girays harnessed the horse, Luzelle took up a hatchet and set about replenishing the woodpile. Expecting argument, she was pleasantly surprised by Girays's complaisance. He voiced no objection, but simply let her finish the task in peace.

The morning skies were dull with leaden clouds, the sun hidden, and the grey world all but devoid of shadows when they set off in Girays's sleigh, retracing yesterday's route. Luzelle's nose tickled, and she caught the tang of smoke on the breeze. The scent strengthened as the vehicle advanced. Long before they reached the site of the roadblock, a detachment of some half-dozen Grewzian soldiers burst from the woods to bar the way.

"*Halt.*" The language was Grewzian, but the command would have been clear in any tongue. Girays pulled up at once.

Where were the civilized faces of yesterday? Half a dozen service rifles were aimed at Girays's chest. Luzelle stared incredulously, almost too surprised for fear.

"Identification." The detachment leader, a sergeant possessed of angry eyes, looked ready and willing to kill.

"Vonahrish travelers." Girays produced his passport.

Luzelle did likewise.

The sergeant checked both documents and handed them back. "No traffic. Clear the road," he said.

"We will go back the way we came," Girays offered.

"Not permitted. Clear the road," the sergeant repeated. "Pull over to the side."

"Please, sir," Luzelle softly braved the angry eyes. "Tell us what happens here, if you please."

He weighed the request, then measured his answer by the syllable. "Rhazaullean terrorist caught wandering the woods last night. Exchange of fire, two soldiers of the Imperium killed. Rhazaullean probably wounded, but he escaped to find refuge in the village down below."

Tchornoi, thought Luzelle. *That brave drunken imbecile.* She lowered her eyes to disguise all knowledge. Girays's face, visible to her in profile, was perfectly still.

"Until this situation has been resolved, the road is closed in both directions. Pull over and stay out of the way, or you will be regarded as enemy partisans and dealt with accordingly." The sergeant turned away, terminating the exchange.

Girays obeyed. At the side of the TransBruzh he climbed out of the sleigh and led the horse through a gap in the trees, across a gloomy shaded expanse to the brink of a sharp drop, almost a precipice, overlooking the valley and the lake. Smoke strangled the breeze, and from this vantage point it was easy to see why. The village of Slekya was burning.

The picture-pretty dwellings spouted flame. Fire sheathed the walls and gabled roofs, wrapped quaint turrets and cupolas, shot from windows and open doorways. Every building in town blazed, and several blackened wrecks had already collapsed. Through the dense clouds of dark smoke blanketing the main street scurrying human figures were intermittently visible, and screaming human voices intermittently audible.

Orderly detachments of grey-uniformed figures roamed everywhere, overturning wagons and carts, plying torches, clubbing civilians. One such detachment, comprising some dozen members, could be glimpsed methodically ripping the clothing off a couple of panic-stricken local women.

Luzelle turned her face aside. "Take me away from here," she requested tonelessly.

"Can't," Girays told her. "Don't look."

But she could not follow his advice, could not forbear watching as the Grewzians marched a large group of male civilians straight up the main street to the edge of the lake, where they halted. The captives, ranging in age from prepubescent boy to white-haired gaffer, were neatly lined up along the bank. One of them—black bearded, right arm bound in a white sling, towering half a head over the tallest of his compatriots—was unmistakable even at a distance.

An order was issued, the grey soldiers opened fire, and Rhazaulleans fell by the score. Several attempting to flee across the frozen lake were dropped in their tracks by sharpshooters, and their blood spread dark stains across the pale ice. The black-haired giant gave a yell and rushed at the Grewzians, whose bullets cut him down in an instant. There was a brief lull as the soldiers paused to reload, then rifle fire resumed and continued until no Rhazaullean remained upright.

A tangle of bloodied bodies littered the bank. Several victims stirred and moaned yet. New commands were issued and the soldiers moved in to finish their work with bayonets. The steel blades worked for a few minutes more, and then their activity ceased. The villagers lay still and the soldiers marched away.

Luzelle turned to Girays. She looked at him and saw that she did not need to say anything. He understood her thoughts and feelings just as she grasped his, despite all differences, because they were made of the same stuff. It was like a rush of clean air to smoke-filled lungs, this mutual unspoken comprehension; it was strength and life. Tears blurred her eyes.

He opened his arms, and she went into them.

· · ·

THE HILLS NORTH OF SLEKYA were free of smoke. From his vantage point atop an icy bluff Karsler Stornzof commanded a clear view of the massacre. He stood there alone, having declined his countrymen's offer of an escort. For the first time since the race began he was attired in civilian garments, for he now ventured on his own deep into enemy territory, where the sight of a Grewzian uniform would incite attack. The Rhazaulleans would rend him limb from limb if they knew what he was; in light of what he witnessed by dawn's light, he could hardly blame them.

Karsler stood motionless as the village burned, as the soldiers herded their victims to the lakeside, and the slaughter commenced. Instinct bade him intervene; intellect recognized the futility of the impulse. By the time he made it down the hills and across the valley to Slekya, the Grewzian force would have finished its work. In any event the men down below were not subject to his direct command, and he had not the authority to countermand the orders of their own officers.

There was nothing he could do, and he knew it, but did not believe it. There was nothing in all his Promontory training to arm him against the necessity of witnessing atrocity and simply turning his back on it. His awareness of events down in Slekya imposed moral obligation incompatible with his duty as a soldier and a Stornzof, and no remotely satisfactory solution to the dilemma existed.

The sensation of powerlessness was unfamiliar and abhorrent. As he watched the mass execution taking place below, shame and disgust that was almost a sickness filled him, but he did not avert his eyes before the last of the victims fell. Then he remounted his horse and rode away.

A COUPLE OF SHOTS RANG OUT and Luzelle started, still unused to the sound, although she had heard it repeatedly throughout the day. Then came the thud of running feet, the crash of another volley, the shouting of Grewzian voices— likewise grown familiar, for the soldiers had been hunting

Rhazaullean fugitives through the woods for hours, and the hills above Slekya were strewn with bullet-riddled bodies.

"Haven't they had enough yet?" Luzelle hardly knew that she spoke aloud.

"They'll have to give over soon, evening's drawing on," Girays told her.

"It's been that long?" Faintly surprised, she glanced up at the sky, grey all day long and now darkening to charcoal. "Think they'll let us go back to the warmstop?"

"Road's still closed."

"We'll be cold tonight."

"Others will be colder."

"I wish we'd gone back to Immeen when we had the chance."

"Perhaps we'll be able to go forward tomorrow."

"Tomorrow seems a long way off."

"It will come soon enough if you sleep."

"I won't be able to sleep tonight. Will you?"

He shrugged. "Hungry?"

"No. Just cold."

"We need more firewood. I'll get some." He stood up.

"Wait, you can't go wandering off into the woods on your own, some Grewzian's likely to blow your head off without stopping to check passports. Maybe we'd better let the fire go out. It calls attention to us."

"Exactly right. We inform the world that we do not try to conceal ourselves. I'm going to collect enough wood to last through the night."

"Then I'm coming with you."

Before she had risen from the log on which she sat, a brace of Grewzian soldiers broke from the trees, rifles leveled. Luzelle hardly flinched, for this scene had repeated itself no fewer than five times within the space of hours. Once again explanations were offered and passports submitted for inspection. Once again the soldiers warned them that the road remained closed, but left them in peace.

The Grewzians departed and their voices receded. Luzelle and Girays gathered armfuls of wood, replenished the fire, and resumed their seats beside it. Night fell and silence descended.

There were no more shots or shouts. Illusory peace reigned. Presently a full moon rose to cast a feeble glow down through the clouds.

Girays fetched a blanket from the sleigh, and together they huddled beneath it close beside the fire. Luzelle leaned her head against his shoulder. He put his arm around her, and they sat in silence. For a while she watched the jumping flames, but soon her eyes began to blur and she let her lids fall. She could not have been physically tired, not after an entire day spent sitting in the woods. But perhaps her mind was more fatigued than she knew, for she drifted off to sleep immediately.

She must have slept for hours, for when she next opened her eyes, the weak excuse for a full moon had switched to the other side of the sky. The fire had gone out; so much for all good intentions of maintaining the blaze through the night. The air was cold, but she felt no discomfort, for Girays's proximity warded off the chill. Girays himself was wide awake, his shoulder tense beneath her temple. Perhaps it was his tension that woke her, or maybe it was the rhythm of human voices uplifted not far away.

Luzelle looked down, half expecting to see and feel the ground quake beneath her. The ground stayed put and she realized that she had momentarily fancied herself back in Xoxo. It was the sound of the nearby chanting that had confused her. A foolish error, for the voices of then and now were not alike; they differed greatly in pitch and tempo, language, style, and every other identifiable quality. Yet there was a similarity, some indefinable intimation of power and mystery linking these anonymous voices of the Rhazaullean night with the jungle shamans of Oorex.

She looked at Girays, but the moon hung low behind him, and all she could see was his dark outline.

"What is it?" she asked, instinctively lowering her voice to a whisper.

He shook his head. For another few moments they sat listening, and then by tacit consent rose to follow the sound.

The source was neither far off nor difficult to locate. Luzelle gripped Girays's arm. For a little while they groped their way through the shadows, the voices intensifying as they advanced.

A flicker of firelight beckoned through the trees. They stole toward the light and seconds later reached a small open space perched at the edge of a steep bluff overlooking the lake, the smoldering town, and the Grewzian camp. There a circle of motionless figures surrounded a jumping fire. Locals, no doubt fleeing the massacre. Now that darkness had fallen, their chances of escape were good.

They could not have been much concerned with concealment though, else they would never have dared to kindle that fire. But then they hardly appeared concerned with much of anything; in fact, they seemed unaware.

Luzelle studied the upright figures. Nine of them, male and female, young and old, handsomely garbed and ragged, robust and emaciated, disparate in every way, yet identical in their remote stillness, their brilliantly blind eyes. Their clasped hands linked the circle physically, but the true connection was clearly psychic, it showed in every synchronized twitch and blink.

A gathering of lunatics? Probably harmless, but sudden fear stirred along her veins.

The voices swelled—moaning manic gibberish somehow resolving itself to an alien music; plaintive, insistent, hovering upon the verge of intelligibility. The music continued for minutes—hours—years—centuries. And when it seemed that she could all but understand the words—when she sensed the imminence of vast revelation—the sound broke off. The fire leapt and dense torrents of smoke gushed.

Silent and motionless now, the nine stood staring into the flames. Their arms remained linked, their circle unbroken. Their faces were death masks. She might have imagined that consciousness had lapsed but for the sense of collective mental activity—distinct and almost tangible—all but sizzling the air.

A center of many forces, Bav Tchornoi had called this place, and he had been right; she could feel the forces at work all around her. The hairs stirred at the back of her neck, and her grip on Girays's arm tightened. The air was coldly suffocating; the smoke was everywhere, dense strangling clouds of

it, far more smoke than a small blaze ought to produce. She
coughed, unable to control the reflex, but it did not matter,
the nine heard nothing. Her eyes were stinging and swimming, her vision playing her false, for now it seemed that the
smoke was filled with human forms, scores of them floating
weightlessly about the fire.

She blinked and rubbed her streaming eyes, expecting to
banish the vision, but the figures sharpened. She could see
them quite clearly now, despite their pallid transparency; they
were distinct down to the smallest detail of feature, form, and
costume. Ordinary-looking people, for the most part. Men,
women, and children with typical Rhazaullean faces and the
serviceable garments of ordinary villagers. The woods were
presently littered with the fresh corpses of just such unremarkable folk.

She had never believed in ghosts. She did not like to start
now, but the evidence hovering before her eyes left little room
for doubt. "Many within our borders have died by violence,
and the site of such death is often haunted by the ghosts of
the slain," Bav Tchornoi had claimed, and she had privately
dismissed him as a superstitious inebriate, but he had been
right. "Our necromancers rule these ghosts, use them against
the enemies of Rhazaulle," he had also insisted, and now she
wondered if he could have been right about that too.

The ghosts evidently shared her bewilderment. Their dead
faces—far more expressive than the tranced live faces of their
summoners—reflected shock, fear, and confusion. Many
gazed about with an air of wondering incredulity, and several
appeared to be speaking, but nothing audible emerged. Two
or three, bent on escape, rushed about the clearing tugging
frantically against unbreakable psychic restraints.

She felt distinctly sorry for them. She was scared to the
marrow, but at the same time found these insubstantial remnants with their staring transparent eyes and their obvious
distress infinitely pitiable.

The night was silent. The ghosts were voiceless, the necromancers seemingly spellbound, but mute communication
must have occurred, for the entire spectral congregation rose
silent as fog to drift off the edge of the bluff into space above

the ruins of Slekya. For a moment they hovered, and then they began to move.

The weightless forms seemed to flow through the air without haste, yet they reached the Grewzian camp within a couple of minutes. A faint cold glow overspread the encampment, and the warning calls of three or four sentries rang through the night, followed by the shrill whinnying of frightened horses. Almost instantly the half-clad Grewzian soldiers erupted from their tents, rifles in hand, to confront the ghosts of their recent victims. A confused shouting arose, then the shouts sharpened to screams as radiant knots tightened about selected grey figures that swiftly fell. Gunfire popped uselessly, and the vocal volume mounted as showers of embers sprayed from scores of banked fires to pelt the walls and roofs of the Grewzian tents.

Flame tongued canvas, leapt for the skies, and sprang from roof to roof. Within seconds the tents were blazing, as the village of Slekya had blazed hours earlier. Fresh screams arose as two or three soldiers, their bodies wrapped in flame, burst from their tents to stagger to and fro at measureless length before collapsing into the snow. Ghostly hands bore blazing debris aloft, and gouts of fire rained down on Grewzian heads. A panicked contingent fled for the shelter of the woods, and the specters followed, hurling destruction. Hair and clothing ignited, black puppets danced in their orange robes. The aroma of grilling meat wafted on the breeze.

A synchronized volley scarcely fluttered the floating ranks. The bullets passed through harmlessly, the fire rained down, and the famed Grewzian discipline broke. The last of the camp's defenders turned tail and fled for the woods. The luminous horde pursued.

Luzelle felt a firm pressure on her arm. She turned her head to face the shadowy bulk that presently was Girays.

"Now," he whispered.

She needed no explanation. The Grewzians were in disarray, their threat temporarily nullified. The TransBruzh was unguarded, the way north relatively clear. Their chance had come, perhaps their only chance.

She cast a final glance at the nine necromancers, petrified

in the jumping light. Would the vengeful ghosts loosed by these people differentiate between Grewzian soldiers and Vonahrish civilians? The marble faces disclosed nothing.

She took Girays's hand, and the two of them groped their way back through the deep shadows to the sleigh and the tethered horse. While he harnessed the animal, she gathered up the few belongings still lying beside the ashes of the day's fire and loaded them aboard. As she worked, her eyes darted, but encountered no airborne wraiths.

It was done. Luzelle climbed into the sleigh. Girays led the horse back to the road, and took his seat. Distant voices and gunfire echoed through the woods, but the TransBruzh stretched clear before them, empty in the weak moonlight.

Not quite empty. A silent, transparent but well-delineated figure hovered above the road. A child it was, a boy of six or seven years, with plump cheeks and thick hair cut in the shape of a bowl. Torn between fear and pity, Luzelle stared into the young dead eyes and beheld terror vastly exceeding her own.

The juvenile ghost drifted from the roadway. Girays, momentarily frozen, recovered himself and shook the reins. The sleigh moved off, heading north.

22

THE SUMMER SUN BEAT DOWN on the city of Sherreen. The air was too warm for comfort, and windows all over the Republican Complex stood wide open in invitation to nonexistent breezes. One such open window, belonging to an office on the third floor of the Ministry of Foreign Affairs, framed a skinny, narrow-shouldered, pasty-faced figure. Deputy Underminister vo Rouvignac stood there looking southeast out over the capital city, eyes blind to the vista of tree-lined boulevards, mental gaze pushing southeast into the distance, all the way to the Haereste border to assess the Grewzian troops assembled there. Numerous, of course. Famously disciplined. Amply equipped. And only awaiting the command to cross the border into inadequately defended Voñahr, a command unlikely to be withheld for more than a matter of days, at best.

Haereste, after all, was part of the Imperium now. And the population of Vonahr's quiet Eulence Province comprised a significant percentage of citizens linked by blood, local dialect, and custom to Haereste, of which Eulence had been a part not more than three hundred years earlier. It was a truth indisputable that all reasonable Haeresteans on both sides of the border desired the reunification of their sundered land, and therefore the government of Vonahr was most earnestly enjoined at this time to cede the province of Eulence back to its true and rightful owners without delay. Such was the tenor of the official correspondence, stamped with the seal of the Haerestean Parliament and ornamented with the Endless Fire of the Imperium, recently addressed to the president and Congress of Vonahr. The letter did not explicitly state, but the implication was clear, that failure to comply with the demand would result in a war wherein the Haeresteans would certainly enjoy the support of their Grewzian brothers of the Imperium.

The letter likewise failed to state the obvious fact that compliance would shortly result in new and even more outrageous demands.

The Vonahrish government required some time to consider the matter; so the official reply ran. Perhaps this stance would buy a few weeks, but in the end Vonahr would inevitably cede Eulence to Haereste; and even that concession would only temporarily stave off invasion. Those seasoned Grewzian troops would stab straight through the heart of Vonahr, probably reaching Sherreen in a matter of days. And afterward? There would be no more Vonahr, that national entity would cease to exist in fact if not in name. The Endless Fire would burn on, expanding until its circle encompassed all the world. There was no possibility of effective self-defense, no real prospect of assistance, no hope beyond the puniest and unlikeliest.

Turning abruptly away from the window, vo Rouvignac returned to his desk, sat down, and addressed the omnipresent mountain of paperwork, or tried to. His mind wandered, however, and presently reaching for a certain leather-covered binder, he opened to the last page, checked the date on the latest entry, and nodded. His secretary was keeping the scrapbook properly current. This collection of articles clipped from newspapers and gazettes published all over the world, with Vonahrish translations furnished as required, traced the progress of the various Grand Ellipse contestants from the beginning of the race to within days of the present.

The account was far from complete, of course. Some of the racers seemed to drop out of the public eye for weeks at a time, their actions and whereabouts during such intervals a mystery. A few disappeared altogether. The two young Travornish contenders Trefian and Stesian Festinette had been spotted in Bizaqh weeks earlier—a dispatch relayed west to Aennorve's *Lake Eev Circular* confirmed the sighting—and after that they had seemingly vanished from the world. And the Rhazaullean Ice Kings champion, Bav Tchornoi, last seen in the Dhrevate of Immeen, had likewise sunk out of sight, his fate unknown.

The ultimate disposition of several other racers, however, was only too certain. Szett Urrazole, victim of a bombing in Lanthi Ume. Porb Jil Liskjil, killed in the Forests of Oorex. Mesq'r Zavune, eliminated from the competition in Aveshq. At least Zavune had survived.

Over the course of the weeks the field had gradually narrowed until only a handful of the original contenders remained. And now, as the race finally neared its conclusion, only three of those remaining few appeared to entertain any real hope of victory.

Two of those three were Vonahrish. Both shared connections to the Ministry of Foreign Affairs.

Vo Rouvignac leafed quickly through the binder. The oldest entries, chronicling the earlier phases of the Grand Ellipse, he skipped over, for he had read them many times and knew them almost by heart. Further into the collection he paused here and there to read briefly, but did not settle deeply into any particular article until he reached the most recent clippings, presenting the latest news of the three front runners. One translation from the Obranese of the *Tuybuv Bvuskit,* or *Midnight Sun,* caught his eye and he read:

It is reported that the Obranese merchant vessel *Walrus,* en route from Ukizik to Port Hjalmos, suffered heavy damages during a storm upon the Sea of Ice. Property of the Yeevo Trading Group, the *Walrus* carried a cargo of oil, ivory, bone, and pelts, most of which was jettisoned. The mishap delayed the ship's arrival in Hjalmos by some thirty-six hours, during which time it was widely feared that the vessel and all aboard had been lost. No fatalities among the crew have been reported, however.

The *Walrus* carried one passenger, a Grewzian national, the Overcommander Karsler Stornzof, currently furloughed from the Unified Army of the Imperium. A contender in the Grand Ellipse race, the Overcommander Stornzof has in recent weeks generally been regarded as probable victor. The *Walrus*'s misfortune, however, has cost the Grewzian competitor his favored status, and several independent bookmakers verify that the odds have altered accordingly. No statement from the Overcommander Stornzof is available at this time.

Vo Rouvignac leafed on through the binder. Mishap at sea notwithstanding, it was clear that the Grewzian continued to hold his own. Clipping after clipping reported sightings of all three front runners. In Obran. In Szar. In Lyuvbrow, where Girays v'Alisante had assumed a small lead for all of twenty-four hours. Then, all three spotted simultaneously in the train station at Hekkin.

Vo Rouvignac turned to the last item in the binder, an article clipped from the latest *Hetzian Gazette*.

GRAND ELLIPSE APPROACHES CONCLUSION

The Grand Ellipse competition, long the object of international attention, is finally drawing to its close. At least three of the racers have now crossed the border into Upper Hetzia, penultimate stage of their journey. Eyewitness reports confirm the arrival of the famous Grewzian war hero, the Overcommander Karsler Stornzof, whose appearance at the Bünckel railroad station was greeted with great popular enthusiasm. The Overcommander Stornzof was trailed by two competitors, G. v'Alisante and L. Devaire, both Vonahrish.

The presence of so valiant a soldier has caught the national imagination, and everywhere he travels, the Overcommander Stornzof encounters cheering throngs eager to honor the visiting Grewzian hero. . . .

Vo Rouvignac did not trouble to finish reading the account of the cheering throngs. He frowned, troubled as always by the political geography of the Grand Ellipse course, whose concluding arc carried the racers through Upper Hetzia, ostensibly an independent ally of Grewzland, but in fact ruled by a puppet dhreve firmly in thrall to the Imperium. In Upper Hetzia, near the end of the race, Karsler Stornzof enjoyed support, cooperation, and privilege, just when he could most use it. The Vonahrish contestants were scarcely apt to fare so well.

Still, it was too early to dismiss their chances. They were determined and resourceful, the two of them. And the presence of a male Vonahrish racer, Girays v'Alisante, doubtless served to deflect enemy attention and suspicion from Luzelle Devaire, granting her a slight advantage of which she probably remained unaware. Perhaps a significant advantage. In the event of enemy action, she would not be the target.

Upper Hetzia. The end clearly in sight. Only a few days' travel south to reach the border of the Low Hetz. Very soon now, one of those three racers would step across the threshold of the city hall in Toltz to close the Grand Ellipse and win the race.

And then?

Deputy Underminister vo Rouvignac rose from his desk. Returning to the open window, he stood there gazing southeast toward Haereste.

"CHILI-OIL EELS," Girays ordered. "And a bowl of lard-smackers. What will you have, Luzelle?"

"Nothing," she returned absently. Her eyes devoured the section of Wolktretz Station platform visible through the window of the buffet.

"You may as well order something now. As soon as my food arrives, you'll get hungry and you'll want some."

"Ummm."

Their waiter bowed and retired.

"If you're looking for Stornzof, you won't see him out there," Girays told her. "He must have picked up the Number

310 in Domi, and that one shunts him off to Kreglutz without ever touching Wolktretz. If he'd taken the Number 444,
now, or even by some miracle managed to get himself aboard
the Number 441—"

"How in the world do you remember these things?"

"Why, it's very simple." Girays looked surprised. "Haven't
you looked at the schedule? Here, I'll show you—"

"No, thanks. The train schedule won't show me if Karsler's
ahead of us or behind, and that's really all I want to know."

"No use stewing. Our own train should be along in forty
minutes or so, and we'll hit Lis Folaze by nightfall. Stornzof
probably won't do any better than that."

"Don't be too sure. Have you seen the way people around
here *fawn* on him?"

"People do that all over the place. Sublime war hero, and
all that. Remember the time in Lyuvbrow when I made the
night run and managed to take the lead? Well, I didn't keep it
long, because the stationmaster at Voyn Junction held the
train for Stornzof's benefit. Then there was that abject coun-
cilman in Hekkin with his champagne and fruit basket for the
immortal overcommander—"

"Yes, but it's even worse than usual in this country. Upper
Hetzia must be a nation of Grewzian worshipers."

"The Hetzians do well to appear so. The good Imperior
Ogron has his heel planted firmly on their necks."

"Yes, and there're probably plenty of them eager to curry
favor by serving the only Grewzian contestant. Karsler will
probably get all kinds of—"

She broke off as the waiter reappeared, bearing chili-oil
eels and lard-smackers. His face was square and so expressionless that she wondered at once if he had overheard any of the
conversation. A curious uneasiness filled her, and she looked
away from him. He placed the bowls on the table and withdrew.

Girays began to eat. "You were saying?" he inquired between bites.

"Only that Karsler's going to get all sorts of help in this
country, and it's not right—"

"No it isn't, but there's not much we can do about it, and

righteous indignation will only spoil your digestion. Speaking of which, help yourself to the lard-smackers. I know you want them."

"Not now, thanks."

"That isn't like you. Better watch that indignation."

"Can't help it. Lard-smackers are unhealthy, anyway."

"That hasn't been proved, and I don't choose to believe it."

There was silence for some minutes until Girays finished eating. Leaning back in his seat, he inquired, "Coffee?"

"No, it would just make me jumpier. I don't see our waiter around, anyway. Where'd he go?"

"Now that you mention it, he's simply disappeared. Fine service. These Hetzians are hopeless."

"Your Lordship is in an ill humor."

"My Lordship could do with a drink of water."

"Water? Plain water? Did I hear you correctly?"

"My glass is empty, and my mouth feels as if it were lined with wallpaper paste."

"Here, have mine." She pushed her glass across the table to him.

"Thanks." He picked up the glass, which instantly dropped from his hand to shatter on the tabletop. Girays muttered a quiet oath. Water began to drip from the table to the floor.

Luzelle contained her surprise. Such clumsiness was uncharacteristic of M. the Marquis; he must be tired or preoccupied. There were no waiters in sight to mop up the spill, the water was flowing everywhere, and Girays, accustomed to the solicitude of servants, was simply sitting there. Quickly she applied her napkin to blot up part of the puddle, and still he never stirred to help her. A little impatient, she commanded, "Give me your napkin."

Very slowly, very grudgingly it seemed, he glanced down at the napkin still lying in his lap. His right hand quivered a little, but otherwise did not move. After a moment he observed quietly, "Something is wrong."

"What do you mean?" Impatience gave way to concern. "Are you ill, Girays?"

"I cannot move my hands or arms. They've gone dead."

"Dead? What do you mean?"

"I tell you, my arms are paralyzed. They have lost all sensation." He appeared to exert effort. A crease deepened between his brows, and he reported, "Legs gone too."

"I don't understand. Are you sick, are you in pain?"

"No pain—no feeling at all. I have been drugged, I believe."

"Drugged? How? Who would—"

"It must have been in the food. Your claim stands vindicated—lard-smackers are demonstrably unhealthy."

"How can you joke at a time like this? What are we going to do? What if—" She did not let herself finish the question aloud. *What if all your muscles are paralyzed?* she had nearly asked. *How will you breathe?* But there was no point in voicing any such ghastly possibility, and his breathing seemed unimpaired. His speech was intelligible, only slower than usual and a little indistinct. No, there was nothing wrong with his breathing. *For now.* Aloud she merely observed, "We'll send for a physician."

"Useless, I fear."

"You don't know that. We may find someone with the right antidote—"

"In Wolktretz?"

"Well, we have to try!" Luzelle raised her voice to a shout. "HELP! Somebody, over here, HELP! We need a doctor, we need a doctor right NOW—"

The uproar drew the attention of every customer in the buffet, and brought the manager scurrying.

"What is this?" he demanded in decent Vonahrish, visibly torn between alarm and annoyance.

"This man is sick," Luzelle declared. "He has taken in something harmful—"

"Our food here is very good! Very fresh! Never has there been a single complaint!"

"Never mind about that. Just fetch a physician, at once."

"Whatever his trouble, it has nothing to do with our food here. I will swear to this before a magistrate."

"Send for a doctor! NOW!"

The manager called out a name, and an underling was

there. Commands were issued in Hetzian, and the underling
vanished.

"The doctor will be here, at your own expense, let it be
clearly understood." The manager fixed a scandalized eye on
Girays, whose face, partially paralyzed, presented a disturbing
spectacle. "He cannot stay here. We will move him to the office. He will be more comfortable there."

*You are all kindness. Your true concern does you credit, you
miserable little worm.* Holding her fear and anger in check, she
answered, "Very well. Call someone to help. The waiter who
served us. I want to ask him some questions anyway."

"Which waiter is that?"

"Young but certainly no boy, heavyset, medium coloring,
square face, sort of droopy-lidded eyes."

"There is no such person working here."

"Yes there is, I saw him."

"This is not one of our employees."

"Are you sure?" The question was rhetorical. Of course he
was sure, and she could only wonder, *Who?*

Just about anyone, really. Anyone set on a Grewzian triumph to conclude the Grand Ellipse.

The manager made noise, and one of his staff was there.
Lifting Girays from his chair, they bore him from the buffet
under the interested gaze of some dozen customers, several of
whom were already pushing their plates away. They carried
him into a small windowless office, placed him in the chair
behind the desk, and then drew back to gawk at him.

"It is an epilepsy, yes?" inquired the manager.

"No," Girays whispered.

"But yes, I have seen such things before," the manager insisted. "It is certainly an epilepsy. This is not the fault of our
food."

"Nobody's accusing you of anything," Luzelle soothed
him. "Nobody says it is your fault——"

"You will sign a statement to this effect?"

"But somebody tampered with his food," she persisted. "If
we could find the man who served it, he might know exactly
what was in it, and then a doctor would have some idea what
to do."

"The doctor will come," the manager assured her. "He will be here soon, and he will tell you that your friend suffers the epilepsy. Or perhaps a morbid degeneration of the spinal cord—this often happens. It is like an epidemic, these days."

"Perhaps it would be best if my friend is given a little peace and quiet now," Luzelle suggested very gently. If these Hetzian invertebrates did not withdraw immediately, she would start screaming at them. "If he and I could just stay in here with the door closed until the doctor arrives—"

"This is very wise," the manager replied, clearly eager to escape. "You keep him here, out of sight. The doctor comes soon. Until then, the door is closed."

The Hetzians withdrew. The stuffy office air seemed fresher without them. Luzelle looked at Girays, motionless in his chair, partially stricken facial muscles twisting his visage awry, and felt the tears scalding her eyes. She would not let them fall, she was not about to inflict her distress on him. Assuming a serene if concerned expression, she inquired, "What can I do to make you more comfortable, Girays? Would you like some water? Cushions? Would you be better off lying on the floor?"

"Water." He spoke with difficulty, but intelligibly enough.

A pitcher and mug stood on the desk. She filled the mug with tepid water and applied it to his lips. He swallowed hard, and part of the water went down his throat, while the rest spilled out over his chin. Conscientiously maintaining her calm demeanor, she patted his face dry with her handkerchief.

"Thanks. Watch," he said.

"Watch what?"

"Time?"

"Oh, your pocket watch." She took the watch from his vest pocket. "Twelve twenty-eight."

"Nine minutes. Train."

"Don't worry about that now. We'll catch the next one."

"No. Go."

"Impossible. You can't be moved before the doctor's taken a look at you."

"You go. Alone."

She lowered her eyes to quench the eager light in them.

Part of her ached fiercely to take his advice. Part of her, equally insistent, rebelled at the thought of leaving him here, in such a state; rebelled, she realized with a certain alarm, at the thought of leaving him at all.

"I'm not abandoning you when you're ill," she returned, almost surprised at the conviction in her own voice. "There'll be another train coming through sometime later today or tonight. With any luck we'll both be on it."

"Stow me in baggage car?" His attempted smile was dreadful.

"If necessary. If you really can't be moved, I'll leave when I know you're being properly looked after."

"No. Stornzof. Win."

She was silent. She wanted to tell him that it didn't matter, that his health and safety were more important than any race, which they certainly were. But the words would not emerge.

"Look at me," Girays commanded.

She met his eyes unwillingly. His face was sadly altered, but his eyes were still his own, intelligent and too observant at times.

"I understand," he said, and did not need to elaborate, for the comprehension was mutual.

"I see that you do, but——"

"Listen. Be all right. Drug wear off. Not fatal, or already dead. Knock me out of race, though. You go on. Win."

He was telling her that it was all right to go, he was telling her exactly what she longed to hear and believe, but it was not all right. The idea of leaving him alone and incapacitated in a foreign railroad station was thoroughly obscene. The tears were starting to well again, and this time she could not control them.

"Girays, I want to stay with you." Her voice was almost as halting and garbled as his. "Do you hear, I want to stay. I can catch the later train, it will be all right. If Karsler draws ahead, I can catch up with him later. I've done it before, several times, and I can do it again. I *will* do it. But right now——"

"No. Too near end. Fall behind now, lose."

"No, no I won't. A measly few hours won't——"

"Luzelle." He held her with his eyes. "You asked before why I race. Remember?"

She nodded.

"Ministry. Vo Rouvignac came. A second Vonahrish racer to draw enemy attention away from you. Did, too. Damned lard-smackers."

"I never let myself think of that, although it should have been obvious. You're you, I should have known. But that's all the more reason why I should—"

"Not waste chance. Waste everything, for everybody. Not now. Go. Win."

She stared at him. Something filled her grip, and she looked down to discover herself squeezing one of Girays's hands fiercely in both her own. The force of the hold would have caused him pain, had he retained the least sensation. She released him at once. The tears streamed down her face.

Voices and scuffling outside. The door opened, and there was the manager, accompanied by a harried individual bearing a black bag.

"Here is the epileptic," the manager announced.

"He is not an epileptic." Infuriated, Luzelle turned to face them. "He's been drugged and poisoned, anyone can see that. You are the doctor?" she appealed to the stranger. Without awaiting reply she continued, "Please, know that this man is in excellent health, only he has been drugged, and now his muscles are useless. Surely your bag contains some strong stimulant that will—"

"Madame, I speak no Vonahrish," the physician announced in Hetzian.

She stared at him. In that speechless moment a whistle shrilled and a bell clanged. The southbound train, scheduled to depart at twelve thirty-seven, was pulling into the station. Her eyes flew to Girays.

"Go," he said clearly. "Please. Go."

"I love you," she answered.

Picking up her skirts, she ran from the office, back through the buffet, pausing only long enough to scoop up the valise still sitting beside the door where she had left it. Then out into the warm summer air and across the platform, sprinting for the southbound train.

· · ·

THE SUN WAS SETTING as Karsler Stornzof disembarked at Lissildt Station in Lis Folaze. Outside the station house the lamplighters were already at work, and the yellow lights were glowing softly through the perpetual mists of Upper Hetzia.

Lissildt Station overlooked the silver Folaze River that wound through the heart of the old city. A river pier some few yards distant accommodated a dozen or more small water-hansoms. Karsler engaged one and found himself once again troubled by the obsequious grimaces of the oarsman, who, like so many of his compatriots, cringed at sight of a Grewz-ian uniform.

And there were so many grey uniforms to be seen. As the water-hansom traveled upstream, Karsler glimpsed them re-peatedly; small bands of his countrymen patrolling the river-side neighborhoods with the assurance of conquerors. Not that Upper Hetzia was a Grewzian conquest. Quite the con-trary, the nation enjoyed favored status as an ally of the Im-perium. Nevertheless, the imperior's ubiquitous peacekeeping forces roused obvious fear.

He did not care to see it. Lifting his gaze from the banks, he distracted himself with a world-renowned vista of tripartite domes and distinctively triple-forked spires draped in fog.

The little boat reached a pier nestled beside one of the numberless red stone bridges spanning the Folaze. Karsler paid the oarsman and returned to dry land. He stood in a re-gion of white town houses boldly ornamented with geometric designs picked out in squares of polished black stone. A fiacre carried him the rest of the way to his destination, and he alighted at the front door of the grand Marbleflower Hotel.

He paused briefly to make inquiries at the desk, then pro-ceeded up the stairs and along a thickly carpeted corridor to suite number 220. He forced himself to knock, heard a famil-iar voice bid him enter, and went in.

For an instant time seemed to reverse itself and he almost fancied himself back in Jumo Towne, for there was another richly appointed hotel room, there was the Grandlandsman

Torvid Stornzof attired in faultless evening wear, there a slim bottle in a silver cooler, a haze of cigarette smoke, and apparently nothing had changed.

"Welcome back to civilization, Nephew." Torvid did not rise from the couch. "Pour yourself a congratulatory glass, if you like."

"Thank you, Grandlandsman." Karsler obeyed. "But congratulations are premature."

"I think not, the thing is all but accomplished. Now sit down, if you will, and tell me what has happened since we parted. I have read the newspapers, but these accounts are penned by idiots and cannot be trusted. I am particularly interested in hearing of your progress through Rhazaulle, whose natives are capable of impertinence."

"They would have been capable of more than that, had they recognized me as a Grewzian officer. I was obliged to adopt civilian dress while I traveled along the Xana."

"Very good. I had feared that your Promontory principles might perhaps preclude such subterfuge. That, in fact, was for a time my chief concern."

"Promontory principles do not ordinarily preclude self-preservation, Grandlandsman."

"That is reassuring beyond measure. But come, your report."

For the next quarter hour or so, Karsler related most of what had befallen him since Jumo Towne. Only a few details he omitted as superfluous. He did not speak of the assistance he had rendered Luzelle Devaire in the midst of the Aveshquian mud. Nor did he mention the Grewzian massacre of a Rhazaullean village, a topic certain to provoke a quarrel. He described the difficulties of driving a team of sled dogs across Ukizik's ice fields, he dwelt at some length on the storm that had so nearly sent the *Walrus* to the bottom of the Sea of Ice, he told of the troublesome plague of carnivorous bats in Obran. At last, having briefly sketched an uneventful progress from Bünckel to Lissildt Station in Lis Folaze, Karsler fell silent.

Torvid considered. "Not too bad," he judged at last. "You

have hardly exploited every possible opportunity, and yet, on the whole, not too bad. Congratulations are surely in order."

"Not yet. The race is by no means over. I do not know the exact location of the two Vonahrish contestants, but they cannot be more than hours behind me at best, and it is not at all impossible that they have already reached Lis Folaze. In fact I would do well to continue traveling tonight, on horseback if necessary, if I am to maintain—"

"You need not inconvenience yourself. The Vonahrish difficulty has been resolved—conclusively, I trust."

Karsler set his glass aside with care. "Explain," he commanded quietly.

"Bah, save your concern." Torvid's brows rose. "I have not maimed or murdered your little Devaire, if that is what you fear. The other one, v'Alisante, is similarly unharmed. They have simply been delayed en route."

"Delayed how?"

"The technicalities are without importance. Enough to know that you have gained an advantage of twelve hours or so—enough to ensure your victory, provided you do not squander them."

"What have you done, Grandlandsman?"

"Served Grewzland and House Stornzof, I believe. That should suffice."

"I hope you will not compel me to retrace my steps in order to investigate. You understand that I will do it."

"That is absurd. Very well, Nephew, since you press me with such zeal, I will assuage your curiosity. I had one of my people slip a little something into the lunch the two Vonahrish ordered at Wolktretz Station. The immobilizing effect is short-lived—a matter of hours—and when it wears off, health and vigor are fully restored. What could be milder or more humane? Even you, with your girlish sensibilities, must concede as much."

"There can be no doubt? Luzelle and v'Alisante both ingested some sort of drug?"

"I would assume that both ate lunch. As far as that goes, however, I have not yet actually heard from my agent."

"And you regard this piece of treachery as a necessity?"

"Victory is the sole necessity. This is a very simple concept, yet one that somehow seems to exceed your grasp."

"It did not occur to you that I might win this race fairly, without benefit of your destructive meddling?"

"It occurred to me," Torvid returned deliberately, "but I was forced to dismiss that rosy hope long ago. You have from the beginning proved yourself unwilling to sacrifice as circumstance demands."

"Sacrifice?"

"Vanity, self-consequence, this deluded self-important preoccupation with the purity of your own character, the pretty juvenile notions of sportsmanship and fair play suitable to the school yard but not the world beyond—"

"In short, honor."

"Spoken like a true schoolboy. Your infinite sanctimony begins to annoy me. You will win this race, and the Stornzof name will gain luster by it, but know this. Save for my meddling, as you term it, you would have lost all possible hope of victory long ago."

"How so?"

"Oh, spare yourself distressing knowledge. Revel on in your spotless Promontory innocence."

"Answer, or I will withdraw from the race tonight."

"How can I withstand such blazing moral authority? Very well, there was the Szarish woman with her peculiar conveyance, at the beginning of the race. She might well have left all rivals far behind, had I not taken the necessary steps. Later on, those twin Travornish cretins assumed the lead and very likely would have kept it, but for me. I did what was needed, then and now. I regret to observe that you cannot say the same. My intervention should have been redundant, you should have overcome all obstacles without assistance, but this you were unable, or rather, unwilling to do."

Karsler's vision turned inward, and he thought of other voices, other places, other realities of his past. There was silence for a time while he remembered, and when he finally answered, his aspect was serene and seemingly untroubled.

"Grandlandsman, I will finish the race, for reasons that I

see little point in explaining to you. It is an obligation to warn you at this time, however, that if I am first to close the Grand Ellipse, I must decline the victor's prize. I will relinquish first place to the next contestant to set foot in Toltz."

"This is childish petulance. I do not take it seriously."

"Take it as you will. I have informed you of my decision."

"Must I remind you that it is scarcely your decision? There is far more at stake here than the integrity of your precious individual conscience. Forget your selfish concerns for once. This is a matter touching upon Grewzian national pride, and it disgusts me to hear a Stornzof speak of compromise. I will not hear it."

"Then I will leave you, Grandlandsman."

"You have not been dismissed. You forget whom you speak to, I think."

"I forget nothing. Otherwise I would not be here this evening."

"Good. Then let us understand one another. As head of House Stornzof, I command you to perform your duty. You will finish this ridiculous race, you will put forth your best efforts, and when you win, you will graciously accept the victory on behalf of Grewzland. You will also accept the Hetzian monarch's offer of an audience, of which there is more to be said at a later date. I trust I have made myself clear."

"I must refuse."

"The matter is not open to argument. You have received your orders, there is nothing more to be said."

"I have notified you of my intentions, and you are right—there is nothing more to be said."

"I do not think you hear me. I order you to serve your House, your imperior, and your nation. You cannot pretend that higher obligations exist."

"I can," Karsler answered, after a moment's pause. "I do."

"Then that sickly monastery of a Promontory has turned the Stornzof blood in your veins to whey. You are a coward, a weakling, and a fool."

"I am a Grewzian recognizing the flaws in an Imperium founded upon the barbarism and mindless amorality of men such as yourself, Grandlandsman."

"Ah? I see you are worse than weakling and fool—you are a traitor."

"You go too far. I have tried to accord you respect, but I will not accept such insults."

"Then prove that you do not deserve them."

"I need prove nothing. I do not seek your approbation."

"Don't you? Take my disapprobation, then." Leaning forward in his seat, Torvid flung the contents of his wineglass into his nephew's face.

Karsler rose to his feet. "Grandlandsman, I bid you farewell," he said courteously, and walked out.

23

HER TRAIN PULLED INTO LISSILDT STATION in Lis Folaze
seven minutes ahead of schedule, but Luzelle hardly appreci-
ated the bonus. Her thoughts were back in Wolktretz, her
mind filled with pictures of Girays v'Alisante, paralyzed and
helpless in that wretched little windowless hole of an office.
And she had left him there in such a place, in such a state. She
had walked—no, run—on her merry way. Of course he had
urged her to do it, and his reasons had been cogent. But she
could not forgive the part of herself that had burned so
fiercely to go.

It was not as if she could have helped him by staying. She
was not a doctor, there was nothing she could have done. Perhaps her presence would have cheered and heartened him,
though. But no, she reminded herself, he had truly wanted
her to finish the race, he had practically insisted.

She wished she could convince herself.

The train halted. She disembarked and made her way from
the lamplit platform to the street, where she quickly engaged
a fiacre to carry her to the nearest livery stable. The vehicle
hurried off through the foggy twilight and she sat inside
twisting her hands, blind to the sights of the city.

The price of a carriage and a driver willing to navigate unpaved roads by night was high, but she paid without demur,
for the expense was worthwhile. Should she reach the railroad
station at Groeflen in time to catch the 4:48 A.M. express

from Ferille, she would cross the border into the Low Hetz hours ahead of any train passing through Lis Folaze tonight.

She paid half in advance, then waited while two grey horses were harnessed to the light barouche she had hired. Minutes later the carriage was brought around and she took her seat. The driver shut the door, raised the collapsible top, lit the lanterns, and ascended to the box. His whip snapped and they were off.

Luzelle settled back in her seat. The tripartite domes and triple-forked spires of Lis Folaze sped by unnoticed. Girays's semiparalyzed face filled her mind's eye. She came within a breath of ordering the driver to turn north toward Wolktretz, and only with an effort of will managed to contain the command.

He wouldn't die, he'd promised he wouldn't.

But he wouldn't finish the race, either—or at least, he wouldn't win it—and neither would she, unless she took care. Whoever had doctored the food at Wolktretz Station, presumably aiming for both Vonahrish Ellipsoids, had partially failed through happenstance. That individual was still out there and would probably try again, perhaps with better luck the next time. Beyond doubt a Grewzian sympathizer, someone supporting Karsler Stornzof's victory. Karsler himself she did not suspect for a moment.

Lost in her comfortless thoughts, she scarcely noted the alteration in the passing scenery, but eventually looked out to find that the city of Lis Folaze had given way to fog-smothered fields and hills. She could barely see anything out there, and there was nothing worth seeing, anyway. She did not care about Upper Hetzian scenery, she did not care about anything beyond Girays's safety and winning the race.

There came the inevitable rest stop to breathe and water the horses, and grudging every lost minute, she did not bother to set foot from the barouche. Fog crept in the window. She watched the swirling eddies illumined by the coach lanterns, and hated Upper Hetzia.

Progress resumed. She closed her eyes and tried to sleep, but her mind revolved unstoppably and Girays's face was with her always.

She shouldn't have left him. No matter what he had said.

He would be all right. And if not, all the more reason to win.

The hours passed indistinguishably until at last the carriage veered from the Dhreve's Highway into the driveway of a vine-covered old inn, where the driver pulled up beneath the porte-cochère.

Shaken from her unhappy reveries, Luzelle stuck her head out the window to demand, "Why do we stop again?"

"We have reached the outskirts of Groeflen, madame," the driver replied. "See, there is the town before us."

She followed his pointing finger and made out a cluster of lights winking in the middle distance.

"Well, the train station, then," she commanded.

"Pardon me, madame," he returned, "but it is only just eleven o'clock. This inn, the Three Beggars, offers a good table. Will you not eat and rest comfortably until dawn?"

She considered. She was not hungry, but she had not touched food since breakfast and she should eat. With appropriate caution. And rest? Far better to spend the remainder of the night, however brief, lying in a comfortable bed, as opposed to sitting upright on a wooden bench in the station waiting room.

"Very well," she consented, "provided you're ready to leave by four o'clock sharp."

"My word on it, madame."

Valise in hand, she alighted from the barouche and walked into the inn.

The evening was well advanced, but the place was still well lighted and well peopled. The innkeeper—a rotund, round-faced, amiably innocuous-looking young man—advanced at once to greet her.

"Welcome to the Three Beggars, madame. Klec Stiesoldt, proprietor." He bowed, all smiles. "How may I serve you?"

No animosity, no disapproval, no disguised or undisguised suspicion of an unescorted female traveler arriving by night. A certain natural curiosity, but nothing offensive in that. Luzelle returned the smile, liking him at once. "Dinner, if you're still serving," she told him.

"We are, madame. Rabbit stew with fennel, lorbers, and my wife's special herbs. My Gretti is the finest cook between here and Lis Folaze. You will be pleased."

"I'm sure I will. And a room, private, and a knock on the door at three forty-five."

"Three forty-five A.M.?"

"Please."

"It will be done, madame. My Gretti will see to it herself. I myself will be soundly asleep at that inhospitable hour. Three forty-five—A.M.! You're for the four forty-eight southbound express, I expect."

She nodded. "You've memorized the train schedule, Master Stiesoldt?"

"Not I, madame. This poor head could scarcely contain so many numbers. Gretti's head, now—that head holds *endless* numbers, you ought to see her with the account books, it's like magic—but mine does not. But I note the four forty-eight southbound, because you are the evening's second guest to request an appalling predawn awakening for the sake of that particular train. Your fellow traveler—a Grewzian military gentleman, you know—is easier on himself, practically a hedonist. He doesn't ask to be awakened until four."

"Grewzian military, did you say? Is he tall and blond?"

"Aren't they all?"

"Well—"

"Believe me, I know. Those Grewzian peacekeepers are everywhere, and I tell you I've never seen so many tall blond beings in my life. I think they must drown the small dark ones at birth."

"Peacekeepers?"

"That's what those ruffians choose to call themselves. But we Hetzians have a different name for them." The innkeeper's voice dropped. "We call them—"

"Master Stiesoldt, the topic is unsuitable."

"Listen, the Grewzian presence in Upper Hetzia is unsuitable, the Grewzian attitude toward the townsmen is unsuitable, the entire so-called peacekeeping force is *unsuitable*. The—"

"Perhaps you could show me to the dining room?" she cut

him off, alarmed at the danger resident in this Hetzian's unguarded tongue.

"Oh, certainly. Forgive me, madame. Sometimes my Hetzian heart gets the better of my head, at least that's what Gretti
says. Here, let me take your bag." He relieved her of her burden. "This way, if you please."

She followed him to a pleasantly old-fashioned common
room with a vast stone fireplace, dark-beamed ceiling, and unevenly worn stone floor, where he bowed and left her. She spotted Karsler Stornzof the moment she crossed the threshold. He
was sitting alone at a small table in the corner, the light from
the old iron chandeliers overhead glancing off his bright hair.
He looked up as she entered, their eyes met, and she was struck
as always by his appearance, but tonight there was a difference.
Karsler was splendid as ever, but this time the image of Girays
haunting her throughout the day did not vanish at sight of him.

She went straight to his table. His eyes never left her face as
she approached, and something in his expression troubled
her, a certain dark intensity of emotion much at odds with his
usual serenity. Disappointment, chagrin that she still kept
pace? Somehow she did not think so.

He rose politely as she drew near, and smiled at her. Her
heartbeat quickened as always, but somehow Girays stayed
put in her mind.

"Luzelle. I am glad to see you here, very glad." Voice and
eyes conveyed the same unaccountable depth of feeling. "You
are well?"

"I am. Girays isn't," she announced flatly. They seated
themselves and she continued, "He was poisoned or drugged,
around noon today at the Wolktretz Station. His limbs went
dead, he couldn't stir, his face was twisted, and he could
barely speak. It was horrible. It was—" Her voice broke.

"He is alive?" Karsler asked.

She nodded, and saw him draw a sharp breath.

"A physician was summoned?"

She swallowed hard. "Yes."

"His diagnosis?"

"I don't know. I didn't stay. My train was pulling into the

station, and I ran for it. I left him there. Girays told me to go, but I shouldn't have. I shouldn't have." Tears spilled from her eyes.

He watched her in silence for a moment, then observed quietly, "That choice was difficult. I am sorry."

"So am I. I chose wrongly."

"I do not think so, nor do I believe that v'Alisante would think so."

"He wouldn't, but I know better. I wish I'd decided differently, I wish now that I'd stayed with him. That's easy to say after the fact, but it's the truth."

"And if you had stayed, then you would have sacrificed all hope of victory."

"There are more important things."

"Never have I heard you speak so."

"About time, then. It's Girays who ought to have heard me speak so. But he didn't, because I wanted to go and he knew it. Now I only wish I had another chance."

"Ah." He regarded her with perfect comprehension. "Matters have altered with you. In more ways than one, I think."

"I'm seeing some things more clearly."

"As you come to know yourself better. I have thought from the start that you might. It was a feeling that I had."

"A little late for self-knowledge, if Girays dies. He might be dead already." The tears were streaming again, and she fumbled for a handkerchief.

"He is not. He will recover fully. You must believe this."

"I wish I could." She clenched her teeth, forcibly containing a sob.

"You are fatigued and distraught. Probably famished as well. When did you last eat?"

"I don't know. Breakfast, I think. I'm not hungry."

"But you must maintain your strength, or you will make yourself ill." He caught the eye of a waiter who flew the length of the room as if magnetized.

Once again almost resentfully marveling at the power of a Grewzian uniform, she watched while Karsler ordered a meal. The waiter withdrew and he turned back to her to request gently but quite firmly, "And now, if it does not too greatly distress you to speak of it, please tell me all that happened at Wolktretz Station."

Her tears had ceased and her voice was back under control. She told him everything, noting as she spoke that he listened with obvious concern, together with something stronger and deeper, perhaps anger or disgust; but no surprise—not a jot of surprise. Nothing she said seemed to strike him as unexpected, and for the first time, suspicion winged across her thoughts. She looked across the table at Karsler Stornzof, willing herself to disregard deceptive externals; she probed his eyes, scrupulously ignoring their color, and despite all mental reinforcements her suspicions died at once. She knew beyond question that this man had never raised a hand against Girays v'Alisante.

Yet there was something there. Karsler himself bore no guilt, but perhaps he knew who did. Into her mind popped the words he had spoken weeks ago in the midst of the Aveshquian monsoon, concerning his Uncle Ice Statue: *Preferring to shorten the tedium of the journey, he has proceeded directly to Lis Folaze, where I shall meet him next.*

Lis Folaze. The Grandlandsman Torvid? Whatever his personal opinions, Karsler would never betray or incriminate his kinsman; the head of House Stornzof, no less.

The food arrived. Luzelle hardly noticed what was on her plate. She ate mechanically, without tasting, but the nourishment must have done her some good, for the sense of lachrymose weakness was passing.

She looked up from her plate to meet Karsler's eyes. "It's not too late," she said. "I could still go back to Wolktretz."

"You could." He nodded. "But is that what v'Alisante would want? Do you think he would be altogether glad to see you? He would be honored no doubt, but would he not also mourn this destruction of your hopes on his account?" There was no answer, and he observed, "The end of the race is very near. Barring unforeseen obstacles, we shall reach Toltz the day after tomorrow. To the best of my knowledge, you and I presently share the lead, and your chance of victory is real. Will you throw it away now?"

The day after tomorrow. As close as that, and it would all

be over. Karsler's point was well taken, it would make no sense and do no good to give up now.

"You and I share the lead." She did not answer his question directly. "Do the rules of the Grand Ellipse include provision for a tie?"

"I do not know. You point out an interesting possibility, however. We two shall board the southbound train together in a few hours' time. We shall change trains in Tophzenk, and the following day step forth onto the platform in Toltz. After that, whoever is first to cover the short distance between the railroad station and the city hall will win the race. It will be a very close thing indeed—but not quite a dead heat, I think."

"Astonishing, isn't it? After all this time, all this distance, all this desperate effort—that it should all boil down in the end to a brief dash through a few city streets, to get back to where we began? I suspect there must be something philosophical in that, somewhere."

"You are beginning to feel better, are you not?"

"Yes. You were right, the food is helping. You were right about finishing the race, too. I wish I could undo what happened in Wolktretz, and other places, but chucking the Grand Ellipse two days from the finish isn't the way to atone."

"You have nothing to atone for. It is the hand and mind behind the poisoned meal that bear the guilt. The hand fouled with crime; the mind barren of moral sense, devoid of honor—"

Luzelle glanced at him in surprise. Karsler might almost have been talking to himself, blue gaze turned inward upon manifestly unpleasant visions. She reached across the table and touched his hand lightly. "Karsler, won't you tell me what is it that you—"

The entrance of a Grewzian military squad cut her query short. Falling silent at sight of the half-dozen soldiers, Luzelle tensed despite Karsler Stornzof's reassuring proximity. She had nothing to fear from the Grewzians so long as she was with him. And the greycoats had probably just come in for a harmless late drink, anyway. Nevertheless her mouth was a little dry, her heartbeat a little quick. Her eyes roamed the common room and she saw that every other patron had fallen similarly silent.

The voice of the Grewzian captain was effortlessly audible as he commanded, "Master Klec Stiesoldt, stand forth."

All eyes shifted to the kitchen door, where the innkeeper stood conferring with the cook. Stiesoldt stood stock-still for a moment, eyes wide and guileless as a frightened child's. He swallowed visibly, stepped forward, and said, "Here."

The captain crooked a finger. "Come."

A brace of customers occupying a table at the front of the room rose and made for the exit. Two soldiers moved to block the doorway, and the customers quietly returned to their seats.

Klec Stiesoldt advanced as if to execution. Halting before the captain, he inquired palely, "May I serve you, sir?"

"Easily enough," the officer returned in practiced Hetzian. "We are told you are a loyal citizen. I trust these reports are accurate?"

"I am a good Hetzian, sir."

"Willing to serve your country?"

"Yes, sir."

"Excellent. And you understand, do you not, that the interests of Upper Hetzia and her allies of the Grewzian Imperium coincide?"

"That's as may be, sir."

"The Imperium has need of your talents."

"I have no talents, sir. Unless the Imperium has need of a good innkeeper."

"You jest, Master Stiesoldt?"

"Not I, sir."

"Then your modesty is excessive, for it has come to our notice that you are quite the local celebrity."

"Many people know me, sir. The Three Beggars offers generous measures and a good table."

"And entertainment?"

"Entertainment?"

"Floor shows for the fortunate select customers. Illusions, projections, conjurations."

"Oh, nothing out of the ordinary way, sir."

"You do yourself an injustice. By all reports your feats are remarkable. Almost magical, it's said."

"I don't know about that, sir. Just a little nonsense to pass the time."

"You have captured my interest. Let us pass the time, then. You will demonstrate your accomplishments."

"Well, I could show you a few card tricks, sir. I've got a couple of good coin tricks too."

"I am more interested in ring tricks."

"Ring, sir?" Stiesoldt moistened his lips. "I'm not sure I catch your meaning."

"Do not try my patience. That ring of yours is famous in these parts, you've made no secret of it."

"I'm not a secretive person, sir. It's true I have a ring, a little keepsake that came to me from my grandfather. It's not worth anything, except for sentiment, and I use it in some of the tricks. That must be what you've heard about."

"You confess the existence of a magical ring?"

"Oh, I wouldn't call it magical, sir. It's only an ordinary little—"

"You will produce this ring."

"Oh, it's around here, sir, but offhand I'm not really sure where. It might not be so easy to lay hands on it. If you'd give me a little time to hunt, maybe come back tomorrow—"

"If you fail to produce this ring, we shall commence our own search, and our methods are thorough."

Looking ruinously reluctant, Master Stiesoldt fished in his pocket to bring forth a small metallic item. The Grewzian officer extended an open palm and Stiesoldt's reluctance deepened visibly, but he obeyed the unspoken command and the object changed hands.

From her chair Luzelle caught a quick glimpse of a small, very plain silvery ring, simple and seemingly unremarkable as its owner claimed.

The captain inspected the ring with care, finally demanding, "What is this thing made of?"

"Silver, I expect, sir."

"I do not think so. There is a curious iridescence there, an array of fleeting changeable colors."

"Got a little tarnish on it, sir."

"The light glints oddly off the surface. I have never seen the like."

"Just wants a little cleaning, sir."

"You will demonstrate this object's capabilities."

"Whatever you say, sir. I know a good one—I can pull a silk handkerchief through that ring, and the handkerchief changes color in a flash. Would you like to see that, sir?"

"I have warned you about trying my patience. Let us speak plainly. This land of Upper Hetzia is rife with legends of magical rings, talismans, aetheric conflations, and the like, imbued with power and capable of marvels. More than one such legend has been authenticated. The power is real, it exists, offering potentially vast benefit to the war effort of the Imperium. We will have that power, Master Stiesoldt. If it resides in your hands, you will assist us."

"Sir, I'll do what I can. But this little ring here, it's really nothing. I just use it for the parlor tricks my grandfather taught me. I don't know what you've heard, but—"

"We have heard from more than one source that you've used the ring to conjure extraordinary apparitions. Such reports have been confirmed by witnesses. As you yourself have observed, you are not a secretive person."

"You know what foolishness some people will tattle, sir. And you know what loony things they think they see after they've had a few."

"It is our conclusion that the reports warrant investigation," the captain observed. He handed the ring back to its owner. "I trust you will cooperate, Master Stiesoldt. The Imperium is as swift to reward loyalty as it is to punish subversion."

"I'm a simple man, sir, I don't know what subversion is."

"Enough of this. You will now conjure an apparition. You will do it before my men and these assembled witnesses here." His gesture encompassed the captive customers.

"Sir, I don't understand what you want of me."

"Then we shall try to make it clear." Turning to his underlings, the captain commanded, "Take him. In there." His finger flicked kitchenward.

A couple of grey soldiers grabbed the quailing innkeeper's arms, and Karsler Stornzof stood up. "Halt," he commanded in Grewzian.

Noting the overcommander's insignia, his countrymen obeyed at once. All six stiffened to attention.

Addressing the captain, Karsler inquired, "Your intention?"

"Persuasive interrogation, sir," the other replied.

"This Hetzian has disclaimed arcane knowledge and ability. There is little sound cause to disbelieve him."

"Sir, the evidence of several independent reports is compelling," the captain suggested deferentially.

"But hardly justifies recourse to, as you put it, persuasive interrogation. You will release the proprietor and withdraw yourself and your men from this inn."

"With all due respect, Overcommander, I cannot obey." The captain's breast pocket yielded a document, which he presented with assurance. "My orders, sir, signed by the Undergeneral Bervsau, commander of the South District peacekeeping force. Please note, sir, I am instructed to investigate this matter in depth and pursue the conclusion by any and all available means."

Karsler unfolded the paper. As he read, Luzelle watched his face closely and detected no visible change. But it seemed as if a current flowed to her from his mind or heart, and she sensed both anger and sadness.

"Follow your orders, then." Karsler relinquished the document and resumed his seat.

The captain saluted smartly, then nodded to his men, who hustled the innkeeper from the common room. The kitchen door closed behind them. A discreet buzz of conversation arose. The exit remained greyly blocked.

Luzelle had lost all vestige of appetite. She found Karsler's eyes and told him, "There was nothing you could do."

"That is true, once again. How often will it be true, that a Grewzian evil arises and there is nothing I can do?"

"At least you tried." Even to her own ears, it sounded feeble.

He said nothing. They sat in silence for a time, until the first cry of pain rang from the kitchen. Luzelle flinched. Another scream, and her hands clenched. The common room was silent. All present listened, and their attention was rewarded with a thud and a cry.

"Come, I will take you away from here," Karsler offered.

She wavered, strongly tempted, then shook her head. "Not unless everyone else in this room is also allowed to go."

"That is not possible."

She averted her eyes, unwilling to look at his grey uniform. She wished she could stop her ears, but at the same time could not forbear straining for every telltale sound from the kitchen. They wouldn't hurt Stiesoldt too badly, she told herself. If they really damaged the innkeeper, then he wouldn't be able to give them what they wanted.

A choking moan issued from the kitchen, and she found herself mentally enjoining the victim, *Give in. Just do what you must to end this.*

Ending this meant handing new power to the Grewzians; as if they needed it.

It seemed to go on for an eternity, although actually no more than a few minutes elapsed. At the end of that time one of the soldiers emerged from the kitchen to stride purposefully from the common room.

Silence. No conversation among the customers, no sound from the kitchen.

Minutes later the soldier reentered with a plump, pretty, alarmed-looking young woman in tow. She wore nothing but a thin summer nightgown. Her hair was falling down her back, and her eyes were puffed with recent sleep.

"What do you want?" she pleaded, as her captor hurried her along. "What is the matter, where is my husband?"

No answer. The Grewzian dragged Gretti Stiesoldt into the kitchen, and the door closed behind them.

"Karsler—" Luzelle appealed desperately.

He shook his head. His face seemed carved in white marble. She could not read his eyes.

A feminine scream shrilled from the kitchen. A confusion of male voices arose within and there came another scream, louder and more anguished than the first. Then silence.

The kitchen door opened. Soldiers, innkeeper, and innkeeper's wife emerged. Master Stiesoldt's face was bruised and bloody. His nose, swollen and misaligned, was probably broken. Gretti cradled an obviously fractured arm. Her nightgown, torn at the neck, gaped suggestively.

The small party halted.

"Our friend Klec Stiesoldt has consented to favor us with a demonstration of his magical prowess," announced the Grewzian captain. "We anticipate an enlightening display. Master Stiesoldt, if you please."

Klec Stiesoldt plodded to the center of the room. Once he turned back to glance at his wife, and ocular communication of some kind flashed between the two of them. He halted and lifted his left hand, the small finger of which bore a silver ring of curiously inconstant reflectivity. Bowing his head, he shut his eyes and stood motionless. Almost he seemed to slumber upright, but the movement of his lips implied inaudible speech and the quivering of his eyelids suggested intense internal activity.

Luzelle watched uneasily. At first she thought some parlor trick in the offing, but when nothing happened, concluded that the innkeeper played pathetically for a brief respite; an ill-considered stratagem, for the lame deceit would only stoke Grewzian wrath.

The seconds marched, a faint chill invaded the room, and a thrill shot along her nerves. The shadows expanded, and the ring on the innkeeper's finger seemed to glow in the midst of the gloom, but perhaps it was simply some trick of the light. Luzelle blinked and rubbed her eyes, but the shadows did not recede. Her hands were icy, and she had to tighten her jaw to keep her teeth from chattering.

Her sense of the uncanny only deepened when Karsler reached across the table to take one of her cold hands in a warm, firm clasp. She glanced at him in surprise and saw that he was not looking at her at all. His eyes were fixed on the innkeeper, specifically on the innkeeper's ring, which was definitely glowing with its own light. His expression reflected an acute awareness that confirmed the promptings of her own instincts. Some inkling of the alien forces at work stirred at the base of her brain, and, grateful for the simple human contact, she clung to Karsler's hand with all her strength.

The air darkened impossibly, reducing the candle flames in the iron chandeliers to a scattering of fireflies at dusk. The shadows gathered about the innkeeper, all but hiding him from view, but through them shone that ring of his, the questionable family keepsake that he would have kept hidden from strangers' eyes, had he possessed a grain of common sense.

The witnesses, both civilian and military, were breathlessly silent. The atmosphere sighed, while the shadows at the center of the room thickened, boiled, and coalesced. A form swirled into sight, blurred and wavering at first, but swiftly acquiring substance and definition, steadily waxing in bulk and apparent solidity. Within seconds it was whole and immediate, a thing sculpted of air and darkness, weightlessly airborne yet overwhelmingly potent.

The apparition was humanoid, but larger and broader than any man, its body sheathed in polished scales, its hands and feet armed with smoky talons. The face was long and evil of jaw as a crocodile's, and the cemetery of teeth belonged to a shark, but the eyes—lightless pits sunk beneath heavy jutting ridges of bone—belonged to no known species. An immense pair of leathern wings fanned from the massive shoulders, and a scaled serpent of a tail writhed at the base of the spine.

A random nightmare? But no, the horrific image was not unfamiliar. She had seen it in a book somewhere, some weighty old illustrated tome. Her memory revolved, and the right recollection clicked into place. The traditions of Upper Hetzia included belief in certain powerful, demonic entities known as "malevolences." The apparition before her corresponded to the illustration in every appalling particular.

But it was only an illusion, she reminded herself in a vain effort to slow the hammering of her heart. A wisp of smoke, a rag of fog, dreadful to behold, but substanceless and harmless as a mirage.

The visitant turned on the nearest grey uniform. Sinking smoky talons deep into Grewzian flesh, it ripped the soldier's chest open, reached into the cavity, and tore out the still-beating heart. Perfectly real blood sprayed from the perfectly real wound, and several flying warm droplets spattered Luzelle's face. Her cry was lost in the midst of overlapping shouts and screams.

Dropping the soldier's lifeless body, the malevolence paused long enough to devour the dripping heart before turning to its next victim, this time the Grewzian captain. A blur of scaled arms, a twitch of saber claws, a jet of arterial blood, and the crocodile jaws closed on the captain's heart.

A babble of frantic Grewzian arose, and several shots rang out. The vaporous malevolence never faltered, but two anonymous customers caught in the line of fire dropped from their chairs to the floor, where they twitched briefly and died. Several civilians, including Luzelle's driver, dashed for the exit. A burst of fire from the guards stationed at the door cut them down. The malevolence seized its next victim, a well-dressed elderly civilian with a wealth of thick silvery hair. That glinting hair must have possessed allure, for the talons stabbed at the silver, there was a jerking blur of motion before the body fell, and then the severed head was momentarily airborne, eyes popping and lips working, perhaps conscious for a last flying moment before the crocodile jaws snapped and the skull cracked open like a great nut.

Apparently aiming to destroy the danger at its root by eliminating the innkeeper, one of the soldiers fired. A revolver shot blasted and Master Stiesoldt fell amid the shrieks of his wife, but the malevolence remained. An instant later the enterprising soldier was dead, rent wide from throat to belly.

Luzelle jumped to her feet. She was not thinking clearly, and recognized only the urgent impulse to escape. The hand still clasping her own tightened.

"Not yet," Karsler advised.

She stared at him, astonished by his calmness. The face still visible through the magical twilight was composed and unafraid. He did not raise his voice, but she heard him clearly despite the surrounding uproar. Her own voice was thin with fear as she returned, "Get us out of here!"

"Not yet," he repeated. "Do not move, you will draw the attention of the Receptivity. You must wait until the focus has shifted, and the perceptions that mold it have altered."

"I don't understand what you mean!"

"I mean that I know what we confront, and I know how to overcome it. Stay where you are."

Believing him on instinct, she nodded, and he released her hand.

"Grewzian soldiers." Karsler's voice filled the room as he announced, "Your captain is dead, I am assuming command. Hold your fire and stand still." The surviving soldiers instantly obeyed him, and Karsler switched to the Hetzian language to command, "Everyone present, stay where you are. Silence, and do not move."

Almost everyone obeyed him, but one of the waiters ran for the kitchen door. The malevolence-shaped thing attacked instantly. Vast leathern wings enfolded the fleeing prey. The talons ripped, blood spurted, the waiter gurgled and died. Releasing its victim, the malevolence hovered, great wings pumping in slow silence, empty gaze sweeping the room.

"Do not look upon it," Karsler commanded, quiet tone powerfully compelling. "Turn your eyes away, direct your minds elsewhere."

Such directions were not easily followed. It took an intense effort of will for Luzelle to tear her eyes from the floating visitant and fix them on Karsler's face. The calm assurance she saw there stilled her terror. He had said that he knew how to overcome this sorcerous horror and she believed him. She understood perfectly at that moment why the soldiers under this officer's command were willing to follow him anywhere.

She looked at his face, not letting herself see anything else.

Karsler himself was watching the apparition and his stance, his stillness, his distant intensity, recalled Master Stiesoldt's concentration upon that unspeakable ring. She did not know what he was doing. Probably it had something to do with the knowledge of arcane forces he had acquired at that Promontory he had once told her of, but she did not understand; she could only trust.

The visitant must have recognized a summons or stimulus of some kind, for it was reacting, its head turning slowly, its lightless eyes seeking the source. The vacant glance encountered Karsler Stornzof and anchored.

Karsler's lips moved, but his words were inaudible. The apparition drifted toward him. Luzelle did not see it, would not let herself look, but she felt the noiseless slow approach through every fiber of her body. Direct your mind elsewhere, Karsler had commanded, but that was impossible. Almost impossible. She thought of Girays, his paralyzed limbs and face, and her attention shifted.

Karsler himself seemed unaware of his own surroundings. He was motionless, eyes unfocused, blind gaze aimed nowhere, and for an instant she wondered if his mental exercises had carried him off somewhere beyond the realm of mundane consciousness.

She stiffened as the apparition drifted into her field of vision. The thing was too near to ignore; she could have reached out and touched it. The air fanned by those great wings stirred her hair, and she shivered. *Turn your eyes away, direct your mind elsewhere.* She could not, she could only freeze into terrified immobility, but that was enough, for the black gaze passed over her without pausing. The scaled form hovered before Karsler, and there it stayed.

It was going to tear his heart out, it was going to rip his head off—

It did neither. The motion of the wings ceased. The apparition floated, still as a weightless corpse.

Karsler's brow was wet with effort. His breathing was deep and measured, his face tranquil. There was an oddly fixed quality to his stare, and Luzelle realized that the seconds were lengthening and he never once blinked.

The endless minutes passed. His eyelids did not flicker.

The dark air was fading, so slowly at first that the change seemed a trick of imagination. The fireflies overhead gradually expanded into candle flames, the shadows contracted, and the supernatural chill grudgingly relaxed its grip. The apparition itself neither altered nor faded, but hovered there, fathomless eyes chained to Karsler Stornzof.

The room remained silent. Karsler's voice, although slow and distant, retained full authority as he directed his listeners, "Exit slowly, single file. Then leave the building. Silence, no sudden moves. Eyes and thoughts turned away from this spot."

Most obeyed without hesitation and without question, stealing quietly from the room one at a time, eyes downcast. Luzelle held her breath in anticipation of bloody mayhem, but nothing happened. One by one they slid through the door, some unable to resist casting frightened glances back over their shoulders as they went, but nobody other than herself lingered.

"Karsler." Wary of blasting his concentration, she kept her voice low, suppressing a score of questions. "What about you?"

"I remain here." His eyes did not turn from the malevolence.

"No need. It's done. Everyone's out but us. Come away now."

"Not done. I fix the Receptivity's attention upon myself. Should that hold fail before alteration in form has occurred, the malevolence goes forth to hunt new victims."

"I don't understand what you mean. Karsler, the exit's clear. Please come."

"When I have changed it; when I have defeated it. Now go, while you can. Go."

"How long do you mean to stay?"

He did not answer. She was not certain that he had heard her. He had excluded her, fixing his awareness upon the contest whose nature she scarcely comprehended. He had somehow managed to engage and hold the apparition's whole attention, that much was clear. Surely he had done enough. She stretched forth a hand, but did not dare touch him.

"Come away," she pleaded, and this time knew that she went unheard. Her hand fell back to her side. For a moment she stood looking at him, then turned and walked slowly to the door, where she paused, unable to resist a forbidden backward glance.

The malevolent apparition—a Receptivity, he had called it—still hung motionless in midair, talons dark with blood, black eyes empty as eternity, but somehow its appearance had altered, and it took a moment to identify the change. The jaw, that crocodile jaw, was neither as long nor as wicked as she had initially supposed. It was big and the teeth were impressive, but hardly crocodilian. Astonishment and fright must have warped her first impressions.

No they hadn't. The Receptivity had changed. Karsler had done it with his mind. She did not understand how, but saw that he would do more before he was finished, if he survived. She looked at him standing there, lost to the present world of reality, and almost retraced her steps. But she could do him no good, her distracting presence would only hinder him. She turned and walked away from the horror and the man who was fighting it.

The foyer was empty. The customers had fled, the Grewzians had withdrawn in accordance with their orders, and poor Gretti Stiesoldt, now a widow, had vanished. She went out through the front door into the mild, misty summer night, where the touch of the fresh moist air could not calm the tumult of her thoughts or still the trembling of her limbs.

She wandered away from the Three Beggars aimlessly and almost blindly. Her feet carried her back to the highway, and on along the road through the darkness and fog into the center of sleeping Groeflen. The windows were dark, the street barely lighted, the town silent, and it seemed to her confused vision that she wandered through a dream landscape. She did not know where she was or where to go, but her feet found their way to a building with a lamp above the door, and the emblem of a locomotive above the lamp; the railroad station.

The door was locked. She stumbled her way around the station house to the platform, where she found a bench and let herself collapse onto it. Burying her face in her icy hands, she sat unmoving.

Her thoughts whirled and warped into dreams or memories, she was unsure which. She sank into unquiet sleep or stupor that lasted for minutes or hours, until the whistle of a train roused her.

Luzelle opened her eyes. The skies had paled to ash, and the four forty-eight was pulling into Groeflen Station. She stood up, cast a bewildered glance around her, and realized that she had left her valise back at the inn. It scarcely mattered now. She still had her wallet and passport safe in her pocket.

The train wheezed to a halt and disgorged two passengers. Luzelle boarded, found a seat, and purchased a ticket from the conductor. The conductor went away. She leaned her head back against the seat and strove without success to empty her mind. The train moved, and Groeflen fell away behind her.

THE MORNING SUN WAS HIGH in the sky when Girays v'Alisante's hired carriage reached the quaint Three Beggars Inn on the outskirts of the town of Groeflen. His southbound train was not scheduled to depart the station for another ninety minutes. There was time enough to pause for a late breakfast, which he badly needed, having tasted no food since yesterday's ill-fated lunch.

In one sense there was all the time in the world, for the point and purpose in exerting himself further was gone. There was nothing more he could do to achieve or ensure a Vonahrish victory; he might just as well relax and finish the race in comfort. But he knew he would not relax, for even now, in the full consciousness of futility, he could put forth nothing less than his best efforts.

The carriage halted, but no ostler appeared to see to the horses, no attendants came forth to assist with the luggage. Curious. The inn appeared well tended, with its neat yard and sparkling windows. The present laxity of the staff seemed inconsistent.

Springing lightly from the box, the driver came around to open the door and assist his passenger from the vehicle. Such assistance was not unwelcome. The effects of yesterday's drug had subsided. Girays could walk and use his hands, but his limbs remained stiff, his hands and fingers clumsy. The Hetzian physician had assured him that full sensation and mobility would return quickly, but the recovery was not yet complete.

He leaned heavily on the driver's arm as they made their way through the front door into an empty, silent foyer. Nobody at the desk, nobody in sight at all. He rang the bell, and nobody appeared. He frowned, puzzled and mildly annoyed.

"Let us leave, sir," the driver suggested.

The fellow was plainly uneasy. "What's the matter?" asked Girays.

"It is not right, sir," was the only reply.

He did not demand explanation. His own nerves were stretched unaccountably tight. There was some sort of butcher-shop odor weighting the atmosphere and his instincts bade him seek fresh air, but he would not listen to them.

"We will eat. This way, I believe," Girays commanded, indicating a nearby half-open door.

"I am not hungry, sir. I will await you outside, if you please." The driver exited at a smart pace.

Girays hesitated, half inclined to follow. Ridiculous. His stomach was empty, he had stopped at this place to lunch, and that was what he would do. Limping stiffly to the doorway, he went through into the common room beyond, where he stopped dead on the threshold. The butcher-shop odor intensified, and the buzzing of countless flies filled his ears.

For a moment he scarcely comprehended the scene before him. The common room was a desolation of overturned furniture, smashed crockery, and sprawling, mutilated corpses. Something like a dozen bodies lay there, perhaps more; accurate count was difficult at a glance. One of them, flung down on its back in a clotted red pool at the front of the room, had been decapitated. The crushed remains of a silver-haired head lay not far away. Blood splashed the floor and walls, even spattered the ceiling, but Girays hardly saw it. His eyes shot to the center of the mercilessly sunlit room, where Karsler Stornzof, upright and utterly still, confronted a floating formless cloud of vapor.

Formless? For an instant Girays imagined the cloud shaped like a man, but the fancy passed at once and he saw only a dark smudge of mist that paled smoothly into transparency as he watched.

When the vapor was gone, or at least invisible, Stornzof staggered, grabbing for support at the nearest chair still standing. He missed it and fell to his knees, head bowed and chest heaving. Girays limped toward him as quickly as partially frozen muscles allowed, pausing only long enough to snatch up an open bottle of wine from a tabletop in passing.

Stornzof looked up, face drawn with exhaustion. Girays wordlessly extended the bottle. Stornzof took it and gulped down half the contents, then offered it back.

"Keep it," Girays advised. "Hurt?"

The other shook his head.

"What happened?" Girays's eyes scanned the room almost unwillingly.

"Receptivity."

"What?"

"Arcane visitant."

Oddly enough, Girays doubted neither the Grewzian's sanity nor veracity. "Did the visitant do all this?" he inquired.

Stornzof inclined his head.

"But it's gone now? It's been driven off?"

"Modified out of existence."

"Modified? By you?"

"It was something I had knowledge of." Stornzof spoke unevenly, his breath still ragged. "This Receptivity's form was molded by the expectations and perceptions of its beholders. By fixing its attention exclusively upon myself, I assumed control of its aspect, which I was able to alter gradually until at last my mind withheld all recognition, and the Receptivity ceased to be."

"Where did it come from?"

"That is a sorry tale, and I am very tired."

"What will you do, then?"

"Sleep. For the rest of the day, I believe."

"Not here, I trust. I cannot recommend the atmosphere. I've a hired carriage waiting in front. It will take us both to the railroad station, and you can sleep on the train."

"The offer is generous and I accept with gratitude."

"Then wait a moment while I find some food. I was ravenous until just now, and my appetite's sure to return as soon as

I leave this slaughterhouse." Girays hobbled to the kitchen, appropriated some cheese, apples, a cold chicken, a couple of loaves, and a couple of bottles, then returned to find Stornzof standing grey faced and shaky, but upright.

"You are injured?" Stornzof inquired, evidently noting the uneven gait.

"No. Some anonymous well-wisher tampered with yesterday's lunch. Doctor doesn't expect the effects to last."

"Yes." Something like a shadow darkened Stornzof's eyes. "Luzelle told me of your misfortune."

"Luzelle? When did you see her, and where?"

"Here, but do not concern yourself. She left hours ago, and she was quite safe. I should imagine she found her way to the depot and caught the four forty-eight southbound, according to her design."

"That sounds like Luzelle. You're certain she was unharmed?"

"Entirely certain."

"Then she's probably on that train and almost to Tophzenk by now. You realize what this means."

"She will reach Toltz tomorrow morning. We cannot hope to overtake her now."

"Barring sudden disaster, the race is hers."

"It is astonishing to you then, to think that she must win?"

"Not entirely," Girays answered. "She has insisted from the beginning that she would."

SHE HAD FALLEN INTO A LIGHT DOZE, but the groan of the brakes woke her. Luzelle turned her head and looked out the window. The train was pulling into the station. The sign above the platform read TOLTZ. She stared at it almost in amazement.

The train halted and the engine cut off. Passengers stood and began pulling their bags from the overhead rack. Luzelle had no bag. Rising to her feet, she strolled unencumbered to the end of the car, waited for the conductor to open the door, and descended three steps to the platform.

The morning air was soft and warm. By afternoon of this

summer day the temperature would probably climb to uncomfortable levels, but for now it was perfect. She made for the station at a quick pace, almost a trot, but halfway there it occurred to her that she did not need to hurry. Her rivals were far behind. She slowed to a walk.

Reaching the station, she crossed the waiting room. Before she reached the front exit, a solid figure clothed in an ill-fitting suit and battered straw hat materialized squarely athwart her path. She halted.

"Miss Devaire, isn't it?" inquired the stranger in the Vonahrish of Sherreen. "Miss Luzelle Devaire?"

She nodded. He reeked of cheap cigars and cheaper cologne. She resisted the impulse to turn her face away.

"Stique Breuline of the *Sporting Gazette,* at your service. Miss Devaire, I offer you my assistance as escort and protector from here to the registrar's office at city hall in exchange for your exclusive statement upon successful completion of—"

"No." Sidestepping the obstacle, Luzelle resumed progress. Stique Breuline stumbled in her wake. He was jabbering at her, probably trying to extract some sort of statement or concession. She hardly noticed what he said, it was meaningless noise, but his persistence attracted attention—of fellow journalists perhaps, or else of the idly curious—and soon a small crowd was following on her heels.

She did not care. Questions and comments were flying at her, but she easily ignored them all. Straight through the waiting room she marched, out the front door, and into one of the clumsy, comfortable Hetzian hansoms that waited in the street before the station.

"City hall," she commanded in careful Hetzian, and the vehicle moved at once. Luzelle settled back into the soft seat. The streets went by unheeded. Only once did she look back to discover at least three carriages following her. Somebody in one of them was waving a bright yellow scarf out the window. A signal of some sort?

More streets, and then the hansom entered Irstreister Square, which she had last glimpsed smothered in black smoke. Straight ahead rose the ornate city hall, with people waiting there on the steps before the entrance. The driver pulled up. Luzelle paid him, alighted, and hurried up the steps. The group clogging her path made way magically for her as she advanced, but she realized that every eye clung to her; that the queries, comments, and congratulations were meant for her—in short, that they knew who she was, and presumably had been waiting for her. Yes, that yellow scarf had certainly been a signal.

She crossed the lofty foyer, her entourage swelling as she went, exited into a hallway, and discovered that the route to the registrar's office remained imprinted upon her mind. She did not need to ask directions, but made her way unhesitatingly along the corridors, the eager audience following.

She reached the office, and a sense of unreality filled her, yet her heartbeat quickened almost painfully. The clerk on duty looked up as she entered, and she saw by his face that he recognized her.

The crowd at her back had gone intensely silent. As she advanced to the desk, she could hear the tap of her footsteps, and even the pounding of her heart. She surrendered her documents to the clerk, who required no instruction. The solidly audible thud of his inked stamp on her passport—the final stamp officially verifying completion of the course—broke the spell of silence, and the cheers exploded as the crowd surged forward to surround her. Luzelle saw enthusiastic faces with open mouths, and the noise beat at her ears, but the words were a jumble. She could not understand them and certainly could not answer, for her throat was tight, her eyes were filling with tears, and the sense of unreality was stronger than ever. She looked down at the passport that was somehow back in her hand, and it was only the evidence of the stamp— *Toltzcityhouse, Lower Hetzia*, with the date and hour, 11:36 A.M.—that convinced her the race was truly over.

24

THE HAIRDRESSER AND COSMETICIAN furnished by the Ministry of Foreign Affairs departed and the door closed behind them. The lady's maid likewise furnished by the ministry curtsied and retired, her services unwanted for the moment. Abandoning all dignity, Luzelle raced through the lavish chambers of the Kingshead Hotel's best suite, back to the bedroom with its great cheval glass in a gilded frame, before which she planted herself, wild to discover just what they had done to her.

She stared into the mirror and hardly recognized herself. Her reflected face was almost comically wide eyed. They had squeezed her into a glorious gown of pale aquamarine silk heavily embroidered with gold around the hem, that bared her shoulders, arms, and most of her bosom. The torturous corset beneath the gown, while reducing her waist to nothingness, was boned and angled to lift her breasts and push them together. The resulting display of rounded flesh threatened to overspill the low neckline.

Tasteless. Common. She could almost hear His Honor's voice. *The vulgarity of your appearance . . .* But no, this revealing mode was the height of fashion, flaunted by stylish women in all the western capital cities, and there could be no denying that she had the figure for it. So His Honor was welcome to say what he pleased; she wouldn't care. Not that her father was likely to say anything at all. In the ten days that had passed since she walked into the city hall in Toltz, accounts of her victory had decorated the front pages of newspapers everywhere. Udonse Devaire must have read about it, but he had not deigned to acknowledge his daughter's accomplishment. Her mother had sent a plaintively congratulatory letter two days earlier, but from her father—nothing. No, His Honor was hardly apt to concern himself with the dress she wore to this evening's reception at the Waterwitch Palace.

Nor was he likely to concern himself with her jewelry, hair, or face, and that was all to the good. The hair—piled up in careless tousled curls with many an artfully placed straying tendril, and dusted with gold powder—His Honor would have pronounced ostentatious. The jewelry—on loan for this one night only, it had been made very clear, and consisting of a magnificent emerald necklace with matching drop earrings—the Judge would have deemed unsuitable for an unmarried woman. And the face—she didn't like to think what he would say about that, she had her own doubts on the subject. Never mind that the cosmetician, a professional from the Toltz Opera, together with the dressmaker responsible for the aquamarine gown, had both agreed that ladies of the highest rank in society were now beginning to affect facial cosmetics. Never mind that the cosmetician had painted with the light and subtle hand of an artist. The alteration in her appearance was marked. The dark stuff delicately applied to her lashes widened and brightened her eyes to a startling degree. The blushing powder stroked sparingly across her cheeks brought her face to almost excessively vivid life. And the rosy, glossy paste smoothed onto her lips ripened her mouth beyond the bounds of proper moderation. The overall effect was unequivocally—she groped for the right adjective—*alluring*.

She had been running from party to gala to reception to party all week long, and she had never dreamed of displaying herself in such a guise. But tonight was the night of the Grand Ellipse victor's audience with Miltzin IX, and the aims of the ministry's minions were only too clear. Well, she had known about that from the start. She had accepted the ministry's terms along with its financial backing, and now it was time to fulfill her part of the bargain.

Luzelle's mirrored reflection frowned. Bargain or no bargain, she did not have to let them paint and varnish her like some sort of mannequin. Nor did she have to let them present her breasts to Mad Miltzin like two tidbits on a platter of appetizers. She still had time to change the dress, to scrub the cosmetics from her face, to pull her hair back into a tight little knot, to *make herself as unattractive as possible.* . . .

She was searching for a cloth with which to wipe the rosy paste from her lips when a knock on the door of her suite halted her and her frown deepened, for she knew at once who it was. He had visited her twice within the last three days, and would certainly put in an appearance tonight. For a moment she thought of ignoring the knock, but that would be pointless as well as cowardly, and in any case the borrowed maid had magically materialized and was already opening the door.

"Good evening, Miss Devaire." The visitor smiled courteously.

"Good evening, Deputy Underminister." Scrupulously suppressing every external sign of irritation, Luzelle produced a smile of her own, for vo Rouvignac deserved civility. The man was only doing his job in checking up on her, and he had traveled all the way from Sherreen to do so. It was not his fault that she had come to dread the sight of his studious face and the sound of his cultivated voice. It was surely not his fault that she contemplated tonight's culmination of her endeavor with a distaste verging on disgust. He had not forced her to accept the ministry's offer; she had done it of her own free will. Not his fault, and she shouldn't resent him, but she did.

"Do come in." Her smile stayed firmly in place.

"Thank you." He stepped into the plush sitting room. The maid closed the door behind him and disappeared. "You are looking splendid."

Good enough to pass inspection? Stifling the hostile retort, she responded correctly, "How kind. Won't you sit down, Deputy Underminister? May I offer you a sherry?"

"No and no. I do not intend to stay. I have called only to offer my best wishes, and to satisfy myself that you are ready and well prepared for this evening's venture."

Come to make sure the automaton's properly wound? Aloud she replied, "I ought to be prepared by now, Deputy Underminister. You've taken considerable pains these past few days to see to it that I am well instructed. I know all about His Majesty Miltzin's favorite books, plays, and poets, his hobbies and interests, his favorite foods, his favorite wines, his favorite dogs and horses, his taste in tailors and bootmakers, his likes and dislikes—loves salmon mousse, *hates* salmon soufflé, loves cockfighting, *hates* bearbaiting—you see? I think I'm reasonably capable of carrying on a conversation with the man."

"And of making yourself agreeable?"

"Yes. I'll be very agreeable. I'll be so agreeable that he'll fancy himself the most fascinating, witty, irresistible monarch ever to grace a throne. I'll be so agreeable that he'll think he's tumbled into a vat of treacle. So agreeable that his teeth start to rot from the sheer sweetness of it all. Is that agreeable enough?"

"Perhaps too much so. You deal with a jaded royal palate, remember. Insipid amiability is unlikely to engage His Majesty's interest. Nor is it in keeping with your own character. You might do better to be more yourself."

And if I were, then I wouldn't offer Miltzin IX of the Low Hetz anything beyond a polite curtsy. She said nothing.

Vo Rouvignac eyed her at length and finally asked, "You are willing to proceed with this project, Miss Devaire?"

"Project. An interesting term. I've given my word, haven't I? Of course I'll perform as promised. I will take advantage of tonight's private audience to secure King Miltzin's promise to sell the secret of the Sentient Fire to Vonahr, at a very handsome price. I am authorized to offer as much as twenty-five million New-rekkoes—"

"That has changed, as of today. You may now go as high as forty."

"Forty. How did that happen?"

"Circumstances press."

"I see." She resumed the recitation, "I will use any and every persuasive means at my command to sway His Majesty in Vonahr's favor."

"Should you fail, however—"

"Then I will do my best, at the very least, to discover the location of the clever Master Nevenskoi's secret workroom. There now, Deputy Underminister. Satisfied?"

"That you have learned your lessons by rote? Quite." Vo Rouvignac studied her perfectly painted face. "But memorization is not the key to success. Nor is pure determination, although it helps. Allow me to observe that the reluctance, tension, and resentment that you presently project in nearly tangible waves are hardly apt to win His Majesty's favor."

"Nearly tangible?"

"I assure you."

"Well, don't worry. By the time I come face-to-face with the king, everything will be fine."

"I wonder. His Majesty's susceptibility to beauty is proverbial, and yet he is not altogether devoid of perception. It is possible, however, that you might reconcile yourself the better to your task if you would pause to recall exactly why you have undertaken it."

Freedom, Luzelle thought. *Fortune, fame, success, independence.*

"Personal reasons, selfish reasons," she answered slowly. After a moment she added, "All along I've thought of nothing but winning the race. I never considered what must follow, never stopped to remember what you explained so clearly the first day we met—that you and the ministry regard my success as purely a means to an end. I knew it, but always managed to ignore it. And now the debt has fallen due."

"Indeed. But if you recall that day in Sherreen, you will remember that I told you of the Grewzian threat to Vonahr. You speak of a debt falling due? Vonahr's long debt of willful ignorance, political misjudgment, and procrastination is falling due with a vengeance. You are aware that we stand upon the verge of ceding Eulence Province to Haereste?"

"I've read that the president and Congress are considering the matter."

"There is little to consider. The Grewzian troops stand ready at the border. We are unfit to resist them, we've neither the manpower nor the weaponry. Submission to the Haerestian

demand purchases a little time. It will not be long, however—
no more than weeks at best, probably less—before another
concession, bribe, or tribute is demanded, one so exorbitant
that we shall find ourselves genuinely unable to pay it. Citing
our defiance, the Grewzians will seize the pretext to launch
their invasion, and there is an end. You've passed through many
nations currently in thrall to the Imperium. What impressions
have you formed?"

"I've seen more than I wanted. I've seen terrible things,"
she admitted unwillingly. "I wish I could forget some of
them, but I never will."

"Soon those scenes you would prefer to forget will repeat
themselves in Sherreen, and in the provincial capitals, and
throughout Vonahr. The brutality that you have glimpsed
briefly in passing will become our daily reality. The Imperium
will expand until there is no place left in the world to hide
from it."

"I know."

"You know, but you do not let yourself think of it, just as
Vonahr has not allowed herself to think of it these past fifteen
years—or perhaps twenty—or more, if you want to take the
larger view. But I ask you to think of it now. I also ask you to
think of what you might do to alter the prospect."

"You've made your point, Deputy Underminister."

"Should you succeed with the Hetzian king tonight, you
are in a position to make a difference, perhaps crucial. Do you
believe that?"

"I know it's not impossible. But not probable, either."

"Forget probability, it means nothing. You overcame all
obstacles to win the Grand Ellipse. That was improbable. You
will similarly overcome the king's resistance to win the Sentient Fire for Vonahr tonight, should you choose. I do not
doubt that you are capable of doing this. The real question is,
are you willing?"

"Yes." She met his eyes. "You've reminded me how much is
at stake, and I won't forget again. I promise to put forth my
best efforts. I'll do everything I can."

"That is all I can hope for. Maintain that resolve and you
will triumph."

Vo Rouvignac's own powers of persuasion were considerable. At that moment she believed him.

There was a knock at the door, and the maid answered. A moment later she stepped into the sitting room to report the arrival of the royal carriage sent to carry the Grand Ellipse victor to the reception.

"May I escort you to your conveyance, Miss Devaire?"

"Should I be seen in the company of a ministry official?"

"After tonight it no longer matters."

He offered his arm. She took it, they exited the suite, and proceeded along the corridor to the red-carpeted stairway, for she did not dare risk her gown in the hugely popular lift.

Halfway down the stairs he remarked, "I nearly forgot. You asked some days ago for news of Mesq'r Zavune, and I've received some. He has recovered his health but remains in Ul-Foudh, evidently uninterested in completing the Grand Ellipse course."

"I'm surprised he doesn't just go home, then."

"He would find life uncomfortable there. Debtors' prison awaits him in Aennorve. His financial obligations are relatively minor, but he cannot meet them, and the Aennorvi law is unforgiving."

She digested this in silence, then observed carelessly, "I'd quite like to help the poor fellow. Any chance that the ministry would advance me a small loan against the profits from the sale of that Hetzian manor house I've won?"

"Perhaps that is possible." He favored her with a keen glance. "Assuming a happy outcome, the service you render this evening places a grateful ministry in your debt."

"Bribery, Deputy Underminister?"

"Motivation, Miss Devaire."

Neither spoke again as he walked her through the lobby and out the front door to the street, where her carriage waited—a royal carriage, big and ornate, blazoned with the arms of Hetzia's monarch.

People on the street were staring. She did not know whether to wave and smile, or to ignore them. She compromised with a dignified nod or two. A grandly liveried attendant assisted her into the carriage and closed the door behind her. She looked out the window to see the Deputy Minister vo Rouvignac's nondescript figure standing motionless before the hotel entrance, and then the carriage moved and he was gone.

The drive to the Waterwitch was not brief, for the palace stood well beyond the city limits of Toltz. Luzelle watched as the cobbled streets lined with tall buildings of brick and stone gave way to unpaved avenues and wooden houses, which in turn yielded to dark stretches of uninhabited marshland. The road—winding through shadowy groves studded with standing pools separated by stretches of increasingly boggy ground—presently became a causeway traversing otherwise impassable terrain.

The carriage reached the first of the three great drawbridges guarding the way to secluded Waterwitch Island. This construction, flanked with fanciful sandstone towers, seemed frivolous enough, yet the winch and chains designed to raise and lower the bridge were obviously functional. Farther along the road the second bridge, spanning an expanse of inky water, was similarly ornate but utilitarian. And the third, connecting the roadway with Waterwitch Island itself, could be lifted to shield the gateway in the high wall of white stone girdling the palace.

This location and design, evidently appealing to His Majesty's sense of whimsy, in fact provide excellent defense. Luzelle remembered vo Rouvignac's description.

His Majesty's sense of whimsy. The Waterwitch almost stank of whimsy with its quaint turrets, cupolas, and spires, its crenellations and flying buttresses, its stained glass and rampant gargoyles. No doubt the place was equipped with camouflaged sliding panels and secret passageways as well. Not to mention a hidden workroom.

The driver pulled up before the gigantic arched front entrance. An attendant handed her from the carriage and escorted her a few paces to the door, where she was relinquished to the care of a footman who spirited her off along a perilously slick marble corridor to the lair of a very tall and very correct chamberlain. This lofty individual led her through a maze of hallways to a small private audience chamber on the second story of the building. He spoke a good deal in fluent, precise Vonahrish and at first, nervous and disoriented, she hardly followed him. Then she forced herself to listen, and the words began to register.

This small audience chamber, she discovered, was part of His Majesty Miltzin's personal suite, which accounted for the relative comfort of the upholstered furnishings. Here the winner of the Grand Ellipse would enjoy the honor of a short private audience with the king of the Low Hetz, and here she would receive into her hand the royal writ conferring the Hetzian peerage that was the victor's prize. The writ required official certification and recording in the Chronicles of the Realm, but this was a minor formality. From this evening on, the Grand Ellipse victress might legitimately regard herself as a baroness of Lower Hetzia.

Is that title salable? she wondered shamelessly, but there was no time to think about it, because the chamberlain was still instructing her.

At the conclusion of the audience, she learned, she would accompany His Majesty down the small private stairway connecting the audience chamber with the Long Gallery, where the guests were already assembled. There she would be presented to Her Royal Highness the Queen Ingarde—

Queen. Strange how easy it was to forget that King Miltzin had a queen.

She would then take a place of honor on the right-hand side directly below Their Majesties' dais throughout ensuing presentations, most notably those of the Grand Ellipse contestants successfully completing the course in her wake.

Girays. Karsler. Hay-Frinl, the Kyrendtish blueblood with the stammer. The Strellian physician, Dr. Phineska. She had not even realized that the last two were still in the race, but they had come straggling into city hall two days apart at the beginning of the week. Nobody after that, however. Everyone else was thwarted, incapacitated, missing, or dead.

The chamberlain was still talking. He was saying something or other about the reception, and she couldn't have cared less about the reception. Her mind focused feverishly on the audience that was to precede it.

His Majesty Miltzin would appear shortly, the chamberlain declared. The Waterwitch and all within extended warmest congratulations to the winner of the Grand Ellipse.

He bowed his way out. She was alone.

She sat down on a damask couch and waited. The minutes expired one by one. His Majesty did not appear. Her fingers began to twist. Rising, she paced restlessly about the room, her short train sweeping the carpet behind her. When she paused beside a window open to the summer breezes, she caught a snatch of music, perhaps wafting from the Long Gallery, where the reception was already in progress. *Girays*. He would be there by now, and she wished him a hundred miles away. She had been dodging him all week long, and although she had encountered him at various social gatherings, she had successfully avoided facing him alone. Except for that first time.

Within hours of his arrival in Toltz he had come knocking on her door at the Kingshead Hotel, and the sight of him standing there whole and healthy had filled her with such joyous relief that she had barely contained the impulse to fling her arms around him. He had asked her to dine with him, and she had assented gladly. They had descended to the hotel restaurant, placed their orders, and then, facing one another across a small table, they had begun to talk in earnest. He had described his recovery from the effects of the doctored eels in Wolktretz, his subsequent progress south, the meeting with Karsler Stornzof at the Three Beggars Inn, their simultaneous arrival at the Toltz city hall, and the coin toss determining Karsler's right to claim second place in the Grand Ellipse, with Girays coming in a very close third. For a while the exchange had been glad and spontaneous, but Luzelle had soon recognized her own growing sense of constraint, whose source had been plain enough. His narrative had inevitably conjured memories of their last parting at Wolktretz Station. "I love you," she had blurted, a moment before sprinting for the southbound train. She had not forgotten it and neither had he—his look of suppressed expectancy had told her as much—but she had found herself tongue-tied, unable to acknowledge, much less address, his unspoken questions.

So she had tossed airy trivialities across the table at him, while watching his eyes and his mood darken. She had gone on chattering for centuries at least, before he had finally met her eyes and observed quietly, "You're uneasy, and there's no need."

She had not attempted denial. He would have known she was lying.

"It would seem that I misunderstood you in Wolktretz," he had continued. "The error was mine, but I won't compound it now. You needn't fear I'll trouble you with attentions that I see would be unwelcome. There, does that reassure you?"

"No." She had replied without thought or hesitation. "You did not misunderstand me, and your attentions are anything but unwelcome. But I'm sorry, I *can't talk of it now.*" Rising from her chair, she had hurried straight out of the restaurant without a backward glance.

And since that day, she had not spent a single moment alone with him. He had been puzzled and frustrated by her elusiveness, she had seen it in his eyes more than once, but that could not be helped. If she had spoken with him, if anything significant had passed between the two of them, then she would never have been able to undertake this evening's task; she could not have come to the Waterwitch at all. If he ever so much as suspected her intentions—

But of course he suspected, she let herself realize for the first time. He knew that the ministry had recruited her for the race and, no matter how little vo Rouvignac had told him, he must have inferred the rest. He could not know how far she would go in order to fulfill her mission, but certainly he must suspect.

Frowning, she turned away from the window and the music. Still no sign of Miltzin and she wished he would hurry. She wanted to get started before her nerve and determination crumbled.

The king did not oblige. Luzelle returned to the couch, where she sat down and waited some more.

THE LONG GALLERY WAS CROWDED and the heat was oppressive. Too many candles for a summer's night, too many bodies trussed into formal evening wear and packed too closely together. Too much noise, too much inane conversation drowning out some fairly decent music. Girays v'Alisante eyed the nearest window, which stood wide open. If only he could reach it, he might draw a breath of fresh air and catch a glimpse of the gardens below. But the way was blocked by a brace of large, bejeweled Hetzian matrons bent on milking the visiting Vonahrishman of Grand Ellipse anecdotes.

"Poisonous snakes and crocodiles in Aveshq?" demanded one of the women. "It's really true? Were you *frightened*, or just *nauseated*?"

"And just what exactly *is* a 'Quiet-fellow,' anyway?" her companion wanted to know.

No escape from the inquisition. Girays replied at polite length. He had told the stories often enough throughout the week that he could almost recite them in his sleep. While he spoke, his eyes traveled discreetly. He saw a sprinkling of familiar faces, a host of strangers, a rainbow dazzle of jewels and silks.

But nowhere did he see Luzelle Devaire.

She was the guest of honor. Perhaps she intended a dramatically delayed arrival, a grand entrance; not like her, but not impossible under such circumstances. Or else her audience with the king of Lower Hetzia could have been scheduled to take place prior to her appearance at the reception. In which case she was probably with Mad Miltzin even now, arguing and pleading, offering Vonahrish millions for the secret of that Sentient Fire vo Rouvignac had described.

And just what else was she prepared to offer?

It was not his place to judge or condemn. Her motives were patriotic. Whatever the outcome, she deserved credit. His intellect conceded as much, but intellect wasn't everything.

Luzelle and Miltzin IX. Right now. The pictures started to roll through his mind, and he would lose his composure if he let himself look at them. He concluded his Aveshquian tale, and his listeners clamored flatteringly for more. A few well-chosen words transported them to the Forests of Oorex and the village of the Blessed Tribesmen. He spoke on, and the objectionable images faded a bit. He permitted himself the occasional quick searching glance around the great chamber, and at length hit on something that momentarily drove all thoughts of Luzelle's royal audience from his head.

On the far side of the room stood a burly, crop-haired figure attired in the black-and-grey livery that he recognized as belonging to House Stornzof. Karsler Stornzof's ramrod grandlandsman uncle had arrived some half-hour earlier, attended by just such a liveried figure. Not this particular liveried figure, however. The servant trailing a respectful pace behind Torvid Stornzof had been medium sized, lean, and narrow faced. Girays scanned the gallery and promptly picked out another loitering Stornzof retainer, this one sturdy and reddish haired. Curious. Most, if not all, of the guests had brought their servants; coachmen, footmen, and the like. But those servants were waiting out in the stables or down in the kitchen, where they belonged. They weren't hanging around the gallery among their masters. And the Grandlandsman Torvid hardly seemed the character to permit his menials unusual liberties.

The anecdote concluded. Girays made his escape and went to stand beside the open window, there to resume his scrutiny of the Long Gallery. He spied three black-and-greys in the crowd, and more than identical liveries seemed to unite them; all three shared a certain compressed-spring stillness and all three faces, while dissimilar in type, were alike in their alert hardness. They looked less like servants than soldiers. A small warning flare went off in his mind.

Accepting a flute of champagne from a passing waiter, he took a thoughtful sip and let his eyes wander. Soon he located Karsler Stornzof; very easy to spot with his height, his fair hair, and his uniform. Stornzof, as usual, stood surrounded by pretty women unabashedly vying for his attention. So it had been all week long, at every party and reception. They clustered around him like aggressive butterflies, they trailed him everywhere, he walked amid polychrome clouds of women. Tonight was more of the same, and the scene was unexceptional.

Or perhaps not.

As Girays looked on, the Grandlandsman Torvid Stornzof forced a passage through the huntress ranks to his nephew's side. The younger man glanced around quickly, and Girays caught a very fleeting, revealing expression of strong distaste, perhaps accompanied by some anger, before Stornzof's face resumed its wonted tranquillity.

KARSLER STORNZOF FELT A LIGHT PRESSURE on his arm and glanced around quickly to confront the Grandlandsman Torvid. Suppressing a powerful surge of dislike, he faced his uncle impassively.

"A word with you, if I may," Torvid requested.

Karsler shook his head. "I do not care to resume our quarrels, Grandlandsman."

"Bah, it is time to finish with foolish squabbling. We are of one House, that is unalterable, and it will not do for either of us to forget it. Have you lost all sense of duty, or will you spare the head of your House a brief word?"

Karsler inclined his head slightly.

"In private, then."

The two of them departed the Long Gallery together. Neither noticed Girays v'Alisante following quietly in their wake.

Torvid led the way down the corridor to a deserted antechamber. They went in, and he closed the door, locked it, then reached into his pocket to withdraw his cigarette case. Extracting a black cigarette, he lit up and drew a deeply appreciative breath, remarking with satisfaction, "There, that is better." There was no reply, and he observed, "Well, Nephew. I am glad you are willing to mend our differences tonight, as it is the last occasion we shall have to do so for some time to come. Tomorrow I return to the homeland."

"I wish you a safe journey."

"And you? I gather your days of leisure are drawing to a close."

"Correct. I have received my orders and I embark tomorrow morning for the Rhazaullean front."

"Scarcely an enviable post."

Karsler shrugged.

"It would seem that you are out of favor with your superiors. That is hardly surprising, in view of your recent highly public defeat at the hands of a woman. No doubt the absurdity of the affair only sharpens the sting of failure."

"Not really."

"I wonder if your fellow officers and the men under your new command will agree. Many will have wagered heavily on your victory, and perhaps hold you accountable for their losses. You are apt to encounter resentment."

"I am prepared for it."

"Well, take heart. A year or so of penance in the chilly wilds of Rhazaulle should properly atone for your blundering, and after that my intercession with the imperior will serve to curtail your exile."

"I do not ask your intercession, Grandlandsman. I do not want it."

"Ah? You prefer a more protracted expiation? Or perhaps you seek to bury your errors in Rhazaullean obscurity?"

"I do not acknowledge specific errors, nor with all the benefits of hindsight would I alter the decisions I made throughout the course of the race. If my reputation has suffered, I will repair it by means of my own efforts."

"Indeed. You cannot know how pleased I am to hear you say so."

Karsler glanced at his uncle. The grandlandsman was smiling with an air of inexplicable approval. The apparent cordiality was uncharacteristic and disquieting. He waited.

"You look as if you've swallowed a bayonet. I assure you, I mean what I say. Your desire to restore the full luster of the Stornzof name delights me, for the opportunity to do so is at hand. You will redeem yourself fully in the eyes of the world this very night. Listen, and I will explain."

THE DOOR OPENED, and Luzelle rose instantly from the couch. King Miltzin IX stepped into the room and she swept a low curtsy. Chancing a quick glance up at him, she saw that his protuberant eyes were fixed attentively on her neckline. She stood, and the eyes dragged themselves from her chest to her face.

"Miss Devaire. I am so very delighted to meet you at last. Allow me to extend my warmest congratulations together with my deepest admiration." Smiling, he extended both hands.

She did not know what she was supposed to do. In anticipation of this meeting she had studied some Lower Hetzian courtly etiquette, but nothing in the books had prepared her for such casual spontaneity. Acting on instinct, she offered up her own two hands, which were accepted at once. He drew her to him, kissed her warmly on the cheek, and released her. His walrus moustache tickled and she fought down the nervous urge to giggle. She caught the odors of expensive cologne and hair pomade.

Not such a bad start. She must have made a good impression. "Your Majesty honors me," she murmured.

"Nonsense, my dear, you grace us with your presence. Do you know," the king inquired, "that I was certain from the moment I first set eyes on you at city hall that you would be the winner? The morning the race began, I looked at you standing there so radiantly resolute, and I just knew. Occasionally I am blessed with such flashes of insight, and they never lead me astray."

"Sire, you astound me," Luzelle confessed. "At the start of the Grand Ellipse I stood in the midst of the racers. I never dreamed that Your Majesty had favored me with your notice."

"Ah, you do not know your own power. My dear, you are all but impossible to overlook. It was all I could do that day to prevent myself from staring, and this evening such an effort is entirely beyond me."

"Your Majesty is most gracious." She lowered her eyes becomingly.

"Not at all, I speak the simple truth." Miltzin planted himself on the damask couch. "Come, my dear Miss Devaire—ah, ruination, but that's so distant, so chilly. I hope you'll not take it amiss if I address you as Luzelle. That is far more cordial, is it not?"

"If it please Your Majesty."

"Indeed it does. Come then, my dear Luzelle—sit here beside me. Let us talk, let us discover one another."

She seated herself with care; not close enough to appear brazen, nor so far away as to seem entirely unapproachable.

"Champagne?"

"Thank you, Sire."

The small table before the couch supported a big silver cooler containing two iced bottles, a pair of long-stemmed flutes, and a document elaborately stamped and sealed. Miltzin IX filled the glasses, handed one to Luzelle, and proposed gallantly, "To victory."

Whose? she wondered. Glass clinked on glass, and she took a small, careful swallow. Not the time to be muddling her head.

"Ah. Before I forget." He picked up the document and handed it to her. "There, my dear. The writ of ennoblement, spoils of the conqueror. Conqueress? I cannot sort it out. Suffice it to say there is no one I will recognize with greater pleasure as a peeress of Lower Hetzia."

"Thank you. It is too great a reward, far more than I deserve. Sire, I am overwhelmed." She scanned the document, which was written in Hetzian, a language she comprehended imperfectly, and further complicated with convoluted legal phrases. The royal stamp and seal were elaborately authentic. All in all, an impressive piece of parchment, but what exactly was she supposed to do with it for the rest of the evening?

"But how thoughtless of me." Miltzin evidently noted her dilemma. "This will be delivered to your hotel tomorrow morning."

"Your Majesty is as considerate as you are generous. I am grateful beyond expression." She smiled prettily and wondered how to work the conversation around to the subject of Sentient Fire.

King Miltzin furnished unwitting assistance. Refilling his empty glass, he urged with enthusiasm, "And now, my very dear Baroness Luzelle, you must relate the tale of your Grand Ellipse adventures. I've caught a few of the stories at second hand, and they're tremendous. But now I would hear the true and accurate version, straight from the lovely lips of the winner herself."

Bless him, he was making it easy.

"Sire, I'll try not to weary you." She meditated a moment and then commenced, "Perhaps it's best to begin in occupied Lanthi Ume, where the local resistance continues to battle the forces of the Imperium. Just at the time I arrived, the Grewzians were engaged in executing a prominent, popular Lanthian citizen—an elderly gentleman who had been badly beaten, loaded with iron chains, and was subsequently dropped through a hole in the dock to drown in full view of his countrymen—"

"Did you actually see this with your own eyes?"

"I did."

"But how distressing!"

"It gets worse. The spectacle of the old gentleman's murder," Luzelle resumed, "incensed the spectators, and there was some public outcry to which the Grewzians responded by firing on a crowd of unarmed civilians. I myself was in that crowd. The bullets passed so close that I fancied I'd been hit. A young boy, little more than a child, standing not an arm's length from me was killed outright."

"Gad, what an episode!"

"Lanthians fell by the score, and even as they tried to flee the dock, the Grewzians went on shooting them down."

"Unnecessary. Absolutely unnecessary."

"Such was my conclusion, Sire. Later that same day," Luzelle continued, "I was contacted by several members of that ancient Lanthian society of savants known as the Select, who offered assistance in the form of an arcane conveyance, a sorcerous glass of transference—"

"Marvelous!"

"But even as the savants transported me and several others from the city of Lanthi Ume, the Grewzian soldiers burst into the secret meeting place and opened fire. I don't believe that any of the Lanthians survived."

"What an unconscionable waste of talent. These Grewzians are running amok. I wonder if Cousin Ogron quite realizes?"

"Sire, I've scarcely begun to tell you all I've seen." Luzelle spoke on. She told of natives tortured by the Grewzians in Xoxo, and of frightful abuses of power in Jumo Towne. She described the massacre and the Grewzian atrocities she had witnessed in Rhazaulle, the ugly incidents in the Mid-Duchies, and finally delivered a calculatedly incendiary account of the Grewzian violence inflicted upon innocent civilians in Upper Hetzia, only a few scant miles from His Majesty Miltzin's own borders.

The king's grasshopper eyes rounded as he listened. He sat quite still, his champagne glass forgotten on the table before him. She had definitely claimed his full attention; in fact, he appeared almost spellbound.

Her narrative concluded. She had daubed the Grewzians in the ugliest colors her verbal palette contained and, she hoped, obliged the king to view them through her eyes. She surveyed him. His expression was not easily analyzed. She decided that he looked stunned.

"Extraordinary," Miltzin conceded in a hushed tone.

She had moved him. Time to exploit that advantage.

"Sire, these Grewzian barbarians are bent on conquest and empire, they make no secret of it. They'll overrun the civilized world," she essayed. "We are all of us their victims, there are no exceptions. Lower Hetzia itself stands at risk."

"It's difficult to credit."

"But true. Your Majesty must believe. They'll crush us all, unless they are forcibly halted." She allowed him a moment to think about it, then suggested quietly, "It's widely believed that the king of Lower Hetzia owns the instrument of our preservation." He said nothing, and she prompted cautiously, "The news of Your Majesty's wondrous possession—the Sentient Fire—has traveled everywhere."

"You astonish me."

"Sire, I thought you knew. The hopes of threatened nations near and far—including my own land of Vonahr—fasten upon the Low Hetz. Your Majesty holds the power to save us all. I pray that you will choose to exercise that power."

"Remarkable. Quite remarkable. Such eloquence. Such fire. Such knowledge of the world. Such luxuriant beauty.

And the places you have been, the scenes you have witnessed, the dangers you have experienced! How fully you have *lived*!" Miltzin's eyes glowed. He took her hand in both his own. "You are a rare woman, the very embodiment of adventure! I do not believe I have ever encountered your equal. Indeed, I sensed from the moment our eyes met and merged that a connection existed between the two of us, between our souls, and now that we finally speak, the belief strengthens to certainty. You feel it too, do you not? I know that you do, you must."

"Sire, what I feel is hope, and confidence in your humanity, your intelligence, and generosity—"

"Ah, but it is so easy to be generous to you, Luzelle. I long to shower you with affection. I confess, I've never found myself so hopelessly smitten!"

"Majesty, if that's true, will you grant my greatest desire?"

"Name it."

"Sell the secret of Sentient Fire to Vonahr. Enrich your treasury, and grant my country the means of self-defense. Do this, and you'll have all my gratitude."

"But you see, my dear, the Low Hetz is neutral. Always. In any event, how can I think of sales, secrets, and warfare at such a moment? You intoxicate me!" So saying, Miltzin IX drew her into his arms and pressed enthusiastic lips to hers.

Luzelle controlled the impulse to push him firmly away. She could hardly afford to offend the king of Lower Hetzia. She could not even afford to disappoint him. And really, the man wasn't so very bad. He wasn't rough or cruel, he didn't stink. He wasn't at all as repulsive as the soldiers at Glozh Station or the night guard in Jumo Towne. Nothing about him that she absolutely couldn't endure. She became aware that she was sitting rigid as a corpse, and carefully relaxed her muscles. Perceiving this as encouragement, Miltzin allowed his ardor to escalate and his hands to stray.

Instinctively she pulled away from him, averting her face, then camouflaged the rebuff by reaching for her glass. A couple of sips bought a tiny respite.

"You are impetuous, Sire," she chided softly.

"It cannot be helped, my dear. You are the most confoundedly exciting creature. And the sweet fervor of your response assures me that our feelings are mutual, as I knew they must be."

"The admiration of a king is stimulating as the best champagne, and yet"—she bowed her head—"despite all temptation I can't forget my fears and I can't ignore them."

"Gad, you aren't afraid of *me,* surely?"

"Never, Sire. Your Majesty is all loving kindness. No, I mean I can't forget my fear for my homeland. It's like a black cloud shadowing my thoughts, quenching light and warmth."

"A young and beautiful woman cannot carry the woes of an entire nation upon her deliciously rounded white shoulders."

"I am Vonahrish, Sire. My country's danger is my own. So long as the Grewzian threat endures, my heart is imprisoned in ice."

"Ice?"

"Glaciers, Majesty."

"That is a tragedy, my dear. It isn't natural, it isn't right, to deny the deeper emotions. Your spontaneous affections must express themselves, else your health is bound to suffer. Allow me to comfort you. Between the two of us, I promise we'll manage to defrost that heart of yours."

He had his arms around her again. His hands were stroking her back while his lips worried an earlobe.

Again she controlled the impulse to shove him away.

"Sire—" she began, but got no further before he stopped her mouth with his own.

"NEPHEW, I'VE OCCASIONALLY slighted your Promontory training, and not without some cause," observed the Grandlandsman Torvid. "But even I can hardly deny certain obvious benefits. Specifically, that curious knack of yours, the ability to sense the working of arcane force."

Karsler Stornzof regarded his uncle steadily. He said nothing.

"This ability remains intact?"

Karsler inclined his head.

"Excellent, for Grewzland requires your services tonight."
Torvid paused, vainly awaiting a query. After a moment he resumed, "This Waterwitch Palace conceals a secret workroom
occupied by one of the Hetzian king's favorites, a certain sorcerous adept of proven talent. No doubt the workroom reeks
to the skies of unnatural activity. It should be a simple matter
for you to find it."

"What do you want with Nevenskoi, Grandlandsman?"

"Ah, you are somewhat informed. Good, that simplifies
matters. You've heard of the Sentient Fire created by this
Rhazaullean adept?"

"I have heard rumors. I cannot vouch for their accuracy."

"I will state the facts briefly. The fire is real, and offers the
greatest weapon of warfare the world has ever known. The
Imperium must have this weapon, but the royal Hetzian fool
refuses to part with it."

"You intend to negotiate directly with Nevenskoi, then?"

"Negotiate? I do not plan to waste time chattering with
some Rhazaullean freak of nature. Listen, I have brought with
me tonight half a dozen skilled Grewzian commandos disguised as servants and guests. When the workroom has been
located, my men will enter and secure the adept, together
with all the arcane writings, records, and paraphernalia of recognizable value that they can lay hands on. These prizes will
be removed from the Waterwitch and packed posthaste off to
Grewzland, where this Nevenskoi will assuredly yield the secret of Sentient Fire, together with any other useful knowledge he happens to possess."

"And then?"

"Need you ask? With such a weapon as this fire at our
command, Grewzland becomes invincible. The present wars
will conclude swiftly, freeing troops and supplies for new
campaigns. Vonahr will fall in a matter of days, opening a
path to the western principalities and all their resources. In
the east, the conquest of Aennorve will establish our total
dominance upon the Sea of Immeen. The Imperium will
grow, waxing in power and splendor, until all the world is

melded at last into a single, eternal whole. And there is an end to the petty rivalries of small nations, the jealous disputes and ignorant mutual fears that retard all progress. There will be a single great state, with one language comprehended by all, one set of intelligent laws governing all, one rational standard of behavior applying to all, one universal religion accepted by all who cannot do without such things, one universal currency, one consistent system of education, one universal philosophy—and one Grewzian imperior ruling over all like a god destined to bring order out of human chaos. You were ever the idealist, Nephew. Tell me if this is not a glorious ambition."

"A very large one, Grandlandsman. Certain to collapse beneath its own unwieldy weight. And perhaps that is all for the best. The world is not some great parade ground whereon all human beings may be compelled to march in step."

"The scope of the project intimidates you?"

"Less intimidates than repels, but that is beside the point. The fact is that your vast endeavor will smash itself upon the rock of practical reality."

"Practical reality is no rock, but a clay that strong men mold as they will. I'm sorry, if not surprised, to discover that you have not the stomach for greatness. Fortunately, your approval is not required, you need only cooperate. You will locate this Nevenskoi's hidden workroom and after that I have no further use for you, and you are more than welcome to slink off to the Rhazaullean front."

"No." Karsler spoke without particular emphasis and without change of expression, but something long held in check had finally released itself. He seemed to taste the words. "No more of this."

"It is not a request."

"Your aims are misguided, your methods contemptible, and I will not assist you."

"Have you lost all reason? As head of House Stornzof, and in the name of the imperior, I order you to perform your duty."

"You sacrificed your right to command me weeks ago,

Grandlandsman. As for the imperior, if he were here in person, I would answer him as I answer you—I will have no part of this latest criminal scheme."

"This is madness. It is impossible." Torvid spoke almost in disbelief. "We have always been at odds. Harsh words have been spoken, the rancor has been mutual. For all of that, you are a Stornzof and I have never seriously questioned your loyalty to Grewzland."

"It is unimpaired. I remain loyal to Grewzland—the real Grewzland, a nation founded upon principles of honor, built and brought to greatness by a people of much courage, generosity, and decency. That true Grewzland still exists, strong in thousands of hearts and minds, but its outward aspect has been distorted by that monstrous entity we call the Imperium. I would gladly die in the service of my country, but the Imperium is not Grewzland. The Imperium is a disease."

"So." Torvid drew smoke deep into his lungs and released it. "I remember I called you a traitor in Lis Folaze. At the time I imagined that I used the term carelessly in anger, but now I see the description was accurate. You disgrace the name of Stornzof, you disgrace the uniform you wear, and I would not accept your assistance now if you pleaded on your knees to serve me. There are other guides to be found. I will succeed without you, and for the sake of our family I will conceal your weakness, but know this—from this day forward I do not regard you as a member of my House. Now stand aside." He made for the door.

"One moment." Karsler did not move. "I cannot allow this."

"You *are* mad; you belong in an asylum."

"You will abandon your plan here and now," Karsler informed him. "You will collect your commandos and leave the Waterwitch."

"Or?" the other inquired softly.

"I will warn the palace guard, and you will be removed forcibly. In view of your rank you will probably escape arrest, but your ejection will be public and ignominious."

"You are in earnest? You oppose me? You threaten me?"

"I will not permit you to carry out this abduction."

"Then I am left with no choice but to defend myself."

A split second too late, Karsler recognized the deep satisfaction in his uncle's voice. A pistol appeared in the grandlandsman's hand, and he fired. Karsler felt something like a great blow to the chest, and he fell without a sound.

Torvid Stornzof put the gun back in his pocket. Dropping his cigarette to the carpet, he ground it carefully under his heel, and walked out of the room.

25

WHEN THE STORNZOF KINSMEN entered the antechamber, Girays shot a quick look up and down the empty corridor, then approached and pressed his ear to the closed door. It did not do much good. He could hear the mutter of voices in there, but they were speaking in rapid Grewzian and they were muffled by the thickness of the heavy door. He could make out a word now and then, nothing more. Both voices were even and well modulated. No shouting, no obvious quarreling. Probably nothing significant going on. His earlier twinge of uneasiness had been groundless.

He would look like a fool or worse if some servant caught him lurking there. Turning from the door, he headed back toward the Long Gallery, but walked no more than ten yards before he heard a sharp pop, like a pistol shot or a firecracker, and some immediate unthinking instinct slid him behind the huge velvet curtains framing the nearest window.

A sliver of space between curtain and wall allowed him a view of the corridor. He saw Torvid Stornzof emerge. The grandlandsman's face was quite expressionless as he glanced right and left, then strode off alone.

Girays waited a minute or so, but Karsler Stornzof did not appear, and a curious trepidation seized him. His pulse quickened as he slipped from his refuge, retraced his steps, and went into the antechamber.

Karsler Stornzof lay near the door. The front of his grey

jacket was soaked with blood, but he was alive, conscious, and struggling to raise himself from the floor.

"Lie still." Kneeling beside the wounded man, Girays saw that the red stain was spreading swiftly. The bleeding was heavy, but no artery appeared to have been touched. "There's a Strellian doctor in the Long Gallery right now. I'll have him back here in seconds. In the meantime, don't try to move." As he started to rise, the other's hand caught his wrist.

"No time." Stornzof's face was white and drawn with pain, but his voice was steady. "The grandlandsman is responsible. Stop him."

"Someone will. Right now it's more important to fetch you a doctor."

"You do not understand. My uncle plans a major coup. He has brought his commandos into the palace tonight and he will use them to carry off the Hetzian king's adept, creator of the Sentient Fire."

"I've heard of it." Girays was listening intently.

"He expected my assistance in locating Nevenskoi's hidden workroom. When I threatened to expose the plan, he shot me. But he will find another guide, he will claim that great prize for the Imperium before the night ends."

"No he won't. I'll inform the palace guards, and he'll be detained."

"Not enough. You thwart him tonight. What then?"

"It will do for now. Don't talk anymore. Lie still while I—"

"It will not do, and you know this. It is not enough merely to deprive the Imperium of the new weapon. This in itself will not save Vonahr, or any other target nation. In order to preserve herself Vonahr must secure this Sentient Fire, and use it."

Against the Imperium? Girays hesitated. He considered the possibility of a ruse, and dismissed it; not from Karsler Stornzof, not now. Confusion or lightheadedness?

"My mind is clear," Stornzof answered the unspoken question. "And I am still a Grewzian. For that very reason I serve the Imperium no longer. These past weeks I have seen its face too clearly."

"That's why you crossed the grandlandsman?"

"It is no time to explain. Help me up."

"Stay where you are while I get the doctor."

"Not yet. I am not so badly off. I am well enough to lead you to that hidden workroom. What happens when we reach it is your concern. Ah, your face, v'Alisante." Stornzof managed the shadow of a smile. "So astonished."

To say the least. Girays considered. If Stornzof could actually bring him face-to-face with the elusive Nevenskoi—if he could talk directly to the adept, bribe or otherwise persuade him to cooperate—then the entire troublesome matter of winning Mad Miltzin's capricious consent could be side-stepped. The adept, carrying vital knowledge in his head, might embark for Sherreen this very night. The opportunity was unique and priceless.

"You think you can find the way?" Girays did not let his eyes dwell on the other's wound.

"To an arcane source, yes. I've a sense of such things."

"I remember. But your wound is serious, and you'd best—"

"Do not concern yourself. Come, you cannot afford to refuse."

He was right. Girays's conscience kicked, and he ignored it. "Here, take my hand."

Stornzof rose with difficulty, assistance notwithstanding. A gasp hissed down his throat and then he was upright but unsteady, obliged to lean heavily on Girays's supporting arm.

"It is down below, I believe," he said. "We must find our way to the bottom of the building."

Girays nodded. Together they made their halting way from the antechamber and along the corridor. A trail of red droplets spotted the floor behind them.

THE GRANDLANDSMAN'S EAGLE GAZE swept the Long Gallery. The place was full of noise, heat, and foreign fools. Everywhere his eyes encountered idiotically animated faces, but nowhere did he spy the one he sought. He did not propose to waste precious time interviewing prospective guides. His aim fixed on the one man undoubtedly capable of leading him straight to the prize—King Miltzin IX himself; an audacious masterstroke certain to provoke international outrage, but justifiable in view of the stakes. The diplomats were welcome to wring their hands, but success would ensure the imperior's approval, and his was the only opinion that counted.

The king, however, was nowhere in evidence. Presumably he would appear at some point, when it suited him, but Torvid did not mean to wait upon Hetzian pleasure. Frowning, he caught the eye of the nearest black-and-grey retainer. A discreet nod, and the disguised commando approached. A terse conversation ensued, at the conclusion of which the liveried figure bowed and withdrew.

Torvid watched as his minion moved smoothly about the room, pausing twice to exchange words with fellow ersatz servants, who in turn approached three similarly ersatz guests. He nodded. His six commandos had received their amended orders. They knew now that the plan of attack had altered, and they knew that their leader required the present whereabouts of the Hetzian monarch. They did not know why the plan had changed. His frown deepened, and an anger too strong to ignore rose to heat his thoughts. They did not know that a member of House Stornzof had revealed himself as a traitor to his country and his imperior. They did not know that a Stornzof of pure blood had manifested weakness, criminal stupidity, and inferiority. They did not know and with any luck they never would, for his own decisive action had saved the day, forestalling disgrace and preserving the Stornzof name.

No one would ever know why Karsler Stornzof had died. His hero's reputation would endure, and nobody other than Torvid Stornzof would recognize the pathetic absurdity of the sham.

It should not have been a sham, there was no sense or reason to it. His sister's son's moral collapse was inexplicable as it was unforgivable, and a swift, clean death with pure fame left intact was insufficient redress. The traitor had gotten off far too easily.

The grandlandsman was impatient with his own silent

wrath. It was too insistent, and he could not afford the distraction. His men were already at work; presently one or another would deliver the information he sought, and then he would act. In the meantime he could not stand conspicuously aloof, he must assume the demeanor of an ordinary guest.

Accepting a glass from a passing waiter, he swallowed Belle of Sevagne and surveyed surrounding faces. Most were unknown to him and he preferred to keep it that way, but not far away stood the Major General Laarslof, kinsman to the Hetzian king and noted military historian, whose society was not intolerable. Approaching the major general, he initiated conversation. Laarslof related improbable rumors concerning the development of new ironclad warships, to which Torvid listened with half an ear while his purposeful thoughts anchored on Miltzin IX. Where was the king, and what was keeping him?

WRIGGLING FREE OF THE KING'S EMBRACE, Luzelle rose from the couch. Flustered, she brushed a straying damp tendril of hair out of her eyes. Matters were not proceeding properly. Somehow the topic of Sentient Fire had lost itself. Miltzin had other things on his mind, and it was all she could do to fend him off without discouraging him altogether. Time to redirect the conversation.

"Where are you off to, my dear?" the king inquired. His face was flushed, his chest rose and fell rapidly. He patted the empty seat beside him. "Come back; I miss you."

"Please, Sire, I must speak with you. I've a message of great importance."

"Do you have to deliver it from halfway across the room?"

"I think I must, if I'm to keep a clear head," she flattered.

"What is the use of a clear head at a time like this? We have found one another. Experience the moment, my dear. Abandon yourself to sensation."

"Sire, I can't allow myself to give way, at least not before I've delivered my message. It is only this: My government has authorized me to offer a great sum in exchange for the secret of the Sentient Fire. Vonahr is prepared to pay thirty million

New-rekkoes." Vo Rouvignac had advised her to start low, allowing the king to work the price up by degrees. Hopefully Luzelle awaited a counteroffer.

"You are a Vonahrish agent?" Miltzin IX sat up straight, and his face darkened. "This meeting is another diplomatic ploy? You've gained my presence under false pretenses?"

"Sire, I'm the winner of the Grand Ellipse. There's nothing false about that." Luzelle's chin came up. "But part of the victor's prize was an audience with Your Majesty, and I, as a Vonahrishwoman, couldn't neglect this opportunity to act on behalf of my country."

"I cannot abide dishonesty, and I am tired to death of this incessant harassment."

"Easy enough to end it," she suggested.

"You are a divine creature, but you don't understand politics. The Low Hetz is historically neutral. This posture never alters."

"May I suggest, Sire, that Hetzian inaction at this time effectively supports the Grewzian Imperium, thus violating your supposed neutrality?"

"Gad, a paradox. I'm not certain it's a sound argument, but it's entertaining."

"King Miltzin IX of the Low Hetz is renowned throughout the world for his sense of justice, his humanitarian vision, and his generosity," she improvised. "In accepting the Vonahrish offer—a great sum of money to replenish the Hetzian treasury—Your Majesty serves both your own nation and the rest of the world."

"I doubt that my cousin Ogron would view the matter in such a light."

"And how long in the normal course of events, Sire, before the imperior's ambitions fix on Lower Hetzia?"

"You don't mince words, do you, my dear?"

"I don't flatter myself that I voice any thought new to Your Majesty."

"Lower Hetzia is capable of self-defense. And yet those Grewzians *are* blighting the world. Cousin Ogron never knows when to stop," Miltzin mused. Pouring himself a glass of champagne, he drank it off in a couple of gulps, and frowned. "What was that sum you named, my dear?"

"Thirty million New-rekkoes, Sire."

"It is fairly considerable."

"Very considerable, Majesty." She studied his abstracted frown, and hope dawned. She was making progress, she was sure of it.

"I am in a position to serve as a great benefactor."

"A role that well becomes Your Majesty."

"You are persuasive, my dear."

"Your Majesty's own sense of judgment is my best advocate."

"Perhaps. The matter cannot be ignored forever. The clamoring only grows louder by the day." Refilling his own glass and hers, the king invited, "But come back, my dear, and sit here beside me. There is much to discuss, and I cannot shout across the room at you. Come, sit down."

She could hardly refuse without giving offense. Suppressing a sigh, she returned to the couch, and Miltzin's hands were on her at once.

BY THE TIME THEY REACHED the barrel-vaulted grey stone corridor deep underground, Girays had lost all sense of direction, but Stornzof evinced no confusion. A couple of times he paused, either to get his bearings or to rest, but the hesitations were minimal. The sense that drew him along a complex obscure path to an arcane source never failed, but the same could not be said of his strength. His pace was slow, he stumbled often, and then it was only the support of the arm and shoulder on which he leaned that held him upright. But his voice was calm and clear as ever, if subdued, when he halted before a stout door veiled in the shadows of a deep recess to announce, "Here."

Girays glanced at him almost in surprise, for the way had seemed endless and the arrival was abrupt. Stornzof's face was ashen even in the warm light of the iron lanterns suspended overhead. Alarm stirred at the sight, but he did not let it touch his voice as he asked, "Sure?"

The other nodded. Girays tried the door and found it unlocked. Evidently the occupant, if any, feared no intrusion.

He opened the door and they went through into a well-lighted, well-proportioned space full of marvels. Another time, the workroom contents would have fascinated him. This evening his eyes skipped over the tall shelves with their myriad glass vessels, the great vats, the dormant automata, the instruments, the Conglomerates, antique folios, pit-of-elements, and all the rest, to fasten on a man who sat alone at the table with a book open before him and a half-eaten bowl of lard-smackers beside him. The stranger jumped to his feet as they entered; a shortish, pudgy-faced figure clothed in the traditional black robe of savant, with the loose sleeves rolled up sloppily. He had sandy hair, thin on top, sandy moustache and imperial, and a look of amazement.

"Master Nevenskoi?" asked Girays.

"Neeper. I am Nitz Neeper," proclaimed the other, without a trace of Rhazaullean accent.

"I want the savant Nevenskoi."

"I've used that name. What is this? Who are you?" He was staring at the blood-soaked Grewzian officer. "What's happened?"

"He's been shot. Can you help?"

"I'm no physician. I can summon Dr. Arnheltz. He—"

"No time." Stornzof's voice was alarmingly weak. He swayed, no longer able to stand. "Set me down on the floor."

Girays obeyed, lowering the wounded man as gently as possible.

Stornzof made no sound, but his eyes squeezed shut for a moment. He opened them and commanded calmly, "Tell him."

Girays wavered, tempted to remonstrate, but there was no time. Turning to the bewildered Nevenskoi or Neeper, he announced without preamble, "We are here to warn you. There's a Grewzian plan to abduct you tonight. If it succeeds you'll be spirited off to Grewzland, where you and your Sentient Fire will enter the service of the imperior, willingly or unwillingly."

"Grewzian?" Neeper's uncomprehending eyes fastened on Stornzof's uniform. "But, then—"

"This officer doesn't condone his countrymen's methods,"

Girays explained shortly. "Now listen. The Grewzian agents present in the palace tonight will take you as soon as they manage to find their way to this room, and I don't think they'll need much time. Your powers are uncommon, perhaps you can defend yourself, I don't know. But I believe your best course would be to remove yourself from this place at once. Seek refuge somewhere. I myself will conduct you from the Waterwitch if you wish."

"The king should know of this," Neeper opined. "If this is all true, the attempt amounts to an act of war."

"It is true," Stornzof whispered. His breathing rasped, and his lips were faintly blue.

He was dying, Girays realized; a truth he had managed to stave off until this moment, and even now would not accept.

"We need a doctor." He scanned the room in futile search of a bellpull. "Where is this Arnheltz to be found?"

"Not here," said Stornzof dryly. His dimming eyes sought the adept. His voice struggled to emerge. "Grewzian commandos. Reception. Looking for someone to lead them here to you."

"They'll find nobody," Neeper told him. "Apart from myself and one very close-mouthed servant, only the king knows the location of this workroom."

"The king himself. Surely not at risk." Girays could hear his own doubt. "Even the grandlandsman would never dare—"

"He will not hesitate. Warn the king." A spasm shook Stornzof. When he could speak again, he repeated, "Warn him."

Unnecessary, Girays reflected, if only he could persuade this Nevenskoi or Neeper character to switch his allegiance to Vonahr. Buy him. Bully him. Flatter him. Win him over somehow, bring the Sentient Fire home. Use this chance that Stornzof had bought with his blood. What could Vonahr offer that Nevenskoi/Neeper did not already receive from his present master? More money? Status? Power? Titles, awards, acclaim? Public recognition? It wasn't easy to think of wooing a capricious adept at such a moment, with Stornzof gasping on the floor at his feet, but there was only one thing in the world that he could do for Stornzof now—use the gift effectively. He drew a deep breath and turned to Neeper, only to encounter an unexpected hint of satisfaction.

"His Majesty is in no danger," Neeper announced. "And neither am I, thanks to your warning. These Grewzian agents are easily controlled. If they're in the Long Gallery, I'll hold them there until they can be identified. There's no cause for concern."

The adept's tone of gratification was unmistakable. Girays could not account for it. "Hold them there how?" he asked.

"They can't pass through doorways guarded by fire." Neeper actually smiled. "Obedient Sentient Fire, commanded by its creator to block all exits while harming no one and damaging nothing."

Luzelle might be in the Long Gallery by now. Girays answered curtly. "No. Too dangerous."

"Not in the least." Neeper drew himself to his full unimpressive height. "The fire is governed by its creator's will. I assure you it is a safe, effective solution to the problem, and wonderful to witness."

The adept's expression reflected inexplicable eagerness. Girays did not like it. "No delay, just come away from here," he urged.

"There is no delay; the thing is done in an instant." Without awaiting reply Neeper turned away and hurried to the pit-of-elements, where a small green fire burned sedately.

Some portion of Girays's mind registered the distinctively hued blaze, quite possibly the Sentient Fire itself, but he paid little attention, for Stornzof seemed to be suffocating, mouth open to gulp down great drafts of air that did him no good. He knelt beside the dying man, looked into the eyes still filled with all their old serenity, and found that he could not lie to them. No false reassurance, no make-believe optimism. Taking Stornzof's icy hand, he held it firmly.

"Is there anything I can do?" he asked. He feared the other incapable of reply, but Stornzof surprised him, somehow catching his breath and finding what was left of his voice.

"Take Nevenskoi and his fire back to Vonahr."

The whisper was barely audible. Girays had to bend near to hear it. "I'll try," he said.

"Succeed. Best for everyone, including Grewzians."

"I'll succeed. I give you my word."

"I do not betray Grewzland. The Imperium betrays Grewzland."

"I know."

"Thank you, my friend. Tell your lovely Luzelle that I bid her farewell."

"She wouldn't appreciate that title of ownership. She's hardly mine, or anyone's."

"Her truest affections are yours. They always were. Once or twice I imagined otherwise, but that was delusion."

"Don't try to talk anymore, save your strength."

"No point, and just as well. I do not suit the world, do not fit comfortably into it, but cannot go back to what I once was. After tonight, cannot go back to Grewzland at all. Exile. Traitor, they will say."

"No. Loyal. You did what was right. If you're ever defamed or accused—and I doubt that will happen, but if it does— then I will defend you to my last breath. I promise that the world will honor your name."

"You will keep your word. I am certain of this. It is a feeling that I have." Karsler Stornzof's breath failed. Another spasm shook him, this one brief and mild. His open eyes emptied themselves of everything.

Girays knelt motionless and thoughtless for an indeterminate span, until a voice impinged on his consciousness.

"It's done."

He looked up into a face flushed with triumph.

"A sentient spark has been dispatched to the Long Gallery," proclaimed Nevenskoi/Neeper. "The situation is under control." His glance shifted reluctantly and he frowned. "But this Grewzian officer—perhaps Dr. Arnheltz might—"

"Too late." Girays's eyes dropped to the still, grey form. Carefully he laid down the cold hand. "My friend is dead."

ONE OF HIS MEN SIGNALED almost imperceptibly. Detaching himself from the Major General Laarslof, Torvid Stornzof withdrew to stand alone. A black-and-grey figure was beside him almost at once, and a whispered message reached his ear. The grandlandsman replied tersely. The liveried man nodded and withdrew to relay fresh orders to his five comrades.

He had the information he needed. King Miltzin IX presently closeted himself alone with the Grand Ellipse winner in an audience chamber connected to the Long Gallery by a small private stairway concealed behind a very unobtrusive door set flush with the wall at the front of the room.

He would go alone, his solitary departure drawing little if any notice. Two of his men would follow at suitably spaced short intervals, the others remaining behind to impose order upon the guests and servants in the Long Gallery, should the necessity arise.

The grandlandsman exited quietly. He found himself in a plain, cramped little stairwell, and there he paused to wait.

LOVELINESS, WHERE ARE YOU? Neeper sent the telepathic query speeding along psychic channels, and the silent, clear response was immediate.

Long place.

Corridor.

Colors under me, but I do not eat.

Good, leave the carpet alone, consume nothing. You know the way?

Yes, in your mind is the way.

That's right, just follow the path in my mind. Has anyone seen you?

No one sees, for I am smallsmallsmall and I go fast.

Perfect.

No. I am small. Wannabe big. Big!

Soon, very soon. I promise. Listen, sweet one, listen to me. This is a rare opportunity. Tonight comes your chance, so long delayed, to catch the eye of the world. Tonight you do not perform to entertain the shallow and ignorant, but serve a far greater purpose. You foil an enemy plot, you protect His Majesty—

Badmeat?

The king. You defeat his Grewzian enemies in full view of all the guests, all the nobility and great folk. Everyone who matters will see, and finally recognize your true greatness. And then at last the glory and honor so long withheld will be ours.

We will be big?

We will be huge.

Goodgoodgood.

Where are you now?

Big place, where you send me. Feet everywhere. Small ones like me eating wax high above, but they do not speak.

Anyone see you yet?

No. I am smallsmallsmall, nobody sees. Big, wannabe big, let me be BIG—

Your moment is at hand. How many doors do you see around you?

Doors?

Open spaces into other places.

Four holes with straight sides.

Good enough. Now, my beauty, my darling, my splendor, it is time. Divide yourself into four wholes and send your selves to the four doors. Fortify yourselves with a little wood and fabric fuel if you need additional strength, but consume no more than is needed to achieve greater size—

BIG!

Yes, big. Spread yourselves across the doorways, the doorways only. Permit no entrance or exit, but eat nothing that lives.

FOUR! Many of me!

Yes, and if any guests attempt to depart by way of the windows, chimneys, skylights, or any other unexpected route, you will spark off new selves to block escape.

No escape. No escape for anyone.

Remember, harm nobody.

No escape.

Neeper stretched his mind to gather the perceptions of Masterfire, and his consciousness accordingly altered.

Big place. High ceiling, bright lights, many colors, and many hundreds of feet in shoes. Four straight-edged holes around the sides.

The Long Gallery, the human portion of his awareness informed him. Filled with guests. King Miltzin's glittering reception in full swing. Four open doorways, potential avenues of exit. Four doorways to cover, demanding four separate selves.

Masterfire, already minute, effortlessly split himself in half and then into quarters, each of which went racing for a doorway.

Far below in the hidden workroom, Nitz Neeper felt the painless shock of the division through every fiber of his being, and the astonished confusion swamping his thoughts threatened to break the mental link with his creation. The lapse was brief. He mastered himself in a moment, the connection held, and suddenly he was in five different places at once. His own body stood motionless in the workroom, distantly aware of its surroundings, while his mind's eye gazed upon the Long Gallery from four separate vantage points. The massive onslaught of overlapping, shifting, and conflicting visual images was almost more than his human mind could support. His intelligence was not designed to interpret such torrents of sensory impressions and it seemed that something must give way under the strain, precipitating him into unconsciousness or madness. He barely knew that he was tottering and that the anonymous Vonahrish visitor was beside him, grasping his arm to steady him on his feet. The Vonahrishman was speaking, but the words were distant and indistinguishable.

The moment passed and his mind adjusted, leaving him bewildered but conscious, mental link intact. And now at last the time had come, the grand and glorious moment, and he could rise to satisfying heights, he could stretch, he could grow, he was tall, he was strong, he was excellent, he was BigBigBig, and the joy and the power surged triumphantly through all five of him.

Masterfire rose, and green flame flared simultaneously in four doorways. Neeper caught the clear sense then of vast surrounding alarm and confusion. The humans in their temptingly combustible garments were backing away from the green glare and the heat, stumbling and colliding and tripping over one another as they went. And there was noise, a great cacophony of shouting and yammering pierced by the shrill, unrestrained shrieks of terrified women. Those women were hard to ignore, with their voluminous skirts of lightweight summer silk begging to ignite, their petticoats of flimsy linen and lace that would flame magnificently at the first touch of a spark. He found himself reaching out toward them, shooting eager green tongues at those billowy skirts, and restrained himself with an effort. Harm nobody. Consume nothing that lives, and those skirts did not live, they were fine and legitimate food, but the meat they covered was bound to cook, so he'd better leave them alone.

For a while he observed the interesting spectacle of the guests in their screaming panic, until he noticed a number of them clumped around the windows along one wall and recalled that the windows offered a potential avenue of escape.

NoNoNoNoNoNoNo.

A new sliver of flame leapt from one of the doorways and streaked for the windows, whose long brocade curtains offered the nourishment and fortification permitting him to growGrowGrowGROW, and now he was BIG, and now he was FIVE, plus the body in the workroom, and now he was mounting higher toward the ceiling, and the humans were screaming, throwing chairs that passed straight through him to shatter the window glass, and that was fine, that was dandy, for the fresh air rushed in to invigorate him and he leapt, shimmied, and cavorted for the sheer joy of it all.

Life was good.

Down in the workroom, Nitz Neeper was bouncing gently up and down on the balls of his feet. An excited laugh bubbled out of him and then he became aware that someone was grasping his arm, jogging it to catch his attention and talking, jabbering at him insistently. At first he tried to ignore the distraction, but the noise refused to go away and at last he blinked and saw the Vonahrishman, who was demanding information.

"No escape," he said, dimly noting that his bright, hot voice was not his own. "No escape."

The Vonahrishman asked something, Neeper hardly knew

what. He shook his head and his consciousness of his immediate surroundings sharpened.

"Masterfire has succeeded," he reported. "The Long Gallery has been secured."

"If you've actually loosed fire in the Waterwitch Palace, we'd better get you upstairs to contain or extinguish it." The Vonahrishman's tone was peremptory.

Extinguish? A suggestion at once ghastly and absurd. The stranger, whoever he was, did not understand. He simply failed to recognize the depth and strength of the bond between adept and creation, nor did he comprehend the totality of Neeper's mastery. He feared imaginary perils, he was concerned and afraid because he was ignorant. *Extinguish.* Dreadful to see what the frightened human mind could conceive.

But this nameless Vonahrishman wouldn't be the only one to contemplate murder. Neeper's divided intellect strove hard to address the issue. *Extinguish.*

Badness? came the telepathic query from the Long Gallery.

Fear nothing, sweet one.

Even now the palace servants might be hastening toward the gallery with their water buckets and their soggy blankets, stupidly eager to turn triumph into disaster. The Vonahrishman was right, Neeper realized. He needed to be up there, he needed to explain, to clarify matters, to protect his Masterfire and his victory. The king, of course, had banished him to his workroom weeks earlier and that decree still stood. But surely His Majesty could condone disobedience under the circumstances; in fact, when the situation was properly explained to him, Miltzin would be grateful. Past transgressions would be forgiven, and the talented Nitz Neeper would regain all his former favor, prestige, privilege, and more.

"Yes." Neeper struggled to focus on the Vonahrishman, whose angular face seemed to blur a little around the edges. "Upstairs. Yes. Come. I will show you."

The Vonahrishman nodded. He cast a parting glance at the dead Grewzian officer on the floor, then suffered himself to be led from the workroom.

Barely aware of his immediate surroundings, Nitz Neeper scarcely knew how he found his way up from the secret bowels of the Waterwitch Palace to the well-known public corridors. His mind was full of fire, he simply let its light and heat draw him. But presently he realized that he was ascending a steep stairway, for the complaints of his own body, impossible to ignore altogether even now, told him as much. His lungs labored, his heart pounded, and there was a stitch in his side. Some part of him wanted badly to sit down and rest, but there was no time, no time, Masterfire needed protection.

Extinguish. The very thought set his innards to writhing. His belly shot a warning pang. He should never have gobbled that mountain of lard-smackers, he should have known better. Now they were catching up with him.

Up the stairs, and his belly was starting to complain in earnest, but there was nothing to be done, he couldn't afford to halt.

Loveliness, how do you fare? He sent the silent query winging, and the response, crackling with satisfaction, came back at once.

No escape. No escape.

Through the storage closet and utility room, out into a corridor, along the hallway and this time down some marble stairs to another corridor, and there before him stood an open doorway filled with green fire, and there stood a gang of sweat-drenched palace servants, plying their water buckets.

A cold wet shower went flying into the heart of the fire, and Neeper gasped and stiffened. For a moment he fought for air, then the flames leapt and his breathing resumed. Shoulders hunched and arms wrapped tightly around his rebellious middle, he stumbled on along the hall. The servants turned to gape at him as he drew near, but he never saw them. Green radiance filled his vision, and he addressed it in silence.

Sweet one, I am here.

IT WAS DIFFICULT TO THINK or speak with King Miltzin's tongue in her mouth. Luzelle flinched and turned her face away. The tongue was gone, but his hands were still on her and they were not so easily avoided, for he had backed her up against the arm of the couch, and he was half leaning, half sprawling atop her. There was no escape without flinging him forcibly aside.

Satisfying as that might be, she could not afford to do it.

Once again the issue of the Sentient Fire seemed to have died. The king had displayed some signs of moderate interest not long ago, but his attention had shifted entirely to other matters and discussion was unlikely to resume unless she took control.

"Sire—" she essayed.

"More champagne, my dear?" he offered amiably.

"No. Thank you." She took a deep breath. "Sire, won't you favor me with an answer?"

"You won't mind if I have some?" Her face must have gone blank, for he added, "Champagne, I mean." Pouring himself another glass, he drained it quickly and poured another.

He seemed to have worked up quite a thirst, she noted sourly. When he set his glass aside and turned an eager face to her, she drew back and pressed gently, "An answer, Sire?"

"What can I tell you, my dear?"

Was he utterly dull, or uncommonly sharp? For the life of her, she could not judge. "Will Your Majesty consent to accept my country's offer for the sale of the Sentient Fire?"

"What was that offer again? Forty million New-rekkoes, was it?"

"That is perhaps not impossible, Sire." Her heart beat fast.

"Hmf. Well. I don't know." King Miltzin heaved a sigh. "Frankly, my dear, I find it impossible to cogitate. Our mutual emotions are too overwhelming, the shared excitement too intense. Let us postpone discussion, let us abandon ourselves to the moment that we both desire."

"No, Sire." She pushed an invasive hand away. "The matter's urgent, we must talk—"

"Later." He was sweaty and panting. "Half an hour or so and then, I give you my word as a king, we'll talk as long as you like about anything you please." He slid a damp hand up under her skirt.

Luzelle stiffened. Half an hour. Nothing, really. She had vowed from the start to succeed at any cost. *You've reminded me how much is at stake . . . I'll do everything I can,* she had promised vo Rouvignac mere hours earlier. . . . *You are in a position to make a difference,* he had told her, and it was true; she might serve and save Vonahr, she might alter the course of history. Half an hour with the king of Lower Hetzia was scarcely a high price.

Time to clinch the sale. Technically all she needed to do was to lie still for him, but Miltzin's satisfaction would be greatly enhanced if she could counterfeit some sort of response; though just exactly and precisely what that response should be she did not quite know, for she possessed no direct experience of her own. No, nor much of indirect experience either. She came from a conservative bourgeois household wherein young ladies were required to cultivate their innocence. Her mother had furnished no information beyond the glum warning that married women owed a certain distasteful but unavoidable duty to their husbands. Her friends, once married, had waxed similarly reticent, and a pall of silence had descended over the intimate aspects of their lives. Curious. Such stringently limited contact as she had experienced with Girays had fostered the distinct impression that the wife's duty might not be so very distasteful after all. In fact— as she would never have dared admit to anyone—during the term of her betrothal years ago, she had actually longed to learn more; with Girays.

Not with this paunchy, pomade-scented stranger presently slobbering over her breasts.

Girays. How would he look at her, after tonight? Would she be able to face him at all? No matter how forgiving he might be, or try to be, matters would change forever between the two of them.

But somehow, for reasons she could not fathom, she found herself thinking less of Girays than of Karsler Stornzof. Her life was not with Karsler and never would be. Yet she thought of him now, thought of his clear eyes that saw what was true and what was right; thought of him in the Three Beggars Inn, sacrificing his chance of a Grand Ellipse victory for the sake of something more important.

Just then she had the strongest, most inexplicable sense of

Karsler's presence. She could feel him standing beside her, feel the current of calm, steady encouragement and reassurance flowing from him, feel it so strongly that she actually turned her head to look, half expecting to see him there.

An absurd fancy. As far as she knew, Karsler was downstairs among the guests in the Long Gallery. Yet she could have sworn that he was near, she could all but see him and all but hear his voice.

No. What she really heard was the king's heavy breathing. His hand navigated an obstacle course of silken underwear to busy itself between her legs.

An angry revulsion so strong that it was almost physical rose to choke her. For a moment intellect lost its ascendancy. She was reacting without thought, hesitation, or conscious intention when she slapped King Miltzin's face with all her strength.

LET ME THROUGH. Loveliness, stand aside, Nitz Neeper suggested, and the curtain of flame shrouding the doorway parted at once. He stumbled through into the Long Gallery, and the Vonahrishman followed.

A single sweeping glance took in the great chamber sealed with fire, the broken windows and overturned chairs, the seething crowd of terrified guests, but nowhere among them did he spy the one he sought, whose recognition validated this entire demonstration. Nowhere did he see Miltzin IX. His insides knotted, and he clutched himself with a gasp.

The gap in the fire guarding the west doorway of the Long Gallery did not escape the attention of the guests, who converged on the exit from all corners of the room. In an instant Neeper was engulfed, crushed among desperate bodies, elbowed, squeezed, and battered. He could not breathe, he could hardly see and barely think. A hurricane of howls and screams beat at his head. He pressed his hands tight to his ears, but the din smashed through into his brain. A pang of exquisite agony stabbed his vitals, and he doubled, grunting.

Masterfire had not forgotten his commission. *No escape.*

The words echoed faintly through Neeper's mind. The gap in the doorway closed itself and the sudden furious flare of light and heat sent the frantic prisoners scrambling backward. Neeper was borne along helplessly as a bit of flotsam, until a violent collision hurled him to the floor. Twice he sought to rise, and twice the crush of frenzied humanity thwarted his efforts. Thereafter he curled himself into a ball, arms laced protectively around his middle, where internal storms raged.

He hardly noticed that Masterfire was expanding. *Big.* He did not see the green flames dancing joyously along the walls and mounting toward the ceiling. *BigBigBig.* Dizzy, disoriented, and in pain, he did not notice that the screams of the trapped guests were waxing in crazed desperation. *No escape.* Nor was he fully conscious that the air in the Long Gallery, heated to oven temperatures, was growing difficult to breathe.

A hand grasped his arm. He opened his eyes and gazed without comprehension into an angular dark face, vaguely familiar.

"Here, Neeper, let me help you up. Lean on me."

Who? *EatEatEat.* Oh yes, the Vonahrishman who had found his way to the workroom. *EatEatEat.*

"Neeper, do you understand me?"

Nitz Neeper offered a glazed smile. "Eat," he mumbled. "EatEatEat."

TORVID STORNZOF HAD GROWN IMPATIENT. His two men should have joined him by this time. They had somehow blundered, and they would certainly suffer his extreme displeasure. Black brows lowering, he stepped to the door and listened. Some sort of commotion was rocking the Long Gallery; he could hear muffled shouting in there, shrieks, a thunder of footfalls. Some sort of problem, obviously. Someone had taken ill and collapsed, a fight had broken out, or else some fool woman had spotted a mouse, screamed, and touched off a panic. Whatever was happening in there could not excuse the failure of his men to follow their orders.

Torvid savored his anger for a moment. It was deep and

strong, promising a rich, vengeful return at some point in the not distant future. Now was not the moment to think of it, however. He could not loiter indefinitely in the stairwell, for it was only a matter of time before some servant noted his presence. He could not afford to wait any longer for his bungling subordinates, nor was he disposed to go hunting for them. He would have to complete the mission on his own. The prospect did not entirely displease him. He was at his best working alone, unencumbered with the incompetence of underlings.

His hand slid into his pocket to close upon the pistol. Silently he mounted the stairs leading to the king's private audience chamber.

"YOU STRUCK ME." Palm pressed to his stinging cheek, eyes wide with disbelief, King Miltzin recoiled. "You—actually—*struck*—me."

Luzelle sat up, automatically adjusting her disordered gown. "I'm sorry, Sire," she said, almost dazedly. "I didn't mean to." Truer words were never spoken. Her thoughts boiled. She had ruined everything, she realized. In one insane, mindless instant she had lost control and ruined everything. Desperation blossomed. She had to fix things, somehow.

"What do you mean, you didn't mean to? Are you trying to claim that you attacked me by accident?"

It had, in a way, been by accident, but the king would never believe that one. "I—I was upset," she confided, adding piteously, "I was very confused, I was frightened."

"Frightened? I think not. You nearly took my head off. You were about as frightened as a tigress attacking her prey."

"I'm sorry, truly sorry. Please believe me, Sire. I—"

"I do not wish to listen. I have never encountered such savagery in a woman. Women should be soft and tender. This is a painful disillusionment."

"It was a mistake, Majesty. A terrible mistake. I'm sorry from the bottom of my heart. Please believe that, please accept my humblest apology—"

"I'm not interested. I am the king of Lower Hetzia, and you presumed to strike me. You don't belong in a royal palace. In fact, you don't belong in a civilized society. I will call a carriage for you. It's time for you to leave."

"Majesty—" She could feel the tears of defeat stinging her eyes, and made no attempt to repress them. Perhaps they would help, women should be soft and tender. She stretched forth an appealing hand. "What can I do to make amends? Only tell me what I can do?"

"You can leave. And the two of us can forget that we were ever so unfortunate as to encounter one another."

"But I shall never forget, Sire. Guilt and remorse will haunt me for the rest of my days. For we stood upon the very brink of something splendid. Your Majesty was about to bestow the blessing of Sentient Fire upon a grateful Vonahr. You had all but agreed to arm the world against the Grewzian menace. Please, I beg you, don't let one woman's folly anger you. Forget my stupidity, and think only of—"

"You are mistaken." King Miltzin regarded her with distaste. His face was still splotched red from her blow. "There was no agreement, either stated or implied. If you chose to believe otherwise, you deceived yourself. And now, Madame, if you will excuse me, I shall ring for a servant to conduct you to—"

"Sire, I entreat you—" It was all she could do to keep from grabbing him and shaking him hard. "If you'll only allow me to—"

The plea, almost certainly doomed to failure, was never completed. The door opened. The Grandlandsman Torvid Stornzof walked into the room, monocle aglint and pistol dead steady in his hand.

King Miltzin rose, wrapped in dignity, to demand, "What is the meaning of this?"

"The adept Nevenskoi—I want him," Torvid announced. "You will lead me to the workroom."

"How dare you? Who are you?"

"That does not concern you."

"He's Torvid Stornzof, a Grewzian grandlandsman." Luzelle locked eyes with the intruder. "Sire, you see for yourself what these Grewzians are, and what they're willing to do. You can't allow these people to—"

"Silence," Torvid advised her. "Another word and I will fire."

She looked into his eyes and saw that he would not hesitate. She said nothing.

"This is monstrous. Leave my presence," Miltzin ordered, beet faced. "Leave my palace. Go before I order the guards to arrest you."

"Your Majesty no longer commands here. That responsibility has passed to me," Torvid observed dryly. "Now you will conduct me to this hidden workroom I have heard of. Its location is not unknown to you, I believe."

"Don't imagine that your rank or your nationality will protect you, Grandlandsman," Miltzin warned. "Your imperior is my cousin. This incredible outrage won't go unpunished. Now go while you can, before you worsen matters for yourself."

"We will go together, Sire. You will lead the way. Refuse, and I will put a bullet between your eyes."

"Have you taken leave of your senses? I am the king."

"Kings bleed, I'm told. Must we put it to the test?"

"You wouldn't dare. I've sentries and bodyguards stationed throughout the adjoining rooms of my apartment. The sound of a shot would draw them instantly. You wouldn't escape capture and execution."

"Possibly." Torvid shrugged. "Your Majesty, however, would not witness the spectacle. Now, enough of this chattering. We proceed to Nevenskoi's workroom. No, not that way," he directed, as his prisoner took an eager step toward an ornate set of double doors. "You have been good enough to warn me of the armed guards and sentries. Therefore we will go down the stairs I have just used, through the Long Gallery, and out into the corridor beyond. You too," he told Luzelle. A flick of his pistol directed her. "Go stand beside the king. Take his arm. Do it now." He waited until she obeyed. "That is good, you are a handsome couple."

"You don't seriously imagine that you can march the king at gunpoint straight through a mob of guests?" Luzelle could not forbear asking. "You're mad to attempt it."

"It is for that reason I shall succeed," Torvid informed her. "No one expects such a stroke, no one perceives it clearly; these fools will not recognize what is under their noses. Now I take my place beside His Majesty and we move to the Long Gallery. We smile, nod, and chat agreeably. It is a pleasant reception, everyone sees that the king enjoys the society of his good friends. But the three of us will know that my gun presses His Majesty's ribs. At the first hint of resistance, the first attempt to break away, the first cry of warning or distress, I will fire. I care nothing for personal consequences. At the very least I will eliminate this Hetzian king whose whims deprive the Imperium of the great weapon. Understand here and now that I will do what is needed."

Miltzin IX nodded stiffly. The red mark of the recent slap had faded, leaving his face altogether colorless.

Luzelle skewered the grandlandsman with her eyes. "Karsler knows nothing of this," she accused.

"Nothing," he agreed with a slight smile.

His expression chilled her. Her eyes dropped before his.

"Now move," Torvid commanded. "Smile. You are enjoying yourselves. Go."

It was impossible. He could not do this thing, couldn't possibly get away with it in the middle of a royal palace crawling with servants, guards, and guests. But somehow they were exiting the audience chamber at Torvid Stornzof's command, he was herding them down the stairs, he was doing as he pleased with them. A sense of furious helplessness filled Luzelle. Gripping the king's arm tightly, she descended.

At the bottom of the stairs she confronted a small, plain door. On the other side of it people were shouting. She hesitated.

"Move on," Torvid directed.

She shot him a glare of loathing. King Miltzin pulled the door partially open. Immediately the shouts and screams intensified. A blast of blistering heat surged into the stairwell from the Long Gallery beyond. Luzelle caught a quick glimpse of impossibly green flames blanketing the walls and tenting overhead before the door slammed shut.

"Move on, both of you," Torvid commanded imperturbably.

"Are you mad?" She rounded on him. "It's an inferno in there!"

"So I see. A green inferno. Very singular."

"We have to go back the way we came, there's no choice!"

"Ah? Let us consider. Did you note the bizarre color of the flames, the eccentric pattern of activity, the dearth of real destruction? Here, I suspect, is what I seek. This is the Sentient Fire, is it not?" Torvid demanded of the king. His victim's pained silence evidently passed as assent. "Excellent. This simplifies matters. The inventor is close at hand, I presume."

"I don't know." Miltzin chewed his lip. "I did not send for him or for Masterfire, I never gave him leave to do *this*. He has gone much too far."

"This Nevenskoi was not summoned to the reception?" Torvid inquired.

"No. He's out of favor; he shouldn't be here frightening people." Miltzin frowned.

"Then Your Majesty must make your displeasure known to the adept. You will find him for me now. Move on."

"No." Luzelle balked. "I won't go in there."

"You would prefer a pistol shot here and now?"

"Better than burning alive!"

"Masterfire will not harm you, Miss Devaire," Miltzin promised palely. "Don't worry, Nevenskoi won't allow it."

His reassurances failed to convince her, but when the door opened again, she found herself moving through it, still clutching the king's arm.

The searing green brilliance, the billowing smoke, and the confusion of cries underscoring the roar of the fire momentarily bewildered her. She blinked, and her vision swam. The heat beat at her like a club, and she raised a hand to shield her face. She dimly perceived that most of the guests clustered screaming near the center of the room, as far as possible from the flame-curtained walls. At once, however, a desperate band broke from the human mass and sprinted for the hitherto unnoticed door through which she and her two companions had just entered. Swiftly as they moved, they were not fast enough. A long, writhing arm of fire shot for the doorway. So blindingly quick and unerring a stroke could not have been random. Almost instantaneously the exit was smothered in green flame.

No way back. Luzelle's stinging eyes ranged. Through clouds of smoke she discerned the fire-choked doorways and windows. No way out for anyone now.

"Over there." The grandlandsman pointed.

Luzelle glanced at him. In the midst of flaming chaos Torvid Stornzof appeared impossibly unruffled, silver hair faultlessly ordered, monocle firmly in place. A small, unconscious curve of the lips communicated satisfaction.

He's enjoying this, Luzelle thought, amazed.

"We shall hunt through that rabble." Torvid's gesture encompassed the cowering crowd. "Go."

Miltzin obeyed without argument. His presence and his predicament seemed to go unnoticed by his guests. The pistol pressing his ribs was unobtrusive, and nobody was looking.

They would never find the grandlandsman's quarry in the midst of such smoky pandemonium, Luzelle thought. But they had barely begun to move before her eyes were drawn as if by instinct to Girays, who stood only a few yards away supporting a smallish, sandy-haired man garbed in an archaic black robe. The robed figure, bent double, was clutching himself around the middle. She curbed the impulse to run to Girays. No good dragging him into the orbit of the grandlandsman's dangerous attention.

Her caution was wasted. Miltzin IX glanced at the man beside Girays and looked away too quickly.

Noting the king's reaction, Torvid studied the robed figure, and stated, "Nevenskoi."

Miltzin shook his head mutely.

"Ah? And yet he wears the costume of an adept. Let us investigate." The grandlandsman steered his prisoners deftly through the crowd.

As they drew near, Girays spotted them, and Luzelle saw his dark eyes widen with a stark horror that startled her, the expression was so uncharacteristic. It took her a moment to recognize herself as the cause. Until this moment he had thought her safe. He had not expected to find her trapped along with him in this fire-swept deathtrap of a gallery.

The robed man lifted a pain-racked gaze to the king's face. "Majesty," he whispered, and succumbed to a fit of violent coughing.

"Neeper," the king returned firmly.

"Forgive—"

"Having another of your attacks? Don't try to talk, Neeper. Better save your strength," the king counseled.

"Neeper? Nevenskoi, surely," the grandlandsman suggested with amusement. He addressed himself to the stricken man. "This green fire about us is subject to your will?"

"It—" Neeper's response gave way to coughing.

The grandlandsman waited.

"Masterfire—consume   nothing—*EatEatEat*—" More coughs, concluding in a moan.

Torvid's brows contracted. "Come, enough of this. I lose patience."

"Mine went long ago. Leave him alone," Girays advised. "This is pointless, Stornzof. You are finished. I know about Karsler, and if we survive this fire, the world will know. You've nowhere to hide. Even your imperior won't be willing or able to protect you."

"What about Karsler?" Despite the intense heat of the atmosphere, Luzelle went cold inside.

"Ah, were you hiding behind a chair, M. v'Alisante? Or perhaps crouching like a little mouse outside the door? No matter. It is just as well to proceed openly, subterfuge annoys me." Torvid turned, advancing his arm slightly to bring the pistol into view.

"And what do you intend to do with that?" Girays arched a contemptuous eyebrow. "Shoot everyone in sight? What happens when you run out of ammunition?"

"By that time, be certain that you and the Hetzian king and this Vonahrish trollop here will all be dead. But in fact I prefer to avoid wholesale slaughter. Rather will I remove the adept, merely." Turning to Neeper, he declared, "You will now accompany me to the nearest exit. When we reach it, you will displace the barrier of fire, only long enough to permit the two of us clear passage."

"I—*Eat*—losing control—" Neeper tottered.

"Do you understand me?"

Neeper groaned and sank to his knees.

"I said, do you understand me? Answer." No reply, and the grandlandsman's overtaxed patience failed. Lifting the hand that held the gun, he struck the adept twice, back and forth across the face.

The blows sent Neeper sprawling. He hit the floor and lay still. A shocked exclamation escaped Miltzin IX. Girays took a purposeful step forward and halted when Torvid turned the gun on him. At the same time something between a rumble and a deep growl shook the room.

Luzelle's breath caught. She could not identify the sound, she had never heard its like before, but it filled her with elemental fear. She looked up. The fire that lined the walls and ceiling was expanding, flinging forth new and longer tongues of flame, their green edged with a furious tinge of red. The roar of the conflagration deepened in pitch, rose in volume, vibrated along her nerves, and she sensed a sudden killing rage, vast and insatiable. Her limbs shook. She was not fully conscious of running to Girays, but his arms were around her and he was holding her tightly.

The fire was plentifully blood streaked now, the red tints almost equaling the green, and the sea of flame overhead was starting to change, its substance shifting and flowing like water stirred by arcane currents. Up above a whirlpool of fire spun into existence, its center directly over the head of Torvid Stornzof. The grandlandsman noticed nothing. He was shouting at the man on the floor, who stirred feebly and opened his eyes.

Neeper looked up; not at his tormentor, but at the ceiling. His glazed eyes widened, and he said something. Luzelle could not hear a word, but she saw his lips form the syllables: *No. Sweet one. No.* Torvid followed the adept's gaze. He studied the fiery vortex with clinical interest.

The revolutions overhead accelerated, and a funnel of fire

whirled down from the ceiling. There was a crackle like a laugh of savage satisfaction as Masterfire seized upon his prey.

Torvid Stornzof screamed. His arms flailed, and he jigged like a crazed marionette. His beautifully tailored evening wear ignited, the fabric burning away in seconds to expose his nakedness to the flames. His silvery hair and dark brows frizzled away in an instant. His flesh began to char, and the aroma of cooking meat drifted through the Long Gallery.

Flinging himself headlong to the floor, Torvid rolled, but the great funnel of flame that enclosed him was not to be smothered. The violence of his contortions loosed showers of sparks, many flying to nearby silken skirts and petticoats, where small new fires blossomed. Fresh cries of terror rose, but none equaled the power of the grandlandsman's unremitting shrieks.

Through the wavering curtain of green and red, Luzelle could see his skin blackening and peeling like the surface of a charred pepper. His hairless scalp was distended with vaporous blisters that nearly doubled the size of his head. His facial features were distorted beyond recognition, eyes lost amid bubbles of ashy tissue, if they were still there at all. Of his genitals nothing remained but a blackened stump. But his voice was intact. Surely by now he must have inhaled fire, he must have scorched his lungs and throat, but his screams never slackened.

It seemed to last for years. Eternity revolved while the blind black mannequin at the heart of the blaze dragged himself upright to lurch through the crowd whose members gave way, stumbling over one another in their efforts to clear the path of the human torch.

Eventually he fell, but his agony was not ended, for he continued to jerk and pule as he burned, and the scrabbling motion of his hands suggested attempts to crawl. At last all movement and outcry ceased. Even then Masterfire did not relinquish his first kill, but lingered fiercely there until the body was reduced to greasy ash and bone.

"Master Neeper." Girays stooped to lay a hand on the adept's shoulder. "Can you hear me?" There was no response, and raising his voice to make himself heard above the surrounding tumult, he repeated the question.

Neeper's eyes opened. *"Big,"* he whispered. "I am Big-BigBig."

"Master Neeper, can you quench or at least diminish this blaze?"

"Big. Big." Neeper blinked, and his eyes focused. "Dizzy. Pain. Can't think."

"Can you clear an exit?"

"Don't know." The adept rubbed his eyes. "I will try. Help me."

Each taking one of his arms, Girays and Miltzin hauled Neeper to his feet and steered him to the nearest doorway, where they released him. Neeper staggered, and Luzelle thought he would fall again, but he managed to stay on his feet. For several seconds he stood motionless, head bowed. Then he lifted his eyes to gaze into the fire, and his face was still, but she caught the intimation of intense mental activity. Long moments passed before the crimson streaks began to fade from the guardian flames. When they had resumed a uniform green hue, Neeper spoke, his words audible to his creation alone. The flames drew themselves lithely aside.

King Miltzin was first to exit the Long Gallery. Luzelle and Girays, supporting Neeper, followed close behind. They emerged into a corridor where a bucket brigade of palace servants toiled. Flying droplets of cold water spattered Luzelle's face. They felt marvelous. Neither she nor anyone else in sight was about to burn alive, and that felt marvelous too, but she could hardly summon undivided joy. She had bungled her audience with the king beyond recovery, and Girays had dropped a hint so dreadful that she could barely bring herself to consider it; something about Karsler.

But she did not have to think about it yet, for the liberated prisoners streaming from the Long Gallery were jostling, shoving, all but trampling her in their haste to escape the blazing palace. No room for thought at the moment, and perhaps just as well. Down the corridor they fled in a terrified stampede, down the great central stairway, through a foyer the size of a marble meadow, and out the front door onto the palace grounds, where a crowd of resident retainers already stood watching.

The Long Gallery emptied swiftly. When the last of the guests had passed through the fire-wreathed doorway, Neeper wobbled, faltered, and muttered incoherently. The gap in the flames closed itself. Masterfire cavorted and roared in mad green glory.

"Nevenskoi—my Waterwitch!" King Miltzin appealed. "Do something, my dear fellow!"

"Sire, I—" The adept's eyes turned up. He collapsed in a dead faint. Girays and Luzelle caught him as he fell.

Gouts of flame lashed out into the corridor. Hopelessly overmatched, the bucket brigade turned tail and ran, ignoring their monarch's frantic commands. Twisting fiery tentacles snaked inquisitively along the hall. A set of brocade window draperies ignited, and then another. The carpeting underfoot began to smolder.

There was no opposing the blaze, at least for now.

"Sire, let us assist you from the building," Luzelle begged.

Miltzin looked at her and nodded. Together they exited, carrying the unconscious Neeper. They bore him as far as the white stone wall girdling the palace, and there in that safe place set him down on the ground. Already the adept was stirring.

They were far from isolated. Hundreds of guests, palace guards, and household servants waited and watched at the foot of the wall. A kind of sighing murmur from the spectators dragged Luzelle's unwilling eyes back to the Waterwitch, where green flame was flaring from the second-story windows. As she watched, the fire expanded, mounting toward the roof and beyond. A mighty roar of triumph reached her as Masterfire arose, reaching for the starry skies.

MUCH LATER THAT NIGHT, when the Waterwitch stood in smoking ruins and the green conflagration was finally subsiding, Miltzin IX spoke up for the first time in hours.

"We'll need to do some sort of a head count to make certain there were no casualties other than that Grewzian swine."

"A search through the debris will reveal the remains of at least one other body, Sire." Girays, illumined by the diminishing green glare of Masterfire, bowed his head. "Karsler Stornzof was murdered by his uncle for seeking to defend Your Majesty."

The tears blurred Luzelle's eyes, but her grief contained no element of surprise. She had known for hours, without letting herself know. Karsler pointlessly dead. Her mission botched, her country doomed. A night of disaster.

"Well. I am sorry about the younger Stornzof." Miltzin frowned. "Not every Grewzian is a criminal, it seems. But my cousin Ogron is, and I can assure you I've had more than enough of him. He's had the bit between his teeth far too long, and it must end. Tonight was absolutely the last straw. I'll teach him to sic his ruffians on me. Miss Devaire, what was that Vonahrish offer you were peddling a few hours ago? Fifty million, was it?"

"Forty, Sire," she murmured, astonished.

"Forty. Well. I cannot haggle. It will cover the rebuilding of an improved Waterwitch, and that will have to do."

"Your Majesty is willing to sell the Sentient Fire to Vonahr?" She wondered for a moment whether her imagination was playing her tricks. Beside her she heard Girays draw in his breath sharply.

"After tonight, do you think I'll hesitate? That fire has grown a little too hot for Lower Hetzia to hold. You may take it, give Cousin Ogron the hotfoot or ram it down his throat, and welcome." Miltzin turned to the still and silent dark figure sitting beside him. "Nevenskoi—I mean, Neeper—are you quite awake?"

"Sire, I am." Neeper's voice was small. "And I wish to express my profound sorrow—my grief and my shame—"

"As well you might, but now is not the time. What you must tell me is this. Given normal circumstances—that is, when you're not dyspeptic, dazed, or smoke poisoned—do you still believe yourself capable of controlling our Masterfire?"

"Sire, tonight was a dreadful aberration. It will never recur, believe me. Ordinarily, Masterfire obeys me willingly, provided he's not overstimulated. But that's something that rarely—"

"Stop there. I'll take you at your word, and if there are conditions attached, that's no longer my concern. You see, my dear fellow—you are about to embark for Vonahr."

Epilogue

ONCE THE KING MADE HIS DECISION, events moved swiftly. There was no time to rest, to reflect, or to absorb the reality of Karsler's death before Luzelle found herself aboard a train en route for Sherreen. Yet another train, but this one special, blazoned with the royal arms of Lower Hetzia and reserved for the use of His Majesty and certain favored guests. Thus she traveled with Girays and the adept Nevenskoi, or Nitz Neeper as he now called himself, along with a muscular squad of armed bodyguards in an absurdly luxurious private car equipped with bulletproof, bombproof walls. The adept, a treasured prize, was not permitted to stir from his seat unaccompanied by a guard.

The moment the train pulled to a stop in Sherreen, Nitz Neeper was whisked away in an anonymous closed carriage. Luzelle assumed that he had vanished into the maze of the Republican Complex, but she could not be certain, for her various questions went politely unanswered. The exclusion annoyed her—for surely, in light of her involvement, she was entitled to some information—but the minions of the Vonahrish government did not seem to see it that way. She was courteously escorted back to her own lodgings and there they left her, curiosity unsatisfied.

Apparently her usefulness was at an end.

It was odd to be back in her old rooms. They were familiar and comfortable enough, but quiet, a bit shabby, and somehow

devoid of meaning. She had no sensation of coming home—
there was little to come home to, beyond a good collection of
books and mementos; even the furniture wasn't her own. But
her mood improved that evening, when she began to sort
through the accumulated post that her landlady had collected
and held for her during her absence. The news of her victory
had preceded her return by days, and the response was impressive. There were literally hundreds of congratulatory letters,
notes, and cards, most of them from strangers, but warming
nevertheless. Less sentimentally gratifying, but of greater practical worth, were the offers—a full dozen communications solic-
iting her services as a lecturer, guest speaker, or writer of articles,
essays, and books. There was even an invitation from the University of Sherreen to spend two semesters as a resident Bulaude
Fellow, an honor never before bestowed upon a woman.

Her success was assured. Never again would she need to
contemplate a return to bitter dependency in His Honor's
household. The freedom she had longed for was hers. It was a
true accomplishment, but somehow she would not fully feel
the triumph, nor would it seem entirely real, until she shared
it with Girays.

She got the chance the next day, when the two of them
were summoned to the Ministry of Foreign Affairs. They arrived simultaneously, and both were shown to a featureless little conference room on the ground floor. Four of the
ministry's officials waited there, but the Deputy Underminister vo Rouvignac was not among them. Perhaps, lacking the
advantage of a royal conveyance, he had not yet made it back
from Toltz. The officials introduced themselves. Meaningless
names and titles flew by too quickly to catch.

Luzelle went in hoping to acquire a little information, but
soon discovered that she was there to answer questions, not to
ask. The interrogation was polite but prolonged. The officials
wanted as complete as possible an accounting of events at the
Waterwitch Palace reception, particularly anything pertaining
to the Stornzof kinsmen, or to the behavior and appearance of
the phenomenon cautiously described as "a quickly spreading
fire of reportedly unusual properties."

Reining in her impatience, Luzelle answered as best she could, and Girays did likewise. His description of Karsler Stornzof's final minutes, which exactly matched what he had told her on the train save for the omission of a few personal remarks, brought the tears to her eyes again. Her own depiction of Torvid Stornzof's assault upon King Miltzin's private audience chamber provoked a discreet exchange of glances among the listeners. The joint report of Torvid's death—singled out for burning among a host of guests, none other of whom was harmed—held them enthralled. The intelligence they gleaned was clearly of interest, but they were not about to return the favor. When she plucked up her courage and dared to ask for news of Nitz Neeper and the Sentient Fire, all four officials went suddenly vague.

At the close of the interview she withdrew frustrated, arm in arm with Girays. They repaired to a nearby café, where they sipped iced coffee in the shade of striped canvas awnings while she told him of the offers, the proposed articles and books, and the Bulaude Fellowship.

"Congratulations." His smile flashed. "It's splendid, you've accomplished wonders. You've so many choices, which way will you go?"

She looked at him. His dark eyes were filled with warmth that was patently genuine. His smile was perfect. "What's wrong?" she asked.

"I'm proud of you, and happy for you."

"And? Something's the matter, isn't it?"

"Nothing to do with you."

She studied him. Three or four months earlier she would have accused him of jealousy, resentment, wounded vanity. Now she knew better. Then it hit her—the bright hopes and plans for the future, the work, the achievement and recognition—all of it was bound to crash in ruins when the troops of the Imperium invaded Vonahr. The publishers would fold or at least suspend operation, the lecture circuit would shut down, even the University of Sherreen would drastically reduce its curriculum, if it continued to function at all. She might, at some point years in the future, attempt to resume her interrupted career, but without great hope of success. There would be little call for a female writer/lecturer in occupied Vonahr.

Girays knew that. He was too kind to remind her. Moreover, he'd even more pressing concerns of his own. His beloved estate of Belfaireau, family seat of the v'Alisantes for generations, was a handsome prize by any reckoning. In the event of a successful invasion the Grewzian conquerors would inevitably appropriate the house and lands. She hadn't even thought of that until now.

Despite the strength of the summer sun, the day seemed to darken. She took a sip of iced coffee and changed the subject.

TWO DAYS LATER she received an invitation to lunch with vo Rouvignac, now back in town. The deputy underminister proved more communicative than his associates of the ministry, but less than thoroughly forthcoming.

"I would answer if I could, Miss Devaire," he assured her between spoonfuls of chilled lobster bisque. "But I myself am kept quite in the dark these days."

She did not believe him, but knew no polite way of expressing skepticism, so she smiled understandingly, allowed an appropriate interval to elapse, then changed the phrasing and angle of her questions. He probably did want to enlighten her, as far as he safely could. When she asked about Karsler Stornzof, he was able to tell her that a thorough search of the ruined Waterwitch Palace had revealed the Overcommander Stornzof's body intact in an underground chamber untouched by fire. The body had been sent back to Grewzland, where the Confraternity of the Promontory would oversee its final disposition. As for the diminished remains of the Grandlandsman Torvid Stornzof, they had been quietly interred in a Toltz cemetery. Despite its fury the fire had claimed no other victim.

And the Hetzian adept, Nitz Neeper? Still in Sherreen?

Difficult to say. Master Neeper had been interviewed by government officials at some length upon his arrival. Vo Rouvignac himself had not been present at these meetings, he declared; in any event, their content was considered sensitive. There was reason to suspect that Master Neeper had recently been transferred to another location that vo Rouvignac could hardly specify; really, it amounted to so much speculation.

And the Sentient Fire? She had seen it with her own eyes, she knew that it was real, but was it practical? Was it remotely reliable or controllable? Could it actually serve as an effective weapon of war?

"As to that, Miss Devaire, I am hardly a competent judge," vo Rouvignac declared modestly. "If you desire concrete fact, I fear that you must do as I do—read the newspapers."

SHE FOLLOWED HIS ADVICE, and two days later her copy of *The Republican* carried the banner headline, HAERESTEAN DEMAND REFUSED.

Her pulse quickened. This was it. She read on. The article was long and loaded with detail, but the gist was simple enough. The Vonahrish president, with the full support of Congress, had responded to the Haerestean Parliament's request for the transfer of Eulence Province to Haerestean ownership with an unequivocal refusal. The Haerestean government had already responded with a formal statement of protest. Diplomatic relations between the two nations had broken off. The Haerestean ambassador had withdrawn from Sherreen, and the embassy was closed. The High Council in Grewzland had issued an emphatic censure of Vonahrish policy, together with a pledge in support of abused Haereste, brother nation of the Imperium.

They would launch that assault within hours. Perhaps, miles to the south in Eulence, it had already begun. Luzelle set her newspaper aside. She did not want to be sitting here alone in her rented rooms at a time like this. She wanted to be with Girays, right now, this minute, but could not respectably indulge the impulse. She couldn't very well turn up alone and uninvited at his town house door, it wasn't suitable.

Too bad. I'm going.

She stood up. Her summer straw hat hung on a peg in the

tiny vestibule. Before she reached it, somebody knocked on the door. She opened it. Girays stood on the threshold.

"Have you seen the newspaper?" he asked.

THEY WENT TO THE NEAREST CAFÉ and found the place jammed, for it seemed the natural instinct of Sherreenians in times of common trouble to assemble, consume much coffee or wine, and talk. Luzelle supposed that the cafés and taverns all over the city must be similarly crowded and noisy. The volume and intensity of discussion was daunting. Strangers addressed one another with the ease of old acquaintance, and everybody seemed to have some theory, belief, expression of hope and confidence, or declaration of impending doom to offer. The rumors flew, and many were presented as statements of absolute fact, but nobody actually knew a thing.

Everyone was in the same boat, all dependent for information on the newspapers, which were in turn obliged to await dispatches from the Haerestean border, hundreds of miles to the south.

Sherreen waited. That evening's special edition of *The Republican* announced in letters two inches high, HAERESTE INVADES EULENCE PROVINCE.

And after that, Sherreen waited again.

TWENTY-FOUR TENSE HOURS DRAGGED BY. Luzelle spent many of them with Girays and others loitering outside the offices of *The Republican*. The stretch of Cliquot Street before the building was choked with pedestrians and closed to wheeled traffic. The offices of the two rival journals— *The Sherreen Messenger* and *The Parabeau Gazette*—were similarly besieged, but the largest crowds gravitated to the city's oldest, preeminent source of news. The men, women, and children gathered there were quiet, orderly, patient, and remarkably considerate of one another. A sense of strong solidarity reigned.

The late-summer sun beat down on Sherreen. Straw hats and parasols offered limited protection. Vendors of chilled drinks and overpriced snacks of every description circled the edge of the crowd, doing brisk business. As the hours wore on, the crowd remained quiet and civil, but certain proprieties began to erode. Men loosened their collars and cravats, and some even removed their jackets. Ladies stripped away their white lace gloves, as they would never have dared under ordinary circumstances. Small rugs, blankets, and mantelets seemed to appear out of nowhere to spread themselves out on the ancient cobbles, and scores of citizens tired of standing seated themselves right there in the street.

Luzelle did not want to sit down in the street, and could not bring herself to ask Girays to do it. When she could no longer bear standing in the sun, they withdrew to the comparative comfort of a doorstep in a shaded entryway, and there she could rest for a while. But her weakness cost them their good position near the front door of the office building, and they could not hope to regain it.

Girays went and brought back chilled fruit juice and cheese pastries. They ate and she felt her energy returning. The sacrifice of their place did not seem to matter much. The hours were passing, and no revelations rewarded endurance.

The sun was leaning on the western rooftops, the shadows were stretching to soothe Cliquot Street, and Luzelle began to wonder what they would do when darkness fell. Give up, go home, and return in the morning? Or wait here along with so many others throughout the night, into the morning, and beyond, as long as it might take? She was sick beyond words of the endless waiting and no doubt Girays was equally fatigued, but she could hardly tolerate the thought of not being present to learn the outcome, and she suspected he shared her sentiments there too.

The emergence of a sweaty, haggard journalistic lackey burdened with a stack of *The Republican*'s scarcely dry special edition resolved her dilemma. The shouting crowd surged forward, up the short flight of stone stairs, and the newspapers flew from the journalist's hands. Luzelle chewed her lower lip in frustration. She and Girays were nowhere near the source, they would never get their hands on one of those early reports.

Hundreds of others shared her plight. A storm of mixed

protest and appeal arose. Some anonymous philanthropist blessed with generosity and powerful lungs mounted the stairs, where he stood waving his arms vigorously. The clamor abated as his compatriots recognized his intention. The crowd fell back and fell silent. Standing alone at the head of the stairs, the philanthropist began to read in a strong voice audible to every listener.

VONAHRISH VICTORY

Eyewitness Account from Carnoche Municipality

Shortly after sunrise this morning, a force consisting of two divisions of Haerestean infantry heavily supported by troops and artillery of the Unified Army of the Imperium, crossed the border into Vonahr to advance upon Carnoche Municipality, capital of Eulence Province. Around 7:30 A.M. the Second Corps of the Vonahrish Army under the command of General vo Lieux-v'Olliard engaged the enemy in the fields to the east of the town. It is widely rumored that vo Lieux-v'Olliard dispatched a message to the Undergeneral Retzlof, commander of the Grewzian units, revealing the existence of a new weapon of inconceivable destructive power and offering the enemy a final opportunity to surrender, but this report remains unverified.

In the midmorning the Grewzian artillery opened fire, which Vonahrish gunners returned. Immediately following the commencement of the exchange, the sudden outbreak in their midst of intense wildfire threw the Haerestean and Grewzian troops into great disarray. The fire, distinguished at a distance by its unusual green color, first manifested itself among the enemy gunners, but in the space of mere seconds expanded to extraordinary breadth and height, spreading across the field to overwhelm the invading troops with terrible rapidity. It was noted and commented upon by many observers that the blaze seemed almost possessed of some predatory awareness, for there were many sightings of fleeing victims pursued, overtaken, and arrested by long, tentacular arms of flame.

Within minutes the entire enemy army was engulfed in a sea of furious green fire—a piteous and dreadful spectacle, never to be forgotten by any witness. The sight of their foes writhing in torment, accompanied by the ghastly chorus of shrieks and pleas, awakened the compunction of many Vonahrish soldiers, several of whom are reported to have begged their commander to extinguish the allegedly arcane conflagration.

The green fire never abated, however, before its work of devastation was complete, at which time the flames dwindled out of sight as speedily and inexplicably as they had arisen. It is believed that every enemy soldier perished, although a contingent of civilian spectators was permitted to depart unscathed. Casualties are believed to number somewhere between forty and forty-five thousand men. There was no Vonahrish loss of life.

The terrifying potential of this new destructive force loosed upon the world is obvious and undeniable. Yet its use in this instance appears justified in view of the immediate results. Upon conclusion of the engagement General vo Lieux-v'Olliard quickly moved the Second Corps across the border into the vicinity of Velque, first of some four municipalities of note standing between the Vonahrish force and the Haerestean capital of Tibille. On the outskirts of Velque, vo Lieux-v'Olliard's advance was intercepted by a Haerestean delegation offering terms of surrender.

The terms have been accepted by General vo Lieux-v'Olliard on behalf of the Vonahrish Republic. The Second Corps is withdrawing from Haereste, having eliminated the threat of foreign invasion in the near or foreseeable future.

The reader fell silent. His listeners were similarly silent for a stunned moment. Then the crowd exploded into prolonged cheers that rolled forth to fill Cliquot Street and the avenues beyond with exultant thunder.

THE BREEZE THAT SWEPT along the River Vir was warm but fresh. Today the air of Sherreen felt cleaner and somehow lighter than it had been for weeks past. Luzelle inhaled deeply.

"Beautiful. Tastes of early autumn," she said.

"About time," Girays opined. They were passing a small pier colorfully decked with pennants. "Care to hire a row-boat?"

"No, it's so pleasant here under the trees. Let's just walk."

They sauntered on along the shady footpath edging the river. Many pedestrians were out upon the path, enjoying the weather. People were chattering, quarreling, playing, laughing. Toddlers were squalling, their nannies shushing them. Vendors were hawking their tidbits and trinkets, while a strolling musician fiddled for coppers. The scene breathed agreeable normality. Hard to believe that the city had confronted the imminence of disaster mere weeks earlier.

On they walked arm in arm until they came to the teeming Waterfront Market, with its ceaseless racket and activity that could grate on ragged nerves, but seemed purely stimulating today. The ancient Bridge Vinculum rose before them, and on the far side of the river loomed the castellated towers of the grim old Sepulchre; fortress-prison and house of horrors in the days of the revolution, but now nothing more than a historical curiosity, one of the interesting sights of Sherreen.

As they walked on through the market, they encountered an urchin selling copies of *The Sherreen Messenger,* and they did not pause, but the big headline caught Luzelle's eye in passing: WESTERN ALLIANCE RATIFIED.

Desperate nations, it seemed, were sometimes capable of blindingly swift action.

The news was already old; she had read it hours earlier in *The Republican.* So had Girays. She knew that he would pick up on her thought without need of explanation when she remarked, "Fine for the Principalities, they're safe under Vonahrish protection now. Kyrendt, Travorn, Ferille, and the Republican-Enclaves as well, but what about Rhazaulle?"

"A little distant for membership in a western alliance," Girays returned, "but not beyond the reach of aid. I don't think it will be long before our Grewzian friends see green fire kindling on the Rhazaullean front. And elsewhere in the world as well. Lanthi Ume, perhaps. Xoxo. Jumo Towne."

"It's horrible. The slaughter—the thousands of men burned alive." Luzelle swallowed. "And we're partly responsible for bringing it all about."

"It is horrible," he agreed. "But the alternative to Masterfire is Endless Fire. Well, the Grewzians have tasted Masterfire. They've no weapon of remotely comparable power, and they know it. It's quite possible that the Sentient Fire will never actually be loosed upon an army of men again. The mere threat will suffice to deter the Imperium."

"Until the Grewzians buy or steal the secret, or learn how to kindle green fires of their own."

"That's always possible. The best Vonahrish course, in my opinion, is for us to use this respite effectively. Strengthen ourselves, avoid repeating past errors, never again allow the Imperium or anything of that ilk to launch itself upon an unprepared world."

"How long a respite do you think we've got?"

"Something between days and decades."

"And then?"

"Indeed. And then."

The Waterfront Market was behind them. The footpath along the river resumed, and they were back in the pleasant shade of the trees. They walked along in silence for a while, until Girays observed conversationally, "You've had weeks to mull over all those offers you received—the speaking engagements, articles, books, and so on. Reached any decisions?"

"Well, I haven't entirely made up my mind yet," she confessed. "So many seem so tempting, but I can't manage them all. The only one I'm quite certain of at the moment is the Bulaude Fellowship. That one I'll definitely accept."

"I see. So you'll be tied to Sherreen all through next year."

"For the most part, yes."

"No doubt you'll be busy."

"Very. I'm looking forward to it."

"Do you think your schedule might accommodate a wedding?"

"Whose?"

"Ours."

"Ours?" She stopped and turned to look at him. He was smiling, the smile that had always warmed her, and she wanted to fling her arms around him. That smile and face were part of the essential terrain of her mind, and always would be. Her heart was pounding, and she let herself recognize at last how deeply and powerfully she had ached for a second chance. Assent almost flew out of her mouth, but she tightened her jaw and held it in. There was more to consider than spontaneous emotion, and she was, as His Honor had pointed out, no longer a green girl.

"I wouldn't marry anyone else," she told him. "But we tried betrothal once already. Remember what happened. Disaster."

"Years ago. We've both changed since then."

"Yes. Some things haven't changed, though. You still want a wife willing to divide her time between Belfaireau and Sherreen. I still want liberty to travel and pursue my work. Even with all the love in the world between us, how long before we'd find ourselves at one another's throats?"

"Even with all the love in the world between us, we remain reasonable, intelligent adults, do we not? We are capable of negotiating a compromise."

"Negotiating?" She tasted the word. A slow smile crept across her face. "Shouldn't we have lawyers or something?"

"We'll represent ourselves."

"You know what they say about that."

"We'll prove them wrong. Come then, Miss Devaire. State your conditions."

"I must continue my career, that's certain. I must be free to travel."

"How free? Be specific."

"Well—" She considered. "An excursion as often as every eighteen months, not to exceed eight months in duration."

"As often as every thirty-six months, not to exceed three months in duration."

"That's ridiculously inadequate!"

"Let's hear your counteroffer."

"Oh. Well. Every eighteen months, six months' duration."

"Every two years, six months' maximum duration."

"Ummm. That's—not so very bad. All right, I can accept that if you can."

"Good, we are agreed. What more?"

"I'll continue to lecture, and endure no complaints and reproaches over the impropriety of setting foot upon a public stage."

"Agreed. Have you ever known me to complain of impropriety?"

"Now that you mention it, no. I'll continue to write and publish under my own name. I will not submit my manuscripts to your inspection unless I happen to feel like it, and you will exercise no authority over the content."

"I have never aspired to editorship. But there is one qualification. Your work will reveal nothing of our lives at home, nothing personal of our family or friends."

"Oh, agreed. I'm no scandalmonger, that doesn't interest me. I'll accept payment for my work, and the money I earn will be mine to use as I please."

"Fine, as long as you don't use it to finance the anarchists."

"All right, no anarchists. I'll be free to read what I like, eat and drink what I like, wear what I like, go where I please without anyone's permission, and choose my own friends, whether you approve of them or not."

"Agreed, so long as you break no law and take no action endangering anyone other than yourself."

"Some laws are unjust and should be broken."

"Should be changed."

"Too slow! But I promise I'll make every reasonable effort to keep myself out of jail."

"I suppose that will have to do. And now a few conditions of my own. First, you may choose your own friends, but you will not inflict upon me the society of anyone I detest as a longtime houseguest at Belfaireau or in Sherreen."

"Reasonable."

"Nor will you cultivate an independent friendship with

any man leading you to meet with him alone, either in private or in public."

"Agreed, so long as you yourself cultivate no such friendship with any woman."

"The disposition of the inherited v'Alisante monies and properties will remain solely in my hands. You will be very welcome to express your opinion or to offer advice, but all final decisions in such matters will be mine. Once such decisions have been made, you'll abandon argument and accept them without complaint."

"Very well."

"And finally, when you find yourself with child—"

"Oh."

"Yes, oh—when you find yourself with child, you will throughout the term of the pregnancy subordinate your own impulses to the welfare of the infant—"

"You don't need to tell me that, Girays!"

"And following delivery, for a period not to exceed four years, you will not absent yourself from the child's vicinity for a period exceeding twenty-one days—"

"Aha, I see what you're about, but it won't work. Following delivery I agree not to absent myself from the child's vicinity for a period exceeding seven days, provided the child is permitted to accompany me on my periodic excursions—"

"What?"

"Well, why not?"

"You can't very well drag a v'Alisante heir off to the Bhomiri Islands or the Forests of Oorex, where he's likely to end in a pot. Don't forget the welfare-of-the-infant proviso. When you stop to think about it, the true welfare of the infant demands the presence of both parents, so you can't drag him away from his father for months at a time. I'm afraid you'll have to consider—"

"You're right, it wouldn't be fair. So you'll have to sacrifice, Girays—you'll have to come along, from time to time. For the sake of the child."

"There is no child."

"You're the one who raised the issue. Come, would it be so bad?"

"Not so bad at all; I've developed a taste for travel. But I couldn't do it every two years. Five, perhaps."

"Four."

"Agreed. Anything more?"

"No, I'm content," she declared. "These conditions accepted, I may by degrees dwindle into a wife."

"Then let's seal the bargain."

He kissed her then in the middle of the path, indifferent to the scores of amused or disapproving spectators. The city seemed to spin around them. When he released her, she was flushed, breathless, and happier than she had ever been in her life.

"You know, it's all out there waiting for us," she said, when she could speak again.

"What is, Luzelle?"

"The world, and everything in it."